THE LIONS
OF GOD

THE LIONS OF GOD

Glenn Feingold

iUniverse, Inc.
New York Lincoln Shanghai

The Lions of God

iUniverse books may be ordered through booksellers or by contacting:

iUniverse
2021 Pine Lake Road, Suite 100
Lincoln, NE 68512
www.iuniverse.com
1-800-Authors (1-800-288-4677)

Because of the dynamic nature of the Internet, any Web addresses or links contained in this book may have changed since publication and may no longer be valid.

This is a work of fiction. All of the characters, names, incidents, organizations, and dialogue in this novel are either the products of the author's imagination or are used fictitiously.

ISBN: 978-0-595-41388-1 (pbk)
ISBN: 978-0-595-90821-9 (cloth)
ISBN: 978-0-595-85738-8 (ebk)

Printed in the United States of America

For John Palmiotti,

For Patricia,
   Who recognizes that understanding is a gift
   With which one should never act miserly.

in appreciation for having been the first set of eyes to wander through the maze,

Love,

Henry Feingold

10/7/07

PROLOGUE

Ensconced in the dunes on the East End of Long Island, the house resembled a bungalow or fishing shack, certainly not the two-, three-, or four-storied sprawling manse that was a common sight in the region. Its weather-hewn exterior, shingled with broken clapboards, revealed that their tan shades had long ago faded to gray and black. As a limousine pulled up to its front door, the passenger in the rear seat rolled down the window.

"Driver, this is not the Aghapos estate!" he shouted into the intercom, making no attempt to hide both his surprise and disappointment over the actual location.

The voice crackled on the other side, then became clearer and rather deep.

"I have been authorized to tell you that everything you want is in that house. The only stipulation that Mr. Aghapos makes is that you play the recording before you start reading."

"Reading? Reading what exactly?"

"The cabinets are stocked with provisions," the driver continued. "Mr. Aghapos regrets the lack of indoor plumbing. There's an outhouse in the rear. You've got electricity, so you'll have plenty of light when it gets dark. There's a cot, too, if you should want to take a nap. I'll stay here all day today, all night long, and the following day, if necessary. If you choose to leave, you'll have no further contact with Mr. Aghapos ever again. I must have your choice now."

"This is absurd. Mr. Aghapos was supposed to meet me … here," he said with a slight choke, as he looked around.

The driver began to laugh loudly. Before he was able to regain his composure, he asked again if the passenger wished to leave.

The passenger got out. After having studied the building's dilapidated condition, he knocked on the passenger-side window of the front seat. The glass rolled down, revealing a very large and very old white-bearded driver, with an open box of donuts next to him.

"The front door is unlocked," the man said, before the passenger had a chance to ask any further questions.

The passenger removed his glasses, rubbed his eyes, looked at the shack, put back on his glasses, then looked at the driver once more.

"You're going to stay here while I read?" he asked, nodding.

The driver nodded as well. He pressed a button on the door at his left, and the window rose up.

The interior of the structure had no walls to speak of, save the wood studs and plywood backing of the outer skin. There was no ceiling either, only the exposed timbers of a wood roof. Of cracked concrete, the floor was riddled with many dark, oily stains. In one corner lay several fishing rods, all broken, next to tackle boxes. A cot and quilt had been placed nearby. A counter-top and sink, with cabinets above and below, lined one wall. In the center of the room a small table had been placed, flanked by a single chair. The passenger sat down in one. A cassette recorder had been placed on the bottom right corner of the table, and a very large volume was lying next to it. The design embossed on its leather cover consisted of two men sitting upon a single horse. He ran his fingers over the symbol. Before he opened the cover, he pressed a button on the machine.

"Good morning to you, Mr. Paine. By now I am certain that this unorthodox encounter may be a bit disturbing. You're probably wondering why I have asked you to come here. I can tell you that it is not part of some scheme devised by a reclusive shipping magnate, despite all appearances to the contrary. As something of an amateur historian myself, I thought you might find it interesting to read a book that has been in my possession for some time. As for the accommodations, well, call me *old-fashioned*, but I have always believed that a quest should end in a place of simplicity, don't you think? As you can see, even after a cursory examination, the folio is genuine. No doubt you recognize the symbol of the Templars on the cover—two knights astride a single horse, emblematic of their vow of poverty. This book may help to answer some questions you have concerning them and their association with one obscure French knight, Sir Guy of Lagery. After you have completed your reading, I think you'll agree that it was impossible for him to accomplish all that you have attributed to him. In fact, your references to an eyewitness account of a Scotsman, Dunstane, and his adventures with this same Guy of Lagery, may be not so much reportage as fiction. The medieval Scots were always fond of their stories, to be sure. Furthermore, as an historian, you will probably find yourself doubting the actual existence of this Frenchman, since his name appears in no other historical documentation. At least, that was the case until I read your recent account of the holy Knights.

"In it you claim that you were unable to find an explanation for the mysterious group of four letters, which appeared at the end of their documents: *D, S, M, M.* In this respect I believe that you will find the folio most enlightening. As to the actual existence of this Guy de—Something-or-Other, well, you will have to draw your own conclusions, won't you? The only stipulation that I make is that you read the entire work here in one sitting. Its text in medieval French, Latin, and English won't pose much of a problem for a linguist like yourself. When you have finished, we shall talk again."

The recording ended. He shut off the machine. Very carefully he opened the front cover, so as not to disturb the delicate binding, and began to read.

PROEM

It is customary, in a work such as this, to give thanks to one's patron, ofttimes in support of one's fiscal responsibilities, and occasionally for those of the spirit. And this practice is performed in the lifetime of said patron, so that he may derive pleasure in the reading therefrom. This, however, is not the case with my humble book. The man in question, my uncle, has been dead for quite some time. So my small attempts at offering thanks may be heard, I fear, only in the Kingdom of Heaven, where, I am certain, he resides for eternity. (Or so it is my fondest wish!) Therefore, dear reader, grant me a moment to share with you a lesson learned at his knee: a life may have little worth, unless it is cherished by someone other than the person-in-question, himself. I trust that you may find these tales of my humble life of some value, for it is my pleasure to relate them to you.

O, but it is good to be alive, is it not?

Sir Guy of Lagery

LIBER PRIMUS

Pater

UNE CHANSON DES GESTES
(A Song of Great Deeds)

*as composed by Sir Guy of Lagery
in the year of Our Lord, 1453.*

CHAPTER THE FIRST,

in which my life is forever altered, and not necessarily for the better.

Arma virumque cano ... Aenidos

Liber Primus
By
P. Virgilius Maro.

As the Latin poet, Virgilius, sang of Aeneas and the founding of Rome, so, too, do I begin my tale with a call to arms; however, the nature of this rallying-cry was not, strictly speaking, a military one. And like all wars, it happened at the most inopportune of moments.

The monk sat atop his horse, tossing pebbles at the window of the rooms above the tavern. A young woman, completely nude, opened the shutters. Atop the sill she folded her arms and placed her ample bosoms upon them.

"If you can wait," she called down to him, "I can be ready within the hour."

The cleric made a face (she told me, and not an altogether cheerful one, I warrant).

"I am looking for Guy de Lagery," he called back to her. "Is he with you?"

She turned to me.

"Are you Guy de ... Something?"

I also came to the window. I recognized the man's huge torso and muscular arms—contradicting the typical conceptions of frailty which one associates with age. His stern face was unmistakable as well.

"Brother Michael? How did you find me?"

"With extreme difficulty. The more things change, the more they stay the same," he bellowed, shaking his head as he looked up at me with the most disapproving gaze that I believe I had ever seen (or would ever see again) upon the old man's face. "You are hereby officially summoned to appear immediately, if not sooner."

4

I looked at the woman, then at Brother Michael, and repeated these actions twice more.

"I shall be down shortly," I shouted to him finally. "In the meanwhile, why not make yourself comfortable downstairs? No need to worry about the payment."

He dismounted, cursing me, whilst I returned to my duties. (I think he cursed me, though I might be wrong; my thoughts were otherwise occupied.) The woman had perched herself atop the bed, resting upon her elbows and knees, and pushing her buttocks into the air. Though she was not a novice at her profession, her flesh possessed such remarkable, unblemished beauty, (and her buttocks were possessed of such an incredibly rounded firmness), that I hesitated briefly to admire it all.

"Are you certain that this will do?" she asked, perhaps embarrassed by her lack of experience with the position (or so I assumed), and more than a little impatient with the novelty of it.

Pulled from my reverie, I tried to assure her that all would go well momentarily:

"A prostitute who had served in Alexandria with several knights showed me what to do. It is much simpler than it looks."

"And you called it, *in the manner of the dog*?"

"Indeed!"

"I think we might be wasting our time, my lord, when we—O. O, my. O, yes. Yes!"

Some time later I had to pull Brother Michael away from *his* duty, which consisted of emptying the tavern of its entire stock of brew. The innkeeper was most gratified; he became a wealthy man that day, and I a poor one.

The little town of *Châtillon-sur-Marne*, in Auvergne, was an insignificant hamlet in all things save one; its reputation as a veritable font of monastic study brought it several degrees of not-unwarranted fame. And it has remained in the memory of men not because I was born there, but because my uncle was. Odo de Lagery was tall, quite handsome, fully tonsured, and possessed of a long nose and thick beard. He also bore a grace in his demeanor, as well as a power of mind, that was most rare for a man of his time. Later portraitists would attempt to convey these qualities of my kinsman as those of the ideal knight. In fact, he never took up a sword or bow. Instead, he was most in love with holy writ. It was his fate to become the church's spiritual and temporal leader, known as Pope Urban II.

Upon the road to the Abbey at Cluny, I devoted much of my time to contemplation, as my companion was determined to say not a single word to me, and not so much as a thing about the weather, my uncle, or even share a bit of knowledge concerning my parents. Of late I had found myself thinking of them more and more. I cannot say why. Perhaps I was simply growing older, (despite the four and twenty years of my youth), and my heart was yearning for their company. Then again, it may have been the sense of dread concerning my possible future that was my other companion upon this strange journey, and thoughts of my old home gave me a bit of comfort. You see, dear reader, both mother and father had given me over to my uncle's care and tutelage from my early youth. I never really knew the reason. After I had grown to manhood, I would learn that it had become a custom amongst all the noble families, especially if the child had evinced any form of unusual intelligence in either his conversations or his actions. I accepted their decision without argument, and was somewhat flattered, though I must confess, there were moments when I craved their attention, especially during those first years in church, when I was often left to my own devices, or rather, I should say, when I was not applying myself to studies. On such occasions I would oft think upon the day that I had been taken. It was, in fact, an interval when the bite of winter had not yet faded. My dear uncle led me from my ancestral castle to a grand church that April morn. And for so long thereafter, I became aware that the word *cold*, had a great many meanings spread throughout each of the seasons, which my childhood would soon learn and sometimes loathe, sometimes cherish.

My uncle had personally seen to my thorough training in the liberal arts—logic, rhetoric, dialectics, especially church doctrine, thence to horsemanship, and even to the practice of war. It was only in recent time that I had fallen into his disfavour. At first I thought it was because I did not follow in his ecclesiastical footsteps. Uncertain as I was, I could not deny the feeling that it was probably due to my determination to waste my considerable life's vigor on nothing of significance. Whatever the cause, on that particular day I could not fathom why my uncle wished to see me. I kept asking Brother Michael about it. Either he did not know, or he had been ordered to keep his counsel to himself. Perhaps he was as displeased with my youthful impetuousness as was my uncle. Indeed, my life could in no way be considered an exemplary Christian one. The Holy Father and

I had not spoken since his election several years previously, and I was convinced that this summons could bode no good, either for my soul *or* for my body.

As we rode on through the main gate, a horse-drawn cart was leaving through it. A cleric, a young woman, and a little boy were seated inside, the child clinging to the woman. The man's eyes were puffy and red. Both the woman and her off-spring were crying.

"Will you tell me now what is happening?" I asked Brother Michael.

He watched the three leave as well.

"His Holiness has pronounced an *anathema* against clerical marriage."

I dared not believe it true!

"That would force these husbands to leave their families behind to fend for themselves. And that would make all children born of such marriages," I said, turning to face him, "bastards! I know that my uncle wishes all men were as pure as he, but we were not created in his image."

"Hold your tongue, boy! It is not our place to sit in judgment of him. Besides, this is only the beginning."

His words weighed heavily upon me. At that moment I knew my life would never be quite the same again.

We dismounted in the east courtyard. Once there, we brought our horses to the stables. The brothers, who had always sought what they took to be an ideal of absolute silence in their daily activities, had, in recent years, adopted a series of complicated hand gestures, all in lieu of speech. I found myself standing there for quite some time, trying to ascertain their meaning, as they pointed, gesticulated, and otherwise mouthed words. Brother Michael folded his arms and fidgeted. At last, they were able to coax the roan from me with a handful of oats. Brother Michael took me inside.

I shall confess to you, dear reader, here and now, that I was never overly fond of church architecture. It always seemed so very *big* to me. My uncle had often mentioned that a church was God's house, and that it had to be very large to accommodate both His strength and spirit. Even then I felt lost in its cavernous spaces, always hoping to catch a glimpse of the Most High lingering there as well. (I cannot say whether anyone else ever saw Him there, though I never did. My uncle always told me that He was there, even though He could not be seen. And yet He had appeared as a pillar of fire and a cloud to the wandering Hebrews of old, and had even deigned to speak to Moses. Why did He not speak to us? My uncle scowled whenever I asked that question, and the conversation would end abruptly.) The sole comfort I found there was in the innumerable recesses between columns, pews, halls, and foyers. I would hide in a secret corner whenever my uncle, during his periods of tutelage, was determined to teach me Greek. It was only later that I would come to regret my decision to forego having learned that language.

I was led past the rows of stone columns, across the stone floors, beneath the vast vaulted ceilings, through the vestibule, the *atrium*, and on into the cloister. At its rear was a library. At the rear of this library was a tiny room. Inside it, surrounded by books, scrolls, and all manner of copious documentation, I barely saw the top of a table that the Holy Father had obviously consigned for his personal use. (It was a modest *scriptorium*, no doubt, for one of so high a station, yet fitting perhaps for a man whose nature was devoid of vanity. I wonder how many still remember that quality of his?) Waiting for him there, inside his study, I became filled suddenly with fear. At the moment when I saw him enter, I decided to ask his forgiveness immediately. He nodded to Brother Michael, who took his meaning and left instantly.

"Holy Father," I began, "if I have done anything to offend you—"

"Nonsense," he interrupted me, raising his hand as if to shut my mouth, and smiling broadly all the while, "your entire *life* is an offense to me. Why select one deed from a list of countless others?"

He was probably thinking of the reputation that I had carved out for myself in the local taverns. In truth, I had become quite the fool since my childhood in church, albeit a deadly one. Long before I was to be called to raise my blade in the defense of Christendom, I would frequently challenge the finest swordsman, (at the first imagined slight, mind you!), only to slay him, only to slay each and every one of those who had the audacity to accept my threats. I decided, however, that the burden of this knowledge was one that I preferred to carry upon my own shoulders, so I spoke not a word of it.

He cleared his throat very loudly as he stood near, which action, (since unexpected), caused me to jump backwards.

"A bit dry," he said softly now, pointing to his mouth before he sat. He removed a bottle and a small cup from a cabinet behind himself, then poured the liquid. He swallowed it in one swift gulp.

I knew it! Damned throughout eternity!—this was to be my fate, thanks to an order of excommunication from my kinsman. So, having climbed to the highest seat of the papal see not two years prior, one of his first orders was to be the sentencing of my soul. And due to a tie of blood, he probably thought it best to deliver the unwelcome news, himself.

He looked up at me whilst still continuing to smile. I found such action highly disturbing.

"I have been thinking about you a great deal in recent days, nephew," he informed me, turning around momentarily to situate the bottle and cup in their former proper positions in the cabinet.

I glanced at a book, turned a page, and did everything that I could not to show him my face, for he would know at once that I was worried about what pronouncement he might make next. My attempt to conceal my feelings was most unsuccessful.

"Are you preoccupied with matters of far greater import than our exchange of ideas?"

I shook my head, returning my attention to his corner of the room.

"I keep telling myself that you are a decent man," he continued. He looked at me askance now, perhaps trying to find something in my face that would convince himself of that statement's elusive truth. "What are you doing with your life? Do you ever think of it?"

Before I had a chance to respond, he went on.

"Have you taken a look at yourself recently? The child you once were has become the man, a man with no wife, by the way. What is worse is that you have no heirs."

"I am a knight," I stated proudly.

He frowned.

"And if you should perchance die during one of your *knightly* excursions, what then? To whom will you leave your holdings? Our relatives are completely worthless. They have less respect for themselves than they do for their own horses. And they treat them far worse than they do the peasants."

"I shall leave it all to you, your holiness, to dispense with, or retain, as you may see fit."

"Of what possible use could your things be to me? You need your family's land for yourself, as the proper place to raise a family, should you ever develop the conception of starting one." He sighed now, and I felt its massive weight more upon my shoulders than I presumed that he felt upon his own. "I promised your parents that I would take care of you, guide you in the course of your life. I fear now that I may not have been so staunch a disciplinarian as I should have been."

"You did your job well," I assured him. "I can translate the Romans as quickly as any scholar."

He continued to ignore me.

"Though you were never the best of students, you learned well and quickly, I must admit. Be that as it may, what is done is done and cannot be undone. You are familiar with church doctrine, perhaps more so than most of your peers. You know full well that the church is not without its numerous gifts, one of which is mercy. You do recall the concept of Christian mercy, do you not, dear nephew?"

Again I tried to respond, only to fail.

"I am hereby duly authorized to grant kindness to those who are determined to do the Lord's work."

That was the second time in my life that I became fearful, and it was also the second time that day. You see, dear reader, I was a knight, a warrior. The last thing that I could have ever wanted was to be a novitiate—not that there was anything wrong with that! It was simply not the path that I would have chosen. Unfortunately, at that moment, it seemed that my future had already been written.

"Would you care to redeem yourself in the eyes of Holy Mother Church, dearest nephew?"

Now it was that he granted me time to formulate an answer. Consequently, I created a question of my own:

"Meaning no disrespect, your holiness; it is not a matter of what I would prefer, rather, it is what *you* would have me do, is it not, dearest uncle?"

"You are a clever one, too much so for your own good, I suppose. Despite that, I have need of such cleverness. I want you to take a trip, a voyage, a journey, one that may become a quest."

O, I had not expected that. Perhaps he wished for me to discover the very spear that pierced the side of our Lord.

"Do you wish me to find the Holy Lance?"

He collapsed into a *paroxysm* of laughter. (Rarely have I ever been so embarrassed to become the source of another's comedy.) It was some time before he was able to control himself again.

"Such a deed is the dream of holy men and poets. You may be many things, nephew, however, a holy poet is not one of them. No. Your task is of a more practical nature, though the dangers surrounding it may prove as great as those in any epic song. You are to make your way to Konstantinople, the heart of the Byzantine Empire, the gateway to the Holy Land. You will accompany one of my dearest colleagues, Archbishop Adhémar de Monteil. He is a just and learnèd man, who is not so easily frightened by the infidel. Once there, he will attempt to use both his wisdom and his vast knowledge of Greek history to convince the emperor that his church and ours must be reunited. You will ride with Hughes de

Payens, of Champagne, a courteous knight, the paragon of bravery. Moreover, he is married to a very beautiful and delicate lady, Catherine de Saint Claire. She has given unto him two sons. Did you hear what I said, nephew? Two. He is your age, I believe, or very nearly so, and he will be a good influence besides."

"But Holy Father, am I so complete a sinner, that you would order a guardian to watch over my every word and deed?"

"This may come as quite a surprise; the universe does not begin and end with you. I have created this brotherhood, not for your benefit, but for our Lord's. Would you prefer to lodge your objections to Him now or later?"

I was sufficiently chastised. I kept my mouth closed.

"Brother Michael and several others will also accompany you. He was quite the swordsman in his youth, and despite his reluctance to admit it, I am certain that he still remembers how to use a blade. The road there is fraught with peril. You will need him."

My uncle may have been many things, but a fool was not one of them. Now, if that were true, why did he select me for this undertaking, when he could have called upon countless others, who would have been only too happy to please him?

"Your holiness, do you believe that I am worthy of this honour?"

He looked at me curiously, before smiling finally.

"This is a new age," he responded with a voice that was far stronger and steadier than I had ever before heard it. "Great changes are coming. As never before, we have the faith and the power to transform a handful of kingdoms into a single world ruled by Christ and His teachings. If a war is necessary to accomplish that truth, then so be it. Only a madman would show a blind eye to inevitability. Due to the seriousness of this age and the future ones depending upon our decisions here, I have had to institute a number of significant changes as well."

"Yes. I saw the family leaving earlier."

I bit my lip, for I knew that the Holy Father would not be terribly happy with my keen powers of observation.

"Is there a negative tone that I hear in your voice, nephew? When a man puts on a cowl, his commitment is no longer to this world, but to the next. How well would that sit, do you think, with his wife and children? Home and hearth can never be his; and their absence in his life comes as no sacrifice to him. He locks himself inside his cloister, so that he may not be battered by mundane concerns. His entire day, as you may recall, is devoted to prayer, from long before the sun rises, until long after it has set. So you see, a *man of God* must be exactly that, first, foremost, always. He may serve only one master. I make no apologies for my decisions, certainly not to you."

Seeing that there was no other way that I might redeem myself in his eyes, or escape this situation with any shred of dignity, I simply nodded.

"You will, of course, earn my eternal gratitude."

I knew exactly what he meant—forgiveness of all past sins. There were many who would have given any- and everything to be in my position at that very moment, so great was the concern with sin and its consequences in those days. However, my newfound spiritual fortune was not for crowds to hear.

"I know that you will be able to convince your friends in Venice, Genoa, or Bari to spare a single vessel." He lifted a scroll that had been tied and sealed. I took it from him. "This should prompt their generosity, even if our holy purpose does not."

Looking at it could not determine its nature. He noticed my curiosity with the object in question, and tried to remove it therefrom.

"A bit more papal forgiveness, no more, no less," he commented with a dismissive gesture. "You would be surprised at how far my words may reach. I am relying upon your discretion in this situation. This will be our conspiracy of silence, in which you are a willing participant. Understand this, my son; life is not about your wishes, nor will it ever be so. You will never have the luxury of simple pleasures, which other men take for granted. Such is the destiny of all sons of the church. As for your actions during this mission, they will be made public only if you succeed."

"Have I ever failed you, your holiness?"

His gaze was stern.

"I would rather not discuss it. So, are you going to stand here all day, or are you going to embrace your destiny? Go forth and show the world how brave and righteous our family can be!"

Though I could scarcely believe it, it seemed that even the Devil might be capable of a holy act. What choice did I have? Without question I accepted …

The church of *Sophia Sancta* was a small one, free from much of the gaudy ornamentation common to the bastions of religiosity, which were everywhere throughout Konstantinople. It was built (as were all the others) completely of stone. A thin layer of dirt had been spread across its floor of pebbles, ending in marble steps, which led to an altar. Its ceiling vault was not high, no more than the height of two large men, if one were standing upon the other's shoulders. Benches were few. Their wood was worn and old. They were placed haphazardly, as if without care (or so it seemed). The sole decoration was behind the altar. Set into its back wall, in tiny multi-hued glass tiles, each one smaller than a fingernail, and perfectly square, was the crucifixion. And everywhere in that representation were images of vivid red: in the blood dripping from the nails in His feet; in the drops pouring from His side, where the lance had pierced; beneath the thorns digging into the flesh at His head. And behind all this vibrant colour were the rays of a sparkling golden sun emanating from him like a gigantic *penumbra*. It was a place of simplicity, of absolute quiet and contemplation, the way that all true houses of God were meant to be.

Now I see that I am forgetting about the massive stone lintel supported by two stone columns. These three items stood at the front of the apse, before the altar. By themselves they might not have been so terribly consequential. It was only because of what was about to happen that their importance—But I am racing ahead of myself, as my uncle used to say of me. And there is much to tell.

Into this silence came the clashing of swords. To our surprise it was not the infidel who fell upon our company; it was our fellow Christians, sent as a special envoy from the illustrious emperor, no doubt—an unmistakable response to the Holy Father's good intentions. The battle had spread from the road outside and into this tiny church. And so great a tumult was raised therein, that the very foundations shook to the Heavens. The benches cracked, the *torchieres* fell over, spilling their flames across the dirt, and dying out with a foul hiss. Adhémar, God's own bishop, the old man with the power of ten youths swelling within him, fought bravely and with excellent command of his blade, even if he could not best the Byzantines. He was led away in their custody. Hughes, a swordsman *par excellence*, fought like a Fury, his golden hair and beard slowly turning red, the mail covering his leathern tunic clanking as each sword struck it. He left many an enemy to bleed out upon the cold floor that day. Nevertheless, he was taken away, still alive. The good Brother Michael, though wounded, acquitted himself well. He, too, was captured. Most of the others were dead. All that I wanted, all that for which I now lusted, was the corpse of the knight bearing down upon me. He was a large man, weighing far more than I, his face full of hair, his eyes bursting with blood—never to be sated except by slaughter, much as the war god, Ares, of Greek fame must have been.

As we fought, I was forced back, nearly tripping over one of the benches. Already I bled from a chest wound. His sword had grazed me, and thanks be to the Most High, that it had not entered the cavity beneath my ribs. But I was losing. He had forced me finally up the stone steps to the columns. Then the tide of battle turned. He tripped upon a shiny surface of floor tile, perhaps worn down from years of genuflection, and fell against that same column. With all my strength gathered, I swung towards him, hoping to behead the *daemon*. Unfortunately, he moved. My sword struck the stone and shattered. In my hand were only the hilt and a small section of metal. I looked down to see a blade plunging beneath my ribs, again, and again. With each thrust I banged against the column, moving it slightly each time. Finally, I fell, and as I did so, the massive lintel above came crashing down upon me. Only, it was not of stone; it was of wood, painted to resemble the masonry that had supported it. It fell upon my chest. I could not breathe. And within this wooden box was a linen cloth. I am uncertain as to what happened next. I can only tell you that the midday sun filled the *rotunda*. I could not see, though I would swear this cloth moved. It covered my entire face and body. And my flesh grew hot. My face began to burn. I did not possess the strength to remove it. As I lay there, I heard my enemy spit upon the cloth over my face, then I heard him leave. I heard them all leave. I cannot say if days passed. Somehow I was still alive.

After a time unknown to me, I was able to rise. I pulled the cloth away from my sweating face, only to see that the lines of my hair, moustache, beard, eyes, nose, and lips had been burned into its fibers. Most strange! I examined my wounds. I brushed aside the dried blood at each insertion, only to find that the flesh beneath was completely closed. Each wound told the same story. But how?

My sword was gone. I saw another nearby. I picked it up. Examining it now, it reminded me of the *frescoes* of gladiators and their swords. I did not know whether this was the Roman *gladius*, though its length and breadth were far greater than was its custom. There were also letters set into it, letters, which resembled the Hebraic alphabet that I had studied only in a cursory fashion in earlier years. The sword may have belonged to a Byzantine, though it was mine from that day forth.

I turned. There was the Son of Man behind the altar, frozen forever in His suffering, more a living sculpture than a portrait. I stood before Him, wondering why. Why had I been allowed to live? For mine own glory? No. I was undeserving of such a gift. For the greater glory of God? If that, then why had He not chosen a worthier vessel with which to honour Himself? I was young then, and the fair lady, Wisdom, and I were complete strangers to each other. At that moment I knew only two truths: I had been allowed to live; I was holding a sword. This sword in my hand, with the strange markings inscribed upon its length and breadth, felt like an extension of my arm. I realized then that, for whatever remaining years the Lord above had given unto me, mine would be the weapon raised in righteous cause, in sacred name.

I bent down upon one knee, holding the blade in front, burnished bright, its tip set between two floor stones. I swore my fealty, my courage, my love—all that I was as a knight, and all that I would ever be as a man.

I left that church in Konstantinople, never suspecting the many circuitous paths, which would lead me back there in the days to come.

And so it passed in the year of our Lord, 1090, that Guy de Lagery tasted death and spat it out. And mind you, it was not so bitter as he thought it might be.

CHAPTER THE SECOND,

in which Pope Urban II rallies the populace to take up both sword and cross.

At Clermont, in the *Massif Central*, in the center of the Frankish kingdoms, Pope Urban II stood atop a high wooden platform, looking around, smiling. The crosier, clasped in his hand, was very nearly taller than he. It was a frigid, gray morn on this the last day of November in the year of our Lord, 1095. There were personages as far as the eye could see—archbishops, bishops, abbots, knights, lay people, all gathered outside the church of *Nôtre Dame du Port*, for its nave could not possibly hold all and sundry who had come to see and hear him speak. Attendants stood at his sides, barely able to hold aloft a vast quantity of red cloth crosses. I was uncertain as to their purpose, though convinced that they would be put to good use before sunset. I looked around as well. Some in the crowds nodded or waved to me, most I had never before seen. I heard one conversation in an Italian tongue that I recognized. Another was, I believed, in an Iberian dialect, though I could not be certain. How far had they traveled to hear his words, I wondered? I watched him standing before them, clad in his mitre, pontifical robe, and all the trappings of his station. He was truly a holy knight. And as he began his sermon, his smile faded away slowly. The crowd grew silent.

"Today I speak not only to you, good people of France, but to all nations under Christ. In a land far away, in a place called Konstantinople, the Saracen is knocking upon the door. Have you forgotten that city and our brethren who live there? Have you forgotten that the lance that pierced the side of our Lord as He wept in agony upon the cross is in *their* safekeeping?"

The crowd gasped.

"Perhaps you do not know what the Saracen is, for he is not yet here," he continued, looking into the multitude of faces. "You spend your time in revels, or hunting, or gaming, all whilst this spawn of the devil burns the churches of Byzantium. They smash the statues of our Lord, urinate upon our altars, defecate in the sacristy!"

Once again the crowd gasped.

"Our brothers have cried out to us, and we have offered to them our deaf ears. When the Most High calls us to account for our lives in His Holy Kingdom, shall we say that His enemies are not ours? Would you say that to the Creator of us all?"

"No," the voices rang back. "Kill the devils!"

Inspired by their angry exuberance, he pressed on:

"What have we done, my brethren? What have we done? For too long have we ignored the tales of pilgrims returning from the Holy Land and all the terrors surrounding it. Dare we forget our sacred duty? Those who have eyes to see, let them see. Christ commands it!"

His voice filled the fields, as he pointed to the right side of the crowd. They echoed his words.

"Those who have ears to hear, let them hear," he shouted, pointing to the left side of the crowd. "Christ commands it!"

Again they echoed his words.

"Today we call upon you, good Franks, and all the other peoples of the earth. Today we call upon you to raise a cross."

At that moment each of the two attendants struggled and finally managed to hold aloft the pile of cloths with one hand, whilst raising a single cross from the top of each pile with the other.

"And with that cross, you will raise a sword. And with that sword, you will march to Byzantium."

A murmur began to swell.

"And when you have cleared the land of all the vermin infesting it, you will march on. With each step you will make the land pure. Then you will journey to Jerusalem. You will walk the roads our Lord walked. And the Saracens, who have held the place of His birth for over four centuries, will be slaughtered. And the land will once more flow with milk and honey. And when you leave this world, Heaven will be your just reward, for this is God's … *holy war!*"

The crowd burst forth with roaring and screaming. "God wills it!" they shouted with one voice. Then they shouted it again, then a third and final time. And they ran up to the attendants and clutched a single cross as if it were their last morsel of food. (Archbishop Adhémar was the first of us to do so. I have rarely seen such strength of will in a servant of the church. I hope that history does not forget the brave man whom once I knew.)

There was not a soul left untouched that day. Even I raised my sword, as did the other knights. Then came the portent that no one could have dreamed possible. The clouds parted. And a few meager rays of sun gleamed along our raised metal. And though blinded and full of awe, we all screamed for the deaths of our enemies, and we were happy.

Inside one of the church's rooms he smiled warmly. The attendants had already taken his mitre and crosier by the time that I entered.

"Did you see it, nephew?" he asked with such unremitting glee, that the entire room echoed with it. "We did not have enough crosses for them all!"

"A rousing speech, your holiness. Everyone is clamouring for you to lead them."

He dismissed that possibility. There was far too much work for him to do here. He had decided, even before the sermon, (should his wish be realized), that the very brave and very capable Adhémar would function in his stead. The archbishop would act as his legate and spiritual guide for the entire noble enterprise.

Ever since he had first informed me of his plans, his words gave me no peace. Was war one means of utilizing the knightly class, that was fast sinking into idleness or seeking petty squabbles at every opportunity? What better way to direct their strength than at the enemy of all Christendom? What better way to transform them into an arm of the church? However, at that moment, standing with him, the two of us alone in that room, I was uncertain as to what the consequences might be, and felt that with no other ears to hear, I could speak my mind freely.

"You have given all this a great deal of thought, but are you truly prepared for what is to come?"

He braced his hands against the desk and stared quizzically. I was no longer the young and foolish boy who had teased his uncle about his lessons in Latin.

"You speak as if I had a choice in this," he responded quietly. "Shall I stand idle, as another piece of land sacred to us is stolen from beneath our feet? Is that what you would have me do?"

His words shamed me.

"The emperor needs us. And he deeply regrets the attack against you. It has been the source of much sorrow and shame for him."

"Regrets his betrayal, don't you mean?" I grabbed the hilt of my sword. "Give me the order, your holiness, and I shall butcher the Byzantine dog myself!"

He studied me now.

"Yes, I believe that you would."

For years now the emperor had sworn to him that I (and my compatriots) had been ambushed by Turks at *Sophia Sancta*. I often wondered how that could be, since the only infidels there were his personal guards.

"They were under orders from the same man who had given the information to the Turks," he went on, as if telling me the old story anew. "The emperor, himself, found the gold hidden in the man's quarters, and sent out his troops, who executed him before freeing the others. At least I think that he wrote that he had … had the man executed. Or perhaps he had done so himself. I wish that I could remember what it was that he wrote exactly. Lord knows, I feel far older than I appear to be these days."

Executed him, he said? How was that possible, when his body was never found? Yet the emperor swore that the man was butchered. So I asked my uncle to explain it to me, moreover, as I was so profoundly ignorant in such matters, how it was possible that in the world's richest city, a Byzantine in the emperor's service would betray his own people for a few pieces of Saracen gold. Such a series of coincidences was virtually miraculous, was it not?

"I cannot deny that it stinks like a Greek trick," he replied after thinking upon it momentarily.

I could not recall his reference. Then I smiled, remembering that a Trojan horse had been a Greek's idea, after all. That Ulysses, he was ever the sly one.

"Why are you always so quick to condemn him?" he asked now. "He may very well be innocent."

Apparently it mattered little what I said to him. We had only the emperor's word that the man in question had been killed. For all we knew, the regent might have sent his loyal soldier to the farthest reaches of his empire, to live out the rest of his years in relative peace and luxury. Still, the Holy Father refused to recognize that Emperor Alexios Komnenos was no man to be trusted.

"Concerning his manipulations, his plots, in any case, they are what I would I would have done, were I in his position," I told him.

I believe that my statement frightened him somewhat. He backed away from the desk as if I had struck him. He regained his composure shortly thereafter.

"If we help him defeat those godless fiends, then the churches of the West and the East will be reunited. We shall once again have a foot in the Holy Land."

"And you will be once more Pope of Byzantium."

That was bad, very bad. I had allowed my anger against the emperor to strike out at my uncle, who had always acted more as my sire than as merely a paternalistic kinsman. Fortunately, the pain did not remain on his face for very long. A wistful look now found its seat there. Strange, I had not often seen him like that.

"It is not Byzantium that I crave, but Rome. Someday, when the political schemes for power are finished there, I shall take my rightful place upon the seat that has been set out for me in that holy city. Until then, I must attend to more pressing obligations. Do you believe that I take these actions solely for my own benefit?"

I could scarcely believe that my opinion mattered to him, though I must confess that he did not wait to hear it.

"Have you forgotten how reluctant I was to assume the rôle of pope? The first *millennium* has ended, and despite the predictions of all the prophets and soothsayers, our Lord has not yet returned to us. Many now believe that He will not come back for another thousand years, perhaps two. And yet the Most High does nothing arbitrarily. If Jesus is not here in flesh, then it must follow that this time belongs to His servants and their deeds. As the representative of Saint Peter, I, too, must build a rock upon which Holy Mother Church will forever stand. That means I cannot bury my head inside a book of prayer, refusing to hear swords rattle in the distance. These are times when even a pope must make alliances with people who are not worthy of his respect!"

For a moment I was unsure whether he were referring to me, though it was obvious that the anger was seething within him, and it was all that he could do to remain its master. He straightened his shoulders, lifted his head, raised one eyebrow, then clasped his hands behind his back.

"Mark well, nephew, what I am about to say; my predecessor, the blessèd Pope Gregory, excommunicated the emperor. Hungry for peace, I declared that order nullified. Without a shred of proof, I cannot reinstate it. Unfortunate though it may be, nevertheless it is still truth, that there be times when enemies must sit together at the same table and speak respectfully each to the other. If it were not so, there would be little left for us except the deaths of our children."

He paced back and forth, his head down.

"This emperor is as much a free man, worthy of friendship, as you or I. If he is indeed guilty, then he will have much to answer for, when the Lord above calls him to account. I want your promise that you will do nothing to harm him—"

I nodded reluctantly.

"When you arrive at his court with the others," he added, raising his head to stare into my eyes.

I was uncertain if I had heard him correctly. My uncle had always followed the *dictum* of Caesar Augustus, *festina lente, make haste slowly,* so as to minimize the possibility of failure in all things, which a man might undertake to do during the course of his lifetime. In his dealings with the emperor, he had acted no differently.

"It has taken me these full nine months to prepare since first his envoys came to me at Piacenza in Italy, in early March. I had to make certain that nothing could go wrong. You are of my blood. Unlike this emperor, I would not jeopardize your life and the lives of so many others needlessly. We both know that many innocent men died that day. You might have died with them," he said, coming over to where I was standing, "except for the love of God. You have been part of and witnessed a miracle." He placed his hands tightly upon my shoulders. "You have been given a higher purpose than ever before you may have had."

I pulled away slowly. How could I know what to say, what to do? And the last thing that I would have wanted was to hurt him.

"Holy Father, I am but one man—"

He smiled.

"It is doubtless that you will ever spend your days, or nights, in prayer, studying scripture. That matters little now. God has touched you, nephew. And whether it is in you to want to live a decent life or not is irrelevant. That choice is no longer yours. Your duty is to perform God's work. Together we shall become the means through which all our people will regain what we have lost. You will accompany our forces, responsible to one brave knight. I believe that you are acquainted with the man."

He called for the person standing outside the door to enter. In walked Hughes de Payens, brandishing his sword, laughing. He came over and threw his arms about me.

"With you there, my brother," he announced, "we shall be doubly blessed."

Even at such a moment he was still a man of noble nature and courtesy, and in vassalage to the church most faithful. In the intervening years we had become friends. And it was during a dinner in his castle one evening that I noticed his wife's languid pallor. I was certain that it betrayed her ill health, and as I was thinking that very thought, she fell from her chair. She never awoke. Her husband and sons wept bitterly all through the night and into the following dawn. It is my belief that he never overcame her loss, and why he rarely left the Holy Land to return to his estates years later. But you, dear reader, must forgive me—I am again rushing headlong into the middle of the tale.

The Holy Father informed me that I would ride with Hughes, Brother Michael, and several other goodly knights. We would likely leave the following August, after harvest. Our preparations were many, and he did not want to add failure to our innumerable sins. He was looking at me, and not at Hughes when he made that last comment. I took no offense. I did not believe that he had spoken in earnest. Of course, I had been wrong before and doubtless would be again.

CHAPTER THE THIRD,

in which the People's March cuts a wide swath on its way to the seat of Byzantium.

Peter (the hermit) d'Amiens, was a tiny, dirty, stinky, hairy man, who did not ride a horse. He rode upon an ass, a temperamental creature that moved forward only when the desire came upon it—a rare occurrence indeed! Many believed that it was his spiritual inclination that led him to ride the same animal that our Lord had upon His entrance into Jerusalem. And no one ever said that his actions could in any way be construed as presumption on his part, for so pure were his motives.

His shirt was of wool. A mantle covered it, falling to his ankles. Certainly his feet were bare most of the time. (I would have expected no less from a holy hermit!) Yet somehow, for reasons, which are beyond my intelligence, the people loved him. (Could it have been because he preached to the sinful and pure alike, seeing no distinction between them, as he always maintained in his sermons that our Lord, Jesus, had done? No thief, perjurer, adulterer, or homicide was exempt from his attentions, so careful was he to seek them out in the hope of purifying their spirits. Never did he concern himself with the state of their bodies either, which could have {on more than one occasion} used a bit more practice with daily ablutions. Then again, he never concerned himself with his own personal hygiene either. More's the pity.) Can you conceive of such a thing? They adored him. They would pull tiny hairs from his mule, and revere them as holy relics, which actions prompted the unfortunate beast to be even more vicious and uncontrollable than was its natural inclination. So when he called upon them to follow him to the Sepulchre of our Lord in the Holy Land, they rejoiced and set out—not very many knights surrounded by vast numbers of the common folk.

As Luck or Fate would have it, this was not to be Peter's first pilgrimage to the fabled land. In point of fact, once there, the Turks had turned him around immediately, after having given to him a great many cuts, which he showed often and proudly to his followers. Now, I am not a holy man filled with lust for a divine presence; I consider myself a pragmatist in most things. (Love is the exception. But tell me, dear reader, what man has not played the fool in an amorous game at least once?) Even I would have been loathe to join this *People's March*, led by an individual who was more at home with a psalter and a pitchfork than with a blade. Would that they had followed their minds instead of their hearts!

As most of the holy army waited to leave until the following year, Peter and the pilgrims set off immediately. They traveled first from France eastward into Germany. A strange people, these Germans. There upon the bogs and in the small villages of the Rhineland they flocked to him. They clung to his every word as though it were gospel truth direct from the Source of all things. Soon these pilgrims (men, women, and even children) swelled into the tens of thousands. (Later, many would think this march exclusively Teutonic in character. I am here to tell you that it was not, despite appearances to the contrary.)

Certainly the cross has been raised by many whose hearts were pure. And a journey requires preparation, the daily concerns for food and shelter notwithstanding. So it came to pass that this tired, hungry collection of souls, faithful followers of Christian mercy, found the first of many potential solutions to their needs in their ages-old neighbours, the Jews.

The situation was becoming desperate. Many were starving. It was proposed that stealing would be permissible, considering the righteous cause of the crowds, which were fast transforming into a single (and very large) mob. Then someone posed a slight variation of that same idea: why steal from a fellow Christian, when one can steal from a Jew? Then again, no one could really call it *stealing*. They had denied the Lord, left Him to die, in pain, alone. They were stiffnecked and uncircumcised in heart. What kindness could they possibly deserve? And rights? No one really believed that they had a right to anything, save perhaps to their own destruction. And upon this point, the many Germans knights were determined to make their unanimous agreement well known.

Peter's protestations could not stem the growing tide of violence.

"God will sustain you," he was wont to say, "through the dark times ahead, as he sustained me when the infidel came upon me and cut me so vigorously."

Such was his adage, indeed, his attempt to soothe the anger in their hearts. What he may have failed to recognize was that the Poverty and Want, which had shaped their lives so utterly, had blistered into the infection of Misery. And as so often happens when stomachs are empty, and a potential source of food is readily visible, Faith, like a tiny sparrow, flew out the open door. And though the populace loved him, they could not obey him. This may have been due in large part to his exceedingly gentle nature; or he may have forgotten (or may have never learned) that a lust for blood, once set to boil, cannot be calmed until it consumes all potential victims, and often itself.

In every city, from *Köln* to *Koblenz*, they fell upon the Jews, beat them, decapitated them, burned their houses of worship, (their *synagogues*), after which they took whatever of their money and jewels they could uncover. Those who had not been slaughtered, were forced to be baptized. Many Jews killed themselves rather than undergo this ultimate solution. (Their children were spared the terrible responsibility for these actions. The parents or relatives assumed the monumental burden of infanticide and any concomitant sin.)

It was in *Mainz* that they met one Emich von Leisingen, a count (or *Graf,* as the word is growled in their tongue). An unusually wrathful man, it was rumoured that he had been born with an equally unusual mark—the Lord's cross emblazoned upon his entire chest. That he, himself, was the source of such a tale could not be verified. He was only too happy to join the other pilgrims, provided that their ideals and his own matched. And if such a match might result in a significant decrease in the Jewish population, so much the better! He claimed that these killers of Christ stole Christian children from their homes, cut out their hearts, and drained their blood; these actions, he further maintained, were evidence of their practice in dark magics, overseen by the ever-present spectre of witchcraft looming nearby.

"We must drive these filthy Jews back into the primeval muck that was their birthplace," he iterated, then reiterated, then reiterated once more.

Christian blood began to boil.

The Jews of Mainz quitted their homes and sought refuge with Bishop Ruothard, hoping against hope that a son of the church, who had always treated them with respect, might be able to dissuade this Christian army from what was becoming a veritable Teutonic diversion. (A fatal error.) He was moved by their pleas. He issued a decree citing, amongst others examples, Pope Gregory I's protection of the Jews. The bishop wrote that the concern for a Christian must be his own salvation, and that the Jews were best left to God and *His* judgments upon them. In keeping with his merciful tone, he allowed the entire population of Jews to remain within or very near his quarters as sanctuary from the mob.

Unfortunately, no one listened to his word, not the laity, not the pilgrims, and certainly not the count. They came in the night, (as all wanton homicides do), smashed through the postern at the entry, broke into the bishop's living quarters, and stormed the gatehouse, forcing all Jews into the courtyard. With arrows and lances, with swords and fists they kept coming. Fearing for their lives, the bishop and his attendants ran off. The first Jew to die was their religious leader, their *rabbi*. They cut off his head. Those who were not killed, killed themselves, lest they fall into the hands of their enemies. Amidst all that carnage and blood, by dawn there was not a single Jew, not even one child, left alive in the entire province.

Though the swamps and marshes about fortified the garrisons, the pilgrims pressed on again. Crossing the Danube into Hungary, they besieged the royal fortress there for more than a month. At last they broke through its walls. The Jewish deaths had done little to slake their thirst for blood. Once inside the towns, they ran rampant, butchering, stealing, feasting, raping, until their bellies and maws swelled to bursting. Then came the soldiers of King Coloman. They rode down upon the invading forces as if they were no more than bothersome flies milling about the town's cesspools.

Frightened, the pilgrims left behind all their possessions, *i.e.*, their stolen booty. The count (and those who believed in his just cause) was the first to flee into Italy. It was then that I became involved. Several reports had reached the Holy Father, not only of the count's actions, but also of his presumed destination. Having incurred the wrath of Pope Urban II, who was determined to preserve the traditions of tolerance and mercy, which his predecessors had instituted, the count was now facing excommunication. (In addition to Hebraic slaughter, his holiness was equally unhappy about the dilemma that had been forced upon the bishop—a respected son of the church.) That, however, was not enough. He was determined to make the man responsible (an unrepentant homicide) learn a valuable lesson, that life is a gift and should be treasured. He repeated an early *maxim* to me, that whilst God's mercy may be infinite, (or so I pray that the forgiveness of a certain unnamed sinner may prove to be a relatively simple task at some undisclosed future date), His sense of justice has been known to lack a particular swiftness. Therefore, on occasion, He has had need of a corporeal instrument, who may, from time to time, exercise retribution, all with a papal blessing no less. The Holy Father sent me to Venice to instruct the man in a newfound appreciation of his life. More of this shortly.

In the meanwhile, the remaining pilgrims, having known but not having learned anything from the count's violent propensities and the consequences of his actions, pressed on. So successful were they in their prowess, that they burned cities to ashes. Onward they marched for some time. Then, of a sudden, they reached Konstantinople. And for a moment, in unison, they did not move. Neither did they speak. Never before had they witnessed such thick stone walls rising high above the highest trees, the façade ending in a parapet cut by crenellations, resembling the single tower of an enormous castle. Built centuries before, the walls now formed a fortification against the rest of the world, like a single fortress, stretching far into the horizon, the length of which was greater than that of an entire nation. And beyond these massive walls stood the spires of churches so high, that clouds gathered around their steeples. The tops of these towers took in all the sunlight, and glittered at the moment before it set. It was the first heavenly kingdom that they had ever seen (and perhaps the only one that they ever did see).

Upon reaching Byzantium, however, the emperor *advised* them to camp in the surrounding environs, at *Kivetos,* the better to await the arrival of their fellow pilgrims, as well as the forces of Pope Urban II. Many refused to listen. From thence they marched on through briars and thickets to *Nikaia,* where their determination to battle anyone who stood between them and their holy goals proved to be their undoing. (So just is the Lord in His judgments!)

As a result of having committed their atrocities, this contentious lot had gained a certain dubious notoriety—in short, they had caused themselves to be noticed. *Sultan* Qilij Arslan, whose forces were already preoccupied in other wars elsewhere in his kingdom, had to take a moment to ponder over the nature of this western rabble. In doing so, he decided to rid himself of these pests, which were a troublesome lot unworthy of the prowess of his brave soldiers. He sent a small portion of his forces to rout them, led by Kerbūgha, the Persian. So violent was this knight (and far hairier even than the hermetic Peter), that his ferocity led to a popular adage that quarrelsome lovers often threw at each other in the ensuing decades:

"Who do you think you are? Kerbūgha the Persian?"

He was only too happy to do his lord's bidding, and by doing so, prove that these were the most powerful fighters in the known world.

On a plain near the Turkish fortress, *Xerogord,* the sultan's man addressed Peter's compatriots, who were fortunate enough to count amongst their number one scholarly interpreter:

"Wherefore do you come to our land, dragging along your god with you? We reject him utterly, as we reject you. This land we took from a cowardly people, who proved unworthy in the eyes of the God. Their blood has watered the fields upon which our children play. If you deny your god, we shall welcome you. If you do not, we shall lead you in chains to serve us perpetually."

Once the Christian forces learned the nature of what had been stated, their representative, the aforementioned Peter, was going to respond when the Turks pelted him with horse manure—undoubtedly an improvement over his usual fragrance. In any case, his sometime-followers responded with sticks, stones, and staves, none of which proved a match for the seasoned warriors. Whilst seeking some avenue of escape, (or at the very least some refuge wherein they might dress their wounds), the remnants of this People's March took the Turkish fortress, which action would prove to have fatal consequences.

When reinforcements came against them, they had no choice but to dig themselves in behind those very same stone walls, which could serve now only as their prison. They did not realize that the structure lacked an internal water supply. A cistern outside its gates, and a single flowing fountain, provided the necessary life-giving elixir. The Turks filled the cistern with dirt and rock and smashed the fountain.

Despite the vast quantities of wine and meats, which had been stored therein, not long afterwards, the inhabitants of the fortress were reduced to slaughtering their steeds to drink of their blood. Shamelessly, some urinated into each other's mouth for a semblance of anything that appeared to be water. So great a weeping was raised therein, that defeat came swiftly. Many were killed. Some abjured their faith, turning instead to apostasy, preferring to embrace the beliefs of their conquerors, rather than accept a very painful death. Still others, particularly the girls of comely countenance and the hairless youths, were chained, to be sold in slave markets elsewhere. The few who did escape fled into the mountains or back to Kivetos, followed by their detested enemy. By the time that the Turks had finished, more than ten thousand souls, more than half of this People's March were dead.

When the Byzantine emperor heard of Peter's plight, he sent out his forces from across the empire. Ultimately they bested the Turks, then delivered one final message: Peter was to return home immediately; if his followers wished to remain, then they would have to wait until the forces of Pope Urban arrived; the emperor would not send aid to them a second time, should the occasion arise.

(He further sent them food and drink with which to sustain their needs.) Peter made his tearful farewells. Many chose to follow him whence they came. Others elected to perform future service to the Lord with a sword in their hands. (These stayed behind.) So, in an abandoned fortress, in sight of a golden land, a small portion of Peter's followers waited. And they waited. And eventually the holy army arrived.

Whilst Peter's pilgrims sat and waited, I arrived at the archipelago called *Venezia*. O, it was good to be back there again, in that most beautiful city, wrought of gold and silver, flecked incarnadine in the summer's twilight. Often had I spent many a wondrous evening there, when—Pardon; the lustrous quality of that place often makes me forget all save its marvels.

It was there that I reacquainted myself with the Contarini family, a grand and noble line, whose *paterfamilias*, the *Doge* Domenico, (both wise and wizened now in his final years), had rebuilt the basilica of San Marco only a few decades before, endowing it with a greater majesty and scope than its original builders had ever intended. (And so profoundly generous was he, that every morning he had alms distributed at his gates—a personal activity that would soon become a family's honoured tradition.) In their *palazzo*, filled with much multi-hued and intricately shaped glassware from one of their local islands, and *eikons* gilded in the Byzantine style, I was received most handsomely like the prodigal son, returning from years-long sojourns to the end of the world. In chambers filled with Frankish tapestries of hunting scenes and *terra-cotta* figurines, I informed my gracious hosts that the pope, *my uncle*, might call upon their resources shortly, as some army would soon arrive. They were most certainly agreeable, especially after I presented the duke with the papal scroll. (Though I was never privy to its contents, the document imparted such an angelic smile upon my host's face, that I would have sworn him, at that very moment, to resemble one of the many *cherubim* or *seraphim* flitting about in church frescoes. And for a brief moment his youth returned to his face. I wondered whether this was what happens to one whose many years have brought him so close to death. Does one return to a former glory, when unencumbered by the infirmities of age?) They introduced me to several shipwrights, who might have had some dealings with the Teutonic count. Though none had seen him, most were determined to give me the benefit of their guild-knowledge in each and every conversation, whether or not I had any desire to learn it, *e.g.*, how alder wood was perfect for a pole or mast, but oak was far more durable for planking. With no apparent success in finding him, I called upon several friends, (and a few others whose watchful gaze was discreetly purchased), to inform me of his arrival. Then, eventually, the man of distinction arrived.

Upon seeing him, I remembered a proverb of my mother's own making, and of which she had been most fond of repeating: "May the Lord save us from short men!" I never understood her until I grew to manhood. Then it was that experience taught me how a man, short of stature, will never seek the path of peace as his first choice. I wondered if the count would fall into the same pattern of behaviour as others of his ilk, as I followed him for several days, marking his ritual movements. He proceeded to ask several shipwrights what it might cost for a single vessel. And each time the price proved too extravagant for his means. He argued with one builder, claiming that the man should donate his services and products to the count's holy cause. The man responded that he might think upon the request seriously, if the Holy Father came to ask him personally to do so. The count cursed him and left.

Within several days, his remaining followers, much disappointed with the recent history of their mutual association, left him to seek their fortunes or futures elsewhere. On a blistering hot day, quite unusual for the early spring, I followed him as he entered San Marco, beneath the sculpture of the Byzantine lion that the duke had installed there. Once inside, within the vast vault, he walked over to the coffin that held the remains of Saint Mark. He did not linger long there in prayer. He was perhaps more taken with the high archways embedded with glittering tiles, and upon which were writ holy verses in the Latin tongue, surrounded by Biblical scenes in portraiture. It mattered little that the sources of light were few, for the entire *basilica* was filled with it, reflecting off and glowing upon every corner of the structure. He sat down in a pew and prayed silently for a short time, then left. I followed him to a secluded path near several residences.

"*Graf Emich von Leisingen!*" I called out to him in his guttural tongue.

He turned around. When he saw my hand at the hilt, he withdrew his sword from the scabbard.

"Who are you? How do you know me?"

I began to walk closer.

"You have been judged and been found wanting," I assured him.

"Judged by a thief?" he asked, laughing.

"By the most holy pope, Urban II, and by the Most High."

He stopped laughing.

"Who are you?"

"Guy de Lagery, the Holy Father's own kinsman."

He sheathed his sword.

"I have committed no sin. I have always performed the Lord's work. It is why I am here now. I have need of a ship that will take me to the Holy Land. Can you help me secure one? I would be most grateful."

"You have killed the Lord's Jews. Blood will have blood."

"You seek retribution for those creatures?" he asked with disgust. "They are not fit to eat slop with swine."

I walked closer.

"That is not your judgment to make."

Once again he withdrew his sword.

"I have no quarrel with you, good sir."

"Most unfortunate. I would have preferred a fair fight, but if you are determined to die without defending yourself, so be it."

He stood there, the Teutonic knight, swelling with pride over his courage to face the church's own swordsman; pride—a profound weakness! Once begun, our quarrel finished quickly. I had heard report of his proficiency with the blade. And I am ashamed to admit that he cut me twice. He fought neither with courage nor heart, however. Perhaps he was ready to die; I cannot say.

With swift stroke, I clove his body in twain, splitting his spine down the middle like a splinter. I wiped the sword's blood with his cloak, then turned to leave. Before I did so, I recalled the tale of his supposèd birthmark. With my sword I pushed aside his bald head, noticing now that he possessed the barest trace of a moustache and beard. His lack of hair reminded me of how, as a young boy, I had prayed for my chin and upper lip to be blessed with a full growth upon them, only to have to wait several years before my wish were eventually fulfilled. With the edge of my blade I removed the cloth covering his chest. Through the oozing blood I saw no such mark, except my own handiwork. I bent down to look at him more closely, then rushed to cover my nose. So it seemed that everything about this man was filled with a wretched stink. I arose and turned to leave. A sword fight was not uncommon in the larger towns then, nor in the very large cities. I knew that his body would not attract unwarranted attention. What I did not notice, until later that day, was that my wounds had healed completely.

On that fateful day in Venice, when the sun came to its zenith, warming the chill of the lagoon about me, I realized that my death might not be possible by any human hand. So I went first to San Marco to offer up a prayer for thanks, thence to the myriad amusements, which one might find only in grand cities. O, but it was good to be alive! Have I not mentioned that already?

CHAPTER THE FOURTH,

in which all and sundry commence our noble enterprise, the First Holy War.

Whilst four armies prepared to leave their homes and holdings, the pope (May he live forever in blessèd memory!) selected that moment in history for a quarrel with Brother Michael, the subject of which I was not to discover until long after its occurrence:

"You will do as I say," the Holy Father berated him, pointing his finger as if the old man were a disobedient child. "As long as I live, I am still your spiritual guide."

Though Brother Michael's desire to help may have represented his commitment to spiritual authority, I believe that it consisted primarily of his friendship with a man whose religious and political legitimacy was never in question, at least as far as Brother Michael was concerned. He would, if necessary, die to protect the pope in the internecine church struggles of the time—an act that his old friend always hoped to save me from doing. (My uncle, weighed down with familial obligations, wanted to keep his belovèd nephew far from his own problems, so as not to risk offending any of the players in the drama, should he lose his position and possibly bring vengeance down upon his house. The false pope, Guibert di Ravenna, had many powerful supporters in Rome. If the Holy Father only knew then what I was to discover later, I might have spared him his pain and brought destruction upon all the generations of his enemies. But he had other plans for me.)

"We were friends long before you became pope," Brother Michael said, smiling. "Is it really necessary for you to stand behind the vestments of your authority at this final stage of our lives?"

The anger that had transformed the Holy Father's face into a horrible mask melted away. His gaze became soft.

"I thank the Lord for your service every single day, my old friend. You must understand that your responsibility is no longer to my person."

"Is this about your nephew again?" Brother Michael asked with no attempt to conceal his impatience. "He can take very good care of himself."

"It is not his physical state that worries me any longer. Despite his having grown to manhood, still is he in need of guidance. His was never the scholar's nature to sit and study. That he ever did so and accomplish as much in his understanding as he has is a miracle that must be credited to the Most High, and not to my very loud voice or occasional slap of the wrist."

From his desk he took now a scroll that had been neatly tied, and handed it off to his old friend, who untied and rolled it open. After a moment or so, he looked up.

"Forgive me, your holiness; I am not the Latin scholar that your nephew is."

The pope told him that Archbishop Adhémar was in possession of one copy; Brother Michael would have another, should any harm befall the former. It was a warning, he maintained, that all who met his nephew would never write about him, under threat of excommunication.

Brother Michael was certain that he had heard incorrectly. He glanced first at the scroll, then at his friend, then at the scroll again.

"No one in the church," the pope repeated, "in the warring brotherhood now assembled, or even amongst the common folk is to write of his existence; no chronicler will leave behind a single document that might become an historical record."

"He is of your own blood. How could you do this to him?"

"Humility is a difficult lesson to learn," the pope uttered between sighs.

"He is no priest. He is a warrior. Let him have his glory."

"The glory belongs only to God. We are all subject to His final justice."

"No greater love has a man than he lay down his life for his friends. He died for you in Konstantinople. He died for all of us. I, myself, saw it with these eyes," he declared, pointing to them. "And he has returned from the darkness. I make no claim to understand how this happened. I am a simple man. Yet happened it did. Let history know him, praise him. With this you will remove him from the memory of man, as though he never existed."

The Holy Father would hear no more of it.

"Like it or not, he is as much a figure of the church as you or I. We have committed ourselves to the threefold vows of St. Benedictus' rule: poverty, chastity, and obedience. He is obedient occasionally; he has a fool's lack of concern for his finances; and the less said of chastity the better. In obscurity he will perform the Lord's work. It is fitting."

Brother Michael refused to listen. He said that despite my many sins, (Many?), I was still a great deal better than most men he had known. (That was kind of him, was it not?) And moreover, why should the pope snatch from me one of the few things, which a man may achieve for himself?

"He has been elevated to a place higher than most of us ever dream possible," my uncle affirmed. "So that he may discover his true purpose, I must do all that I can to forge him into the proper vessel."

For Brother Michael that was the final insult.

"What pride is this," he asked, "that makes you believe he cannot find his own way, and that only you are fit to lead him there?"

The pope's face grew as red as a hot coal.

"If any other man had spoken those words to me, I would have had him drummed out of the church and sent away, excommunicate, exiled!"

"O," Brother Michael exclaimed, jumping back, pretending that he had been struck, "save your bluster for your sermons. In these last years of my very long life, the only thing that I fear is God's *judgment!*" He pointed upwards. "That is something no one can call upon to use for his own benefit."

The pope was livid.

"Blasphemer!"

"Yes, and idolater, too. So there! Look at me, the world's greatest sinner," he said, raising both his arms and jumping up and down. "Excommunicate me. Do it! Maybe in Hell I shall find the peace that you denied me in this life."

They both glowered at each other for some time. Brother Michael was breathing heavily, when, finally, the Holy Father shook his head.

"Were you put upon this earth to torment me?" the latter asked.

"I think that the Lord put us both here to prevent us from being the prideful creatures we so often attempt to become."

His holiness laughed heartily.

"With you at my side, brother, I could never be guilty of that sin."

"Then my work here is done," his friend said with a smile and a bow.

But the pope was not yet finished with him. He was determined to convince Brother Michael that his decision would prove the best for me in time. Still, the latter was not convinced.

"If you, with all your love for him and the power of your station could not change him, of what possible use would an old war-horse like myself be? My place is here with you."

The pope would not be swayed from his convictions. After Brother Michael's wife had died, the old man came to his friend, the pope, asking to contribute the service of his remaining years to the greater good of the church. It was then that a stern warning was delivered: when one assumes the cowl, his obligation is to carry out church doctrine, whether one agrees with it or not; that is the terrible responsibility of the good Christian, especially of one devoted to a higher calling than most others. Brother Michael frowned.

"Are you reminding me of the past to silence my objections?" he asked.

"One should always remember where one has been and what one has learned whilst being there."

"I always believed that when you turned around to look at what was behind you, you turned into a pillar of salt."

Now it was the Holy Father's turn to make a face.

"Lot's wife never could behave, could she? Thanks be to God that you are not that woman, and that we are not standing before the cities of Sodom and Gomorrah, awaiting their impending doom."

"Are you certain that we are not?" Brother Michael asked.

The Holy Father made no response to his friend's query, except for this:

"You will do as I say, for I have asked you first as the church father, and finally as your friend." He walked over and stared sharply into the other's eyes. "I can tell from his letters and the good bishop's reports that his general understanding has deepened. That matters little. He has still so very much to learn. The demands of my position prevent me from being with him. I cannot be the angelic voice whispering in his ear each time that he thinks a sinful thought."

He looked at Brother Michael, perhaps to confirm his assessment. The latter turned away.

"You know that I am correct, old friend. You also know that our Lord did not spare him so that he might indulge himself in that way."

"He is a good man, worthy of your lineage. Never doubt that."

"He can be a better one. It is my fervent prayer that, like the sainted Augustine of Hippo, he will one day renounce his passions for great responsibilities. For all that we know, he may be the seeker who finds the Holy Lance."

Brother Michael stared at him, his mouth fully open, then recalled his friend's earlier statement to an assemblage outside upon a field.

"Confused is what I am," he said. "Did you not say that it was being kept in Konstantinople?"

The Holy Father shook his head and laughed.

"O, that was no more than a bit of speechifying, as a traveling player would orate to an audience. The truth is, I have no idea where the Lance is, nor does anyone else. I grant you, the idea of my nephew finding it sounds as foolish to me as it does to you. Still, I so wish to believe that he will achieve great things," he spoke with desperation, looking upward.

"Your wishes have outdone themselves is my fervent belief." Now it was his turn to place his hand on the pope's shoulder as a gesture of comforting. "I can only function as your substitute, in the faint hope that when he looks upon me, he will see his belovèd uncle. I can do no more."

He had no way of knowing if the action that my uncle was about to take, *via* the use of his scroll, would be the correct one; nevertheless, he had made a vow to obey the wishes of the church's own prince.

"I shall do what you ask of me, but my heart shall not be in it!"

He began to walk away, then stopped. Without turning around, he spoke:

"Did you ever think that God spared him out of pity for you?"

Once again my uncle sighed.

"More times than I can count. May the Lord go with you, my old friend. *Dominus vobiscum.*"

In a curious way Brother Michael knew that there was something in his friend's good-bye that had seemed so final. Nevertheless, he ignored it, for he was still determined to show dissatisfaction. And he left without turning around, unaware that he would never see him again in this life. And so, he bade him farewell:

"And with you. *Vobiscumque.*"

Godfrey de Bouillon, duke of Lower Lorraine, it was who, with his brothers Baldwin and Eustace, set out with many in their company as the first Frankish army. It was fitting that they should be first, since they could claim as their ancestor the greatest knight of Christendom, Charlegmagne. Despite their ties of blood, however, Godfrey and Baldwin were two so complete contradictions, that the world had rarely seen the like. Godfrey was the eldest and tall; Baldwin was the youngest and far taller. Where Godfrey was blonde and fair, Baldwin was dark and ruddy. Where Godfrey's features were sharp, Baldwin's were fleshy, though his nose was aquiline. Where Godfrey dressed in mail and leather, Baldwin dressed in monkish robes. Yet, where Godfrey was pious, ascetic, kind, Baldwin was—More of this shortly. (Eustace stood in the middle between the two extremes, and was, essentially, a curious combination of the two, as if both halves had been sewn together in a patchwork cloth that somehow never fit quite right. Perhaps that was why the man was never satisfied with anything. He, too, will be examined further.)

Bohémond, the Norman prince of *Tarentum* in Italy, and his nephew, Tancred d'Hauteville, left with the second army. (He it was in whose company Hughes de Payens, Brother Michael, and I were to make our way In point of fact, when he met Brother Michael for the first time, he said: "A holy man with a sword—my favourite type of prelate!" Then he laughed, more taken perhaps with his own observation, I believe, than with any of the old man's habits or characteristics. But that might have been an unfair assessment of the man's character. Only time would reveal the truth.) This Norman was the tallest man whom I had ever seen, (or would ever see in my lifetime), a veritable giant even. Despite his great height, he walked with a slight stoop. Unlike the rest, this knight kept his fair hair quite short, exposing his ears, and he wore no beard. (In truth, he looked more like a Roman *senator* than a Norman knight of the current era.) With shoulders broad, and skin like milk, he conveyed a frightening image to any and all who would call him *enemy*. This very brave warrior had fought with his father, the noble Robert Guiscard, against that same Byzantine emperor into whose kingdom we would eventually find ourselves encamped. That was not five and ten years prior, and the Byzantine had bested him—something that the Norman would never forget. Very much more of this later.

The third army had two leaders—one temporal, the other ecclesiastical. Raymond IV, Count de Toulouse and St. Gilles, shared equal control with Adhémar, the pope's belovèd archbishop. Whereas most of the leaders had years in their thirties and forties, both of these men were in their sixties. Despite the rigours of the campaign, their age belied their determination to succeed, as well as their expertise with weaponry. These men led the Provençals.

Four men took charge of the fourth and final group: Hugh, Count de Vermandois and brother of King Phillip I de la France; Robert de Flandres, a bold man much in love with conquest, and an acquaintance of the Byzantine emperor; Robert de Normandie, whose father, William the Conqueror, had taken England as his own not thirty years prior, and the final player in the drama—Stephen de Blois, who was married to Adela, the daughter of that same conquering William. And if you, dear reader, will permit me a moment's digression, I would prefer to say a few more words about these individuals.

Hugh and the Flemish Robert, were knights first and *carriers of the cross* second. By this I mean that they lived for the glory that only war might offer. (A holy purpose to any possible conflict was a mere *adjunct* to it all.) It was not the possession of new territories or the lure of fabulous jewels, which tempted them;

it was the spilling of blood. They believed that victory over one's enemies was the nobleman's obligation both to his society, and to his Maker. Anything less would confirm the man's unworthiness to his position as bulwark against the unseen foe, who was always sniffing about, ready to pounce, ready to steal all that society had named as its treasures.

Though the son of that war-like William, Robert de Normandie was always the first to espouse these ideas of knightly conduct, and the last to take up a sword in defense of anything. He had no love for the heat and dust of travel, and often made certain that everyone was aware of his displeasure. In this respect, he was more akin to the husband of his sister than to his own blood.

And speaking of that same sister's husband, we come now to Stephen. For him life was somewhat different than it was for the other leaders—filled with merriment and celebration, it was. In his court the minstrels sang, and there was much of dancing, and no less of jubilation. He so enjoyed the festivals in his lands, that he really did not want to join the others upon this *crusade* (or *croisade* as his dear wife had come to call it). Unfortunately, as the adage goes, there are three things which might send a man out of his comfortable home and into the cold, dark night: a leaking roof, a blocked chimney, and a shrewish wife. Whereas his castle was always maintained in pristine working condition, his beloved helpmate was known for her very vocal means of letting her husband know her wishes. (Some have said that she was very much her father's daughter in that respect, but I have a feeling that the sire's desire to leave home and amass foreign territories may have had less to do with his own violent behaviour, and more to do with some rather profound vocal exhortations to do so, courtesy of *his* lifemate. Certainly, I assure you, this is mere conjecture on my part.) Ultimately, Stephen realized that he had little choice except to go. Such a conclusion made his wife very happy. She said not a word when she kissed him and bade him good-by. (It was rumoured that he wept a tear or two when he left his home behind; not so his queen. He would later spend the entire winter lolling about Italy in relative luxury and comfort, whilst the rest of us were being fêted in Byzantium, or already engaging the enemy in surrounding territories. A letter containing a word or two from his wife finally prodded him into leaving there and achieving the fulfillment of his righteous mission.)

And there you have it—the royal fresco of personages riding through foreign lands towards the unknown. (No one ever really knew how many souls had taken up the cross for this blessèd pilgrimage. The Norman assessed the number to be several hundred thousand. Based upon observations and discussions, I think that count a fairly accurate one. I have, since those fateful years, heard accounts of millions. I assure you, such wishful thinking would have served no one's cause, save the fool's, who was determined to transform his fellow Christians into a seemingly endless source of battle-fodder.) Of them all, only two had experience fighting what we had come to call the *infidel*—Raymond, who had bested and been bested by Moorish Spain, and Bohémond, who, with his father, had defeated Arabic *Sicilia*. They were the perfect choices for such an expedition. The Norman, however, felt differently from his comrades about his forthcoming journey. Perhaps it was because of his adopted home and the Italians' long naval history, that he and his forces struck out by vessels. And there on board, sharing our company with brave soldiers, the finest horses, grand provisions, and numerous bows, axes, and all manner of armaments, beneath multitudinous banners arrayed across our bow like shields of crosses, we had plenty of time to acquaint ourselves with the essential men we were.

Our early-morning ritual never altered. Bohémond, Tancred, and I always found ourselves at the prow, exchanging greetings, as we relieved ourselves into the ocean. Of course, one had to be most careful, lest the wind (A fickle mistress indeed!) decide to change direction; in which case our own waste might have a tendency to find its resting place upon our faces. Thankfully, this never happened to the three of us. (Other knights, or so I have been told, were not so fortunate.)

Shortly after the dawn of one particular day, I decided to put into action an idea upon which I had been ruminating in recent times. I had always loved the sea, and thought that if I had not become a knight, the prospect of becoming a ship's captain held equal fascination for me. Growing up bounded by farms and plains, I yearned, even as far back as I can now recall, for a landscape whose breadth and majesty could feed my spirit in a way that was far different from the one to which I had grown accustomed. As much as I gazed with awe at streams and rivers, nothing could compare with the moment when my uncle first took me to the sea, and I stepped upon sand, watching the waves break near my feet. My heart soared! There was water everywhere, as far as the eye could see, roiling, crashing, all the way to the ends of the earth. I would laugh as the wet salt scratched my face, and the seawinds yanked at my hair. And as I stared with child's eyes in wide amazement, I wondered what lay beyond the horizon. I wondered if I would ever see what was out there.

So after I tucked away my manhood safely, I climbed up and jumped. Bohémond's mouth fell open, as his nephew grabbed him by the arm. But instead of watching me swim around in the morning sun, surrounded by strange sea creatures, they saw a bold knight bounding back and forth over the oars, and laughing wildly.

Tancred could not believe what had happened.

"May God pity our most Holy Father," he said, "for his bloodline is infected with lunacy."

His uncle simply smiled.

"Mark him well, nephew. It is one of the few times in your life that you may see a man who is truly without fear. He once spat in the face of Death when the shade came to take him. Why, if I had had twenty knights like him years ago, Byzantium would now be mine. This is a good omen, a very good omen. I can taste the blood of victory upon my lips even now."

He walked away laughing, as Tancred continued to stare.

Others came and looked over the edge into the watery abyss. I have no idea what prompted them to do so, but they laughed, then jumped headlong into the depths. Soon there was a veritable crowd below me, swimming about (or nearly drowning as the case may be), and roaring with amusement like children. How could I begrudge myself their joy? Of course I jumped in. Tancred, however, failed to participate in our current situation and stayed rooted there in that same spot, staring. (I do not believe that the nephew ever liked me; not that I ever cared about that particularly. I simply thought that I would mention it in passing.)

Of a sudden the flocks flew off, when the salt-air became filled with an almost palpable sense that something was about to happen. And so it did! There was a great commotion in the distant waters. They bubbled up, as if a mountain peak were about to burst forth from the deep. Then it came. I dared believe that my eyes had betrayed me. He was dark like the bottom of the ocean, and must have been longer than the length of ten men lying end to end. It was him—Leviathan, in all his frightening majesty, the monster of countless legends, as old as the Holy Word, Itself. His skin was so black, that it shone in the early morning light. The streams of water fell from his flanks swiftly, as if he were covered with pitch, and the drops could not cling to him and dry away in their own good time. As he sailed upward, his arms spread wide like bird's wings, or English longbows flattened and smeared white upon the underside.

When the men saw what I had, they swam back to the ship, faster than sight, fearing (I supposed) that they would be swallowed up like poor Jonah of old. Many screamed; others shouted to be rescued. Brother Michael called to me from on board, though I could not make out a single word in the watery din. Ropes and rope ladders were slung over the sides, so that the men could climb up and away to their safety. I chose to stay and watch. Somehow I knew that I would remain unharmed, that he would take no notice of the tiny creature so far away. In fact, no sooner had he flown into the air, when he came back down with a crashing thud onto the glimmering surface. A mountain of water flew up and about him. He sank beneath, as his long tail shot up and splashed his farewell to me. That such a giant was content to share the world with people and insects filled me with awe at God's infinite majesty, grandeur, and variety. And I was humbled.

The others called for me to return. Finally, after seeing no more of him, save the dark hump of his back cutting the waves, I swam back slowly, savouring every moment of my grand adventure upon the sea. This was truly an age of miracles, was it not?

CHAPTER THE FIFTH,

*in which all and sundry arrive at the fabled empire of Byzantium,
only to discover that it appears to be like every other place, where one
is not wanted.*

In Arlona, at the foot of the Byzantine realm, we disembarked and struck camp. Having arrived without any fanfare, (I was uncertain if the emperor were expecting us or not), nevertheless, the preparations took most of the day and on into the night. It was dawn of the following morn when the Norman prince rode out to survey the troops. High atop a hillock he looked about, wearing the same mask of intense seriousness that he always did, whenever he was addressing those under his command.

"We are God's pilgrims in a Christian land," he began. "That means we must do what is proper, what is just. We shall take what we need from this place and its people so that we may live. Anyone who wishes to glut himself will have to answer both to God and to me. Whilst the Lord's mercy may be infinite, you will find that mine has its limits. I am not so forgiving of unnecessary cruelty."

We rode into the valley of Andonopoli, met with its people, (most of whom, we soon discovered, were afraid that these strangers in their midst might kill them wantonly), and traded for supplies and foodstuffs. In their marketplace, (their *agora*), we found dried meats and fruits, numerous grains, fish, and live fowl, the latter squawking riotously.

"Truly a wonder to behold!" remarked Brother Michael, gaping at the bounty before our eyes.

And verily it was so, for livestock and grain were all in abundance. There were books to be had as well. I leafed through one that had caught my eye because of the three distinct shapes etched into its cover: a square, a triangle, and a circle. Inside were all manner of figures bisected and measured in fragments. Since the writing was Greek, I was able to determine only the author's name: Euklid. So this was one of his studies on the subject of *geometria*. I wanted to purchase it for my uncle, (who, I think, sometimes preferred the logic of mathematics to the seeming insanity of church politics), only to discover that the seller would not agree to any form of currency or item of trade. I thought that most unusual, however, I decided not to argue with him, lest my company evince little patience for one of their own haggling with a bookseller over no work of war machines, mind you, but one of numbers.

So I walked on and saw many cloths of strange design. There were fabrics so fine and transparent, that they might have been spun from spiders' webs. And they were soft to the touch, as if they bore no weight upon the body of its wearer. Rarely had I seen the like.

I noticed Hughes exchanging a few coins for two pieces of cloth—one black, the other white. I could not fathom his purpose, so I walked over and asked him of it.

"I thought that I would stitch together my personal standard of two plain colours," he explained, "in comparison to all the rainbows, which everyone else feels necessary to hold aloft as a symbol of personal honour. I thought that, when we reach the gates of Jerusalem, our Lord might prefer to see something less garish. Do you think it a foolish notion, my friend?"

I did not think so at all. (In truth, Hughes de Payens was one man who was the least concerned for his own matters of fame. In that was he most humble.)

As I made my way through the crush of people, I noticed that our purchases (or trades) were not what I had initially expected them to be. Though the inhabitants appeared friendly, it was obvious to all of us that the lambs, pigs, and chickens were really the runts of their respective litters. Surprisingly, rather than cause any fighting over this matter, Bohémond chose to make do. (I can only assume that with the enemy before us, he did not wish to expend his forces against a potential foe behind us as well.)

Not one day had passed when, only moments before sunrise, a guard ran into the prince's tent, hoping to awaken him from his deep slumber. The man, himself, was already up and about.

The whispers of something looming in the distance spread like midsummer fires through fields of dried brush. We all ran to see row upon row of knights, neatly arranged up to the very line of the horizon. A short, stocky knight of perhaps fifty years or so rode up in front of the others. His armour was well worn. He carried his helmet in one hand, (a peaceful gesture, I assumed), exposing his thick shock of mussed, dark hair.

"I am Tatikios, captain of the guard," he proclaimed. "The illustrious Emperor Alexios Komnenos welcomes you to his lands, and orders you to take a vow of fealty to him. This you must do; then I shall convey you into the most beautiful city in all the word, Konstantinople, where you will make your vow to the illustrious Emperor a second time."

There was much grumbling from our men. Tancred's face turned red.

"I shall swear him an oath," he spoke quietly.

The Norman giant did not remove his eyes from the Byzantine captain, as he reached over to his nephew's shoulder and clutched it tightly. Tancred pulled back in pain.

"How many times must I teach you how to behave in front of your enemy?" the uncle asked through clenched teeth. Then he held his head high and smiled to the captain once more.

Brother Michael, who had been standing nearby, whispered into my ear:

"These Greeks speak our language," he said with much wonderment. (I loved the old man, even when he did have a gift for stating the obvious.)

"For a soldier he spends a great deal of time upon ceremony," I commented.

Our leader continued smiling at the captain, though he addressed me:

"Noticed that as well, did you? You must have some Norman blood in your family's history. Tell me, did you also notice that it is not the finest armour that one might wear for a ceremonial occasion? It is of the sort that one has worn to many battles. This soldier may have other plans."

"The emperor's preparations for us have been quite thorough," Hughes de Payens added, looking over the knight as well.

"Go to him, Sir Guy," the prince told me. "Mount a horse. Sit straight when you ride up to that servant," he spoke with mild offense. "Welcome him into our camp. Never stop smiling as you do so. I want our guest to be comfortable when he is eating and drinking from our stores."

I do not believe that the Byzantine captain was prepared for the sumptuous feast that our leader had spread before him, as his look of disbelief betrayed his feelings. (Or it could be that he did not expect to see that his own people had been so *generous* in their trading.) At any rate, his stomach was quite full when our leader began his attack:

"We shall make our pledges, though only to the emperor, himself."

"I have been told that you must first swear the oath to me," the captain insisted.

"I could care less what you have been told. The emperor has asked for our help. We are here to provide it, unless he would rather not have it." He stood up. "When he asks why we left, you can tell him that it was your fault."

All of us were smiling, anxiously awaiting the captain's next response.

"Mine?!" he asked, exasperated. "But I have said what I was asked to say. Please sit."

The Norman looked down upon the captain for a moment or two before complying with his request.

"You must understand," the Byzantine continued, "this is an imperial order. All will obey."

"We are not his vassals. We are his allies. The subtlety of that difference may be lost upon you, not upon us. It is unreasonable to ask us to pledge an oath, when we have come here in fellowship, not enmity."

The captain informed the Norman that it was not the former's position to judge if an edict were unreasonable; he simply did what he was told, which was any soldier's duty.

"Is it also your duty to demand of foreign princes how they should act when upon your soil?"

"I demand nothing of you, Prince Bohémond. I am a messenger only."

The Norman was not pleased with the response.

"What sort of message are you trying to convey with your ranks of armed men?"

"It is custom, my lord," he answered with some hesitation.

"We are not Saracens."

"I have done what I—"

"What you have been told. Yes. I shall tell you something, my good and dear captain of the guard; we have come here from the other side of the world. Many of us have left behind everyone and everything we have ever held dear. And many have died along this journey. There is not a soul amongst us who will not pledge to anyone except the emperor, himself. If that is a problem for you, then you will have the privilege of watching our backs, as we return whence we came. The choice is yours."

Said choice (repeated once again for the captain's benefit, lest he fail to remember its import from the Norman's previously veiled threat) did not sit well upon the captain's shoulders. He began to sweat. Then, as he pondered his options, he began to sweat more profusely. His discomforture was as painful for us to witness, as was his experience of it. After several very long moments, he reluctantly agreed to give the Norman entry through the city's gates.

"We shall make preparations to leave at dawn," the prince said, smiling.

The captain feared that he had not explained himself fully; only the prince was permitted entry.

A hush fell over the entire assemblage. We all stared at our leader, waiting for what he might say next. He smiled again as he looked down upon all of us.

"*Alone*, you say? How interesting! Your emperor must realize that he is making an unreasonable demand. Don't you think that he is being unreasonable, captain?"

"It is not my place to question my lord."

The Norman demanded to know what the emperor had said would be a *reasonable* number of men. The captain was visibly uncomfortable, perhaps embarrassed that the Norman had uncovered the truth of a conversation to which only he and his master had been privy. Nevertheless, he pressed on with some sort of explanation:

"We never discussed numbers," he insisted.

"Is one hundred an unreasonable amount?"

The captain laughed.

"Then will five and seventy suffice?" the prince asked.

"No more than five and ten," the captain spoke with a final shrug.

"O, a fine number! Is that the one your emperor gave to you, or did you create it all by yourself?"

The captain's hand reached for the hilt of his sword, or so I thought. As he did so, I also reached for mine. But there was no need. His hand moved over and rested upon his knee. I caught the Norman's eye as he watched me pull my hand away from my sword. He shook his head ever so slightly. The captain did not catch either movement, I believe.

"On the morrow then," the Norman concluded. "It will be a fine day, one that may change the entire world. Wouldn't you say so, captain?"

The captain said nothing as he looked around at all of us, who had followed our Norman leader's example and were also smiling quite broadly, some even open-mouthed, mind you!

CHAPTER THE SIXTH,

in which we witness all manner of Byzantine wonders.

At the time of the First Holy War there was a saying being bandied about: two-thirds of the world's gold could be found in Konstantinople, whilst the remaining third had been scattered by the Four Winds to the ends of the earth. We had all heard of its untold riches. A few of the company had even witnessed the wealth firsthand, either through trade or in time of war. But there are no words sufficient for me to describe what it felt like to pass through that golden city, where could be found the largest church in the world—*Hagia Sophia*. As we rode by, it reminded me of the *Colisseum*, except this structure possessed an enormous dome-shaped roof, covering its soaring columns.

Tatikios stopped us a moment, that we might admire the handiwork of Byzantine craftsmen.

"Only a great empire can build a church like that," he declaimed proudly.

"Only a great empire can afford to do so," Brother Michael whispered to me.

A short time later, we arrived at the humble quarters of the illustrious Emperor Alexios Komnenos and his fortunate family.

Unlike the castles and fortresses throughout the world at that time, many of which I would come to see, and many of which I would hear tell, there was no gaping hole in the earth surrounding its foundation. (The typical access into such a structure was usually a drawbridge, thus making it far more difficult for any invading army to breach its walls, so high was the actual entrance above the earth-proper.) There was only level or stepped ground stretching out onto the boundaries of imperial territories. And gardens everywhere! There were orchids and lilies and roses, the colours of which fought against their own sun-dappled shades for supremacy. I would never see their variegated enticements in my life again. There were acacias, fragrant cedar, oak, and willows so tall, that their branches overflowed like water from mountain falls on high. There were orchards spread out before us across terraced levels sparkling green. I smelled the perfumes of flowers and fruits, fig trees and pomegranates, apples, and an arbor covered with grape vines. It was a heady mixture, and very nearly overwhelming. Of course, guards were all about, eying us suspiciously, as we made our way. A moment before I crossed the imperial threshold, I espied several tiny stalks of *dianthus* bending towards the sun, and the sight reminded me, I had almost forgotten that it was early spring.

Once inside, what surprised me was the lack of a centralized tower or corridor. The palace consisted of pavilions all tied together by a series of barrel-vaulted audience-halls. Everywhere were standing *torchieres* or censers suspended from the walls, filling the vault above and all things around with more light than I had ever thought possible to be contained within a single room. And each large chamber or corridor was filled with colonnades. I had not seen that much marble in one place since my visits to the Italian kingdoms. And the tops of these columns, so high above, were *acanthus* leaves, no doubt in imitation of the ancient Greek models, all impeccably gilded. Above these were the vault-murals. I thought it strange that the subject matter was ever the same—a naked warrior battling gigantic, fantastical beasts with a short sword, (much too short for the task at hand, I thought), a maiden watching her belovèd from a safe vantage point in the distance. And not a single image was remotely Christian in character.

Hughes de Payens, Brother Michael, and I were amongst those who followed the Norman past the battlements and on into one of the great halls. (Tancred had been ordered to stay behind, which fact initially displeased him, until his uncle informed him of the absolute trust that he had in the former's abilities to lead the army, should the need arise.) Engaged in walking, almost falling over ourselves as we stared at the ornate decoration and furnishings, (all except our leader), we barely noticed the Count de Toulouse standing near one of the columns, his arms folded, the faintest shred of a smile crossing his thin lips.

"This is truly an age of wonder," he began, as our leader passed him. "The mighty warlord, Bohémond, has deigned to grace us with his presence at last."

Across from where Raymond stood, near another column, Robert de Normandie wore a sour expression.

"Do you have any idea how many weeks we have been wasting our time here?" he asked of the Norman.

Bohémond pursed his lips then smiled.

"Calm yourself, my friend," he told Robert. "There will be time enough for killing."

"We have been entertained by a royal hospitality that knows no limits," Raymond added. "It would appear that excess is a Byzantine failing."

"Don't you mean, *sin?*" the Norman asked, looking around.

Whilst the three laughed then debated the nature of sin and politics, I made acquaintance of Godfrey and his brethren. I was received warmly, though Eustace spoke barely a word. I had come to know (and would later come to know) men, who would wear *melancholia* in the same fashion that a knight would his favourite armour that had carried him safely through many a campaign. At the time I was uncertain if this were true of Godfrey's brother, but I thought it to be. He was morose, sullen, his face forever downcast, his only humour saturnine. If he were capable of any *modicum* of happiness, it was clearly not visible to me (nor to most of the others who shared our company).

But none of us had time to ponder these sicknesses of the soul. We had a war to win, and much planning ahead. So after conferring with me upon my uncle's health, the archbishop took me over to a corner, where he probably thought it best to share his thoughts concerning our Norman leader in private.

"Never forget that notwithstanding his princely station, he is first a warrior. And such a man always remembers who gave to him his losses in battle. He is still waging his father's war. These Byzantines will never be anything more to him than potential victims. Be suspicious of his judgments, is my advice to you. Despite his hatred and concomitant mistrust of them, I fear that he may be correct. I know that the Holy Father wishes to believe the best of them. So do we all. The truth, however, may prove that they deserve far less than we may be all too willing to grant them. Tread carefully in this land, my son. Trust only your blood."

After having imparted his advice, he joined the Norman and the others for a meeting of strategy and tactics. Instead of asking me into the session, Bohémond bade me survey the castle and its grounds, and to familiarize myself with the locations and numbers of troops, after which time I was to report to him personally with all the details. As I walked away, I realized the full import of the archbishop's advice. Who was here from my family? No one. Did that mean I should trust no one here? Not even Brother Michael or my old comrade, Hughes? Verily, I was a stranger in a strange land!

All about were the empire's standards, most of which were mounted upon poles higher than a man—the red cross of Saint George in the center, handsomely wrought against a white background, with the Greek letter, *beta*, or *b*, in blue, sewn into its four corners. (It would be a long time before I discovered the ancient motto that those letters represented.)

As I walked past them, what suddenly struck me as odd was that no guards accompanied or followed me at a safe distance. In truth, I cannot say why. Perhaps it was because of my uncle's position. Though the more I thought upon it, the less I was inclined to believe it so. Over the years the emperor's unflagging insistence, that an attack by a guard in his service had never been prompted by him, served only to inflame my anger and resentment, not quell them. Whatever the reasons, I knew eyes were upon me somewhere, watching my every move.

Throughout the palace there were women strolling about, their faces covered by sheer black veils, wearing fabrics which shone with intricate beadwork. I believed that they were gossiping about us in half-whispers; not that it would have mattered if they had used their normal tones of voice. Very few of us spoke Greek, and even fewer understood more than a handful of phrases, myself included. As I walked past them, I noticed something curious—a young girl was poking her head around various columns. (Strange that her face was uncovered!) I supposed that her curiosity prompted her to do so, and perhaps it would have been a breach of etiquette, had she appeared without her veil.

At one point I felt someone staring at me. I turned quickly to behold the blackest eyes, which I had ever seen. They belonged to this same young girl, who, upon meeting my gaze, flew off, the train of her gown trailing behind her like some forlorn lover. But the peculiar feeling of being stared at did not disappear with her absence. I turned again, this time to see those selfsame dark eyes peering into me. They belonged to the emperor, himself.

The captain made the necessary introductions. The empress and her various female attendants were all veiled. At the emperor's right side stood a young man quite proudly, and who, I was to discover later, smiled as often as our Norman leader. He was a much more youthful version of the emperor, possessing both his strong jaw and eyes of ebony. Our forces had been gathered together in an enormous hall, so large in fact, that when the emperor spoke, his voice echoed through it completely:

"All those who come in peace are welcome to Byzantium," he announced, and ended as abruptly as he had begun.

His entire retinue turned and left. We all exchanged glances, wondering if there would be anything further. The captain informed us that there would be a feast served in our honour that evening, where we would be joined by the empress and the imperial children, whose names he related: the Empress, Irena, the son, Paleologos, and the daughter, Anna. I found the boy's name most rare, due to its length and sound, as if it belonged to a scholar of legend, and not to a potential ruler. (It had been my experience, until then, that most regents could never, in any fashion, be considered scholars of anything. Unfortunately, time would never alter that assessment.) As for the girl, her name was deceptively simple and direct—qualities which I would later come to associate with her in every way.

The captain had servants show us where we could stay. As we followed, Brother Michael shook his head.

"To think that I would live to see Byzantium! Now that I have, I see that it is a bit too rich for my blood. I hope at least we will not have to sit near that little Greek," he said, watching the captain walk off.

"Why?" I asked.

"His breath smells like feet."

At that, Bohémond's hearty laughter bellowed from his large frame and filled every chamber with incessant echo.

CHAPTER THE SEVENTH,

in which the feast begins and ends, in more ways than one.

Guards led us into the dining hall. As we entered, we heard no bard singing of love's agony or the glories of war, all whilst strumming his lute. Instead, we were greeted with the clarion-blast of trumpets everywhere. I grabbed at my ears, for I was momentarily overcome with deafness. Both Raymond and the archbishop gritted their teeth. I can only surmise that their lack of youthful endurance had betrayed them at last. And how cruel it was of our gracious host to stir the physical agony of these two fine (though quite old) men.

The table was long. (And I have seen many an oak board spread out for feasting in many a castle, mind you!) I had never seen one *that* long. (Nor would I ever again. In point of fact, Brother Michael's gaze spent quite some time in the perusal of its length, as he stood there, his mouth agape.) I thought fifty or sixty individuals could be seated quite comfortably around it. The emperor assumed his customary position at one head. Instead of assuming the other side, his empress sat down in a chair over in a corner with her daughter; both were still veiled. (I found out later that the women of the family only sat and ate unveiled at this table when there were no guests or dignitaries about.) The son was at his right hand, the captain at his left. I had hoped to position myself as far from the regent as possible, but my desire was not to be. One of the guards, upon his master's order, made certain that I be placed next to the son, with the Norman prince at my right. The others of our company were placed in what I believed to be a random arrangement, save the archbishop, who was shown the chair next to the captain.

As we began to take our places, I noticed how the empress was watching her husband. Though I could see only her eyes, I knew that she was staring at him with what might have been considered a visible concern. Perhaps she worried that his Frankish guests would slip the contents of a draught of poison into his forthcoming wine. In a curious way I supposed that I envied him her devotion.

Though only the upper portion of her face were visible, I knew that she was lovely, her body well-formed in her tight clothing, her arms and legs supple. Indeed, she was much younger than he—a marriage typical of the age, wherein an old man, once infatuated with a much younger maiden, would then become affianced to her. Nevertheless, she had borne him two children, come to care for him, nay, even love him. Was ever a man so fortunate?

Before the food had arrived, or any conversation begun, the guards left the hall, as musicians entered. They carried cymbals, flues, a viol, and other stringed instruments, the like of which I had not previously seen. They sat and began to play a soothing melody (not one of celebration). Its tone was somber, elegiac. I thought it rather an odd choice, though not unexpected, when I saw that there were no dancers about. I wondered if it would stoke the embers of Eustace's humours. He did in fact sit and say nothing—a markèd improvement over his appearance of perpetual dissatisfaction.

As they played on, the musky fragrance of cooked meats began to mingle with their music. My stomach growled with anticipation. I smelled lamb, most likely clad in onions and garlic. The prince, who was a friendly sort, though not overly so, assured me that my initial impression was correct, and that it was his favourite food as well. (An amiable boy, I wondered what sort of man he was destined to become.)

Serving-men appeared, bearing tiny bowls filled with water. I learned that we were supposed to wash our hands in the liquid provided, prior to the commencement of our meal. An unusual request, even if some of us did so without too great a deal of complaint. (Several, however, carped bitterly and thought this ritual cleansing to be one more filthy custom of these strange Byzantines.) When the bowls were removed, the servants appeared again, carrying intricately wrought goblets and bejeweled chalices for our use. No one could believe the extravagance, especially Brother Michael, whose mouth had never before fallen open to the degree that I saw it that night. Maidservants, (veiled, of course) brought out flagons of wine, and poured the contents into our magnificent cups. Then the cooks entered with all manner of foodstuffs. Having arrived on silver chargers were partridges and hens, wild boar, and very many lambs, both their legs and heads. Several of the meats were covered with herbal sprigs, which (whilst resting now upon the heated flesh of the animals) released an aroma that only added to the flavor of the entire experience. It was the perfect perfume for dining. (And ah, the meat would be so succulent! Though I cared little for animal heads interspersed amongst their legs, I had been told that the flesh was a Byzantine delicacy.)

I can assure you that, whilst not unpleasant, it was far from my favourite form of nourishment.)

As we prepared to partake of the feast, we were suddenly delayed. The emperor pointed to the small bronze replicas of knights upon horseback, which we all assumed was a curious means of honouring our presence at his table. Little did we suspect that each knight could be removed from his saddle to reveal a belly full of water. (These ewers, called *aquamanile*, {after an influence that I discovered to be Venetian}, were to be used in conjunction with the small cloth beneath them to wash and dry our hands, all during the course of the meal.) Never had I seen the like, nor have I ever heard as much stifled grumbling about the activity as I did that day.

After having contemplated an entire evening of feasts and ablutions, we were all grateful that our attention would now be called to the food at hand, when (much to our chagrin) it was diverted to several metal utensils, which had been laid out before each of us. One was shaped like a blade, though much smaller. The emperor informed us that we would use this instrument to cut the meat. And the other unusual item was how we would lift each piece to our respective mouths. (This second one resembled a pitchfork, though not much larger than the length of a man's middle finger down to his wrist.) It seemed like a most efficient means of eating, if one were practiced in the art of its use. I must confess, however, that its appearance flustered the archbishop to no end. He refused to use it at all costs.

We were shown how to hold the meat steady with the pitchfork-like tool, simultaneously slicing it with the other. Not an easy task, mind you, though I used these implements throughout the entire seven courses. Quite clever these Byzantines! Why had a Frank not thought of it, I wondered?

The Norman took one look at the utensils and pushed them aside. (There was only so much in the manner of polite decorum that he was loathe to suffer.) He lunged for the meat, lifted it to his mouth, and shredded it. Its blood flowed across his teeth and down his chin, as he smiled.

I supposed that the emperor's stares prompted him to make some sort of explanation for his unwillingness to attempt to practice their customs:

"If these are truly the products of an advanced civilization, I wonder if we are not better off to have remained ignorant barbarians."

Several guests found the Norman's statement amusing. The emperor, however, (if the expression upon his face were any indication of it), did not.

Throughout the long evening meal I found myself watching the princess. She was terribly uncomfortable. And she so hated the wearing of her veil, that she squirmed in her seat all night long, occasionally grasping at it, perhaps to make it appear that it had fallen of its own accord, *per accidens*. Her mother had little patience for such fussing, and slapped her wrist several times. During one such encounter, the daughter's eyes met mine. The momentary glance pleaded with me to rescue her. How could that be? No. I must have been mistaken, I thought.

Though almost all of us were focusing our attention upon the meal, our gracious host seemed determined to present us with a synopsis of Byzantine history. I cannot recall all that he said, for the focus of my thought, (as I have already stated), was elsewhere. Some of his recitation, however, has stayed with me:

"When the great Emperor Theodosius died, the Roman empire split in two—an eastern and a western half. Konstantinople was the eastern empire's most powerful city, and consequently became its capital. As Germanic hordes overran the western empire and plunged its traditions into darkness, they ignored Byzantium. This wondrous place remained the fountain of faith, knowledge, and art. It has continued in that tradition for these past seven hundred years."

No one responded to his statements, though I saw both the Norman's and count's faces redden.

"Tell me, your highness," Godfrey asked, "is Konstantinople truly a city of holy relics, as the stories tell?"

"O, we have all manner of those—bones of saints, precious objects, and the like. And all of them are authentic, in markèd contrast to similar artifacts in many churches around the world, which play upon the ignorance of the faithful. Certainly many relics have found their way here since Rome fell, however some were of such a sacred nature, that only the emperors of Byzantium have known of their existence."

Staring at me, he had spoken those words. I had no idea to what purpose.

At this point I cannot say if the archbishop looked upon the imperial response as an insult, and though he spoke now with a calm voice, his face wore a gravity of spirit that I took to mean a type of cloaked anger. I believe that he did his best to hide it as he spoke:

"Many current tales mention the lance that Longinus held, the one that pierced the side of our Lord on that fateful day long ago. These same tales say that it is in your possession."

"Alas, no. It has been lost to time."

"That is fitting," I said between mouthfuls.

A hush fell over the entire company, as all eyes were upon me. I stopped eating, my mouth still open, then gulped, nearly choking upon unchewed food.

"Why would you say that?" the emperor asked.

"Yes. Why?" the archbishop also asked, his facial gravity fast becoming a rather visible combination of impatience and anger.

Very nearly did I gag upon some wine before I made my response:

"It seems to me that a holy relic is something that people should admire. It should stir their faith. It should not be a weapon, least of all the one that provided the final stroke that took our Lord from us that fateful day in Calvary. It deserves to be cursed by all Christians. Better it should be gone and out of our sight!"

The entire company either nodded or smiled.

"Amen," Godfrey agreed.

"Spoken like a true son of the church," Bohémond offered, as he placed his hand upon my shoulder. "Amen to that."

Though the emperor said nothing, he wore a most curious expression. I could not determine if he were simply pleased with what I had said, or if it had somehow touched his heart, for there was something of a spiritual nature in his look, of the sort that I would have imagined a saint to wear in a moment of religious ecstasy. Perhaps it was nothing, really.

Once finished, as abruptly as when first we met, the emperor bade us all a good night and left with his family. Servants showed us to our various rooms. I was not tired, so I lingered for a time near the entry to the great hall. Only the archbishop came over to wish me a restful slumber.

"Did you hear him, my son? Does speech ever fail him? I shall confess to you here and now, that, in truth, I do not fear the infidel as much as I fear the emperor entering my dreams this night to pontificate ever further upon all manner of Byzantine glories."

I laughed.

"May the Lord rescue us from all regents!" was my addition to his fears.

"Well said."

I watched the old man leave. And for a moment there was only silence or the occasional distant rustling from someone so far away as not to matter at all. Strange that it should remind me of my childhood spent in a cavernous church. Then it occurred to me once more; perhaps that was where God could be found—only in the sheer silence of a given moment when we are alone. And if one listened carefully, whose voice might he hear?

I, too, was about to make my way to a bed, when I felt again that someone's eyes were upon me. I turned. Standing next to a column was the emperor, himself. I cannot say if it were his sudden reappearance that prompted me to forget all manner of polite behaviour, for I found myself speaking my mind freely in any case:

"You have been staring at me all day, sire. Do you wish to stare at me all night as well?"

He did not speak immediately. Like all leaders, he was weighing his words, lest their burden prove too much for him to bear.

"The pope and I have been corresponding these past few years. We have become great friends."

O, those words must have been one horrible affliction to his soul and to his body, and their enunciation must have provided him scant comfort.

"Really?" I asked.

"I have the highest respect for him and his position."

"He would be grateful to hear that."

I could see that he was not having an easy time of it, which surprised me, since I had rarely seen someone in a position of power who was ever at a loss for words.

"He writes frequently of you," he continued, "never short of praise, yet no written word could prepare me for what I felt when first I saw you."

And why was that, I wondered?

"You have survived a death that would have been terrible for any man. Did you know that I, myself, killed the traitor?"

"My uncle informed me that you gave credit to your soldiers for that deed."

"He was mistaken."

Indeed!

"However, before the coward departed this world, he told me everything that he did that lethal day, and everything that he saw."

He eyed me in the oddest manner. I could not be certain if he were seeking a response regarding that statement or not.

"Following that incident, I saw to it that the survivors were conducted safely out of my empire."

I wondered if he could barely wait to rid himself of them.

"Yet you made it all the way back home by yourself, and without incident, if what he wrote to me is accurate. Commendable."

What exactly was his point? This story was old. Did he hope to add to it a new wrinkle? Then I felt my face grow hot and red, as I realized that the emperor may have (at this very moment) accused my uncle of having lied to him.

"Then all accounts between us are balanced, are they not?" he asked.

Ah, that was what he was struggling to remove from his mouth! What could he have possibly hoped to gain by this? If he had wanted redemption, better he had sought a priest instead of a warrior.

"So it would seem," was my response.

He was about to leave, when he stopped and turned to me again.

"I know that you and your forces will liberate Jerusalem."

"They are not mine. They are their own men."

He smiled.

"Once free, and the concerns of daily warfare are behind you, even if only for a short time, I want you to return here."

"And why is that, sire? Do you have another war in which you would like me to engage an enemy upon your behalf?"

He shook his head.

"Nothing of the sort. I have a gift for you, one that you may recognize. We shall talk more of this when the time is fitting."

I was completely baffled. What could he possibly have for me, other than some sort of additional betrayal?

Before he left the hall, he turned to me one final time.

"I have also been admiring your sword. It is most unique. The last people to wield it were *centurions*. However, the Roman Empire fell long ago. It is either an imitation excellently wrought, or it is excellently real. How did you come to possess it?"

"I found it when I needed it."

"Thus the Lord provided it for you."

"Even so," I said, bowing.

He turned to walk away, finally, thanks be to God!

"You are a fortunate man, Guy de Lagery, far more than you can possibly know."

I shut the door to my bedchamber and began to remove my garments. Not several moments later, the door flew open, and in rushed the princess carrying a taper.

"My lady?!"

"Shh," she whispered. "No one must know that I am here."

"Exactly. You should not be here. Your father—"

"My father will never know of this, if you will only keep quiet!"

A bit haughty for one so young, I thought, and not unexpected in an imperial daughter.

As she walked towards me, the thin fabric of her gown shimmered beneath her robe in the palest of candlelight. It was the barest hue of red, and it hugged her curves ever so softly. She saw that I admired it, and informed me that a Venetian trader had found it at the other side of the world, in the empire of the *Chin*. The material was *silk*. (I had often heard of it; this was the first time that it had ever been presented before me, and in so delightful a manner, no less!) The people there had sallow skin and slits for eyes.

"I have rarely seen the like," I commented, running my fingers over the sheer quality that the cloth possessed. It felt like water.

"I wore it especially for you."

Certainly the many paths of desire were not unknown to me, yet each time that I found myself down one of those familiar roads, the excitement would stir, ready to burst, as if I had never before experienced its sensation. Not so this time. I kept telling myself that it was a girl's body, though I could have sworn that it belonged to a woman. I have no idea why I did what I did next. Perhaps I was flattered by her attention and thought best to focus it instead upon something else for her pleasure.

I removed a small brooch from my purse.

"I have a gift for you as well," I told her.

"For me?" she asked, her eyes wide with anticipation.

"The Contarini family of Venice gave it me. They said that I would know which lovely maiden was worthy enough to receive it."

Held by its golden prongs was an amethyst. She could not remove her eyes from its sparkle.

"Are all Franks equally generous, my lord?"

I had no idea how to respond, nor did she give me the opportunity.

"My father says that your people have come here not to redeem the Holy Sepulchre in Jerusalem, but for some other purpose. He refuses to discuss with anyone the nature of that purpose."

At first I wondered if her comment were anything more than a child's curiosity. Then I noticed that her playful manner had given way to a markèd change in her stance, her carriage.

"I am here because of the blessèd Holy Father, who asked me to come, princess. I cannot attest to the purity of another's motives; though, because of the vast numbers of us, I think it fair to say that not all are here to carve out a piece of the Holy Land for himself, if that is what you were implying."

She closed her eyes and clasping her hands, she held them tightly to her lips as she bent her head slightly. After a time she looked up at me.

"You address me as a *princess*," she spoke with equal wonder and satisfaction.

"It is your station in life, is it not?"

"Just so. I believe that I can trust you, not so this Bohémond. His laughter frightens me," she said with a shiver.

It was then that she told me of a conversation that had passed moments before between her parents:

"Did you see how she looks at him?" asked the empress whilst removing her veil.

"The Norman warlord, you mean? Yes, she was staring at him for quite some time."

"Not him! The pope's nephew."

"O, *him*. It is nothing more than a girlish fascination. He is handsome, young, and powerful. Is it any wonder that she finds him pleasing?"

"She wants him."

"Don't be ridiculous."

"My concern for my daughter is improper?"

"I never said such a thing!"

"You have spoiled that child, allowing her to march around unveiled, for all common eyes to witness her beauty."

"Where is the harm?"

"She has always done what she has wanted, and she always will. It is all your fault, exposing her to those corrupt ideas in the literature of our ancestors."

"Yes," he said, laughing. "Sokrates and Platon should be left to gather dust in some forgotten library in some even more forgotten corner of my empire, I suppose."

"Say what you will, but she will have that damnèd Frankish creature."

"She is a child."

"Not anymore. We are superior to these wandering fighters, these strangers to courtesy and all manner of civilized behaviour. Did you see how they eat? Boars have more dignity. Our ancestors dreamed of and created the Akropolis. At the same time, theirs ran naked amongst the beasts of the forest. They are no different now. It matters very little that her years are five and ten. These barbarians marry young girls, regardless of their ages. They are far too impatient to wait until a girl has blossomed into the woman that only her maturity can impart to her, beginning at the age of eight years and ten, of course. These people are not Byzantines."

"Lacking your wisdom and experience does not make of her a fool. Have faith that she will always do what is proper for herself and for ourselves."

"Pray instead that we do not become grandparents nine months from this night!"

She could not stop laughing.

"They have no idea who I am and what I know. They think that I know nothing of how to prevent conception."

"And you are learnèd in this art?" I asked, quite amazed that the Byzantines would have made this knowledge part of a female child's education in the royal court.

"I have read everything in a treatise by Aristotle that my mother has always kept hidden in her chambers. I find everything that she keeps tucked away safely beneath her bedclothes."

She giggled. For a moment I found that action endearing. Then I saw how she looked at me. Her eyes became two black stones—polished ebony in the candlelight. My heart began to beat heavily. I did not know if I should attribute its cause either to fear or to desire. I gulped before I could speak again:

"What was Aristotle's recommendation?"

"Olive oil."

Most interesting. I had not thought of that.

"How can you be certain of its efficacy?" I asked, trying to determine if she had had a former suitor with whom she had attempted its use.

"Only experimentation will prove that true or false."

Apparently she had never used it before, though she had every intention of doing so now, I surmised.

She removed a tiny flask from an inside pocket of her robe. It was filled with a greenish-yellow liquid, the aforementioned oil.

"I have brought along an *amphora* with which to aid us," she informed me, then ran her tongue across her top lip and giggled once more.

I walked closer and held her face in my hands.

I tried to make her understand by telling her that I was deeply flattered. In doing so, I had hoped to deny her request with the least amount of agony.

"I am your father's guest. It would not be fitting."

What I neglected to tell her was that I did not want a servant to find the blood from a ruptured *hymen* upon the bed sheets the following morn, and report the occurrence to the emperor. After all, a war with his forces over a sexual dalliance with his daughter would have proven too absurd for anyone to conceive. And despite all rumours to the contrary, I *did* have my uncle's best wishes at heart, even if it meant passing the night in my solitary meditations, very much the cleric.

She pulled back.

"Is this the great Frankish warrior of whom my father always speaks?"

"Does he really?" I asked with more than idle curiosity.

"O, yes! You are the one who defeats Death, very like our Lord. He says that you will defeat the Turks as well—a veritable Alexander!"

It appeared that my reputation had preceded me. I had no idea that that would be a good thing.

"What is it that you fear, Guy de Lagery? My mother says that you hate us, because you are jealous of our relics, wealth, and power."

"I hate only betrayal."

"And have you never betrayed anyone?"

I would not answer, though I remembered one or two women who had expected my affections to be solely theirs. After my time spent with them, I began to take up with prostitutes, who were not so demanding of one's attentions.

"I would never betray you," she spoke softly. "Nor would I marry you. I would marry only another Byzantine. Your people are very vulgar. Instead, I know what I shall do for you, my lord. I shall become your muse. Yes. That is what I shall do, if you allow me."

"And to what will you inspire this very vulgar man, my lady?"

"To greatness, of course!"

We laughed together at her witticism.

"What if I were to tell you that I would love you all my life?" she asked, coming closer, reaching up to touch my face.

I stopped laughing.

"What if I were to tell you that when I first looked at you, I knew that no other man would ever have my heart?"

I pulled away.

"I would say that your youth betrays you into thinking that you could ever love a sinner like myself."

She made no attempt to hide her pain, or it may be that she had not yet learned how to conceal it.

"You must have known so many beautiful women. Compared to them, I must seem a mere child."

She touched her cheek and began to whimper. I came closer to comfort her. I held her fast to my chest. She looked up at me, as I looked down. She reached up and kissed me.

"No," I told her.

"What do you fear?" she asked again, only this time she did so whilst massaging my member through my clothes.

I moaned, then pulled back.

"Do you fear the unexpected?" she asked with a smile now. "I always do the unexpected. It is a torture for my mother. She cannot control her disobedient little girl. Do you know that I always do what I want?"

I had no doubt of it.

She walked over to the bed very slowly.

"My mother has a fascinating treatise that dates back to Roman times. My father calls it, *pornographia*."

I was unfamiliar with the term.

"It is a manual of positions in the art of love-making," she explained. "She also owns a collection of artificial penises. Did you know that Athenian leather-makers created artificial penises of animal skins for their customers?"

I had no idea!

"Yes. It is absolutely true. But the Romans preferred them of wood."

That did not surprise me. Often had I heard it said that Roman women preferred their men to exist in a state of perpetual excitement, or the household would degenerate into a singularly hellish world of mutual recrimination; or so had I heard.

"Roman women were always being left alone because of constant warfare," she went on. "Sometimes they needed a bit of comfort. My mother has an entire collection. I found them, too. She can never hide anything from me for very long. I have practiced with one. It is made of wood—long, firm, yet delicate to the touch. I used it to take away my own maidenhood and gave it up to the ancient god, Hymen. The action scratched me. But the price was worth the experience," she added, nodding vigorously.

As she spoke, she rested upon the bedclothes, bathed now in golden candlelight. She lifted up her gown, exposing that soft nest of pubic hair, and ran her fingers across it. Then she opened the vial of oil and allowed it to drip slowly onto her index finger. I watched as that finger crept delicately, smearing her hairs and on between her *vulvae* and deep inside. Then she pulled it out, licked it, and lifted up the gown further. Exposing her little belly, then her round, young breasts, the sweat glistened across her skin. She licked both index fingers, then rubbed them in a circular motion around her nipples. These grew hard, firm. (And so was I.)

"Why do you stand there wearing your clothes, when I am so hungry for you?" she asked now. "I want what is real. I want to be loved for the woman I am. You will be Ares to my Aphrodite. Will you not conquer me, my lord?"

God forgive me! I was a man, and like any true man, I attempted to lead a dignified life whilst hurting as few as was necessary (except for the unjust!). In this particular situation I had done all that was possible to send the young woman back to her room. She would hear none of it. As I went to lay with her, I naturally assumed that even my dear uncle would have forgiven me this momentary lapse from chastity. Moreover, I was quite pleased with the idea that I would be her first. My first was a plain but sweet girl named Rose, who—But that is a tale for a different moment.

I had barely removed my clothes when she fell upon my member like a ravenous wolf. I allowed her as much time as she wished to enjoy her meal. Besides, it would have been ill-mannered of me to offend a hostess so determined to show her hospitality to her guest. And O, she was very good, so much so in fact, that she took me into her mouth and did not choke once. Then it struck me; exactly how often had she done this before?

She looked up at me now.

"I adore the way that it grows inside my mouth," she whispered.

Her flesh burned to the touch. And mingled with her sweat was perfume in all her sweetest recesses. Her body cried out for mine. She suckled me to her bosom, then bent down and took me full into her mouth again. This time it was my fingers, which sought out her *vulvae*. As I touched, massaged, and played with them, a tiny moan sprang from inside her full mouth.

Then of a sudden, I was about to scream, when I thought better of announcing ourselves both to the palace guards and to my comrades in the adjoining rooms.

"It is not a piece of roasted lamb," I told her through clenched teeth. "Be gentle."

Afterwards, she climbed atop me, rubbing her *pubes* into my lips. My tongue sought out her tender bud. It was so sweet, so succulent. As I licked it, she moaned further. I reached up to place my index finger into her mouth, hoping that she would suck upon it and so maintain some degree of quietude. Thanks be to God that she did! In fact, she sucked upon it very slowly. Soon after, her body began to quake. Then she moved over and atop my shaft. I held fast to each buttock as she rocked up and down. She bent over slightly and let her long black hair spill across my face. Its soft fragrance thrilled me, excited me more. (It has never left me.) Finally, she burst, and her warm juices soaked my belly. As I felt the same, I lifted her up. She twisted round her body and took me full into her mouth. She swallowed every drop of my milk, then she smiled, as it glistened across each tooth.

She nuzzled against me, covering my face with kisses.

"Shall we try it again, my lord?"

"Not yet, my lusty wench. Soon."

"But I want it right now!" she demanded of me.

"Very soon, I believe."

Though the rest of our time together had proven to be of far greater enjoyment than that first painful moment, when I examined myself the following morning, I pulled back the foreskin and saw teeth-marks all over the helmet atop my shaft. It was not a pleasing sight, mind you, and I had terrible dreams about it for many a night thereafter, but I must admit that what she lacked in experience, she more than made up for in enthusiasm. Her ardor had grown with the night's passage, and she had become insatiable.

Our bodies lay entwined. She held onto me so tightly, I could barely breathe. We began to fall asleep (not an easy task considering that there was nary a dry spot to be had anywhere), when she stirred. She left me at some point, though I could tell that she did not want to. She did, in fact, want more. (Impetuous girl!) But we would have certainly been found together in the morning. So she kissed me and crept off down the corridor. (And she would creep back to me for every subsequent night that I spent in that heavenly kingdom.) I fell asleep with her smell all over me. She was my first princess, and she was absolutely delicious. O, but I can taste her even now!

CHAPTER THE EIGHTH,

in which a Byzantine emperor seeks an oath, and a Frankish disputation ensues.

It was on the following day that we learned more of Peter's failed *crusade* and the whereabouts of his army. Our gracious host had seen fit to lodge the survivors in various towns throughout the empire. (We would soon pick up the tattered remnants of the hermit's vainglorious attempt to be the first holy army to enter the blessèd city of Jerusalem, and add whatever was left of their strength to our own.) The Norman was convinced that the emperor had done this to keep our forces separated and thus minimize the possibility of an attack upon himself.

"It makes no sense," Godfrey insisted. "Why would he do this to his fellow Christians?"

The Norman looked at Robert de Flandres.

"You know our host very well, I am told," he said. "Do you think that he really believes in our success?"

"Certainly. Why else would he have sought our help?"

Though the Norman nodded in agreement with the Flemish nobleman, the former, nonetheless, exchanged glances with several others who surrounded him. Its *eirony* was not lost upon me, I assure you.

"You may not agree with me upon this issue," the prince continued, "but I believe that we are no better than Turks to them. The Holy Father has sent us here in their hour of need," he added, staring at me, "and this is how they repay our kindness and sacrifice. I should have killed this emperor years ago. If he had fought alongside his army, as any real leader would have done, he would be dead now. I believe that if he ever held a sword, he would have no idea what to do with it."

The entire company (except for Robert de Flandres and Hughes) laughed.

"We are on a holy mission in a Christian land," Hughes added, "allied in a single cause against a common enemy. Can he truly believe that we would attack him?"

Our archbishop proceeded to respond before his friend, our Norman leader, had an opportunity to do so:

"You will find that the Byzantines respect one thing only: the blood of their own. Despite the unimaginable fortunes spent to glorify Christ and His works, they have changed little from the ancient Greek lineage that spawned them. Remember, it is Greek glory, illuminated through Christian eyes, that feeds their souls now. We are not Greek, and *ergo*, we are nothing to them except barbarians."

I would not have hesitated to argue, had I truly believed him to be incorrect. The truth of it was, I had to agree with him. Their distaste for us was as close to hatred as any emotion that I had ever witnessed in anyone. (I had discovered that fact about them years before in a small Byzantine church, and I had no doubt of it now.) It had also been my experience that people in power do all that they can to mask everything that is within their hearts; in short, there may be much of deceit and guile, but little of truth. It was nothing that the emperor said or did specifically to us; rather, it was his glance from the side, that lingered long after the deed in my mind. It was the way that he lifted his nose in the air, whenever he stood close either to a Frank or to a Norman, as if the man reeked from each pore. There was nothing of kindness, respect, friendship, or anything that could be remotely termed *affection* in his feelings for us. There was, however, subtlety.

Whilst it appeared that the head of the royal family had asked for and accepted our help, another member, his daughter, represented perhaps the possibility for change. We were all convinced that the son was far too perfect a replica of his sire to hold a different opinion. Of course, the son was the rightful heir, yet I was not ready to dismiss his sister's power of influence. Only time would tell if she were to foster that same illwill that the Byzantines appeared to have for those who were not Greek, or if something were to alter her forever. Time, the great leveler, held us all in His firm grasp, (or so I was then convinced), and would ultimately release us to go about our business only when It saw fit to do so.

Though our Norman leader spoke and did everything from a position of righteous indignation, he was not readily able to convince everyone that swearing an imperial oath was the correct course of action. In fact, it proved to be no easy task, as the very long day wore on.

Hugh, Count de Vermandois, often racked with doubt concerning the emperor's sincerity in these recent days, revealed little patience:

"Now under Turkish rule, these Byzantine lands are forfeit. We shall risk our lives in order to rescue them from their barbarian captors. A great many of us will die. Who here can argue that they should not become ours by right of defense and conquest?"

The others agreed, and quite vocally, I might add. Robert de Normandie was one of the first to echo the count's position:

"New lands and resources might go a long way towards justification of the monumental expenditures which have brought us here."

It was obvious that such a simple thing as this minor delay was too great a weight for Robert to ignore. He was not to discover until long after this evening had passed, what the true cost of this holy war would be for him personally, *i.e.*, his financial ruination. If he had had any inkling of what was to come, I wonder if he would have ever left his home.

"With all due respect," the archbishop began, "we must not lose sight of why we are in this land. It may be true that some of us may not care for its strange customs. (There were several murmurs of assentation at this.) It is, nevertheless, the final bastion of Christianity in an Eastern world that is losing ground to the infidel with each passing day. What happens when Konstantinople falls? Do you believe that these Saracen creatures will be satisfied? The sea will pose no barrier to them. They will cross it, invade our lands, take your women, enslave your families and friends, that is, the ones whom they have not yet killed. (This statement prompted more than one audible gasp). They will not stop preaching their blasphemy until their accursèd beliefs become our own, or until the entire world is drenched in Christian blood. No, my comrades. This enemy of the church must be wiped clean from the face of the earth. If we must make a pact with a Byzantine devil in order to accomplish our holy task, then do it we shall!"

We cheered the old man, who bristled now with the fire of youth.

Though reluctant to become anyone's vassal, save the Lord's, Godfrey was willing to take a broader outlook than most concerning our current situation:

"An oath will bind him to the very real fulfillment of a promise that we must extract from him: provisions and ships. Does anyone here truly believe that we shall *not* need him as an ally?"

Robert de Normandie agreed, albeit reluctantly:

"We have not come all this way, braved all manner of hardships, solely to turn back now. This mission has already cost many of us several fortunes. Let us do what we must and be done with it."

Eustace, perhaps bored with talk of strategy, betook himself from our company. As he did so, he looked around at the cavernous chamber, then spat upon the floor tiles and left us. Godfrey shook his head disapprovingly. Baldwin watched and said nothing.

"Our prince has remained unusually silent upon this issue," the archbishop pointed out, returning our attention to the matter-at-hand, and staring at Bohémond.

The Norman returned the former's glance as he began to speak:

"Good *seigneurs*, my friends, we must be practical, not stupid. We have no idea how long this holy mission of ours will endure." (This statement he had made whilst looking at Robert de Normandie.) "For that reason, we shall need his supplies. His armies, on the other hand, are not impressive, though they always look filthy, as if they have come off a battlefield several moments ago. Of course, if he chooses to send Byzantine soldiers out to die upon Saracen lances, who are we to argue with him? If he wants an oath, let us give him all the oaths which we possibly can."

We all laughed, and none more heartily than our Norman giant.

Unbeknownst to us, the oathtaking became a matter of high ceremony. (I suppose that I should not have been surprised, considering how things were done in this world of ritual.) We stood in the center of the grand hall, flanked by guards at either side. The entire family was present, as was the entire court. All were clad in the finest of fabric (some in embroidered cloth, mind you!), and the brightest of metal. The captain, himself, wore a suit of polished armour. And I believe that his hair had been washed. (Or so it appeared.) And lo, their footwear was bejeweled! Though our faces were clean, we were dressed for battle, our finery deposited safely in our homelands far away, waiting to be used in a more peaceful age than the one in which we now found ourselves.

Since their faces were veiled, only the women's eyes were exposed. I could feel Anna staring at me. I turned and smiled slightly in her direction. It was not a wise deed, for it had occurred beneath her mother's notice. And for a moment my heart froze. What if the empress had discovered the truth of our liaison? No, such confessionals were for the befriended servant girl or the antique crone, who would care for a female child as if she had sprung from her own loins. In any case, a conspiracy of silence would be the typical course of action in those circumstances. No, these were no more than vagaries of intellect, I kept telling myself. There was no cause to believe that I had jeopardized our entire mission. I was being foolish, was I not?

Then the matriarch put her arm around her little girl's waist and pulled her closer, all the time staring at me. O, that simple action spoke volumes, veritable libraries even!

Atop his platform (at least ten steps, if I remember it correctly) the emperor looked down upon the rest below. His entire family walked up the steps and took their assigned places next to him. His empress and daughter stood at his left hand. He held out his right hand—a signal to his prince to remove a scroll from a small gilded box. The young man did so, continuously eyeing the court and smiling. The proud father received it from him and began to read.

I shall not bore you, dear reader, with the overly florid diction of the regent. Nor shall I trouble you with each word of that long tome. I found myself thinking of Cicero, who could orate for days in the Roman senate upon a disagreement beginning with the word, *but*. But I think even he might have been hard pressed to follow all of those words, which seemed to blend into each other like the first brushstrokes of a painter's apprentice. I shall simply repeat the ending, which stayed in all our minds for many years to come:

"—That any and all lands, fortresses, and structures extant within the territories of the earlier Roman Empire be turned over to that most illustrious Emperor Alexios Komnenos of that most illustrious empire, Byzantium; moreoever, said soldiers, warriors, knights, laity hereby do vassalage to said Emperor Alexios Komnenos of that most illustrious said empire, Byzantium."

There was not a single face in that great hall that day that did not become flushed with anger. Bohémond was standing next to the archbishop, and whispered in his ear:

"Jerusalem was once part of the Roman Empire, was it not?"

"So were all the cities of the Holy Land," the archbishop added. "We have been separated from the Romans for a thousand years, yet, to stand here in this royal court, one would never know it."

They looked at each other, nodded, then looked back in the direction of the emperor.

Godfrey and his brothers were the first to swear the oath. They were also the first to receive a small bag of gold coins from the emperor. Whereas formerly our leaders appeared angry or indifferent, at this time each one left the throne with a smile. (And it was now I understand why his royal highness had been continuously portrayed in the *eikons* of his empire as holding a purse. There had been no mistaking the artist's perception of typical royal events.)

"Is our emperor not the most generous regent in all of Christendom?" the captain shouted, smiling.

After everyone else, the archbishop and I followed last.

"Well done of the family Komnenos, is it not, my son?" he whispered to me as we walked up the stairs together to the throne.

Before I had an opportunity to comment, the emperor stopped us. He brought the archbishop over to stand at his right side; I took position at his left. (This action put me between the emperor and his wife. As I stood closely to her, I could feel her eyes peering into the side of my head. I said neither a word *to*, nor did I glance *at* her; instead, I looked out over the entire court, hoping against hope that she would stop. Alas, she never did.)

"I ask no man of God," the emperor announced, "to swear fealty, when it is his very nature to do so."

The emperor bowed now to the archbishop, which action stirred several murmurs within his court, though it touched the latter deeply, or so he told me later.

"I ask no servant of God," he continued, "whose blood is the blood of popes, who has raised his sword in sanctified name, I say again, I ask no such man to swear justice, when justice is all that stirs his life."

And at that moment I could not believe that the emperor bowed to me as well. There was practically a deafening chorus of loud shouts when this action occurred.

"These men cannot swear to anyone, for they have already sworn themselves to God. They are vassals of the church, and the church is enriched by their presence."

For a time I allowed myself to believe that the man had tried to make better his sins of the past. I surveyed our leaders, proud men all. And my heart stirred, until I caught sight of the archbishop's smile, barely tinged with a bit of *eirony*.

CHAPTER THE NINTH,

in which our forces besiege Nikaia, the first of many sieges.

Nikaia. (Nicaea.) More than seven centuries had passed since its former glory as a center of the Christian belief in the Eastern Empire—an historical fact whose importance was not lost upon our archbishop. Perhaps that was why he, more than any other, regarded our first holy battle as the wisest possible choice. Several of our leaders, however, were blind to all things, save the gates of Jerusalem. The Norman offered that the idea of fighting our entire way there, with little or no possibility of respite in hostile lands, was a war that only a saint could win; and since there were none but sinners amongst ourselves, with the exception of the archbishop of course, it was probably a better idea to begin with a city nearby. (Most of those present laughed.) The emperor, himself, recommended that we make preparations for an attack upon Nikaia. It was large enough to attract the sultan's attention, (as it had with Peter's followers), and small enough to mount a powerful defense whilst maintaining risk at a minimum level. The Norman agreed. A skirmish with which to test our mettle was necessary.

"Our prowess as warriors is something that needs a constant foe," he stressed, "if it is to remain as sharp as our swords."

Moreover, we had to prove that our united force would be capable of eventually taking the fabled (and quite well-fortified) city of Antioch—a daunting task that lay ahead of us in the very near future, a very necessary step prior to the retaking of Jerusalem; for without Antioch at our backs, safely in our hands, the chance of holding onto the holiest city in the world would have been an impossible feat. So, Nikaia it was.

Before we left, a young servant girl passed me by, slipping a missive into my hand. I walked away to be alone to read it. A fragrance had barely passed my nose to confirm my suspicion that its message might be coated with perfume. I hesitated to open it; I did so nonetheless.

"Where you rest your arm," it began, "there shall I make my pillow."

O, yes! I knew it! She loved me!

There were many soldiers about, so I had no opportunity to continue reading the remaining portion of her amorous confession. My eyes rushed through the lines down to the signature. It was Anna's, as I had suspected. And a more beautiful hand, full of tiny, elegant flourishes I had not seen. Still, there would be time enough later to admire it and linger over the remembrance of our nights together.

I stuffed the letter into my purse, as I saw the emperor draw near. He had been looking for me. He had a surprise that he thought I might appreciate.

We went out to the royal stables where he presented me with a horse—a black stallion. An *Arabian* was what he called it. And he also said that it was the only good thing that ever came out of the Saracen world. I thanked him for his generosity. In time I would refer to the beast as *Nigrum*, which was Latin for *swarthy*, and we would both become great friends over many years. (Of all the steeds, which I had been honoured to ride, she would become my favourite.)

The Norman came over. He admired well the imperial gift, and touched the horse's rear flank. Then he called upon one of his men to inform the archers that they were to shoot at the rear flanks of the enemy's horses during the inevitable battles to come, thus bringing down both horse and rider swiftly. He thanked me for the inspiration.

As I prepared to ride off, I turned to see him now with the emperor, laughing and conversing apparently on all manner of subjects. If I had not known better, I would have sworn the Norman to be the most officious courtier in all of Christendom. I presumed that taking the emperor into his confidence must have been his plan all along. And if this behaviour were so obvious to me, was it not equally self-evident to all others?

At one end of Lake Askania arose the city's mighty western wall, and as it rose, it spread out with over two hundred towers looming above to guard it against invasion. (I think it were as many as that number, though I must confess that I did not count them all, nor have I ever known anyone who did, despite some later reports which have claimed hundreds more.) The city, itself, was composed of two walls. Its outer one was thick and imposing. It was not, however, beyond any liberator's military capabilities. It was deceptive. It might lull one into believing that it could not sustain a protracted assault. And in truth, this outer wall would never stand strong indefinitely. Unfortunately, once past its defense, the warrior would have to face another one, much thicker, much more solid. And few, if any, had ever breached *this* wall, let alone broken it down completely.

It was during the first week of May, on a cool morning full of sun, when Godfrey and his brethren were to unite their forces with those of Robert de Flandres on the plateau at the eastern wall. Together they would become the initial thrust into the enemy's territory. They arrived without incident and encamped there.

The southern wall awaited the arrival of Raymond, the archbishop, and their forces. No sooner had the standard-bearers dug their poles into the earth, when a loud noise distracted them. All looked up. Screams descended from the surrounding hills. A virtual caterwauling was carried across the winds. It was nothing that anyone had ever heard before; it was unearthly.

The Turks rode down hard, some with their blades clasped in their jaws, others twirling them overhead like swift (albeit deadly) strings.

"Archers!" the count cried out.

And the men pulled the arrows from their quivers and let them fly again and again with such alacrity, that their hands could barely be seen. (Of all the forces there, Raymond had the best bowmen in Christendom, having selected them himself from very many who had sought to join his campaign.) One by one the Saracens fell like dolls from the fingers of a bored child.

In the meanwhile, Raymond sent a messenger to Godfrey in order to inform him of his situation, and the man arrived thereafter with a vast number of his troops. Our forces engaged the enemy, who fell upon them with mighty roarings. Horses whinnied as they tumbled. Swords thrust through leather and mail cracked bone and tore flesh, as blood flew into the air and soaked the soil. A Saracen galloped about, holding a Frankish head, and laughing riotously, until a Frankish arrow pierced his eye and toppled him to be crushed beneath his own horse's hooves. As for the leaders, Raymond's cuts were minor, whilst the archbishop suffered a severe wound in his shoulder, though he pressed on, ignoring much pain.

The battle was not long. The Turks soon returned to the hills as quickly as they had descended therefrom.

The clouds of dust began to settle, as the figures on the ground took on more recognizable features. It was apparent that there were far more of the enemy's dead than ours. The archbishop saw to our men personally, administering last rites to those who were still breathing, though not for very much longer. (Raymond would say later that this first battle in the Holy Land was probably nothing more than an attempt to see if our forces could be as easily defeated as Peter's had been. "Woe unto the unbelievers!" the archbishop was wont to say in those days.)

Raymond ordered the construction of siege-towers armoured with shields to protect the men inside, as others dug around the wall's foundations with which to weaken them. His wounds being dressed, the archbishop overheard this, and suggested to his comrade that, in any ensuing attacks, the knights place their shields across their backs, crouch down slightly, and move in unison, tortoise-fashion, to keep themselves safe. Though initially glad to have the company of a holy man on a perilous journey, the count had no conception of how well versed the archbishop truly was in sundry facets of militaristic experience.

"A novel idea!" the count exclaimed.

Actually, it was a rather old one. The archbishop had read of this *testudo* in the works of the Roman general, Flavius Renatus.

"Most unusual for a man of God to be also a scholar of military history," Raymond remarked further, quite pleased with his comrade's acumen.

"Are we not, all of us," the archbishop asked with a smile, "soldiers of Christ?"

Having wasted no time in questions of conscience concerning an oath of fealty, the much unremarked and unsought Stephen de Blois made his pledge without hesitation at court, then of a sudden appeared with other northern Franks at the western wall. He was amazed to hear that many had already fought one battle. Once there, he met with the emperor's captain and his troops, who had all settled in comfortably for what appeared to be a very long siege. (I have included this historical fact, as I thought it might bear some mention. He was, after all, one of the military leaders of this campaign, was he not?)

Some time later Bohémond and his army arrived at the north wall with plenty of fresh supplies for all, courtesy of our generous host. One of his first orders was to send the scout out along the roads to ascertain the location of enemy troops. But once apprised of the attack, the Norman, himself, rode out to survey the dead. As a result, he formed an interesting notion. It appeared that our enemy had a newfound respect for the act of beheading. Bohémond decided to counter with a reaction of a similar nature. After conferring with the others, he ordered our massive wooden *trebuchets* to catapult the heads of our attackers into the city proper.

"Let them have no doubt," the Norman said, "that we shall respond to their hatred with enough violence to consume all their lands!"

The deed done, he also ordered the construction of even more numerous siege-engines.

By the night fires Raymond informed our Norman leader that it was Ker-būgha, the Persian, (about whom there were already scattering numerous legends of his nefarious crimes against Christians in the Holy Land), who had led the sultan's troops against him.

"How do you know this?" Bohémond asked.

A young scholar, proficient in the Turkic tongue, who had once accompanied Peter, recognized him.

The Norman began to ponder. If this Persian were killed, and his forces were without a commander, then victory might be swift.

"I have faith that we shall endure," the count said, "though the speed of our accomplishment is open to question. This Persian was the first one into the fray, and the first to lead his soldiers out of it to safety."

"It sounds as if they have no stomach for long sieges," I offered, not realizing that I had given voice to my innermost thoughts.

"Very like," the Norman added.

"It may also be their entire method of attack," the archbishop pointed out.

The Norman was very interested in this observation. He turned immediately, hoping for a new viewpoint that would, nonetheless, confirm his own.

"How so?" he asked.

"They enter the battlefield, flailing about in a maniacal fashion, then depart as quickly as they arrived."

"Yes and no," Raymond added. "That is only how they appear. We are correct to concentrate our attention upon this Persian. He has trained his men to strike terror into the hearts of his enemies by feigning madness, thus taking them by surprise, all the while keen in their swift strokes against them."

"And yet, despite all that," the Norman countered, "we killed far more of them than they of us."

Raymond barely smiled when he gave his final response of the night:

"We are competent warriors, perhaps blessed by our Lord in our holy mission. Nevertheless, we cannot forget that these Saracens will refuse to relinquish so much as a single handful of dirt from these lands, without the blood of their own as its defense. That they will take many of us with them in the process should surprise no one here."

As the others left, I wished them well. Tancred came over (which action took me aback; I had not seen him for several days), ignored me as I greeted him, then entered our leader's tent. I did the same in order to determine what activity the Norman would prefer for me to do upon the morrow, not suspecting that I would be witness to an argument between the uncle and the nephew. Tancred had foresworn the oath by sneaking through Konstantinople under cover of darkness. I was uncertain which action spurred on the uncle's anger more.

"What have you done?" Bohémond asked. "What have you done?" he asked again. "How could you be so stupid?"

"That Greek is not my lord. Would you have me bow before him, as the rest of you were so eager to do?"

The Norman shook his head.

"You have spoiled any opportunity that we may have had to convince the emperor that we are his loyal subjects."

Now that his uncle's plan had been made abundantly clear to him, Tancred grew embarrassed and even more confused.

"So all that was—"

"The game of politics. How much easier it is to defeat an enemy once convinced of friendship! Now your actions will reflect upon me. How can my words be trusted, if my own sister's son refuses to obey them?"

Tancred insisted that his uncle could have told him of his plans and indeed, *should* have.

"Why should I share them with a boy, who refuses to listen to his elders?"

Tancred's face reddened. He insisted that he was no child!

Ignoring his nephew's reaction, the uncle stormed out of the tent, followed both by his nephew and myself. The man walked up a hill, then stopped to survey the palaces of Byzantium in the distance.

"Someday those castles and all of their adjacent lands will be mine." He turned around to Tancred. "No one will spoil that truth for me. Save your anger for the Turks. I hear tell that you will need to call upon it to defeat them."

He pulled me along as he ran down the hill, leaving Tancred behind to ponder the import of all that he had most assuredly done.

Ever since the first time that I had found myself in this empire, I no longer required so much sleep as previously. Often I would ride or walk about, long before the earliest morning prayers or sunrise. On one such excursion, not several days later, I chanced to pass our encampment and ride close to one of the city's gates. It was then that I heard the rumble of a mechanism. The noise lasted but momentarily, and long enough for one hooded, cloaked figure to leave through the now-open gate on horseback. I followed. Nigrum raced into the wind. She overtook the horseman with all deliberate speed. When I reached him finally, I slammed my sword against his back, knocking him off his mount.

A short time thereafter, I returned to camp, my prisoner's screams having already roused my fellow fighters from quite a distance. I tossed him and his small sack into our leader's tent.

"Pardon me, my lord," I told Bohémond. "I have brought a gift for our cause."

With his hood pulled back and his face now revealed, his years appeared to be perhaps no more than thirty, and though his features were not so very different from the faces of the Turkish dead, I would have assessed this man to be simply one more Greek.

Tancred ran in. As he was anxious to know the truth, he was the first one to ask the all-important query:

"Are you Saracen?"

The prisoner was quite sickened by the question.

"Hah! They are barbarians, not unlike yourselves."

Our leader came over, picked him off the ground with one hand, studied his face, and said:

"This is no Saracen."

Then he tossed the frightened fool (his face now completely ashen) back down onto a blanket.

"He is Byzantine," the prince continued.

A moment later the Norman left the tent and called to one of his men.

"Ride swiftly. Bring all our commanders back here, that they may bear witness to Byzantine plots. But speak no word of this to that filthy Greek captain."

It was not long before the tent was crowded to bursting. Few could believe the outrage that this man seated upon the ground was in the monarch's service. Once all were present, the Norman opened the sack and removed a scroll from it. He unfurled it and looked over its writing before handing it to me.

Knowing of my facility with languages, he wondered if I might be able to translate any of the scroll's Greek. I found that I was only able to determine the nature of the occasional letter, thus making gibberish of all that I saw. I did, however, give him the name at its conclusion.

"It is signed by someone called, *Boutoumites*," I told our company.

Bohémond stuck his face right next to the man, who shrank back and nearly fell over.

"Who is that?" the Norman asked of him.

"Commander of the fleet."

"This scroll was fixed with an imperial seal," I added. "It is placed next to the name."

"What imperial order has brought you here?" Bohémond asked.

Reluctant to reveal any secrets, which must have accounted for the man's hesitation, nevertheless, he spoke haltingly at first.

"Lord Boutoumites has met many of the sultan's forces in battle. The emperor knows that even though they may detest our faith, they respect the commander as a warrior. They believe him when he writes that he will guarantee their safe passage out of the city."

Count Hugh could not believe what he had heard:

"Why go through all the trouble of giving us two thousand of his own men, if this were what he had planned all along?"

Our prince said nothing. He placed a finger across his lips, as if to silence his ally, who had allowed his anger its full expression.

Robert de Flandres was aghast.

"Some have called the emperor *ruthless* in his consolidation of power. It is what one would expect of an empire surrounded by its enemies. I confess to you now, Prince Bohémond, that I was ill-prepared for this revelation."

The Norman smiled before picking up the thread of his last round of questions:

"What has been your purpose here?"

"I am a courier. I want no trouble, my lord."

Our leader's face bore an expression of some distaste as well for now.

"I have been here for less than a month," the courier went on, "attempting to negotiate a peace with these devils."

The Norman looked over his compatriots as he continued his questioning.

"And have you succeeded?"

"I thought so, until I learned that they had sent word to their sultan, who is leaving behind one war to return here for another."

"We have already met them," Raymond spoke with much bitterness.

The Norman wanted to know how many of the sultan's men were still inside the city, to which query said courier claimed that he knew nothing of the numbers. The Norman was not pleased.

"We are fast learning that Byzantines are often much more than one would assume them to be. Give me the tally, courier, or the failure of this mission will be upon your head. I have heard that your illustrious emperor, as enlightened as he believes himself to be, rewards failure with the most ancient forms of torture, which his people have created during their long and proud history. I have heard it said that he especially adores *that* tradition."

Perhaps the threat of what might happen prompted the man to speak further. In any case, it was enough.

"No one has given me that information directly. I heard discussions of perhaps four- or five-thousand. I cannot be certain."

"So few to protect an entire city?" Count Hugh asked.

"I, myself, thought it most unusual, considering that his wife and children still reside here," the courier added.

Bohémond stood still. "Whose family?" he asked.

"The sultan's, of course. Who else have we been discussing here?"

This was one of the few times when the Norman made no attempt to conceal his anger:

"And did you not think this piece of information vital to our cause?!"

The courier shook, as he denied any offense.

"You are a most polite, meddlesome, little creature, are you not?" asked the Norman of the quivering mass below.

The courier looked agitated but said not a word. Our prince pressed on.

"And where is this commander and his fleet now, this Bowto—Bitou—"

"Boutoumites. I am not privy to that information, my lord."

"This son of a whore lies with every word that he utters!" Eustace shouted.

"I swear by all that is holy, that I spoke the truth. May I leave now, my lord?"

Our leader looked into every one of our faces. I do not know what he sought or found there, (if anything), until he turned back to the courier momentarily and gave his response:

"You may, but you will have to return to your emperor alone. We can spare no one to accompany you. We shall, however, offer you a horse."

The man could not leave the tent fast enough to satisfy himself. Before he was outside, he received one final piece of advice from our prince:

"Beware of the dark, courier. There are many creatures, which haunt the forests by night. And some of them are even human."

The man hurried off, as if rabid dogs were snapping at his heels. The Norman laughed as he ordered one of the men to see to a horse. Raymond, who had been restraining his anger, now let it burst forth.

"Are you mad? Why should we let that coward leave?"

"Shall we take him prisoner? How do you think the emperor will look upon that course of action?"

"Who cares?" asked Count Hugh. "He has already betrayed us. I expect that his captain must have known about this all along."

"Not necessarily. It has been my experience with these Byzantines that sometimes the hand does not know what the head is thinking. The emperor will learn shortly that we are familiar with his plans. He will become very unhappy. As for betrayals, was there ever any doubt? No, my good, dear friends, despite his manipulations, the emperor wants us to succeed as much as we do, even when he may not be convinced of our expertise in battle."

"Or there may be another reason," the archbishop offered. "He believes that we shall keep these stolen kingdoms for ourselves. He is convinced that the oath is meaningless to us, for the custom in his court does not carry the same hallowed respect that it does amongst our peoples. It is nothing more than a legal means of tying us all to his ambition. Everything that he does originates from one simple basis only—fear. It would seem that our allies are a most duplicitous race."

"The chess pieces are still being placed in their proper positions on the board," our leader said. "The game has barely begun."

Eustace revealed once more how impatient he could be, regardless of the circumstances.

"Your *metaphors* will not aid you, Norman prince. You have made a foolish mistake."

"And how, exactly, have I acted so foolishly?"

"One should never let an enemy live. Invariably he will return to finish the struggle that he began. You will regret this day."

As Eustace left, Godfrey tried to apologize once more for his brother's actions.

"Forgive my brother; he has been known to speak his mind at all times, in all places."

"Despite that, he may not be wrong," Baldwin countered. "Our brother's lack of decorum belies the fact that he is first and foremost a grand warrior, who can see betrayal in war-time as clearly as a falcon does its prey, from high atop the clouds. One should always hesitate to dismiss his words."

"What shall we do if this toady returns to complete his mission?" Raymond asked the Norman.

"We shall kill him like the vermin that he is," Bohémond responded. "Execution is always an option, is it not?"

At that point I left the tent for cool evening air that would hopefully be free of argument. After a time, our leader came out to me.

"You have done well this night, Guy de Lagery. You honour the bloodline of your forebears. When our Holy Father reads of this in the archbishop's letters, his heart will swell with pride. Sleep well, my dear friend. Tomorrow we shall begin our war anew, when there will be much bloodletting and many honours to garner for our children's children."

CHAPTER THE TENTH,

in which our forces are educated in the true meaning of the Greek Expression, a Pyrrhic victory!

Midday belonged to the sun. With searing heat at its highest, full upon my face and body, I drank from a skin, then poured the water over my head. Its relief lasted momentarily, but was enough.

"Do I have the privilege of addressing Guy de Lagery, the pope's own nephew?" a voice asked.

I wiped the water out of my eyes. The man was not much older than myself. (No more than five or ten years, I surmised.) And though he was not what one might consider a particularly ugly individual, nor was he a particularly handsome one. He was slight of beard, which I found most unusual, considering that his hair was thick, dark, and curling. And he was remarkably thin, his armour and garments far too large for his modest frame.

"You have that distinct privilege, sir. And who might you be?"

"Stephen de Blois at your service," he said with a bow.

The infamous Stephen! And here I thought his existence merely a rumour.

"You may have heard of me," he continued. "My father, by marriage, is that William who conquered England."

"Though your name is not unknown to me, I have heard more of him and less of you."

Nevertheless, he had been determined to find and see me, to assure himself that I was not a fictive character, but quite real.

"Your survival is miraculous," he told me. "Everyone should be entitled to one miracle in his life, don't you think?"

He began to laugh. I have no idea why his laughter irritated me so. It was then that I set out to quell it.

"Your joy will be of great use to all of us today," I informed him, "as you help with the construction."

He looked about at the numerous men who were building siege-machines, myself included.

"This work is not fitting for you, Sir Guy," he spoke in a hushed tone, presumably so that others around us would not hear. "It is unseemly in a man of your station."

"Is this not honest work?" I asked quite loudly.

The others stopped what they were doing. They became mightily interested in our conversation.

"Indeed it is!" Stephen shouted, looking about at the others, who were staring now at him.

"Then how is it unfit for me, or I for it? Are you saying that some men should not dirty their hands in the performance of holy work?"

"Nothing of the sort. I never said—"

"For you should recall, Stephen de Blois, that the Son of our Lord was Himself a carpenter, and remember furthermore, that every single person here will do what he must in order to restore the lands of our Lord into the bosom of Holy Mother Church. Are you too good for such labour?"

"Certainly not! That is why I am here."

"Then remove your jerkin. And rub your hands with dirt, so that the ropes do not burn, as you twist and bind them."

The others around us cheered, as Stephen removed his hauberk then buff-hued tunic. And when I saw his scrawny chest finally, revealed for all to see, it was I this time, who laughed as heartily as the Norman was wont to do.

Early on the following morn, shortly after sunrise, many troops appeared on a hill, carrying what must have been long timbers and much rope.

Bohémond stared at them, not with contempt, rather with boredom.

"O, look!" he uttered with an audible growl to whomever might be standing near. "Here comes something that we desperately needed—more Byzantines."

The commander rode up to the Norman and introduced himself. He was uncommonly tall for a Byzantine, (though not quite so tall as the emperor, himself), and his eyes bespoke a vibrancy of spirit.

"I am Boutoumites, commander of the fleet."

"And where is this invisible fleet, commander?"

"We have brought it with us."

He pointed to the innumerable items, which his men had carried across land. Apparently they were to construct their vessels here upon the shore of the lake.

"A blockade by water," the Norman said aloud, presumably giving voice to his ruminations. "Does his highness truly believe that our mutual adversaries will arrive by water instead of by land?"

The commander became confused. Is that not why he was here?

"Very well then. Build your ships. From their high decks you will have the perfect vantage-point to watch us down here on the land below, killing *your* enemies."

Our great labour completed, we stood back to admire our efforts. Animal pelts covered the high towers, the better to protect the men inside. The machines moved in place now against the city's walls. The soldiers concealed within began to dig away the ground from its foundations, hoping to weaken the structure. Turks on the parapets shot their arrows. Most of their efforts proved ineffective. (Our archbishop had told us to keep the skins loose, not taut, in hopes that arrows would seemingly strike, only to fall to earth against the thick rippling effect, which would mimic the ocean in turmoil.) Our good men toiled away for many hours, ignoring the tapping noises from up above. As they did so, our engines lobbed dirt, rocks, boulders, and anything else that could be strapped into the mouth of the scupper. And for most of the day the siege continued.

Late in the afternoon one of the men came running up to the Norman and informed him that we had broken through a small portion of the outer wall. But before we had an opportunity for celebration, a terrible accident occurred. With no support, a section of the stone structure tumbled, crushing one tower and twenty of our men inside it. (Though most of our forces were capable fighters, we had, however, proven ourselves to be less than adequate carpenters—a tragic revelation that would repeat itself more than once over the next few hours and days.) Robert de Flandres was standing near our leader when he remarked upon the event:

"A most inauspicious commencement."

Upon hearing that, the Norman's face reddened. He decided to bare his soul to his comrade-in-arms:

"Whilst it is impossible for a leader in battle to weep over every life that has been lost under his command, it is most fitting that he show his respect for the dead."

Robert was silent. He walked away with a curious expression. I could not define it really. There was something of a smile about it. Then again, it might have been the mask of embarrassment that every child wears when berated by father or mother. Who can say?

As word of the event spread throughout the encampments, a Lombard came forth to offer his skill as a manufacturer of weapons for defense. Having served in many a battle, his reputation was assured. It was a simple matter of elementary arithmatics, he informed all. The walls would need very strong timbers to shore-up the existing structure, as the masonry below a given point be removed slowly. Elementary, he repeated.

The Norman could not argue with his logic, so the former left to secure the strongest wood that he had seen in this land. That said timber was already in the hands of the fleet-commander was no obstacle for him.

With several hundred of our troops, Bohémond came to the lake's shore to inform the illustrious Boutoumites that he would have to make do with less vessels than originally planned. There was some hesitation in his response. He agreed, albeit reluctantly. (I am of the considered opinion that he had far fewer soldiers than the Norman, if I remember the event correctly.)

Our troops carried away the timbers, and our new project began to assume a definite shape.

Perhaps the forces of Darkness were not content to slake their thirst with our misery, for within several hours came the sultan's men, again led by the afore-mentioned Persian. And for the first time I was witness to the man's fighting prowess. He twirled his sword as if it were weightless. That was only the first oddity. Its shape mimicked the crescent of a moon. And its length was quite thin and sharp. He sliced through metal, leather, and flesh as easily as a grandmother (with hands shaking) would her onions for the family's meal.

His soldiers did their best to imitate their leader, but it was soon evident that they were pale copies of his skill. Despite their best efforts, however, my blade would soon taste their blood. On Nigrum's back I rushed into the fray.

Following the Norman's order, our archers shot at the hindquarters of the steeds, bringing many down and crushing the legs of their riders in the process. In the excrutiating heat I was covered with perspiration. I wanted to tear off all my garments and fight nude, as the ancient Greeks did in competition of their games. When the salty water coursed into my eyes, burning them, I knew it was time. I threw my helmet to the ground. My dark hair, soaked and shining, flew about me as I turned this way and that, cleaving one enemy then the other in the vast crowd.

The Norman and his nephew were fighting at each other's side, (I was to find out later), when the uncle nudged the latter to look over at me.

"There he is—a veritable Mars on the battlefield. Jerusalem will be ours soon. God wills it!"

As our leader roared, the rest of our forces took up the call and repeated his words. I have no way of knowing what impression that action created in the minds of our enemies, though I, myself, witnessed many of them grow silent in the wake of our unified and most terrible shouting.

As for Tancred, he had nothing to say regarding his uncle's observation. I have been told that he watched me many times throughout the rest of that afternoon.

After we routed the enemy, (Thanks be to God in the highest!), we turned our attention once more to the city's walls. As I helped bury our dead, or watched wounds being dressed, it struck me that we all knew so little of this place. O, it was of great strategic value, due to its proximity to Konstantinople, no doubt, but what was it really? Seven centuries earlier church fathers had gathered here to compose their Nicene creed. But today? Besides remnants of a Roman theatre, bath, and several aqueducts, it contained little else of very much value, historical or otherwise. We were supposed to take the city and protect its churches. (That it also contained our enemy's houses of worship, their *mosques*, as I was to learn their terminology later, never occurred to any of us.) Yet there we were, so many who had fallen beneath its grand walls. And it was only the first of countless cities along the dusty roads in these ancient and fabled lands.

During one of our typical evening discussions, Bohémond put forth the idea that the sultan's family could be ransomed.

"Once they are returned safely to him, he will have to realize that we are a people who are true to our word, in markèd contrast to these pretenders to Greek glory. He will want us as his allies."

Baldwin could not agree.

"Do you honestly expect him to deal with you in any way, after you have captured and ransomed them? How is this behaviour any different from anything that we have witnessed in this hellish part of the world? We are far from home. Everything about this place tells me that we must do everything differently here, especially the act of warfare. This sultan is as treacherous as the Byzantine. He will trust no one, with the possible exception of his own band of accursèd fighters."

The Norman was silent—a most unusual moment for him. I can count upon the fingers of a single hand the few times when I witnessed his loss of an argumentative bent.

With new, stiffer timbers in place, the work was once more begun. And this time the Lombard's experience proved invaluable. Whilst our enemy fired down at us from their parapets and towers, and we up at them from our grassy plain, the outer walls began to crumble. All through the night we fought against each other, until the first rays of dawn began to spread across everything. The Norman, his eyes burning like coals, raised his sword high.

"We shall take them this day!" was his battlecry.

We were about to follow him forward, when we all noticed something unusual. As the last vestiges of the night's sky began to dissipate, I beheld banners flying above the towers. Strange, I thought. I had seen none before. The inhabitants of the city must have put them up throughout the night. What I failed to notice, until the brilliant dawning had made its presence truly felt, was that they were the colours of the Byzantine Empire.

At that moment the gates opened, and out walked the commander and the courier, surrounded by Turks, and all were smiling quite broadly.

Brother Michael, who had been riding near me commented that our Greek host had denied us the possibility of ransom. Robert de Flandres also decided to pass judgment over our current situation:

"The emperor has taught us what it means to have a *Pyrrhic victory.*"

The Norman did not know the meaning of the terms. Robert was only too happy to explain.

"It means that we have won, despite the loss of very many men. Too many, I might add. As you may recall, the reference hearkens back to the Trojan War."

"Do you know what rankles in my very soul, Flemish count? People who spout quick judgments at the most inappropriate moments."

"Now I fail to understand *your* meaning."

"Worry not. You will."

And with those final words and the flat part of his sword's blade, the Norman slammed the metal against Robert's face, knocking him off his steed.

"This is war, not literature, fool!" the Norman shouted, then shrugged.

Even if initially inclined to agree with the others concerning the emperor's traitourous conduct, I later found myself wondering if the Byzantine were not taking the first steps towards what he might have believed to be a very necessary truce with the Devil. Barely tolerated as guests in these lands, we were nonetheless strangers here. We were not unlike Caesar's *centurions,* sent out to defeat the Gallic populace—some here because of duty, others adhering to the call of a faith, still others scheming after avaricious dreams which seemed so near, so real. Despite all that we may have felt, this was not our home; it was the great Empire of Byzantium, that had flourished for many centuries. And now this empire was surrounded by those who were intent upon its destruction. Was the emperor playing at cards? Perhaps it was what he had planned all along—something that he was holding in abeyance to use as a last resort in whatever game he had been playing. Perhaps he felt that any action could be legitimized, if it resulted in the future security of his empire. Whatever reasons there were for his actions, like them or not, in the end we would all have to live with them.

He was the first man whom I would ever know to wield great power over a nation. As God, or Fate, or Fortune would have it, he would not be the last.

CHAPTER THE ELEVENTH,

in which we proceed to journey inland, taking several small villages, (during which some of us die), and we also take Dorylaeum, without much Byzantine aid, mind you!

After what happened, none of us were disposed to adhere to the emperor's recommendations. (He wanted us to travel along the coastline all the way to Antioch.) We decided instead to make our way thorough the Anatolian lands, with the imperial captain as our guide. The man was unhappy with our choice, and he let everyone know of his dissatisfaction immediately.

"If we had followed the illustrious Emperor's suggestion, the fleet-commander could provide us with fresh supplies as we need them."

"Better we should starve or die of thirst," Bohémond insisted.

The Greek ignored him and rode onward. The Norman smiled, and to those who chanced to be riding at his side, he said:

"Someday the family Komnenos and their great empire will be crushed underfoot."

He was correct, though it would not happen in his lifetime.

As we passed through several towns, what surprised me was their inhabitants, though primarily Christian, were indifferent to our presence; nor was the archbishop greeted warmly by the local priests. He was viewed as an interloper, poking around in the affairs of those whose lives were of no concern to him. A symbol of the Roman church, the Western church, he was unwelcome in the East. Why come to their land now, after so many centuries? Had their lives somehow gained in value that he sould take notice of them? He was bewildered by their reaction to him, and, I believe, deeply pained.

Despite a lack of mutual agreement, our leaders eventually decided that a token force would be left behind at strategic points along the route. Primarily footsoldiers, they would help guard our rear as we moved onward to Antioch. The rest of us continued along our journey.

My uncle had once told me that there is a price to be paid for every action that a man takes, and that nothing worthy can be had without struggle. We learned quickly that every bit of soil upon which we trod ever further towards our ultimate goal (*i.e.*, Jerusalem's restoration as a Christian kingdom,) would be purchased at a terrible price. We came upon many wells, only to find them blocked up with stones and dirt. Crops had been burned, leaving only scorched stalks. Ewers full of wine or oil were left in shards. Our leaders were unusually quiet during those difficult days. Godfrey was one of the few who was able to find his voice:

"Our Lord has put a test before us to see if our faith will sustain us."

"I never liked tests," was Brother Michael's reaction to that statement.

In truth, if not for the supplies, which we had taken at Nikaia, or traded in towns, many of us would have starved. Little did we suspect how much more difficult would be our trek up the mountains.

At one end of the Anatolian plateau the land rose high. Its craggy forms and sheer rock faces depleted our reserves of strength long before we began our arduous climb. Since there was no way to circumvent the obstacle, we had little choice but to push forward along our path, or return whence we came. I can tell you most assuredly, that no one elected to pursue that latter course of action. (Praise be to us all!)

So dangerous was our ascent, that several of our men (and far more of our steeds) were lost to us. Stephen almost toppled over with his mount. The Norman noticed him in time enough to reach out and hold both rider and horse aloft, until the animal was able to reacquire a sure footing. As for myself, I thanked the Lord for Nigrum, who, perhaps because born and reared in these lands, took the mount as easily as if it were in her blood. Once upon a solid footing, Godfrey and I helped many others, who would not have been so fortunate as we, had they remained without assistance. I feared instead for Brother Michael, the archbishop, and Raymond, all of whom could not call upon their once youthful vitality. Each struggled with his task, yet survived. (More than one younger knight was embarrassed by the skills of his elders that day.) Of the three, only Brother Michael was often the one most out of breath afterwards. By the time that I saw him reach the top, I was convinced that his heart would simply cease to function. I was most relieved that it did not. He looked upon this event with his typical equanimity of spirit:

"Age is as merciless as it is relentless," he managed to utter with a smile.

One evening, after we had all made do with a meal culled from our meager stock of provisions, I walked about, as was my custom, this time accompanied by Brother Michael. We had no idea that we would come upon Godfrey and his brothers engaged in heated debate. I may have been wrong, but I believed that Godfrey was trying to soothe one brother's temperament. Eustace, on the other hand, was the first to spout his venom:

"What can you possibly know about my feelings? In time you will learn how to live with your pain as I have learned how to do so with mine."

Incredulous, Godfrey stared at him.

"What pain can you possibly call your own? You are the son of landed gentry, and a brave and fearless knight with much fame. Wherefore do you wear this mask of tragedy? It is unseemly in a man of your station."

"You have never understood who and what I am."

"Who and what you are is my brother. Now conduct yourself with that same dignity that our forefathers have passed down to us. And in the name of all that is holy, wipe off that frown, even if such action gnaws at every fiber of your being. Looking at you in this way sickens me."

Baldwin stared at Eustace, simultaneously speaking to his other brother:

"The devil has possessed him again and is using his voice to torment us. Do as I do and ignore the creature. In time he will drag himself back under the rock, where he continually wastes his days in self-loathing."

"If we are lucky."

Two brothers laughed; the third scowled. I was going to walk up to them and say something in hopes of quelling both Eustace's rising ire and his brothers' disrespect, when Brother Michael saw what I was about to do and restrained me.

"Never put yourself between brothers," was his advice. "This is their problem to resolve. It will, in time. If not, they will kill each other. Best leave them to their fates."

"Or their choices."

"As you say."

Only later was I to discover that the source of this argument was a prophecy of Eustace—one that his brothers consistently dismissed out of hand, and one the veracity of which I would recognize too late.

We had not encountered our enemy very many times after Nikaia. The Norman believed that they were gathering their forces for a single major confrontation. Not until we reached *Dorylaeum* did a large force come to bear down upon us. As soon as their infernal wailing began, the Norman ordered us to dismount and set camp.

"If it pleases God, today we shall kill our foe and become rich with his plunder," he began. (Everyone cheered. Seeing their reaction, he continued.) "This day we shall send the Turk screaming all the way down to Hell with their thrice-damnèd leader, Mahomet!" he cried out. (Everyone cheered again.)

They came down upon us with an infernal fury. Though far outnumbered, we met their ambush with an equal ferocity. We matched them sword for sword. For every one of us they killed, we killed two. Death was everywhere.

The battle had not proceeded for very long, when we saw our relief. Raymond, the archbishop, and their forces rode down to us, taking many of our mutual enemies with them as they did so. By the end of the day we had made the Turks taste their defeat over and over again. I believe that none of us had ever fought so hard as we had, for we knew that once defeated, our enemies' supplies would become ours. And so they did.

Whilst the Persian took his handful of survivors with him, ("Gutless swine!" we all shouted after him), we betook ourselves to their former encampment, where we found much of gold, no less of silver, an abundance of foodstuffs and drink, and most especially, some of the finest horses we had ever seen. Like so few days before this one, we were grateful for its end, despite the vast numbers of our dead, whom we now began to bury.

As I began my late evening ride, I passed a tree and stopped. I turned to see Baldwin smiling. I had no idea why he sought company or conversation, if at all. In any case, I was in a foul humour with him, after having witnessed the sorry treatment of his brother at his hands. Still, he persisted.

"This is your custom, is it not?" he asked.

"I never sleep very much anymore," I gave as explanation for myself.

"A wise course of action in a time of war. It occurs to me that you and I have never spoken, and it might be a good thing for me to talk to someone whose wisdom has grown far beyond his years."

"And you have waited here all night to tell me that?"

"Only a little while," he said, laughing. "Tell me, Guy de Lagery, what is a knight's purpose?"

I thought the question unusual. Was this some form of test? Nevertheless, I addressed it.

"To protect his church, his king, his country, and the maiden."

"That is only secondary to his real purpose, which is to kill. How fortunate we knights are to be here! With the Holy Father's blessing, we can kill all whom we desire, whilst deluding ourselves into believing that our actions are holy. What does it matter if we capture Jerusalem? Its restoration as a Christian kingdom will not cleanse our souls. We have all killed, and it was not always for the defense of our bodies or our homes. It takes only one innocent life to ruin the essence of who and what we are. For us there can be only land and empire, women and drink, for there can be no redemption. That is what it means to be a knight. What choice do we have but to accept our inevitable damnation?"

"I have never killed a man who was not seeking to take my life."

"Keep telling yourself that."

Strange, sad words to pour out of the mouth of someone dressed like a monk. I remember thinking that despite his proficiency in swordsmanship, he was (most likely) profoundly lacking in the ability to comfort anyone, including his fellow soldiers who had died within his environs.

If we had been ignored or treated in a less than kindly fashion by Christian townspeople before, in the village of Dorylaeum we were viewed as veritable saviours. They were kind, respectful, and generous. For a moment we forgot the hardships, which we had endured—the inestimable loss of comrades, to say nothing of this land, that was so often so unforgiving.

Shortly before we left, I was about to place a water sack on Nigrum, when Tancred came over. (A rare wonder indeed!) Even more wondrous was his apparently affable nature. What *could* he have wanted from me, I wondered?

"My uncle has done well by all of us, has he not?" he asked.

"A most capable warrior," I offered, uncertain if the nephew were referring to our leader's military skills or not.

"He has also led us to much heathen booty. We shall become wealthy before this war is finished."

So *that* was his reference.

"You have never cared about the fate of Jerusalem, have you?" I asked.

"How dare you say that to me? Do you think that because you are of the Holy Father's blood, that you have license to speak to your betters in such a disrespectful manner?"

So very much did I want to cleave the braggart's head in twain. My *better*? But an internal squabble would have served to disrupt the fragile alliance between many different men, to say nothing of how such an action would have been a betrayal of my dear uncle's trust.

"Mount your horse, Tancred, and ride off. I shall choose to forget your insolence."

That statement was exactly what he must have sought all along, for when I turned to tie the sack, he reached out with his blade and cut my cheek.

"Is that how you fight?" I asked, touching the moist cut upon my face, "with a coward's stroke?"

At that moment I cared nothing for the Holy Father's vision. Blood will have blood, I thought, and I raised my sword high. Tancred did the same, then stared, and stopped moving altogether.

"It is healed!" he shouted, pointing to my face.

I touched my cheek again to discover the truth of his statement. I smiled now.

"What are you?" he asked.

"A man most beloved of God. You, however, are not."

He grabbed at his chest, his blade falling to the dirt. Finding it difficult to breathe, he backed away, frightened, his eyes never leaving me.

"Unholy thing," he struggled to say.

I made no response, though I must confess that I laughed heartily. I cannot say if what he saw disturbed him further, but I hoped sincerely that it did so.

I rode on with the others. Neither Tancred nor I ever spoke a single word of what had transpired between us. After all, everyone might have said that we were as mad as Eustace, and no one ever wanted to be *that* mad.

CHAPTER THE
TWELFTH,

*in which we come to Antioch but have no idea what to do, so we wait
for quite some time, hoping for a miracle, and would you believe it?
All good things come to those who wait.*

From the direction of Dorylaeum spread three armies; the first was the Norman's, in whose company rode Tancred, Baldwin, Robert de Normandie, Hughes de Payens, Brother Michael, myself, and many others. Godfrey led the second group, and most of the other personages of power rode with him. A third group that consisted only of Robert de Flandres and his men headed toward the port of Laodicea. Perhaps because both he and the Norman had not maintained a mutually respectable discourse for quite some time, did the former choose to take the route that he had. Everyone hoped that he would make good use of his time there and send supplies to us by means of ships. But that never happened. The cause might have been the Turks' thoroughness in not allowing any items for our use to find their way to Antioch; or it could have been the Flemish count's considerable anger against our prince, so much so in fact, that he was intent to make everyone else suffer with him. I cannot say why it happened. I can only tell you, dear reader, that Bohémond never forgave what he perceived to be another form of betrayal.

The Norman and I were riding next to each other upon the road through Arabic *Suriya, (Syria)*, when we were accosted by fellow Christians. They commanded that we stop to hear of their plight.

"Hail and well met, my lord," one of the strangers addressed us in Latin. "We are an embassy sent from our leader, *Thoros*. The story of your successes has spread to our kingdom of *Edessa*. We are desperate for your help against the pagan. Will you come?"

I translated his request for my comrades. The Norman wanted to know if he were addressing a clergyman, a knight, or a scholar, since so few of the laity ever spoke Latin. (Actually, so few of any class knew even the simplest verbal declensions.) The man responded that he had never learned the Frankish tongues and apologized profusely for that particular lack in his education, and moreover, he had been a knight sworn to protect his lands all his life. Despite that, Bohémond dismissed his plea out of hand. Once Jerusalem were secure, he would be happy to help transform the entire eastern world into a Christian one, but not until that time. The Edessan advised him that there would probably be no Christians left in his kingdom by that time. Baldwin offered to go, which surprised everyone except me. (I surmised that since his was not a holy purpose, ambition was the only thing that truly mattered to him. What better opportunities than those presented by war?) Tancred then offered his services as well, which action surprised and visibly pleased his uncle far more than it did any of us. (Make no mistake about this; we were all {to a man} quite happy at the possibility of seeing far less of the intemperate Tancred. I must confess, however, that the motives for his actions were open to speculation. I cannot say if the cause were his hatred *for* or fear *of* me, or if it were his own vaunting ambition. Only the Lord could reveal such an answer, and once more He preferred to maintain His silence upon that issue.) So the two left with a number of our forces that was divided equally from amongst the original four sets of armies.

What you may find most interesting, dear reader, is that within several months, the brave Tancred was returned to our company. (Will wonders never cease?) Baldwin's prowess in battle impressed the Armenian ruler far more than did his companion's. (The former captured one town after another as he carved a path east towards the Euphrates.) For that reason, Baldwin was adopted by the old man and made his heir, whereas Tancred was asked to be on his way. (In truth, I cannot say if the better or the worse man won.) Not long after Tancred's return, Baldwin deposed his regent and benefactor with the aid of the king's own daughter. In March, in the year of our Lord, 1098, Baldwin became Count of Edessa and subsequently ruled over it with his Armenian princess. Many believed that it was a matter of political convenience—the triumph of pragmatism over romance. I cannot say if that were true. His actions would be repeated by others frequently in the ensuing decades, for it appeared to be the best way to soothe the dissatisfaction growing within the potentially warring factions of each respective country. Some have said that love can transform the universe. Others have said that a chest of jewels, a heap of gold, and the occasional plot of land can accomplish quite the same. What I can say is that in the few times during which I witnessed him looking at her, there was an unmistakable lust in his eye and love in his heart. For her part, whenever she noticed his stares, her face would become flushed, like a young girl awaiting her first suitor come to call. Draw your own conclusions.

As for her paternal affection or affiliation, only Baldwin was privy to those emotions (or lack of them). I can tell you that his was the first of the Christian warrior-kingdoms in the Holy Land. And he would sit upon his throne, offering to help us both in Antioch and subsequently in Jerusalem, even though he never did. He came only after his brother, Godfrey, had died. But I see that I am rushing the narrative ahead of itself once again.

We crossed the Anatolian Desert, the sole inhabitants of which were some previously unknown type of rodent scurrying about, as well as the occasional spiny thistle, that proved quite inedible. In that terrible place more than one of our brave knights succumbed to its rigors. Then it was that we saw our enemy holding the iron bridge that crossed the River Orontes. We met them with courage, and many of us accepted death with honour. We finally routed them, but at great cost. The living amongst us reached Antioch a day after this latest battle, towards the end of October, 1097, I believe.

Upon seeing that there were far more towers than we had previously witnessed at any city's boundaries, (four hundred, I was to learn later), Bohémond realized that no amount of weaponry or siege-machines would bring down this place. A more devious method of liberation had to be utilized. No one was really certain what that might be, so we settled in for what would doubtless become a very long contest of wills. Whilst the Byzantines were glad to have struck a blockade at Nikaia's lake, we preferred instead to blockade the gates at Antioch. No one could enter or depart without our knowledge of it. None of us suspected that we might be there for many months, and very nearly a full year.

"We must persist," Brother Michael told me regarding our current situation, "for fortune favours the bold."

"But evil to him who evil thinks," was my response.

"How is that related to what I have said here and now?"

"I have no idea. I simply thought it time for me to begin to dispense my own sage counsel."

"In that case," he said, laughing heartily, and slapping me upon the back, "well done!"

So often have people claimed that the holy land might be like a palace shining in the desert. Needless to say, the air would be clean, the breezes gently brushing the face and body. None of us expected the brutal winter to force our encampment outside of Antioch's walls. The conditions there were often so terrible, that barely had a day passed, when I did not miss possession of the coats of otter and ermine, which had warmed my frame through many a harsh season. Food and drink were also in scarce supply. I found myself dreaming upon the imperial repast—the aromas, the garlic, the onions, and all those bloody viands. I had hoped that the images might lessen the desire gnawing away at the pit of my stomach. I must confess that they did not. So my mind reached out to search for something that would satisfy it in some form or other.

There were times, even during the day, in the midst of fighting, or constructing our engines of war, when I would think of the women whom I had known. And, of course, the one who kept coming to the forefront of my mind was Anna, my Anna! I ruminated upon the sweet taste of her youth, how soft were her kisses, how hot and moist she felt. I allowed myself the possibility of a waking dream or two, in which I would return to her in triumph to ask her father for her hand in matrimony. And we would have many children. And my uncle would be so proud of his formerly profligate nephew. And the dream would make me smile. Then the cold or the hunger would slap me out of my reverie, and I would struggle to breathe the chill of the ever-graying days.

As the final frost of winter began to lose its bite in the longer daylight of early spring, we continued a tradition that had commenced during recent months: we counted the dead, then buried them with respectful (though concise) ceremony. Most had fallen victim to starvation, others to disease. In our weakened state we were all painfully aware that a man who wiped the *mucous* from his nose at night, might never awaken to wipe it again the next morning. Our only consolation was that the great city of Antioch, as large as it was, could not contain enough supplies to feed its hungry population indefinitely. But I must admit, it was a cold comfort indeed!

It was during these difficult times, after the savage winter, that many of us became quite exhausted and sickly. Every attempt to forage met with little or no success. I am ashamed to say that some did desert us. Whether they lived or died, I cannot say. At any rate, I held no hope for their survival. Even the emperor's captain (who, I must confess, had fought bravely at our side for every step of our path since Byzantium) was not immune to despair. He went to the Norman and told him that he was leaving with his men, what few were left. Had he seen a means of entry, or so much as the possibility of one, he might consider staying on, but—. Bohémond needed no further explanation. For him the captain's actions were typically Byzantine: never see anything through to its conclusion; never fight a war in which other Christians can die for you; never—. That was enough for the captain! He was too tired, too disgusted to allow the Norman's vile temper to bait him. He bowed to our leader as a sign of respect for his courage and leadership, then left. Whether the Norman was pained by the man's departure, or glad of it, he revealed no emotion in his face. The one person who betrayed his true feelings about this sudden change in our routine was Stephen. As he watched the captain and his troops leave, he wore a most curious expression. It was not fear exactly. It was more of a concern, possibly about his own future, and, I trust, that of his men. Or it may have been nothing more than the seed of an idea that was beginning to germinate. Only time would reveal how it would flower.

That very night I decided to walk around the camps. (Nigrum had grown thinner in recent months, and I had not the heart to ride her and so add to her travails. I often wondered if the poor animal were as hungry as was I.) Of a sudden I espied a man's face at one of the tower-windows. I watched that location for a time to make certain, but saw no one. This same happenstance continued for several evenings thereafter. Then, during one particular occasion, I saw something most unusual. Out of that same window appeared a pair of hands. They tossed a long ladder of rope over the side. It appeared to be secure at the window's ledge, for its lowest rung fell to a man's height and stopped. Shortly afterwards, the man inside the tower held up two torches and crossed them. I thought that he was trying to fashion the shape of a crucifix. Instead, the figure became an X. His signal must have been for me, since there was no one else about, save the guards at the gates. (And one of those was fast asleep, being watched by the other.) I had no idea if this were a trap, perhaps to capture then ransom me. Nevertheless, I decide to test Brother Michael's adage; I had rarely seen fortune favour the coward.

Once at the top, arms reached down to pull both me and the ladder inside. In the torchlight I could not determine if this man were a Christian. The one lesson that these lands had taught me was that one could never ascertain a man's faith simply by staring at the colour of his skin or the roughness of his features. The man had a squat frame that surrounded a very large stomach. I could not guess at his years, though I believed him to be relatively young. (His eyes, on the other hand, appeared very tired and very old, if what I was able to see of them proved accurate.)

There was no difficulty in making myself understood. He spoke my language flawlessly, due to the many Frankish pilgrims who had often passed through the city's gates. He introduced himself as *Fairuz*, a tower-guard ordered for the night's watch, and he was no Christian. He said that he had often seen me as I was scouting about in the earliest hours before dawn. Occasionally, when he would first begin his duty at night, he noticed that I had as my companion a giant.

"Is this giant your leader?" he asked.

"Yes."

"I never knew that the *Franj* had a giant in their midst."

I was unfamiliar with the term. Apparently it was what everyone called the Christians from beyond the sea.

"We detest the *Franj*," he made certain to let me know.

"Does that include you?"

"I make no distinctions according to race. I detest everyone in equal measure. Take the Turks, for example. They call themselves, *ghazis, brave warriors of the faith*. I call them, *pigs*, which is exactly what I call your people. Do you think I care a fig for anyone who is not of my family? I sit here all night, looking out of this window, the brave soldier who will protect his beautiful city. I piss on this city and everyone in it. Does anyone here care if I or my family starve?"

Why had I never met a rotund man who carped about little else save the fact that he was starving, I wondered?

"Shall I assume, then, that you will help us?"

"I like gold. I like big heaps of it, so big, that they are too heavy to carry. Tell that to your giant. O, one more thing that I may have neglected to mention. I also make swords in my spare time, what little I may have of it."

He went over to the far end of the room and came back with a sword, fashioned in the shape of a moon's crescent. Its handiwork was as fine as, if not better than, any of a Christian manufacture.

"What do you think?" he asked, smiling now, the eagerness in his eyes glowing.

"It is most excellently wrought."

"*Allah* be praised! I *knew* you would think so. If there is one thing that a good Christian appreciates, it is a good weapon. My prices are very reasonable. How many shall I make for you?" he kept asking, nodding all the while.

I was dumbfounded by his question.

"Actually, I am quite happy with my own."

"I see," he said with great disappointment. "But you will let me know if you have a change of heart."

"Without hesitation."

"As you say."

Climbing back down, I wondered what group was his *progenitor*. I discovered later that he was an Arab, and that his people had an alliance with the Turks, which, though often strained, had lasted and would continue to last for very many years to come.

When I apprised the Norman of what had occurred, he became ecstatic. He brought me outside of his tent, threw his arms about me, and roared to the entire camp:

"We shall soon enter the city, thanks to this bold knight. Is it not as I have always said? The Lord is with him, and will be with him until the end of time!"

"Praise be to the bloodline of the Holy Father!" the archbishop added.

I hurried Bohémond back inside using the pretext of working upon a plan of victory. Initially, I was not comfortable standing at the center of such fulsome praise. In addition, I was far more concerned about seeing the hopes of our forces smashed to bits because of someone's foolish error. This was our only chance, first and last, and it required diligence, not arrogance.

That night we ate together. (O, that it could have been a sumptuous feast! But we had stripped the land clean of its *flora* and *fauna*, and we were forced to make do with what little we had stored away.) The archbishop brought up an issue about which most of us had wondered though had hardly given voice to, namely, what would happen after we had finally captured Jerusalem? The Saracen would not be going anywhere. Hughes de Payens then mentioned the necessity for an army of knights to remain behind in the Holy Land to protect pilgrims, whether or not we succeeded in wresting Jerusalem from the infidel. (Whilst the rest of us could see only the possibility of war on the morrow, it was my good friend, Hughes, who saw far into the future. In truth, I have to say that I believe he always did.) The archbishop promised that he would write to the Holy Father, asking for formal recognition of it. Brother Michael could not understand why it was necessary at all.

"Knights have been traveling through these lands with pilgrims for centuries. They are already here. *We* are already here. Do we need more?"

"There is no single military order," Hughes insisted.

"Perhaps there *should* be an army," I offered, "a holy army."

The others stared at me. The Norman seemed intrigued with the idea. He asked me to continue.

"Christians need an escort in this land. That should be the first rule of obedience in a new order. We need an army whose sole purpose is the protection of pilgrims, as friend Hughes has mentioned. This will be especially true after we liberate Jerusalem. More Christians than have ever been here will flood this entire part of the world for a glimpse of the city where our Lord lived."

The archbishop stared wildly, as he voiced his innermost thoughts:

"A spiritual army above reproach, appropriate for a new Jerusalem in a new Christian age. The concept is brilliant!"

If I had not known better of him, I would have thought the old man enraptured.

Bohémond believed that the idea had merit. He turned now to Hughes.

"You proposed it. You should head this new order. Once Jerusalem is in our hands again, we shall speak more upon this subject. I want to know all your plans."

Hughes was embarrassed. It was not his nature to seek a position of so much worth. The Norman could not agree. Hughes was as good a man as any for the task, and a great deal better than most. My friend was pleased by the compliment, though I could see that he was still uneasy about the future appointment that we had all asked him now to fill. He then looked at me helplessly. I think that he wanted me to say something or create a new idea that would further expand upon the one previously mentioned. I must confess, I had much more to say, but knew that it should wait for a later, more opportune moment. I shrugged, and Hughes sighed.

I left afterwards to check upon our guards at the gates. The moon was golden, not its usually pale white. And so clear was it, that I could perceive every detail of the man's face etched into it, roaring with laughter. I wondered if that were God's face, amused about the future that we were hoping to shape here, or if He were simply mocking us about the future that He had already written—the one that none of us ever expected would actually happen. In my very long life I have never been able to answer that question.

CHAPTER THE THIRTEENTH,

in which our forces face their foe at the fabled city of Antioch, where there are miracles abounding, though some might be of a rather dubious nature.

The agreement that I had struck with Fairuz involved the delivery of several sacks of gold coins, (*bézants*, as our currency was then termed), as well as a number of gold goblets and miscellaneous jewels, which we had taken from our good Saracen neighbors. He would have preferred more, but once I informed him that we were placing an order for several hundred swords, (to be fashioned in the straight, Frankish manner certainly), he was most pleased. I was to deliver the items personally to him upon the morrow, under safe cover of darkness.

The early morning sky had only then begun its first tentative steps into the light, when I reached the Norman. He was standing absolutely straight, his fists clenched at his hips. He was watching Stephen, Robert de Flandres, and Count Hugh, with their respective troops, ride off.

"We have come so far," he said. "Now, when we are so close, they choose to believe that we shall fail. I refuse to blame the count. He is easily swayed. And the loss of Flemish vermin is no loss at all. I have no doubt that poverty awaits him, for he has spent far more on this holy mission than all the wealth that he might have ever been able to accrue. What a shame! But it would appear that our precious Stephen has always had little stomach for long sieges. I knew I should have let that coward fall off the mountain."

"He is most precious, my lord, is he not?"

Bohémond turned his face towards mine. Its sneer transformed into a smile, and he soon filled the air around us with raucous laughter.

"What says the heathen sword-maker?"

"Tonight."

"We must make ready. There is much to do." He began to walk away, then turned back to me. "When our work here is done, I hope that you will consider staying on."

"In the Holy Land?"

"In Antioch."

"I am at the Holy Father's disposal. If it is his will, I shall stay here."

"Your will is of no less value. You have proven yourself most worthy. It is an honour to kill at your side."

I wondered what was to become of me in the near future. Would I stay to help secure these territories against a relentless horde? Would I return to my belovèd Paris? I put my faith and my life in the Creator's hands, in the hopes that, even if He did not always cherish me, He might not always reveal to me His mighty anger. And that was all that any man could hope for, was it not?

Shortly thereafter, a strange incident occurred. During the afternoon of the following day, (one that was already uneventful), I chanced upon a man in the group that Stephen had brought with him, and who had chosen to remain with our forces. Fulcher de Chartres was young and thin, his face quite drawn. (I began to wonder if every man in Stephen's company were nothing more than a representation of the man, himself.) This chronicler had set before himself a large piece of wood upon which rested a sheet of *vellum*, a small bottle of ink, a quill, and a pumice stone (presumably for erasure). He was engrossed in his writing when I disturbed his concentration. Jokingly, I suggested that he make certain to spell my name correctly. He apologized, then informed me that de Blois had ordered all chroniclers to omit my name from any recorded tale, and that was due to the Norman prince's firm order. I ignored all else that Fulcher may have been saying, as I ran to the Norman to have him explain this grievous insult.

Bohémond told me that there must have been some mistake, and that he would take care of it immediately. At the time that was enough for me, though I related the entire event to Brother Michael later on. That was when I saw the most unusual expression there, upon my old friend's face. In point of fact, I had never seen anything like it before that moment. I should have pushed him to reveal something that he was obviously trying to conceal. But I thought that its revelation might have eased his pain, and at that time, I wanted him to suffer with the keeping of it, especially if he were keeping it from me.

Then came the evening, so late in fact, that it was barely dawn—the third of June, 1098, a seminal date in this war, for as I presented Fairuz with his newly acquired wealth, I watched our troops, one by one, climb up the tower, and then down into the city proper. They opened the Gate of St. George, and in rushed our forces like a monstrous wave upon a sea at storm. The city's ruling governor, *Yaghi Siyan*, awoke to our clarion-blasts. I have never believed that he suspected his force of approximately four thousand to be so quickly defeated. (It turned out that their supplies had also diminished considerably over time; consequently, said soldiers were probably not at their peak of strength.) Since the city was predominantly Christian, he thought it advisable to depart with a token group of guards. But when an unruly mob came for him, his faithful company miraculously disappeared, and he was forced to defend himself. (Not a pretty sight, I assure you.) By late afternoon the city was ours. We cheered each other, celebrated our astounding victory, praised God. That was when I discovered the vast numbers of Christians whom we had killed in this place, and their blood mingled with that of the Saracen in the dirt at our feet.

The day wore on, forcing us all to remember its most unwelcome burn. I found the archbishop resting comfortably upon a pile of tattered carpets in the shade between two small buildings. He was looking up.

"May I bring you fresh water, your holiness?" I asked, also looking up.

"I have had my fill, thank you. Have you noticed how many birds there are, flying about this city?"

The truth was, I had not. However, he had. And he proceeded to tell me of how, as a boy, he had seen a group of itinerant players, jugglers, and the like, who were passing through the town of his birth. Of them all, the only one who fascinated him was a man who termed himself, *the master of the animals.* He it was who pretended to speak to his coterie of beasts in their specific tongues, after which they performed various tricks with little balls, or who ran around chasing their own tails. There was only a single bird that the archbishop had never forgotten. Its master tied a tiny scrawl to its claw, containing a message that the reader should raise three fingers. It flew to another member of the troupe, who was standing upon a hillside. This man untied the note, read it, raised three fingers, then sent the animal away to return to its master.

"My vision is not what once it was," he continued, "though I believe that I may have seen several birds with very large feet pass over. Inform the Norman that the governor may have sent a message to others for aid prior to his untimely passing. The prince will need to rally our troops. When you are finished, come join Raymond and myself in Saint Peter's Church. We shall pray and give thanks together. Do not allow the Norman to convince you to help him organize. I have been unduly lax when it comes to your spiritual training, and the Holy Father will never forgive me my lapses of judgment. I shall be awaiting your return."

He struggled to arise. I offered my hand. He refused it. He walked away from me with steady (and very slow) steps.

We worked far into the night to bury so many dead. I, myself, had slept not at all when I thought of the archbishop's mention of secret messages. In the early light I took out Anna's letter, the perfume of which had long since dissipated. I was so engrossed in it, that I did not see Brother Michael standing nearby.

"Is that hers?" he asked.

"Whose?" I asked, quickly shoving the item into my tunic.

"You know how much I hate it when you pretend to be the naïve innocent. Have some respect for your elders."

How did he know? I had always been so careful not to be noticed.

"The Holy Father has asked me to keep a watchful eye upon his young charge, for all the good that it has done both of us."

"During our first night in Konstantinople the archbishop told me that no Byzantine could be trusted. I wonder what he would say of their women?"

"He would tell you that they will break your heart."

I further wondered if he would take my feelings for her into account. He smiled wryly.

"Which feelings are those—the feeling of your shaft hardening each time that you remember how you felt whilst inside her, or the feeling of spilling your seed upon the ground, for she is nowhere nearby to swallow it?"

His words cut me deeply. I cannot say if it were because they cheapened what had passed between the princess and myself, or if he were most correct in his perception.

"Is that everything you believe she means to me?"

"You forget, young one, that it was I who paid the prostitute who gave you your first taste of what it felt like to be a man, may God forgive me. Were you at all careful this time, or will her large belly be the spark that sets fire to an imperial crisis?"

I was most apologetic when I informed him that I had been quite careful, more so than ever.

"Must you tell him?" I asked, referring to the Holy Father.

"We shall see. First, I am willing to wait until some time in the distant future, if you are contrite."

"O, I am most contrite!"

"Very well. Now you must confess to me all your sins. And omit no detail, upon pain of excommunication!"

So I sat there for a very long while, relating any and every moment of our time together. It was not so painful an experience as I believed that it would be, though I must confess further that Brother Michael's constant smiles bothered me more than once; nor did he cease to ask for ever-more details.

We had not spent more than a day or so in that place, when, as the archbishop suspected, Kerbūgha came with a vast number of men, greater even than he had ever brought before. We threw ourselves into the fray.

Death was the sole victor that day.

There came a lull in the fighting, and we were all grateful for it. During this time a monk in Raymond's company approached both him and the archbishop. He was of a most calm demeanor and spoke (as I was to discover he always did) in quiet, measured tones, as if it were a conversation to which no one but he could possibly be privy, despite the presence of others. He measured each word with deliberate decision, I thought. This Peter Bartélémy claimed that visions from Saint Andrew had come to him during the past month. Before he had a chance to explain what they were, the archbishop questioned him in some detail. How did he know it was a saint? What did the man look like? Was all this nothing more than a fever brought on by hunger? Peter described how the saint told him of his preaching in Capodocia, Galatia, and the Scythian deserts; he spoke of how Nero had cheered when he discovered that his governor had bound the saint to the cross, that the man might die slowly in the hot sun of midday. Raymond was mightily impressed, less so the archbishop. Raymond pressed him to describe his visions. In essence, this is what they constituted:

The saint had told him that he could find the Holy Lance in the Church of Saint Peter here in Antioch. The archbishop laughed. He had prayed in that very church earlier in the week. If a holy relic were there, it would have had to be buried deep within its massive stone foundations, for there was no place of honour that any of its adherents had ever created; nor did any of the surviving Christians, who had worshipped there all their lives, mention a single word of it. Moreover, tales of Saint George had been in abundance for centuries, and more than one claimed that his body could be found in that selfsame church. Unfortunately, the archbishop could find no trace of his presence there either. Peter thought that they should go together to the church, but he agreed to abide by their decision, should they elect not to do so. He excused himself. The archbishop looked over at me and made a face twisted with disgust.

The Norman and I both entered the small house that our compatriots were using for their quarters. After having been apprised of the current situation, we could not believe that the monk had somehow brought dissension into the friendship between the archbishop and Raymond.

"Is his vision real?" the Norman asked.

"I am loathe to think that he is anything but mad," the archbishop offered.

"Do you believe that the Holy Spirit speaks to him?" Bohémond asked of Raymond.

The latter had no opportunity for a reply, as the archbishop interrupted, which action pleased Raymond not at all.

"I have known people like him all my life. They believe that they burn with holy fire. Trust me when I say that, whatever they may feel, there is nothing holy about it. For them it is no more than a need to sustain themselves throughout all the years of their empty, wretched lives. These insignificant men have a vision one day with which they hope to transform the world, and sometimes people begin to listen; for so great is the need to have the presence of God in our lives, that many follow even a false prophet whose aspect of holiness may be no greater than the absence of shoes at his feet. Invariably his vision is about war, the war of Good against Evil. And invariably many die because of his holy calling. This Peter, supposedly beset by saintly visions, he, too, will fail. Shall we fail with him?"

As I say, Raymond, however, was impressed, and offered to go with this Peter to the church, and, if necessary, dig, himself, to uncover the truth. The archbishop, perhaps because he was fatigued, reluctantly gave his blessing.

That very night we were all witness to an event that could be considered only as miraculous. We saw a ball of fire in the sky. At first it was far away and quite small. Then we noticed it grow larger, which meant that it was coming closer. Brave as our men were, some of them yelped like dogs, or wept like infants. Some cried that it was the end of the world. Somehow I remained calm. If it were time for me to die, then so be it. None of us can escape our Lord's judgment. Better now than later. Then I saw something that I had not suspected would happen; it appeared to change direction, ever so slightly, yet quite perceptibly. It was going to bypass the city.

Everyone fled. I stood alone in the town's center, watching it pass overhead. I could not believe what it actually was. It was the largest boulder that I had ever seen, yet fire surrounded it, forming a long tail in its wake. It carried its unspeakable heat over the city's walls and directly into the camp of our enemy. It landed with a thunderous crack, sending many of their soldiers high into the air like broken dolls, burning to cinders. Dirt, dust, sand—these billowed up and swirled about, spilling pieces of vegetation (and flesh) everywhere. In the midst of all that horror, I realized that someone had to know the truth of what was happening. I ran to one of the towers. Through its window I could see that Kerbūgha's army was in shambles. I raced back down. The Norman had to learn of what I had seen. A swift victory in Jerusalem was assured!

I found Bohémond with many others in the Church of Saint Peter. Its vast, firm structure was the only thing that gave everyone a sense of safety. And all that mattered so little now. I told him that he must take our forces out of the city and attack what was left of our enemy's camp. He hesitated. I had never seen him hesitate about anything. But when I saw the archbishop, who was crouching in a corner, being held in comfort by Count Raymond, I knew that something terrible had transpired between all concerned.

"We shall dig for the Holy Lance," the Norman told me. "It is the archbishop's will; it is God's will. When we have found it, we shall raise it aloft in parade before our enemy, and we shall smite him like the insect that he is."

I had come to know that the prince was a man deeply in love with the sound of his own voice. What I had not anticipated was that I would come to recognize finally how hollow was its echo.

He left without another word. Raymond lifted up the archbishop and led him to the entry doors. It was there that the man of God looked at me.

"I was arrogant," he said, "prideful. The Lord above has burned those sins out of my spirit."

The two men walked off. I went out of the church to one of the many gates at the city's walls. I had no idea why I was doing so. I simply needed to leave everyone and everything, if only for a brief time, hoping to make some sense of it all.

When I arrived at the gate, I thought it unusual that it was already uplifted. Eustace was standing outside of it, watching in the distance, where all of the surviving foe were now gathering. I could have walked away, perhaps should have, though I cannot always be accused of having taken the wisest course of action, may God forgive me. I came up to Eustace, who was standing now upon a small mound.

"Do you see it?" he asked. "It crouches right there," he said, pointing to a clearing between trees. "I have never seen anything so huge."

I squinted, then stared again.

"I see nothing but trees, grassland, and the desert beyond."

"How can you be so blind?!" he shouted, grabbing my shoulders. "How can you not see … the dragon?" he asked once again, his eyes wide at the horizon.

I looked again, and again I saw only branches moving.

"He is taller than the tallest tree," he continued. "Each scale is the size of a shield. His form glistens in the sun. His claws rend the earth. He belches flame. Or does he laugh? He knows what is to come." He turned once more to me. "He holds this land in his sway, and he has no need of our worship." He began to walk away. "He is waiting for us."

"Where is he waiting?"

"In the holy city upon the hill," he called back to me. "He will join us there."

CHAPTER THE FOURTEENTH,

in which the preponderance of Antiochene miracles knows no bounds.

On an early morning in the very middle of June, Count Raymond and the monkish Peter began to dig up the stone tiles of the very large and very old church. Long after the sun had set, I came by to see their handiwork. When I entered, I barely escaped falling into one large hole adjacent to the entrance. It was then that I saw the entire floor riddled with more of those same holes than I could count. Raymond was sitting in a corner, covered with much soil, his face so drawn, I thought it would fall to his knees. The monk was begging him to stay.

"I cannot. No more of this. Whatever your dream was, it was not prophecy."

"If you will but permit me to dig in this last place," Peter implored, pointing to the hole nearest his feet, "I know that we shall find it herein."

Raymond ignored him momentarily, before acquiescing finally. The monk jumped down. With no implements, he dug feverishly, his hands bleeding as he cut them, deeper and deeper. What happened next is something about which I have never been assured. Either he pulled the piece of a broken lance from below his robes, or he actually found one that had been left in that place a long time before. Whatever the cause, he jumped out, holding the broken tip of iron high. Raymond fell to his knees and wept.

Early of the next day I came to the archbishop's quarters. He ran his hands over the lance. He did not look at me as he spoke:

"I have long dreamed of this moment, when I would touch the very spear that had pierced the side of our Lord. When we sat together at a Byzantine feast, I thought your opinions childish; what good Christian would not want to seek out all manner of holy relics? However, I have come to understand that wisdom may not necessarily discriminate against the very young."

"I am not so very young, your holiness."

"O, my son, believe me when I say that you are." He sighed now. "Despite your youth, you have much of value to say to those who have the sense to listen. Finally am I able to hear your voice. It tells me that no object, forged by a human hand, and utilized for an evil purpose, should ever be revered. Wherever that lance may be, it is not here."

He picked up the object, turned it over in his hands, then tossed it aside.

"That piece of metal is no more the lance than is the sword that you wield."

"How can you know this?"

"I wish I knew. Perhaps it is because the time granted to me has diminished of late."

When I tried to convince him that he had many more fruitful years ahead of himself, I was asked to speak no more of it.

"My Creator has taken pity and granted me a moment of the purest clarity. This knowledge cannot be gleaned from any book. I know now that the discovery of the true lance was never meant for any mortal to make."

Though he knew it a false thing, the archbishop ordered us all to march in procession through the streets, carrying the relic aloft. But this was no mere ceremonial activity. We marched in two long rows, as the Norman had suggested. Then we marched out of the gates. Then we marched towards what remained of Kerbūgha's army, each row twisting itself to surround them. Then, with swift stroke, we engaged them. And then I realized the reason for the archbishop's actions. Our men fought with renewed vigor. Though still hungry, they fought as if the stink of their own sweat and the taste of their own blood were all they needed to sate their growling stomachs. And with the lance at the forefront of the battle, what army could lose?

I noticed several men, who appeared to be leaders of rank equal to (if not greater than) the Persian. Within a short space of time, they betook themselves (and their soldiers) from the field. (Perhaps they were his allies, but no more.) The Persian's forces were dwindling. I knew it, (and I assumed he did as well), that this would be his final campaign.

Nigrum bore me through their ranks, where I swirled my blade, as I had seen the Turks do, and I circled around them, cutting with each thrust. I had lost sight of the Persian, until I saw a curved shape coming towards me. I bent down to let it pass above my back, as I lunged, cutting off a small portion of the attacker's sword-hand. Then it was that I stopped to see Kerbūgha's face. Etched into it deeply were neither fear nor pain, but absolute bewilderment. Bleeding to death, I expected him to fall over. Instead, he reined in his horse and turned to leave the field. As he galloped off, he turned round to look in my direction again. Some of his men followed. Most fell to the ground. Still others, bowing to us, placed their swords upon the ground before themselves, and awaited our mercy.

I dismounted, then led my trusted steed back towards the city's gates. Out of the clouds of dust I walked past Godfrey, Brother Michael, and the Norman, all of whom were standing near each other.

"The Lord has made you indestructible, my brother," Godfrey said, watching as the wounds upon my face and body began to heal themselves. "Behold, I have seen the Lord's own lion sent amongst us to protect the true faith."

Brother Michael rubbed his eyes, then stared.

"Blessèd is he who is witness to the Lord's wonders!" he exclaimed. "I had no idea."

"Neither did I," I spoke quietly.

The Norman said nothing, though he never took his eyes from me.

We had finally captured Antioch, and there was much celebration. Stephen was doubtless conspicuous by his absence. Some even marked him with the title of *deserter* and *coward,* but I believe that the former remembrances of his comforts had called to him in sirensong, and he could naught but follow their tones all the way homeward. Unfortunately for him, he ran into a Turkish garrison along the way, who smote him and his entire company most terribly, and consequently, they all died. I must confess that history has never been particularly kind to his memory. And who am I, after all, to attempt to stem the tidal forces of historical inevitability? I often wonder what profits a man to seek his comfort but lose his soul, as well as his flesh? I wonder if he were thinking of that question as he lay dying? I wonder.

Barely had we spent several days or nights in victorious celebration, when the Norman chose that unique moment in time for his own annunciation, *i.e.,* he was to take possession of Antioch as his personal fiefdom. Raymond was aghast! (He spoke now with the full confidence of all the others who supported him.) If the city were not being returned to the emperor, as their original agreement had stipulated, then the dispensation of this place was a matter for all parties concerned. The Norman laughed. The emperor could have ten thousand pledges; how would he enforce them? As for the other leaders, they would have to recognize that the Norman would stand his ground, regardless of the cost.

Thus began a rupture that would never completely heal. As Raymond and Bohémond argued, the days lingered on into months. With so much time available, and no constructive outlet for them, our forces grew restless. Fights broke out, often prompted by the local tavern's ale, or the heat, or not much of anything else. It was during this time that I found myself one day in a brothel that several of my compatriots swore was quite satisfying. I had not been with a woman since Byzantium, and I thought it high time to release the fire in my loins once more. But when I saw the bevy of beauties, I must confess that I could not alter my member's flaccid state of being. They were not unattractive really. In point of fact I had once been with a woman, both plain and large, in Siena, one whom everyone thought most hideous, though I found her not unappealing. She was the best who—I digress. The workers in said brothel were wives, daughters, sisters, widows. Most could not pretend to smile, let alone enjoy their duties. And when I saw one girl (whose years could not have been more than ten) being groped by numerous men, whose hands had become like paws upon her sad face, I knew that I could not stay here; nor could I stand idle whilst the child was being so wrongfully abused.

I pushed the men aside, and held fast to her little arm. But I could not leave. A woman jumped in front of me. She slapped my face.

"Where are you taking my daughter?" she shouted. "If you want her, you must pay for her."

Surprised, I allowed my grasp to loosen. The child wiggled freely from it, as her sadness changed to a veritable hiss of anger, then she kicked me in the groin and ran crying to her mother. Crouching now, I soon fell to the floor. The customers spat, hit, and kicked me. Brother Michael (whose presence there I shall discuss not at all!) picked me up. He brought me out of that hellish place of mischief and cruelty.

"Are you mad, boy? These men would wrestle with God, Himself, if He denied them the right to that glorious patch of hair between a woman's thighs."

I pulled away from him.

"She is no woman!" I insisted.

"Her services can be purchased. That is all they need to know."

"And you as well?"

His face turned a deep red.

"I would never do that to a little girl," he spat between clenched teeth. Then he calmed himself as he spoke further. "Even the Holy Father knew what these men were. What would you have them do? Shall they savour each other's buttocks like the accursèd Sodomites of old? A man will have his needs. That is how we are made. If God had wanted us to be perfect, He would have made of us angels. Instead, we are the lowly creatures you see before you. As for these women, how do you think people will behave when food is so scarce? The child will have a full stomach. Maybe, if God is kind, she will forget."

"She will never forget."

"At least she will not starve!" he shouted.

I dragged myself back to my quarters, where I had been keeping a small jug of wine. I drank myself to sleep, clutching it as if it were my sole salvation.

The sometime-pleasure for many continued, until the searing heat of August came, and they succumbed to plague. During one of those pitiable days I went to see the archbishop, who had been ailing. He was barely able to lift his head from off his chest. I stared at him. Never had I seen the like. His skin had a grayish, greenish pallor. Beneath his eyes were two dark wells. The particular sickness from which he suffered was one that we had termed, *aigu-morts, the chill of the dead.* And often he shook with a quaking so terrible, that it seemed as if God's (or the Devil's) hands were upon him. He shook for hours, his saliva spilling across his bedclothes. We laid innumerable skins upon his person, all to no avail. He was beyond all warmth, all comforting.

I cannot say if he knew where he was (or who he was) anymore, for his hands reached up and about haphazardly. His time was almost gone. Brother Michael performed the final rite of extreme unction for him, even though the poor unfortunate was incapable of response. I bent down to kiss the old man's forehead. At that moment his palm brushed against the hilt of my sword, and he let out a faint cry. I turned over his hand to examine it. Its flesh was emitting smoke. And into the palm was burned an imprint of the hilt. I touched the handle to see how my body would react. Nothing happened, as nothing had ever happened during the ten thousand other times when I had held it in my firm grasp. The archbishop looked up at me. The cloudiness in his eyes had fled.

"It was you," he strove to speak. "All this time you have had it. How did I not know? How did I not see? Most blessèd ... amongst men...."

I had no idea what his ravings meant, if anything at all. I knew only that I pitied the once great man brought low by his weakness. And when his body ceased its palsied movements, he let out one last loud gasp, and his chest sank down, as if crushed by loss of air. His spirit fled its frail dungeon only moments before dawn's light filled his chamber.

Many were sickened by his loss. I, myself, was not immune. But only Raymond, our brave count, wept piteously for the servant of God, whom he had come to know as a friend. (And he would honour Archbishop Adhémar's memory for the rest of his days.)

Not long afterwards, Peter came forth to enumerate another dream. In this one Saint Andrew (who apparently had far more time for prophecy in death than ever he had in his short life) informed the monk that the Norman should be given Antioch; as for the archbishop, his spirit would rot in Hell for having initially denied Peter his holiness. Every one of us stared at each other, incredulous, wretched.

On that particular night, Peter had a visitation from a most unusual creature. Clad in black, the spectre (for so it must have been) cut his cheek ever so slightly, neither with talon nor with claw, but with sword, before it fled into the night. No one else ever saw that creature. I can tell you, dear reader, that Peter's wound never healed. On the following morning he related the previous night's unique events, and claimed that the phantasm responsible for his current pain was St. George, himself. (How and why he conjured that name is one mystery that I have never been able to solve.) He added that it was the saint's way of illustrating how vital it was for the monk never to allow his special visions to make himself prideful; for such was the sin by which the angel fell.

I was not at all pleased. Only this monk could twist a warning into a cautionary blessing. Somehow the mysterious visitor had done his job improperly.

I cursed myself greatly.

Finally, in the following year, in January, in the middle of a very wet winter, many of the soldiers (and several of their leaders) swore to follow the count, if he would but lead them to Jerusalem. And it came to pass that these *carriers of the cross,* or *crusaders* (as they had taken to calling themselves with greater frequency) departed with Raymond at their head, whilst the Normans elected to stay behind and create a new (and entirely Christian) Antioch.

On the night before we left, Bohémond came to me. Fresh out of the rain, his cloak and breath steaming in the chill, he endeavoured once more to alter my course of action.

"I offer you one final opportunity to cast your lot with me; stay here. With Baldwin in Edessa, and we at Antioch, the Holy Land will soon be ours. Let the old man go to Jerusalem. We can always take it from him later. Ally yourself with me, and together we shall make the very earth quake! What say you, my friend?"

I was sorely tempted, though I suspected that he was thinking only of his belovèd (and most detested) emperor. There were so many cities, towns, villages, any number of which I might have made my own; for what had seemed only the slightest of possibilities before, became now quite real. But the possession and governance of such territories—was that my true nature? Was it my nature to take from the count something that he had sought so desperately, and not for his own glory? No. Nor would I do to him what the Norman had done. I declined, even if the Norman would hear none of it.

"Everyone believes that simple spear is responsible for our achievements. You and I know better, Guy de Lagery. It was you. It may have always been you who has made all the difference."

"Perhaps you have never truly known me, Prince Bohémond. I am now, I have ever been, and will ever be ... a son of the church."

"Poverty? Chastity? Obedience? These are not the paths you seek."

"The blood that flows within me is the blood of Christendom. I may never be anything more than its sword, but I cannot deny my blood its responsibility. It is my duty to go to Jerusalem. I shall be there to witness it, to become a part of it, to create it. I may have been commanded to do this by our Holy Father, whom God has seen fit to allow to walk in the footsteps of the sainted fisherman of old, but I shall not deny him, as I shall not deny myself."

He unsheathed his sword. My hand immediately grabbed my own. He raised the sword high, swiftly, then brought it down slowly to be held in both of his hands.

"I never thanked you for having introduced me to your dirty, little Arab. His blades are the finest I have ever seen, the sharpest I have ever used. He could teach a thing or two to our Christian manufacturers, who have yet to learn his skills. He will make a fine addition to my new kingdom. You would have as well. I think I shall dub him, *royal swordmaker*. I think he will like that, providing his title comes with a few more gold pieces."

Laughing, much taken with himself, he nodded, then walked back out into the pour. I did not know that he would fail to bid me farewell of the following morn, though I suspected it. What surprised me far more was that I would not see his face again for some years. And when he saw mine, he was so grateful—But I am rushing headlong once more, and the tale has barely begun.

CHAPTER THE FIFTEENTH,

in which we liberate all of Jerusalem's children, whether they desire it or not.

On the road to Jerusalem we passed many cities, all of which had heard of our coming, and all of which gave no battle as we marched through them: Tripoli; Palestine; Beirut; Jaffa; Ramleh. It was in this last place that emissaries from Bethlehem appeared, seeking our aid to free them from the Turk—a story that was not unfamiliar to any of us. Tancred (who had grown ever more sullen than was his usual nature) informed the men that he would be only too happy to go. And so he did, only to return several days later, having succeeded in his mission (much to everyone's surprise); nor had he sought to make the city his own. (I thought that the possession of Biblical cities was a family trait; I might have been wrong about that.) Only in Acre did we find a city that refused its surrender. When we settled in for another siege, we had not expected it to last until April.

During that time Peter decided to bless us with another vision. This one consisted of all of us throwing ourselves simultaneously against the city's gates. And *finally*, (thanks be to the Lord in the highest!), not a single soul believed that his vision had any veracity. And he was mightily offended. He asked for an ordeal by fire, the result of which would proclaim that he had had no mere dreams but visions. Raymond knew this to be a bad thing, yet he could not convince the monk otherwise.

Two parallel rows of timbers were set afire. Holding his fabled lance, Peter jumped into the blaze at one end, then emerged from it at the other. I did not know if I should praise him his courage, or condemn him his foolhardiness. You see, dear reader, he was horribly burned. There was barely an *iota* of skin left free from the flame's char. (The only piece left unharmed was the patch of it surrounding the cut upon his cheek. It was as if the wound had to remain clearly visible for all to see.) And yet the man stood there, grinning broadly. As his legs caved in upon themselves, several of us grabbed him, lest he fall back into the raging mound. He lingered on for twelve more days in unremitting agony. After he left this life, no one ever spoke again of him, until the chroniclers began to write of these events long after they had transpired. As for the lance, we all decided that it should receive its proper burial with the man who had uncovered it. I offered my services as part of the detail, and was, in fact, the one who laid him to rest in the earth. As I placed his wrapped body upon the soil, I concealed the remnant of the spear beneath my tunic. I did not believe that anyone (especially he) would miss it, and I wanted it now either as a remembrance of our heritage, or as a token of one man's overweening pride. (I could not determine which inclination were the stronger.) No one ever discovered what I had done. And I possess the object to this very day.

Afterwards, in the forests outside of Acre, we left him and the city still unliberated (or unconquered, as the case may be) behind.

By early June we had struck camp outside the walls of Jerusalem. Unlike the previous city-governors (or *emirs*, as I would later learn its Arabic terminology), this one had expelled all Christians, had stocked the city with provisions, and had poisoned the wells in the surrounding region. Whatever acrimony we may have felt for this leader, we had to admire him his thoroughness. Then we made our assessment of our current situation, and it was not good. There were thick walls, and there were many towers. And the possibility of finding another Fairuz was too rare to consider. What was far worse was our lack of any siege-engines. These, doubtless, would have to be built. That posed a further problem. We were in a desert. A lone reed at a very rare wateringhole would not provide us with anything, save the occasional bit of laughter at our own expense. We had no choice but to return to the nearest forest to cut down timbers. Unfortunately, the trip was several days' journey. Robert de Normandie volunteered for the task. As soon as he heard this, Tancred piped up that he would go with him. So they rode off with a large force to the forests of Samaria.

Our men worked vigorously at their labour for several weeks. In the meanwhile, one morning, after Brother Michael and I had finished our ride around the city's boundaries, hoping to find some possible means of unguarded entry, we were stopped by Raymond. He needed to tell us something that only we, with our ecclesiastical backgrounds, could appreciate. During the night he had had a vision. (Brother Micheal and I exchanged glances, which betokened our exhaustion with our apparently holy companions, and said nothing.) The archbishop had appeared to him. The archbishop? No! Truly? Verily, he said unto us, it had happened. And what information did the sainted man wish to impart, I asked? All of our forces would have to march with their feet bare around the city's walls, all whilst praying loudly. I was dumbfounded when presented with this dream; consequently, I could say nothing. Brother Michael had no wish to insult the memory of the good archbishop, but was it really necessary to march on hot sands, without the protection of good Christian footwear? The count insisted that it be so.

And it came to pass that the Christians fasted for an entire day. And they chose no feast for its conclusion, but rather a holy procession, where they (we) marched, barefoot to a man, chanting as loudly as they (we) could, whilst enemy soldiers on the parapets above derided us, mocked us, spat upon us, threw rocks down at us (me), all whilst laughing at us (me!). Once finished, we made a final prayer at the Mount of Olives. Though Brother Michael's feet gave him much pain, he was as moved by the experience as was every single one of us. I smiled. Perhaps my uncle's dear friend had returned, after all, to shore up the tumbling morale of these most blessèd soldiers; for if God is infinite, and His capacity for forgiveness equally infinite, did it not follow that a Christian deed might provide these men with their sole source of redemption? I wanted so very much to believe in the essential dignity of our cause, to believe in us. And at that juncture in time all doubt in me fled, if only for a moment.

On the following day Raymond asked me to ride to the others to determine their progress. I knew this would not please Tancred, so, without hesitation, I agreed to go. When I arrived to present myself as the courier to whom he would have to convey his information, I discovered that he was nowhere to be found. I questioned the soldiers, who began to laugh. Of late the Norman's nephew had developed a most rare and rather unusual problem with his bowels, *i.e.,* he could not control them. No matter what he ate or drank, each item fled between each buttock with all deliberate speed. And the noises of this activity were like nothing that had ever been emitted from a human body, (if what the men said were true), and the smell of it was something that truly defied description. Nor did he care for it, when his forces lingered about the hidden spot in the woods to which he would rush to claim for his privacy. Consequently, he might drop to his knees near one rock, notice the rest of the men attempting to stifle their laughter, then rush to another spot, thence to another. It was during my unscheduled visit to him that he was in the middle of this rushing about, when he chanced upon a cave. Within it were thirty timbers already hewn, and piled neatly. Having clothed himself once more, and with a modicum of dignity, he ordered the others to remove the *cache* of items and begin construction. After conferring with him for a short and strained discussion, I mounted Nigrum.

"You are most fortunate, Tancred," I told him. "The Lord has answered your prayers. You have prayed, have you not?"

I gave no time as courtesy for an answer. I turned and rode off.

By the time that Tancred and the others rolled the machines into place before the walls, it was not soon enough. We had reports that a Turkish garrison was on the way. For two days the battle ensued. It did not appear that we would have much success. Then, during that third and final day, the fourteenth of July in the year of our Lord, 1099, at the very hour of noon—the time of the crucifixion—thunder cracked in a bright summer sky. But it did not rain. Our forces looked up. Our enemies upon the parapets above us did the same. What happened next was a dream so real and so great, that it encompassed each soul who was its witness that day.

There was a sound that flowed about us. More than hear it, we could feel it wafting across our skin, caressing our faces. We heard the heavenly host, whose breath was song. And the light that descended from above blinded me. When I was able once more to see, I noticed that our entire force was staring at me. I could not have guessed why, until I looked to my sides. At both right and left was a single line of white stallions. And upon them sat knights in white armour, whose skin, hair, and eyes were equally white. There was not a sound to be heard anywhere from any man, bird, or insect. I looked over to my left. One of the knights, who had been staring ahead, as the others had done, turned now to me. He nodded whilst smiling. I knew that the moment had arrived.

I raced to Hughes, seized his black and white banner, raised it aloft and was about to give forth our battle cry, when I realized that I did not know what to say, so I simply shouted the word for *banner*:

"*Beaucent!*"

The knights and the rest of our men did the same, then turned with me and began to ride hard. Somehow we knew; somehow we all knew that the gates would not hold us back. They began to glow as if afire from an unseen source. Then the glow ebbed, though the metal continued to sizzle and melt. Eustace, who was closest to one of the gates, jumped from his horse with his sword drawn. As he landed upon his feet, he jumped up to the hot metal, thrusting at it. The locks and chains cracked and fell. He still held on, as his flesh sizzled against the hot bars.

"Go, my brother!" he called to Godfrey, holding on in his agony. "Take the devils."

Godfrey was the first inside. I followed, leading the charge.

Amidst the swirling clouds of sand and dust, I passed the stone relief of a Roman eagle near the entry wall. It was surrounded by a lion at each side, about to attack it. I cut a sharp line through the bird. The only voice that I heard belonged to Eustace in the distance:

"Blood cries out for blood!" he roared, and we all roared with him.

We attacked with all deliberate force and speed. There was no plan to any of it. It was as if we were scattering across the entire earth, itself. Tancred took over the structure known as *the Temple of Solomon*. (It stood over the rock where Isaac had offered his beloved son, Jacob, as a sacrifice unto the Lord.) Its commander did not fight bravely, but rather gave over the entire place, and pled to be saved through conversion. The Christian conqueror placed his personal banner upon its highest point.

Our angelic assistants were immune to attack; (blades passed through them as if through air) yet they began to accumulate very tiny drops of blood along their armour and capes. They smiled at me. I smiled back. Then one of them opened his mouth as he smiled. And I saw nothing but blackness, a horrible emptiness without end. I had no time to react, as my enemy came at me, and I thrust the blade between his ribs.

I cannot say how long we fought. It may have been moments, though it seemed like very many days. Still did the brilliant flame of conflagration burn, leaving only charred remains of the blackest ash in its wake. By early evening we had the Tower of David as our own, the Jaffa Gate, each single piece of the city. And some of us were on horseback. And some of us were standing. We looked about. The streets, the byways, the paths, these were all covered in blood. There was so much blood, that it soaked the horses' limbs and splashed along our thighs. Our horses did not gallop, but swam in all that blood. Our hands were covered in it. Our faces were soaked with it. It was all that we saw, all that we breathed. What we had unleashed upon the unsuspecting world of men, I dared not think.

Our assistants gathered together near the Holy Sepulchre. Their once clean garments covered now in blood, their faces smeared with it, they raised their swords aloft, then disappeared in a flash of light, a crack of thunder. No one took very much notice of their passing.

Whilst we basked in the glory of our homicidal rage, we neglected to take further note of the aftermath that was beginning to form itself. We had killed so many of Jerusalem's inhabitants, that there seemed no one left. Each victim's faith had been of no concern to us. Saracens, Jews, and even fellow Christians all died at our hands. The chroniclers would soon begin the tales of our heroic, valiant struggle. The Turk, the infidel, the pagan, these would come to look upon us as no better than beasts, creatures without honour. I was to discover only later that the city was sacred to them as well.

Whilst slaughter and rapine consumed the day, Brother Michael and I had made our way to the Church of the Holy Sepulchre. We stood upon one of its roof outcroppings, surveying all the dead. The wind picked up and brought their carrion-stench across the verdant land now run red. He tried to smile, though the odor would not let him.

"God has given to us Jerusalem this day," he said, covering his nose, coughing.

"And we have repaid Him with a city of death. That is why we shall lose it another day."

He stared at me, amazed, frightened perhaps that my words possessed the sound of prophecy. Of course, I was neither prophet nor seer, merely an observer and participant in man's noble deeds.

"We should burn the dead and salt the earth," I continued. "We have made of this place … a desolation."

"Is there no possible way for any of us to find redemption?"

I could barely believe his question. For the first time he looked to me to find solutions for problems of the spirit.

"There is always hope," I responded. "Whether any one of us seeks that path remains to be seen."

My clothing and skin were drenched. Standing there, battered by the fierce wind, I could see only the swirling sands. And then it seemed as if the dust gathered itself all around the city and rose before us as the serpent, the great worm, the dragon. I swear now that I saw it raise its scaly head and belch flame. And the flames engulfed everything about us, including the heavens, themselves, awash with fire. And we were all inside of it. We had become its talons, its life's blood, its beating heart. I could hear it shriek its terrible roar as the fire flew from its maw. And then (I have no idea why) I burst into a *paroxysm* of laughter. And my laughter drowned out all else.

At that moment Brother Michael gagged. The *vomitus* flew from out his mouth and mingled with the deafening din of the storm, as it tore at our faces.

Here endeth the First Book.

LIBER SECUNDUS

Filius

CHAPTER THE SIXTEENTH,

in which Godfrey is called upon to lead the New Jerusalem.

I wonder with what conviction a man will burn down the entire world, all the while convinced that his actions are the sole means of purifying the truth of an ever-sinful populace? Is there ever any room for doubt?

Respected by some, detested by others, and loved by none, Pope Gregory IX lived a full life, nine and ninety years to be exact. He was a man possessed of a long nose and an equally lengthy chin, both of which strove for union with the other. And he had little or no patience for heretics, the number of which increased daily (somehow, miraculously) during the years of his papal tenure. Of them he once told me:

> "We kill them," he said, holding up the open palm of his right hand, "and they kill us," now holding up the open palm of his left. "Perhaps they believe this to be an equitable arrangement," he said, folding his hands in front of his belly. "I do not."

So greatly did their presence mock his stature, that he set about the creation of what he termed his *sacred obligation*. It consisted of a series of tribunals to be conducted in every corner of the then known world, (administered by Franciscan friars, who were generally considered to be above all reproach), where various people (sometimes from the nobility, but more often than not from the peasantry) would be judged for their crimes against God. In the decades following its inception, Pope Gregory's labour would assume the name of *Inquisition*, and no one would remain untouched by its presence.

There in Rome he stood before me, in a grand cathedral, the soaring vault of which pierced the very firmament itself. Below a portrait of Christ's ascension into His Father's kingdom, he scowled at me, and ranted, as was his wont.

"You speak of the essential nobility of the human spirit, though nothing changes. Charlemagne fought the Vikings. You fought the Saracens. I fight everyone. Man is nothing more than a contentious bastard, ill-bred for nought, save the destruction of his own kind. This is one lesson that you have learned all too well, is it not? You will do as I have ordered," was his commandment. "I shall hear no more of it."

"I shall not," was my curt reply.

I do not believe that he expected me to deny him his will, for the look of bewilderment upon his face betrayed the secrets of his heart.

"You are the vassal of the church."

"I am its sword."

"And I am its commander! Whither I point, there will you strike."

"I have followed the wishes of the papal line, for it has pleased me to be of service. What you ask—"

"What I ask is the service that all men must do for their pontiff. The Templars have agreed to participate. It would not be fitting, if you refused to fight at their side."

I thought momentarily upon his judgment, uncertain if there were a grain of truth in his statement.

"They have lost their way," I responded finally. "The sin is not mine. I shall never slay a fellow Christian simply because his life does not conform to the tenets of church doctrine."

His face was flushed now.

"Who are you to make that assessment?" he demanded to know. "It is my prerogative and obligation to do so. You forget your place, Guy de Lagery."

"And you would place me in the midst of the slaughter. Is that where I belong?"

"Ours is a holy mission. If you fail to join it, you risk excommunication, and your soul will be damned."

"I died long ago. My God judged me then, and granted to me resurrection and immortality. And one who cannot die fears nothing for the loss of his soul."

"You may think that you died, but the truth was that you had barely a taste of it. I pity you. You will never know what it means to take that final slumber, only to awaken in the arms of our Lord."

He stared now at the statue of the bleeding Christ set behind and high above the altar, before turning to me once again to make his feelings known.

"This holy battle will take place with or without your involvement. It is my God-given duty to protect the church and its believers. I shall rid God's green earth of this infestation of traitors to the true faith. His will be done!"

"When the fog of Ignorance lifts, who do you believe will be the one left standing? Good day to you, pontiff. Forgive me; I cannot help but wish you *bad* hunting."

I believe that he thought his deeds would prompt his own canonization. Shame that he could not grant himself such an honour in his own lifetime.

That year of our Lord was 1233, and as I walked out of the pope's illustrious presence, I began to ruminate upon the long road that had brought me hither. And a very long road it was indeed!

With Jerusalem now in Crusader hands, the next task fell to the selection of its new Christian ruler. And in this holy city, everyone was agreed that he would have to be both wise and just, as well as deeply spiritual. There was only one man whom all believed evinced these three qualities: Godfrey de Bouillon.

When the crown was offered him, his modest response endeared him to the hearts of every citizen and became the stuff of legend:

> "I shall not wear a crown of gold or silver in the same city where our Lord wore one of thorns."

Everyone cheered then wept, then went about the business of survival or conquest, depending upon one's frame of reference.

Instead of *king*, he bore the title of *Defender of the Holy Sepulchre, Advocatus Sancti Sepulchri*. Once so christened, he took up the unenviable task of having to secure his city's borders against all invaders, foreign and/or domestic. I fear the burden that he assumed weighed most heavily upon him, for the kind spirit, whom we had all come to respect, soon traded his genial manner for the incessant sneer of his dear brother, Eustace. (And even *that* failed to make Eustace happy. Was there no pleasing the man?)

After numerous discussions with Hughes de Payens, I agreed that there was no more fitting time to put into action his initial idea concerning a group of warrior guardians, who would protect visiting pilgrims in the Holy Land. (I prayed that something of fertile consequence would bloom from the soil that we had soaked so thoroughly here.) Consequently, together we went to the Advocate to broach the subject, only to discover him overly cautious (or reluctant) to commit any number of men to our purpose. Hughes attempted to assure him that volunteers for the task at hand were too numerous to count. That fact mattered little to the new ruler of Jerusalem. More than once we asked him only for his permission, (as regent), so that the knights might have a place of refuge as their own, and the support of noble families from each Christian nation. He did, however, keep putting us off with various excuses.

Since most of the Christian leaders had either left for their respective homelands and properties therein, or gone off to create one or two new Christian kingdoms of their own, all but a few knights and several thousand soldiers remained behind. If ever a Boutoumites and a fleet were needed to protect against access from the sea, it was now.

Godfrey's prayers were answered in the form of a Pisan bishop, Daimbert, and a massive *flotilla* controlled by the ruling families of that city. As recompense for his support, (and that of his compatriots), the bishop was given the *Patriarchate* of Jerusalem. As God or Fate would have it though, when Godfrey learned that Daimbert's ambition was to rule over the city as head of a new *theocracy*, the former asked me to intercede with the help of my old comrades in Venice. And when both fleets eventually faced each other, they, too, were compelled to join in a discomforting alliance, this one of maritime-power. In short, Godfrey was far more concerned about retaliatory strikes against Jerusalem, than he was about any Christians who might be harmed in any occasional skirmish along the way to the places of pilgrimage.

Hughes and I would have to wait for the fulfillment of our mission, though not for long.

Brother Michael secured a small residence for us, the former occupants of which never returned to reclaim it. (Raymond had seized it originally, upon his entry into the city, but soon lost all desire to retain it, as no one had thought to ask him to wear the crown. Offended by the apparent lack of respect for his leadership and age, he believed it fitting to be elsewhere. He had thought initially to begin his return journey to the Empire of the Byzantines, thence to his ancestral properties in the southern Frankish kingdoms, stopping at various points along the way to carve out a piece of territory here, a bit of farmland there. After all, he had no wish to appear *empty-handed,* so to speak, in front of the emperor, should he decide to make an appearance there. It would have been most unseemly, would it not? Only after careful consideration did he decide to stay in the Holy Land and mark out a city for himself. Without much resistance, he took Tripoli, where he ruled for some years, prior to his death.)

I descended the stair to see a messenger, much haggard and worn down by his long journey, as he handed a message to Brother Michael. The latter's face took on an expression so sad as to be tragic. I did not think that he had ever revealed so much pain even upon the discovery that his dear wife's agèd heart had ceased to function during the night that they had been sleeping together. When he raised his head, he espied me, then turned to the messenger to dismiss him forthwith. When he returned his gaze to mine, there was no mistake as to the import of the words held now in his hand. His misery was not for his own anguished heart. There was no need for further explanations. I could feel each part of my body freeze over, as if I were a cold, dead thing that had once been a man …

CHAPTER THE SEVENTEENTH,

in which the church, once again, becomes something of a new home, before I return to the place of my birth.

I had never been in Rome. I preferred the Italian north, the sea-faring *Veneto,* to the clustered *campanile,* broken aqueducts, and other Latin ruins of the south. Yet it was here, in the former capital of a pagan empire, that the papacy had taken its first tentative steps in the world, and constructed its churches, like the *arenae* of old, in every corner of each land.

After having bowed and crossed ourselves, Brother Michael and I made our way to the end of a colossal chapel in the grand house that was built to honour the disciple, Peter. Much overladen with statuary and bejeweled decoration, there stood an enormous headstone. It marked the place where my uncle's body now lay buried beneath the marble floor.

"He would not have liked all this finery," Brother Michael commented, staring about. "Still, I am happy that he has finally found a place to rest in this sacred city. It is what he would have wanted after all."

"*Salve, Caesar. In tua patria magnam famam habes.*"

My statement confused Brother Michael. I had to explain, though I had not the strength for the task at hand.

"*Hail, Caesar. You have great fame in your country.* It was the first lesson in Latin that he taught to me. I have lived all of my life inside of the Church-Militant. My uncle should not have been so surprised that I found myself more suited for war than for prayer."

I recalled a time when, as a boy, I would sit with him at table. One or two burning tapers provided the sole light. There I would recite my lessons in Latin—the language of the Caesars that had become the language of the church. An entire universe was opened to me, as I studied Emperor Julius' lessons in warcraft, Cicero's arguments for liberty in the senate, and Vergil's poetic tale of the founding of a nation. Those moments provided me with the only true comfort that I have ever known.

"He always said you had more intelligence than all of the church fathers combined. Not an easy thing for a pope to admit, mind you."

"Why did he never tell me, himself?"

"Open your eyes, boy! He was no knight. He hated it when you strutted around, all full of your own arrogance. He wanted you to have a bit of humility."

"O, my old friend, I am many things; humble is not one of them."

We stood together in silent meditation for a time. It was broken only when Brother Michael laughed, then tried to restrain his impulse to do so again.

"He was very good at dice," he spoke finally, in so low a tone, that none might hear his words, "or maybe the good lady, Fortune, was with him always as he tossed the cubes about."

I never knew!

"Certainly not! He had to provide a good example for you. He knew that you would need that sort of guidance. And he made me give up not only dice, but all games of chance, when I took the vows. I never regretted my decision, though I think *he* may have, once or twice. Is it not strange what you recall when a friend, who has been as close to you as your own flesh and blood, should no longer be ... near?"

"He was the only real father I have ever known."

"Never doubt that he loved you."

"I never have. I regret only that I was a disappointment to him."

"How can you say that about yourself? He was proud of the man you have become."

"I am no priest, nor could I ever be. I desire too much the touch of a woman."

"A common enough sin, my boy. I would not whip the flesh from my back because of it."

"I never thought that he would die."

"No one ever thinks about the death of a loved one, until it is too late. Unfortunately, no one lives forever. All that matters is what one does with the time granted him. He was a good man. I did not always agree with him, and I made certain that he knew of it each time. But a hundred years from now, no one will remember me; they will remember him."

He was wrong, of course. I can see Brother Michael as clearly now as if we had made our good-byes only yesterday—the sparkle in his eye, the way he raised his brows and squinted whenever he smiled. I can still hear the raucous laughter that would shake his entire large frame. And when I recall the sternness in his voice during those occasions when he had a very good reason to grow angry, I still look around, hoping to find some secretive place where I might perchance escape his bile.

O, my old friend, are you sleeping peacefully in the earth, or do you fret somewhere in the heavens above, watching over the rest of us, poor fools that we are, straining to make our way? Perhaps we shall meet again, even if only in the dusty corridors of the memories, which you helped forge within me. *Requiescat in pace.* Rest now. There will be time enough for your laughter later on.

My comrade and I took our audience with the new pope, Paschal II. (Much given to self-deprecation, he had believed himself unfit for the demands of so exalted a position. Despite his misgivings, the conclave rendered unto him their unanimous approval. In truth, I believe they recognized his most capable gifts.) He was a man slender of form, not gaunt necessarily; neither was he given to the partaking of frequent meals. And he wore a beard, the whiteness of which would virtually sparkle in the light of the high forenoon. What I remember most of him was the dignified manner in which he carried himself, for he was as affable a pope as the images, which his pastoral name might inspire.

We were welcomed into his presence as if we were long-lost brethren suddenly rediscovered:

"Your names have spread throughout the world. You are heroes! And here in St. Peter's palace, you have found a place of refuge."

I looked over at Brother Michael, whom I assumed would be as ecstatic as was I, only to see that a curiously sad expression had found its home upon his face. I could not fathom its meaning.

The Holy Father assured us that the church would look after our financial needs, though it would be useful if my own family were to provide a *stipend*, perhaps, to alleviate the *onus* of costs for myself. (Brother Michael, as a dependent of the church, would receive a sum twice yearly.) And we were to obey his word, alone. Whilst in the Holy Land, it would be fitting that we adhere to church doctrine and conduct as delineated by the appointed papal representative, Daimbert, though the final decision on all matters was to originate from Rome, should any pertinent questions arise. I was to assume a new standing in the church hierarchy, and with it came a new title as well, *Defender of the Faith*. The pope maintained that it was the proper course of action for him to take, as I had proven myself many times in battle, and moreover, I was the only descendant of that most holy

Urban. Then he whispered to me how he would seek my uncle's canonization, though not so quickly; these things took time, I had to understand.

Whilst grateful for his promise regarding my uncle, (despite his reluctance to commit to a particular point in future-time for its achievement), I found his statement about me to be somewhat disturbing. Was I to be bound in service to the church for the rest of my days?

"No specific religious order can claim you as its own," he went on, "yet you occupy a unique position amongst all men. It is my belief that someone who has been the recipient of a miracle should devote at least a portion of his life to the church."

"You know about my ... *experience* in Konstantinople?"

He walked over to me and placed his hand upon my shoulder.

"Dear boy, everybody knows about you. Your most reticent uncle could be circumspect about many subjects, however, his admiration for his nephew was never one of them. And yet, despite your achievements, I cannot compel you to do this. Think awhile upon it. I shall await your response patiently. Do not take overly long to decide. As you know, there is much work to be done in the new Jerusalem."

The Holy Father walked away, as Brother Michael whispered to me:

"Do you see now? I *told* you how much you meant to him."

"Your holiness!" I called after the pope.

He stopped and turned to me. I walked over to him and apologized, for I had forgotten to broach the subject of what Hughes de Payens had considered to be a holy excavation. My friend believed that the Ark of the Covenant had been buried beneath the Temple Mount, and wanted permission to be able to dig there and hopefully uncover it. The Holy Father was uncertain how he had arrived at that conclusion, since there were only stories about that possibility. I had no idea how I might respond. I told him, at last, something that I believed was no lie; for Hughes this was a matter of faith.

"And you, my son," he asked, "do you believe that he will find it there?"

I did not wish to lie to the Holy Father; nor did I wish to call my friend's belief into question.

"I believe that it may be there," I spoke finally.

Pope Paschal eyed me curiously. Perhaps he saw that I was not saying everything that I had concealed in my heart. Nevertheless, he did not think the activity would be disrespectful, so he agreed to give us a letter for Godfrey, as evidence that permission to commence the project had been granted formally. He apologized now.

"Forgive me," he said upon coming closer. "My memory is not what it was in my youth. I may have also neglected to mention something; the Byzantine emperor has written to me to congratulate the bold knights for their efforts on his behalf."

"His?" Brother Michael asked, making no attempt to conceal his distaste for that imperial assumption.

"Apparently he is not without a certain comical sensibility. On the other hand, he may have taken his own comments quite earnestly, and now expects all others to do the same. In that case, his false pride might become the undoing of his own people. As you can see," he said, turning to address me, "he knew that you were coming here, and he hoped further that I might prevail upon you to return to his empire. Apparently, you promised that you would."

I told him that I had agreed to return only when my work in Jerusalem were finished.

"You do realize, I trust, that a stronger alliance with him might be beneficial to the church. Forgive my lack of familiarity with political concerns. I believe that your uncle, himself, knew this to be true. We should continue all that he had hoped to achieve. It is his legacy, is it not? Only God knows what result your presence there may yield. The reunification of the Western and Eastern Churches is certainly within the realm of possibility, in the new Christian age that you have helped found. I would consider it a kindness, therefore, if you were to present yourself at the Byzantine court as my personal envoy."

I was about to tell his holiness that I was probably not the correct choice for such an onerous task, but at that very moment I heard someone call out my name. I looked about to see who had done so. The voice was like a whisper, though quite loud in my mind. Why was no one else twisting his head around to seek out the person of its origin?

Brother Michael eyed me quizzically. No, the voice had not been his. A woman had called to me. Was it Anna, tempting me to enter with her into that languid kingdom of Remembrance? Or was it simply the wind and my own mawkish notions?

"I would not be opposed to that request, your holiness," was my response.

"Very well. Make your preparations to return there within the next few months. That should grant you sufficient time to complete any tasks, which currently lie ahead of you. God go with you."

After having left Rome, we returned to the nation and province of our births, to Champagne, and to my family's estates. I had not been back since first I bade farewell, prior to my involvement in the holy battle. It would be good to see my parents once again.

After the servants took our horses, I wondered why no one had come out to greet us, as was their custom whenever I returned from my *peregrinations*. Were they not well?

My mother met us in the great hall. Her face was somewhat more drawn than I had remembered it. And her garments hung upon her. This was not the robust woman, full of life's power, whom I had seen manage my father's lands with such determinate will. I was most glad to see that still her very long hair was thick and full, though each strand of it was white now. When had it all turned?

She stood there, hands poised upon her hips, shaking her head, as if about to punish me for some foolish action, though smiling. (Perhaps it is true, that even if the entire world comes to sing one's praises, to one's parents a man will never be more than the unruly child who caused them so much unnecessary grief. I suppose the Lord has constructed the world in that way, so that we may never grow too foolishly proud *of* and arrogant *about* our accomplishments. It is, perhaps, a type of balance for us, prideful fools that we may be.)

She ran to Brother Michael, took his face in her hands, and kissed it.

"It has been too long, old soldier. Have you been keeping my boy safe from harm?"

"I promise you, my lady, he needed no aid from these withered hands."

"And you," she addressed me, "have you no comforting embrace for the woman who bore you in the oppressive heat of an August summer?"

I hugged her, resting my head upon her shoulder, as she kissed it.

"And your husband," Brother Michael asked, "the master of this domain, has he hunted every last grouse from the forest?"

She pulled away from me and smiled once again, albeit bitterly.

"He will hunt no more," she said.

It seemed that my father had died several years previously. Brother Michael wondered why the Holy Father had never written him of it.

"He was sick for most of the year," she explained, turning to me, "and did not wish his son to have to return home whilst occupied in the midst of God's mission. And well that he did not! Jerusalem is Christian once again. Do you not see how wise was your father's decision to conceal the truth of his illness?"

I found no words, for an emptiness began to gnaw away at my bowels. It took all of my strength to keep it at bay, though it succeeded in devouring each bit of speech that might have tried to escape from me.

That evening we dined. A seat at the head of the table was left empty.

I looked over at my mother. Her spirits seemed well enough. And though my sire had been gone for more than three years now, I knew that she had acquitted herself well in the management of property and goods. Despite my concerns, I knew that there were potential problems, which might arise. I suggested that she remarry. (It was never a good thing for a woman to be alone.)

"With my new position in the church, I may not be able to return here for many years," I informed her. "Who will look after you?"

"Have you decided to accept the offer from his holiness then?" Brother Michael asked.

"I cannot say. Perhaps."

As for my mother, she refused to hear of having another man in her life. She was too set in her ways, she maintained. Besides, she had had one of the best men she ever knew.

"But life is for the living," Brother Michael suggested.

"And a woman's bed-mate is her own choice," my mother offered as a response, most assuredly, I must say.

"Forgive me, lady; I am unfamiliar with that adage."

"And well should you be! I created it even now as I sat here with you."

"I see where your son has acquired his wit."

"I refuse to take any responsibility for what emerges from his mouth," she said, looking at me. "In that he is very much his father's son. And it is likely that my dear brother's spirit will probably not rest, until his nephew has learned to speak more properly than is his custom."

She smiled at me. I smiled back, then sank to my knees, hands folded, looking up.

"Our Father, Who dwells in Heaven ..."

Both my mother and Brother Michael shook their heads, before laughing most heartily.

After Brother Michael had received my mother's kiss upon his forehead and gone off to rest, she and I sipped wine near the fire and spoke of my dear father.

"Of what did he die, mother?"

"It became increasingly more difficult for him to breathe. I never discovered the cause."

I had heard of such an ailment, even if I never knew anyone who had personally suffered from it.

"It is not so rare a thing as you might conceive," she continued. "The change of seasons made no difference for him either. In spring and summer his breathing was horribly laboured; so, too, it was in the crisp air of autumn. He died on a winter's evening, full of a storm's furious snow. He would not have had it any other way, I believe."

She sipped from her goblet and stared into the crackling wood.

"Were the physicians of no use to him?" I inquired.

"Mountebanks, one and all! I threw every single one of them out. They gave him elixirs, which weakened him further. They bled him almost to death with their cursèd leeches. No one deserves such cruelty. I should have killed those knaves. At the very least *I* would have felt better about that, even if your father did not."

And had he suffered very much?

"From the first twinge to the final gasp, it persisted for a full year. You knew how strong your father was, but by the time that he was ready to leave this world, he was so frail, more bones than skin."

Her eyes began to water, though they did not shed a single tear. I could not say why. I believed that if she had allowed herself the depth of that anguish, but for a moment, there would have been no end to the déluge.

And what about him had she missed?

"O, too simple a question! Your uncle would have scolded you for not having commenced a *colloquy* on the very nature of love. Is this not the proper circumstance for that sort of inquiry?"

I allowed her to go on, as it seemed her need was to move her mind into abstractions, which were, doubtless, far less painful than recollections.

She looked at me, her head to the side, and despite her smile, her face was very sad.

"What I miss most," she admitted finally, "is that he made me laugh."

"He made me laugh as well."

Before the night was finished, she told me that the estate would yield enough monetary gain for me to thrive, as it always had; (my father, and his fathers before him, had provided well for us) therefore, future fiscal matters need be of little concern. And should I ever require a substantial sum at once, there was always the property in the land of the Scots that could be sold. What? Why had I never been told of this? My father had been ashamed of its possession, since he won it from its previous owner in a toss of the dice. Nevertheless, its sale might yield considerable gain.

Word had it that the greenest hills in Christendom could be seen there, and the seas surrounding it were mighty and ferocious. And its people were said to be some of the bravest ever to raise a sword. I would have liked very much to see that land. I wondered if I would ever go there.

She rose, as I thought, for her departure to her bedchamber; instead, she removed a small scroll from what I took to be a sort of jewel-box or ancient reliquary, that had been set upon a small table. She presented it to me. I recognized the impression of my uncle's papal ring set into the wax seal.

"He wanted me to give it you after his death. Do not ask me what it contains. Its words are for your eyes only. Rest well."

She bent down to kiss my cheek, then left.

In my chamber I broke open the seal and began to read:

To Guy de Lagery, Defender of the Faith, greeting.

If you are reading this, my son, it is because your mother, my dear sister, has learned of my death. You will forgive an old man his sometime-cowardice, I trust, for I have had not the strength of will to relate these words to your face. The sin is mine.

You never discuss your parents. I know that it is because you harbour a resentment against them for having placed you in my care, when you would rather have been hunting on your estates with your father. Since it is likely that I shall not pass through the night, I shall use this moment to make my confession and ask your forgiveness for having spirited you away from their tender company.

You have been told that your birth was a difficult one. What you did not know is that it very nearly killed your mother. Though she lived, the damage to her had been so great, that she could bear no more children.

It had been raining that day—a powerful storm in late summer that threatened to wash away half the countryside. At the moment of your birth, the rain stopped falling, and the vicious summer heat, that had taken its toll on so many in recent weeks, cooled long enough for everyone to appreciate a sunrise. It was a portent. There was no mistake. Even your father, who was loathe to believe in such things, had to agree with his wife's judgment, that their child was blessèd, that he had to be reared in God's house, so that he would grow up to do honour to Christianity. As much as it pained them, my sister and her husband gave me the child, hoping that he would assume the cowl, very like his uncle. The child, however, had ideas of his own.

The church has been the salvation of many, though a true home to a scant few who are devoted to its rigorous demands. And whilst on a mission for God's works, pain ennobled the scoundrel you were. You have commenced to conduct your life with honour. I am more grateful for that truth than you can imagine. My only anguish is that you are without family. You have never stayed in one place long enough to set down anything that resembles roots. Perhaps you will find your proper home in the Holy Land, walking in the very steps that our Lord, Jesus, walked. I know that you will find peace there. May the love in my heart comfort you during your darkest moments! If it is the will of the Most High, perchance we shall meet again in Eternity.

Dominus tecum,
Pope Urban II
Né Odo de Lagery
In this year of our Lord, 1099.

The letter dropped from my hands as I began to weep. In all this time I found that I could shed not a single tear. Especially at the gravestone, beneath which his body was interred, I thought only that the uncle with whom I had lived and whom I had loved was a lifeless lump of flesh; his spirit had fled him, and the man whom I had come to know so well was no more, certainly not the thing entombed in the depths of Holy Mother Church.

It was only now, when his words rang in my ears and touched my heart, that I recalled his comforting in times of sickness, his gentle words of faith, in my darkest moments of doubt, when I could see neither avenue of resolution nor surcease of pain. And I wept until a voice within me cried out, and the agony had passed unto his spirit and freed mine own.

I lay upon the floor of my bedchamber, my strength spent. I did not move until dawn of the following day.

CHAPTER THE EIGHTEENTH,

in which I receive an imperial gift, that was destined to become both blessing and curse.

Having realized that my responsibilities in the Holy Land would only increase with time, I decided (several days later) to take leave of my mother and set out for Konstantinople. But before I could depart, she had a question that she wanted me very much to answer. She found me with Nigrum at the stables.

"Will you not see your father's crypt before you leave?"

I said nothing.

"A father who has loved his son," she continued, "should not be punished for having sought only the finest of futures for him."

"This story is old. It is best forgotten."

"If he deserves your continued anger, how much more of it should be mine?"

I ceased grooming my steed, though did not turn to look into my mother's eyes.

"If you bear any affection at all for me, mother, you will leave off this subject."

Still, she would not be dissuaded from her purposeful speech.

"Your inability to forgive detracts from all that you have accomplished."

"I regret that I have been a disappointment to you."

"Foolish boy! No mother could be more proud. Despite that, you are a babe no longer. My brother's lessons were filled with the word of God. Unfortunately, in trying to teach proper forms of conduct, he may have forgotten how many petty things of childhood one must forego in order to become a man. No father is perfect, but most deserve a bit of forgiveness from their children. Men are such fragile creatures, after all."

I turned to her. Without saying a word, I knew that she would recognize my decision. She shook her head, twisting her lips into a most horrible expression of anger or disgust, (I could not say which), then turned from me and walked away.

No, I could not forgive my father that day. In truth, I never have.

Brother Michael was unhappy about the prospect of lingering upon the imperial grounds of Byzantium for any appreciable period, despite his recognition that it would have been dishonourable to break my pledge to his highness, had I not returned. (My old comrade put no trust in the Byzantines when first he had met them, and he was not about to do so now. I could not blame him really.) I promised that I would not linger overly long there. I believe that he doubted me. Perhaps he recalled the fondness that had been previously exchanged between an imperial daughter and myself. I know that I did.

Mother bade me take care of myself. (It was the last time that I would ever see her alive.)

Upon our arrival, (without a fraction of fanfare), we were led to a very large and ornately decorated room. Though his highness loved feasts of all sorts, he had apparently decided not to grant us one. I found that odd. I was reluctant to believe that an imperial daughter had made confession of our passions to the imperial mother, thus antagonizing the seemingly placid nature of the imperial father; nevertheless, that might have been her action indeed! And would I now suffer the execution that his previous slayer had failed to achieve? Then I began to feel most terrible for Brother Michael, who was innocent of any wrongdoing. He would suffer my fate, simply because he had accompanied me out of friendship. If I were to die, then so be it. But my comrade as well? (And Anna was conspicuous by her absence.)

Before I had an opportunity to warn my old friend of what might transpire, guards entered. These men were different than the typical martial contingent. Their uniforms were coloured over with a hue of royal purple, signifying their positions as members of the emperor's personal protectors. They asked Brother Michael to stay behind, (and he did so despite his reluctance for same), as I was led out of the palace to a section behind it—one that I had not previously seen. There was a structure consisting of four very thick walls, each composed of thin layers of rock, (free of any mortar), fitted together in a perfectly symmetrical pattern of increasing layers. Said walls were also one and one-half times the height of a man, so tall were they erected. And atop each of the four boundaries of the manorial garden (contained behind them) stood a bronze horse, poised, as if to gallop. (I was to discover later that the steeds were the emperor's fixed and joyous response to the future four *apocalyptic* Horsemen, who were to be released when the seals would break at crack of Doom—a triumph, perhaps, of Hope over Inevitability.)

I was brought through a single archway to see some of the most wondrous botanicals I had ever witnessed. The flowers, hedges, trees, multi-coloured all, with many leaves of that selfsame deep royal purple and blood red, were planted in various geometric configurations, leading to a central fountain. His highness was seated upon a stone bench facing this fountain. He bade me sit next to him. It was then I noticed an object at his right hand, covered with a cloth. The guards left us.

"This is one of the few places where I am able to steal time for myself," he remarked, staring into the falling water.

"*Steal*, your highness?"

"A regent's life belongs to his nation. It is sometimes a burden for one who enjoys studying the *logic* of Aristotle far more than enacting the intricacies of rule. Nevertheless, we must all carry our burdens with a certain degree of satisfaction, for it is how the Lord made us to be. The farmer who toils in the field should be happy with his lot in life, should he not?"

I had never known very many farmers who were happy to toil until their backs broke in twain. And why was he going on in this fashion? Was it my lot in life to sit here, surrounded by sumptuous foliage, listening to birdsong, whilst interrupted by one emperor's analysis of the world's *strata*?

"I believe that it is your place to carry on the sacred traditions of our ancestors," he continued.

Mine?

"A mighty burden, sire! You do me too much honour."

"Not enough. In time you will probably become one more *eikon* in the great *pantheon* of Byzantine worship."

Really? Me? This fulsome praise grated upon my very soul.

"Whilst your words stir my heart," I said, attempting to make him understand some of what I was feeling, "I must confess that I do not seek to become an object of veneration."

My verbiage, unfortunately, did not produce the effect (or the comprehension) that I had sought.

"Not only do you share His power to punish evil, you share His humility as well."

"If by your statement you refer to our Lord, the Christ, then your judgment of my place in the world is as wrong as your gestures are bold. I am not now, nor have I ever been, nor shall I ever be a deeply spiritual man. I know how to do one thing well—the killing of my enemies. That makes me a poor successor to the legacy of our Lord."

Still he could not grasp the essence of what I had made most evident to him.

"I believe in you. From the first moment that I saw you in my court, I knew that you had been chosen, deemed worthy where others were not. I saw it in your face. Your eyes burned with a sacred flame that would consume the world of its wicked, whilst cleansing it for the day when our Lord returns to us. I feel it in these bones that that day is near."

He pulled the cloth away and handed me the curiosity. It was a golden bust, a perfect replica of his belovèd daughter's head, as she looked upon the day that she first entered my bedchamber.

"In all the world she is the most precious thing to me. In this manner I make a gift of her to you. Carefully placed within it, resting comfortably, is a burial cloth, one most precious to all. Our Lord was wrapped in its linen after His body was taken down from the crucifix. It has been kept safely in this land for over a thousand years. It was in a small church when it found you."

The shroud? Is that what kept me alive as I bled to death?

"It found you when you needed it; therefore, it belongs to you. You have already displayed your worthiness for its possession."

I had no words; for by the presentation of this gift, he had elevated me to a plane of being higher than most, whilst simultaneously denying me his daughter's affections. He was an able ruler; I had expected that. What surprised me far more was the extent of devotion for his child. Child? Was she not a young woman now? (And where was she keeping herself?) But with his partial smile and piercing eyes, albeit without uttering a single word of it, this emperor had informed me that the only way to possess his belovèd Anna was to call this replica my own. Its cold metal casing would be the closest manner in which I would ever come to know her touch, or so he thought. What he may have forgotten was that in our world, then, love and proximity to one's beloved were ofttimes complete strangers. Knights might be called upon to join campaigns, which would transport them to the other side of the world, sometimes for months, only to have those months fast become years. During their absence, respective spouses might occasionally grow lonely and seek the comfort of another. But love was love. And men needed their castles and their families and their traditions and their legacies. Knowing that she would always be there waiting could soothe anyone's longing, despite the numerous trysts, which both husband and wife might be prone to undertake. That was the way of things, was it not?

I declined his offer.

"I cannot accept so precious a thing, your majesty. It is a relic for all men to revere."

"There is none more worthy. And someday, when you look upon her face, you will realize, as have I, that you are what is most decent in man. Take good care of it, Guy de Lagery."

I suppose I knew that he would refuse my denial of its ownership.

"I shall treasure it always," I agreed at last, taking it from his hands.

As Brother Michael and I left the following day, with a battery of guards who would take us out of Byzantium's treasured territory, I looked back at the palace shining golden in the sun. What I did not learn, until much later, was that Anna's mother (with the father's assent) had decided to keep the princess sequestered in one of those towers, as she was to have discourse with no man prior to her marriage, (with some Byzantine), within the year. Yet despite her imprisonment, she had been watching me the entire time that I was present in her father's *imperium*, including the very moment of my departure. And as I rode off, convinced that she wanted nothing further to do with me, (I had assumed this because of the forbearance with which the emperor had received me, whilst his daughter was nowhere to be found), I had no idea that somewhere in one of the structures above and behind me was a young woman whose tears were becoming a veritable cascade.

Some years after, she admitted to me that a piece of her heart had died that afternoon; and try as she might, she would never again be as tender with any man, as once she was.

CHAPTER THE NINETEENTH,

in which the reign of Godfrey passes into history in order to make way for the reign of Baldwin.

Into the heat of battle he rode, cutting and carving with each equine stride. So much of his life had he spent in battle with his enemies, first at his father's side, against the sire's adversaries, then by himself, against his own. Nor would this combat be his last. He knew it. And the burden of that knowledge did not weigh heavily upon his heart. He was prepared for war. He was born into it. And he savoured each and every contest of wills as if it were his last.

And as he pressed on valiantly, convinced that the wedge, that he and his warriors had thrust into the midst of the opposing army, would shatter his foe's defenses, he failed to notice (or may not have conceived) that an entire legion of troops had begun to surround them.

At the end of the day, all his militaristic preparations, all his bellicose posturing, all came to naught, as the forces of *Malik Ghazi* of Anatolia swarmed, tightening their circle ever more around Prince Bohémond, formerly of Tarentum, and now of Antioch. And though the Norman was incredulous that he had been captured, nevertheless, he would not taste liberty again for three more years.

By the time that we returned to Jerusalem, we learned of Bohémond's imprisonment. (No one knew why the Norman had sought to take over that piece of land, though I wondered if its proximity to Byzantium might not have had something to do with his decision to seek sovereignty over it.) Tancred, who had gone off and made of Galilee his personal fiefdom, inquired of Godfrey and several other rulers if they would aid him in freeing his uncle from a Turkish prison. Most maintained that it was a difficult time, what with the possibility of Saracen invasions a constant threat. There was also the inevitable burden of having to raise sufficient finances; the cost of war was very dear. With each passing year, it grew only larger. Surely Tancred could understand the demands of their positions, could he not?

Having been denied the participation of others, the nephew wrote to the Byzantine emperor, as well as to Count Raymond, both of whom were less than enthusiastic about having the Norman free to roam about and create all sorts of mischief. Both declined to be of service, citing Saracen threats or the exorbitant expenditure involved in guarding against same. As a result, Tancred decided to wait and see, whether a ransom-demand were forthcoming or not. And whilst attending a Turkish messenger, he took over the administration and leadership of Antioch, no doubt to hold it secure until his uncle returned, if ever.

Since Godfrey sought alliances with surrounding cities and nations under Saracen governance, (which decision pleased both Daimbert and the Holy Father not at all), he chose to attend a banquet given by the Emir of Caesarea. After having conferred with the Patriarch, our leader informed me that I was to join him for the feast in the capacity as one of his personal guards. He also told his brother, Eustace, that his presence in Caesarea would not be required. This revelation resulted in a considerable amount of argumentation. Nevertheless, the brother agreed. (I never found out why this was Godfrey's decision. He may have felt that his brother's company was best suited for war, not for peace. That is my assumption only.)

As concerns Daimbert, a man of ponderous frame, he had the rare habit of reeking perpetually of onions. As a result, it was often difficult to stand in anything that remotely resembled proximity to him. Most would amble off to the side, straining to hear all that he had to say. Totally devoid of an even temperament, he spoke in clipped phrases, his curious manner of speech often at the commencement of a new sentence, before he had completed the prior one, occasionally punctuated by something of a stammer:

"What? You? Ye—Yes. The papal defender? Why not? Wholeheartedly. You were saying?"

I assure you, dear reader, that I am not given much to *hyperbole*, for such was the way of his tongue. Yet somehow, miraculously, (even though we stood far enough away from him to avoid being down-wind of his particular fragrance), both Brother Michael and I were able to deduce that the former was to stay behind, since his considerable experience in battle would aid him in conference with others concerning the best means of protection for the church and all of Jerusalem's holy relics. (Daimbert was most pleased with this decision.) Hughes de Payens offered his counsel as well.

The Emir's palace, though barely a third the size of the Byzantine emperor's, contained many tall towers as the majority of its design. And into its masonry skin was cut much fenestration. It differed from Christian castles in that there were no long rectangular or *rhomboid* figures, nor circles even, but onion-like shapes pulled up and ending in a spire (in imitation of the roofs of these selfsame towers). Once inside, its walls were covered in tiny glass tiles, of the deepest blue that I had ever seen, written over (in various locations) with gilt lettering. I assumed that these were words from their language, an act in imitation of the practice in their mosques. And a most strange tongue it was indeed! I had never before witnessed so many curling and twisting lines, ending in overly long flourishes. I had a sparse knowledge of Hebrew, and I assumed that, since Jews and Turks had grown up together in the same part of the world, their *alphabets* would be similar. I would learn this to be true of much of their vocabulary, though the appearance of their words was markedly different.

The table was set as it might have been anywhere in Christendom. And the food was quite the same, except that its taste was richer, more pungent even. (I noticed also that roasted chickens were laid before us with pieces of sliced fruits, dried plums, and the like. I had never thought to add fruits to charred foods. I had to admit that I found the idea and its execution quite appealing.) And there was an endless source of drink.

I cannot say which issues of a political nature were discussed, as my head was befogged with the brew, but I believe that all ended well, for there was much laughter and embracing by meal's conclusion.

Within a day or so following Godfrey's return, two of his personal guards complained of stomach pains. No physician's elixir could stem the tide of their increasing plaints. At the end of a week, the loyal men succumbed. There was a great deal of talk about poisons, even though I had eaten of the same food and had drunk of the same wine and was yet unharmed. Shortly thereafter, Godfrey revealed that he, too, was not immune to the mysterious ailment that had claimed his trusted men.

The Advocate lay now upon his deathbed. Since unmarried and childless, (as much as anyone knew of him), when asked who should assume the leadership of Jerusalem, he wasted no time in response:

"There is only one whom I trust absolutely to govern this city. Send word to my brother, Baldwin of Edessa. Jerusalem will be his before this day is finished."

For the entire time that Godfrey was bedridden, his other brother, Eustace, never left his side; nor did the latter partake of food or drink. And at the moment when the spirit left the former, the latter wept piteously for him. (I had never seen the living brother reveal any emotions, save his perpetual dissatisfaction and impatience. In a curious way, I was relieved to learn that he was still human.)

Daimbert gave to the first Christian ruler of Jerusalem his final rites. And the entire city fell into mourning.

The reign of the Advocate, Godfrey de Bouillon, had endured not one full year.

Barely had a messenger time to complete his task, before Baldwin, and a considerable number of his army, were upon the road. (The kingdom of Edessa he left in what he believed were the very capable hands of his cousin, also called Baldwin, a Burgundian, and known ostensibly as *Le Bourg.*) As Godfrey's body was wrapped for burial, his brother was not far from the gates of the city.

The body was being placed inside a coffin for its final rest, as Brother Michael and I stood near. Suddenly, I detected an odd odor.

"Can you smell it?" I asked of him in whispers.

"The dead always have their own particular stench. I thought you would have grown used to it by this time."

"This is unlike anything else."

"Be strong. It is not so horrendous as some of what we have previously smelt."

With gates open, the first to enter were the heralds, signaling (with their clarion-blasts) the coming of their king; then rode on the standard-bearers, then the knights, (vain and victorious), surrounding his highness, himself, and his queen, herself, followed by more knights, themselves. The entire royal retinue marched on towards the Church of the Holy Sepulchre, where the Edessan king and his deceased and cherished brother would be united once again.

Eustace stood near the stone coffin. Once he espied his sibling coming towards him, he walked away from the dais, upon which the encasement was situated. By the time that Baldwin placed his hands upon the carved reliquary, he noticed that Eustace had departed with not a single word. The Edessan royals knelt and prayed.

Though I admired Eustace's conviction neither to mask nor to betray the depth of his sensibilities, I did not think his action a wise choice. Baldwin would now reign in the most coveted position of leadership in all of Christendom; many would soon come to believe that Eustace's disappearance was a foolish decision that would soon stir his living brother's already bilious temperament.

By twilight of evening, Baldwin did not hesitate to let everyone know that he would be proud to wear the crown of Jerusalem. (Daimbert was most dissatisfied.)

At the hour of noon, upon Christmas Day, in the year of our Lord, 1100, amidst much pomp and celebration, Daimbert placed the crown upon Baldwin's head. The queen could not have worn more glee, so joyous was this day for the man she adored!

Brother Michael, who stood at my side, watching the pageant, and who never bore much affection for the now former Edessan ruler, whispered to me:

"The king is dead. Long live the king?"

After numerous dignitaries and functionaries made their praise known, I stood before the royal head of state. The difference in him, from the time that we had last met, was noticeable; the warrior had stepped aside for the monarch's entry. And he carried himself with as much honour as his station demanded, and a good deal more than I would come to see in any who were either born into or had assumed that position.

When he regarded me, he smiled and bowed his head ever so slightly.

"We are most pleased to see you again, Defender of the Faith."

"I have done what I was asked to do, sire, no more, no less."

"Always the humble and holy knight. Your uncle would have been gratified. Christianity lost one of its most eloquent spokesmen, when the Lord took him to His kingdom."

Though I had never come to know Baldwin well, the one lesson that our time together had taught me was that the man never excelled in masking how an individual might say one thing whilst meaning another. This day was no different. And since he was determined to speak in the formal diction of kingship, I decided to perform an antique ritual, cloaked in the form of a request.

"King Baldwin I of Jerusalem, I have come here today to ask of you a *boon*."

He was taken aback by the formality of my statement, even if it brought another more curious smile to his face.

"We acknowledge your respect. It is so ordered. What would you, Guy de Lagery?"

I asked for a small structure to be set aside as a meeting place for a new military order. (There were several orders then in existence, though none had satisfied all the *criteria*, which Hughes and I had agreed should be present.) He was fascinated with this idea, however, a question concerning it now bothered him.

"Why do you not join the Knights of the Hospital, this Order of St. John, as it is called?"

I had already spoken with their master, Peter Gérard, an ancient man quite set in his ways. Our views concerning the purposes of a military order differed considerably.

"They are physicians, care-givers, and monks," I explained. "They take up the sword in defense of the sick only if they have exhausted all other choices. Such was the recommendation of their Genoese merchant-founders, and they have never strayed from it. Our order will protect the travelers."

He wished to know who would become part of it. I informed him that both Hughes, myself, and several other goodly knights would participate. And were we to assume any vows? We had agreed upon St. Benedictus' rules regarding poverty and obedience. Chastity … was a matter still open for discussion. Even though we had not yet sufficiently deliberated upon all the details, it was crucial that we begin our first duty as soon as possible. Surely he could see that.

He acknowledged the mission as a holy one. And as a gesture of generosity, if not for us, then for the sainted memory of my uncle, he would set aside a section of the Temple of Solomon for our usage, and would furthermore see to the construction of new stables behind it.

"We think it appropriate," he added. "You have already been digging there for some time. Please let us know if you find the Ark. It would be a symbol of God's blessings upon us for all that we hope to accomplish here in His name."

And if he were so bold as to make a suggestion, he thought that our new title should be, *the Poor Knights of the Holy Temple of Jerusalem*.

I could not have agreed more. And before I did so, I made a suggestion of my own.

"The followers of Muhammad refer to us as, *the knights from beyond the sea*. Perhaps *Outremer (Beyond the sea)* should be the word everyone uses instead of the expression, *the Holy Land*."

He thought upon it a moment or so.

"An excellent recommendation! Henceforth the word will be used in all civil documentation and royal correspondence, the one Frankish term surrounded by all others of Latin origin. It will do honour to the land of our birth, and will, moreover, compel future historians to recognize all that we have accomplished here in the name of God. Amen."

Everyone present repeated the *amen,* including the scribes, who immediately set about to place their master's each word to vellum.

"It is so ordered."

(*Outremer*—this is what the Holy Land came to be called in common parlance during the decades which followed the First Holy War. In short, the very real territories and their respective peoples developed into a *mythos*—a collection of legends fit for storytelling around the hearth at eventide. I can thank Baldwin I of Jerusalem for having made real what had been until then a momentary thought.)

O, yes; he needed to clarify one or two more pieces of business. He would write to the current pontiff to make his actions known, as a matter of formality. (Upon hearing this, Daimbert eyed him with suspicion.) And he could foresee an occasion when he might have to call upon the knights of this new order to defend their new home.

"But, sire, our first obligation must be the protection of pilgrims," I insisted without hesitation.

He mentioned that he would probably never have to use our expertise in any martial endeavours, for he had all the forces necessary to defend our new kingdom. He urged me to recognize that, unlike the commandments, the Future was not written in stone; it was fluid. And there could be times when we should all be forced to wet our feet within it.

"Do you concur, Knight of the Temple?"

I thought I had no choice in the matter. I had no idea how my decision would return to haunt me again and again in all the years following.

CHAPTER THE TWENTIETH,

in which Baldwin's court reveals something of its true nature.

About Baldwin's new court skulked a Venetian doctor, Fausto di Rofocale. This lank, little man with the enormous hooked nose and mere handful of teeth in his jaw, had the thickest, blackest hair that I have ever seen. Only the dense flesh about his eyes and the absence of any fatness in his cheeks (which thing might have prevented his face from appearing so drawn) told the tale of his extreme age. His decades were more than seven, though one would have never known it from a cursory glance. And he never smiled, except when someone regarded him.

The new king believed that his man could be trusted with absolute surety, for he was a physician of the utmost discretion and capability.

Baldwin's next royal act was to invite the Emir of Caesarea for a sumptuous feast. When finished, all except Baldwin and I had left the hall.

"That went well," he commented.

"I wish I were so convinced."

"O? What have you seen in our guest's behaviour that no one else has?"

"He is concealing something."

"As do all rulers."

"Not like this. He has agreed to come here for one reason only; he wishes to appear amiable to his good Christian neighbors. And whilst he wears his smile, gaining their trust, his forces are gathering."

"The Norman prince always admired your attentiveness to the details of observation, as I recall. Did you know that all lies are betrayed by their odor? In point of fact, each one has its own particularly loathsome stench. Did you smell how the rooms reeked upon his entry? Your concern is unfounded, however. I have taken precautions to avoid any argument. There is nothing more stupid than a pointless war, don't you think?"

I had no idea why he was being so cryptic. What I discovered only later (for the truth of any given situation can never stay hidden from the eyes of men indefinitely) was that Fausto had prepared a potent draught composed of vegetable extracts and floral tinctures, most of which was added to the leading guest's repast only. The Emir may have realized this, for he had brought royal tasters with him, who partook of the first sips of wine and bits of meat and fowl, prior to their master's gluttony. (Rarely had I seen so obese a man devour the enormous quantities of nourishment, {during a single meal}, which he did.)

But upon his return home, the Emir and his tasting-minions suffered horrid stomach-cramping, which resulted in all retching continually, until nothing was left inside their bellies, not even a drop of blood.

King Baldwin I of Jerusalem was most pleased with the services of his faithful medical practitioner.

The king's Venetian had requested my presence in his chambers of examination. For that reason, I found myself passing through the dimly lit corridors beneath the royal castle. At one end was a door that opened into an extensive vault, filled with all manner of oddly coloured liquids in even more strangely shaped retorts and flasks. Some of these sat positioned above a flame and were emitting a noxious vapor. Upon one table, and tied to a small block of wood was a dead rat, completely eviscerated. Upon another rested a small lookingglass, partially covered with a diaphanous fabric. The back of the item had not been silvered over, as was customary, but had been blackened. If one were unable to glimpse one's face therein, what purpose could it possibly serve? For that matter, what might one see therein? I could not fathom why this thing had been so wrought.

Looking about, I realized that this was a self-contained, hermetic world into which I had stepped. I wondered if it were not better to leave immediately, rather than see or learn more of its secrets.

He was wearing a white mask when I saw him at last. Though the facial representation was expressionless, a black mass surrounded its left eye, forming what appeared to be a large star, dotted with tiny globules of white, in imitation of a cluster of stars, I supposed. He removed it, revealing a broad smile.

"A gift from one of my many Venetian admirers. Welcome to my humble *donjon* of study," was his greeting.

"Why do you find it necessary to inflict these tortures upon yourself?" I asked, covering my nose.

"If I did not, then I would be uncertain as to their efficacy. They are a useful means of ridding the entire palace of vermin."

"And of all humanity as well, I should wager."

He laughed a bit.

"And how goes it with you, sir knight?"

A most unusual query. The man had never before shared any form of polite conversation with me. In fact, the only contact that we had ever exchanged was a mere nod in a corridor passing, or the like.

"Fair to middling," was my response.

"Now I find that strange. A man who has been as blessèd as you have been should always find an occasion to smile."

"There is very little reason for me to smile about here," I said, sniffing the room.

"I have been thinking of you a good deal since my arrival. Did you suspect that of me?"

"Should I have suspected anything of you, physician?"

"I am fascinated by you."

I had no idea how to interpret that statement.

"Really? In what manner do I linger in your thoughts?"

After careful study and a good deal of meditation, he had determined that God had treated me with kindness, because of who I was.

"Who I am is a knight."

"Yes. And knights kill."

"We defend," I begged to differ, correcting him.

"You kill to defend something or someone, a nation, an idea. Even so, after all is said, you are a killer of men. From what I have heard, you are quite accomplished in that field of endeavour. The Lord has rewarded you for having rid the earth of a significant portion of His enemies. Does your place in the scheme of things make you feel more powerful, or more cherished to be the left hand of vengeance?"

Doubtless he was baiting me in order to elicit some sort of reaction. I chose to maintain my rational approach to this *meeting of the minds,* so to speak.

"I am a man, no more, no less."

"You have helped to wrest Jerusalem from the talons of its former pagan captors. Do you believe that any ordinary man could have accomplished that feat?"

Uncertain as to what his point was, my patience for this conversation had worn thin.

"I did not fight alone in order to be here. Now, you requested my presence. Is your assessment of me to be the sole subject under discussion?"

"I have requested your presence as a curiosity merely."

"For someone who seems to know so much about me, your curiosity seems oddly misplaced."

"Actually, I thought you would feel that way about yourself. You have no doubt determined that you are indestructible."

I was taken aback by that conclusion, for at that moment in my life, I was still reluctant to accept that which had become so evident to all, except to myself.

"You should not believe every story about which strangers chatter like clucking chickens."

"O, you would marvel at what I know about you and so many others, and even more would you marvel at what I have forgotten in this very long lifetime," he spoke quite softly now.

"Since your knowledge is so extensive, you must know what I am about to say next, and that is, *good-bye*."

I turned to leave when he reached his hand to touch mine. He brushed against my skin, and the act was chilling. Never had I felt something so unrelentingly cold. I stood still.

"Please do not go. We have so much to learn about each other. I can, for example, tell you more about yourself, if you will but permit me to take a sample of your blood."

Unbelievable! Never had I heard uttered such a request. I simply stared, wide-eyed.

"O, it sounds far worse than what it actually entails," he tried to assure me. "I cut away a small piece of flesh. That should pose little problem for someone who has the capacity for regeneration. You do realize that it is one of your gifts as well, do you not?"

I looked down upon him with all the repulsion that I could cull for the action.

"I am no rat for you to study!"

"You misunderstand. I have been watching you, learning about you, from your first visit to Konstantinople, until the moment when you entered this chamber."

I walked over to him and came very close to his face. He backed away.

"I can give you everything that you want, sir knight. You have only to ask."

"And what do you believe that I desire most of all?"

"Why, a family, after you have taken possession of the world for yourself, of course!"

"You are labouring under the most ridiculous of illusions," I said, walking away.

"There is so much about yourself that you do not understand."

I turned back to him.

"And who are you to teach me of it?"

"I have made the study of esoteric knowledge my life's work. Believe in me. I can help you."

"You can do nothing for me, except waste my precious time."

I turned once more to leave. He spoke loudly now, hoping to keep my attention gathered upon his self-importance.

"I can teach you that it is a fool who does not yield to the calling of his blood. You kill, albeit reluctantly. This I have seen in your face whenever you have left to join the royal campaigns for conquest."

"Someone who has lived as long as you should endeavour to recall that the face is merely one piece of a man's life. And the story that it tells is not always easy to interpret."

"Give yourself over to the voice of Slaying that calls out to you each time that you raise your blade."

"This I have done more times than you, with all your wisdom, can count."

"Never have you laid your soul open to it. Do you not see the truth of what it means for Jerusalem to be Christian once more? The enemies of Christ must be expelled from this world. These *Muslims*, as they call themselves, follow a cursèd faith that, in their foul language is known as *Islam*. That word means *submission*. They submit themselves to their prophet, Mahomet, who claimed that he received his revelation from the archangel, Gabriel, Himself. Have you ever heard any statement that is so patently false? As if the archangel, who spoke with Mary about her Son's destiny, would have anything to do with such creatures! These vile Muslims must be destroyed. You, alone, are capable of this."

"I?"

"With all your power you can stand astride the world like a *kolossos*, stepping upon these betrayers of the true faith, as if they were mere insects. This you must do. Then you should kill all the Jews for their betrayal of Christ. Then the entire world will thank you and bow at your feet. It is your Christian destiny to rule over those who are weaker than you."

This final statement he made to me as he held fast to my wrist.

Repulsed and enraged, I lifted the little man and held him against the stone wall.

"Now you will listen to me, physician. The next time that you touch me, I shall cut off your hand. I am certain that it will make a unique specimen for your dissections. And the next time that you speak with me, it will be with a civil tongue in your head, or I shall rip that out as well, and force you to eat of it!"

As I tossed him aside and left, I heard him call out to me:

"Remember; a few drops of your blood is all that I need. I shall be here waiting. Call upon me anytime, day or night. No appointment is necessary. I am here to serve!"

Unlike the Advocate, Baldwin was never comfortable in the presence of truces, and the treaties, which were generated invariably therefrom.

First came the business of Daimbert, whom the king considered far too meddlesome for his own good. Accused of financial irregularities, (*e.g.*, having stolen from the church's funds), the archbishop was sent away from Jerusalem in disgrace.

"But innocent am I!" he exclaimed. "A newborn babe could not be more so!"

Apparently the crisis had enabled him to overcome his verbal frailties, not that any of it made the slightest difference.

The pope ordered him into exile, to preach to the Sicilians of Messina, where his efforts would meet with little success. (The former legate never looked upon the people there as much better than heathens, I fear. Did that fact have something to do with his inability to create the results, which he had so labouriously sought?) There he died, some years after he had fled his patriarchate, ashamed, and very much alone. (It was said that the Venetian had put his hands into the concocted scheme of this dismissal, even when no one was ever able to prove it, or cared to, as much as I could tell.)

Then continued the further labour of kingship, that meant the subjugation of surrounding territories. Caesarea was captured. Germans landed at Jaffa (calling themselves *Crusaders* now), and when the English followed them, we (including Hughes, Brother Michael, myself, and even Eustace) who had been fighting at all fronts, took that city as Baldwin's own. Leading his troops, and with the aid of a Genoese fleet, he claimed the port city of Haifa (a much sought-after jewel). After that, he took Arsuf, and either cast out its Muslim inhabitants, or butchered them, enslaving only the more comely young maidens, who would serve him perpetually.

New Christian armies kept arriving each year in *Outremer*. And with the *addenda* of Christian-controlled territories began the construction of monolithic fortresses for the protected boundaries of same: Petra, Shaubeck, Montréal, to name a scant few. In ensuing decades these would number far into the hundreds. There were more than a few failed campaigns, to be sure. Despite them, our determination overcame each setback with renewed success. And in each battle I wielded my sword, neither for the glory of Holy Mother Church or for the righteousness of our mission, nor for the possession of a plot of land or a hill or a village that I would make mine own, but for the sensation of the blood that flowed within me with its deliberate rapidity and dominion. I could feel the last flicker of life flee each victim's body, as it shook, twitched, then ceased all motion. I was master over the fields of all the dying, and I was happy … once again.

CHAPTER THE TWENTY-FIRST,

in which faithful alliances prove themselves rampant with lies.

By 1103, Tancred had secured enough capital to cover the ransom of one hundred thousand gold *bézants*, and his uncle was set free. (Many, such as Baldwin, for example, did not think it a particularly good idea for one of the former leaders of the Holy War to waste away the rest of his years in captivity. The truth of that action would be a stain upon the honour of all good Christians, he affirmed, so the leaders tallied up a portion of the booty that they had acquired, and donated it to the funding for the freeing of their former comrade.) But before the Norman uttered a word of gratitude to his nephew for the efforts on his behalf, he made a statement that was carried by the winds to the four corners of the world:

"I shall not rest until I have planted a spear into the side of Byzantium, itself!"

Most people thought his behaviour somewhat odd, for the Byzantines had had no involvement whatsoever with his failed campaign. And what was even more peculiar was that he chose not to return to Antioch. Instead, he traveled first to France, where he was determined to woo the sister of the king, which modicum of romantic activity was a wonderment to me. (I say this only because I never saw the Norman express interest in anyone or anything, save the destruction of the Emperor Komnenos and his entire empire.) His attraction for her might have been little more than a desire to possess her dowry, that most believed to be substantial. And Bohémond was able to wed rather quickly, as the royal sister (more than a little plain) was exceedingly anxious to have so courageous a suitor (albeit uncommon in appearance) as her own. Moreover, her lack of height (the top of her head stood far below her newly belovèd's heart) bothered none. And all were grateful for the marriage of both houses.

After a rapid period of a few short months, he and his newly acquired princess returned to Italy, accompanied by many Frankish troops. In the nation that had acted as his home for so many years, there he hoped to raise a new army, not to rule over more Saracen territories, mind you, but to conquer Byzantium. Even stranger, perhaps, was that many knights, burning with a novel *crusading* fervor, joined him, though it would be several more years before all preparations came to fruition. (And the result was to become one more disappointment that he had never anticipated.)

Eustace was invited to return into his brother's good graces, though I cannot say if the invitation were simply a gesture of good will to the only surviving brother, or if it involved Baldwin's assessment of the former's loyalty; for Eustace was ferociously faithful, in the manner that a dog might bite off the hand of one who raises a clenched fist at its master; moreover, he could kill as good as any man, if not better than most. The king knew well these truths, and doubtless rewarded him with significant riches and property, for which Eustace cared little.

On one occasion I was at court with the king and his brother.

"We have received a letter from the Veronese," Baldwin noted, smiling.

"There are only two kinds of people I detest," Eustace averred, "the ignorant and the foolish."

"That includes almost everyone!" I exclaimed with surprise (and, I hoped, an equal amount of wit).

"Is it any wonder that I am never happy?"

Confused, Baldwin stared at his brother.

"About what possible thing are you speaking?" he asked of him.

"Nothing of significance, brother."

"Apparently. Now, as I was saying, they wish to be of service in any or all of our campaigns. Notwithstanding their wishes, they are of a land-locked city, and therefore without ships; they would be of little use to us."

"They are fine horsemen, your highness," I suggested that he recall.

"To be sure, but as the physician has informed us, the Veronese prefer the eating of their horse-flesh to the riding of it."

"I had no idea that he was given to much witticism."

"He is a man of many hidden talents."

"Indeed!"

"I am tortured incessantly by the inadequacies of others," Eustace added, somewhat tangentially.

Once more Baldwin stared at him.

"If that be so, brother, then you should probably leave us and wallow in your misery, all by yourself."

"Wherefore does the king not require his physician to attend mass?" Eustace asked with marked impatience. "Is he no Christian then?"

O, I did not expect that blatant anger from Eustace. And why had I not noticed the absence of the Venetian at prayers? A most curious thing, was it not?

"Di Rofocale is consumed with his work."

"And of what nature is the work that he creates day and night in that cesspool of a room? Is it something diabolical?"

"He is trying to prolong life, if you must know. It is his *credo* that King Baldwin I of Jerusalem should live one hundred years in the full bloom of youth, and with perfect health. He considers the discovery of such an elixir, that would enable us to endure, his holy mission."

"God forbid!" I exclaimed.

"God may have forbade it," Eustace added, "but not so my brother."

"Stop it, both of you. This is a palace, not a cathedral. Leave your religiosity at the gate, when you enter herein."

Actually, Baldwin was incorrect. Upon first seeing this church's grandeur, he discussed with the new patriarch, (whose appointment he had somehow, miraculously convinced the pope to approve), that the possibility of declaring said *aedifice* unsound, structurally, was a task of paramount importance. Consequently, it would have to be abandoned. Shortly thereafter, the king claimed it for the good of his kingdom, and set about the commencement of all necessary repairs. Strange that no single workman ever appeared there to fix anything during his entire reign!

"This is no man, my brother; this is a viper, an unwholesome thing, whose soul is so corrupt, that it is incapable of assuming a pleasant appearance. It can only befoul everyone and everything around it. It has already begun to eat away at the roots of your kingdom. Why else do you think it finds the chambers of torture below so appealing? Beware. It can only take you down with it, when it leaves, and leave it will."

Eustace fled, as if he were being chased by some unseen force. Baldwin watched him go.

"He has not been the same since our dear brother succumbed," he said, still looking back at the empty space where the living brother had recently been standing. "I fear for his mind."

"It would be so much easier to dismiss everything that he says, your highness. Experience has taught me that one man's friend may be another man's monster. Sometimes it is difficult to recognize that one person might be both."

He eyed me curiously, even though he said not a word.

I cannot know if Baldwin ever were afraid, for I never once saw an expression of fear upon his face. And whilst he had a deep appreciation for his brother's expertise with a blade, he began to look upon the latter as a liability—something for which he could ill afford to tend and care. For that reason, I believe, he sent Eustace home to their ancestral estates, there to live out the rest of his days in a manner of relatively peaceful ease, far from *Outremer* and its existence of eternal warring. And though displeased with this turn of events, Eustace, ever the dutiful brother, obeyed, as he always had, shrugged, and left by Genoese vessel, never to be seen again anywhere near his brother's kingdom, with exile his recompense, until the day that he lost his wits and slaughtered all about himself, screaming against some Venetian doctor or other, upon hearing of his brother Baldwin's death.

But that is a matter for a later time.

When I returned to Temple, Brother Michael pulled me along for evening prayers. My lax attitude about its practice had begun to trouble him of late. He thought it only fair that I never forget my uncle's legacy and its demands upon me.

Afterwards, we walked past the other members of the Order and stopped near a baptismal font. Of the whitest marble that I had ever seen, I ran an index finger along its rounded rim. Without realizing it, I must have been wearing a troubled expression, as my friend inquired of its cause. Though I had not intended to speak my mind, I went on, at some length, about betrayal and mistrust and the victims of the two. Brother Michael took on that singular look of sadness that I had seen upon his face only once before, in Rome. He stepped closer to me and placed his hand upon my shoulder.

"All men are flawed," he began, "especially the great ones."

Both his comment and downcast appearance were unusual for one who had drunk from the cup of life so completely. Of whom was he speaking?

"Your uncle, the Holy Father, was a good man. Though friend, I loved him with a brother's love. Though loving, I cannot deny his flaws. No one has ever had as much faith in your abilities as he did. But when he sent you against the German Count, Emich, he was afraid."

Afraid that I would fail to punish the fiend for his wickedness?

"Afraid that the sinner might succeed in rallying others to his cause, and that you would never escape from Venice alive."

I had listened to each word that my old friend had stated. It did not strike me through the heart, as did the realization of my dear uncle's cherished motives.

"Are you saying that he sent me out to die?"

Brother Michael hesitated to respond. Finally, he told me that everything my uncle had planned was threatened; he could not risk the lives of any foreign princes or the other allies of the church for what many believed to be the inconsequential matter of the Jews.

"Yet he could risk mine own life?"

My uncle believed, in part, that, if necessary, the Lord would again rescue me. He also believed that if the Lord chose not to do so, then, regardless of the consequences, the judgment of the Most High would be, of its divine nature, just. In that case, he would have had no choice but to seek another who might complete my mission.

"I want you to know that he prayed day and night for your safety, even starving himself as penance, until he heard that you were well."

Whilst I knew that the significance of the holy war would be profound, I had no conception of how much my uncle was willing to sacrifice for its success.

As I ruminated upon same, Brother Michael bespoke further revelations. He related the final conversation that the two old friends had exchanged concerning the absence of my name in all historical matters. At the conclusion of the story, I could feel my anger boil and surge through every piece of muscle and flesh. Howling, I flung my blade at a wall, where it sank almost to the depth of its hilt.

"Calm yourself, boy! This is God's house. He will see what you have done here, and will curse us both with torments everlasting."

"Calm? You want me to remain calm in the light of this defamation?"

"Your uncle cast no insult upon your dignity."

"And what would you call it? You knew what he was doing. You admitted it even now. If you deprive a man of his fame, you steal from him his honour."

"It was a lesson."

"Should I laugh at that or weep? Ever the dutiful teacher, was he not? And what shall I have learned from all this? What? I shall tell you what. Poets will sing epic songs of the saint-like Godfrey, who trusted all his enemies with a child's blind credence. They will wax poetically upon the heroic Tancred, who mistrusted and detested all about him. For Baldwin, the first Christian king of *Outremer*, they will say that he was the bravest of fighters, whilst he bathed his hands in more blood than any man had ever before him seen. And I? I shall be unnamed, a shadow on the periphery, haunting the dreams of tired, old men."

"There may yet be wisdom in his decision."

"Speak no more, friend. Your words ring hollow. You, yourself, cannot even believe in them."

I suppose I should have guessed, long before those moments, that my uncle was as much a political leader as a spiritual one. I had thought him different, better than other men. The truth that he was not was a burden that would weigh heavily upon me, even unto this very day.

CHAPTER THE
TWENTY-SECOND,

in which the new landscape that I explore has a particularly feminine curve to its boundaries.

In the ensuing months, as Baldwin laboured tirelessly to return the city to its former glory, a class of people, hitherto unknown, began to take shape. They called themselves *entrepreneurs*. Some had lived in Jerusalem all their lives. Others (from amongst a new wave of migrating treasure-seekers) hoped to take a foothold in the new possibilities for business and/or services to the ever-increasing populace. Through the city's gates now passed warriors from far-off realms, mages and sorcerers, carpenters, bakers, cobblers, tradespeople of every stripe, thieves, homicides, and the occasional dwarf—good Christians one and all. Of these the only ones who concerned me were the panderers, whose stables of prostitutes provided intriguing ways of occupying a weary swordsman's precious time.

I must confess to you, dear reader, that a majority of the women were adept at a significant number of techniques. I learned from their treasured experiences, and they learned from mine (if their statements held any truth at all).

And perhaps here is as good a place as any to discuss what of a woman pulls a man so hard to the place where her bosoms meet (along with other caverns of mystery).

Poets write always of a cherished one's long tresses, the softness of a cheek, the full lips opening slowly, making themselves ready to receive the passionate embrace of her lover's kiss. They tell of how the curvature of her back moves ever so slightly beneath the man's firm hand. They will sing many stanzas of the application of perfumery about her neck, and its fragrance fading about her bosom. (I, for one, was ever grateful when the woman in question smelled nothing like my trusted horse.)

And there are those who will wax on with sheer delight about the manner in which her thighs grow tight about him with each successive thrust. (Even so, these scribes are few and are much detested, though their works are related with lascivious admiration by all.)

And what will she do for him, for the man she loves? She will make him stay behind (when Duty calls upon him) to smell the rainfall, and taste of pollen from springflowers. He will caress her beneath the apple blossoms of autumn, and plant a kiss upon her hand in the garden replete with the majestic white roses of May. And she will dance around the pole, twirling her long standards behind. And she will smile. And that is the one aspect of her femininity that will linger with him long after the taste of her lips has lost its heat. What is it of a woman that the man carries with himself all of his life? It is the smile of recognition, of comfort, that cleaves two hearts, only to stitch them back together each with the other's half. And was there ever a man who loved as well as he?

No man would ever admit such a thing.

"It will cost extra for swallowing," she said, upon removal of my shaft from her mouth.

I nodded.

She resumed her work. But before she could bring me to a rousing finish, I heard Brother Michael calling to me from somewhere outside and very close by.

"I am coming," I shouted back to him. "I am coming!"

A woman's body is an endless source of mystery, that I have never grown bored with the exploration thereof.

In the next several months following, I indulged myself at the numerous flesh-pots, which sprang up in the Holy City like a verdant copse overrun by strangling weeds. And I made no distinction between the various goods available therein for purchase. Thin or fat, tender with her speech, or pragmatic concerning the financial transaction about to take place between us, each woman was a means of forgetting. And when they could not make me forget, I sought out more bizarre couplings. Two women would search each other's recesses with their tongues. Sometimes I would watch; sometimes I would join them. And when even these could only excite me momentarily, (though never mollify my soul's torment), I could ever find one lady who would be willing to do a bit more for her coinage. One swore that she could swallow a significant portion of a horse's member, if I but cared to witness the act. This vision, I must confess, (though curious about it), was one that I decided to forego. (It might have been a source of pleasure for the beast, though not really one for me.)

Of late during one particularly wet evening, after a day that had sapped much of my masculine strength in the bedchambers, Brother Michael and Hughes found me in a tavern. Together, they wanted me to leave with them. Of course I refused for no reason other than a wish to be indignant for it's own sake. Seeing that I was drunken, shouting, wretched, into the now muddied road they pulled me from the tavern. Hughes, who had taken to calling all of the Order's members his *brethren*, now addressed me:

"What are you doing, brother? You bring dishonour upon your name and upon all who believe in you."

"My name? What name is mine? Obscurity is my name!"

"There is no sense in this. Everyone knows of you. Everyone always will. This is not the same man who fought at my side in Antioch."

"Antioch happened years ago. We are all much older now."

"Come out of this damnèd rain!" Brother Michael ordered, grabbing at my arm. "I shall put you to bed, like the ill-mannered boy you are."

"Take your hands off me!" I shouted, pulling away. "I am not going anywhere. I shall drink all night, if I so desire it. Who are you to tell me what to do?"

Hughes shook his head. I had never witnessed that much pain upon his face. Though my vision was blurred, much from the falling water as from drink, I could see it all. He bore the onus of embarrassment for everyone present upon his shoulders.

"You cannot fight a spirit," Brother Michael averred. "It is like spitting into the wind."

I knew of his reference to my uncle, yet that knowledge gave me no peace at all.

They left me there, all by myself. And for the first time in many months, I was most heartily ashamed.

Never again would I allow my own pain to diminish me as it did that night. Thus I swore, and I have remained faithful to that promise (regardless of the cost) ever since.

CHAPTER THE TWENTY-THIRD,

in which the Byzantine court proves itself an endless source of revelations.

On a warm afternoon of an early spring day, I set foot once more onto the stones of the Palace Komnenos. I had so much desired to forget the last time here, that I rid all dates of it from my mind. To this day I cannot claim to know that season, nor its very month. I calculated temporal concerns only in the knowledge that five years had passed, since Bohémond won his liberty. Five years of preparation had yielded a final battle with Emperor Alexios Komnenos, only to witness the incessant slaughter of Frankish and Italian troops, and the continuing spread of Byzantine *hegemony*. The Norman did not think of himself as a shamelessly defeated man, however. He could see only that Byzantium was everywhere. There was no safe passage to escape from it. It was suffocating him.

Despite all that, the emperor treated his prisoner with the due respect and honours akin to a royal guest—not an uncommon practice of the time, especially if the captor sought significant remuneration for the safe release of his prisoner. And the Norman strolled about the royal domicile and its adjacent grounds with seeming abandon, giving rise to his new practice of spewing drunken bluster and vague threats, none of which appeared to bother the emperor. (That may have had something to do with the many guards present, who were forever watching said guest's motions and habits.)

We dined in the typical luxury that I had come to expect from my host. Brother Michael, Hughes de Payens, myself, the Norman, several other goodly brothers of our new Order, and the royal prince, (whose *pedagogical* name still irks me so, that I refuse to write of it here and now!), were fêted with glorious abundance. (Both the empress and the royal daughter were nowhere to be seen this time. Where could they have been? Were we not fit to be in their royal presence?)

And during the infinite display of courses, the conversation turned often from the possibility for a lasting peace to the inception of a new war, or wars, as was so often the case. Whilst we dined, whilst we spoke, Bohémond often drank, often laughed, his jovial manner most raucous. I had never seen the Norman act with so little decorum, though he had never been much for adhering to the rules of civilized conduct. If his behaviour disturbed his host in any fashion, one would never know it, for the emperor expressed no seeming dislike throughout the meal. In fact, he never altered the smile that had been painted upon his face from the first moment that I saw him again.

Hughes mentioned the enormous sacrifices necessary to maintain our positions. The royal prince (who had grown into an older replica of his father than when last I saw him, beard included) offered a small contingent of Byzantine troops for Jerusalem, if we so desired it. (I could see that the father was most pleased with the son's suggestion.) Hughes was gracious enough to say that he would be happy to ask King Baldwin if that were his desire (though he would later admit to me that he would not even mention it; the option would have been dismissed out of hand. Byzantine troops in Jerusalem? Perish the thought!). When he thanked the prince, he added that the human cost of *Outremer*'s possession had been very dear. The Norman stopped drinking when he heard that statement. He looked into his chalice, revealing for the first time no smile at all.

"In war," he said, "sometimes one sees so many dead, that he no longer feels much of anything."

The entire hall grew silent. The balance of our meal contained only snippets of discussion. We, too, had all grown quite weary.

As we were led out of the vast chamber, Bohémond's massive bulk resting upon the shoulders of one or another of the palace guards, both Brother Michael and Hughes had several opinions, which they felt they needed to share with me, quietly, of course, lest the volume of their speech attract the unwanted attention of the guards.

"The Norman giant has been reduced to the size of a dwarf," Brother Michael was the first to say with more than a little empathy. "The emperor must have sorcerers at his disposal."

"No, my friend," Hughes countered, "the only magic here is the result of ignominious defeat."

And to me he said:

"You must convince the emperor to set him free to return to his home in Italy."

"Why do you rest the responsibility for his life upon *my* shoulders?" I demanded of him, then looked around to determine if anyone had heard my rather vociferous question. "Where were the kings of *Outremer*, who allowed him to languish amongst the Turks for years, rather than pay his ransom?" I continued more quietly now. "This is not my sin, yet you wish for me to redeem him somehow. You lavish far too much praise upon my capabilities, if you believe me clever enough to accomplish that deed."

"Brother Hughes is most assuredly correct. You were the honoured guest at the imperial table. Did you not see how the emperor deferred to you, even when you had nothing of consequence to mention?"

"I always have something important to say!" I insisted.

Hughes motioned me to keep quiet. The less heard, the better.

"The rest of us there," Brother Michael continued now in a low tone of voice, "were no more than your retinue. Listen to me, boy. This is one game that should not be lost. You must force the imperial hand."

"If he is not released shortly," Hughes added, "he will wither and die. A former leader of the Holy War deserves better."

"It takes no prophet to see this," Brother Michael agreed.

"No," I had to admit, "it takes no prophet. It takes a soldier."

I bade goodnight to all as I entered my bedchamber. I had begun to remove my clothing, when, shortly thereafter, another guard knocked upon the door. He came to inform me that my presence was requested in the emperor's personal garden, and that I should follow him forthwith. I sighed. All this ceremonious gesturing only added to my fatigue. (It had been a very thorough day, and so stuffed was my stomach, that I longed only to sit or sleep, certainly not to move in the slightest from what I took to be a most comfortable bed. Perhaps that was why I had not noticed that the guard was absent the usual purple raiment of the personal imperial troops.) And why had the emperor not asked me to stay behind, if conversation were his wish? Reluctantly, I followed.

I walked over to the fountain and looked about. No one else was there.

"Your highness?" I called.

From the shadows emerged a young woman clad in what could only have been gossamer. Still was she without veil. Still was she most beautiful. And her dark eyes swallowed all the moonlight, there to reflect its luminous presence evermore.

"I am here, sir knight," she whispered.

"As am I, my lady," I struggled to find my voice, and bowed to her.

"You have changed not at all."

"The same cannot be said of you, princess. You are most wonderfully made, and even lovelier than I remember."

"I am no longer that love-sick child, Guy de Lagery."

"Thanks be to God that you are not. You are now, in all things, a woman."

"And as a woman, I have married."

I was silent.

"Did you not hear me?" she asked. "Was I not honest with you when I said that I would marry only a Byzantine?"

"In that were you most honest, my lady."

"He is Nikephoros Byrennos, a brave fighter. And he is far from here, keeping the borders of our empire safe against the pagan. He is our symbol of victory made flesh. Though prompted by my elders, my marriage to him was my wisest choice. It is fitting for a woman of my years to have a husband, and for the Byzantine Princess to have her consort, is it not?"

"As you say."

"Not only is he brave, he is also handsome, like the ancient *kolossos* of the sun-god, Helios. And his strong arms are like stone."

"He sounds like a monster, half rock, half skin. How could you care for such a creature?"

"Are you displeased because I chose marriage, or because I chose not to marry you?"

"Thinking that you would love me for the rest of my life was a foolish notion, and would have made of me the King of Fools, had I believed it. I am far too wise for such nonsense."

I began to walk away.

"Where are you going?" she asked. "I have not dismissed you."

"O, but you have, my lady," I said, and left her there all alone.

CHAPTER THE TWENTY-FOURTH,

in which the Norman's liberty is purchased at the price of his humility.

"If anyone else had attempted to trade upon our friendship for this, I would have had him tossed out of the empire, thence to find his way home on foot!"

The emperor paced about his sacred garden, digging his heels into the grass as he stepped this way and that.

Friendship? Is that what the emperor convinced himself that we were sharing?

"Not only did he raise an army against me," he went on, "but it was also a holy war!"

"I beg to differ, your highness. He had no papal blessing for his misdeeds."

"So, has he become the Lord of Misrule, a court jester perhaps? What is to prevent him from taking up arms a third time?"

"Prince Bohémond is not the same man who led his armies at Antioch. Never again will he raise his sword, especially in the manner that he has previously done."

"Prophecy, my young man?"

I gritted my teeth.

"No longer am I so young nor so naïve, your majesty."

"To an old man like myself, the entire world is young, or at the very least, somewhat younger. Concerning naiveté, you have always proven to possess an experience beyond your years. That much about you is true. Nevertheless, your trust in him may be misplaced. I, for one, never believed that he would want to usurp me again. Decades have passed since that former failed attempt. I thought that he had lost all desire for regicide."

"He is unwell. His family members will tend to his needs now. Release him to them. They will be most grateful for your kindness."

I bit my tongue after those final words. There had been no mention of a ransom, and I may have inadvertently planted the seed for one in my host's fertile mind.

Agitated, his hands clasped behind his back, he continued to pace about. He turned to look at me to begin another of his official pronouncements:

"I cannot say which truth angers me more: the presence of an old enemy in my kingdom, or your wish to carry politics into my sole refuge of contemplation."

Dear Lord, did this man ever do a thing that was not infused with ceremony, the expression of his anger included?

"If I have offended you in any way, emperor, I beg your indulgence, and ask your forgiveness. My concern is for a Christian warrior, who has acquitted himself with victories upon the field of battle."

"If you believe that he has ever placed the legacy of our Nazarene before his own ambition, then you are truly a naïf."

He sat upon the bench, motioning for me to take a place near him. He put his elbows upon his knees, clasped his hands, and rested his chin upon the latter. Whilst I had no desire to disrupt his mental processes, (which were continuing for some time), I found myself growing bored. The view was not unpleasant, but I had far more important work to perform than contemplation of this sylvan scene.

"I might be willing to free him," he offered finally, "if he were to sign a truce, of sorts."

To what sort of *truce* was he referring exactly? Bohémond would have to agree that, should another attempt be made upon the emperor's life, all of the Norman's possessions and properties would be turned over to the Byzantine crown, should the Norman lose, of course. That agreement would include the kingdom of Antioch. I reminded his highness that Antioch was now under control of Tancred, who would be far less willing to lay that realm at the foot of a Byzantine than ever his uncle was. The emperor agreed; he would omit the mention of Antioch. And he had me understand (in no uncertain terms) how generous he was being with his former adversary; all this he would do (he reiterated) solely for my benefit.

I wondered if this were no more than a pretext for him to commence his own war anew.

"Do you wish possession of his lands, then?"

"Why should I care about *Sicilia?* I have heard that its people are hard-working farmers and are nothing like their coarse, vulgar Norman masters. Byzantium is quite large, and it requires my full attention. A war to conquer that isle would be the most horrifying form of indulgence. I would like to think myself a better man than that."

And perhaps he was, for the agreement was one that the Norman would have never conceived.

Upon the following afternoon, (when the documentation had been completed), and after a long morning full of very loud argumentation between the Norman and myself concerning his future, Bohémond signed the document with the seal of his ring, imprinted in wax, for he could not write otherwise.

Several years later, he would confess to me that he had signed it that afternoon in his own blood. But there was no blood, nor swordplay, nor chorus of weeping women. Any tragedies that day were of the quiet sort—the ones, which people keep always to themselves, except perhaps in nightly prayers, when the only one who will listen is God, even though He will give no other voice to one's pleas.

The Norman was escorted out of Byzantium several mornings thereafter. I was to see him only once more in Apulia, some years later, merely days before his death, where he would ask of me to grant him one final kindness.

Amidst the gentle breezes of an early autumn morn, Hughes, Brother Michael, and I were escorted as we rode along the hills on the outskirts of the city. Hughes stopped to admire the many church spires rising high above the line of trees about. It was then that another group of riders came amongst us. They led the princess, who appeared as comfortable astride a stallion as any horseman. (And her face was uncovered for all to see, even when surrounded by palace guards. Was this a new custom that she had instituted?) Clad in pale blue, her thick, long tresses were pulled back and separated into two twisted braids of hair. These were tied together into a larger single one very near their base, and tossed over her right shoulder. (I can only assume that their length might have interfered with the swift motion of her horse, and would have probably thrown both animal and rider, had her hair been allowed to remain free.) Around her neck she wore a single jewel, an amethyst.

"Good day to you, men of Jerusalem," she greeted us.

We welcomed her into our company as well.

"Has my father been regaling you with stories of his many exploits and conquests?"

"Now there is one emperor who knows how to tell a tale!" Brother Michael was quick to say.

Hughes, somewhat off-put by my friend's statement, stared at him. Brother Michael stared back, mouthing the word, *what?*.

"You are most welcome, my lady," I greeted her.

"Really?"

"Indeed."

"If that is so, then perhaps you will accompany me, as I ride. I do so enjoy the morning air. Take your place at my side, Guy de Lagery, whilst the rest follow at a safe distance."

The last half of that statement she had made to the leader of her guards, who took her meaning, and nodded.

Once ahead of the others, she broke her silence:

"How many beautiful women have you loved?"

"I have loved no one else since."

"Since?"

"Since last I beheld you. There. Are you happy now that I have said it?"

"Somewhat."

"Do you love him?"

"He is wonderful. He is my Caesar."

"And is he as ambitious as his namesake?"

"In what manner do you mean?"

"The Roman, Julius, longed to rule the *imperium*, though he once refused that position when offered. It was the game of Roman politics, I suppose. Does your husband desire to do the same?"

"He is a loyal subject."

"So are we all. That does not mean he will forego his ambition at the expense of your father's precious life. Did he marry you to bring himself closer to an unsuspecting emperor?"

She reached to slap me, then thought better of it, as the captain of the guard was watching us quite carefully.

"He loves me. He has loved me since we were children."

"Do you love him?"

"Why do you ask me that? Do you love me?"

"My love is so great, that it cannot be measured."

"It is a rare thing when a man loves the woman more."

"And why should that be so?"

"When a woman loves, it is completely, and for all time. Long after he is gone, she is still soothed by the memory of his touch, or the smell of his tunic. Men may love deeply, though they will never learn the ecstasy of suffering that can trample the human heart."

"Perhaps the man is stronger. He is, after all, the sword that brings the wild boar to the feasting-table. His heart may be hardened by circumstances which he cannot control, yet love he will."

"Is he, then, no more than his labours?"

"Labours? Much of *Outremer* is ruled by Christian kings. Was that labour no more than the toil of a poor farmer in the fields from dawn until dusk?"

"I thought that our discussion was on the male component of civilization in the abstract, not the specific."

Now it was I who wanted to reach for her, though to give forth a caress, not a slap. Instead, I simply gazed upon her.

"Do not toy with me, my lady. Would you have the gift of my heart only to crush it under foot?"

She looked around us quickly.

"Who do you think you are? Kerbūgha the Persian? Have a care, sir knight. I belong to another."

I began to laugh, recalling the famed warrior whose swordhand I had sliced so swiftly.

"What do you find so amusing?" she asked, quite irritated with my reaction.

"Nothing. I am laughing for no apparent reason."

"Then you must be touched in the head."

"Where a woman is concerned, that may be more true than not."

"If that is your best example of a courtly love ballad, you will need considerable more practice at songmaking."

"My uncle always believed that my skills in poetry were poor. He would have agreed without hesitation."

"He was a very wise man."

We rode on, she taking in the floral perfumes, and I sniffing only at the woodland dampness. Would she ever love me as she loved the man who had taken her to his bed?

"Do you love him, my lady?"

She stared at me.

"He has always been here."

"You mention comforting, a bit of affection perhaps. Where is the ecstasy of which you have spoken? Where is the pain that no balm in Gilead may heal?"

She began to ride away from me. Momentarily, she stopped, though did not turn around.

"A woman learns how to live with her pain," she explained. "Sometimes, when the night is cold, it is the only thing that may comfort her."

CHAPTER THE TWENTY-FIFTH,

in which a princess and a knight find each other once again, for a time.

I awoke, wondering when, if ever, the emperor would tire of my company, and so, allow me leave of his realm peaceably. (I had not expected to be here more than several days, and nearly a fortnight had already passed.) My companions were equally anxious to be on their way, and they let me know of their impatience in no uncertain terms. At this point they were convinced that only I might able to liberate us from this soft prison. With the Lord above as my witness, I undertook to do so often, without any degree of success.

As I dressed, guards came to inform me that I had been summoned once more into some imperial presence, or other, the author of which I could not say. I followed, dutifully, as I was brought into a small chamber at the farthest corner of the east wing. There I was left to my own devices for a short time.

Then from behind a large wooden screen, ornately limned with golden representations of Mary and our Lord, I heard a rustling.

"This *eikonostasis* provides a perfect form for concealment, does it not, Guy de Lagery?"

A woman's voice had emerged from behind the standing canvases. Though similar to that of the princess, it did not belong to her.

"Indeed it does! And who, may I ask, is concealed there?"

"Empress of Byzantium, wife of the illustrious Emperor Alexios Komnenos, and mother of Prince Paleologos and Princess Anna. You may address me with all the respectable titles to which I am most assuredly due."

O? What did this trickery portend?

"I shall endeavour to please, your highness."

"I had always promised myself that I would never speak directly with a Frank."

"Pardon my ignorance. Is that a custom of your people, or is it simply your choice?"

"You have a bold spirit, Guy de Lagery."

"My uncle believed that as well."

"Did he tell you that it borders on insult?"

"Not that I am able to recall. Be that as it may, I meant no disrespect, empress."

She informed me that my uncle had trained me well in the ways of proper courtesy, despite my apparent unwillingness to avail myself of them. I bit my lip. I informed her that he would have been most pleased to hear that.

"You are not like the others of your kind," she added.

Was she about to bestow a compliment upon me whilst insulting my people?

"In what way or ways am I different exactly?"

"You know how to respect your host. I never trusted that Norman who led your company. He has brought shame upon himself and upon his nation."

"I believe that he will bother you no more."

"My daughter is happily married now," she said, apparently thinking nothing of having altered the subject of our discussion. "Did you know that?"

"The emperor may have mentioned it in passing."

She wanted me to know that her daughter's happiness was precious to her. She did not wish for anyone or anything to disrupt the routine of her child's days.

"Do you take my meaning in the spirit in which it is intended, Sir Guy?"

I knew it! Somehow she had learned of that fateful tryst between her precious daughter and myself long ago, or she may have guessed at it. And that supposition would have been enough to confirm her seeming distaste for all foreigners, especially this Frankish knight.

"It needs no further explanation, empress."

"You are dismissed."

Dismissed, was I?

"Farewell, empress," I said, bowing, then cursed myself, for she could not even see the respect that my action had presented to her.

Reluctantly, the emperor agreed to allow us departure several days thereafter. (He had fallen into the habit of contemplation of miracles, and felt that I was the perfect companion for this process; nor did he believe the Byzantine patriarch capable of illuminating all the intricacies of faith, history, and human frailty, which often combined themselves into various permutations for any analysis thereof afterwards.) Frankly, I was glad to be leaving shortly; my mental processes had exhausted themselves in dealing with his favourite topic and its any and all confusing combinations.

On the night before I left, she came to me, unexpectedly, as she had done years before, the moonlight pouring in as it had done so as well. And though her beauty was luminous, still did I take well her mother's meaning, and decided that I would prefer to leave this land with my head intact.

Upon her entry, I arose from the bed to address her:

"I am surprised yet relieved that you have come," I told her. "I am to depart on the morrow, and I wanted only to wish you well in your marriage. May you have many healthy children, who will bring honour to your name."

"So formal are we now? And so soon are we leaving? Barely has a week passed since your arrival."

I thought that behind her questioning lay a pained voice; I might have erred in that judgment.

"Actually, two have passed. And my responsibilities lie elsewhere. I have not time to indulge my pleasures in the wonders of your kingdom. Besides, your husband will probably be returning to you in the near future. I would prefer not to look upon that *paragon* of Greek perfection."

"Why are you unkind? He has done nothing to you."

"He has taken you as his bride. Is that not enough?"

"He has always been here. You left me," she uttered with scorn, coming closer. "After I had tasted love for the first time, you left me!" she accused me, now raising a tightly clenched fist at me. "How could you leave me?"

"War is my life. I did not flee from here to seek glory. Lord knows, that will never be granted me now. I went to defend everyone and everything Christian, including you. It was my holy mission."

"Were you a priest, then?"

"Those who cannot save souls with words must take the souls of God's enemies with a sword. So has it always been."

"The pope was your uncle. You could have convinced him to let you stay here, if you did but try."

"And what excuse would I have created for my seeming cowardice? O, I suppose I could have told him that I was planning to marry the royal daughter. He might have accepted a delay for that reason, and I believe your family would have been equally ecstatic about it!"

"Marriage? Who is talking about marriage here? Not I, most assuredly!"

"Yes, I forgot; how could you possibly marry someone who is so beneath you?"

"Stop that. You are not beneath me. Not yet anyway," she added, finishing her statement with a coy smile. "O, I hate this! I wanted so very much to make you suffer the loneliness that ate away at me each day and night."

"And did you think that I, who held you in my arms and tasted your lips, could bear the separation so easily throughout all the summers and winters of those lost years? Remembering you brought the misery of days to its swift end. Only at night, when I lay half-awake, dreaming, did I think I could hear you calling my name again."

She stood still, her eyes and mouth agape. Then began the flow of her tears.

"I curse you that you ever left me," she choked. "I bless you that you have returned."

"To taste your wrath?" I asked, smiling.

She laughed along.

"Will you love me forever, Guy de Lagery?"

"All the days of my life."

"Liar. But lie to me once more. It would not displease me."

She reached to touch my face. We embraced, then kissed.

Slowly did I linger, planting kisses upon her neck, as its fragrance wafted up to me. I caressed her cheek. She moaned slightly. My fingers touched her lips. Supple, they pecked at my fingertips. Her tongue crept out and licked them. Then it sought my face, my lips, my throat, where we thrust at each other's tongues.

She jumped up, wrapping her legs about me, as I held her fast, each buttock nestled in my palms. I carried her to the bed, still kissing her all the while. We clawed and tore at each other's garments. I placed her down, then kissed her neck. Opening her red silk robe now, I began to lick her, creating a path gently down along her breast, until I found her nipple. I licked, then sucked. She moaned. I reached up and thrust my fingers into her mouth. (It was my attempt to quieten her, lest her vociferous manner call attention to our activities once again.) She proceeded to suck upon them forthwith.

With my other hand, I massaged her tender bud.

"I adore it when your fingers are within me," she whispered. "Enter me," she pleaded.

I climbed atop her. Soaking between her thighs, she took me in with little or no effort on both of our parts. (There was no olive oil this time. That was a curious thing.)

Her body tightened everywhere, her legs wrapped around me, beneath me, above me, all over me, becoming one with mine, matching push and caress, moan and whimper.

She pulled from me, moving around to place her perfectly rounded buttocks before me. Verily I obliged, as I mounted her from behind. But as she shoved against me, slapping against my scrotum, my hands hard upon her hips, each thrust brought along the very real possibility that the young novice had become quite the adept. And the many hours of practice had not been with me!

I could not permit myself more than a momentary flash of realization, lest our ardor cool, and the night descend into a hellish den of mutual recrimination.

I began to pull out (not as a result of jealousy, for I was above such childishness, but because I could feel myself about to burst), as her legs tightened about me, refusing to allow me leave to go. I have no idea why I forced myself back and away from her (despite her best efforts), spilling my seed across her belly, as she fell upon the beclothes, revealing her nakedness once more. Perhaps it had been an habitual action, for I had done the same often before. Not until I had finished, did I realize that she had loved me so much, that she would have given me a child. No! I was deluding myself. I knew it even then. Our babe would have grown up in Konstantinople, most likely reared by another man as his own. And I would have had nothing, except the memory of this night.

She stuck her fingers into the sticky mound upon herself and licked from it.

"Never shall I forget your taste."

I kissed her long.

We lay, bound by each other's arms.

"I shall remain with you tonight," she said, after a time.

"Is that wise?"

"A woman in love is a stranger to wisdom."

"Of a man is that statement no less true, my love. We shall be discovered."

"Do you fear that?"

"I fear only the wrath of the Lord. Everyone else be damned!"

"Will our Creator punish our participation in this adulterous act, do you think?"

"Love is a truth that possesses a logic all its own. If the Lord, our God, has granted us the ability to feel, then He must have known what He was doing."

"Did He suspect everything that we *might* be doing? I wonder. Come. Softly now. Do not fear. I shall not bite."

I felt her hands grope for my crotch.

It was very early when I arose to dress myself. As I did so, I looked back at her, resting there upon the pillows. She was scowling. But why?

"Give to me not your anger, my lady. It would be most sinful to recall your harsh face when no longer together."

"Would it not be most sinful to recall that you took another man's wife, as if she were your own?"

"Wherefore do you punish me, after I have loved you?"

"You will leave. All men leave. They race to war, as if it were their sole reason for being. Forever to remain behind are the wives, sisters, mothers, forever to weep for their cherished ones. O, stay with me, Guy de Lagery! Stay here in my arms, in my bed. I shall make every moment precious to you."

"If only I could!" I said, caressing her cheek.

"Then go," she countered, slapping aside my hand and throwing herself back upon the pillows.

"My shoulders will bear great burdens. I would prefer to depart with a tender kiss."

"Would you have my heart as well? Like all invaders, you would steal everything that is Byzantine."

"I cannot steal what has been offered freely."

"There you are wrong, thievish knight. What was offered to you comes at a very high price. It costs everything that you feel, and most especially everything that you are."

"Everything that I am is yours."

"How precious a thing that would be to me, if I still desired it."

She could not have struck me more deeply, if she had slapped my face with all deliberate force.

"I see now that I was foolish to come here," I declared, disgusted with myself and everyone and everything about me.

"You should know me well enough to ignore me, when I am angry. Do not leave me again. I offer everything that I am freely to you."

She pulled aside the bedclothes, and lifted up and spread apart her legs. O, my Lord, everything about her was beautiful!

"Your husband might have a problem with another man in his bed, or is that a Byzantine custom of which I have not yet heard?"

She covered herself.

"Wherefore do you always leave me? How can you not know how much you mean to me? If you leave now, we shall not see each other again for many years."

Had she become a new Oracle of Delphi?

She stared at me for some time, before she spoke again:

"I have a sense of things before they happen. I knew that you would be my first love. I saw it in a dream."

"And what do your dreams reveal to you now?"

"I shall be old," she said, rubbing the back of her hand softly against my cheek, "whilst you remain forever young."

"Truly am I blessèd among men."

"This is no farce!" she shouted.

I tried to calm her; the guards would have come forth, running, had they heard her outburst. But they did not, or perhaps they were paid to turn a deaf ear to all sound that would occur herein.

"I cannot shirk my responsibilities," I insisted.

"What of your responsibility to me? Is love so common a thing that you can pass it by without another glance? If you leave here, you will change our lives forever."

"I must go."

"Then go! Leave, before I have the guards escort you to our borders."

I gathered myself together, then turned to look upon her one last time.

"Stare long at me!" she demanded. "When next you see me, I shall be too old to appreciate the warmth of your passions, belovèd. Long will you regret that you have left me this day."

"You will always be at my side, for my heart is no longer my own."

"Liar."

And in the years to come, we proved each other most correct; may God forgive us both!

CHAPTER THE TWENTY-SIXTH,

in which a German leader becomes besotted, whilst drinking from a cup of Might.

Much have I noticed that the Germans are a people obsessed with the conception of empire, or *Reich*, as is their terminology. Perhaps that was why, in the century prior to my birth, they took to the calling of their lands, *the Roman Empire*. I can only surmise that this action was their attempt to align their history with a Latinate power and glory. However, Rome had also produced Vergil's poetics and Cicero's orations, whilst Teutonic fighters, clad in animal skins, their faces brightly painted, smothered Roman achievements with a scarlet hue; and with them they carried upon their shoulders a Darkness, that spilled over into each piece of adjoining territory for centuries to come. And now they believed themselves harbingers of the light of Civilization throughout the world.

Really?

After Charlemagne had united the kingdoms of the Rhineland, Germany was born. The then current ruler of this second Roman Empire, Heinrich V, a man fair of hair and blue of eye, wished to appoint bishops, for then he would be able to control bishoprics, and all the ecclesiastical wealth that they might be capable of bestowing upon their respective communities. The pope refused him this desire, since it had always been a portion of his own ecumenical prowess, and that fact made Heinrich a most unhappy man.

So the ruler of the *Reich* marched into Rome with an army, seeking papal approbation for his wishes. (He always did have a problem accepting a negative response, I have been told.) Bearing witness to the might of one contentious emperor, the pope decided that it would probably not be the most opportune occasion to stand his ground for what he knew to be the proper choice of action. Then, when preparing to render into ecclesiastical law whichever suggestions had

189

been asked of him, the strangest of things occurred. No one knew why. It may have been the authority of his position, or the hand of God that prompted him, but Paschal II refused to accede to the demands of the *Reich*. And consequently, he was carried out of Rome like a carpet-weaver's goods tied to horseback. And though the emperor may not yet have been happy, he believed that he was on the true path to that much sought-after goal.

"Who does this swine from the Rhineland think he is?" Brother Michael roared. "I never thought I would say this, but the Holy Father would benefit from a standing army in Rome."

"We should have thought of that previously," Hughes agreed.

I motioned for the others to keep still, as Baldwin, who had granted us audience, was about to speak:

"As always, you are most welcome, Knights of the Temple. Have you come to discuss the situation concerning our pope?"

I nodded.

"These Germans have ever been a contentious lot," he continued. "If it were unnecessary to strengthen our borders here, we, ourselves, would lead the force against them, taking their empire for the glory of all. They are a most detestable people."

The entire court nodded in unison.

"We can offer you no more than a single garrison."

Hughes and I exchanged glances. We had not expected even that much from the king.

"We would be most grateful, your highness," I offered as thanks.

"We wish our assistance were more generous. We fear your meager forces will be quite inadequate for this task. Despite your growing numbers, you should redouble your efforts at proselytizing."

"We are inundated with new candidates for membership each day!" Hughes affirmed.

"And are they the finest of swordsmen, brother Hughes, or have we stolen all of them away?" Baldwin asked, smiling.

"They are the finest of *men*," Hughes corrected him.

I was proud of his statement, for I knew it to be the truth.

"A victory will not be easily attained, your highness," I maintained. "Though many innocent souls may die, we shall not fail."

Baldwin smiled.

"As my physician has told me more than once, *no one is innocent.* Is that not true?"

The entire court nodded in unison, as did my comrades. I, however, did not.

As we rode away from the court, we all agreed how difficult our task would be. It was Brother Hughes, (after having conferred with Brother Michael), who thought that our efforts would benefit from the creation of fear.

"Why should Fear not be as mighty a weapon as any *trebuchet*? If we shake loose their firm wills to power, we shall fight an enemy who has no more heart left for battle."

"Or stomach either," Brother Michael added. And he would make it known to all and sundry, that the Knights of the Temple were coming to free their pope, and riding along with them was an indestructible knight.

An indestructible knight? And who, pray tell, was that supposed to be?

The two men smiled at me.

Now really! That was a bit much, was it not? Why should the Germans believe such a tale, if I, myself, were no more inclined to do so? Besides, they were not so gullible as all that, were they?

"Why not?" Brother Michael asked in response. "We have been victorious in every campaign since the retaking of Jerusalem. And everyone has heard of you, even those filthy Teutons!"

"Forgive me, my brother," Hughes said. "We may have to cut only a few wounds into you to prove how special you really are."

"This is absurd! They will think it a trick by some traveling band of players, no more, no less."

"Have faith," Brother Michael assured me. "The sight of swords and blood will make them very excitable. They will believe almost anything that they see, so anxious are they for miracles of any sort."

"Is it not better to win a war with a few choice wonders of our own before it has begun?" Brother Hughes added.

I could not disagree, even had I wished for it.

The German forces, who rode to protect their borders, were ill-prepared for the sight of one enormous Venetian vessel sailing close to their shoreline. Even less did they expect ever to see the Holy Knights of the Temple of Jerusalem. Prepared for battle, (as ever we were), we set upon them like the finest of huntsmen. Heedless of our safety, we bounded from the deck. Our sole armor being our breastplates, we were fleet and lithe. With their metallic-clad horses and their bodies virtually hammered into their own clanging garments, the knights of this Holy Roman Empire could barely move. Indeed, they had sacrificed their agility for protection, and were about to pay the price for that choice now.

Once thrown from their horses, they staggered about, slicing the air with haphazard strokes, as they sank into the peat-covered soil. (O, dear reader you should have seen Brother Michael that fateful day! He ran and jumped through the enemy's lines like a boy during his first lessons in swordcraft. Each time he plunged his blade into a chest or cut off a head, his smile stretched from ear to ear. So happy was he, that he ignored the fresh wound upon his cheek, that would become one more of the scars he would wear proudly in the days to come.) Eventually (to a man) they fell like thick oaks, mired deeply, and splashing the mud all about their visors. Hah! As if German might were ever something that a Frank should fear!

We had heard that their nation had a long tradition of hunting, and would sometimes let loose a slave, (or some other poor wretch), into the dense forest, and once located, there he would be brought down by their swords like a feral animal. We were far less brutal. We simply killed, when no one would tell us where the king was. One swordsman, however, begged of our mercy. And he was most voluble. In fact, once he began to speak, we could do little to keep his mouth shut. Fortunately, Brother Michael was able to accomplish what the rest of us were unable to achieve.

"Go tell your king," he began, "that the Knights of the Holy Temple of Jerusalem have come unto him this day, led by a warrior that no sword can destroy, Guy de Lagery." (He pointed to me now.) "We have come for the return of our pope. If he is unsafe, then the wrath of God will be upon the heads of every German! Do you take my meaning, varlet?"

The man's eyes widened in fear. He nodded slightly.

"Then go. Go now! But first, remove everything upon your person."

"Everything?"

My old friend refused to allow the brave soldier to leave safely, until the latter had removed each piece of armor and clothing. Denuded, the now-shamed man mounted his horse and left us. I turned to Brother Michael.

"I had no idea how much you were given to the gift of *hyperbole*."

"O, I was not overly demonstrative, was I, Brother Hughes?"

"Somewhat."

"Is there no appreciation for a good tragedy here? Verily am I a sparrow among a horde of ravenous wolves!"

"Exactly as I said," I added further, "*hyperbole* to the extreme!"

We rode beneath the *lindens* in their dark forests, where witches and sundry other cursèd creatures were supposed to dwell. Despite all fantastical tales, I saw no monsters. There were robins only. And the rare falling leaf did not occasion inclement weather or unknown roarings. All was peaceful in this realm, perhaps deceptively so.

When I saw the royal palace rising from the mountaintop, I could not help but wonder why it was that kings have ever been so determined to outdo the castles of their neighboring rulers in the gaudiest of ornateness (or most ornate of gaudiness, as the case might be). Besides possessing an overwhelming desire to control everyone and everything around them, (whilst surrounded by every possible comfort), all rulers shared this quality in common. I did not think that it said very much for the legacy that all men would leave behind as their mark upon history. Then again, what would a poor servant of the church, like me, know of such complicated matters? Still, did this king really need *that* many towers?

The cowardly knight must have related Brother Michael's warning well, since the drawbridge was down, and there were no guards around it to bar our passage inside.

Behind the throne was a massive shield, emblazoned with an imperial eagle thereupon. And upon that throne sat the king, surrounded by very many of his guards and a goodly number of the nobility. Rarely had I seen that many fair-haired, blue-eyed *simulacra* gathered together in one place. I thought that I had fallen into a golden sea. Nevertheless, instead of allowing myself to feel disconcerted by this bright strangeness, I stood straight and announced my intention:

"The Knights of the Temple of Jerusalem have come to you today, Heinrich, King of Germany, to demand—"

"*Ach*, the Roman Empire," he spoke, correcting me.

"What?"

"The Roman Empire. This is the new Roman Empire. Actually, it is not so new. It is approximately three centuries old now. Have we calculated our *chronology* well, Stillwulf?" he asked an antique advisor, who stood nearby. The man nodded rather slowly in response.

More than once did I look upon his counselor's face, for his features were not unlike those of Baldwin's physician, albeit considerably older.

"We are here to demand that you set free the Holy Father!" I made him understand in no uncertain terms.

"Do you mean to say that you have come all this way for *him*?"

I stood there, my mouth agape.

"Did your knight not tell you of our approach?"

"A most useless nephew. If he were not so dear to our sister, we would have had him killed when still a spoiled child. Families, you see, they demand everything of you."

"Where is the Holy Father?" I bellowed.

A hush fell upon the entire court.

"Now, is there a need for this uncivilized behaviour? We are perfectly willing to discuss the current papal situation. Please try not to raise your voice again. We find it quite irritating."

My face had grown so red and hot with ire, that I could feel the chain mail about my chest begin to smoulder.

"It is not every day that our court is graced with the presence of an indestructible knight. Are you said knight? We would very much like to see evidence of this amazing prowess."

"Give to me your dagger."

"What?"

"Do you not carry one, as all other royals do? Give it me."

He pulled it out and held it in front of himself.

"Why do you wish this, sir knight?"

"Give it me," I demanded, walking closer, my hand outstretched.

The guards began to surround me. I growled at them. They stepped away.

He held it by the tip of its blade, offering me the hasp. I took it, then unbuckled my hauberk, throwing it to the floor. I lifted the knife high for all to see, before plunging it into my chest. Its silvery-gray shading turned a deep red. The entire court gasped.

"*Gott in Himmel!*" cried the king, recoiling from me.

I pulled out the blade and threw it to the floor, where the blood, now upon it, dried and disappeared. Everyone looked at my chest, as the wound closed and the carnelian (that had stained my clothing) now faded as well.

"Those who have eyes to see, let them see. Christ commands it!" Brother Michael announced.

Cautiously, the king approached my chest.

"Do you not possess a beating heart?" he asked of me.

"If I slice my breast, I may reveal it to you. Would you care to see it?"

"*Nein!*" he shrieked, raising his hands before his eyes. "I would prefer *never* to see it." Somewhat dazed, he took a moment to gather his wits. "I hail you, holy knight!" He raised his hand to me, as if in some sort of a salutation. "Pope Paschal may leave with your company. I was going to release him within a day or so at any rate."

I thought his final statement a poor explanation for the sacrilege that he had committed against the Holy Father. Nevertheless, I was about to discover that it were true.

Upon the ship that had set sail now for Rome, the Holy Father and I communed over the waves, which were gleaming in the sun like sapphires.

"I must confess myself to you," he began. "Of all the people whom I know, I believe that you will understand me, when I say that a man's word carries with it all his dignity."

I had no idea to what he was referring. He clarified his point when he told me that he had granted the emperor freedom from excommunication. (Perhaps that was why Heinrich had been wearing a smile when we left.)

"He should be quartered!" I ranted. "At the very least, should he be disemboweled. This I would have done, had you not prohibited me from doing so. I would have offered you his head."

"Yes, I know that you would have taken Germany as the rightful possession of the Poor Knights, or given it to the Church, or handed it over to King Baldwin. I know all this, yet none of it can satisfy me. You see, my son, he and I had made peace together. I was set to leave on the morrow, when you and your brethren came."

That I had not known. I doubted that it would have altered our plans at all.

"I shall not ask forgiveness," I told him, "for your safe return was my sole concern."

"Bless you for your kindness and courage. I fear that none of it will matter anymore now. The emperor can claim a number of Roman families amongst his dearest friends. They will use my decision to vilify me. My fellow prelates will condemn me for what they believe is my cowardice in this; nor will history act any differently. My life has become a most peculiar form of comedy. All that I have ever wanted was to pray to our Lord in the peacefulness of my cell. Instead, I have been thrust into this rôle like the player of a traveling troupe, who complains bitterly about the loss of the part for which he has practiced so diligently."

I turned to see Brother Michael, Hughes, and the others laughing, congratulating themselves for a task well done. Indeed, it was the first taste of victory that our Order savoured, even though it remained (for some time thereafter) as bitter upon my tongue.

CHAPTER THE
TWENTY-SEVENTH,

in which the Norman fights one more battle.

Humbled before his Byzantine *nemesis*, Bohémond had returned home, ashamed. There he would sit all throughout the day in the garden of his palace, surrounded by the chirping of many birds and the scratchy clatter of insects. The tender ministrations of his wife, his physician, and several sisters of mercy, endeavoured to make him feel comfortable there, for he had grown quite ill, and often could not stand anymore without resting his enormous weight upon someone else's shoulders. No one ever discovered the source of his deterioration, though his wife confessed to me that she was certain of it: he had lost his very will to live.

Making my case, Baldwin prevailed upon the Genoese. One of their vessels provided passage for Sicily. No sooner had I landed in Apulia, when servants of the prince brought me to his palace. Once there I had the good fortune to make acquaintance of the Norman's wife, whose concerns for her husband had become her sole reason for life, itself.

When first I saw her, I was taken aback, for I had had no idea how truly small she was. With little effort, I looked down upon the top of her head. Mostly gray now, one could see that the sheen of her dark curls had not left her completely. Did her giant of a husband ever greet her without having to carry her about? And she had the tiniest of hands, not unlike those of a little girl.

She raised her head to look at me. The lines in her face betrayed a gentleness of spirit, a naïveté really, that had been forced to harden itself, (the better to protect itself, I assumed), thanks to the innumerable disappointments over what must have felt like very many years. Of such things was the love for this Norman of hers made.

After having welcomed me, and having attended to my needs from the weary route of travel, she began to speak more freely, certainly less formally.

"You must prepare yourself before you see him," she advised.

I knew not what to think. Would he appear any more monstrous than was his custom?

"He is not the man he once was."

I entered the grounds with a degree of hesitation. And when I looked upon her husband, I knew exactly how to take her meaning. Seated in a large chair, (that had been evidently constructed in order to support his massive frame), and covered with heavy, dark fabrics, (the better to warm his constant *ague* presumably), he was a fraction of his former size; O, not in length certainly, but in breadth and depth. The skull beneath his face had become more pronounced. Tiny caverns had formed beneath his eyes, which wore no smile anymore, not even one born of viciousness. And his powerfully thick fingers were bony now, their surface hatched by the numerous tiny vessels pulsating beneath the flesh. What disturbed me most of all was his pallor. Its whiteness had given way to a grayish-green hue that seemed so horribly familiar. Momentarily he espied me, as I came around the hedgegrowth. With the sun in his eyes, he squinted before he finally recognized me. A smile soon became his greeting.

"Is it you, holy warrior? Come closer. My eyes are not what once they were."

I stood near him now. He grasped my hand tightly; I thought it would snap.

"It *is* you! Blessings upon us all, now that you are here."

I reminded him that he had written of how he wished to see me upon a matter most grave, to which none else would be privy. Yes, yes, he had not forgotten of it, but there were other matters to discuss.

"Those kings of *Outremer* never think of anything else, save their own importance. By the by, *Outremer* is a fine word. You did well to coin that term. Everyone uses it. I hear that even the Byzantines have spoken it … reluctantly."

He laughed. I was grateful that its usage pleased him.

"What was I saying now?"

"You were referring to Baldwin and the rest, I believe."

"Yes. A miserly group, the lot of them. They should share the wealth. Finally, there is a Christian presence in *Outremer*. We are all good Christians here. Those Turks are stupid. They are incapable of self-governance. That is why we should control all their lands. They kill each other daily. They are incapable of governing themselves. Have I not mentioned that already? This world would be so much better, if we were to rid it of their foulness. I am weary of their constant attacks. We should kill them. Kill them all!"

I wondered whether a new holy war was the reason why he had requested my presence. He placed his forefinger against his closed lips, tapping it against them, then looked about with great caution.

"Is anyone out there listening to us?" he asked in a whisper.

I shook my head, also after looking about.

"No one must know!"

I did not think that problematical, as I, myself, still knew nothing of his wishes.

He motioned for me to bend down, so that he could whisper it within my ear. I did so. After hearing what it was that he said, I straightened my back.

"You cannot know what you are asking, my prince," I spoke now in a normal tone of voice.

"They think me mad, but you know better. Look at me, Guy de Lagery. I am cleaned and fed gruel from the wrinkled hands of old women. Is this any way for a warrior to spend his final days?"

Though I searched my soul, I could find no words to gainsay his degradation.

"All my life I have been surrounded by men who were neither as intelligent nor as capable as I have been. I have had enough of fools to last a lifetime. I did not think I would be so anxious for sleep all the time. It is strange really. I had no idea this would be the outcome."

Nevertheless, I tried to dissuade him from what I believed to be a foolish course of action. When a man is young, often will he follow in the direction whither his spirit leads him. If he is fortunate, he either lives and/or thrives.

"But when a man is old," he countered, "he needs to recall the stupidity of his youth, so that it may inspire him once more to an even grander foolishness."

"It will cost you dearly."

"Everything already has."

I agreed to help him in what would become his final cause, only if he were to tell the woman who loved him everything about his plans.

"Either she will agree to this, Prince Bohémond, or I shall not."

He was not happy with my proposition, I can tell you. (And the angry voice that left his withered body was not so very different from the one that had rallied troops in Nikaia.) Despite that, I left, and returned with his wife, there to stay and hear exactly what he was hoping to achieve. It was not the wisest of choices that I have ever made, for the afternoon had completed the day with much of wailing, beating of the breast, and perhaps even some gnashing of teeth. All in all, the Norman received his wife's blessing, though I was certain that she had imparted a curse or two for the peace of my soul. In truth, I would not have blamed her for her actions. As the Lord is my witness, I certainly blamed myself for what was about to occur.

Several days thereafter, an old fisherman informed me that a storm would arrive shortly after sunset. And it would doubtless be a thing most terrible to behold. Strange; there had been no sign of its forthcoming in recent days, not in the behaviour of fish, nor in the sparkle of the stars at night, nor in the rush of winds in the day. (Perhaps God had taken pity upon Bohémond, and granted to him this one wish.)

I found the princess seated in the large hall, near the burning hearth. Her red eyes had not paled any less since that fateful garden-conversation previously. Upon hearing what it was that I had had to say, she nodded slightly. I was uncertain if she understood my meaning.

"Do you not wish to bid him well upon this journey?" I asked.

"I have already done so."

"I have known many brave men, princess. Compared with yours, their courage means nothing."

I turned to leave. She bade me stay.

"Wait, sir knight. Tell me; how does a man enter God's kingdom?"

"In truth, I have not the wisdom to answer that, my lady."

"He must have been thinking about this for a very long time. He could have pleaded with me for his cause, or asked any number of servants to assist him. Instead, he waited for you, for he believes that you, alone, are God's fortunate servant, and he felt better of the plan, if you were to be with him."

"I am a soldier only, my lady."

"No one believes that of you, not the Prince, not me, and certainly not the King of Jerusalem, whom you serve."

"It is only God, Whom I serve."

She smiled.

"Exactly as I thought."

"What would you of me, princess?"

"Call upon our Lord to forgive him."

"Every man must do that for himself."

"Whilst to others He grants a deaf ear, the Creator of us all will hear you. My husband knows this; so do I."

"And so does the King of Jerusalem?"

"Very like."

"I shall endeavour to do my best."

"I expected no less from the pope's own nephew."

Somehow, miraculously, the Norman took to horse without benefit of grooms or squires. And his back was straight now, as he took the reins with pride. Only once did I see the frailty of his body claw at his face, as he winced. Then the weakness fled as quickly as it had come upon him. He looked at me and smiled.

"The warrior chooses his fate. Come with me, Guy de Lagery!" he bellowed. "The sea awaits."

Down to the waters we rode upon this gray day, the stormclouds threatening to unleash their fury against us at any moment. The old fisherman had placed a small vessel, with two oars inside of it, at the point where the sand and stones met the sea. The Prince dismounted slowly, handing me the reins, then went over to place several coins in the old man's hands. The fisherman denied him his gift. The Prince insisted and would brook no refusal. I, too, dismounted. As I looked into the darkening horizon, once more I wished to have him alter his course of action.

"There is a good woman who loves you!" I shouted above the winds. "Your decision will cost her everything as well."

"She has always been a woman of great intellect. She knew the price of marriage to me. I might have died a hundred times before. Perhaps I should have. Help me, my friend. Help me to correct the mistake of which Nature and Circumstance have deprived me. Help me regain my lost honour."

He looked into the distant clouds.

"This storm will be fierce," he commented, then he laughed most heartily.

As the rage came closer to shore, I helped him into the boat, and handed him the oars. The rain began to fall.

"You can still return with me," I told him.

"And give up the opportunity to taste God's own fury? That is the path of the coward. Prince Bohémond is a warrior! Never forget that."

And he rowed out to sea with the strength of ten men, for never had I witnessed such alacrity of a vessel, small or otherwise. And he cut through each rolling wave that slammed against him. And as the rain drenched his hair and body, I saw him, I tell you now, I saw him throw away the oars and stand erect, laughing riotously in the eye of the storm!

And though his remains were never found, the tale of Prince Bohémond's final battle was embellished by most of the chroniclers of his age. One has mentioned a war at sea against a German ship set for an invasion, whilst another speaks of his death at the center of a Byzantine plot, filled with poisons and the like. The one aspect that none of them could have known was my presence there. You see, dear reader, I stood upon the shore, the wind whipping at my face, and howled all the way up to God, that the man should be forgiven for this and all his other sins. I cannot say whether the troubled spirit of the giant ever discovered a lasting peace. I know only that those he left behind have not.

CHAPTER THE TWENTY-EIGHTH,

in which the god of War makes a mighty laugh at the expense of others.

Upon my return to Jerusalem, my brethren informed me that we had been called upon to ally ourselves with both Baldwin's forces and those of the Norweyan King, Sigurd I, all of whom were besieging Sidon. (I was right glad to hear of it, for never had I met the fair people who dwelt in the frozen waste that Vergilius had termed, *Ultima Thule*.) Brother Michael told us that it was one campaign that he would be unable to join, for he was most tired.

"I knew it!" I shouted, hoping to goad him. "The ancient one finally uses his age as an excuse to seek out a comfortable chair and a tankard, rather than a broad sword and an enemy's throat."

We were on horseback, near the Temple, when Brother Michael reined in his steed and turned to face me. Turning red, he fumed, and I was overjoyed at the sight of it!

"Had I but five or six years less upon my head," he spat out, "I would thrash you like the insolent child you have always been!"

And with that, he turned to leave. I did not believe it. I had expected far more insolence.

"Never have I seen him so disinclined to continue the act of insulting," Hughes commented. "He is most weak, I fear."

"No. He is not weak. He is Michael! And like his namesake, he will wield the sword of Justice eternally."

My comrade wanted to add something more, though may have thought better of it. Together we watched the old man ride away.

The road to our victory was arduous. Well did I learn how fearsome were these descendants of the Northmen, for they carried themselves into the campaign with no fear for loss of life. (I wondered if anything at all could frighten them.) With five and fifty ships of his fleet, the king had arrived at the port of Jaffa. Once the necessary victuals had been provided the crews, they sailed off to besiege the city. With Baldwin, his knights, Templars, and Hospitallers on horse, and the Noreweyans asea, Sidon could not withstand any point of attack. It fell soon after our arrival, though with very many casualties on both sides. (Perhaps this people of *Outremer* had not yet lost all taste for war. That fact would change very soon under Baldwin's leadership, as the king had no wish to subjugate them, only to control their port as his own.)

Their king and I developed a mutual respect for our considerable martial abilities. In the process, we became friends. He was proud of the honour that Baldwin I of Jerusalem had rendered unto him, for the former had presented him with a sliver of wood reputed to have been cut from the Holy Crucifix, itself. Sigurd swore that he would place it amongst the venerated remains of St. Olaf when finally at home. (I had no heart to tell him that it was not the first time that the King of Jerusalem had been so generous with an ally. Still, I marveled at how many ancient pieces of wood {which bore little or no relation to any crucifix at all} Baldwin had secreted away for such an occasion.)

This Norweyan cut an imposing figure. His moustache was so long, that its ends hung below his chin and were tied into braids. The same was true of his long beard. And his hair fell fully about and covered his shoulders. His eyes appeared to be of the palest blue, when one could see them, for ofttimes he squinted. (I had the distinct feeling that God's sunlight and his own brightness were in a state of constant combat, and our Lord was the usual victor.) The helmet he wore was of animal skins fitted with horns—an ancient relic of his people. The fair warrior-king, with his face hewn ruddy from his many years at sea, spoke our tongue well, even if he were disinclined to chatter overly much. Whenever he did, it was usually of something significant, like the *sagas* of his *Viking* ancestors.

And oft over nightfires (with his eyes beaming as were the Norman's when in discussion of wars) he related how their leader of the gods, *Odin One-Eye,* had strapped himself to an ash tree, there to suffer for seven days and seven nights, where he sacrificed a single eye, as the price to gain wisdom, that he might better rule over the world of men in a just manner. (A noble deed. If only the kings of the earth had as much conviction and fortitude!) And moreover, the god-king sent out two ravens, *Thought* and *Memory,* that they might always learn of man's deeds and misdeeds and tell him of such. But locked forever against him as his antagonist was the ruler of the underworld, the daughter of a giant. Her skin was both white and black, and her name was *Hel.* Her kingdom was no infernally burning world; it was a cold, dark land of ice. She dwelt in a great hall named

Misery, waiting for the last skirmish between the forces of Light and Darkness. She would lead her rebellious troops against Odin in this final battle, a twilight for the gods, in which all would be consumed in fire, only after the great *Fenris-Wolf* had devoured the moon. And only after all were dead would a new universe dawn, much greater than the one that had come before.

More than once (I had to admit to him) I thought I saw the devilish canine with its hairy snout and glowing eyes and maw spread wide to reveal its twisted canines covered with black spittle. He confessed that he, too, had seen it racing like a storm across the night-sky.

"Only here, in this land have I seen him," he said quietly, "only here."

His people were Christian now, though there were still times, of an evening, when the old songs filled the warm air about the hearth, or surrounded the fires in battle-time, when warrior maidens would ride between the clouds, and gods would cross a rainbow bridge from their lofty hall in the heavens above, only to wander amongst and observe the world of men. It was a tale most terrible to tell, though not without hope, for the warrior-god had always looked after the wellbeing of his troops, and all would be ultimately rewarded for his efforts on their behalf.

Indeed, there was much of magic and legend surrounding his people. And little did I realize that one such manifestation would become an essential part of the future of all Templar brethren.

At another time, as we stood at the prow of his commanding vessel, we drank a honey-wine, a *mead,* more potent than any that ever I had quaffed. As we emptied several skins and felt our heads swirl, I beheld strange figures, which he drew into the air, using the lantern, that he had raised, like an artist's brush. Never had I seen the like.

"What are those?" I asked, watching the lines of smoke and light disappear.

Runes they were, and so enchanted, that they were more than letters; they were numbers as well. He cautioned me to heed his warning, that all words have the power both to heal and to destroy. His people believed that they could predict the future, for the divine hands of the gods of old (the *Aesir*) had fashioned them.

"Will you teach me?" I asked.

From his belt he removed what I had taken to be his purse. Actually, it was a small sack that held a number of tiny stones (five and twenty, I was to learn). And inscribed into each was one of these *runic* symbols. Certain elderly women (the blessèd witches) of long ago were wont to use them in the act of divination.

Today, only ship's navigators found them serviceable, the better to learn of coming victories or defeats in their quests.

It was his tradition that, when a person came of age, he would pluck a stone from such a sack as this, and learn of its guiding principle through the course of life. He invited me to reach inside. I did so and brought forth a sign of an arrow pointing upwards. He laughed upon seeing it, for it was the sign of the warrior, the letter *T*, *Teiwaz*.

"The *Aesir*, themselves, know who and what you are," he realized, nodding and laughing.

Much respected in the days of yore, Viking warriors painted it upon their shields, in hope that their deaths would be honourable. It also stood for the number *tenthousand*, and much of his people's documentation held combinations of these and the other symbols.

"It is your destiny to be always a leader of men," he informed me further, "perhaps a leader of the ten thousand warriors who are not yet born."

I was uncomfortable with that pronouncement, and changed the matter of discourse. A leader? The Lord in Heaven above knew that I was many things, and certainly not fit to be one of those. I laughed at the king's suggestion, then thanked him for the gift of these enchanted stones.

And when the war in Sidon was done, and the Norweyans had sailed away, I wondered how proud would be this king to learn that the bards of his land were to make him the hero in their song of the poetical *saga*, *Heimskringlä*:

> Brave was he in battle, Sigurd, the bold,
> Master of men, swordbound on barks
> Riding for strife, with seasteeds roaring
> On strange hillocks to see, in hills of skulls.

So Sigurd achieved immortality by becoming the hero of an epic poem. (Alas, no songs were sung for me.) And what did King Baldwin receive from this little war? Was it simply one more port city to call his own? Actually, it was the promise of profit from the crop-yield of local farmers. Many good men died to secure for him that pledge. Was that cost sufficient enough to satisfy him? Would it ever be?

Our labours completed, we returned home, where one of our brethren informed both Hughes and myself that a significant number of donations had accrued.

"It appears that an influx of capital has doubled from the previous year," Hughes commented, upon an examination of the records. "I think it behooves us all for you to create a secretive form of records-keeping for the Order."

I? Keeping records?

"You are as comfortable with numbers as you are with swords, though you refuse to allow anyone to recognize another of your gifts."

Absurd! Was there no one else who could make a good accounting?

"Very few of us can write letters, to say nothing of numbers," he informed me quietly, as he looked about.

"O," I remarked, nodding in shameful agreement.

Moreover, it would not do for others to learn very much of our daily functions. Kings might believe that they had a right to any and all currency within their borders, regardless of its sanctified purpose. I could not disagree with him, yet why did he appear to be so terribly sad? People everywhere had finally begun to recognize our contributions to the safety and security of a Christian Jerusalem. Is that not what he had always hoped?

"Still we are not recognized as an official order by the church, with all the rights and privileges thereto. However, you might prevail upon his holiness to change all that."

I had to disagree. I believed that he was not of a mind to grant dispensations of any sort, or contemplate little else, save his own continued survival.

"Heinrich has sworn fealty to him. He will not threaten him again. At the very least, I do not believe that he will."

I informed my brother that there were many ways to defeat an enemy. The kindest was to kill him. Far worse was it for the victim to continue his life, stripped of his dignity. From such a defeat few could ever recover.

"We should have destroyed that king," he maintained. "One must never let an enemy survive another day. He might decide to return."

"Even if he does not, he is unworthy of the gift of life. No matter. We have made our decision."

"You mean the pope has made his decision, do you not?"

"And we are ever his servants all, are we not?"

Pondering over the uses and misuses of leadership, we neglected to keep an eye upon Tancred. It turned out that he had become embroiled in a struggle between the illegitimate heir of Raymond, (Illegitimate? Was I the only one who knew nothing of the old man's indiscretion?), and his own vaunting ambition to control Tripoli. In fact, the Norman's nephew had secured a significant portion of the city for himself. In the process he had also captured an enormous Muslim fortress—*Hasn-al-Akrad*. And when Brother Hughes learned of its size, he turned his eye towards Tripoli. Tancred had a multitude of palaces in Antioch and elsewhere in which to reside, he argued. Who deserved better a single structure as a base outside of Jerusalem than our brethren? I thought his idea had merit; consequently, I wished him well upon his journey. He asked me to accompany him; I thought it better for all if I stayed away. (I did not wish to dash his hopes, were Tancred to see me.) I stayed behind to tend to other business, including the welfare of my very old friend.

Not long thereafter, Hughes returned with others of our fraternity. I was sitting with Brother Michael, who was resting abed, when the Knight of the Temple burst in.

"Damn him!"

"And who do you wish to condemn?" Brother Michael asked calmly.

Hughes had it on good authority that the Norman had donated his huge fortress to the Knights of the Hospital, to use as they saw fit.

Brother Michael and I exchanged glances.

"But Bohémond is dead!" he called out with more than a little surprise.

"Not him. His nephew."

I began to laugh, and quite loudly, I might add.

"Do I amuse you, my brother?" Hughes asked.

"Forgive me. I apologize not for my mirth, but rather for being the most probable source of his decision."

I explained further that the Hospitallers had grown envious of the respect which members of the knightly classes in the known world developed for us. Consequently, I had made no efforts towards friendship with the Order of St. John. That fact, once combined with the obvious dislike for me that Tancred had always evinced, led me to my conclusion.

"No," Brother Michael insisted, "the Norman's nephew would not punish an entire group simply to insult you. Would he?" he asked of Hughes.

Hughes simply shrugged.

Within the month, King Baldwin let it be known that Tancred was dying, and the latter wished to see no one except me.

"Why is that, do you think?" Baldwin asked.

"Verily I cannot say, your highness. Perhaps he has grown bored of those who would fawn over him and wishes to spend his last hours with someone who will speak only the truth."

"Raymond's bastard will soon become a new force in *Outremer*. When this business with Tancred is at an end, we shall have to acquaintant ourselves with this new master of Tripoli. Perhaps you will make the necessary introductions for us; you have a certain artful manner with words, I have noticed. And the crown is most appreciative of your service."

An *artful manner*? Me? I began to wonder if this king were truly as intelligent as everyone believed him to be, myself included.

Not far from the capacious citadel now in the hands of the Hospitallers stood a small palace. Unimpressive either in design or construction, it was to provide a final resting place for the Norman's nephew. Once inside, I marveled at its filth. Geese and chickens squawked about in riotous tumult. And not a single spot upon any floor had been swept in a very long time. The air was rank. And its entirety was a disgrace, a dishonour even unto the memory of his uncle. I could not believe everything, that my eyes had sworn to reveal as absolute truth.

A servant came over. His hands were filthy, his garments no less so. He led me to the royal bedchamber, where the stench of urine choked me.

Wearily, Tancred looked up from beneath the soiled cloths covering him.

"You?! What do you wish here?"

"I heard it said that you were dying. I have arrived to determine if it were mere rumour."

He studied me for a short while.

"Have you come to spit upon me?" he asked finally.

"Now why would I demean a figure capable of as much grandeur as you have achieved?" I inquired, looking about.

He did not alter his expression of repulsion.

"I have detested you," was the most honest thing that I believe that I had ever heard him speak. "Before I die, I think that a necessary confession."

"Our Lord must be pleased with your candor. If the truth be told, I have never cared very much for you either. The Lord is probably pleased with my honesty as well."

"I have never pretended to be anything more than what I am. You, on the other hand, with your lofty position in the church, should be clad in monkish robes. Make certain to soak them sufficiently in blood, so that all who see you may never forget your true purpose."

"Do you wish me to administer your final rites, or to cleave your head in twain? I am here to serve, after all."

"I have more than enough priests at my disposal, who would be all too willing to do either. Find a chair and sit at my bedside. I wish to spend this final night relating everything about you that sickens me."

Taking a chair, I brushed loose feathers off its seat, and placed it near his bedside. And he went on, and he went on, and he continued further. First it was the mere accident of birth that had made me a kinsman of the pope. Why had I been so deserving? Really, I knew not what to say. I told him that it should be his first query upon arrival at St. Peter's Gates.

Then came the miracle of my rebirth. Who did I think I was to dare to return from the ranks of the dead? (As if I had had any choice in the matter!)

Then was mentioned the incessant affection that others bore me. (Incessant?) I reminded him that not everyone whom I had met felt that way about me, himself included. Reluctantly, he had to agree.

When the time for his departure arrived, he held fast to my arm, thrust his face close to mine, and frowned. I tried to pull back, as the odor emanating from his mouth was a thing that I have neither the courage nor wit to describe.

"You think yourself so fortunate. It will make no difference at the end. You will never save them all. Do you hear me, Defender of the Faith? Not even you can stem the tide of evil in men's hearts. Of what use are you, then? Hmm? Tell me. Tell me!" he shouted, then stared out of the portal, howled at the moon, and gave up the ghost.

I could not say if his passing were a pitiable thing, however, it fled as quickly as it had come upon him. For that reason, I hope that his soul was most grateful when it met its Maker. Moreover, I hope that he was able to set aside his anger against me, for I have heard it said that the Lord, our God, prefers peaceable men in His kingdom. Of course, Tancred may not have possessed enough will to overcome such weakness. In that case, his soul may have found itself elsewhere. Pity, that.

CHAPTER THE TWENTY-NINTH,

in which I endeavour to be of service in the Templar manner to the empire of the Byzantines.

In the years after the conquest of Sidon, the burden of our deeds (though infused with righteous cause, or so we told ourselves) began to weigh heavily upon my soul. Rarely did I find any peace anymore.

At the Temple one afternoon, Brother Hughes returned from a meeting with Baldwin, and the face he wore now before all and sundry was far from one of pleasure. Our brethren knew well enough to leave him be. Whenever he was like this, I was the only one who would dare approach him with impunity.

"Why so disappointed, brother?" I asked.

Baldwin had promised a significant portion of the booty from his latest campaign.

"And he has suddenly created an excuse for not handing it over? Why am I not surprised?"

"He has been generous to the Order before."

"He has donated only a small portion to the Temple. The stables, which he, himself, had promised to build for us, we, ourselves, had to erect. Though not his primary force, we have become his secondary one. And upon our heads he lavishes much praise, and into our purses he pours nothing, save his vocal gratitude. Yes, he is much appreciative of us, for we are an army that conquers, without benefit of pay. What ruler would not be grateful to call upon our services?"

"I cannot argue against you, brother. It may be that we have lost our way. I suppose the protection of pilgrims does not mean the destruction of every Saracen in the world."

"*Muslims.* They are *Muslims.* How many times must I tell you that? If one is going to defeat one's enemy, one should know who and what he is."

"You speak in the manner of the Norman, though with a deeper insight, I believe."

"I have grown sick of compliments."

My statement hurt him terribly. He may not have been the source of my general dissatisfaction, even if he were its recipient.

"Do you not see the truth of us, brother?" I continued. "We began as protectors of pilgrims, and are now become killers of men, all with a papal blessing, no less. What have we done?"

I walked away.

"Where are you going?"

"You wished to lead us, so tell the others what your commandment is. I shall be elsewhere."

Once more I sought solace from the company of women. Brother Michael reminded me often that if it were a family I desired, I had only to let it be known. He believed that I would have my choice from the many lovely maidens both here in Jerusalem, and elsewhere, certainly amongst the Venetians or Genoese. And from time to time I granted myself the indulgence of that thought, only to think better of it after careful contemplation. Unlike other knights, I came to agree with my uncle's *dictum*, that a man cannot serve two masters. Though he was speaking of the reasons for his prohibition against clerical marriage, he may have been most correct about the manner in which other classes of men should live out their lives. I say this, for Hughes de Payens had two sons. One had taken to wearing the cowl, whilst the other sought out the glories of knighthood. And though his children ofttimes corresponded each with the other, and had made visits to their respective homes from time to time, the father had not seen them in very many years; nor had he been present to watch them grow. His care and guidance for their difficult journeys into manhood were mere words upon a page. (Or so they told him, I am ashamed to write.) Not a week passed, however, when he failed to mention them to me. But if they were ever in his thoughts, why did he not return to Champagne to be with them, if only for several months? Why did he not allow them to come here? He may have hoped that he was keeping them safe from intrigues and the inevitable harm that follows such events, for it was obvious to me that he did not want them involved in any of his labours. Or was it that he felt a degree of shame for what he was trying to accomplish in the name of God? Perhaps he felt that he needed to sacrifice all that was most dear to him for the success of his mission, namely, the pleasure that a father may discover in the laughter of his children. I cannot say which of these (if any) should have been applied to him. He never discussed his reasons with me, or with anyone else, as much as I know that to be true.

Nevertheless, his choices shaped themselves into a standard of measurement, against which I would compare and erect my own life. What sort of man sacrifices the simplicity that everyone craves? Yes, it was a knight's duty to defend the realm, or the cross, or both. Still, why did it have to be at the expense of all joy? There were times when I wished to have been anything but that which I was, as trivial as it may sound to me now, writing this.

The truth of it was, I would not sacrifice fatherhood for my other responsibilities. At that time I was not always happy to be different from other men. Even so, I knew it was not the proper conduct for me to keep a family in Champagne whilst I dwelt herein, or create one in *Outremer*, where the only way to live was to wage war or die. (Other knights often thought and acted differently, however. Some had even married Muslim women, who converted to the faith of their husbands. Some of these marriages had even produced children, as well as some happiness.) Perhaps in ten or twenty years it would be more appropriate to think of such things. I would, after all, be older, perhaps more malleable in my ways, thanks to the touch of a young bride's caress. Or would I be no more than a foolish ancient, turning a blind eye to the dalliances of a wife whose heart could never become part of mine, no matter how much I craved for it to be so? Now *that* would have been a curious turn of events, would it not?

And still did I long for a moment with Anna. What did it matter that she shared another man's bed? He could not make her feel as I had. Whatever of herself that she gave to him, it would always be less than the merest touch of her lips. Never had I doubted it. Never would I. And then appeared an object most unusual, for it was most unexpected.

Pondering the possibility of marriage and children, (or the lack thereof), a missive arrived, and gave to me a renewed hope for a much finer future. Anna was its author. When I saw her hand upon the page and sniffed at the delicate fragrance arising therefrom, I refused to believe it. My hands shook as I held the item. What promise did it contain? Had her Greek god of a husband died in some terrible manner? Not that I prayed for such an event, but I would not have wept piteously, were that truth to become evident. I began to read.

No, he did not die. In fact, he was very much alive. And they were very happy together. How marvelous that was for both of them!

I wish I could say that each line was filled with a desire for me so great, that mere words would only lessen the depth and grandeur of her emotion. I wish I could say that, for it was not so. All that she ever mentioned were her disagreements with her brother regarding his conceptions of kingship. (In point of fact, I do not recall that she ever asked me once about what was transpiring in my life, or how I might have felt about anything.) Indeed, I received no more than the pleasantries of introduction to the real cause for having broken her silence to me after years of separation. (No, I had never written to her either. In that action was I as guilty as she. Still, how could I know whether any letters would ever reach her? I had not been cruel to omit the expressions of my love, had I?) She sought my help, even pleading with me for it. From time to time her father's occasional cough had grown into a far more regular fit. And neither the royal physician, nor others of his ilk throughout the empire, was successful in little more than temporary relief. She believed that the very air was leaving his chest in a deliberately slow manner.

And whether or not I sympathized, I could not possibly be of any use to him. What did she want from me exactly?

After I continued reading and discovered the true cause of this letter, I was tempted to tear the page to bits and cast it to the Four Winds. Never would I respond to anyone else the plea that she had asked of me. Then again, she was not anyone else, was she?

Upon entry into the caverns below the palace, I gulped my pride. It seemed that Fausto's reputation for curative ability had spread as far as the Byzantine Empire. If anyone could aid her stricken father, should she not attempt to prevail upon his generosity? And of course, that meant my involvement. She was certain that I would probably know him, as I was so often at court (when I was not fighting at Baldwin's side elsewhere, no doubt).

I knocked upon the thick oaken doors before me.

"Enter, welcome stranger, whoever you may be," came the voice from behind them.

When he saw my face, a broad smile spread across his own like a crescent-shaped moon.

"O, it has been far too long since you have graced these humble surroundings with your presence!"

For me it had not been long enough.

"What misfortune has brought you here, or have you decided to pass the time in amiable conversation concerning the nature of things? There is much that we have left unfinished, since last we met. And despite the passage of some years, you look not a day older. Is that not most unusual?"

"For that matter, neither do you, physician."

"Did you know that there comes a point in a man's deterioration, when his body is so old, that his face barely ages a single moment anymore? The same is true for women, I have observed."

Whilst I informed him that I was appreciative of his having illuminated these matters, I was here to seek to prolong someone else's life, not my own.

"O, you are full of surprises today. Who is the pertinent subject-in-question?"

I told him that it concerned the relative of a friend.

"How has the affliction manifested itself?"

I related all that I knew, still continuing to conceal the identity of the ill one involved. He thought upon it, pacing to and fro, his hands clasped behind his back, then he stopped and turned to me.

"I know of no noble family whose member is suffering so."

"This is a private matter. I … rely on your discretion."

"Certainly! We would not want King Baldwin to know of such things. He might misunderstand why the time that his physician normally devotes to *ana-tomical* research for the King, himself, is being spent in other pursuits."

I knew exactly in which direction he was leading the conversation.

"How much do you want for the cure, and how much more for your silence?" I asked.

"Very good," he said, laughing. "There is a price to be paid, rest assured, for nothing in this life is free."

"I shall ask you again, how much?"

"No currency. My fiscal needs are well provided by our illustrious leader. You know all that I require."

"I am afraid that you must enlighten me."

He took my hand, turned it over, and poked at it with his forefinger.

"What truth lies herein?" he asked, smiling again.

I jerked my hand away from his promptly, and stepped back.

"Why so modest, defender of the realm? One would think you a virginal maiden, loathe to relinquish her closed portal to that most appreciative of gods, Hymen, after a much-pursued courtship."

I must admit, I never did care for the way in which he used his metaphors.

"I feel rather like *Prometheos*, chained to a rock, whilst eagles tear at the flesh of his organs."

"O, I am not so bad as all that. Your use of metaphor tends towards hyper-bole, did you know that?"

I stood, debating with myself if I would stay, or perhaps kill the creature that was smiling over there, in that damp, dark corner.

"What must I do?" I asked, finally.

"You must return after nightfall. By that time the solution of *veronica*, combined with other medicinal extracts, will be ready."

"I am unfamiliar with that substance."

"Then you are fortunate that I am not. Until later then."

When I entered his chamber again, I saw a large flask resting upon a table. The colour of its liquid shifted back and forth between a pale green and a deep purplish-red. He watched as I noticed the change.

"A play of the candlelight, nothing more," he said.

"And how can I be assured of its efficacy?"

"I have been in the service of many a great man. I never lied to them about what I was capable of achieving on their behalf."

"How do I know that I have found a single honest man, simply because he tells me that he is?"

"O, I have never stated that I was honest. I said simply that I have never lied about my medicinal practices. All other aspects of life, however, are fair game."

I could not help feeling that if I were to behead him, the rains of September might not always seem so gray. Then again, I would probably have to quarrel with an enraged king, and Brother Hughes and the Order would be forced to defend me, and the entire situation would grow into a violent misunderstanding. No, I was far too busy with Temple business to allow my own pettiness to be as great as that of the other man standing in front of me. And a woman was depending upon me. How could I disappoint her?

"How do you propose to gather my blood?"

He removed a tiny, thin strip of glass from a table.

"I think it best that you cut your own skin."

Initially repelled by his request, I elected not to hesitate to allow this man the satisfaction of his morbid curiosity. After all, like Heinrich, he would soon discover that the contents of my body never lingered long in the light of day.

I ran my sword across my palm. He placed the glass under it to catch the few drops of blood upon its face. Barely had a moment passed, when those red drops dried, then turned to ash. Fausto's barest breath sent the fragments flying.

"It would appear that our Lord does not wish for anyone to have His secrets," he uttered with a laugh. "What a pity that He is so miserly with His gifts!"

He then set his eyes upon my wound, studying how swiftly the skin closed, ultimately leaving not so much as a single line of scar.

"I have done what you asked," I told him, then took the bottle and turned to leave, when he stopped me.

"You must understand that the person involved may be beyond any cure. The elixir can only grant an individual no more than a single year. At the completion of that time, the disease will strike with a virulence hitherto unknown. It will take his life within the month."

"I never said that it was a man."

"No? At any rate, the person will be better for a time. In the words of our Muslim enemies, *Al-hamdulillah*."

"Which means—?"

"*Thanks be to God*. You really should learn a bit of Arabic. You never know when it will come in handy, so to speak."

"In what manner should this be taken?"

"One drop only, each day after dawn, preferably with a bit of fruit, the acidic nature of which will help to dissolve the bitter flavor."

I opened the doors.

"There is no need for you to be a stranger," he added. "We are friends now. We have done acts of generosity for each other. Never forget that, holy defender, for I shall not. Remember, you are always welcome … here."

And as I stood in the corridor, looking back now at him, I watched how the great doors next to me closed shut, seemingly of their own volition.

I returned to the Temple to discuss with Brother Hughes the voyage to Konstantinople, that would needs be undertaken for the safe delivery of the items, for I had now in my possession not simply the flask, but also a letter of mine own. (I had written to the Emperor to wish him well, explaining that Byzantium had many songbirds, which often flew from one end of his realm to all other parts of the world, telling of what had transpired in their country of origin. As I already knew of his ailment, I thought that I could help him, as best as I was able. And I further cautioned him of what would transpire after a year of its usage. I was to discover later that he wept upon the reading of it, thanked the messenger, told him that I would be ever in his prayers, and spoke not a word to anyone of what the letter contained.)

As messenger I chose one from amongst us, whose courage in battle had garnered praise by all. Andrew de Montbard's years were no more than six and thirty, as I recall, when I selected him for the task. Though relatively young, his black beard was thick and full.

Hughes thought better of his selection, however.

"I believe that the emperor would much rather see you."

"I cannot go there now; perhaps at some future time."

"And is this your final decision, brother?"

I nodded.

I presented the items to Andrew. On bended knees, his head down, he swore his fealty.

"I shall not fail you, my lord."

"Arise," I ordered, lifting him up. "We are all your family here. God, alone is my Master."

"Did you not hear him, brethren?" Hughes announced to all who chanced to be about. "What say you?"

They repeated my phrase in unison.

"Again," Hughes ordered.

They repeated it again.

"Again!"

And this they did for a third and final time.

"Never forget our brother's teaching," he admonished all. And to me he said: "How would one repeat this phrase in Latin?"

I needed no more time to think upon it, as the words escaped me forthwith:

"*Dominus solus magister meus.*" ("*God alone is my master.*")

And from that day forth, all documentation of the Order was signed with initials representing the four words of my Latin phrase:

D.S.M.M.

Long after this day, the lawyer for a king would spend many hours of study, perusing these initials, convinced that they held strange and terrible secrets. But he was never to learn the truth of that most simplistic of sentences.

CHAPTER THE THIRTIETH,

in which King Baldwin I of Jerusalem is presented with many intriguing possibilities.

Baldwin's queen was dead. She had fallen off her chair in the midst of dining, still clutching a goblet of wine. Upon examination, Fausto declared that she had been most likely suffering from a rare stomach ailment, nearly impossible to treat, for it often escaped detection. He would doubtless learn more, if he were able to secure permission from his highness to dissect her corpse. The king, who often indulged his cherished physician his each and every desire, refused adamantly! No one was to touch her, save servants who would prepare her for a proper burial. The royal physician excused himself to continue his research into a variety of esoteric matters again, whilst Baldwin began a very public display of three full days of mourning, with all the weeping and acts of contrition attributable thereto. (He never did wash the feet of the poor, as he said he would, when standing over her lifeless body, however.)

No sooner was the dear woman entombed, when word of her demise spread like swarms of locusts. And so began a veritable procession of daughters from royal families everywhere, come to *Outremer* to march before the king. So numerous were they, that I could not relate to you, dear reader, an accurate summation of all. They were enrobed in the finest silks, or cloth-of-gold, or Tyrian purple, or the bloodiest of scarlet shades. Nor was a single nation absent (except for Muslim lands, of course). And whilst some of these women were gentle of face, others were lascivious in the manner that they sauntered about before the man who might become their king. Most smiled coyly. Several licked their lips. And the entire population ran from home and gathered near the steps of the palace to witness this most rare occurrence. Even Brother Michael suddenly rediscovered his strength, for he, too, dragged himself out of a sickbed to see what was being offered. In truth, the entire processional reminded me of the finest houses of

219

prostitution, where the women stand about, revealing their wares for potential purchase.

Of this mass of pulchritude, only one was so different in form, that she remained in the minds of all who looked upon her, sometimes as the recipient of insult for her large frame, though more often for the promise of what she might bring to a marriage, *i.e.*, a considerable number of children. And when Brother Michael looked upon her, he could state simply the obvious again:

"An exceedingly large woman, is she not?"

Adela of Sicily may have been squat in height and sweeping in width, but she possessed the largest breasts and buttocks of any woman whom I had ever seen (or would ever see, for that matter). With hips so expansive, she was bound to bear a litter of mewling runts. And everyone's suspicions about this were not lost upon Baldwin, for of all the majestic, fantastical visions of femininity, he selected this little Sicilian princess, whose own shy smile masked her own rigorous, wanton manner in the bedchamber. (I heard that she put him through his paces often there, after which the man's exhaustion was quite visible to all at court. What a terrible burden he must have borne!)

Whilst Baldwin attempted to prove his vitality night after night, (in a new marriage barely six months after the queen's death, mind you!), I tended to the health of my old friend, who had taken to bed once again. And sitting with him, there in his chamber, I neglected to notice Brother Hughes nearby. He chanced to see a curious object from the corridor. As it intrigued him, he walked into my chamber and removed the cloth that covered it. When I left Brother Michael to the care of others, I saw Hughes holding the metallic bust. I ran in forthwith.

"What are you doing?" I asked, grabbing it from him.

"Who is it, brother? It looks very like the Byzantine princess, though a much younger representation. Could it be—No! Is it Mary?"

"How dare you look upon what was meant for my eyes only?"

"If she is the Holy Mother, then all should see her. If she is not—" He hesitated as he thought about what he would say next. "If she is not, then she might be the representation of a lost love. If that be true, I hope that my dearest friend will forgive me, for having indulged my curiosity at his expense."

"She may not be Mary," I told him, looking at the bust, rotating it in my hands, "but she is a symbol of the promises, which youthful beauty, alone, may grant. How fitting that such perfection should house the shroud of our Lord, Who is ageless."

Hughes stepped back and stood there, his mouth wide open.

"The holiest of relics!" he exclaimed. "Brother, where did you find this?"

"It was a gift."

"A gift?! And who, on God's earth would ever possess such a treasure?"

I was disappointed with his lack of wisdom, and the scowl upon my face let him know so in no uncertain terms.

"Where does one find holy relics in this terrible, godforsaken age?" I asked with little patience.

He thought about it for a moment or so.

"Konstantinople?"

"Where else?"

"O, tell me you did not steal it."

I gritted my teeth.

"I have never taken anything that was not first freely offered. The emperor believes that I, alone, am worthy enough to look after its safekeeping."

"I knew that he regarded you with kindness, however, I had no idea that he held you in his highest esteem. You must mean more to him than the Byzantine church fathers, or even his own son. He believes, I think, that you are blessèd."

"No one else must know of this."

"But brother—"

"In *Outremer* the only other person who is aware of its presence here is Michael, and he will take that knowledge to the grave, when he leaves us, which I hope is a very long way off."

"I beseech you, brother, do not keep this from the eyes of men, whose spirits cry out for redemption. The cloth will heal all wounded souls. His most precious blood is saturated in its very fibers. To look upon it will be to know His pain."

"Has our faith grown so feeble, that it needs miracles to give it renewed vigor?"

"That is a strange question from a man who has arisen, Lazarus-like, from the dead."

"It has been placed into my hands; therefore, the decision either to reveal or conceal it is mine. I ask you to respect my wishes."

"I shall do as you ask, even if every fiber in my being tells me that you are hoarding it for your own unfathomable purposes. I love you, brother, though I thought you a better man than this!"

I sat at Brother Michael's bedside. It would not be very long now. Together, we spoke mostly of the past. I reminded him of how he taught a young man to hold a sword. (I was not very adept in the use of the blade at that tender age, I must admit.)

> "Not like that, boy. It will only speed along your death.
> That is how a girl would hold it. Are you a girl, boy?"
> "No, my lord. I am a brave warrior!"
> "Indeed you are!" he said with a smile. "Never forget that.
> Now lunge at me. On your right foot, boy. On your right foot!"

He slipped into and out of sleep. His forehead was hot, and the bedclothes were soaked with the water that had seeped from each pore. Towards nightfall he looked up at me.

"Of all the things I have done in my sinful life," he admitted, "the only regret is that I have to leave it all behind."

"You cannot go yet, old friend. I shall be lost without your guidance."

"Of course you will, arrogant pup. But you will fare well. I have faith in you."

I bent down and held his old, grizzled face next to mine own. A moment later he pushed me away.

"Now leave!" was his order.

"Never. I shall be here always."

"Leave!" he roared, rising slightly from the bed. "You stubborn whelp. Your uncle should have taken a whip to you. You always did what you wanted, regardless of what your elders may have wished for you. You will leave now, or by God, I shall throttle you myself!"

I stood up and walked towards the doorway, for I knew that he was very much a man of his word.

"And try not to waste your precious life," he warned, his finger pointed at me, "or my spirit will return to haunt you, ill-mannered child!"

"Whatsoever you wish, my lord. Fear not; I shall make you proud of me."

"My lord, indeed!" he called after me, laughing.

I left him there in his bed. By morn I returned to find that he had gone to a better place during the late night hours, a better place than the one in which I now dwelt. It was the first time that I could recall myself feeling quite old, too old for a world, that was endeavouring sedulously to leave me behind.

CHAPTER THE THIRTY-FIRST,

in which the passage of the year, 1118, weighs most heavily upon one and all.

The year of our Lord 1118 began with a crushing truth—the Holy Father had passed on. (Though a tragedy for the Christian world, I believe that, for him, this was a blessing.) And once again the cardinals found themselves with the unenviable task of having to search high and low for a candidate, who would fill the exalted position. Only this time they had to make certain that he would not be a supporter of that most vile creature, Heinrich V.

Cardinal Giovanni di Gaeta, a quiet, old soul, was in prayer at *Monte Cassino*, when they came to give him the glad tidings of his election. Immediately he refused. He never sought this; he never wanted this; did they know what they were doing?

Within days of his selection, a political party loyal to the German cause, and led by one Frangipani, (a Roman, mind you!), stormed the monastery and dragged the agèd pope to a castle dungeon, in which the poor man was enchained. The Roman populace, however, egged on by the conclave, refused to stand idle. And when the friends of Frangipani saw the size of the mob coming towards them, they ran away, lest they be disemboweled with their former acquaintance.

Before the castle's doors were struck open, Frangipani released the pope. He pleaded with the elderly Giovanni for his forgiveness. And the Holy Father forgave him. And for a short time there was peace once more in Rome.

The Italians had barely escaped a civil war. And all this had occurred within the first few weeks of January. What did the balance of the year hold in store, I wondered?

With early spring came what many would consider to be a betrayal, of sorts. Everyone knew that Baldwin's former belovèd had never borne a child, and as the years progressed, it became evident to all that the current occupant of his bed would prove to possess a womb equally barren. (Or it may have had something to do with the ruler and all the medicaments, which his physician had requested that he take daily, for the supposèd prolongation of his own existence. Of course, no one dared mention *this* possibility.) But he was a king. And what was a king to do? Simply by appearance, Adela had seemed to be *quite ripe for the plucking*, as one might say. And still there were no bawling babes about. This turn of events was unexpected. It pained him deeply. Then it made him wrathful.

After an evening, when the song of the nightingale had set the queen's eyes to flutter and close, and she had taken to bed alone, (as she had been doing for some time now), she awoke to learn that her husband had cast her out of his kingdom. Serving-women barely had enough time to clothe her, before royal guards took her to be escorted away. A few coffers of precious gems, gold, and costly raiment surrounded her, though their numbers were considerably less than the amount she had once brought along as her dowry. And she was placed on board a Venetian galley, (large enough to be worthy of her station), that transported her to the royal court of the Byzantines, where she was welcomed for a time, before her final voyage home. There she waited, hoping for a word or so from the man she had come to love. Alas, he never wrote to her. Instead, he wrote to her family, attempting to explain the reasons for his actions, and how it would be simply a matter of time, before the Patriarch of Jerusalem, or even the Holy Father, himself, would declare this marriage void. All in all, the entire situation was a thing most terrible for everyone involved therein.

Many believed that Baldwin had found another younger maiden, who might give him the child he had sought. The truth was that he had little wish for dalliances of any kind, and he certainly did not care to see another feminine processional before the royal palace. No. He was concerned only with the continued growth of empire now. He did not care if he had stoked the flames of Sicilian ire against him. He did not care if other nations would come to look upon the Franks of *Outremer* as a vile, contemptuous race with whom, nonetheless, they would probably still conduct the business of trade (if they were fortunate enough to be a party thereto). He cared only for conquest, or was it simply *defense*, as he called it?

That first oppressive heat of summer began with word that some *caliph* or other had died. Briefly did royals, their standing armies, and the church stop all their respective activities to take a moment of appreciation for that report. (The common folk, on the other hand, went about their business as usual, undeterred from daily goals, regardless of which leader was alive or dead.) Baldwin took this as a good omen. He marched forthwith into Egypt. But he did not have our Order with him. This was the first time that we had refused participation in a royal campaign. (Our forces were occupied along the borders, where there had been numerous raiding parties. Indeed, many an innocent Christian pilgrim had perished there.) He was most displeased with us, and he swore to discuss his dissatisfaction at some length upon his return. Brother Hughes thought that the king might cast us out of the Temple and send us into exile. I assured him that he had no reason to worry, for our Order had been forged like a burnished blade, into one of the most disciplined group of fighters anywhere. Our participation in the fulfillment of the king's plans had contributed to that truth, and he would have to live with our continued presence here, like it or not. Hughes was uncertain that we could make a successful stand against him, if ever it came to that. I, however, had no such doubts.

Then arrived a little bird from Byzantium to say that the emperor there had fallen ill.

I put away Anna's letter, wondering how much pain her father must be suffering. I took no joy in it. O, I had not forgiven him for what I still believed to be his involvement in that first attack upon me, nearly thirty years prior. (Had it really been that long?) Despite that, I realized how he had attempted to make amends, in various fashions. And I felt far worse for the woman I cherished, who adored her sire so deeply, and who commiserated with him through each prayer for more breath in his weakening body.

Autumn began in the first weeks of the September of her mourning. Anna's father had perished, and there was sorrow everywhere, for the man had been much loved by noble and commoner alike. And though I was illdisposed to bear considerable affection for him, I had to admit that there had been none like him. His predecessors had created an empire. Of that there was little doubt, except he was the one who made it virtually impregnable, as it spread ever further from its ancient capital, Konstantinople. His death was a turning point in Byzantine fortunes, and one that none had ever expected. The son had been well groomed for his rôle as leader—a fact that served only to pique Anna's dissatisfaction with her brother's choices of action. (Or was it jealousy that the father had placed the son's importance before her own?) As the new emperor took time out from governance to weep over his father's funerary bier, old enemies watched from a safe distance. Nothing would ever be the same for anyone else again.

Anna requested that our Order came. I debated with myself for some time about whether I would go, before I realized that I could not. Brother Hughes refused to accept my decision.

Inside our stables I fed Nigrum from my palms. Whenever I could, I, myself, preferred to look after her. She had been faithful to me all these years; how could I be any less? Brother Hughes was watching me for a time, before I noticed him standing near.

"Tell me, my brother," I asked, "is there a more noble steed in all the world?"

I kissed the snout, hugged the head, and smiled at my equine companion.

"She was a gift, was she not?"

"The finest," I assured him.

"Brother Andrew has told me that you wish to stay here, whilst a good portion of us go to Konstantinople to pay our respects. Is that true?"

I turned to face him.

"Are you asking me as head of the Order, or as my friend?"

He backed away as if I had struck him.

"I had no idea there was a difference."

Nigrum neighed.

"You see, brother," I pointed out, "even a beast has enough sense to realize that the two positions are mutually exclusive."

"And when did you begin to suffer from this *melancholia*? Shall I call upon Baldwin's physician to bleed you?"

I laughed.

"I would rather not disappoint the Venetian twice."

My old friend eyed me curiously.

"Your meaning, brother?" he asked.

"Nothing."

He walked over and ran his hand across the thick black mane.

"She is most beautiful," he offered, smiling. "I see no reason to insult me, simply because you do not wish to accompany us. Nevertheless, I believe that you owe me an explanation why, both as friend and as head of the Order."

This I refused to give him.

"That man loved you as if you were his own son. Will you not show his family the same respect by mourning his passing with them?"

"He will be in my prayers, in church," I told him, walking away.

"Verily, I cannot understand your reluctance to go along."

I turned around once more.

"Ask anything else of me."

He studied me for a time. I looked away from him, lest he discover the truth that lay hidden behind my gaze.

"What you are concealing cries out with a deeper voice than does your silence. We are family here. You, yourself, claimed that. If one cannot speak the truth amongst the members of his own family, then the universe has grown dark indeed!"

I had tried to maintain a quiet, dignified manner, nevertheless, I wanted to confess the truth as much as he wished to hear it.

"I *cannot* go!" I shouted at last. "She will be at his side," I spoke now in a normal tone of voice.

"Calm yourself," he admonished me, walking closer. "To what woman do you refer?"

"Anna will be there. And her husband will be with her."

He stopped.

"O, my Lord in Heaven!" he was barely able to enunciate, his eyes gaping. He looked down at the dirt near his feet, as he held his hand over his mouth.

I stood there, marching back and forth, like a soldier eager to leave for his next combat.

He dropped his hand and looked up at me.

"How long have you loved her?"

I stopped moving as well.

"I feel as though I have loved her all my life."

He jumped towards me, his hands tight upon my shoulders.

"Leave the courtly poetry for the bards! How long has this continued?"

"Since our first days in Konstantinople."

He grabbed his head and paced back and forth.

"Do you know what you have risked? The entire holy campaign might have fallen apart. It very nearly did so, without any help from you, thanks to the petty ambitions of each man there. That it somehow remained a cohesive group is a miracle. Yet our holy mission was threatened simply because you could not keep yourself clothed?"

"You know what I am, brother. I am an unrepentant fornicator. I am not exactly proud of it, and yet … there it is. You see," I explained, holding my arms open wide in order to better illustrate my meaning, and fashioning the curves of a feminine shape in the air, "when a woman saunters before you, in the glory of her nakedness—"

"Enough!" he pleaded, holding up a hand as if to cease my speech. "No more descriptions, brother. Tell me instead, who else knows of this?"

"No one, as much as I can say."

"Then you might be in error?"

"I do not believe so. But what is so terrible about it? Really? We loved each other long ago. And she has gone on to marry, whilst I pass away the decades of my life amongst my brethren. Of course, there was that last sojourn in her homeland. I do not believe that anyone discovered us."

"Have you lost all reason?!" he shouted, thrashing his hands about, his face a strikingly deep red now, digging his feet into the place where he stood. "I—I—I have no idea what to say. This is not some tavern girl gone off for the night with the most generous patron. This is the daughter of an empire. Her father could have sent legions after you, and all of *Outremer* would have been embroiled in a pathetically stupid war! And what of her husband now? Do you think him generous enough to allow you to partake of his wife's passions free of reprisal? In the name of all that is holy, what *could* you have possibly been thinking?"

Initially I was uncertain how I would respond. I nodded, I shook my head, I had no idea what to say. Then it occurred to me:

"And would it have been so terrible, if she and I had married before she became the wife of that pathetic substitute for a Greek god, or whatever he may be?"

"Dear Lord in Heaven!"

"Enough! If you keep calling upon Him, He might decide to appear, as a pillar of fire, no less. And that would not be a good thing for any of us, especially the horses."

A little stool had been placed next to one of the wooden stalls. He took it now and sat down. It was of such a tiny size, that his buttocks remained close to the ground, as his knees rose high. It must have been terribly uncomfortable for him.

"Who and what do you think you are?" he asked. "A knight is not a king, despite the ties of his lineage to the throne of St. Peter, as you can proudly claim. Moreover, you are no Byzantine. Freely do I admit ignorance of their customs, yet even I know that she would never marry anyone who was not of their blood.

Your behaviour was not only reckless, it was dangerous, to say nothing of its tragic nature."

"However—"

"No *howevers, in additions,* or *whethers*! I refuse to listen to any of them!" he howled, standing up, kicking over the stool, and struggling to straighten both his spine and legs.

"Nevertheless—"

"O, *nevertheless*! I forgot that one."

"I love her, brother. And she loves me."

"And so?"

"So?"

"So, we are the Poor Knights of the Holy Temple of Jerusalem. And you are the Defender of the Faith. The rules, which govern our lives, are different from those of other men. Our souls may not be pure, however, that is the ideal to which we must aspire. Have you forgotten every lesson that your blessèd uncle taught to you?"

"I love you as if you were of my own flesh, but not even you can tell me how my heart should feel!"

He stood there, his stern gaze burning into me.

"Ours is a holy purpose," he began his pronouncement. "It has been that way from the first moment of the Order's existence, and it will stay that way until the Order exists no longer."

"Amen," said Andew, who had come in upon our disagreement. "Forgive me, but the others have been waiting outside, and both your voices carry rather well. I thought you might want to know that."

He excused himself and left.

"Thanks be to God that they have sworn an oath of silence concerning all that transpires herein," Hughes said. "Very well then. I shall depart without your company."

He walked to the doorway.

"If she should ask of me—" I called after him.

"If *anyone* should ask of you, I shall speak the truth, that you are leading our brethren on a mission of protection against the infidel."

"Muslim."

"Whatever! It may not be the complete truth, yet it is no false tale. By the way, you have not loved any other princesses, have you? Either of Baldwin's wives, perchance?"

I shook my head.

"I am most relieved. Be well, brother. Try not to reap any whirlwinds, whilst I am gone."

As the year settled down into what had always been a *torpor* of mind and body in the land of my birth during the first chill of winter, it brought with it here mild sprays of rainfall, which were soon replaced by torrential downpours. Everyone grew wet and disgusted, especially our glorious king, who believed that he was above such petty concerns. Perhaps the Lord believed otherwise.

Leaving a failed campaign in Egypt, (a rare occurrence!), Baldwin took ill upon the muddy roads homeward. Never did I see the man sick. Reports of it amazed me far more than those concerning his losses. Several fathersconfessor, whom he had taken along, told him that it was a portent of ill tidings. He refused to lend to that possibility the slightest bit of credence. It was nothing more than a lack of success for two decades worth of a *serum*, that his physician had plied to the royal body. So, how did the liquid come to lose its potency? He would take it up with Fausto upon his return. And what had they meant by *portent* exactly? As soon as they mentioned Adela's name, they were forced to endure royal shouting, the likes of which had never before assaulted their ears. God had not grown angry because a king had set aside his wife. The idea was preposterous! Still did they have the courage to speak the truth that was in their hearts, for they urged him to remember that he was not simply one more ruler upon the earth, but the first Christian King of Jerusalem. And with that exalted position came a certain mode of behaviour, a standard, perhaps, to which the Lord did not hold others so stringently. And though he wanted to shout again, Baldwin found that he had no voice for such an activity. Indeed, much of his strength, and not a small portion of his will, began to dissipate slowly. He found that he needed to remain silent, if only to keep together the frail fragments of himself. In this moment the truth of his entire life became to him an open book. And the revelation thereof proved too extravagant a weight for his once-mighty shoulders to hold aloft, as Atlas had the entire world.

He called all to his side, that they might bear witness to his wishes: first, he wanted to be buried next to his dear brother in Jerusalem. (These Saracen creatures would only dig up his bones and defile them, should he be left to rot in the hot, stinking sands of Egypt.) More than one of his subjects suggested, (and all others present agreed), that he had lain an impossible task to achieve before them; this selfsame heat would destroy his royal frame, long before any heathen were to do so. For that very reason, he insisted (with more determination now) upon a second command: that his *viscera* would have to be cut out, and the inside of his trunk salted and spiced, only to have those same organs placed back inside, there to be sewn up again. It was a task that his cook would be most proficient in the accomplishment thereof. And as a third order to all: he would have to be wrapped in linen to be borne away to rest in *Outremer* for eternity. (Where anyone would find linen of a quality excellent enough for burial, no one could say. But no one thought it proper to burden their leader with this bit of concern either, so they decided to keep their own counsels once more.) Finally, he let it be known that his cousin, who now ruled Edessa, the other Baldwin, (and who was to assume the title of *Baldwin II* immediately, upon receipt of word that his cousin had departed this world for the next), would call Jerusalem his own. All present agreed.

Within three days, shortly after dawn, King Baldwin I of Jerusalem was dead. And his knights wept for him, as they conveyed his body to the Chapel of Mt. Calvary, that would serve as its final place of rest.

On one unusually bitter morning, shortly thereafter, I left the Chapel only to see the royal physician in the distance. He was walking towards the city gates. I found that most unusual, for how far could a man travel without benefit of a horse, to say nothing of his lack of any sack or possessions, save the clothes he wore? I ran swiftly and overtook him, before he had any opportunity to depart the holy city.

"Why are you leaving?" I asked upon reaching him.

He did not cease, but rather, continued on.

"The reason for my stay no longer exists."

"How far will you go on foot?"

Now he stopped and turned to me.

"O, I have traveled a long way upon these weary feet."

I studied his appearance as he smiled.

"It occurs to me," I said, "that you have not aged a single day since first we met."

"I was born old. What is your excuse? Now, if you are finished, I have somewhere else to be."

He turned to leave.

"At the side of how many kings have you stood, physician?"

That query prompted him to cease his movements once more.

"What makes you think that they were solely kings? Why not popes, bishops, or the wealthier counts? I have watched them conquer, listened to their night-fears, stoked the embers of their dreams. They never change. They are as ruthless and as wretched now as when they drew their first breaths as sobbing babes in swaddling clothes."

He began to walk away again.

"Who are you?" I called after him. "What are you?"

"No more than the conscience of a sinful humanity. I bid you well, faithful defender. We shall meet again someday, if only as two faces in a bloodthirsty mob."

He passed through the gates and turned to the left. I rushed up to him. I cannot say why. Perhaps I wished to continue our discussion, or rather, it may have been to see what I actually did see that day.

By the time that I was through those gates, I noticed several people in the conduct of their daily tasks, and not one of them was the physician. He was nowhere to be seen or ever to be found in the years following that most unusual of days.

Brother Hughes and I stared at the bust of Anna, that had been placed upon a low wooden platform.

"Are you certain that you wish to do this?" I asked of him.

"It is fitting. We commit ourselves to Christ. His mother deserves our worship as well, does she not?"

"This is no replica of the Holy Mother," I continued to insist.

"This contains the Holy Shroud, or so you have told me."

"That is what *I* was told. And if one lifts it up and shakes it about, one may hear something falling back and forth against the metallic sides. O, something is definitely therein."

"Is it safe to assume that its contents are of fabric?"

"The emperor never lied to me about relics."

"Did he, however, lie about else?"

"Shall we continue?" I asked, ignoring his question.

He looked once more at it and sighed.

"She will always be for us what is most pure in woman—the ideal Feminine," he spoke softly. "In all the dark places, she will be a light unto the world."

I smiled.

"She might take a curious satisfaction in the knowledge that you think of her in that way."

"Your meaning, brother?"

"Nothing. Before we begin, I must secure a promise from you. I beg you, brother, whatever you may ask of us, no tonsures, please."

He laughed.

"A full head of hair is one more aspect of appearance, that will separate us from the monks of any other order, though it should be kept short. It would not do to have hair of the same length as is the custom. Rest assured. You may retain your marvelous black locks for as long as you wish."

"Like unto Samson, I shall be strong and powerful."

"Pray that you do not fall victim to the wiles of some wench who will cut your hair and steal your strength from you."

"I thank you, brother, for your warning. It is time. We should call in the others and begin."

"Not yet."

From a table next to him he removed a cloth, revealing a robe. Though apparently well-crafted, it was of a blue so deep, as to be almost black. He gave it me.

"It is yours now, my brother."

"Mine? And what am I to do with this?"

"Wear it, certainly."

Why was it not of an earthen hue, like every other piece of monk's clothing throughout Christendom? He told me that man was born of dust and dirt, and that sometimes his clothing should reflect his humble origin.

"You are unlike the rest of us, Guy de Lagery, for you have returned the Order to its True Path. We are not the arms of kings; we are the defenders of the helpless. You have understood that truth better than anyone. And with this revelation you have brought along the blessings of Mary. Only you have felt the hand of the Mother, as she held you in a manner like unto the caress of our Lord's mortal frame, dead beneath her tears. It is fitting that you, above all others, wear a robe of her colour. Now we may begin."

Emblazoned upon the white tunics we wore was the red cross of St. George, (in markèd contrast to the black robes and silver crosses of the Hospitallers I might add), and presented as the uniform of our Order at my suggestion. (I suppose the image of the Byzantine standard was more of an influence upon me than ever I dreamed possible.) And over almost all (save one) were brown monk's hoods and robes, which covered us warmly, gently. Standing now in the chamber, we took our places, one by one, and formed a circle around the metal bust. Only nine of us were present: Hughes de Payens; Andrew de Montbard; Geoffrey de Bisot; Roland de Chinon; Archambaud de St. Agnan; Gondemar de Poitiers;

Payen de Montidier; the sole Flemish knight, Geoffrey de St. Omer; and finally, myself. (In the ensuing years, all documentation of the order was to list only eight names; I made certain to omit the ninth—mine own.) Most of us had been in *Outremer* from the earliest days of the Holy War, and had acquitted ourselves well as the bravest of soldiers. All of us were far different from the other knights of our age, not simply because of the pledges, to which we were about to dedicate our lives, but because we had left the West, most never to return. To this day I do not believe that the Order could have come into existence, had the circumstances, which surrounded its birth, been any different; for Necessity had been its father, and Faith its mother. And here, in the East, where we had spent more than two decades, it was born in the forges of War. And now we were to take our rightful place both as defenders of the wandering multitudes, and as the sword of Holy Mother Church.

One by one we kissed the brow of the statue, as one would that of a mother or a sister. Brother Hughes told us that from this moment on, we would adopt the Rule of St. Benedictus. (My heart sank. Poverty and obedience perhaps? But chastity? No. This I could never do, had I even cared to.) He said that he had struggled with this question for many years, and had often called upon our Lord for guidance. He knew that the Rule would be our most proper form of conduct, since we were all monks, essentially. And he knew this to be true now more than ever, he affirmed, glaring at me. Our labours were sanctified, and if we could not be the holiest of men, our sins would corrupt the Order, debasing it before the eyes of man and God. (He said the last half of this statement whilst eying me again. Now, really!)

"And with the threefold rule that governs the purity of our lives, we must remember to avoid any woman's touch, be it even from mother or sister."

Now had I lost *all* patience. The woman under whose heart one rested before birth's painful voyage into this world, or the maiden whose friendship and concern provided the comfort that only a sibling can, deserved far more than the avoidance of a touch. Even a sole hermit, disdainful of all human companionship and living in the fetid squalor of a forest-cave, would not deny himself a caress from his own bloodline. To what absurd extreme had Brother Hughes forced the purity of others? Had he revealed a representation of the Holy Mother, only to deny himself and everyone else all feminine kindness? Was I the only one present, who saw something horribly wrong with this? He and I would have much to discuss after this night.

"We are the Poor Knights of the Temple of Jerusalem," he continued, "but henceforth shall we be known as the *Knights Templar*."

He walked over to me.

"Brother, we call upon you to intercede with the Holy Mother, to seek her beneficence for all that we may do in Her Son's name."

He walked back to his original position on the arc. I stepped into the center, near the platform, bent down upon both knees, clasped my hands, and lifted my head to pray aloud for the universe to hear. I had no idea about what I might say, therefore, I settled upon a statement that was not altogether uncommon for a son of the church.

"*Mater Dei, refugium hominum, ora pro nobis.*" ("*Mother of God, the refuge of man, pray for us.*")

Brother Hughes looked at me in a most disappointed fashion. (Perhaps he had desired something of greater originality. I was equally disappointed that I had not been able to prove worthy for the task at hand.) The brethren repeated my sentence three times, then left the chamber, one by one, as Brother Hughes and I stood together with that replica of a beautiful young girl, transformed by faith, into a relic of the most immaculate adoration.

Nevertheless, still am I convinced, to this day, that she would have laughed about it all, had she but known.

CHAPTER THE THIRTY-SECOND,

in which the church grants its formal recognition to the Order of the Templars.

Hooves dug deeply with each gallop, churning up the mud along an empty stretch of road. With successive gales, the soggy robes of the riders slapped against the flanks of their steeds, shoving them on ever further into walls of water.

And when the horses could no longer gallop, nor take one more step even, they halted before the gates of the small wooden structures, which (altogether) had become known as the Abbey at *Clairvaux.*

The three horsemen dismounted. One of them knocked upon the door. Several brothers within had been awaiting the arrival of the strangers, and when the door opened, they ran out to lead the tired animals to the rear stables. Once inside, each pulled off his hood. Of the first, the lines in his face were deep, the golden hair of his beard flecked now with gray. The second wore a beard that was still almost completely black. The third rider revealed a visage far younger than his years.

A young man come forward, holding a taper in front of his face. Remarkably emaciated, the few hairs of a child-like beard clung to his chin, perhaps with the knowledge that they would never grow into a mature fullness. His brown eyes were forever widened in wonderment at the infinite variety of our Lord's works. This little monk was the voice of his generation, calling upon all good Christians to enter the abbeys and monasteries, which sprang up more and more with each succeeding year. Many have said that he spoke with a truly divine diction. I cannot say if his words were originally those of our Creator, though he spoke them heartfully, and with full credence in the righteousness of their cause.

This sainted abbot, Bernard de Fontaines, rejoiced, for he recognized Hughes de Payens, Andrew de Montbard, (his uncle), and myself immediately. He took his uncle's hand and smiled.

"You are most welcome in this humble house of God, my brothers. It is an honour most especial to meet you," he addressed me. "My uncle has written of you often. Come in. You may dry yourselves by the fire."

I turned to Andrew.

"Why do you write of me?"

"Why not? Like Christ, you have been resurrected. The entire world is curious about you. Surely you must know that."

"Notoriety and I have been sometime-strangers. The older I become, the more I believe that I would prefer it if everyone were to leave me be. Please refrain from any further narratives about my life, brother."

"That might prove difficult, as you are one of the Founding Nine of our Order. However, I shall attempt to do as you wish."

Upon entering, Brother Hughes handed a letter to the abbot, who excused himself. (He was going off to find dry clothing for us.) I sat down in front of the hissing timbers, rubbed the water from my hands, and held their open palms before the flames.

"Must you be so miserable?" Hughes asked me. "I never thought that you would enter your mature years with nary a smile upon your face."

"You are most assuredly correct, brother, for why should I not smile? Not one of us can claim that the tiniest portion of himself is dry. Most comical, is it not? Nor should we forget the amusing reason why we are here."

"I do not understand," Andrew interjected. "The church is supposed to grant formal recognition to us for seven long years of faithful service."

"It has been much longer than that," I corrected him.

"No, brother," Hughes made certain to emend my statement, "one should not count from our first days in Jerusalem."

"Why not? After twenty-five years there, tell me what has changed?"

"I cannot reason with you when you are like this," he said, walking to the other side of the room, and as far away from me as he could.

Andrew was concerned about that letter, for he thought that he had seen King Baldwin's seal upon it. What did it mean?

"Tell him!" I demanded, jumping to my feet. "He has a right to know. So do the other six founders. So do all our brethren."

Reluctantly, Hughes tried to explain, (in a way that only he could), how best to cleanse a filthy situation. Only he and I knew of Baldwin *Le Bourg*'s desire to align our soon-to-be blessèd forces with his own. And who better to approve of this alliance than a man whose purest thoughts and deeds were admired by all, namely those of our kind host, Bernard?

So he stood now before Andrew, detailing a pointed issue that had been contained in the missive: how the king wanted the Order to be a permanent addition to his own army.

"And how is this any different from the wishes of the first Baldwin?" I asked.

"He has been very generous with us," Brother Hughes countered. "Do we not have our own Temple now?"

"Solomon had seven hundred wives and three hundred concubines, to say nothing of his large retinue at court. If the Temple that he built was adequate enough for the worship of his needs, why has this copy suddenly become too small for ours?"

"Baldwin's unflagging support has already given us greater opportunities than we could have ever imagined. There has been talk amongst the English, that they would prefer a Temple of their own in London."

"English Templars?!" I exclaimed. "Now *that* is comedy."

"O, will you never shut up?"

"Why berate him," Andrew asked of Hughes, "when he speaks only the truth? I am no servant of a king. God, alone, is my master. Wherefore do you conceal Baldwin's martial wishes?"

"We must defend the holy city. It is our very purpose."

"Do you not hear yourself?" I asked. "You stand ready to sacrifice all that we have accomplished."

"A knight must be practical. Faith helps feed his soul; currency helps feed his horse."

"You speak like a tradesman! Never did I imagine to hear such words from your lips. So old have you grown, my brother."

Hughes lunged at me. I shot my hands forward as defense. Andrew threw himself between us.

"If you wish to beat each other," he ordered, "go outside! You bring disgrace upon us all in God's house. There will be no violent quarrels here."

"If pragmatism is your first concern," I shouted at Hughes, "then know this: throughout the world there are noble families ready to give us their support. We do not need this Baldwin and his demands, however subtle you believe they may be."

"Would the Doge and his family be one of those willing to open their coffers, all without recompense? How naïve you are, if you believe that anyone else will act differently."

"With a Temple in each land, what real power can any of them truly possess?"

"Exactly! With Baldwin's help, I, myself, could go to London and begin the fulfillment of our holy mission there."

"We do not need him for such work," Andrew said. "Christians have been setting foot upon the road with nought save a small sack of foodstuffs and rags as clothing for more than a thousand years. Wherefore do we need gold *bézants* from any king? Ever this concern for the acqusition and hoarding of wealth! I look forward to the day when the entire world will walk about with letters, in lieu of metal fragments, for transactions of trade."

Brother Hughes and I stared at each other, then broke into a fit of hysterics.

"No metals?!" I struggled to speak, laughing riotously, and pointing at Andrew.

"Letters instead!" Brother Hughes spat out, also pointing at him. "Poor Andrew. The man must be touched."

(Would that I could laugh about all that now! As the Lord or Fate willed it, I was the one who kept most of the records of the Order then. But between the *ones* of the Greek, Arkhimedes, and the *zeroes* of the Muslim, Al Khwarizmi, I had a most difficult time of it. In addition, since all brethren were determined to keep secret from any king the exact amount of monies donated, I utilized *runic* letters for most of the documentation, as each letter corresponded to a number. And despite the grief that so very many of these numbers caused me, I believe that I acquitted myself well in the meticulous accounting thereof, or at the very least I hope I did. Who knew that time would prove Andrew ultimately correct?)

We laughed again, not so Brother Andrew. He refused to be deterred from the earnest point that he had hoped to make. He turned now to Brother Hughes once more.

"That you have led us for all this time is a privilege, not a right. Do you consider yourself another ruler, ready to abuse, simply because you have the power to do so?"

Most unexpected, *that* was! Brother Hughes ceased his laughter. His face became quite pale. I would have thought him about to fall over dead.

"Listen to us, brother," I urged him. "Listen well."

"You are foolish, the both of you. How quickly you have forgotten the lessons of our faith. Should we not render unto Caesar that which belongs to him? We are of flesh, and we live upon this soil, not in the clouds above. Where would we have been, without the generosity of kings, whom God has seen fit to allow to rule over us? This is the way that it has always been, and will no doubt always be. Everything that I have ever done was for the benefit of this, our mission. If I have proven myself unworthy, then I shall not continue. There are several better men, who could easily replace me."

Before Andrew began to argue against that final point, he had to stop, as Bernard returned to us. We took the clothing from him, rendering unto him our thanks for an end to our wet misery. Looking at us, he knew that something of a foul nature had transpired.

"Are you unwell, good sirs?" he asked.

"We are old," I responded, "and therefore much given to an argumentative nature. Ignore us. It will be best for everyone if you do."

Brother Hughes shook his head, perhaps revealing that he was the most aggrieved of all present.

Bernard agreed that the mission of the Order, and the manner of its conduct, would needs be codified formally. He, himself, (after long conversations with the three of us) sat down to write a document that would ultimately contain more than seventy precepts. They concerned each aspect of Templar life, from the type of bedding used (straw of course, with a single sheet and two blankets per Templar) to the military hierarchy (Grand Master, *seneschal*, draper, and at last, the knights). Of them all, the most obvious were these three: we would protect the pilgrim; we would defend the land in which we resided against all non-Christian invaders; and the most important point—only the pope could make the final decision regarding the correctness of what we should or should not do. (And the supremacy of the Holy Father over our order would not sit well with many regents throughout the decades to come, I can tell you!) Doubtless, we had been following these rules since the day that Brother Michael and I had first met with Pope Paschal II in Rome, but nowhere were they written down as part of official church records. Our time had come at last.

After several days with the abbot, we returned to Champagne, and my ancestral lands. Exhausted from the rigors of travel, Andrew preferred to sleep, rather than sit with Brother Hughes and myself by the fire. Servants showed him to comfortable quarters, whilst we two praised each other and the Order. Hughes was especially fond of the furnishings about. He admired the hunting tapestries most of all.

"My mother would have been grateful to hear you say that. She always prided herself upon her sense of decoration, though the scenes of the hunts were my father's suggestion."

"You should stay behind a while longer. Hopefully, with future support from the church canons, we may now found Templar houses throughout the world. And I beseech you, brother, no more argumentation upon that point. Thanks be to God that we may be able to fulfill those many requests, which have inundated us for same. You can go to Paris for that purpose. You would be most welcome there."

What a strange and beautiful city that was! Did Brother Hughes know that it had been in Paris, where I first learned the pleasures of the flesh? Brother Michael had not yet taken his vows. He was leaving for it on family concerns, when my father, with whom I had pleaded to remove me from all things ecclesiastical, if only for a short amount of time, asked him to bring me along, the better to broaden my education, in a manner of speaking.

"My uncle was most displeased with him," I concluded, stifling laughter.

Brother Hughes stared at me.

"Perhaps journeying there was not my wisest suggestion," he commented.

"Brother Robert would be better suited to the task. The man loves to pontificate. That will impress the royals, no doubt. And this is not my home anymore. I shall donate it to the church with the stipulation that your son be appointed its priest."

He smiled proudly.

"He would be honoured."

"There is one other request that I would add: a full two-thirds of the land should be set aside for the cultivation of wine-grapes."

"A vineyard?"

"In my mother's memory. She would have been most happy about that, and I have the distinct feeling that the monks here will find some happiness in the partaking thereof as well."

He laughed.

"And what of your father?" he asked me now. "Will you go to the family crypt this time to forgive him his decisions?"

"Sons can never forgive their fathers the sins committed against them. They can only pretend to do so."

"Shall I take my own life, then, in the hope that this act will grant to my sons a moment of peace?"

"Your mistakes have never been so horrid as you may believe them to be. In time your sons will come to honour your name, as will History, itself."

He smiled again.

"Now you are making too much of me. We are not here for my familial obligations, but for yours."

I supposed that I should go to see my father, if for no other reason than it was my mother's final wish. Long had I carried resentment in my heart for having been denied his company during the earliest years of my childhood. Though I felt it a punishment, I refused to accept then, that kindness and concern had prompted his decision.

"It is never easy between fathers and sons," Brother Hughes commented, staring into the burning embers. "My eldest has gone off to tend to your property in the land of the Scots. I wish that he had not made certain to be absent whilst I was here."

That was not to happen for at least another month. I had no idea that he had departed so soon.

"In truth," he continued, "he should have been your son. Whenever he deigns to write me, an action that is most infrequent, his voice is strikingly similar to your own. Likewise, he blames me for not having been there to watch him grow. He has even begun to sign all documents with his mother's family name, *de Saint Claire*. Did you know, brother, that I tell myself every day of how my life's devotion to holy works represents the best choice that I could have ever made for mine own life? However, there are times when I recall the passing of my belovèd Catherine, and the tears of my sons mingling with my own that night. It is then I wonder if my son's disgust with his father is truly misplaced."

He sipped his wine.

"Not every decision may have been the wisest," I assured him, "even when you did everything that you thought was best for them."

"I wish I could say that were so. All that I have done, I felt compelled to do, for my faith. My sons were of secondary importance at best. That is a thing most terrible for any father to admit."

I wanted his anguish to cease. I told him that he would have to stop punishing himself. None of us could return to a former time and alter the circumstances of who and what we were. We had little choice except to live with the consequences of our decisions.

"Your regret now, my brother?" he asked.

"They may not have always agreed with or respected your choices, but they are your sons. Wherever they may be in the world, they are still here. With the passing of my mother, the last of my family is gone."

"The Order is your family."

"My fellow Templars are not the children of my loins."

"Will you complain *now* about all the opportunities, which you tossed away? There was that daughter of the count from Padua, as I recall."

"A lovely maiden, to be sure, but her feet were enormous! Did you ever see them? They were longer than Prince Bohémond's, and I always thought that his resembled two large boats."

"What of that Norweyan *earl's* niece?"

"*Jarl's* niece, you mean."

"Whatever. Regarding the lady, she was far taller than any man, with arm-length flaxen hair. She stole the eyes of everyone who gazed upon her."

"Perhaps. Not a woman of considerable ardor, however. She would simply lie there, unmoving, waiting to be serviced, as a mare would her master's stallion. A spoiled child, no doubt."

He stared at me.

"Brother! Did you have to bed every woman who entered Jerusalem?"

"Exaggeration does not become you. And the less said of my mating habits, the better."

"Still, you have always been determined to find fault with any of them who paid you the slightest attention. Is that because not one of them was Anna?"

Now it was my turn to stare at him.

"I have asked you not to mention her name to me."

My manner and face were downcast, though neither prevented him from berating me. He wanted me to leave off this childish pouting, and unburden myself. He knew how it pained me when I learned of her failed attempt to usurp the throne from her brother.

"If she had succeeded, the world today would be very different," I assured him.

"Yes, and the outcome would have been tragic. The glorious Byzantine church of *Hagia Sophia* would have been overrun by Muslim armies, who would write their devilish script across all the *eikons* therein. They would have laughed at the idea of a queen in command."

"Her husband would have been regent."

"A sister who would take her brother's throne, is not disposed to allow any husband of hers to assume the reins of power. That much is certain."

"I suppose so," I said, thinking about the possibility and laughing.

"I love you, brother. It grieves me to say this, however, I would not wish for you to stay within the Order, whilst you grow more miserable with each passing year. If you want children, then you should not deny yourself the possibility of having any. Go forth and multiply, if that is your wish."

"There would be no sense in that, for the children would not be hers."

His face downcast now, he stared into the fire.

"Hughes?" I asked, after a time.

"Yes?"

"Why does it always seem that everyone is dying?"

"I believe that is part of what it feels like when one grows old."

"O."

Within a single year, in that year of our Lord, 1128, Pope Honourius II convoked a Council at Troyes, at which Bernard was to assist the cardinals. It was a bitter January morning as clerics gathered from everywhere to attend. Hoarfrost had settled upon each piece of cloth, depriving all present of even the slightest chance for warmth of any kind. Still did they remain unmoving, anxious to hear each salient point. The humble abbot arose to speak.

So greatly did he impress all present with his understanding of matters ecumenical, that he was able to put forth his idea concerning an existing military order. And everyone gave to him again his undivided attention:

"A sacred army has been forged in the heat of battles. Within the ancient city of Antioch, and in the glorious Jerusalem, now liberated, dwells the Order of the Temple. These knights, clad in *argent* tunics, emblazoned with a crucifix of *gules*, as the heraldic terminology of their Order refers to them, are the first and final bastion of the Christian faith. With their blood have they returned Jerusalem to the bosom of Holy Mother Church. Three decades have passed into history since those terrible days, and they are still standing, sword in hand, at the city's gates—a stern refusal that no enemies of God may enter therein. They have sacrificed families, homes, property, everything, in order to protect the hapless pilgrim and the roads upon which our Lord trod so long ago. For all their sacrifices, it is fitting that the foundation of their beliefs, the Church, itself, today recognize all that they are and all that they will ever be. Today we grant to the Order of the Templars its fundamental right, not only to exist, but to continue in its service as the first and last line of defense between liberty and oblivion. Let us honour them, for they are Heaven's own army made flesh. In the name of the King of Heaven and its Prince, His only begotten Son, and Our Holy Mother, it is so written. Amen."

The entire body present rejoiced.

Shortly thereafter, the codicil was adopted into church law. By the time that one more year had passed, Christian kings and noble families everywhere were donating currency and/or land to the former Poor Knights of the Holy Temple of Jerusalem, now the Knights Templar.

CHAPTER THE THIRTY-THIRD,

in which the first Grand Master of the Templars, Hughes de Payens, faces his final days.

The dirt had mingled with our sweat and turned to mud. Exhausted, we tried to wipe it from our eyes, without much success. Since my earliest conversation with Pope Paschal II, I had been granted permission (as representative for our Order) to dig beneath the remnants of the original Temple, in hopes of finding the Ark of the Covenant. After more than three decades, (and the movement of considerable debris), we had little to show for our strenuous efforts.

"It is not here," I coughed out finally, loading the last of the muck into the cart. "This is the final passageway. If we dig any deeper, we shall uncover Hell, itself. There can be no more labour for this task."

Brother Hughes lifted his head, and wiped the sweat from his brow with the side of his arm.

"Then we shall dig elsewhere," he maintained.

"We must put an end to this, brother. We have done all that we can. This is the last of it."

"It is here. It *must* be!"

"Then it is God's will that we do not find it. Perhaps some things should simply stay hidden forever from the eyes of men."

"Is its discovery not our holy obligation?"

"Justice is our obligation. So, too, is our survival. Leave relics for the Byzantines."

He looked at me. I do not believe that I had ever seen his eyes so saddened.

"No more then, brother?" he asked at last.

"It is time to leave off this quest and resume the fulfillment of our obligations."

"Amen," the brethren surrounding us said in unison.

We threw our spades aside and began to leave.

"I was so certain," Brother Hughes said quietly to me.

"Have you not yet realized that we are the blessèd soldiers of the Lord? What more does the rest of humanity need?"

"It was not for our glory; it was for the hope of all men."

The realization of how futile our efforts had been weighed most heavily upon him. At that time he was not much given to the participation of any sort of joyous celebration (nor was he ever, actually). But he grew more despondent than was his wont. And no one and nothing could alter the disconsolate manner in which he now began to carry himself throughout all of his daily tasks.

Of late we had had many new arrivals for potential membership. Most were unworthy. Together, he and I would welcome them, after a fashion. Brother Hughes allowed himself a single pleasure, and that was his speech of entry.

"Would you care to watch as I frighten off would-be candidates?" he asked, smiling.

This I knew would be most joyous for him, so I consented quickly. (He could be a master at sending away the weak-willed posthaste.)

"The sight of their fear is most agreeable to me," I concurred.

"Shall we enter?"

In a dark chamber, lit by a sole torch, the men were lined up, shoulder to shoulder. The Grand Master marched in front of them, back and forth, then again, speaking his perfected oration all the while:

"So, you would become Templars, would you?" he asked in a normal tone of voice, before assuming a full stentorian one:

"Who do you think you are to stand in this holy place, where better men than you have begun their sacrifice?! O, did you not realize that *that* was what you were doing? Do you think you are brave? You have no idea what that word means, until you have stood, watching ten thousand infidels riding towards you, screaming for your blood! Do you think you will live comfortably herein? Do not be fooled by our wealth, or the size of the Templar Houses, which are growing across every nation like fields of grass, for we are the poorest of the poor. The clothes upon our backs, the few crumbs in our bellies, even the palfreys we ride all belong to the Order, and are no more than gifts for our occasional use. All these things are transitory, as are our pathetic lives. You must ask yourselves: is this what I really want? But wait! Your misery is not yet complete. Do you think your deeds here will bring you lasting fame? No one will remember you when you are gone from here. Your name will not endure. You will most probably die in a desert, parched, bleeding, and all alone.

"If anyone wishes to leave, he may do so now. There is no shame in realizing the truth of who and what you are (Several knights turned and fled.) ... though it be a coward!" he shouted after them. "For those who stay behind, know this: the agèd, the very young, the helpless, the infirm—these are the reasons why we raise a blade in defense; the word of our Lord, that awakens us from our dreams, that we may use our lives to do honour to His name, this is the reason why we don the cross of St. George. Have you forgotten the noble deeds of that valiant soldier of Christ, how he, a fighter in the Roman legions, refused to execute Christians and even adopted their faith and died in their defense? St. George is the patron of all who would raise a sword against the enemies of the faith. He taught unto us that to the greater glory of our God do we bring all that we have, and all that we may become. We are significant in that we are His instruments only.

"As Templars, we do not retreat from battle, unless the forces against us are three of them compared to each one of us. When we fight, it is to the death; for God's warriors, there can be no ransom. When we face death, it is with head held high, for there can be no fear, knowing that we are soon to journey to our Father's Kingdom. Now, enter that chamber," he ordered, pointing to a closed door. "In it you will find a relic most sanctified—a representation of the Holy Mother. Kiss her brow with love, as if she were the matron who bore you, then take your stand here, at our side, that we may fight the Darkness from now until the end of time. You are most welcome, my Templar brethren."

The candidates entered in a single column. Brother Hughes walked over and whispered into mine ear:

"This group was not so quick to depart as the previous one. I used to be able to send them all away with the first few words. Now the majority stays behind. I tell you, brother, I have lost my ability to generate fear. That truth makes me feel absolutely ancient."

Brother Hughes rushed into the stable, where he found me sitting upon the ground next to my treasured steed, Nigrum. She lay down upon the hay, breathing heavily, jerking to and fro. Like everything in Konstantinople, she, too, had proven herself one more miracle from there. Whereas rarely had I seen a horse live past a single decade, she had borne me upon her back through many a campaign, for what had become almost four. And the only marks of her age were the few white hairs surrounding her dark eyes. In strength, speed, and agility, nothing else about her had changed.

I had been riding past the Temple, where we had placed a heap of rocks from the recent excavations, when one large boulder fell down from on high. There was no time to escape its path, and Nigrum had stumbled over it, cracking the bones in both of her forelegs. Nothing could be done to heal her now.

I ran my fingers over her mane, holding back my tears. Hughes put his hand upon my shoulder. I pushed it away. I wanted no comforting. I wanted only to feel each twinge of her pain. I wanted silence. And even that could not be mine. Perhaps the other horses somehow knew of the torment that their comrade was undergoing. They neighed, they whinnied, and they snorted. Some raised their heads, as if in the act of nodding, they recognized the truth of the moment. Hughes may have as well, though I could not look upon him. I could not avert my eyes from the grand old lady who had been so much a portion of my life. Could I sit here all night and watch her wallow in agony? Did she not deserve a better fate?

I arose. Hughes touched me again, this time to call my attention to him. I looked into his eyes, and he nodded to me. I raised my sword, and with all deliberate strength, brought it down upon her head, cleaving it in twain. Her palsied movements stopped instantly. Only then did I begin to weep.

Upon a new horse (this time a white stallion) I rode out, accompanied by Brother Hughes, to the plains of *Har-Meggido*. It was here that the final battle between the forces of light and dark would contest at some future time. Strange, I thought. It was most peaceful. Filled with hyssop, myrtle, rue, and pomegranates, one would never think to call this place a veritable *inferno* upon the earth.

Hughes stopped to pluck a fig and taste of it.

"Rarely have I eaten of anything as sweet," he said, breaking the silence, and smacking his lips. "As we discussed, I have informed Robert de Craon that he will lead the order after I am gone."

There was no denying the finality of that statement, and it bothered me to hear him speak it.

"The choice of a successor should not sound your death-knell, my brother."

"I have walked this earth for five and sixty years. I am so very tired lately, tired of wars; tired of living as well, I suppose. I shall not stay here indefinitely, thanks be to God."

"Linger a while longer, if not for yourself, than for me." I turned to him now. "I am a selfish man, for I believe the world better that you are in it."

"You are an excellent swordsman, as fine at this age as when first we met. I should have guessed that you would deflect the important matters by appealing to my vanity."

"I have never uttered a false statement to you, and I am pained that you would think so little of me."

"Now comes the one note of falsity. Perhaps you have spent too much time in royal courts and learned their bitter lessons well."

"If you wish to insult me, wait until I leave; then you can cut the air with a sword's flourish, ranting against my many weaknesses for as long as it may please you. Perhaps a sojourn into this place was not one of your better notions."

"You must be confusing me with Prince Bohémond, may he rest in peace. I am not so overly dramatic, brother. You know that Robert is not my initial choice."

"Robert? And why not Andew, who is much more capable, in my estimation?"

"Not this again. How many times must I remind you that he is far too young?"

"And Robert can barely remember his lost youth."

"If you are so dissatisfied with my choice, then you can assume the leadership yourself. You were always my first successor."

"Absurd! I am not even a Templar, not strictly speaking, at any rate. I am more like a ... *muse*, who inspires the Order, and fights at its side, and gives to it the benefit of his exceedingly brilliant intellect."

He laughed.

"And your vanity as well, it would appear. You are a great mystery to me, brother. You have always done what you have always wanted, and the Order of St. Benedictus be damned! Though you prefer the company of women much of the time, your heart has never strayed from the gaze of our Lord. Look at me now. There is no mistaking the distance that I have journeyed. Each step is a line carved into this old face. Only for you is it different. Brother Andrew has always believed that you would outlive us all. Of late I have come to agree with him. What if Guy de Lagery, who does not grow old, who does not bear the slightest of scars, can never die?"

In no manner would I accept such a ridiculous conclusion.

"Such is not man's lot in life," I assured him.

"There is the key point that I have been trying to make with you for some time now. You are not subject to the same rules by which other men's lives are measured. A man who cannot die would be the perfect leader for the Templars. He will see to it that our holy work continues until the end of time."

"Why would I accept that position now, if I have refused it from you before?"

"I have come to realize a truth concerning you, my brother. If Jesus is the Lamb of God, then you may very well be the Lion."

A wind rose up. I thought I heard a woman's voice call out my name. But that could not have been, could it?

"I have listened to this foolishness long enough," I shouted, hoping that my own noise would rouse me from my revery. "We should go back now."

"It is a shame that you see the essence of everyone except yourself. This is my final request. After today, I shall never again ask it of you. Will you lead the Templars when my time here is finished?"

"No."

"Very well. Then make me a single promise: that you will always look after the brethren, as if they were of your own flesh."

"This I swear, before all that is holy."

He looked about.

"In such a place as this, your pledge will have its most profound meaning. Now am I able to rest easy."

His heart stopped one fine morning, much like any other, surrounded by his cherished Templar brethren, who were ill prepared for the sudden fall that he took from off his horse. All this would happen in less than a year's time from our conversation upon those plains. But he did not depart wearing a frown. There was not a single city in the known world that lacked a Templar House, and in some cities there were two. By the time that Hughes de Payens, first Grand Master of the Templars, drew his final breath, his dream had been fulfilled.

We were everywhere.

CHAPTER THE THIRTY-FOURTH,

in which the fall of Edessa becomes the rallying-cry for the Second Holy War.

Overly much has the word *Crusade* been misused since the retaking of Jerusalem. In point of fact, each time that a Christian king had an argument with anyone deemed of a significant station at the time, (usually another Christian king), he would demand an official papal condemnation, to be followed by a call to arms for a new pious war against the offender. Unfortunately, sometimes the Holy Fathers did exactly everything that they were told was most just, whether or not it actually was.

I had never been to Edessa. I had no idea how vast were its holdings; and bordered upon almost each side by Muslim nations made the continued possession of it increasingly difficult, as the decades had passed. But when *Imad al-Din Zanghi*, Muslim leader of Aleppo, captured that city in that year of our Lord 1143, a call went out, and both French and German kings took the oath to punish the devils, who had dared to besiege a Christian nation; except this time, it was the abbot, Bernard, with ardent papal approval, who convinced the rulers that it was their holy obligation to fight. And whilst Louis de la France accepted his new position as one of the military leaders most readily, (thanks, in part to the influence of the monks who had raised and educated him), the German ruler, (or *Kaiser*), Konrad von Hohenstaufen, was less inclined; the significant expenditure of resources involved, including the best of men and very much of monies, was indeed burdensome. Despite his initial misgivings, he agreed to lead as well. (After all was said, he had no wish to stir up papal anger and risk excommunication. In this he was very unlike the accursèd Heinrich.) Bernard had made an especial trip to Germany for the very purpose of convincing him of that, as well as to avail himself of an opportunity to quell the persistent Teutonic habit of slaughtering as many Jews as could be found in one place during a sacred call to arms. Ultimately, Bernard was most pleased with his results, and his holiness far more so.

Several years thereafter, when I rode to meet with Brother Bernard this time, I was alone. And it was not to the abbey at *Clairvaux* that I had come, but to the cathedral at *Vézélay*. Past the white and black stone columns, beneath its soaring vault, I found the abbot at the opposite end of the structure, looking through a portal east towards *Outremer*. Aware of my presence, he turned to me.

"We have lost this battle," began his confession, "for we have fallen from grace."

And why had this become true? Was it due to a lack of leadership, or a miscalculation in the number of armed men? Was God determined to humble us, using the power of our most detestable enemies? No. It was all due to the presence of women.

Really?

Did not Pope Urban II, my dear uncle, advise strongly against bringing them along on the First Holy War?

"He knew how weak men would indulge their passions at the expense of their martial concerns," Bernard urged me to remember. "What man would not avoid a bloody engagement in combat, simply to spend the night with a serving-girl or a prostitute?"

"Perhaps their concerns were more marital than martial. Most of the men there did bring along their wives, as I recall."

"And that, as well. Husbands and wives rutting like hounds in their tents, in the midst of a glorious campaign against God's own enemies? The whole matter was disgraceful!"

I had to stifle my laughter. So close was he to the truth of that situation, (as I had heard it to be), that I thought he had seen it firsthand. In point of fact, nine months to the day, many of the women who had been there (and survived) gave birth. And all the progeny were children of Christian fathers, as much as I had heard it so.

"These concerns never appeared in the first generation of warriors, who sacrificed so much when you were with them. Their descendants are cowardly, weak-minded, and weak-willed. O, to have had men like Godfrey or Bohémond fighting for us!" he shouted, looking upward, his hands clasped together. "We would have never lost."

I knew that generation quite well, it was true, including all their faults and foibles. Whether they might have acted differently was a question that I could not answer.

He asserted that King Louis should have never brought his wife along. Like all foolish husbands, he could not bear to deny the indulgence of his child-bride her every whim, no matter how ludicrous or dangerous.

Child-bride? She had but one year less than her husband, and both were in their mid-twenties. To what tales had the abbot been listening? Or was he simply so disheartened by reports of her deeds, *i.e.* that she could never be more than an uncontrollable little girl?

"That Eleanor of his is no better than the Whore of Babylon. Have you heard the stories about her behaviour?"

"People say a great many things. They say that Louis has the heart of a clergyman, not that of a soldier. Some have said that our Grand Master, Robert, was not up to the task, for, though seasoned, he lacked the bite of violence that youth, alone, may claim as its personal possession."

"Do you believe any of it to be true?"

"I cannot say in which direction the truth may lie."

"Your experience upon the field should tell you more than you may be inclined to discuss, though your loyalty to both men is admirable."

I hesitated. Anything that I might have said had the potential to lay the groundwork for a war between a French king and the papacy. There was no doubt in my mind that Bernard would report each word that I might speak against any of them, especially Eleanor, if only to use it to force a possible end to Louis' marriage, and thereby strengthen the influence of the Holy Father over the crown. (Not that any of my concerns mattered, really, for some time thereafter, the unhappy wife would seek and ultimately obtain an annulment from her devout husband.) At this time, however, it was most difficult for me to say anything.

"She is a woman given to ... great passions. Yes," I affirmed, continually nodding, "she is a woman given to passion for the sundry aspects of life."

I did not think my assessment of her character to be particularly convincing, nor did I wish to lie to a holy man, even if my statement did possess a ring of truth, however small; nor did my assessment please him.

"From what I have heard, her greatest sin was her complete lack of discretion—a detestable quality in any woman, whether royal or common. However, it appears that you are unwilling to condemn her. I have the distinct feeling that you are revealing a great deal, whilst simultaneously relating nothing at all. With all due respect, brother, I believe that you should spend less time at courts, and more time amongst the commoners. Usually they mean what they say."

I knew that the abbot could be a man of little or no patience when it came to matters of heresy; I had no idea that he could be so short-tempered when not presented with the immediate answers, for which he yearned.

"I have journeyed a long way in order to be here, and despite what you may believe of everyone else, I have ever fought to the best of my abilities. If for no other reasons than those, I deserve your respect, brother."

His face reddened, not with anger, but with shame.

"I beg your forgiveness. The fault is certainly not yours. I shall not permit my displeasure to become my master once again. It was misplaced."

"Then by all means, place it where it belongs."

He went on about how some deed of an inviolate nature would have to be accomplished, if we were ever to deserve better of our Lord. He wanted me to set out upon a quest. A quest? And what was to be the sought-after object? I was to find the cup from which Jesus drank at the Last Supper—a *sangréal*, or *grail*, as he called it.

"You wish me to find a cup?" I asked, incredulously.

He nodded. I refused to believe mine own ears.

"With all due respect, brother, I am the Defender of the Faith. My sword-arm belongs in *Outremer*. Wherefore do you send me away upon this search, when my responsibilities lie elsewhere? Have you forgotten that I arrived late to the war for that very reason? Should I now wander God's very vast earth in order to locate a small cup? Do you know how many cups there are?"

He turned from me. O, I had struck him so very deeply with those words.

"It is the symbol of healing," he uttered at last, in an attempt at explication.

I could not comprehend how a cup, from which our Lord drank at a meal, would heal the world. I knew that Bernard was well versed in spiritual matters, but *this!*

"If all that we may need be a symbol," I stated firmly, somewhat impatiently, "then we should enter the nearest church and contemplate the crucifix. That is the ultimate truth for any Christian."

"Sometimes a holy relic can transform the very souls of those who have lost their faith. How can you not see this, brother?"

I began to walk away.

"If men are so weak, then they should pray to our Lord for strength. I shall waste no more time in this."

"It is your obligation to defend the helpless. This is part of your holy duty to your fellow man," he averred, lifting a scroll that he had been holding.

Noticing the papal seal upon it, I walked back, and took it from him, before cracking open the wax closure thereupon.

"His holiness concurs," he added.

I perused the Latin contained therein. Most of the syntax and portions of the vocabulary were less than perfect, though there was no question as to the intent of the author. I rolled up the scroll once more.

"And shall I be informed of where my journey is to commence, or is that information, too, a matter of *faithful* speculation?"

"A wry tongue does you no justice, my brother."

"Forgive me. My anger was misplaced."

He told me that I would find a hermit living in the forest outside of the city of Toulouse, in the south. And how was I to recognize the man, since the possibility existed that there could be more than one errant clergyman, who had grown disgusted with human company, and had made himself a home amongst the wild animals and greenery? It turned out that I would be looking for a man named *Waldo*. Waldo? Yes. He was a man of French, German, Spanish, and some other unknown ancestry; hence his unusual appellation. Still, I was undecided if I should begin at all.

"There is none better suited for this task," Bernard concluded.

"If it be God's will."

"As all things are."

Walking away from him, I wondered exactly how many times our Creator might have rung His hands, whilst witnessing how His children have been determined to satisfy their wishes at His expense. O, my Lord, have any of Your children ever cried for *You*?

My tardiness in arrival at the above referenced war was due in large part to the ruler of Antioch, another Raymond. He had written to any- and everyone, including a pope, a Grand Master of the Templars, and the Patriarch of Jerusalem, all to secure my services in the defense of his city, for he wished to have at his side in battle the Templars' most blessèd soldier of the Lord, or so had he written. (He feared, and not without good reason, that Muslims from neighboring Aleppo might try to conquer his sovereignty.) And each recipient of each letter was not without a certain degree of sympathy for the ruler's circumstances. So, it was requested formally, advised kindly, and entreated passionately to go thither and use my sword as I saw fit, which action I proceeded to do posthaste. (I believed that Raymond might be in immediate danger. I was to discover quickly how most assuredly incorrect I had been.)

I had not returned to Antioch since my first days there. I was ill prepared to see how greatly it had changed. Its palace was like a hundred others throughout *Outremer*, though this one was much overladen with servants for all manner of civilized concerns: from the putting on and taking off of *cuirasses,* to the removal of footwear and the washing of feet therein. Raymond had transformed the Antiochene nation into a curious reproduction of a French royal court, replete with all the conceivable appetites now fulfilled. Whilst I had been prepared to enter the fray, upon my arrival, alone, (as had been asked of me and of everyone else I knew), I found, to my utter consternation, that Raymond was occupied with the feasting of his belovèd niece, Eleanor d'Aquitaine and her husband, King Louis VII de la France. (His own young wife he had sent home to France for an extended visit, to last at least as long as his niece and her husband where enjoying his hospitality.) If anyone here were concerned with the possibility of war, no one evinced it.

Raymond's years were a bit more than fifty. Both hair and beard were completely white. His belly was not overly fat, though his cheeks were round and quite red. (Or perhaps that was due to the wine that he savoured so much.) His nephew (by marriage) was a lean man with that curious look in the eye that said it was never staring directly at one, even when one were speaking with him, but flitting about in a search for the Great Mystery, wherever It might be. O, there was no doubt in my mind that the man had the temperament of an ascetic. Often that was most unfortunate for the women who loved such men, who were forever looking everywhere except at their comely wives. Usually, these matings resulted in unhappiness for both. When I espied Raymond's niece, I knew that my judgment was indeed borne out.

How can I describe her in a way that would permit words to do justice to her form? *Beautiful* is so paltry a term. She was not overly thin or fat, only a perfect combination that allowed each supple curve to give a moment's pleasure to a man's eye. Her auburn hair, lit only by candles and torches, (and not yet witnessed in the brilliance of the day upon my first glimpse of her behind the castle walls), gleamed like flame. And nary a strand of it was out of place. Her green eyes were otherworldly. If I were ever to see a queen of faeries, she would stare at me through those selfsame eyes, or so was I convinced. But beyond their shades of colour, they revealed a characteristic of their owner that was wondrous strange; they were lit by a ferocious intelligence and will to live. It would take a man of very rare gifts to appreciate the many aspects hidden within this lady, if any were ever deemed worthy of that appreciation at all. And when I looked over at her husband, Louis, who was visibly uncomfortable in the midst of all this drinking and dancing, I knew again that her marriage was doomed.

As was my custom, when most were asleep, I took to walking about in the lateness of an evening. Upon the castle ramparts I conversed with one of the night-guard concerning the possibility of any recent appearance by invaders. There were none, he informed me. Not a single one? No. The previous border skirmish had been a relatively minor affair, and that was four years previously. And nothing since? No! I thanked him and went upon my way. Before I descended the stair, I paused, my hand upon the stones of the parapet, and looked up into the black sky. The moon and stars were its sole sources of illumination. And there was Orion, club in hand, and nearby was Sagittarius, about to let fly an arrow. How fitting! Was this not the time of year for the rise of the Hunter's Moon?

Back in the corridors below, I found myself disturbed by the possibility that my presence here was little more than a means of allaying the fears of the ruling monarch. He had not requested aid from Jerusalem, or from the Order. Why? Many soldiers would be far more effective than a single one; unless, of course, there were some reason, other than the threat of war, that had prompted him to ask for me.

Struggling to comprehend his motives, I heard a noise. Quickly I withdrew my blade. (Perhaps there were enemies here after all!) My back against the walls, I edged forward slowly towards the direction of the sound. When I discovered its source, I stood still. Not far from me, at the other end of the hall, were a king and a queen. Rather, I should say, Raymond, his garments around his ankles, was thrusting into Eleanor, whose thin gown was pulled high, up to her very neck. It must have been exceedingly uncomfortable for her to have her spine pushed against the cold stones with such vehemence like that. I thought, at first, that the man was the sole recipient of pleasure, but her moans betrayed her enjoyment as well. And I had to grant the old man his due, for he kept at it quite some time, before he ultimately pulled out and spilled his seed all over both their feet. And they laughed, kissed, hugged. And whilst she held him now, his head resting upon her breast, she peered into my direction. I backed away, hoping that the torches upon the walls did not betray my presence. I suppose that they must have in any case, for she looked directly at me. (Of that there was no doubt in my mind.) And she smiled.

In each possible way was their action wrong, yet why had they not selected one of the very many bedchambers in which to fulfill their incestuous yearnings? Apparently, she had thought it safe to leave her husband by himself. The poor cuckold must have been sleeping off his cups, or a possible draught of somnolescence that had somehow, miraculously, found its way into his wine. Despite that, it was also evident that uncle and niece may have wanted to be discovered. Surely that was not so, was it?

In the early morning following that most eventful night, I walked about the ramparts once more, searching the horizon for enemies, who appeared not to be coming hither. Eleanor found me there. And in that effulgent light after dawn's rise, free from all possibility of shadow, her hair framed her face, and took on a life all its own. Perhaps she was like a female Samson, holding her strength in her locks, and possessed of a fury beyond words.

She approached me, smiling again. Before I had an opportunity to greet her, I felt her hand grab at my crotch (gently, mind you). She would not let go. A guard saw this, stared, then quickly averted his glance and walked on.

"You will let me know when it is you discover all that which you seek, my lady, will you not?"

She laughed, releasing me.

"A respectable length and girth, Sir Guy de Lagery. You should be proud of your ... gifts. And to that may I say, you appear remarkably youthful for someone so old. The Lord has been generous with you more than once. If ever you tire of your duties in *Outremer*, I would be honoured to welcome you to the Aquitaine. Someone like you could be a great asset to our needs. Likewise, your achievements there could be limitless with our support."

"I have the support of my Templar brethren. That is enough for me, for now."

"I have no doubt of it. However, should you change your mind, you would be most happy there. Our lands are the finest in the entire nation. All manner of crops grow there with little effort. And the women who reside there are unlike any upon the earth. Even their hair is beyond words. Whereas the women of other nations have thick wool, we are possessed of the finest of silken strands. That is equally true of ... *all* our hair."

She smiled coyly. I supposed that she was much taken with her bawdiness. A queen she may have been, but to me now, a randy wench was she. Perhaps it was an enticement, perhaps not. Regardless of her intent, I smiled back. I did not wish to disappoint her.

"You should learn that lesson for yourself," she continued. "I have always believed that personal experience is the finest educator."

In truth, I had no doubt of it either.

It took no more than a day or so before reports of Eleanor's behaviour came to light. (I assumed that my eyes were not the only pair that had witnessed her curious tenderness for her uncle.)

I found her, her husband, and her uncle in the main hall. Clad in a golden breastplate, (into which two recesses had been hammered out in order to support her breasts), Eleanor appeared very like a female warrior set for battle. It was obvious that she and her consort had been arguing. Together they were silent now. What struck me as a singularly odd behaviour was Louis' refusal to confront his host. The man spouted no insult, no threat; nor did he raise a sword, or dagger, even. He simply turned to his wife and ordered her to leave with him immediately for Edessa. And then it happened. That was the moment when the marriage was finished, despite the absence of any official declaration for such. She *stood her ground*, as one might say. She maintained that she would not leave, and that French troops must stay behind and defend Antioch instead. Louis was livid! (From what I have been told, it may have been one of the few times in his life, when he had allowed himself a degree of passion, albeit of a violent nature.) He refused adamantly. She asked for a divorce. She, herself, would petition the pope, if necessary. And she reminded him further that, as part of their matrimonial agreement, the Aquitaine would revert to her control and ownership. (That had been a clever ploy by her father, I had to admit, since I had known no other women to retain their property in similar circumstances; moreover, Louis, himself, had agreed to such at the time of nuptials.)

There was absolute silence. No one moved. After the husband and wife stared at each other for a time, unblinking, it was the husband who took now the first steps to leave. He lunged for his wife, and grabbed her hair. Dragging her across the stone floor, he pulled her out of the palace. Her screams were terrible. I ran to rescue the maid, when her uncle reached out and stopped me.

"This situation cannot be resolved at your hands."

I could not say if his statement to me were a recognition of some deep truth about marriage in general, or a simple warning to stay away from this one specifically. I pushed him aside.

"She is of your own flesh. Will you not go to her aid?"

"I think that I have done more than enough for both."

He walked away from me, deep into the recesses of his castle. He said not a word to them upon their departure, not even one of apology.

I had continued to think upon all the effort that had been responsible for having brought me to this place. And when I surmised the reasons for his actions, not a day hence, I went to the king.

He stood upon the ramparts, looking over his verdant lands.

"How goes it?" he asked.

"I shall be leaving on the morrow, your highness."

"What? You are supposed to remain until we give you leave to go!"

"There are a great many knights who patrol your borders, and the number of your personal guards are no less numerous. You do not need me here. The truth is, you never have."

"Why else would we request your presence, unless it were needed?"

"I have been asking myself that very question, since my arrival. And it was not until your niece's husband had been apprised of your activities, that the explanation became evident to me. You, yourself, are the probable source of the rumours. You wanted him to know the truth."

"Now why would we possibly want that?"

"Louis is a good and pious king, even if he is not the consort that you would wish for her. That is probably why you did everything in your power to put an end to that marriage. This does not negate the Muslim threat to your lands, nor does it mean that you are unconcerned for the lady Eleanor; it means only that you have indulged the worst aspects of your nature to lay the groundwork for the dissolution of her marriage to a man, whom you detest."

He shook his head, and upon his face he wore an expression of the deepest sadness.

"We do not detest him. Actually, we admire him his piety."

He had an unusual manner of showing his admiration. Nevertheless, he wanted her to be happy. I could respect that wish. The means to grant her that happiness, however, left something to be desired. I especially did not care for his urge to have me bear witness to his—how shall I put this?—to his methods. Obviously his highness must have heard of my need for less sleep than is typical of other men. That characteristic of mine was well known. But what were he hoping to gain by this? Did he think that I would tell the pope, so that he might force Louis' hand to leave off his wife? If that be so, then he was in error. Rarely have I exposed the secrets of others, to which I, alone, had been privy.

"Really?"

"Verily."

"Perhaps you are not aware that you have an arrogant way about yourself. Wherefore do you address a king in this manner?"

"You brought me here to legitimize your actions. You tried to use me as a witness to them, knowing that the worst fate you would have to face would be papal censure, no more. Your wish to bring me here was a mistake."

"Will you threaten me now, sir knight?" he asked, his hands upon me.

Guards nearby began to unsheathe their swords.

"Tell them to leave here," I said rather quietly, "or you will never see the sunset. This I swear."

He did as I had requested. They retreated down the staircase.

"Now take your hands off me."

Again, he did exactly as I told him.

"Never be fooled by my appearance," I made certain to inform him. "I only look as though my years were four and twenty. I have walked this earth far longer than you have. You should treat your elders with respect."

"What are you, then, unholy knight?"

"Yes, I suppose you have no idea who and what I am. The truth is, I am the Lion of God."

He stared at me, then he stepped back. I thought I saw fear in his widened eyes, though I might have erred in that assessment.

"Will you forgive me my many sins?" he asked at last.

The question surprised me. Perhaps there was some hope of his redemption after all.

"Go to your chapel," I told him. "Ask that of our Saviour. I am incapable of granting forgiveness."

I left for Jerusalem the following day. Raymond said nothing to me as I rode off, though he was no longer wearing the smile that had greeted me previously.

Upon my return, I discovered that all forces involved in the conflict had gone off to Damascus. Why to that city, and not to Edessa? Apparently the retaking of Edessa was considered a lost cause, and someone or other suggested that wealthy Damascus might prove an easier conquest. Of course, no one bothered to recall that its *emir* had sought alliances with Christian kings against Muslim Aleppo for years, fearing the loss of his own realm. And when faced with the approach of a

Christian army, he realized that he had only one possibility left open. And he took it, much to Christian chagrin.

(And in the conflict that waged thereafter, it was Konrad's nephew, Friedrich, whom history would come to term *Barbarossa* for his red beard, who was the sole warrior capable of having distinguished himself with any degree of honour there. More of him later.)

I decided to take off upon that famous road to Damascus as well. But by the time that I neared the city, it was too late; the wounded survivors were making an *exodos* out of the hostilities, for their retreat to whatever place they referred to as *home*. And rarely had I seen such anguish on faces so drawn, so old before their time. They had lost more than a war; they had lost the absolute faith in their own invincibility; for who would dare to think of the possibility of failure, of loss, after Jerusalem had been secured? Their belief in God, so long taken for granted, had left them betrayed. What would they do now? In what would they believe?

Throughout the Muslim world, Zanghi's name was championed. Some said that he had won revenge for the many who had been butchered by Christian hands in Jerusalem more than forty years previously. And not two years hence, he would be stabbed unto death, courtesy of his own servant's hand. It was rumoured that an insult had been the cause. All that I could imagine was that if it were true, its nature must needs have been a thing most terrible to hear. The ruler should have probably exercised some restraint in his rather voluble manner, if he wished to live a long and relatively safe existence in the eyes of *Allah*. But he was never one for restraint, as far as I learned of it to be true.

For Raymond, the Muslim threat, (whether real or imagined), that had prompted my appearance in Antioch, became fact prior to that year of our Lord, 1150. He entered into a war with Zanghi's son, Nur al-Din, and lost. Raymond was beheaded. Several Templar brethren were with him when he met his Maker. I had elected not to be at the side of the Christian king, for which I heard that he had been most ungrateful. In fact, he called out to our Lord for me to die a horrible death. Despite his best wishes, I have lived to see him (and so many other rulers) return to the dust from which we are all made.

CHAPTER THE THIRTY-FIFTH,

in which I begin a quest, of sorts, for a holy cup.

The *sangréal*, the *graal*, the *grail*—legends about it took hold in everyone's mind from the beginning of the twelfth century onward. Most were promulgated by more than one Frankish chronicler eager for notoriety. And there were as many variants as there were authors. In one tale Joseph of Aramathea had taken it with him across the mighty oceans to secure its final resting place among the French, the Germans, the English, or whomever. In another, the Holy Mother, Herself, brought the cup to the region of the author's birth (wherever that might happen to be); or it somehow, miraculously, appeared in a nation whose people God had deemed worthy of its possession. And who had actually seen it? Absolutely no one, as much as I knew it to be true.

The forests around Toulouse possessed some of the densest brush that I had ever seen. And more than once was I cut by thorny vines. So vast was the growth of trees, that I thought it would be overly long before I would be able to return with the sacred cup.

The first day there yielded no positive results, nor did the second. Only on the third did I find an enormous tree, the trunk of which revealed a lair, apparently scratched- or hollowed-out in some fashion. Odd, I thought, that this one had no birds upon its branches. Nearing it, I realized why that were so, for I had to back away; the stench emerging from it was atrocious. It had been my experience that no animal could ever produce a spoor like that. The occupant must needs be a man. At the portal I called inside.

"Leave me alone!" a voice called back.

Exactly as I believed, the hermit wanted nought to do with his fellow man.

"Are you Waldo?" I asked anyway.

"Everyone is a *Waldo* here. We are Waldensians in this part of the world. From where do you originate, Paris, that home of arrogant ignorance?"

It was the one time in my life that I was convinced that the Lord would forgive me, if I took the life of this monkish Christian. Unfortunately, I thought better of that deed.

"Actually, I come from Champagne. Are you Waldo, or not?"

"Who cares to know?"

"An emissary from the pope."

"Do you expect me to believe that nonsense? You look like a fraud or a cutpurse. Who are you really?"

"Then you are able to see me from deep inside that dark recess?"

"Do you think I make foolish statements as a matter of course? Do you take me for a fool, sir?"

Verily I did not wish to answer that question.

"Again I shall ask, who are you, or who do you pretend to be?"

"I am not one for pretense, hermit. I am Guy de Lagery."

"I have heard the name. It carries with it an unusual story. Is there any truth to that story?"

"There is always a bit of truth in the greatest of lies. Tell me, where can the grail be found?"

"How should I know?"

I shook my head in a futile attempt to relieve it of its ache.

"I meant, do you know of its location?"

"I am not privy to that knowledge, but I know someone who is."

"And where might I find this fountain of knowledge?"

Silence.

"You have a nasty attitude," the cavedweller uttered with conviction. "Has anyone ever told you that?"

"More than once. Please continue."

"Do you know the ruins of the ancient Roman Cemetery, in Rome, not the one in Padua?"

I did not. He explained that the cemetery was located adjacent to the ruins of the Coliseum.

And what was I supposed to do when I reached that place?

"Its caretaker, Lodovico, the Bald, can tell you what you need to know. Are we finished here?"

I nodded, assuming that he could see me somehow.

"Good. Never return. You look like a cutpurse to me."

I assured him that I had no intention of crawling into his den in order to steal away his amassed wealth.

"I am most relieved to hear it. You may go now."

So enraged did I become, that I bent down to put my head into the tree's bole, reach my hand therein, and grab him from inside of it, when I jerked my entire body back out again. There was no manner in which to enter that den without retching for days thereafter. I decided that a cautionary departure was the best for all concerned.

In Rome, after having apprised his holiness of the status of my activities, I went to the *cimitero*. I found the man in question removing the wild *flora* from around grave-markers for the recently departed (those who had died in the past three or four centuries or thereabouts). He was kneeling when I called to him.

"Are you Lodovico, the Bald?"

He arose and turned around. I cannot say which feeling burned within me, whether extreme heat or cold, for I recognized that face. It belonged to Fausto, though this one was considerably younger. Moreover, his pate lacked a single strand of hair. Perhaps because he noticed how I stared at his crown, reddened no doubt by many years spent in labour beneath an unforgiving sun, he patted the top of his head.

"My parents gave to me the name of Lodovico," he said warmly, "after a German uncle of mine, one Ludwig. And God took my hair from off my head when my years were barely three and ten. So I suppose I am he. What may I do for you, my lord?"

I was silent for a time, studying his appearance. His manner, I had to admit, was quite genial.

"How may I be of service, my lord?" he asked again.

"Bernard de Clairvaux told me to see Waldo de Toulouse, who in turn advised me to confer with you concerning the whereabouts of this grail."

"This Bernard I do not know, though everyone speaks well of his piety. And how is old Waldo?"

I winced.

"In truth, I cannot say. We spoke whilst he remained concealed in his cavern, thanks be to God."

"Once a hermit, always a hermit, as they say. And what did you require of me again?"

"The grail."

"Ah, that. I must confess to you that I do not have it."

I stared at him.

"You do not?! Then I have come all this way for nought? In God's name, where is it?"

"I shall tell you where it may be found, only if you will deign to answer a single question for me."

"What do you wish to know?" I asked, quite exasperated.

"Of all the books which, together, form holy writ, which one is your favourite?"

A query most strange, I thought.

"It would have to be *Genesis*."

"Why that one, if I might ask?"

"That is a second question."

"Please indulge me, good sir."

"I am more partial to beginnings than to endings."

He smiled, thinking about what I had said, savouring it perhaps.

"I do like that response overly much. Do you mind if I use it in daily discourse?"

"By all means, please do. Now, where might I find this cup?"

"O, everyone knows the answer to that question. It can be found in southern France, not far from the city of Toulouse, at the Tavern of the Three Sisters."

Near Toulouse, where my journey had originated?

"What is this *tavern*?"

"It is a tavern owned by three sisters. Was I not clear in my statement?"

"I thought—you understand—prophecies and all, they are usually rather vague."

"I was not vague, was I? I apologize if I were."

"In truth, you were not. So, I must look for a tavern—"

"Owned by three sisters, yes. Is there anything else that I may do for you, my lord?"

"No, I believe that I am done here."

"Good fortune to you upon the rest of your quest."

He returned to his gardening. I walked away, thought about it momentarily, then walked back to him.

"Explain to me one thing, if you will," I asked of him. "Since you knew where it was all this time, why did you not go there to acquire it, or for that matter, why have these sisters not revealed their secret unto the world?"

"You will understand that when you hold it in your hands, if you are deemed worthy of that special consideration. Fare well, sir knight."

Finding the location of the tavern proved a simple task. Apparently everyone knew of the unusual group of sisters who kept it. Once inside, I introduced myself to the proprietress, the eldest of the three sisters, (perhaps with an age of four decades or so), one Callipaea. An exceedingly tall and large woman, (in any and each capacity imaginable), she would have frightened Brother Michael, I think, and no one had ever frightened him. Her dark hair was loose and wild about her head and face, sometimes sticking to the sweat upon her full cheeks. But it was an honest sweat, and she was as proud of it, as she was to be the mistress herein. (Her husband had died a decade previously to the very day of my arrival. Initially, I could not say whether it were a satisfying marriage or no, though the sour expression upon her face led me to believe that it might not have been so, and furthermore, had left its telltale mark upon her—the presence of a single eye, whilst the other remained concealed by a dark patch of cloth.)

The middle sister, one Lacitenne, also with dark hair, though tied back and quite long, revealed to all a thin face with high cheekbones. She it was who had a glint in her eye each time that she looked upon a man, and with her tight garments, exposing much of her breasts to them, she was not averse to taking one or two upstairs to an empty chamber for whatever might come to mind, hopefully with a degree of appreciation for her exertions, in the form of remuneration, of course. She, too, had only one utilitarian eye, for the other was concealed by a dark patch of cloth.

The youngest, one Arcanthia, had cut her dark hair very short. Her single eye (yes, she, too!) was like a black fire raging within a white universe. And her hands were always filthy. She served all quite slowly in her walks to them, and when a man looked upon her, he decided never to lodge a complaint against her service, or lack thereof. In fact, each one made certain that she saw him smile as she left him to his food and drinks.

"We have been expecting you," Callipaea informed me.

She spoke loudly above the raucous noise, I thought, only to learn that it was her usual tone.

"Where is my ale?!" shouted one impatient customer.

"Shut your mouth, before I tear out your tongue!" was her rather adequate response. "Men," she said to me now, "are such pigs. Mine did this to me," she added, pointing to the location of her patch, "and he did the same to my precious sisters, until I cut out his heart. He was a typical man, and even died weeping like the scared little boy that all men are. You we shall have to see about."

I asked how she had come to know of why I was here. She pointed to Arcanthia, explaining that the youngest sister was a seer, of sorts.

"Visions and all that misery," she went on. "It is a terrible burden not only for her, but for all of us. There are days when she scares me. Have you ever been scared?"

"Once or twice perhaps."

"A brave knight like you? A Templar and all? You must not be all that special, are you?" she asked, obviously disappointed with my appearance and everything else about me.

"You must also know why I am here."

"O, yes, that misery-filled cup."

Misery-filled?

She called Arcanthia over. It was some time before the young woman arrived.

"Take this one down to the cellar, and try not to fall and break your neck this once."

Inside the dark cellar, lit only by the torches we carried, she brought me over to a niche, that had been cut into a wall. I put my torch closer to the recess, that I might better see what was inside of it. And when I did, I laughed. The cup was small, misshapen, bent, and falling into pieces.

"Where is it?" I asked.

"There."

"No. Really. Where is it?"

"That is it. That is what you seek."

"This thing? I would not give it to a child for his misuse."

"That is the main reason why my sister, Callipaea, wants someone to take it out of here. Her son, my nephew, is a curious little boy. He touches everything. God forbid that he should ever touch this!"

"For what possible reason should anyone be afraid to hold it?" I asked, looking back at the object once more.

"Do you not know? I thought Templars were smart. You should know about holy objects and all sorts of things like that."

"Only God possesses all the knowledge of the universe. It would appear that I am His ignorant servant."

"O," she agreed, nodding. "I thought as much. You do not look overly gifted in the mind."

"Really? I thought I possessed a certain air of intellect, as well as bravery, about me"

"I am afraid not. Very well. Since you have no idea about what it is that you are doing, I shall tell you. No mortal hand may touch it and live. In each generation, one of my male ancestors has thought the story ridiculous, so he took hold of it to disprove any belief in its miracle. Immediately thereafter, he choked unto death."

I stared at her, then at the cup.

"And *this* killed them?"

"Each time."

"How long has it been in your family's possession?"

"No one really knows. Some say that it appeared miraculously one day in the rootcellar of one of our ancestors. Some say that Mother Mary brought it to our shores after the death of Her Son, and how it came to be in our keeping is a great unknown to us. But I prefer to believe the story that Joseph of Aramathea's dearest friend was one of our ancestors, also a tavern-keeper, and was given the relic to keep until the day, when an immortal hand would take it from his safekeeping."

"But I am not immortal."

"Then, when you touch it, you will probably die."

"O."

Not very comforting, I had to admit; then again, I did not seek, (nor think that I would ever receive), anything that could remotely resemble comfort from any of these three. Still, I had given my word that I would complete this task, in whatever way was necessary, regardless of the consequences. I had lived a relatively long existence and did a great number of things of which I had been proud, (and some of which I had not been so proud). Still, there was much else that I had wanted to accomplish. And is that not true of everyone?

I reached for the cup and touched it.

At that moment, the cellar was replete with light. I heard a gentle singing, dulcet upon the ear, as from a choir of angels. And I heard a woman call my name. I did not know if the voice belonged to the mother of Jesus, or to my very own mother. The sweetness of the cadence was unmistakable. And the cup, the cup, itself, was gleaming silver, fully formed and fashioned as it needs must have been upon the first day that the smith had struck it.

I turned to my companion to show it to her, only to discover that she would not have seen it. She was upon her knees, her hands clasped, her head raised, her eyes closed, uttering quietly her prayers. As I stared at it, I realized how absurd was this entire situation. Many had sought it, died for it even, good men, holy men, yet here I was, a profound sinner, standing here, holding it. Suddenly I felt an overwhelming urge to laugh. And I did so, quite loudly, I believe.

I placed the cup in my sack, and the darkness returned. I helped Arcanthia to her feet. She embraced me and cried upon my chest.

Back upstairs in the tavern, only Callipaea and Lacitenne were present. The eldest, her hands upon her hips, grumbled at the sight of us.

"They have all fled when the lights came. Did you see how bright they were? Everyone thought the world had come to an end, and they immediately wanted to be home with their families. You would not believe the tears that men can shed when they are afraid. And what of you, brave Templar? Did you touch that thing and live?"

"I am quite certain that the grail was responsible for having emptied your establishment of its paying customers. I am also certain that if Jesus were here, he would beg your forgiveness."

She shook her head. "Probably not. All men think that the world is theirs, and women exist for their use and abuse. Would He be different, simply because He is the Son of God? I think not. So, you have what you came for. Good. Take the damnèd thing away, and maybe the rest of us will have some peace."

Before I departed, I let them know, in no uncertain terms, that should anyone inquire after the chalice, (even though it be a pope), not one of them was to reveal all that had transpired herein. Lacitenne was somewhat reluctant to agree, however.

"I shall shut my mouth for a price," or so she informed me.

"Is coinage the only thing that you whores understand?" Arcanthia asked of her.

"It keeps the wolf from the door, dearest sister."

Immediately did Callipaea take offense; she did not wish to appear that she had not provided well for her siblings.

"We may not be rich," she stated proudly, "but we do not starve here either."

"Receiving my share of a fair pittance is no way to live. I use what I have, and that is worth its weight in gold."

"That is not what I hear," Arcanthia added.

I tossed several coins upon a table and left the three of them in their tavern amidst the shouting and mutual recrimination, for, like it or not, it was my decision where the best home for this relic would be.

I journeyed to the land of the Scots, and to the manor that had formerly belonged to my father, and was now cared for by the son of Hughes de Payens. An elderly man, gray of beard, (and gray of eye as well), Sir Richard still carried himself with the same dignity that reminded me so often of his father's courteous, noble manner.

We stood in the caverns beneath the chapel. I placed the chalice (that I had partially covered with a cloth) upon a rock ledge, and wrapped it even more carefully now, so as not to touch it again. We both stood there, silently, regarding the piece or so that was still somewhat exposed. Its vision was not a particularly pleasant sight, as my companion's mouth was agape.

"It is a thing most disgusting to behold," he admitted. "Are you assured of its authenticity?" he asked, turning to me before he returned his sight to the loathsome object.

I had no doubt of it.

"As you may recall, Brother Guy, I have never disagreed with any of your decisions. This is something else again. To keep it here, away from the eyes of men, is to defeat its holy purpose, is it not?"

All rulers would claim hereditary rights to its possession. They would use it to justify any horror imaginable, most especially the conquest of other lands and the enslavement of other men. This could not ennoble the human spirit. Man was not yet worthy.

"You touched it and lived. God judged you and found you worthy."

"I am no angel made flesh. I am a servant of the Lord only, an unholy fool trying to find his way. Believe me, my friend, this is best for all."

"Brother Bernard will be most unhappy, I fear."

"I shall have to lie to him about it, as I shall do with the Holy Father, may God forgive me. You are the only other person who will take this secret with him to his grave."

"I shall not fail my father's dearest friend. After the object has been sealed behind walls of rock, will you perhaps stay a while and tell me of my father's adventures with you?"

He placed his hand upon my shoulder and walked along with me.

"I find it curious that the older I become," he continued, "the more I miss him, and the more I like the hearing of a tale well told."

"It will be my very great honour to do so."

And lo, it came to pass, that behind boulders and stones, rock and dirt, the chalice was sealed from the eyes of men, until such a time when they might grow into their worthiness for its possession and its use, whether they like it or not!

CHAPTER THE THIRTY-SIXTH,

in which I return to Princess Anna for the last time.

I regretted an omission in my personal education, *i.e.*, I had never learned Arabic, though it was a language spoken by the Muslim world; therefore, I began to take lessons in it from a Muslim prostitute, Amalia, who had converted to Christianity, left her chosen profession thereafter, found it extremely difficult to surmount the economic demands of the new Jerusalem, so returned to her former means of eking out a bit of currency necessary for survival. With hair of ebony and eyes so dark, that I would often be reminded of Anna whenever I stared into them, she had offered an arrangement that had always proven itself mutually beneficial for both. And there was more than a small degree of friendship and concern involved, during nights filled with an endless supply of drink, shrill laughter, much of caressing, and tender confessions. It was only when, after a single year, that she brought up a topic of conversation for which I was ill prepared; said topic was the possibility of marriage ... between us!

Marriage? With me? Surely she was jesting. Unfortunately, she was not. O, it was not a question of her origins that concerned me (lest you, dear reader, think it so). Since those first days here, many Christians had married Muslim women, who had converted to our faith. This practice had gone on for more than five decades; therefore, the novelty for such an event had long since worn off. And the topic concerning her varied experience was a quality that I found ... intriguing, shall we say? She would, after all, be quite capable of keeping the greatest enemy of all marriages, Boredom, far from our bedchamber. But you see, dear reader, it was the idea of being married at all. I had, for some time now, decided that it would not be a practical choice for someone who possessed neither castle nor lands as a legacy to leave behind. (I had recently given the manor in Scotland to the descendants of Hughes, with all the proper legal documentation appertaining thereto.) Besides, I thought that children should make their own way in the world, with a bit of help certainly. Moreover, I was not growing any older in appearance, nor did I feel any less vigorous. The idea of watching a wife age, whilst I would not know the thousand tiny aches of that experience, frightened me a little. I did not yet know everything that I was, or was becoming. I thought it best to leave things as they were, with a slight variation perhaps.

I proposed a new arrangement. Marriage was out of the question; providing a comfortable existence for her and any offspring that she might bear was not. (I found the prospect of raising a child and teaching him all that I had learned was more than a little satisfying, even though he would probably never be as proficient a swordsman as his father. {Who was, really?} There was still the possibility of a daughter though. And I knew that I would show her how to be bolder than the bravest knight, which fact would probably not be an easy thing for a husband with which to live. I supposed that all children would always suffer in some fashion, despite the father's best intentions.) Though my suggestion was not everything that she had desired, she agreed that it would be best not to have to work, as she tended to the child (or children) in a life of relative comfort and ease. Once agreed, we commenced our activities. Imagine my surprise when nothing happened. Rather, I should say, we kept each other busy, but there were no offspring. None appeared within the year, nor in the year following that one. Consequently, after two years of endeavouring to create a life, (and after three years together), we came to a mutual conclusion that our arrangement should cease. Instead of returning to her former occupation, however, she found a previous client, a stonemason, a diligent labourer and honest soul, (though plain of face), who had always cared for her and wanted her to be his betrothèd. She agreed to marry him, only after having confessed that her womb was barren. He did not care, for she was his alone, and he was happy with that arrangement. Imagine my surprise to learn that she had a son not two years later, then another, followed by a daughter, and several more thereafter. It would appear that her womb was not so barren as all that. It was then that I began to wonder about myself.

After hearing that Anna's husband had died, (not in war, but in the comfort of his own bed, damn him!), I decided that it was time for his widow and I to meet once more. She had been writing to me through all these years, alternating between pleas to return, and promises never to see her again, whilst her husband lived. As much as I desired to go to that fabled Byzantine city, I came to realize that no good could come from a meeting between the man who held her as his own and the man who did not. Reason had prevailed—a rare thing to be found in *Outremer*.

I decided to visit Byzantium. Brother Andrew advised against it. He saw how reluctant I was ever to speak of my experiences in that empire, and rather than press me upon the issue, he had respected my wishes and allowed me space enough for my privacy. (That was his way in all things.)

He had recently become Grand Master, when I congratulated him.

"It has taken twenty years, but the legacy of leadership that began with Brother Robert's installation, and that of his successors, has ended, thanks be to God!"

"Do not insult his memory, brother. That behaviour does not become you. And this position does not become me. It should be your tenure, not mine."

"Have I ever told you how much you remind me of Brother Hughes?"

"Once he told me that the Grand Masters can hold that position only temporarily, until the day when you realize that you should assume it."

My foolish friend could never take *no* for an answer, much like the aforementioned Heinrich.

Andrew worried that I was leaving on the morrow; there were no Templar Houses in that kingdom. If I should have need of currency, I would not be able to trade one of the Templars' *letters of coinage* for actual monies there. (These pieces of vellum had originally been his suggestion, though I must confess that I am the one who created the first of them, simply on a whim, hoping to dissuade him from their usage, once he saw how foolish was the execution of his initial conception. Lo and behold, he found instead the idea quite to his liking, much to my chagrin.) Being compelled to take gold with me was an antiquated practice, and most dangerous, was it not?

"I am touched by your concern; it is unnecessary."

Reluctantly, he bade me leave to go, though he demanded that I bring along several letters anyway, whether they could be traded for currency or not.

At Brother Andrew's suggestion, our Order had instituted the practice of using said letters to signify that a portion of someone's currency had been deposited with us, so that it could be shown to a member of our Order at a chosen destination. There it would be redeemed for the same amount. Moreover, he and I had struck upon the idea of creating numerous devices, approximately the size of small mallets or cudgels, which bore on their large flat sides several sharp, miniscule metal spikes in various numerical forms—*runic* letters. At the point of departure, a brother would slam the end of this hammer upon the letter. At the point of arrival, a brother would pour out a powder (or grains of sand, or whatever item was available), the better to see the amount. The carrier would then be given the monies, which the various patterns of holes represented.

The institution of this practice had been long and difficult, especially the tutorials in Norse letters for all members of the Order. Nevertheless, without the necessity for the transport of currency, voyages had become considerably safer. And most made good use of Brother Andrew's dream of a world filled with paper currency. I must confess, however, that paper neither shines like gold nor gleams like gems, and I miss terribly how pleasing to the eye those latter items used to be. What has progress wrought, I wonder?

Brother Andrew was a good friend and a capable leader, though a trifle too worrisome for my taste. Despite that, I miss his concern.

Anna now lived in a monastery, that her mother had ordered to be built some decades previously. I was not surprised when I saw it, for it resembled the Palace Komnenos in most aspects, except one of size; this structure was considerably tinier by comparison. The nuns were initially reluctant to lead me to her cell, until I introduced myself. They had heard much of me, and related that their prioress wanted to speak with me about the Holy Father, (and his assessments of the current state of Christianity in our very troubled world), after I had finished my meeting with the Princess Anna. They took me to a hallway and to a door, that looked altogether like every other one near it. But when I opened this door, I was not prepared for the capaciousness of the chamber into which I had stepped. I thought that I was back in the great hall of the palace, and it was then that I noticed the other doors again. There were six both to the right and to the left of the one that I had used for entry. A clever ruse, I thought, for they all led into this single room. The nuns excused themselves and left me to my own devices.

Surrounded by intricately designed cassocks, and enrobed in velvets and brocades, I saw her resting there, the starlight from a window full upon her. Was this how nuns of the present time were living in Byzantium? Espying me, Anna put her hands in front of her face.

"O, do not look upon me. I am so old! And still you are so magnificently young, as handsome as the day when first I saw you."

Despite her protestations, still was she lovely, though more the fading rose than the blossom of youth. I walked over to her, took her hands, and placed them down upon her knees; then it was that I knelt and caressed her cheek.

"I cannot find the words to tell you how enraptured I am at this moment. Verily, a woman's loveliness is beyond time. You have always been my most beautiful girl."

"O, I hate it whenever you know exactly what to say."

We stared into each other's eyes, then at each other's lips, then we kissed.

She pulled away.

"What do you want with an old woman like me? I have been the source of your pain, as you have been the author of mine. What can there be between us now, except an ancient anguish?"

"Anguish is much overrated in these difficult days. And I think that it has been easier for you than you are willing to admit."

"You know me so well, do you?"

"I know many things about you, except how you have fared these past few months. Why have you stopped writing?"

"Have you returned to me now only to torture me with your youthful beauty, as well as with your false accusations?"

I refused to be put off.

"Why have you not responded to my letters?" I asked once more.

"And still you write them, to commemorate that night so long ago. I think that your uncle was very wrong about you. Though you may not be a blessèd poet, you have the heart of one."

I stood up and walked away.

"I did exactly as you requested; I never returned whilst he lived."

"My memory may not be so acute as once it was. I am certain that I asked you to come here several times, despite his living presence."

I smiled at her.

"That was not what you desired truly."

"Foolish boy! Like all of your sex, you think that you understand everything about a woman's heart. The unspoken truth is that her heart will always remain a mystery to the man who loves her. That is why he seeks it out. It is the only time in his life that he is ever attracted to the unknown. And after he has lain with her, and grown old along with her, still is he convinced that he knows all there is to know about her. What blissful ignorance!"

"Though I may not be the wisest of God's creatures, I have endeavoured to do the best for everyone concerned in this situation."

"So my husband's feelings were as important to you as mine, or your own?"

I knelt at her side once again.

"I shall not fight him for you, my lady. His spirit should rest in peace. In truth, I have come here to offer you only tenderness. If you would rather that I leave, then I shall go, never to see you again."

"No! No!" she shouted, grabbing my hand. "Stay with me a while. I have so few visitors these days. My children have been by to sit with me only once, since I have locked myself away within this tomb."

She had, as I recall, four children; and that fact meant four times the usual grief for a parent, I was certain.

"Not even your youngest?" I asked.

"Daughterly devotion is not what it was wont to be in better times."

A strange truth, I had to admit. It was a common enough occurrence between fathers and sons, but between mothers and daughters? I thought it a thing most rare, especially considering that the mother had suffered the birth agonies, and a female child would understand (if not sympathize with) her matron's experience of them. Anna began to sob, admitting to me now, that she had not been the true mother of birth for her children; a serving woman had borne all of them, with the aid of the mighty Nikephoros certainly, and all three parties had agreed that Anna would become the mother.

For *this* I was ill prepared. It struck me dumb. She had never written a word of it, nor hinted at such a thing. How had it come to pass that she had not had children of her own body? What had prevented it? Accident?

She began to relate a story from her past, one filled with more pain than I had thought possible, both for herself, and for my participation in its cause.

The Empress had come to her, after the first holy warriors left, and I along with them.

> "Stupid girl! Have I raised you to believe that I would learn nothing?"
>
> "What have you learned?"
>
> "Play no innocent with me. I was your age once. I know how sweet a man can taste."
>
> "What are you say—"
>
> "Keep still. What excuse you have to make is of no consequence. The only thing that these barbarians have in common with us is their Christian faith. They are not fit to touch the hem of your garments. But you have let this papal nephew touch far more, have you not?"
>
> (At first uncertain as to how she would respond, the royal daughter decided to tell the truth that was hidden within her heart.)
>
> "I would never marry anyone, save a Byzantine."

"O, yes. And that day *shall* come to pass; make no mistake of it. But the matter at hand has nothing to do with marriage, does it? Either you have taken him to your bed, or he has taken you to his. I saw your face the day after at our morning meal. Did you think that I would never notice how much your life had changed in a single night? I have waited until he left. I saw how you watched him from the window of your room, and I saw the tears in your eyes after his departure. This man has defiled you. I shall not allow him to rob you further of your purity. You will never see him again."

"Never?" she asked, pained by what she believed was an irrevocable truth.

"Our court physician will come to you this evening with all manner of medicaments. You will eat nothing before his arrival."

"Why is he coming to see me?"

"No daughter of mine will give birth to a Frankish bastard!"

For many days thereafter she retched. Her stomach ached terribly. She could not control her bowels. If felt as if her womb had been shredded. She feared that she might never bear a child. In fact, this Venetian physician was so proficient in his duties, that he made certain as to Anna's lack of pregnancy. I have no idea what items he concocted for her dosage, but in time her worst fears were realized, as her womb was to prove forever barren.

And when, after the First Holy War, I returned, her mother had kept her prisoner in her chamber, where she could see me again only through the windows so high above me.

She could not have children, as much as she yearned for them, as so many women do. She was willing to do anything, make any arrangement. In the midst of her tears, the Lord took pity upon her, and gave to her Isola. More than a servant, she became a friend, yea, a sister even. This dear sister never betrayed the confidence that Anna had placed in her, not even upon the woman's deathbed. Ever good and devoted to her, she worried that Anna might become jealous that Isola lay with another woman's husband. Anna assured me, it was never a problem for her. She knew that Nikephoros loved her, that she was the great love of his life. Perhaps she did not mind, for he was not the great love of hers. Her only regret was that he had had a sense of that truth.

She ran her fingers through my hair.

"From our first night on, the memory of its event has given me no comfort. I loved my husband deeply. But when he spoke to me in gentle words of how I filled his heart all the more each succeeding day, it was your voice that I heard. When his body ached for mine, I remembered the taste of the sweat upon your skin. Easy for me, you say? I have watched my body grow enfeebled, my breasts hanging, my firm stomach wrinkled, fattening over a span of years. Yet you stand before me now, bound together with a timeless beauty so real, that it can exist only within a dream, the dream of my youth, when I was a girl filled with loving desires. Tell me, after so long a time, why do you come back to me now? Would you know all my secrets, my belovèd?"

"I shall never leave you. This I promise."

"Liar. But lie to me again."

We kissed.

In warm whispers bespoke our bodies each to each. So familiar, their touch was the path towards home. The tenderness of her lips confessed mercy now, beckoning me to taste of them as never before had I done. I caressed them, licked them, barely brushed against them with mine own. I took them, took her cheeks, her brows, kissed her eyes, smothered them, pecked at the small half-circles of her ears. Her little moans assailed then comforted me. I lingered long over each portion of her frame, neck, fingers, arms; they were all mine. Her breasts waited for me, called to me, as I took the nipple of each into my mouth. Softly I began, then hard I sucked upon them, wanting to taste each entire breast at once.

I kissed her belly. Flat now, (as she lay supine), she gave it up to me freely, without hesitation. I rubbed myself across it, hardening ever more. Slowly I left it, kissing along the path of tiny, pale hairs, which grew ever darker, the further down I traveled. I found her bud, caressed it, kissed it, licked it, took it into my mouth tenderly, as her moans echoed now throughout the vast chamber. There I stayed for a time, then twisted myself, placing my knees near her head. She reached up, taking me full into her mouth. Momentarily, she pulled me out and whispered to me:

"I adore how you grow when inside my mouth!"

Taking me back inside, she thrusted, as I did the same. Finally, when I could feel her about to burst, I pulled myself out from between her lips, then tickled her bud with my member. I lunged forward, inserting it between her *labia*, thrusting once again. More and more I pushed myself against her. More and more she returned each thrust. She welcomed me inside of her with an ardour that had never cooled, one that she had given to no other. I knew it. I would know it forever.

I sat up now, holding her as I moved myself, keeping myself inside of her. We sat, caressing each other's backs, lingering over each other's lips. I could feel the fluid rushing forth from me. I wanted to pull away. Her legs tightened around me, clasping my body to hers, refusing to give me leave, until I had poured myself completely within her, and she upon me. Then it was that she loosened her limbs, as we lay entwined, around, atop each other, kissing, caressing. The wanderer within me had fled, for this was hearth, this was home.

So the two of us were together once more. I think that we both knew it would the final time for us.

I did not want to leave her. (I never wanted to leave that night.) She told me that it was quite late, and perhaps I should really go. I tried to argue against it. She would hear none of it.

"For you certain things will never change," she said. "There will always be a spring and an innocent maiden at your side, as the two of you stroll through a field of wildflowers. You will bend to clutch a handful of blooms, present them to her, and receive your kiss of gratitude. You will be her first love. She will never forget you, when her hair is no longer fair, only gray. For you she will be but one more bit of pleasure or kindness. For her you will be a dream of a bygone age that was most pure, golden even. That is your gift ..., and your tragedy."

She caressed my cheek, then kissed me softly thereupon.

"You should leave me now."

"Do you not wish me to stay?"

"I wish it with all my heart. That is why you should flee from me. If you stay, my heart will break."

I dressed myself, watching her as she watched me. Fully clothed now, I turned to her again. She lay there, smiling coyly. I did not realize that I had been staring at her.

"What?" she asked softly, smiling.

"I was thinking that the one aspect of a woman that lingers with a man all of his life is her smile."

"Is that all? Nothing of my beckoning breasts, my languorous gaze? Where is the poet who stepped into this chamber previously? You have grown weary of me. Perhaps it is best that we have not lain overly long with each other."

"Say what you will of me, lady. You know that I love you."

"Foolish boy, coming here to a faded rose. Go home. Return to wars. Think upon me, if it pleases you. Do try to forget the bad things. I would like to believe that somewhere there is someone who recalls me fondly. Never forget that from now until the end of time I shall always be the one who embraces you in the darkness of the night. I pray that the remembrance will be a comfort when you need it most."

Even then her farewell was so much more than a matter of formality. Even then she could not bear to let me go, for the fingernails of her one hand were dug deeply into the flesh of mine own, as she bade me leave her with a dismissive gesture from the other.

It was the last time that I would ever see her alive. Over the years her fame as an historian was assured, thanks in large part to the voluminous biography that she wrote of her father, *The Alexiad*. She had refused to translate a copy of it into Latin, (it was a gift that she offered me freely), thus forcing me into a protracted struggle with her native tongue. After many months, my endeavours met with success. I enjoyed her work, though I did not always agree with her assessments. Somehow, miraculously, Emperor Alexios Komnenos makes no wrong decision, and is forever the victim of these vulgar creatures, these *Crusaders*. I was not in the least surprised at his portrayal. As brilliant as her writing is, it functions primarily as an *apologia* for the only man whom (I was then convinced) she ever truly loved, the only one who never disappointed her—her father. Noble in spirit, courageous in heart, and handsome in body, what man, after all, could ever hope to compete with such perfection?

She died in that monastery some years later, much revered, much admired, and certainly much remembered. Despite all that we meant to each other, we were tied together in flesh, memory, and spirit. I may have haunted her all those years, yet she haunts me still.... Still.

CHAPTER THE THIRTY-SEVENTH,

in which the Old Man of the Mountains requests my presence.

Not far from the gates of Jerusalem, (upon my return from Konstantinople), stopped a horseman before me. He sat tall atop his steed, and his skin was black as night. There were small scars upon his face. I did not think them to have been caused by wounds in war, as they appeared to have been wrought in intricate patterns. He stared for a time, then let fly a phrase that I have since come to recognize as having been uttered by the Turks during my first campaigns here so long before:

"*Allah akhbar!*" he cried out. ("*God is great!*")

At that very moment a chorus of horseman echoed it. I turned around to see a dozen more behind me. How had they appeared so quickly, and without having made a single sound to betray themselves? It did not matter. They would not take me willingly.

I raised my sword aloft.

"For God, Jerusalem, and St. George!" I shouted.

"We have greeted each other honourably, Christian," the man before me spoke now in Arabic, in a normal (though sonorous) tone. "You may put away your weapon. We are not here to fight. Our master requests your presence. He wishes only to speak with you."

"Who is this master?"

"All in good time."

I was taken to a castle somewhere in the mountains of Suriya. (I did not recognize a single bit of land or a tree, that would allow me to find my way back again, so remote up the steep cliffs was this structure.) *Masyaf* was its name. It reminded me somewhat of the Palace Komnenos, though this one was not overly wrought with decorative carvings; in point of fact, it had none at all. What it did possess were very many *donjons*, circumscribing it, and from which there were guards watching whoever dared to come near these keeps.

Inside I was brought to a very large room filled with many large pillows. Across several lay a rotund, little man, smiling broadly, revealing each of his teeth. His hair and beard were fully white. He reminded me of Fairuz, that irrepressible sword-maker, though this man was considerably older in appearance. Behind him stood dozens of men, hands at their swords, patiently awaiting their master's next order.

"Sit. Sit. By all means, make yourself comfortable! Would you care for a date?" the master asked, proferring a handful of the fruit to me.

I knew that if I were to decline, such action would be taken as an affront to his hospitality, therefore, I ate of one.

"I know who you are," he went on, "so you need not introduce yourself. Besides, I detest names. Our sires give them to us without knowing the great men or fools we may become, so they never really say anything about what a person is. Have you not found that so? I think that when a man begins to make his way in his lifetime, he should take a name that reflects how he thinks of himself. Take yourself, for example. When I look at you, I immediately think of the word, *asad.*"

(This was the Arabic for *lion.*)

"A lion is a noble beast. Unlike man, he kills only when he is hungry. From what I have observed of you, and heard about you, this is exactly how you kill—only when necessary. I like that. I like that very much. You do not waste your skills or your efforts. That is a valuable lesson from which all my boys would do well to learn. As for names, I have offered you a single suggestion. You may choose to ignore or revere it as you please. I really do not care. Where I am concerned, you may refer to me in conversations as everyone else does, as, *the Old Man of the Mountains.* That title is something that I like as well. It sounds mysterious. A man should have an air of mystery about himself from time to time, should he not?"

I nodded.

"And what is your preferred manner of address?" I asked.

"You are most respectful. That is a good thing. It has been my unfortunate experience that Christians do not respect those of other faiths, and sometimes not even those of their own. Somehow I knew that you would be different. You may call me, *my lord.*"

"My lord, why have you sent your men to bring me here?"

"How much will it take?"

"For what exactly?"

"For you to join us?"

I found the possibility more than a trifle off-putting.

"Why would you want me, a Christian, here? And what is your business exactly?"

"I have been thinking often of diversifying my membership, as I have diversified my list of clients. I used to take commissions from other Muslims primarily out of a sense of loyalty to the faith of my father and his before him, and so on. But it has never made much sense to me. To my people, yours are heathens and are cursed by God. To yours, mine are heathens and are cursed by God. If it were up to me, I would toss all these heathens into a single field, where they can kill each other. I think, maybe then, we would all have some peace. As much as your people are concerned, these days there are so many Christians about, that a good businessman would have to be a fool to deny himself gold, silver, or jewels simply because of a difference in faith. As you can plainly see, your people have been very generous."

He stretched out his hands, and the men stepped away to reveal a horde, the likes of which I had never seen. For every jewel, there were ten pieces of silver. For every piece of silver, there were a hundred of gold. And the torches reflected off each item, blinding me with their sparkle.

"Desperate men do all sorts of silly things, do they not? But let us conduct a bit of our own business, shall we? I have had my boys bring you here, so that we may speak freely."

He dismissed them. Once alone, he turned to me.

"As good as you are, you can become better. How would you like to learn to be so silent, that no one will see you, until you have your sword at the throat of your prey? If that does not appeal to you, how would you like to learn the art of poisoning? There are poisons, which can inflict pain in whichever part of the body you may choose to harm, leaving all others completely untouched. Some may cause your victim to retch. Some may deprive him of his life in a matter of moments. All these choices are open to you. Someone like you, who is virtually indestructible, may still find them of some use."

"Why would you call me that?"

"*Indestructible*, you mean?"

I nodded.

"O, that is one of the better stories about you, and there are many of them. I had to determine if that were true of you, so the date that I have offered to you was one that I had laced with poison."

He laughed. I jumped up, placing my sword at his throat.

"Now, now, let us not exhibit a short-temper with each other, whilst partaking of nourishment."

"What?! You tried to poison me!"

"It was merely a test to see the extent of a portion of your power. You cannot condemn me for that. Everything in life is a contest to see who is the stronger, or the more easily adaptable to change. I had to know what type of man was brought before me here into my kingdom."

"And what if I had died?"

"In that case, Christianity would have been deprived of its most powerful warrior. Many of my people would have been happy about that, to be sure, whilst many of yours would have mourned for years, I believe. But if it did not do its proper work, then such a warrior would indeed be the most dangerous man upon all the earth! Who would not want to have him at his side and call him ... *friend?*"

I held my sword there for a time, staring at his smiling face, before I removed my weapon from his neck and sheathed it once again. I sat back down.

"I serve the Creator of all things, and through Him, the Holy Father of Christendom, the pope. I cannot serve both them and you, though your offer is intriguing."

"I realize that you do not receive an offer like this one each day, so spend some time amongst us. Learn our ways. Give to us a single year, no more. If you are still determined to leave, then you may go with our blessing, providing that you keep secret the location of this castle."

"I have kept secrets for more years than you have been alive."

"Yes, I thought that about you, though I was uncertain if those stories were true either. You are most welcome here, *Asad.*"

I would have to write both to Brother Andrew and to his holiness in order to explain my forthcoming disappearance. Andrew might better understand my desire to become more skilled, but the pope would never approve. The latter would be convinced that I had become an apostate, and excommunicate me. The necessity for a tale might have to suffice, say, an opportunity to gain the confidence of the infidel, and thereby learn all of his secrets, including the locations and numbers of troops, as well as plans for future conquest. Yes, I thought that his holiness would understand that the most effective means of destroying an enemy might sometimes be burrowing under his skin like a loathsome insect, and weakening him, and sickening him unto death. Yes, the acquisition of any information that might facilitate such an action was a thing that he could support wholeheartedly, I believed.

So I agreed to spend time in Masyaf, wherein I came to know the Old Man's loyal followers as the *hessessim*, the *men without law*. Later history would come to know them by the work that they performed—the *Assassins*.

My training began under the tutelage of the very man who had stood before me in the road, one *Shabako*, a warrior from the ancient land of *Nubia* (the biblical *Cush*). I could not believe it when he informed me that his people had been practicing Christianity for more than six centuries. (In truth, I was somewhat glad to learn that I was not the sole Christian here, though equally surprised that we both were.)

"Why do you marvel at such a truth?" he asked. "Is it because of my blackness? Is it so difficult to believe that Christians may have more than one color? It has been my experience that people with pale skin tend to look upon those with dark skin as no better than animals."

Were his words true? After thinking about it, I had to disagree.

"I do not believe that God makes mistakes. If He has seen fit to populate His world with peoples of different hues, then He must have His reasons. Who are any of us to judge Him for His actions?"

He eyed me curiously. I was uncertain whether he thought that I had made a neat statement, or all that I had uttered were heartfelt.

"I cannot say that you and I will ever become friends," he mentioned at last, "but I find that I dislike you less today."

An improvement, I suppose.

Meanwhile, we continued with our lessons, the first of which was acquiring the skill to climb sheer rock faces.

Whenever the Assassins climbed, it was always with the aid of two ropes tied tightly together, and a third one tied only at one of its ends, the other at the climber's wrist. In this manner they would provide the necessary support for those who were not so lithe as were their comrades, whilst simultaneously promising additional security, should one fall.

For very many days did we both mount the steep cliffsides. I stumbled several times, though quickly recovered. Only once did I fall. (More of this soon.)

I came to learn that the forces housed in the mountains numbered perhaps ten thousand. The exact amount varied from time to time, as one or two might not return from a scheduled mission. These were the men only, for all of them had families, spread across the ranges. In caves or outcroppings, mimicking villages or towns, generations had made their homes. No one really knew how much time had passed since settlements had arisen in those places. Some mentioned a century, but most had no idea at all. Some said that the Old Man was the original founder, one *Hasan,* who had begun this holy mission long before, and that he had discovered the elixir for the prolongation of life, so that he would lead them forever. Some said that the Old Man was a new one, who took over each time after the death of the former. No one was certain about anything regarding histories. It did not matter. They were safe in this insular world, away from the petty plottings of petty tyrants. And they were happy.

Amongst them now I learned a portion of the tenets of their faith, that there were five principles, (or *pillars*), upon which it was based: that one had to believe both in Allah (God) and that Muhammad was His prophet; that one must pray daily (at least five times); that one must fast (at the requisite times), and obey the special dietary considerations, such as the prohibition against the consumption of swine (in this respect were they not unlike the Jews); that one must give alms to the poor (there was even a tax in place for this in each Muslim nation); that one must make a pilgrimage to Mecca (the place that Muhammad declared the *holy city of Islam*, after his armies captured it in that year of our Lord, 630). But what I found most interesting was that for the Muslim, the just, upon death, would enter into a sensual paradise, unlike any upon the earth. Once there, men would be fawned over by very many lovely virginal maidens. (No mention was ever made of how any women would be treated there upon entry.) I had to admit, its appeal was not lost upon this Christian, who would (hopefully) enter into a glorious realm of angelic chorus and much brilliant light at the specified time. As peaceful as my faith seemed to me, it was definitely lacking in the presence of lovely, nubile maidens. Ah, that was a most pleasant thought, was it not? And, I had to admit, I was more than a little envious of their steadfast beliefs on this particular issue.

Moreover, I discovered that Islam had split into two factions shortly after Muhammad's ascension into Heaven. There were a number of differing beliefs between the two; the primary one had to do with the position of their religious leaders, their *imams* and the like. The *Sunnis* believed that the word of Allah, as spoken by his prophet, Muhammad, and written down to form their holy work, the *Q'ran*, was of paramount importance. No one, no matter how blessèd, could alter the meaning contained therein. The word was of primary and ultimate truth.

The *Shias*, on the other hand, believed that their religious figures were the interpreters of their prophet's words. These priests were held in the highest esteem, for their views were the *alpha* and the *omega* to their adherents. And neither side was ever willing to acknowledge the possibility that some of its beliefs could (or should) ever be altered; *ergo*, religious civil war.

I must confess, neither *credo* seemed all that unusual to this Christian.

On one particular occasion, Shabako and I were practicing the art of making sturdy knots in the ropes. We were standing upon a vast mountainous ledge, that functioned as a temporary resting place for families. One of the children, (a little boy), had been rolling and smacking pebbles along the dirt, when he came close to the edge. His mother called to him, to roust him from his playthings, but like most youngsters, he ignored her, moving closer to the end of land and the abyss beyond. I was watching him, ignoring my tutor, who now lost all patience with me, and demanded that I pay closer attention. Then it was that I saw the boy stumble over a rock. I leapt for him, tossing him back towards the location of his family, as I fell over the cliff. I heard his frightened cries and the shouting of all about, as I saw projections of rock below me reaching upwards to pierce my flesh. At any moment I was to be impaled upon them, until I felt a powerful yank at my wrist. So strong was it, that it wrenched my shoulder from out its socket. I cried out in agony, as I felt myself being pulled up, and my arm throbbing. When I reached the ridge once again, I saw that it was Shabako who had pulled me to safety. (He had been holding the ropes at the time.) When he saw my shoulder, he warned me that it would hurt. What could possibly hurt more? Then he pulled and shoved my arm back in its proper place. I fell to my knees.

The boy's mother asked Shabako if I were in very much pain.

"He is stronger than he appears."

I stood up now, rubbing my shoulder.

"My body has already begun to heal itself."

"Allah is great!" he said.

"And merciful," I added. "I thank you, Shabako of Nubia."

"You would have done no less for me, Asad of Jerusalem."

When the Old Man met me after this event, he embraced me and kissed me upon both cheeks. (It turned out that the boy was his great-grandson.)

"You have saved my little one. You can ask me for anything, and it shall not be denied you. Riches? Women? Tell me. Young boys can be provided, if so desired."

I made him know, (in no uncertain terms), that I would have normally preferred women, except that I believed, (in my current situation), that they would interfere with my concentration. I was here to learn, and nothing should impede that process.

(I realize now, as I write these very words, how atypical my behaviour must have been, placing larger concerns before my pleasures and all. Perhaps I, too, had grown quite old, or even more serious about myself. Was such a thing possible?)

"Attention must be paid to each detail. I quite agree. So be it. You can ask anything of me at any future time, and it will be given."

He was indeed grateful, and was soon to become amazed at how quickly my body healed itself. But before he was to begin the lessons in the use of certain medicaments, he chose to share a particular herb with me.

The item he referred to as, *hashish*. (He laughed at how the rumour stood that his followers burned it and breathed in its smoke so often, that they were referred to as, *hashishim*. Of course, if that were true, not one of them would ever do anything except occupy himself with puffing it, in lieu of the performance of his labors. So foolish are the rumourmongers and historians!) This herb was placed inside a round glass object, where it was surrounded by water. A flame heated both. As the water vapours mixed with the smoke produced by the burning item, the two commingled. A long tube was attached to the top of this *hookah*, and one would inhale the smoke and puff it out. He showed me how to do so, and bade me try as well. It was a rare courtesy, and I could not deny him his willingness to share it. Often had I heard of the practice of inhaling smoke amongst certain peoples, though never attempted it myself. I inhaled and puffed out.

At first I coughed. Then began the most curious flood of sensations. My fingertips and toes felt as though ten thousand honeybees had stung them, yet my arms and legs were like water, still and undulating simultaneously. I could not see clearly. Each object upon which I brought my attention was as if surrounded by streams of hues in multitudinous variations. The entire chamber receded from me. Though the Old Man was seated near me, he appeared to be upon the other side of the world, and I was very much alone.

Was this a poison far more effective than the previous one that I had imbibed? I felt his hand upon my shoulder.

"There are many ways to see the world, Asad," I heard him say from afar. "We are in Masyaf, and the day is warm and full of sun. But you can journey from here. Can you see to the ends of the earth? Can you see the white water on the mountaintops there?"

I strained my eyes. Yes. Yes! I saw it. I was standing there, my feet growing wet, the winds whipping about me, blinding me. Everything spun.

"Return to me now," I heard him say.

I could see that he was staring into mine eyes.

"Are your feet firmly upon this ground, Asad?"

I felt myself floating, but yes, I had returned.

"Next time," he said, "you will go further. I have no doubt of it."

And travel far I did whilst in his kingdom, though occasionally without moving at all from a single spot!

He had set aside a room of Masyaf for research into various liquids and their effects. Everywhere were cabinets filled with vials and *philtres*. He brought one before me. It contained a greenish-bluish liquid that appeared to be constantly undulating. He opened it and waved it beneath my nose. I had to hold my stomach, so foul was its stench.

"First learn poisons by their appearance. Then learn them by their particular aroma. Each is different."

"And how is that one used?"

He lifted it up, watching its peculiar liquid move about.

"This one will empty a complete castle of its vermin in no more than a day. Should it find its way into a person's mouth, in even the slightest amount, it will be most unfortunate for the poor wretch. Exercise extreme caution with its usage. I cannot stress that enough."

He allowed me to smell of other substances. Only once did I linger over a specific one.

"You recognize this," he remarked, observing me. "How have you come to know it?"

I stepped back, marveling at its colourless quality. It could have been water, placed in a goblet by any of a dozen servants. No one would have known the difference.

"It was once used to kill a king."

I recalled the odd odor that had surrounded Godfrey's body. The rumours had proven true. If Baldwin were with me now, he would have smiled, satisfied that he had poisoned the *emir* in kind. Then an idea about that struck me.

"Some poisons leave a tell-tale scent," he went on. "Usually that means the practitioner was something of a novice. The professional never makes such poor choices. A substance that is odorless, colourless, and tasteless is always the best selection. A professional understands this, and would rather die than utilize such obvious *chemicals*."

I was unfamiliar with the term, *chemicals*. I was informed that the word was used to represent substances of a liquid nature.

"My lord, did you ever provide Baldwin I of Jerusalem, or any of his servants, with a chemical?"

Shaking his head, he frowned, but it was not because my query had insulted him, I was to find out.

"Never ask me about my past business. That information is strictly between myself and my client. Do I ask you how many Muslims you have killed? We are all friends here, and our pasts are our pasts. Look around you. Today is the world a different place. Here, in the mountains of Suriya, an old Muslim businessman shares a pleasant talk with a Christian knight. That bodes well for the future of all men. Is that not so? Be at peace."

The final lessons were those involving the ability to be somewhat invisible. Since most attacks were during the night, the obvious choice was to be clothed in fabrics of black or dark blue, or if one hoped to disappear in dense brush, green; if one had to contend with the desert sands, a golden-brown usually sufficed. That initial step was the easiest to take. It was a movement, that demanded far more in each possible way.

How could one step (let alone *run*) across any surface in absolute silence? This educational process did more than teach me how to do so; it taught me that one could do almost anything, if one believed enough in himself to accomplish said goal.

First I was to walk across sand, then across forest foliage (including leaves, branches, and tree trunks), then lastly across stones. Shabako told me this part of the training was the most difficult. Many took a great deal of time to learn how to do it, and some never succeeded. Most were simply not agile enough to perform the activity. It demanded more than a pair of nimble feet or hands, otherwise any juggler in a troop of itinerant players could have performed the necessary deeds in question, gaining the cheers of his audience and their coinage as recompense for his strenuous efforts. What it required was the determination to think altogether differently. One had to concentrate upon a redistribution of weight from the heel to the toe. And one had to do this with so much repetition, that it became an activity that seemingly required not so much as a casual thought.

That was how it was for me for months: practice, repetition, precision. It was far from easy. Many times did I fall and appear quite the comical fool. (And many times did Shabako shake his head, believing that I would never become the student worthy of the teacher's efforts.)

Eventually, I was to prove him wrong.

After the year was finished, I went first to Shabako to inform him of my departure. He had never been forthcoming about his personal history, and I hoped that now was the proper time to ask him of it, that I might better carry the memory of our association throughout the rest of my years.

"Will you tell me now, how you came to be here?"

He turned from me, then stared into the mountains.

"Only because now can I call you *friend*."

He went on to say that far from here lay Nubia. The crops had been plentiful there, and its people kind. Peace ruled at its borders. Then one day rode in a *caliph* and his army. He did not like the idea of a Christian kingdom in a Muslim world, so he decided to destroy everything that he saw. He burned the people and the buildings, and scorched the earth of its crops. Those who lived were scattered to the Four Winds, later to become some of the finest warriors this world has ever seen (of necessity, no doubt). The Master found Shabako as a boy, wandering in the desert, starving.

"I have been with him ever since," he concluded.

So, the Old Man had allowed the child to continue his original religious practice, though it was different from the rest of the community here—more evidence that this Hasan (or whatever his actual name was) had a far broader outlook of the world than that of anyone else whom I had ever known.

Initially, I wanted Shabako to accompany me, then thought better of it. Such a desire would have been selfish. This was the only home that he knew, and who was I to offer him another, in which he might always feel himself more of an outsider than he did amongst the families here?

I wished him well, as I took my leave, thanking him also for the benefits of his experience.

"We shall see each other again," he told me.

"Prophecy?"

"A feeling."

"May Allah walk with you through all the days of your life."

"And with you, Lion of God."

I went to the Old Man to bid him good-bye. He was saddened to see me leave. He gave me one more bit of advice, should I ever need his services:

"Find any *bedouin* trader anywhere. Make certain that he is with camel. If he is with horse, ignore him. It will make no difference in which nation you will find this trader. Go to the man and tell him that a message must be sent to the Old Man in Suriya, and that the messenger is Asad. You need do no more."

I thanked him for the education and the generosity. It was difficult for him to allow me to leave his company.

"Is there nothing that I can offer to change your mind?"

"My commitment is to my men. Should I be any less to them than you are to yours?"

I knew that he would understand. Still, it pained him.

"You will be in my prayers, Asad. Allah has been merciful with you, and He will continue to be, I think, until the end of time. May you never know anything, except His blessings!"

I took my leave, grateful for the experience, and both of us knowing that it was the last time that we would ever see each other. I hear that he still lives in those mountains. Perhaps he always will.

CHAPTER THE THIRTY-EIGHTH,

in which my Templar brethren (and so many others) are skewered upon the Horns of Hattin.

Nur al-Din had a lieutenant, in whom he had placed his full trust. This man was quite short of stature, (despite differing Muslim and Christian descriptions of him since his demise), with thick, black hair, eyes of the deepest brown, and a head the shape of which I always thought to be very nearly circular. (Odd form, that!) About him had grown many rumours (and legends). It was said that he was the wisest man upon the earth, and the most ambitious. It was claimed that he could look into the grains of sand and know instantly where, in *Outremer* he was, at any given moment. I cannot verify each tale, however, I discovered that he was intelligent and far more ambitious than any of his brethren, for he wanted not only the power to control his destiny and that of others; he also wished to unite all Islamic rulers under his own personal standard, thereby creating a lasting peace (or so he had hoped). Such a task would not be easy, for he was neither Turk nor Arab; his blood was Kurdish. And such a man might not be so readily accepted as the one ruler of legend who would bring about the creation of Paradise upon the earth—the *madhi* (or so the Islamic tradition went). Their reluctance to accept him was simply another obstacle in his path towards what he believed would be his own greatness. In a short amount of time only would he surmount their refusal.

This man was born in the city of *Tekrit*, on the border of the Eurphrates River. Upon his entry into this world the name given unto him was, *Salah al Din Yusuf ibn Ayub*, but history would come to know him by another—*Saladin*.

A string of victories brought him to the forefront of Islam. He conquered Alexandria, thereby assuming secure routes of pilgrimage to Mecca. When Nur al-Din died in that year of our Lord, 1174, no ruler wanted a mere Kurd to be in a position of control over so many territories, as the Kurdish lieutenant had

always believed that his supposèd allies would think of him. Despite their animosity, (or perhaps to quell it), he married Nur al-Din's widow. (And so fecund
was her womb, that she bore him seventeen children. Seventeen?! How did the
man ever leave the marriage-bed to find time to wage war?) The widow's acceptance of him meant nothing to the other rulers. They quarreled with him and
waged wars of their own against him. Moreover, they paid the Assassins to
remove him from his post, in whichever fashion that they might see fit, certainly.
To the dismay of all, he survived the attacks. In the end, his critics lost everything. Consequently, he soon commanded Suriya. By 1176, having attained
supremacy over Damascus and most of Egypt, he knew that everyone (including
those of Muslim birth) realized what was coming. Many of those in positions of
power, however, (both Muslim and Christian), refused to believe that a single
Kurdish warlord would accomplish what no Arab or Turk had ever been able to
do. So, they ignored him. That was their undoing.

At that time a young king sat upon the throne of Jerusalem, and had taken the
name of Baldwin IV. He was intelligent, clear-minded, and possessed of a thorough grasp of militaristic and political concerns. In all things was he well fitted to
assume his rôle. Only one impediment stood in the way of absolute acceptance
by all; this king was a leper. Despite his crippling disease, he was able to gain the
respect of many who came to know him. Only one at court made a pretense of
that respect. (Whatever he genuinely believed about Baldwin did not become
clear until later.) This man was the Patriarch of Jerusalem, one Heraclius, a man
of fierce determination and belief in the absolute will of the Church to accomplish the impossible.

Baldwin was in Ascalon with a goodly portion of his army, several Templars,
and some Hospitallers, late that year, 1177. The trip had been most trying upon
the ailing regent. It was becoming evident to him, (and to anyone who chanced
to be near him), that his arms and legs were weakening. It was a temporal concern (as it so often happens to be when one is ill) of how much time would pass
before he would be unable to use his limbs in any capacity. His pain did not deter
him from his appearance in that city, however, for it was an attempt to foster alle-
giances in a world that was changing far too rapidly for anyone's satisfaction. And
whilst engaged in pleasant discourse, word arrived that Saladin was marching
north. In Ascalon everyone girded his loins for battle. Soldiers stood guard at the
city's walls. Each man was prepared to meet the invader. But Saladin never
arrived there. It became evident to all, that Jerusalem was far too tempting a tar-

get to concentrate one's resources upon less important places. Finally, a Leper-King, his army, several Templars, and some Hospitallers, all watched, as Saladin and his army rode by in the distance, ignoring them, as if the city and everyone inside of it had never even existed.

I was in Gaza with others of my Templar brethren when we received word that Baldwin wanted us to join him in Ascalon. Apprised of the reasons, we wasted little time. We began our march north. Not far from Baldwin's encampment, we met our enemies in the ravines below a mighty Crusader citadel, *Mont Gisard.* In its shadow began a fierce battle. We were, I believe, equally matched with the numbers of our men. I wondered with what overweening pride had Saladin convinced himself that he could take the Holy City with a scant three thousand armed soldiers? Is that why he failed this time?

We surrounded their ranks, circling them as once their ancestors had circled me upon the arduous road to the Damascus Gates. And in our open palm, (so to speak), where they now stood, we began to close our hand upon them. They fought well, I had to admit. Yet it became apparent to me that they were determined to protect their leader at all costs. That ferocity was in their every stroke, each cut. Yes, they would die for him in this ... holy war, this ... *jihad.*

Despite their best efforts, for them, all was lost. They died, throwing themselves upon swords, axes, and arrows, in short, anything that would allow their leader to depart the field of battle safely. As I killed each man who came near to me, I caught sight of Saladin riding away. For a brief moment our eyes met. And each realized a truth about the other, (I was assured), that neither one of us would ever stop doing that which we both believed was essential to our lives. Revelatory it may have been for both of us; peace it could have never granted to either one of us. That is what it means to wage war, persuaded by rulers, friends, kinsmen, that the destruction of one's enemy is as inexorable as the mountainous tides in a tempest. And what fool would ever dare to stand against their onslaught?

As prideful a man as Saladin was, he never allowed his conceit to blind him to the truth of a failure. All things were lessons to him. And from his defeat at Templar hands was he to learn much.

298 The Lions of God

After three more years of incursions and mutual slaughter, (including the capture and subsequent death of one Grand Master), Baldwin proposed a truce. Somehow, miraculously, both Christian and Muslim agreed to it, for a time.

During the process of the aforementioned continuing negotiations, Heraclius took it upon himself to cross both sea and land for the sole purpose of convincing England's Henry II to take over as King of Jerusalem, since young Baldwin's disease would eventually prevent him from ever seeing full maturity. (The other noble families and Christian rulers would have never supported him in this, had they known; not that it mattered to the Patriarch, who would move Heaven and earth to maintain what he believed would be a potent Christian leadership in the Holy City. He was also quite disheartened by the endless machinations of those already in power in *Outremer*. He believed that an *outsider* might have a different and perhaps less ambitious outlook.) And perhaps this is where I might say a few words about the king in question and his rather famous queen.

In the ensuing decades since I had last seen Eleanor d'Aquitaine, she busied herself with considerably varied experiences. At first overjoyed at the official papal annulment from her dull (and devout) husband, she sought about for another man, whose temperament might be more akin to her own unique one. She found him in the personage of the King of England, one Henry II. Robust and passionate, (and given to an occasional bit of self-mockery), he was everything that Louis was not. And to this man she pledged her faith in marriage, and gave unto him seven children, two of whom (one of each sex) would never live to see their senior years, whilst two of the sons were apparently destined to become kings. It appeared that she had finally achieved a degree of happiness that she had so long sought. Yet despite her joyous satisfactions, she chose to ignore Henry's sometime-capricious, wanton, and violent nature. And after she had grown revolted by the presence of all the other women whom he had taken to his bed, (for this was one man whom she had allowed herself to adore beyond all possible limitations), as well as his political ambitions, (or lack of them), she led a campaign against him for possession of his throne, only to fail miserably. (I supposed that she had no idea how strong was her husband's desire to hold onto his territories, even though he was disinclined to increase them through conquest.) The consequence of her action was that she would spend fifteen years locked inside of a tower as belovèd prisoner of English hospitality. And it was to her husband that Heraclius had come in hopes of saving the Holy City, that was obviously headed towards its own ruin.

Initially intrigued by the prospect of so important a position, Henry contemplated the possibility for several days. No one knew with what inner debate the king eventually reached his decision. Had the offer been made to anyone else, (to Barbarossa for example), it would have been snatched up immediately. Henry was different. He liked England. In point of fact, he loved it. He loved the muck of the roads after a rainfall, and the squealing of pigs in their styes, as much as the blaring of geese faraway, and the neighing of his horses nearby. In a word, he was ... *comfortable*. Besides, had he not supported both Templars and Hospitallers twice yearly with revenues from his kingdom as penance for having ordered the execution of his former childhood playmate, the Archbishop of Canterbury, one Thomas à Becket? (So had the papacy ordered!) And when his advisors told him to decline the generous offer, since they felt that guardianship of that faraway city was far more trouble than it was worth, he concurred, most especially pleased with their counsel and relieved at his sagacious decision.

The Patriarch was quite unhappy. He returned to the Holy City, more assured than ever that it was now in its final days.

By 1185, Baldwin had become completely immobile. No longer could he see. No longer able to feed himself, he refused food from other hands. He decided to allow starvation to run its course. From what I have been told, his passing was not so horrific as it might have been, for he had lost almost all feeling throughout his limbs and trunk. Often for the infirm have I seen Death come to them as a blessing. When It arrived in his bedchamber, he was most thankful for Its appearance.

The first decision that Saladin made (after Baldwin's demise) was the dissolution of all treaties. What prompted this was the fact that he would have to maintain it with a woman, Baldwin's sister. And could he trust an emotional, headstrong female as much as he had trusted a weak (albeit honourable), clearheaded Christian king to keep the peace? Absolutely not!

It had turned out that, as a matter of form, Baldwin's throne was now occupied by his eldest surviving relative, namely, his sister, Sibylla. Along with her husband, Guy de Lusignan, (who had served as an advisor to the king), she proceeded to rule over a city that was now constantly being threatened. Though everyone was enamored of the goodly queen, (for she was gentle of manner and kind also to the poorest of the poor), they watched as this dutiful wife conducted herself with the utmost reliance upon her husband's assessment of current events. In any other situation would this fidelity have been a thing to admire. Unfortunately, Guy was never the wisest of men in the easiest of circumstances, of which these certainly were not. When his good friend, the Count of Tripoli, ordered a Muslim caravan to be slaughtered, (to whom Guy had given his assurance of complete safety whilst passing through the Count's territories), the foundation was laid for another battle.

When the truce was ended, Sibylla called upon her husband for his advice. He, in turn, called upon the Templars, whom he trusted completely. It was Gerard de Ridefort, our bellicose Grand Master, who urged him to present Saladin's head to the Patriarch, when the time came. Guy de Lusignan pleaded the case for war, and Sibylla agreed. Unfortunately, no one else in the surrounding kingdoms of *Outremer* thought that the nobleman's suggestion had any merit, for they knew of his distinct lack of political acumen. As God or Fate would have it, this was the one particular circumstance when Guy was most correct. Pity, that.

By 1187, three Christians were tossed into Saladin's tent. Only one was tied up with a cloth stuffed into his mouth. Gerard de Ridefort, Guy de Lusignan, and I (the one trussed up like a partridge at feast) were all upon our knees. One soldier stood over us. Saladin asked him which one was the man who could not die? The soldier pointed to me.

"He looks like any other Christian. Are you certain this is he?"

The other man nodded.

"I would never know that his age is more than a century. Allah has been most generous with him."

He gave the soldier leave to go, then walked about me, studying me for a time, before staring into mine eyes.

"It is said that you are fluent in my tongue. Good. Then you will understand my every word. You have killed very many of my men today. They were fine warriors all. Had you been any other man, you would have been my first execution. But Allah has seen fit to grant to you a kindness that He has given to no other. For that reason, you are, perhaps, a holy man. I do not kill holy men, unless they have taken up a sword against Islam. That is a prohibition from our holy book. I would not risk Allah's wrath against me by committing that atrocity. Yet you have used your gift against us. I cannot so easily forgive your presence here today. Helpless, you will watch quietly, as I dispense my swift judgment upon your brethren."

Brother Gerard looked over at me. His lip was split, and it must have been causing him utter anguish. Nevertheless, he spoke to me of his shame, for having ignored my warnings.

"Forgive me, Brother Guy. I have allowed my pride in my judgments to disregard your own. For that reason, today am I brought low. I shall accept my punishment with head held high, as all Templars should. Look after our brethren. Go with God."

He began to pray now. Saladin watched him and said not a word to me. (I was to discover later that the ruler understood many languages, including my own, however, he spoke only Arabic; all other tongues, he believed, would be a sacrilege for a faithful Islamic adherent to utter.)

"Surely goodness and mercy will follow me all the days of my life, and I shall dwell in the house of the Lord … forever."

Saladin turned to me.

"Has he finished his prayers now?"

I nodded.

With swift stroke, he removed the Grand Master's head from off his neck. Blood splattered across both myself and Sir Guy.

"I never liked that man," Saladin spoke quietly, looking down at the head, as it was tumbling across the ground. "He never had anything nice to say about my people. Ill-mannered, was he not?"

He then assured us that any surviving soldiers were now being beheaded outside. However, inside this tent Guy watched the head slow its pattern of rolling. The colour had fled his face. I had no doubt of it that he believed himself to be next.

Saladin bent down and removed the cloth from my mouth.

"Tell this king that the two of you are free to go. If you are wondering why I have allowed him to live, you may tell him that I do not kill kings, unless no other choice is open to me. My men will lead you away from here. Once past our borders, they will cut loose your bonds. It is said that you are a man of honour. I want your promise that you will not harm them."

I promised him that I would not.

"There is one other request that I would ask of you."

After he told me what it was, he asked if I would agree to this as well, which I did.

"Tell this king further that it was not I who defeated his forces today; you are all the victims of your own betrayal. I have no doubt that we shall see each other again," was his form of final farewell.

"When we do, you may address me with the name by which my Assassin brethren know me—*Asad*."

"You have made a curious choice in your friendships along the winding path of your life. As concerns your name, I shall not forget it. It is one that we have in common."

Once at the border, the soldiers cut my bonds and rode back in the direction of their leader. Guy turned to me.

"What did he say to you at his camp?"

"He wants official chroniclers to write that upon this day, Saladin captured you and held you for a single year, before you were ransomed and returned to your people."

"Of what possible use could that lie be to him?"

"Do you not see? He wants control over history, including our versions of it. And in this history will he appear as the mighty defender of the true faith."

"We shall certainly not give this power to him. Who does he think he is?"

"We shall!" I averred. "We are men of honour. He knows that. I gave my word. It is one of the reasons why he allowed us to leave."

"O, this has been a most terrible day. Surely there is more that we could have done—"

"I beseech you, my liege, leave off this oration. No words will ever be fitting enough."

"Quite so. Quite so."

Before the Sea of Galillee lay the vast open plain of Hattin, containing two large hills, or mounds. Whenever I rode past, I considered them as the nurturing breasts of Mother Earth, not a pair of deadly *horns*, as everyone else called them. And it was there, upon the fourth of July in that year of our Lord 1187, that many Christians would make the final journey to their Maker.

Sibylla's husband, the Grand Master, and I were at the palace in Jerusalem, proving once again that among three proud men one might ofttimes find four opinions. (We had word that Saladin was amassing his troops for a major battle within the week.)

"This is lunacy!" Gerard bellowed. "We shall lose valuable days, if we go around the Horns of Hattin. It makes perfect sense that we cross over them."

"And what if this information is wrong?" I asked.

"Conrad of Tyre swears by it," Guy interjected.

"If he is so certain of his facts," I urged them to recall, "then why is he so reluctant to join us?"

"That is a fair question, Grand Master. How do you respond to it?"

"He is concerned with the security of his kingdom, as are many others. He is sending us one thousand of his finest troops, despite that."

"A thousand from him," I averred, "two thousand from someone else, and when Saladin comes to Jerusalem with twenty thousand, shall we go out and welcome him with song and dance?"

Guy was most unhappy with my demeanor.

"Man for man shall we match him equally," he swore.

"With the addition of our brethren and the Hospitallers, will this heathen face his mightiest foe! Victory will be ours."

Perhaps, I could not help thinking, but at what cost?

Throughout many decades had I been fighting, and still a Grand Master argued with me over who knew more about the tactics on positioning of troops in war. If my appearance were older, perhaps he would have lent my judgments more credibility. Moreover, he refused to listen to my advice that the brethren should not be clad in full armour in such oppressive heat. And when row upon row of the enemy surrounded us, closing in to form a single fist of their own, how much did Gerard regret his choices?

With enough troops to flood an entire nation, Saladin rode into the holiest city. Upon the Temple Mount he stopped to begin his oration:

"As the boy-king, David, united his tribes to form the Hebrew people, so, too, have I done the same for my blood. Jerusalem was the center of his kingdom. Today we have made it the center of Islam!"

And the roar of approval swelled across the city and traveled the world over.

The *débâcle* of Hattin still afresh in our minds, Guy and I rode away from Saladin's guards. Since we could not return to Jerusalem, we took refuge in Gaza, where we set to commence a period of mourning for our lost comrades. We bewailed their deaths for more than a year. The loss of Jerusalem haunted us for the rest of our lives.

CHAPTER THE THIRTY-NINTH,

in which commences the Third Holy War.

Of Eleanor's sons who had come of age, it was only her eldest, her first, who would achieve a notoriety as great as that of his mother, though for completely different reasons. This man, Richard, would be held dearly in the hearts of the English for centuries to come. They would know him as, *the Lionhearted. Eironic* as that may be, (for rarely did he speak a word of the English tongues in his lifetime), he preferred instead the French nomenclature given unto him by his dear mother—*Coeur de Lion.* And it was this Richard, now king, (upon the death of his father), who would journey to *Outremer* to fight perhaps the last heroic holy war, and so leave his mark upon history for all men to see.

Of him I shall say that his hair was russet, interspersed with flecks of his mother's red; and he was quite tall, taller than his own sire, though shorter than the Norman giant. He carried himself with the dignity that befits a true soldier of the realm, for he was in all things a knight, with the most erect posture that I have ever seen, even when astride a horse in the midst of battle, even with full armour.

He stood now in the cathedral in Rome, that had been built to honour the fisherman, Peter. Beside him was a much smaller man, somewhat bent by his age—Pope Urban III. The latter was holding a scroll.

"I have completed the canonization, as I told you that I would. Henceforth will Bernard de Clairvaux be known as Saint Bernard. I think that he would have appreciated the efforts, which so many have made on his behalf. I cannot understand why none of my predecessors saw fit to do this. The church takes overly long to make a decision, does it not? Of course," he whispered, "never repeat that last statement."

"I regret that I shall not be here to witness the ceremony tomorrow, your holiness."

"Nonsense! You must stay. Please write to your mother and tell her that you are old enough to make your own decisions."

"She has never been wrong about Barbarossa. He will not be happy until a German standard is planted upon French soil. I have little choice but to return."

Before the Holy Father had an opportunity to respond, a Templar came running down the aisles, brandishing a scroll, and shouting:

"Your holiness! Terrible! Most terrible!"

He thrust it into the pope's hands, then stopped and struggled for breath.

"Calm yourself," the pope told him. "Who has sent you?"

The tired man swallowed, then spoke:

"The Patriarch of Jerusalem. O, it is terrible. Most terrible."

"You keep saying that," Richard commented. "Has something happened in Jerusalem?"

"Everything. It is no more. Saladin has captured it. Your holiness, Muslim armies are in the Temple!"

Pope Urban III perused the message, then looked at the messenger, then back again. This he did for several times.

"What shall we do?" the man asked him.

Before he could speak, Pope Urban's face turned a ghastly white. His mouth fell open, as he clutched at his chest, then fell into Richard's arms, never again to take another breath.

"O, my God in Heaven!" the Templar shouted.

"Leave now. Tell your Templar brethren that King Richard will soon be fighting at their side."

It was the year of our Lord 1187, and Richard knew that *Kaiser* Friedrich would have to wait; Jerusalem needed him, and unlike his father, he was more eager than the sire had ever been to rescue it.

Whilst the revelation of a holy war's necessity had struck Richard in Rome, in Strasburg, Barbarossa, now a ruler in his sixties, had assembled his knights, many from the noble families, together with his bishop. All were present to take up the cross as emblematic of their will to wrest Jerusalem from the hands of that most detestable infidel—Saladin. Before a word was spoken, or a ceremony begun, a mystic entered the grand hall. Hildegarde von Bingen was clad in shredded garments of a blue so dark as to be black. Unkempt, her hair was multi-hued, like forest-growth in mid-autumn, before the first chill of winter has stripped the foliage from each branch. Her feet were unshod, naked. And her eyes, O, her eyes were a sight most terrible to behold! Of those who were there to witness her appearance that day, some remarked that her eyes burned like scalding timbers piled high for a funerary bier; others commented that there were two empty orbits, where once had eyes made their home; still others saw nothing of consequence in a pair of darkling eyes in the brilliant light of morning.

She walked up to the Holy Roman Emperor, (the *heiliger Römischer Kaiser,* as he called himself), and stopped before him. She began to speak, and her voice was like a whisper, yet audible to all:

"The end of days has begun. The wolf has ravaged livestock, and the farms have been cleared. Still he comes. The floods do not drown him; the winds do not whip him; still he comes. In the blinding sun of noon will he spit his bile upon the Templesteps. Only the Son of Man will rip his head from off his neck and smear Himself with the creature's blood. And day shall become night, until the holy brotherhood has redeemed us in the eyes of the Son."

She collapsed. Several went to attend to her. The bishop turned to the ruler.

"The Templars?" he asked.

"The Templars," Friedrich replied, nodding.

With a fleet of five and twenty ships, Richard landed at the isle of Cyprus, where he drank, perhaps, from his first cup of betrayal. The Greek governors there never treated the Franks well. (They continued that hoary Byzantine tradition of ridiculing anyone who had the misfortune to be born of any blood other than Byzantine.) Upon his appearance there, Richard had no idea that word had already been sent to Saladin to inform him of the current situation, courtesy of the governor. Since the man made no pretense of his disaffection for the French/ English regent, Richard admired him his sheer honesty, before beheading him. Thus began the first battle in *Outremer.* It did not last very long.

Shortly thereafter, the isle was Richard's to do with as he saw fit. Since my Templar brethren wished to retain it as another base of operation, (due to its proximity to Byzantium), I was asked to negotiate with Richard for its purchase.

There, in Cyprus, at a palace that had formerly belonged to its governor, Richard and I met for the first time. As a fit place for our discussion he chose a simple room, small, with a low ceiling, free of decoration, and designed to be little more than a functional area. We sat together at a small table, his guards posted outside, as were my comrades.

His manner was affable, his conduct respectful.

"It is a distinct privilege to meet you. My mother has spoken of you often."

I did not know if this were an introduction to a swordfight for what was an offense against his mother, whether imagined or not.

"O? What—what has the queen mother said of me exactly, if I may ask?"

"She has never forgotten your kindness to her. Though other lords, as well as some of your brethren, treated her most disrespectfully, you gave to her a kind word. You are ever in her prayers."

"I am most relieved—I mean, most *grateful* to hear that."

"Often she has told me that, had circumstances been different, the two of you would have become great friends."

"I shall always consider her a dear companion. When you write her, please let her know that."

He spoke proudly of how his mother and the other wives of nobles, (and all serving-women), had come to *Outremer* dressed as Amazons, a sword in each hand, gilded sandals upon their feet, and a single breast exposed. In truth, I had no wish to shatter the illusion that he had either created or heard, especially since it gave him so much obvious pleasure to relate the telling of it. But as unique as Eleanor may have been, she was no Penthiselea, Queen of Amazons. Would that she had been!

"If I may prevail upon you, Templar, would you tell me one quality of hers that you recollect with fondness?"

I struggled with a number of possible responses before relating a truth, even if it were not a complete one.

"She was, if I remember correctly, a most passionate woman. Yes, she was passionate about all possibilities, which Life has to offer."

"You are most kind. She will take joy in that assessment, I am certain."

Our greetings done, we began our negotiations. Initially, he tossed out the extravagant number of eighty-thousand *dinars*. After several discussions, I was able to convince him that forty-thousand were the more appropriate figure. He agreed (without much argumentation, I might add). Now in our hands, we did not retain it for long. In time this isle would prove to be too tenuous a thing to hold forever, so we sold it eventually to Guy de Lusignan, who was most generous with his purchase. (I negotiated that transaction as well, and for far more than I had paid for the item!)

Saladin feared our transactions, for a Templar foothold so close to Acre posed a continuing threat. Finally, Richard had agreed to the price, for all Christians took delight in doing anything to the Muslim regent that was even the slightest bit irksome.

As Richard sailed off for Acre, he did not know that, at the very same time, Barbarossa was nearing Antioch. (Against the advice of his nobles, the German warlord had decided to cross to *Outremer* along a territorial route, as many armies had done during the First Holy War.) And during a pleasant day, not very different from any other, really, he ordered his cook to prepare a meal that was fit perhaps for two kings (or emperors). It was an unusual request, however, the regent was a rather large man, whose appetites for war, women, and food were not unknown to all. The cook complied. Once completed, the varied dishes were set within his tent. There he sat down and devoured the entire enormous repast, as if he had been ravenous for very many days (which thing he was not). Then he betook himself to a lake nearby, as he wished to feel the mud of its bed oozing between his toes and the splash of cool water upon his heated frame.

At its deepest point the lake was no higher than the length of the lower portion of a man's leg from toe to knee. The emperor's clothing lay upon the bank, as he walked into the beckoning liquid. He bent down and lifted it into his palm, then poured it over his face and shoulders. He was laughing when a sudden ache struck him in his stomach. At the time there were no soldiers about, for their leader wished always to wash in absolute privacy, especially when completely unclad. For that reason, they were afar, and it was some time before they heard him calling for them. When they arrived at last, they found him with his face down in the water. They pulled him out, yet could not save him.

His loyal followers did not know what to do next. Since he had never placed a second-in-command to lead his troops in the event of his death, (which may have had something to do with his reluctance to share even the slightest portion of his authority), there were as many ideas posited as there were men present. Eventually, some began the trek homeward; some saw their master's death as an omen from God, and left to join Muslims in their fight against the *Christian* infidel; still others wrapped up his body and began the journey towards Acre, whereat they hoped to unite with Richard's forces. Thus ended *Redbeard*'s mighty excursion into the path of holy war.

I cannot say if the emperor were the victim of a poisoning, for you may recall, dear reader, that such activity was not unknown in that part of the world at that time. I can say (with absolute conviction) that I have never taken to water following so quickly after a meal, since I learned of the events during that fateful day.

Richard arrived at Acre during the first week of June, the week of Pentecost, with all his ships, soldiers, and supplies. Trumpets blared along the shore, and at night, bonfires blazed throughout the Christian encampment. Everyone believed that a new Christian age was dawning, led by the man whom everyone called *Coeur de Lion*. Now began the siege against the city. It lasted one month only.

Decades previously, when Barbarossa first came to *Outremer*, he had brought with him a young knight, poor, (without benefit of family or its support), whose ambition was almost as great as that of the Teutonic emperor. And when said emperor decided to return to the land of his birth, he left behind the young knight, who was actually reluctant to leave a potential source of riches. In time, the poverty-stricken Conrad de Montferrat became the wealthy Conrad of Tyre. And it was he who negotiated now this truce of Acre.

The Muslim-controlled city would have to agree to the following: the city, its inhabitants, all ships in the harbour, several hundred Christian prisoners, a ransom of two hundred thousand *dinars*, and four thousand gold pieces to be given to Conrad (for his magnanimous efforts on behalf of the holy warriors of Christianity). And the *emir* agreed. It was rumoured that Saladin wept upon hearing this. I am here to tell you, dear reader, that he confessed to me the absolute truth of *that* circumstance.

Shortly after this, Saladin sent his brother, Al Fadil, along with a translator, to open negotiations with Richard, primarily for the release of several thousand of his troops, who were in Acre when it fell to the latter's control. After having conversed with him, Richard sent for me. I rode cross the field, and entered the large tent, as he asked me to sit with him. He had been thinking a goodly while upon my accomplishments, most especially my ability to speak a number of different tongues. This *Arabic* grated upon his ear worse even than the guttural German of his former adversary, or the English of his peasantry.

"This English patter, with its incessant usage of *goddamn* this or *goddamn* that, as harsh as it may be, is pleasant compared to this Muslim equivalent of a language. I cannot fathom how you have ever been able to comprehend any of it."

I assured him that I had had a great many years in which to study it.

"I hope that I may call upon your fluency."

"How may I serve, my liege?"

I was to open negotiations with Saladin, first through his brother as intermediary. Al Fadil related that his brother wished to speak with me personally. Any negotiations would have to be handled in that manner. I was invited to be his brother's guest in all the lands controlled by the *Ayubbid Dynasty*, as his brother called the line that he, himself, had founded with his own assumption of royal power. I accepted readily.

I led a contingent of no more than twenty of my Templar brethren to *Kahira* (*Cairo*), at the outskirts of which we entered a former Byzantine palace, (eight centuries old, I was to learn, where, it was rumoured, several early drafts of Holy Mother Church's Nicene creed were put to vellum), that now housed the royal court of the *Sultan* of Egypt, Saladin.

"It is welcome to see you once more, Asad," he proclaimed from high atop his throne.

"Your highness has honoured me with an invitation. How could I resist it?"

"We have much to discuss. Your brethren will be attended." He clapped his hands.

I watched as guards led them away, along with everyone else, who had been standing nearby. Initially wary, I nodded to them that all would be well. The entire hall grew suddenly empty, save for the two of us. He stood up from his throne and began to walk down the steps leading to and from it, bidding me to walk beside him.

"Your people are much concerned with ceremony and position," he said, pointing to the seat of power. "My predecessors have been equally guilty in that they have kept it for so long. I am afraid that the more I sit upon it, the more I forget our custom of sitting upon the ground, as all men of humility should position themselves before Allah, when not prostrating themselves before His glory, and the more I like to walk up to it and stare down at others, who would set themselves higher before me. More than any other of your customs, that creation is the most dangerous, I fear."

As we moved up the staircase to the battlements, he remarked that the winter would be a bitter one, for all the signs had been present to reveal it thus. Once outside, we gazed across the grassy plains.

"So, you know the Assassins," he commented.

"I have known their friendship."

"Tell me, does the Old Man still lead them?"

"He does, as much as I know it to be true."

"An independent people, they are. I have sent councilors and soldiers from time to time to the very mountains in which they are reputed to dwell. I had hoped to enlist their services as good Muslims for the glory of Allah. None of my people ever returned."

I informed him that they were without mercy for all whom they believed had committed offenses against them. And they were likewise fiercely loyal to each other, and to their friends.

He stared at me.

"I have no doubt of it."

He spoke proudly as he pointed to several new bridges in the distance, the construction of which had been recently completed.

"I have hoped to be worthy enough to bring honour to the legacy of my fore-fathers," he averred.

"Is that why you have declared *jihad* against my people?"

He eyed me curiously, perhaps confused by the question.

"Your tone is accusatory, Templar. You should make certain to use your words properly. The first *jihad* of any Muslim is the one against his own weaknesses. If he cannot conquer those, then he brings dishonour upon himself, his family, his entire people, his Prophet, and Allah. The sin is fivefold, like the fingers of a hand. If a single finger is broken, how can one grasp at anything? The entirety becomes useless. In the heart of a sinner are all things rendered useless."

That might have explained the first *jihad*.

"What of the second?" I asked.

"Each succeeding generation should never forget the insults given to its forebears. Understand this: we are as proud of our fathers, as you are of yours. It was your holy father, a pope, who declared holy war first. However, I am certain that you know these wars have never really been about fundamental differences between two faiths. The story is about sultans and kings. One ruler wants another's land, in order to create an even larger empire than the one that he governs currently. Faith is a tool that we use against each other to stir the anger of our respective peoples, so that they may fight our enemies and thereby help our empires to grow. It is the same dream for all men who would hold sway over all other men. As difficult as it may be to believe, despite our worst ambitions, we create these kingdoms for the purposes of order. Without the guidance to be found in them, all men would be little more than beasts. It is a terrible truth, though a necessary one."

"Is that how you conceive of civilization, as a product of kingship? Where is your respect for other faiths and all which they have done in the name of God?"

"You read your holy books, yet do not understand them. Judaism is the source, the wellspring from which all else came; Christianity is its child, the seed that grew to nourish the world with belief in a divinity made flesh; Islam is its spirit of absolute faith and sacrifice. In Islam we nourish the cultures of others, as well as our own. In what Christian kingdom can a Muslim or a Jew build his house of worship free from persecution?"

"Not every Muslim ruler believes as you. The *Almohades* of *Córdoba* have long waged war against both Christian *and* Jew."

He shook his head. "That is their sin, not mine. Abraham was the father of many nations. From him came all the Hebrews and all the Muslims. Though our mothers may have been different women, we shared that same father. In our lands Jews have always lived peacefully. We have respected them, as well as the Christians, until the latter tried to take our land."

"You claim to rule with absolute concern for all others, whilst charging a tax to those of other faiths who live in your lands, since it is not the faith of its ruler."

"We may tax them, but we do not force them into the position of moneylenders, as you have done with the Jews, only to vilify them for doing the only work that your kings and priests allow them. It might interest you to know that the court physician here is the finest in the world. He is also a mathematician, an astrologer, philosopher, and *rabbi*. So great is my trust in his knowledge and abilities, that I would have no other man, less capable albeit Muslim, tend to the health of my family and that of the entire court."

Had he been any other regent, his pronouncements concerning his acceptance of other faiths might have made me laugh. From the stories of him, and looking into his eyes now, I knew that each word of his was absolutely true. For that reason I accorded him respect. Yet such a man had already remade a portion of the world in his own image, despite his undeniable fidelity to Islamic doctrine. And his hands were quite bloodied with the results of his slaughter of so many of my brethren at Hattin. For those reasons, it was only to God I would give mine own unquestioning fidelity. It was a curious thing, really. I could have killed him instantly. I think he knew that. He knew also that I would not have dishonoured myself so, since guest I was here.

"It is obvious to me, your highness, that you are a man of deep understanding, where it concerns questions of reverence. A ruler as reasonable as you are should be able to discuss a treaty that is of mutual acceptance to both your faith and mine. King Richard has proposed that—"

"What would be acceptable would be the departure of your people from all territories," was his interruption.

I had hoped that he would say something different, something that would open a bit of negotiation. Apparently, that was not what he wished.

"My people have been here for a long time," I told him. "I, myself, called Jerusalem home for almost nine decades."

He understood my reference immediately, though he took no offense to it.

"A holy man like you would be most welcome there at any time."

"Not so my people?"

"Your people are not like you at all."

"How do you know this, if you do not know them?"

"At a later time that might come to pass. For now, you must tell this King Richard, and all the rest who are with him in this action, that the troops in Acre are loyal. I want the promise of their safe conduct out of the city. If no harm comes to them, then perhaps there is an opportunity for an end to our mutual distrust and hatred. You must tell him further that the Sultan of Egypt will no longer tolerate the presence of the enemies of the true faith in his kingdom. You and your Templars may leave now, Asad. I promise you safe departure."

"Before I take leave of you, your highness, would you tell me how you came to know of when we were crossing Hattin?"

He laughed.

"I thought I made myself quite clear at that time. Your people had betrayed themselves. Did I need to break any further confidences? I told you that much, for you are a holy man, and not all men are so loyal as you."

Upon my return, I shared the points of conversation with Richard.

"This man wants no peace," he maintained. "That is unfortunate. Many lives will be lost."

He looked over at me, noticing that my concentration were elsewhere.

"He told you something else, did he not, something that has disturbed you?"

"All those loyal soldiers died at Hattin, for there is a Christian traitor in *Outremer*."

"Lies! He would like nothing better than to sow discord between your Order and the kings of *Outremer*. How sly of him to plant this doubt in the mind of one of the Templars' own founders! He must have hoped to foment a civil war."

"One thing that I learned about Saladin is that he does not lie, not even to a Christian." I laughed. "He would consider the deed a dishonourable one."

"Have you no doubt of this?"

I did not, I told him.

"Did he give you a name?"

"No. To do so would have been a dishonourable act."

Richard appeared to be wondering about the exact nature of his adversary.

"A most unusual man, is he not?" he asked of me.

"Though he calls himself *sultan*, his sensibilities are royal."

"You must pardon me. When I look at you, I forget that you have walked this earth far longer than any other man, and that you have known many kings. Why does this one seek the release of our prisoners? Do you believe it is simply because he cares for the lives of his comrades under his command?"

"He values the life of each soldier. I have no doubt of it. But these men are tools to be used in his war. He seeks an end to Christian kingship in this part of the world."

"Exactly as I thought. Tell me, Brother Guy, how many of your Templar brethren lost their lives upon the Horns of Hattin?"

I stared at him.

"Far more than ever I could count."

"We should remind the great Sultan of that, don't you think?"

In late August, Richard ordered that two thousand seven hundred hostages (primarily Turkish) be brought onto the plain outside the city. He granted to me the honour of leading my fellow Templars and his troops. We stood proudly upon our horses, our heads high, and we shouted to the ends of the earth:

"For Hattin!"

Then it was that we beheaded all of the prisoners. And we rejoiced as the blood soaked our hands and splashed upon our smiling faces. All in all, a very good day was had by all!

Not two days had passed, when Richard led the army out of Acre. And by the first week of September, we were all at the port of Arsuf, wherein battles ensued. By the time that the month was finished, it was ours. Word came that Saladin was worried. I had no doubt of that either.

During the first week of October, Richard sent me to open negotiations with Al Fadil, which actually consisted of the former demanding the return of Jersualem and all the lands between the coast and the River Jordan. He knew that this *negotiation* would never be acceptable to the Sultan. I believe that he was hoping for a delay, since these wars had exacted a great price in terms of the loss of so many soldiers. There was also the ongoing debate among the other Christian kings as to the efficacy of Richard's plans. Whilst he concerned himself with the possible restoration of Jerusalem as a Christian city, Pisans had already taken over Acre in the name of King Guy, and were being besieged there by the Genoese, who had allied themselves with Conrad of Tyre. The Italians had created their own little private war, and Richard and his forces, (along with the Templars and Hospitallers) were left to fend for themselves.

I led a contingent of troops as escorts for Saladin's brother and his guards during their return home. When we passed a forest, we were set upon by a pack of wolves—the human variety. Members of a large armed band (who, I was to discover, would turn out to be the raggèd remnants of Barbarossa's forces) surrounded us. We shouted for them to put down their weapons. We were ignored. Having no choice, we defended ourselves. I must admit, it was not much of a struggle, as they were starving and weak. Only in one last act of desperation did a knight throw his sword in the direction of Al Fadil. Though I pushed him out of the way, there was no time for me to do anything, save replacing him as target. The sword penetrated my chest up to the hilt. No one moved. I groaned, yanking on the handle, as I pulled it out. Grasping it now, my hand blood-soaked, I ran over to the knight responsible for my agonizing pain. He stood still, staring at me, as I began to beat him with it.

"How many times did I tell you to put the damnèd thing away?!" I shouted at him.

I stood over him there, his head broken, bleeding upon that grassy field.

Al Fadil came over to me.

"Well have you deserved your name, Asad. I would not want to fall beneath *your* talons. You have given to me my life today. I shall not forget how you have acted with honour. Allah be praised!"

Several of his men mounted their horses. Two of the cutpurses began to argue with each other.

"I told you that he was Guy de Lagery," one said.

They fell to their knees.

"We pledge our blades and lives to you, Templar," the same man spoke, as if in prayer.

I eyed them with not a little disgust.

"Arise, before you join your fallen comrade!" I ordered.

They did so immediately.

Still breathing heavily, I looked down at the poor wretch, who had risked his life for what he believed was a noble act. But how could I have allowed him to do it, when the object of his hatred was under my protection? It was the last desperate act of a desperate man. If only he had stopped to question me (or himself) first! Would that have made any difference? Perhaps not. I found this kill to be completely devoid of even the slightest pleasure.

I returned to Richard and the onset of a winter that was to be every bit as wet and miserable as Saladin had informed me that it would be. Soon would come torrential rains, then the mud, then wet clothes, which never dried in the dampness of the air. Thus, trenches had to be dug around the camps, siphoning the run-off. And war would have to wait both for Christian and Muslim, for the principal arm of each, the archers, would never be able to let fly arrows from their quivers when the bowstrings were wet and useless.

By the end of March it had become evident that neither party would be able to stop the other from any incursion into the foe's territory. Perhaps for that reason, Richard asked me once again to seek a truce with Saladin. When I heard in detail all the terms, I refused to believe that the prince was serious. I was certain that the *truce* was actually little more than an attempt to bide time until a more detailed plan of attack could be created. I suggested this as a possibility, only to discover that he neither denied nor comfirmed my suspicions. And I led my Templar brethren to Kahira.

In the Sultan's palace I discovered a secret that Saladin had been keeping for some time.

"The Templars have offtimes been the bane of my existence. Led by you, they have killed many who were loyal to me. My anger has been great. And when I think that I can feel nothing for you except hatred, you put yourself between a Christian blade and my brother's life. How can I hate such a man?"

He asked me further about what it was that Richard were offering? Jerusalem would stay in the Sultan's possession, I explained, but Christian pilgrims would be allowed access to the Holy Places and to Christian priests the guardianship of them. In addition, all properties and structures currently occupied by Templars and Hospitallers would remain under *their* control. (This last point was one of my own making.)

"I shall need time to think upon this proposal. You should know that I would never agree to that matter concerning your military orders. You, however, as I have previously stated, will always be welcome and safe in your travels through Muslim-controlled lands. The same will never be true of your brethren. Moreover, you should know that as a punishment for your actions, I have ordered that my chroniclers omit your name from the history of my deeds."

"The only honour that a Templar seeks is in the eyes of God."

"I am glad to be of service."

The Sultan kept his counsel for several months. In early April of 1192, a council of royals convened to decide who would wear the crown of Jerusalem. In point of fact, this action would be no more significant than mere decoration, since control of the city rested with Saladin. Nevertheless, everyone approved of the ritual, regardless of its lack of efficacy. Richard favoured Guy de Lusignan. The entire council, (almost to a man, or to a noble), voted for Conrad of Tyre. Richard ultimately went along with its suggestion, even though he had far more faith in Guy than anyone else (including myself) did. Shortly thereafter, Al Fadil came to Richard to inform him that his brother had agreed to most of the precepts, which I had earlier presented to him. (He reiterated the denial of Templar and Hospitaller lands and properties, however.) And he had a private message for my eyes alone.

I thanked the brother, who left. I turned to Richard.

"I suppose that we can we trust him to act honourably," I offered.

He must have noticed my great displeasure, for he smiled and shook his head.

"I know that you are unhappy with this decision; so, too, is the council of royals. However, you should realize that you have been its architect."

"I?" I asked, quite exasperated.

"You have convinced me, and I have convinced the others. Unlike several Muslims *and* Christians, Saladin has never broken a treaty. That will make his holiness very happy. If the Sultan is willing to secure the places of pilgrimage, there may be hope for future discussions. He is ruthless, as all leaders should be. Despite that truth, he possesses a quality that few of his contemporaries do—he acts with honour."

"What are you saying?"

"If we kill him, we may find that his replacement is a creature far worse. Is it not better to fight a known enemy than an unknown one?"

I could not believe what I had heard him speak.

"Have you forgotten how many of your people, *and mine*, were skewered upon the horns of Hattin?"

"They are ever in my prayers. Yet today we stand at the edge of a precipice. If we turn around and go back, the war will continue. If we move forward and jump, then we must pray that the Lord, our God, will not allow us to fall."

"Shall we make of their deaths a meaningless comment in a chronicle? Those were our brethren, my brethren."

"The road to Peace is one that is rarely traveled. How necessary it is for a man who has lost everything to take his first steps upon that path! Is our commitment only to ourselves? Do our children's children deserve no better from us?"

"And you believe that it is fitting for you to put our faith in this man?"

"He has never broken a promise. You have assured me of it, and you are most correct."

I paced about, awaiting a moment of deeper clarity. Then it came to me.

"Though I cannot easily accept his continued existence," I said, "there may be the possibility of hope. If I can make him agree to a resolution of conflicts, we both know that he will do everything in his power to maintain that position."

"It is exceeding strange. I never believed that I would jump at the opportunity to seal a treaty with a Muslim."

"Perhaps that is what is meant by a *leap of faith.*"

He laughed and pointed now to the message that was in my hands. Since I had obviously neglected its presence there, I began to read it. Almost immediately, he must have noticed my face growing red and hot.

"Pardon my curiosity, but does it contain anything that you might be willing to share?"

"He says that Conrad is loyal to his ambition only."

"That is a revelation to no one. Simply speak with the man, and it will become evident that he yearns for currency and kingdoms far more than he does so for his own wife. Do you think that the Sultan fears him?"

"He fears only God's wrath. You misunderstand his meaning, my liege. Conrad is not to be trusted. Conrad is the man whom I have sought. *He* is the liar in *Outremer.*"

"You cannot slander him on the word of a Muslim."

"Do you not see? He must have been the one who betrayed us to Saladin when we crossed Hattin!"

"The meeting of your forces with theirs was mere chance."

"Have you no faith? God created the world, and everything in it has its purpose. His children created the idea of *chance,* the better to delude themselves into thinking that there are situations over which our Lord has no control. The Sultan writes further that there will be no Christian king in Beirut. It all fits together perfectly, like the stones of a castle."

"I do not take your meaning."

"That city was the price asked for his betrayal. Conrad must be destroyed!"

"Calm yourself, Templar. We have already repaid the Sultan in kind for those needless deaths. What is more, you have no proof, except the word of the one Muslim ruler who has snatched Jerusalem from our grasp. The council will believe not a word of it. I know that you trust the word of Saladin. I, myself, am not without a certain appreciation for his military skills. Yet, have you asked yourself why he would reveal this supposèd truth at this very moment? In point of fact, he has stated very little. His words only hint at a possible past or future betrayal. You want to believe him. I understand this. An enemy who has neither face nor name is a recurrent nightmare. Saladin may be playing upon your need for justice."

"That is not so, your highness. You see, he was bound by honour to keep that secret. He has broken his silence for one reason only: I saved the life of his devoted brother. That bound him to me, whilst breaking his vow to a Christian liar, whom he detests."

Richard paced about again, his hands folded behind himself, ruminating upon my final words.

"Conrad is an important man," he spoke at last. "For that reason, he cannot be disposed of arbitrarily. If you attempt to do so, you will smear not only your name, but that of the entire Order. I ask you to give yourself a bit of time. A treasonous creature like that cannot always be so careful. When he slips and falls, I have faith that you will be there to catch him."

I promised that I would not *personally* commit an act of regicide, which promise I did not break. It was not the last time that someone would ask me to forego my wish to punish the wicked, much to my regret.

Our meeting concluded, I road about until I found a bedouin trader atop his camel, and passed a few select words to him. Within the week appeared a stranger at our encampment.

A knight entered the tent, complaining bitterly.

"We have a problem with a persistent beggar. He keeps repeating, *Alms for the poor, alms for Allah*, but he never leaves, even when he has been given a coin to move on."

I decided to tend to this situation myself. Outside, I went up to the man, whose head and face were covered. His back was bent, perhaps riddled with some unknown disease. As I neared him, his back straightened. He was quite tall now. He looked at me. He pulled back his cowl. The face was unmistakable.

"Shabako?" I asked.

He wasted no time with greetings, (as he never did), and wanted instead to know the particulars. I gave them to him.

Within the week, Conrad of Tyre was found with his throat cut, and curious designs carved into the flesh of his cheeks. (This last has been omitted from all chroniclers, I believe, though some do mention the possibility that the Assassins were somehow involved.) There were all sorts of rumours, of course, though no one ever found the man or men responsible.

Thus is the traitor to liberty rewarded!

Within a week of his death, his widow married a nobleman, Henry de Champagne (with whom, it was said, that she had been making a cukold of Conrad for a considerable number of years). Richard (and the entire council) recognized him as king. And all breathed a sigh of great (albeit temporary) relief.

Not a month passed when Richard heard terrible rumours concerning his ministers in England and their support of his brother, John. He felt ashamed to tell me of how the latter must have recently usurped the throne and taxed the populace beyond words. He confessed now that his mother had often taken the younger brother's side against the father, even when it was obvious that the boy were guilty. And his crimes had always been petty—mere theft of trinkets and the like. Perhaps Eleanor saw in him that profound lack of maturity that would never grow therein, and pitied him his continuing failures. Even so, her efforts had proven ineffectual. O, yes, the boy had grown into manhood, despite the truth that he would never be more than a shadow of his elder brother's glory.

I wish I could say that when Richard sailed from Palestine in October, he returned home forthwith and punished his wicked sibling. Unfortunately, life rarely provides so neat a story as that.

During the journey, his ship was wrecked in a storm. It was not in England that he had found himself, rather in Germany, with his entourage, all dressed in monks' robes and cowls. Eating at an inn, the Tyrolean innkeeper noticed how tall one monk was, and how the other monks deferred to him. The innkeeper had heard of his ruler's arguments with the English Richard, (as did most of his countrymen), so he sent word to the ruler of the eastern *Reich*. As a result, Richard was seized and imprisoned. The ransom was set at one hundred and fifty thousand silver marks. The chests containing the coinage were borne in a procession.

A royal processional, heavily armed, and clad in the finest of armours, some of which were themselves bejeweled, bore the chests. And they surrounded a royal litter, intricately wrought with carvings of many lions and *fleur-de-lis*. Inside it sat a woman of perhaps seven decades or so, scowling. Her hair was white now, and nowhere near as thick as once it had been. Her face was ferociously lined, as if felines had rent her flesh, and her jowls were long. She was angry about her ill-chosen decisions, and contemptuous of all who had never continually cherished her each word and deed. The only emotion that she could feel was disgust. And it was said of this monument to sorrows, Eleanor d'Aquitaine, that she smiled rarely anymore.

Barely had a year slipped by when the Muslim world was rocked by the death of their belovèd Saladin. Once again Shabako made a mysterious appearance. The Old Man had wanted him to deliver a message:

"The Master does not like to leave any business of his unfinished. He also thought that you would benefit from the work completed."

Shabako disappeared before I had any opportunity to question him further as to his reference. All became clear shortly thereafter, when word arrived that Saladin had died suddenly from an illness; it was something to do with his stomach, I believe.

Now it was that I understood why the Old Man had taken the original contract. What better way to illustrate one's faith, than by ridding the world of a powerful enemy of the true beliefs? I suppose he had never relinquished his Shiite leanings. That was most unfortunate for the Sunni known as Saladin.

The Ayubbid Dynasty ruled the Muslim world for several decades thereafter, before their Turkish slaves (the *Mamlukes*) destroyed them, in order to establish and secure their own path of succession.

Richard died in that year of our Lord, 1199. He had been watching his archers, when one of them shot his arrow in order to bring down a partridge as a gift to the king. Unfortunately, the man missed his mark, and the arrow pierced Richard's shoulder. The king laughed at his wound, and the cause of it, for such was the nature of his good fellowship. Then the wound began to fester, and still did he ignore its occasional twinge of pain. Eventually, it killed him. His brother, John, (whom he had forgiven for his transgressions years earlier), now took the throne as his own.

Upon the death of Eleanor's son, I met the mother again at the Abbey of Fontevrault in Anjou. It was a common practice among royals to have artisans create sculpted ossuaries, in which were held the bodies of the honoured dead. Upon the lid of each lay a figure, supine, called a *gisant*. Stonemasons had fashioned one into a remarkable likeness of her son. Despite their best efforts, his mother barely recognized the figure. And when she looked upon me, I, too, was as much a stranger as was her own flesh. Only momentarily was there a sudden flash of acknowledgement, that dissipated as quickly as it had come upon her, leaving her eyes empty now, her mouth open and free of any voice.

When she died, a *gisant* was fashioned of her in her more youthful days. She is reading a book—an activity from which she derived great pleasure. And she is lying-in-state next to her husband and son. Finally, the three are at peace with each other and will continue to be so for many years to come.

CHAPTER THE FORTIETH,

in which my health is tended by the Sultan's own physician.

It is perhaps a common enough human failing that the more one is denied the possession of a thing, the more one desires it fervently. In the years since my arrangement with one or two women, I had made other arrangements with other women, all for the possibility of a child. And all mutual efforts had proven futile. I suppose that I should be grateful that not one of them attempted to present me with a child that was not of my body. I was fortunate in that I had selected honest women for the task. I must confess, however, there were times when I might have thought it a blessing, if I were to put on an act of pretense and accept another man's infant as mine own. Yes, it sounds foolish, as I write of it herein. But oft-times a particular truth is far more difficult to bear than is the opportunity to delude oneself.

I had no way of knowing whether I would ever become a father. Nevertheless, I realized that the only person, who might be able to tell me of this possibility, was the finest physician in the then-known world. As it turned out, he happened to have been Saladin's own.

The man had agreed to enter the Sultan's service with one stipulation: he was to spend each night in the home of his own family, and not within the environs of the royal palace. Saladin had always thought it a most unusual request, though agreed to it without hesitation, so much did he desire the man to attend both to himself and to the royal family; nor did Saladin dismiss so easily the man's desire to be surrounded by his own wife, children, and grandchildren; a man who preferred the company of his family to that of the royal court was a man whom any regent could rely upon to aid in the maintenance of a nation's stability. He liked that quality. He liked it very much.

And now the royal physician tended to the family of Saladin's brother.

Across the desert sands I rode, past bedouin traders shouting out lists of their wares from high atop a camel's hump. I was ill prepared to find myself so soon in the shadow of the great pyramids. Even in such a place as this, where the asp and scorpion reigned, could one observe the glorious result of arithmetic concerns. A triangle with a square at its base (an unremarkable design really) had planted itself in the minds of men from the first sighting of it. For the Hebrews it was a symbol of slavery and unremitting toil. For their *pharonic* masters it was a marker, not simply of their tombs encased therein, but of the human spirit surging ever higher towards a heavenly kingdom. Perhaps that yearning was not so very different from the sort that brought forth a cathedral's spires in my former homeland so far away.

In *Misr,* the old section of Kahira, stood a long and wide structure, not at all representative of how other (smaller) homes surrounding it were constructed. Covered by the dark blue monk's habit that I had long before adopted, I knocked upon the door.

A bearded man of middle years opened it. Upon his head was the round, cloth skullcap that Jews wore, the *yarmulke.*

"What is your business here?" he asked curtly.

"I seek the physician."

"As do many people. Why should he take the time to see you, especially at this late hour?"

There was a rustling from inside.

"Barak, who is there?" a voice called.

"Rest, father," the man at the door called back. He turned now to me again. "Return shortly after dawn, if it is an emergency. He sees only Sultan Al Fadil's family during the late evening hours."

Before I had the opportunity to say anything further, an old man walked up and pushed Barak away.

"Who is here?" he asked.

"Father, I have already told him to leave."

"Who are you?" he addressed me now. "What do you want?"

"I seek Abu Amram Musa."

"That is how the children of Muhammad refer to me. Among my own people I am known as, *Moshe Ben Maimun.*"

"A Moses to your people?" I asked, amused by his name.

"I am a Jew. And though this is not the land of my birth, I can see something in your face that tells me the same about you. I cannot say what it is though. To whom do I have the privilege of speaking?"

"I have been told that you are not unfamiliar with my name. It is Guy de Lagery."

His eyes widened.

"The immortal knight who fights with the Templars? I never dreamed that I would live to see you!" he spoke with no attempt to conceal his excitement, his arms raised high and opened in a gesture of grand welcoming.

Immortal?

"Yet here I am."

"Come in! Come in! You will share our evening meal with us."

He hurried me inside, whilst Barak frowned.

"Father, it is very late."

"O, be quiet already!" he informed his son. And to me he said: "Ignore my son. He thinks me an old man," and to Barak he concluded quite loudly: "and that I should rest like the dead!"

Through the antechamber, we walked into a large room filled with benches. I took this to be the area where the patients would wait prior to treatment. Then we stepped into a hall. (I would soon learn that each meal served in this chamber had indeed become a feast, prepared by his dutiful wife and their daughters.)

After an introduction to all the occupants herein, and especially to the rabbi's grandchildren, (who were too numerous to count), we ate. Later on, we walked outside, and sat upon a small bench, where the rabbi enjoyed looking up at the night sky and its stars. There we spoke of my reasons for having come.

After having listened to my tale, he gave me the benefit of his experience:

"Perhaps the problem was not yours. By your own admission, some of these women belonged to an unsavory profession that has often spread disease. Several of these illnesses have been known to result in a woman's inability to bear any offspring. It is also conceivable that they may have passed on this disease to you."

That was of little concern. My body was quite capable of healing itself.

"Yes," he agreed, nodding, studying me, "I suppose that it would have to, in order to keep you healthy and young. How many decades have you witnessed, if I may ask?"

"More than ten."

"Amazing! You have seen one century end and another begin. In several years, you will see that pattern of time repeat itself. You may be the most unique man in the entire world. Do you ever think about that?"

"Only when I am witness to the foolish acts of stupid kings. Only then do I feel myself very old, and wonder why it is that I have lived so long. If you were given this opportunity now, would you be grateful for it?"

"If it had come to me forty years ago, or even thirty, I might have praised our Lord for His very rare generosity. If it came to me today, it would be a curse. Who would want to live for eternity as an old man, after he has already spent his life?"

"Believe me when I say that there are times when I often ask myself that very question."

He laughed, then concluded that I must have wanted a child very much. He wondered if there were one woman of whom I was particularly fond, who wished to become a mother. I had to admit there were none. Not a single woman? I reiterated that there was not a one.

"Then you are hoping for a future possibility, are you not?"

"Can you help me?"

"I cannot answer that question. I shall, however, try."

Adjacent to the house stood a tiny structure (a room actually) in which could be found any number of glass vials neatly arranged along shelves, and burned sheaves of wood in one corner, functioning, I supposed, as a hearth. There were also several scrolls lying about. For a moment I thought myself back in the catacombs with Fausto. Only when I looked into my host's face and beheld the absence of all malice therein, did I dismiss my initial impression.

He gave to me a thin strip of glass.

"I shall need a sample of your blood placed hereon."

I turned the sliver over in my hand. I explained to him that another physician had once asked me for the same thing, only to see the first few drops turn brittle immediately, before they disappeared like fragments of dust.

He laughed at Fausto's seeming lack of experience.

"You need no more than the large dosage of a potent *anti-coagulant*."

I was uncertain as to his meaning.

He poured water from an ewer into a small cup, then shook out some powder from one of the vials, before mixing the two together. He proffered the combination of substances. Initially reluctant, I reminded myself that no poison could ever harm me, so what could this medicament do? And there was no malignity in this man. That much was evident.

I drank of it. He lit a small taper. We sat there, waiting until it burned itself out. Having admired the vast numbers of the Maimun progeny, I chose to break the silence with a simple enough compliment:

"You must be proud of so large a family."

"O, the thanks should be given to my wife. If not for her, the entire household would have descended into *chaos* long ago. Unfortunately, we all do everything in our power to create that anyway, despite her best intentions."

He smiled, watching the last bit of flame flicker and die away.

"We may begin now. Make a clean incision, if at all possible. That will produce the largest quantity of blood whilst omitting any of your flesh. It is the blood, itself, that requires further examination."

I took out a small dagger, and cut across my palm. I made a fist, squeezing tightly, until several drops of the telltale liquid fell upon the glass. To my surprise, they remained in an *aqueous* state. It was then I noticed that he was staring at my hand.

"Do all your wounds heal so quickly?"

I held open my palm. He marveled at how the cut was already closing, as if it had never been made.

"I think it a tragedy that the Lord did not grant this gift to all men."

"Why do you say that, rabbi?"

"If He had, there would be no wars. Without the threat of death, everyone would have to live in peace with his enemy. If that were so, what honour could there be in the spilling of blood? Far more honourable would be the man who put away his sword in order to forge a treaty. Such a man would be hallowed in the eyes of God."

I was uncertain if he were laying an insult at my feet, nor would I allow him to undermine all the beliefs, in which I had placed my utmost confidence. I said nothing in response, however. I did not wish to stir his animosity, and thereby cause him to turn a blind eye to a possible cure. Nevertheless, I may have betrayed some of my feelings upon my face, for he stared at me.

"It is also my belief," he continued, "that if the Christ were standing here now, He would weep for all the innocent souls who have been killed in His name."

Perhaps He still does.

"I have known several Templars," he went on. "They all wore their swords with great pride. Do you have any idea how many times you have touched or held the hilt of your sword, since your arrival?"

I looked down at it, removing my hand therefrom as I did so.

"It is a most unusual weapon, in that I have never seen its like. It appears to be the sort that the Romans used in the time of their empire, though yours is far larger, as if it had been fashioned for a giant's hand. Did I see correctly that there was lettering inscribed upon its face?"

I removed it and placed it upon the table before us.

"I had thought it the Turkic tongue, when found. I have since learned that it is unlike anything that I know. It resembles Hebrew somewhat, though if it is, it is one that I have never seen."

"Besides Arabic, you speak Hebrew?" he asked, apparently quite surprised and pleased.

"Only a bit. My uncle made certain that I would learn some of it, though I fought him at every turn. I am sorry about that now."

"Since you are here, it would be my pleasure to teach you the language of my ancestors."

He reached to touch the blade. I pushed his hand away. Hurt, he stared at me, questioning why I had done so.

"Forgive me. It has been my unfortunate experience that no other hand, save mine, may wield it, let alone place a finger against it and live."

"A thing of wonder!" he exclaimed, smiling. "Is there no end to the miracles which are you, Templar?"

He bent down his head, moving closer to it, the better to see and examine each letter.

"In all these years, has no one ever told you what language this is?"

"Everyone has feared to be in its proximity, and rightly so. Do you recognize it?"

"It was spoken in these lands over a thousand years ago, in the time of the Christ. This is Aramaiac."

"Can you translate it?" I asked, excitedly.

"Not immediately."

He walked over to the burnt wood, took a small piece, then snatched a vellum from a shelf. He proceeded to rub the ash across the face of the cloth. Now he placed it across the blade, and used the burned stick to press it hard against the surface. A moment later, he lifted up the cloth, revealing all the letters across it. He held it in front of himself.

"Now *this* I can touch, and study."

Continuing in what had now become two objects of research, he bade his entire family treat me as a very important guest. Despite Barak's misgivings, everyone evinced only warmth and friendship. They were a vociferous lot, given to frequent assertions, which resulted in argumentation of an equal volume. Rarely did I see the rabbi and his wife disagree, though when I did, their voices were so loud, that all and sundry would flee at the onset of their shouting. I can recall one such occasion when he came to me to unburden his soul over some point or other that I found to be of minor concern. In his quiet manner now, he said unto me:

"My people have a saying: to live alone is to have a pure soul. Are you ready to relinquish that peace?"

Then he smiled … somewhat sadly, I thought.

And as I watched the entire family, I wondered if life would ever vouchsafe me similar routines, or was my rôle as Defender in direct conflict with any happiness to be derived therefrom?

In the days following, I witnessed his manner with the ailing. He made no distinction between wealthy and poor; all deserved treatment of equal measure in his eyes, whether the complaint were as grave as the goring by a bull, or no more than the minor scrape of a child's elbow.

At night he would ofttimes tell stories of the ancient patriarchs, brave Moses demanding that his people be freed, and the hardened heart of Pharoh maintaining only denial, or Samson pulling down the columns of the Philistine temple upon the enemies of the Jewish people. Sometimes he would relate a story of his own making, or so I thought.

There, surrounded by his large family, one granddaughter upon one knee, a grandson upon his other, he pondered the question that the girl had asked of him:

"Grandpa, when did love first appear?"

He smiled broadly.

"Let us see. I believe that God first caused love to appear in His heavenly kingdom. From his Hall of Souls he took a single soul and split it in half, as you have seen your mother do with a gourd."

"He cuts it?" the boy asked.

He laughed.

"No. He is God. He does not need to cut anything. He simply wishes it to happen, and it happens. So great is the power of the Lord! After that, He looks down at all the babies, who will be born, and He places one half of the soul into one child, and into another He places the second half. This He does with each soul. Years pass, and the two babies are now grown. Somehow, God created the world in such a way, that these two people meet. When they do, they immediately know love for the other. And how does this happen? When they look into each other's eyes, they see the other half of the soul that they did not know they were missing, until they recognized it inside the other person. Love is when two souls come together to form a single one. Love is the most important gift that one person can give to another. The Lord created His children, and the earth for them in which to live, both out of love. When two people love, then do God and all the heavenly host rejoice! Now to bed; it is quite late."

They kissed him, as their mothers lifted them up and carried them off to sleep. His wife bent down and kissed the top of his head. He looked at me.

"Did the tale please you?"

"O, rabbi, if it were only that simple!"

He laughed.

Only once did I have to disagree strongly with him. It was concerning the nature of women in general, and their beauty in particular. Not a day after his tale of the origin of love did he begin his assessment:

"The most attractive aspect of a woman's youthful, physical beauty, is its ignorance of life's agony. The only thing that it understands is the continued cultivation of itself. It attracts us, for it represents everything that we have lost or will lose along our journey."

"I cannot agree. I have seen beauty in the faces of women, regardless of how young or how old they may be. It is far more than a reflection of naïveté. It is the essence of everything feminine brought forth to the surface, a signpost only, revealing itself to a man in a very small portion, with the promise of a further, greater mystery as yet undiscovered."

He looked at me curiously, in what I took to mean a cursory assessment of my character.

"O, you must have loved a great many women."

"Quite the contrary. There has been only one."

"My wife has been that for me during these very many years. However, beauty can exist in many different forms, not simply those, which are pleasing to one's sense of aesthetics. Sometimes the soul can be entranced. Would you care to see what I find most beautiful of all?"

He walked over to a shelf and removed a small scroll that had been resting thereupon. He began to unfurl it.

"This is sheer beauty in its purest form."

The scroll had been painted white, after which a coating of black had been put on top of it. The black had been scratched out meticulously so as not to disturb the white beneath. I saw what appeared to be many different Hebrew words.

"What is their significance?" I asked.

"They are the names of God."

I multiplied the top horizontal line by the vertical one and arrived at a figure that was more than seventy.

"So many?" I asked.

"A small portion of Infinity only."

As I looked at them, I noticed that each letter appeared to be undulating. I rubbed my eyes. Regarding them again, I realized that there had been no mistake; still they moved.

"It is as if—"

"As if they are alive?" he asked, looking at me. Now it was that he turned his attention to the scroll. "Indeed they are! Words are very powerful things. Either they heal or harm. They are anything but arbitrary. These are reflections of the power of our Lord. Since He is alive, without beginning, and without end, but life continuing, they, too, are alive. These names are how we, who are terribly finite, may know him. They are an attempt to understand His essence. You pray before a crucifix. The contemplation of these names is one of my forms of prayer."

I placed my fingers upon them, and felt them move beneath.

"And the word was God," I spoke with awe.

"Amen."

I began my Hebraic tutorials as if I were a boy once again. When all the others had gone abed, and little fires still burned in the hearth at eventide, the rabbi would teach me the language that God had written into stone with His own hand. And despite my assertion that I knew some of it, I could not convince my tutor that I knew anything of it. So, he began at the beginning, from the simple *A, B, C,* the *Aleph, Beth, Gimmel,* to the essence of philosophy—God was *without beginning, b'lee ray-sheeth,* and *without end, b'lee sakh-leeth.* And like the runes, themselves, these letters also functioned as numbers. (This lesson I would remember later, as I saw to it that all of the recordkeeping of the entire Order was written in Hebrew.)

Once, of an evening, it was quite late when the rabbi came out to find me sitting, looking upward. He sat down next to me.

"Do you never sleep?" he asked.

"Only for a short time. And you?"

"The older one becomes, the more erratic are the patterns of sleep. Doubtless you know this better than I."

I wondered if he had uncovered any of the secrets inside my blood. He had seen several unusual things, though was loathe to discuss their nature in any detail, until he were finished with his study of them. Then he informed me, regretfully, that he would need another sample.

"I have given you two already. Why do you need it this time?"

"I must complete my work, or what I have to say will be only partially correct."

"Why are you not telling me how this sample became corrupted?"

"In truth, I cannot say. Initially, there were fibers of cloth. This time I saw plant filaments. I have no idea how this is possible. I can assure you that I took great care."

I agreed to do as he asked, albeit reluctantly.

"Saladin once told me that you were the finest physician in the world. I hope that your expertise is as great as your reputation."

"I shall attempt not to disappoint you."

"And he mentioned that you were an astrologer," I added, staring upward. "Do you believe, as others have said, that the movements of the stars govern our lives?"

He laughed.

"The stars merely reflect patterns of the lives, which we *may* create. Over there," he said, pointing upwards to the right at the sparkling constellations, "you can see the pincers of the scorpion. Nearby is the great bear. In what month were you born?"

"In August."

"Then you are of the lion's brood. There he is," he remarked, pointing to a group of stars at the left, "exactly there. And here you are, fierce, proud, and, I have no doubt, at times quite deadly. Whilst its accuracy might not be free from flaws, the study may have merits, which should not be ignored."

"I think that a man would have to have great wisdom to look into those constellations and see the future written therein."

"Wisdom is nothing more than the ability to recognize patterns. That is how God constructed the universe. Nothing is arbitrary."

I, too, had come to believe that nothing occurs without a purpose.

"The wise man sees with his heart and his mind. The study of mathematics and Aristotlean logic have taught me that something can result only after other things have caused its occurrence. The study of the human body, and by extension the natural world, has taught me that there are patterns of birth, maturity, aging, disease, and death common to all things. This is true, whether it be the babe in a mother's arms, or the timbers of our homes, or the insects in the dirt beneath our feet. The very air that we breathe is alive as well. And what is the source that propels these rhythms of life, if not its Creator? Have you never wondered if the vessels, which carry blood in our hands are any different from those, which carry water in a leaf? I have devoted my entire life to an understanding of the natural world, for if I am able to see its truth, even if only a small portion of it, how much closer am I to understanding the mind of God? All creation is one in God's universe. And that is why all life is precious to Him, including the life of one's enemy."

I elected not to argue, for neither one of us would have been able to convince the other of an opposing view. Instead, once more I looked up into the sky.

"Do you think that we shall ever set foot upon those stars?" I asked.

"In God's universe all things are possible. I regret that I shall not be here to see that day, though I have no doubt that you will."

In the short time that I spent with him, I found myself growing ever more curious about his perceptions, particularly as they related to other faiths.

"Like Judaism and Christianity, Islam was born in anguish, at a moment when an oppressed people reached out for something to grasp, that would become its answer. Regarding Judaism, the revelation of the one God was given to us at Sinai. With the presentation of His commandments came forth all law and all civilization. In that moment we knew that we were born to become better than the worst aspects of ourselves, for we were born to become like unto angels upon the earth."

"Is that our purpose, then, to become perfect?"

"God, alone, is perfect. All else is flawed. However, it is to perfection that one must aspire."

"And how does one go about doing that?"

"One must endeavour to do his best in all things at all times, to create the world, to nourish the souls of one's brethren."

"And if one fails?"

"Would you punish your child simply because he was not able to achieve his goal, though he had done everything within his capabilities to do so? The attempt must be from the heart and with absolute conviction. That is what is crucial for all faith."

I asked him why it was that he thought the Jews could not accept that Jesus had been the Messiah. Was He not born of the House of David?

"Often have I heard Christians refer to Jesus as, *the Son of Man*; however, that is not strictly accurate, is it? He was actually the son of a woman, as all men are. According to your beliefs, God was the father. His paternal lineage contradicts our prophecies, for the *Moshiach* will be born of two human parents. Whilst true that God is the source of all things, and that a child may have many fathers in the course of his life but only one mother, in this situation, it is the seed of a human father that will help to create the Saviour. As far as lineage is concerned, I, too, am able to trace it back to the House of David, however, my wife will be the first one to tell you that I am no one's saviour. I suppose that is as it should be."

"Then you do not accept His miracles, or anything else about him that the sainted scribes have mentioned?"

"I have no doubt that he may have performed those acts of wonder. He was a prophet, as was Moshe before him and Muhammad after him. Such men transform the world. Yet as unique as they may be, they are men of flesh, as much as you and I are. They deserve our praise. Whether or not they deserve our worship is the choice that everyone must make for himself."

He saw that I was not comfortable with his judgment.

"In all this time," he asked, "have you never wondered why God had allowed only you to live so long? Is it because you are a type of prophet?"

"I would never presume to delude myself in that manner. I always thought that I would live to see peace amongst all peoples. The older I become, the less I believe in that possibility. Rabbi, do you think that there will ever be peace in the Holy Land?"

"The greatest tragedy of man is his refusal to believe in the interconnectedness of things. All life is one. Differences in religious practice, or the colour of the skin, or the language spoken, are nothing more than God's variety made manifest. We should revel in our differences, embrace each other, for are we not, all of us, children of God? Judaism is the revelation, Christianity the sacrifice, Islam the submission. These three are the paths which one must take in order to embrace and understand the mystery of all creation. On the day when the Jew, the Christian, and the Muslim remember that brotherhood is more than a vague concept, on that day these three faiths will teach the world how to create peace."

The next day I was with the rabbi in his chamber of study when one of the elder grandchildren entered to tell me that I had a visitor.

"I thought that you said the only one who knew you were here is the Sultan," the rabbi commented.

"No one else does, as much as I know it to be true."

We walked to the entry, where I met a Templar brother. He was in a troubled state, which was probably why he had forgotten his manners and spoken to me directly, without leaving but a moment for the amenities of introduction. I ignored him at any rate and made certain that he exchanged pleasantries with my kind host. I excused myself and walked outside with him.

I was angry that I had been found, especially since I had assured the Grand Master that I would be returning shortly, after an *excursus* into the Sultan's empire. My brother informed me that the search put before him had not been an easy one. But God did provide, did He not? What was so important that it could not wait a month or so until my return? Pope Innocent III had written to the Grand Master concerning holy war.

"Has he declared one?" I asked.

"Not exactly."

"And what do you mean by that, *exactly*? Was there no formal declaration? Was no papal bull or encyclical issued?"

The Holy Father wanted to know if the Grand Master *and I* believed that a renewed push into Muslim territory might possibly yield the recapture of Jerusalem. He had sincerely hoped (since the time of his election) that he would be the pope to leave behind the legacy of a Christian Jerusalem for his flock, after having departed this painful and most wretched existence, or so my Templar brother informed me.

I would have to return to the Order soon, though not today. My brother was most displeased with that. (The Grand Master had hinted that it would be a very good thing if he were able to convince me to leave, when presented with official papal concerns.) He made me promise him that I would return to them within the month. This I promised. He handed off a letter from the Grand Master—one that was intended for my eyes alone. For that reason, he had not opened it, despite his curiosity. I asked him to stay. He would not, could not. There was much work ahead. He departed with a smile that reminded me of someone else's, though I could not immediately recall whose it was.

I returned to the doorway, only to see the rabbi standing there. I turned. We both watched my brother ride off. I began to laugh.

"That conversation appeared to be a serious one," the rabbi noted, "yet he amused you in some fashion."

I explained that he looked so very like someone I once knew, and there were times when I forgot the person who was speaking to me, as I often recalled Brother Andrew's equally pleasant and brusque manner of speech now.

"Our Lord takes a curious pleasure in providing a certain number of souls to accompany us upon our life's journeys. Though one of these people may disappear from us, or even die, another then appears who is very much like him. Perhaps it is our Lord's way of seeing to it that we are never alone, even in our darkest moments."

I watched as my brother Templar rode off in the distance.

"Odd that you should say such a thing! I find that his presence is both equally irritating yet comforting."

"His manner is one of deference to you as well."

"It is a gesture of respect only."

"I think it far more than that."

On the very next day, Barak informed me that his father wished to see me immediately. I rushed outside to his chamber of study. Therein I found the rabbi, standing over a table, looking at several documents. He invited me in.

"What have you learned?" I asked, eager for any clarity.

"You are a great mystery to me, Guy de Lagery. Everything about your life is as simple as it is complicated."

He revealed that the message upon my sword was carved by one *Yehoshua bar Yasef, Joshua, the son of Joseph.*

"Do you recall that name in your studies?"

I did not. Apparently, it was a common name in the biblical age.

"It is also the name of the Christ."

I unsheathed my sword and placed it upon the table, staring at it the entire time.

"Are you saying that Jesus, a carpenter, forged my sword?"

"I have no way of knowing if that be true. Is it a possibility? I remind you that he came to baptize with fire and with sword."

"But He was a man of peace."

"There is another possibility. The object may be formed from the metallic point that pierced the side of Jesus. An armourer may have heated the remnant from that spear of Longinus, along with other metals, in order to forge your blade."

That was impossible. Many times had I heard popes and kings claim that it was in their possession. Then it was that I realized what I had said a moment previously, as I lifted up the blade and stared at the lettering inscribed therein. Perhaps none of them ever really knew what they had.

"I knew one Turkish trader who sold the remnant of some spear or other to Conrad of Tyre, who, whilst believing it to be this holy lance, purchased it for his sole edification. That happened shortly before his murder."

I corrected him.

"His *execution*, you mean."

He eyed me in an odd manner, as if he were seeing something in my face that he preferred not to discuss.

"If you know more about that than you are saying, please keep your counsel to yourself. I need not know everything that you do. Being ignorant is a state that is sometimes full of bliss, especially when one is old enough to choose to remain so."

"Tell me, rabbi, what is the message?"

He was reluctant to translate it for me. Despite that, I pressed him; I had to know, regardless of what it might be.

"*Use this sword of justice in righteous cause, in sacred name.* It also warns that only the hand of a dead man may wield it."

I stared at him, then at the sword, then back at him.

"But I am very much alive!"

"From what you have told me, you died in Konstantinople. Moreover, you have suffered many wounds, which would have killed any other man. You live, yet you have died. You wield this blade with no harm to yourself. It may have been forged by a simple weapons-maker, or by the hands of a prophet. In either case, it is yours to render justice and defend the innocent, or to indulge the worst aspects of your nature; for though you have been touched by God, you are very much a man, subject to all the weaknesses, which conspire to destroy one's dignity and that of others. It may be that only a man who has been touched by God has any right to its possession. I do not envy you your position. To wield this sword is a responsibility both great and terrible. It seems to me that your purpose is not simply to defend the faith or foment a rebellion, but to rescue the weak and helpless."

"Though you may not accept Jesus as the Messiah, I do. The world already has Him as its Saviour."

"Despite our differing beliefs, I want you to know that I have no problem with the entire Christian world praying to a rabbi."

I laughed.

"This world is a very big place," he continued. "And sometimes the Lord needs help from lowly members of the multitude. That is why He created prophets. Perhaps we are *shomrei hashalom, protectors of the peace.* Do not be so hesitant to dismiss the possibility that your future may hold for you."

The time had finally arrived. I could delay no more. I went into the chamber to ask if he had discovered something that would help cure my ailment. Before he would answer, he asked me whither I might go. I told him that I would return to the Order. And to the possibility of war? I had to agree that *that* was a very real consideration. And so began the last of our argumentation:

"Where is the honour in taking another man's life, no matter how just the cause?" he asked.

"If someone points his sword at you, should you allow him to thrust?"

"It is no sin to defend oneself."

"Is it only a sin to seek the death of your enemy before he has the opportunity to slay you?"

"You speak like a king, full of determination to strengthen the borders of his land at the expense of others' lives."

"You, yourself, translated the inscription. I do what must be done. Shall I betray the very essence of who I am?"

"You have taken pleasure in the deaths of others, as you believed in the righteousness of your cause. Is this why you have been granted immortality?"

"I have done all that I have had to do. In that, we are both alike. You have tended to the Sultan's family. Under their protection, you and yours have prospered, yet you are very much aware of the blood upon their hands."

He laughed, bitterly.

"I have no illusions about them, or myself, actually. I know how their beliefs and actions have limited them. I, too, am a child circumscribed by time and all the daily nuisances and terrors of existence. Despite all their limitaitons, they have given me the opportunity to help their people *and* mine. I shall always be grateful to them for having allowed me to be of service. Only for you can there be no limitations. A man like you can transform the world. Should it not become a better place for *all* His children?"

I recognized that he did all that he had had to do for the continued survival of his family. Would it have been any different, had a Jew possessed a kingdom of his own, I wondered?

"The world already has its Saviour," I maintained. "And I am His sword."

"How fortunate that you cannot see beyond the edge of your blade! Otherwise, what purpose could you possibly have?"

"Killing my fellow man is what I do best. It is, in fact, all that I do."

"And did the Lord bestow immortality upon you merely to use you as His means of vengeance upon the wicked? Are you nothing more than the sword that you carry?"

"It is a gift. Shall I not use it?"

"A man is more than blood."

"Though he bathe in it?" I asked, whilst looking at my blade. Then I stared into his eyes. "Though he yearn for his next kill?"

He stared back into mine eyes as he responded:

"You were put upon this earth to learn, as all must, the laws of life, which the Lord has given unto us in His commandments. You were made immortal not to kill men, but to lead them. Long after the mistakes of others have left behind their scars upon the innocent, still will you be here to make all things right."

"O, my friend! My heart is not so pure as you would have us both believe it to be."

"O, my friend, if you could but see your truth, as all others do!"

Upon his table, set before him were two scrolls. He opened one and perused it.

"I have performed every examination known, and quite a few which have been only suggested in several obscure texts of the ancients. Inside your blood may be found bits of linen cloth and remnants of flower petals. I cannot explain the presence of either of those items. Perhaps they were in the ground at your feet, when that first stroke of Death overtook you."

I smiled.

"*For dust you are, and to dust shall you return,*" I quoted.

"That may be so for the rest of us. But you are unlike all of us."

He continued with the results of his research. Matching the filaments to an actual plant was not an easy task. His botanical skills were not so expert as he would have preferred them to be. Perhaps he was wrong about this, however, he had found remnants of dianthus therein.

"A flower?"

"I am not finished. There is also a substance of an acidic nature in your blood. I have tested it on several insects, only to discover that it kills them instantly. I applied it to a plant, and the results were similar. This substance destroys all life, yet I believe that it preserves your own. I have been unable to learn what it is exactly. Perhaps in five hundred or a thousand years physicians will be able to examine the very structure of blood, itself. Then they may be able to tell you what I cannot. I wish I had more to reveal."

He must have seen the expression that had etched itself into my face, for he said then:

"I realize how difficult this must be for you. I am sorry."

Though I had suspected what his answer might be, the foreknowledge of it could not prevent my heart from breaking.

"You need not apologize. You have done me a service. For that, I am most grateful. I shall be leaving in the morning."

"I have something else for you, Templar."

He opened the other scroll. Upon its surface was illustrated a tree with ten spheres at various points upon it, and a series of interconnecting lines between them, and Hebrew names upon each. He called this, *the Tree of Life*. Apparently, if one were to recite the names of the five thousand angels who exist at each of the ten *sephirot*, (or spheres), until one were able to reach the highest level, *Keter*, there, one would be able to speak directly with God.

"And each sphere creates its own melody."

"So that is the true music of the spheres!"

"I believe that all things possess their own particular music, even the sphere upon which we live."

I laughed.

"Everyone knows that the world is flat."

"Is it? Were we not created in God's image? If the angels, themselves, dwell upon spheres, why should we exist upon a flat surface?"

"This is ludicrous! Next you will be telling me that the sun is the center of the universe."

"In God's universe are all things possible."

"Indeed!" I replied with more than a touch of mockery and disdain.

"You must understand," he explained, "one cannot simply read and recite the names; one must announce them from memory. I have never been able to achieve more than the first level. You, on the other hand, have eternity in which to dwell. Surely, in all that time, you should be able to recall them. I give this to you," he said, proffering it. And from his shelf he took another. "Upon this one are listed the fifty thousand names. I wish you well in this great journey."

The next day, as I prepared my horse, I decided that Rome was to be my first destination, despite my promise of return to my Templar brethren. Upon my arrival there, I met with the Holy Father, Pope Innocent III. Elected to his exalted position at an age of less than forty years, he possessed a young man's determination to have his wishes made real, despite any who would dare to argue with him against his own will. With very straight brown hair and a long face (with slight growth of beard thereupon), his gentle appearance belied his somewhat contentious temperament.

"Let us understand each other," he began, after having thought a time upon our discussion. "You, the swordsman and protector of the church and all things Christian, have come to plead the case of a homeland for the Jews, these killers of Christ. I, the regent of the church, must decide whether there is any logic or wisdom in your unusual request. Some have said that their race is being kept alive so that it may endure ignominy and suffering until the end of time, for having denied our Lord's only begotten Son, and that they are a lost people, as are these accursèd followers of Mahomet, of course. Have I summarized the issue adequately?"

"Our Creator constructed all peoples from the same clay. To several He saw fit to impart skin as white as milk, whilst to others He gave a complexion as darkly ebon as the night's sky. God revels in infinite variety. And from the blood of the Hebrews in the House of David, He fashioned His own Son. Their once powerful kingdoms are ruled now by others, or have passed into dust. Their entire population has been scattered to the Four Winds. Yet there is no place upon this earth lacking at least a single Jew. For whatever reasons, our Lord has seen fit to keep them alive. And there is every possibility that He always will. Perhaps granting them a piece of land for their use is in keeping with His wishes. Who are we, after all, to argue with what our Lord has decreed?"

"The nephew of Pope Urban is a man much given to theological debate, or so it has been said. Like all true orators, his arguments are unique and clever. He knows exactly what to say to sway the mind of his listener."

I was not at all pleased with his assessment of me. His comments sounded as if I were no more than a manipulator of language. Surely he must have realized that I was pleading the case for a people, who deserved a piece of soil to call its own, did he not?

"How long do you think it will be before a prince decides that he must have their land for his purposes?" he asked. "Moreover, how long before a disgruntled tradesman convinces his family, friends, and neighbors that these Jews have no right to live anywhere in peace? It is a very old story, I grant you. And whilst it may be possible that God wishes for every single one of them to atone for the crimes of their ancestors, I do not believe that He would favour their gathering into a single place. They might provide too easily accessible a target for the less enlightened amongst us. No, this cannot be the wisest of actions."

"They will be made aware of the risks involved."

He looked at me now with full knowledge that my will could be every bit as determinate as his own.

"Still you persist in this. It is a noble quality to defend one's beliefs. I wonder what Pope Urban would say, if he were standing here now, listening to his nephew champion the cause of the Jews."

I maintained that he always believed that they should be left to the Creator, and His judgments upon them, and that it was not any man's place to condemn them relentlessly and punish them violently.

"Many will think me mad, or worse, traitorous to the true faith."

"On the other hand, they may welcome the absence of Jews from their vicinity."

"I had not thought of that!"

"It may be one of the finer points to argue in a papal bull."

"O, I think not. The entire world will come to learn of my decision eventually. Why rush this sort of thing. No, this is a question of ... I suppose I am uncertain as to what it may be a question concerning, however, it is in the spirit of ... a ... *trade agreement*, if you will. Yes, that is what it is exactly! It has to do with territories and lands, and things of that nature. I shall give you what you have asked of me, with one stipulation. If the duke agrees to set aside land for this purpose, I shall agree as well. There you have it."

I spent several days at the *Palazzo Ducale* in Venice, sharing the company of the Doge, Enrico Dandolo, and that of his family, whilst marveling at the city's most golden and most serene sunsets, as well as passing time with one or two lovely Venetian women. My host was a man of nine decades or so, his face framed by a flowing white beard and an exceedingly large hooked nose—a trait common to many of the ducal line. Whenever I looked upon him, I was reminded of Fausto's comment that people cease to age after a certain time (and that quantity differs for all). Indeed, his mental acuity and vigorous manner belonged to a much younger man. And his appearance was of a man with perhaps sixty or seventy years, and not a day or year more.

We had arrived at a mutually agreeable figure for purchase of a good many ships—thus the contents of the Grand Master's letter to me. In this manner, the Templars would soon have a fleet of their own, for their purposes and usage. Initially reluctant to make a sale of said ships, (for his family had made quite a fortune from our Order for the temporary usage of same), the Duke finally acquiesced.

To celebrate, we rode together in his official *gondola*—the very large red one that required two *gondoliere* and exceeded the proportions of a small ship. We were concealed behind two tiny wooden doors in imitation of a type of carriage, I always thought. The Doge began to discuss a number of issues. I wondered if the two men rowing would speak of any of them. My host assured me that they could not, for he had had the servants' tongues cut out. I winced. In addition, he claimed that they had always been amongst his most trusted servants and had allowed this to happen to themselves voluntarily:

"It is a very great honour to be in my service."

Yes. But at what price?

Seated comfortably abreast, we looked out of the small circular portals at the lagoon. The waters were not so placid as I might have hoped, for numerous vessels passed us. He eyed them with joy, relating that when the shipwrights were at their busiest, they could fashion as many as a hundred in four months' time.

That was the ideal moment, when he was filled with pride for his city and its achievements, that I made my request. He was taken aback by it.

"You have been a friend to Venice for all of your life. I would be illdisposed to begrudge you any desire. What you ask is not impossible, however, it will not sit well with the church or with other Christian rulers, for that matter."

I disagreed, about the church, at any rate. I presented him with a scroll from the Holy Father, whom I had stopped in Rome to see, prior to my journey hither, I informed him. He smiled.

"I should never be surprised by your thoroughness."

After having read the document, the Doge agreed, though wondered, whither these Jews might be relocated.

I was looking out of a portal, when I noticed a large strip of land.

"Why not there?" I asked, pointing to it.

"O, that is not sound ground to till. Several farmers live there. I have no idea how they manage to survive, yet they do."

"The Jews are an industrious people, never shirking their labours. I know of one who is not only a religious guide for his people, but also physician to the Sultan of Egypt."

"And this ruler places his trust in a Jew's knowledge?"

"Every single day."

"He must be the finest physician in all the world! If he ever grows tired of that royal court, or if he is ever mistreated, please tell him that I would very much like to have such a man in *my* service."

He went on now about how he felt that I needed an additional warning as to what we were about to accomplish here.

"You should probably remember that the hearts of men do not so easily change. What you hope to achieve may be little more than a temporary measure. I can foresee a time when my family, in order to maintain the peace, may be compelled to send these people once again into exile. I want your promise that you will not bear ill-will against my children and their children, should such an occasion arise."

I swore to him that I would not bear them my anger.

Later that day, he wrote and signed off a declaration.

I returned to the Maimun household and related to its patriarch that which I had accomplished. Both the Holy Father and the Doge had agreed to set aside a small, largely uninhabited island in the Venetian lagoon to be used as a homeland for the Jewish people.

He was overwhelmed. He began to sob.

"That you have done all this for my people is a kindness beyond words. For the first time in my life, I am struck dumb."

In time the island would take its name in memory of the Jewish population that had once lived there—*Giudecca*. For the Pope and the Doge had been most correct; the day would come when no Jew was welcomed in that city, despite our best efforts to alter the hard hearts of men.

A few years later, in 1204, in a wet and cold December, Moshe ben Maimun died. Not only did the Jewish people come to pay their respects; so, too, did many Muslims, including the Sultan and his entire family. And the Sultan wept piteously for the man whose expertise and kindness knew no boundaries.

This century had commenced with my participation in the recapture and creation of a Christian Jerusalem. It concluded with my participation in the creation of a homeland elsewhere for its original Jewish inhabitants. There was a curious sense of balance about everything, as well as a horrid emptiness that so much and nothing at all had really changed.

CHAPTER THE FORTY-FIRST,

in which begins a Fourth Holy War, though not against the infidel.

With the commencement of a new century arrived a summons to appear at the Venetian court. The Doge had suddenly found it necessary to question my affiliations.

We sat across from each other at the very long table often used for royal functions and feasts. The hall was grand, its ceiling overladen with meticulously wrought *cherubim*, which circled portraits of Greek (or perhaps Roman) deities cavorting or lolling about, courtesy of Bacchus' fruit of the vine.

"They call themselves *Byzantines*," he began, after sipping of the goblet, "when they are little more than Greeks with a few coins in their purses. My ancestors entered into trade with them centuries ago, and the arrangement has proven mutually beneficial, I must admit. However, we, in the West, have had to endure their schemes and betrayals. I have heard it said that with the death of Emperor Alexios Komnenos, their dignity has faded into little more than historical remembrance."

I, too, sipped from a goblet.

"Though not perfect a man," I let it be known, "he granted to me much honour."

"That is why I have requested your presence. I thought that you might bear them a certain *fondness*, shall we say, and with it a degree of loyalty."

A curious statement. What did he seek from me?

"Theirs was once an empire ruled by men who were honourable, most of the time. Today it is only a fragment of its former glory. To my family have you been more the faithful son than the loyal friend. Should war erupt between the West and Byzantium, at whose side will you stand?"

"I shall stand where I have always stood—next to the pope."

"Well said!" He arose now. "Come. The vintners have blended several new varietals, and I knew that you would be as anxious as I to partake of the first drops."

After Pope Innocent III's renewed call for a holy war, the first to take the cross (in 1199) were French nobles. (Most of these came from Champagne, I was proud to discover.) A treaty was then negotiated with the Doge; his city was to provide extensive transport plus six months worth of provisions for the entire army (or fleet), for a fee, of course, albeit at a reduced and very fair market-price—in excess of eighty thousand silver marks, if I remember it correctly. But something happened, that no one had ever expected would occur; there were simply not enough nobles attending, who would be able to pay off the full sum. By the time that ships were ready to sail, there was still a shortage of more than thirty thousand. I do not believe that the Holy Father was prepared to hear this truth. (When he did hear of it, his face took on a distinctly purplish hue, whilst he clenched and unclenched his fists in a silent tirade, the words of which only our Lord heard.) He had had no idea of how the current strain of noble rulers preferred instead to concern themselves with the problems of governance within their own kingdoms. Not even the papal assurance that the souls of all participants would journey to Heaven immediately upon death, thereby passing any time in Purgatory, would sway their hearts.

The forces now milling about Venice had no idea of where to find the additional monies. The Doge had been very generous, everyone agreed. How could anyone ask him to be more so?

At that point Enrico took it upon himself to guarantee to all present that he would be magnanimous once again. It was (he made certain that everyone knew) one more example of Venetian *largesse*. He would supply transport and provisions, providing that the knights join his forces in one or two wars, which he was currently waging. With a goodly portion of reluctance, they agreed to his terms.

The only person who did not agree (when he learned of it) was the pope. Fearing that (from the very outset) this holy war had begun to transform itself into something else altogether, (*i.e.,* something that he would not be able to control), he sent letters of excommunication to Venice, that all the knights (and the Doge as well) would suffer the infinite anguish of eternal damnation! Yet somehow, miraculously, these letters never arrived. So, the Venetians and the rest went off to war.

I cannot say why the holy warriors found their way to Konstantinople, since the Doge had not been at war with his trading-partner. Perhaps it was the promise of untold riches that spurred the knights on to their attacks. (This was one story that had never lost its excitement, despite its extreme age.) Perhaps it was an attempt to place back upon the throne a deposed emperor, who had promised to the pope that he would unite the church of the East with that of the West; the monarch also promised to appoint a Latin patriarch to the city, and rid it of its soon-to-be former Byzantine one. But the pope did not trust these *Greeks*, (as he was wont to say), and so had forbade this conquest.

The Venetians and the others arrived at the city on the fourth of July in that year of our Lord 1203. The Doge, fully armoured, stood at the prow. He lifted high the Venetian standard. (Upon its face had been stitched a golden lion holding two golden tablets. These stones carried a Latin phrase that may be seen everywhere upon buildings and statuary throughout Venice even today: *Pax tibi Marche evanelista meus*; *Peace unto you, Mark, my evangelist.*) And beneath the crimson sail of his ship, raising the standard of peace, the Doge ordered the knights to attack in holy cause. They did so immediately. And they ravaged an empire.

They tore down the great doors of *Hagia Sophia*, cut them apart, stripped silver from all the columns inside, and with axes cracked the variegated jasper of these same columns into large chunks, still small enough for a single man to carry. They smashed the censers, walked away with pavers of white marble from the altar, and tore out precious stones from everywhere about. Then the marauders spread their violence to the homes of the wealthy. Then began murder and rapine. Then their leaders carved up the surrounding territories, until each one had secured for himself his own piece.

I heard that the Doge was most pleased. So pleased was he, in fact, that the four bronze horses, which once stood atop the walls of a Byzantine *arboretum*, were spirited away to Venice. For a time stored in the *Arsenale*, eventually they found a new home. They reside now upon the low roof of the *Basilica di San Marco*. When I stood before its entrance, several years thereafter, I fought to restrain my tears. It was the first time that I ever felt any sympathy for the achievements of Emperor Alexios Komnenos and his people, and all their arrogant pride, and all their lost beauty.

The Doge died in Konstantinople in 1205, at the age of eight and ninety. His marble tomb was placed in Hagia Sophia, the restoration of which he personally oversaw. A few days prior to his demise, he watched as a Venetian was made Patriarch for the city, which action pleased His Holiness deeply. So much did it do so, that the Holy Father and the Doge were reconciled. All was forgiven, for a time.

And whilst Venice raped Konstantinople, the Templars and Hospitallers awaited the arrival of bold knights who would once again attempt to retake Jerusalem. But they never came. It would be years before Christian knights would heed once more a papal call to arms. Unfortunately, the only result of these future endeavours would be more deaths. Of such blood is much of glory made!

CHAPTER THE FORTY-SECOND,

in which more than one pope makes the Cathars the object of new holy wars for years and years and....

So frequent were the holy wars thereafter, that their numbers blur in a constant battle between a sacred wish to regain Jerusalem for God and Christ, and a more secular concern for the conquest of nearby territories.

Perhaps the one holy war that overshadows all others in that century was the one against the Cathars. The Holy Father condemned them as *heretics* for a number of their beliefs. Central among them were these:

1. Evil was as potent a force as Good was.
    (And such an insult to the Lord's might should never be tolerated!)

2. In religious ceremonies, women were allowed to officiate as priests.
    (As if a woman could be every bit as good in a man's rôle! Unthinkable!)

3. Both men and women could lie with others of their respective sexes, without fear of reprisal.
    (Damnèd Sodomites, the lot of them!)

And what prince of the church could tolerate this heresy? Certainly not his holiness, Pope Gregory IX! He responded to their insolence with as strong a command as the ancient Romans had against the Carthaginians:

"The Cathars must be destroyed!"

And so began another holy war.

The Northern and Southern French had ever been in contention each with the other. The former thought themselves industrious and the latter lax in all things. The latter had ever felt that the former knew nothing of how to appreciate each exciting moment found, especially since life was so transitory. This became a matter of language as well. The Northern and Southern tongues constantly warred for supremacy. Over time, it was the former that was fast becoming the victor, in no small part due to the location of Paris (the seat of government) in the north. Finally, none of it really mattered. This war was destined not to see its completion so readily.

In 1208 a papal legate was murdered in the largest city of southern France, Albi, and against their most troublesome group, the Cathars, King Louis IX of France took the cross immediately. He had only one problem with his rash action: he had not thought long about how much his decision would actually cost. He queried the Holy Father for a possible solution. The answer was an obvious one; the king should borrow the necessary funds from the wealthiest group in Christendom—the Templars. However, the idea of lending money without a fee was one that his holiness found irksome. He did not wish his Templars to do so without benefit of some form of additional currency for their troubles. Of course, he could not permit usury. It was enough that the accursèd Jews were doing so. (But not even all their wealth could finance an entire war.) On the other hand, a church tax would not be out of the question. That was when it came to him suddenly. The Templars could not charge a *church tax*, for they were not of the church hierarchy proper, but they could certainly charge a *usage tax*. And if Holy Mother Church were to receive a meager tenth portion of said tax, (a usage tithe), where was the harm in that?

So, the king went to the Templars, who were only too happy to lend a portion of their wealth to a needful sovereign. Unfortunately, said king was often slow in his repayments—a disgusting family trait that was to repeat itself again and again among his spendthrift descendants.

One war became a series of wars, which continued for twenty years with little or no result. It was not until four years after its commencement, when Pope Gregory IX was pondering how he might rid Christendom of the heretics, that a novel idea struck him like a thunderbolt. In that moment was born the Inquisition.

At the beginning of this war I found myself in Paris, where Templars (from all lands), Hospitallers (from all lands), and as many knights as could be found were ordered to meet. At the Parisian Temple I met one brother, a young man, bald, with much fire in his belly. This Brother Benedictus, a German of large frame, came into my presence with so ferocious an anger, that one could feel it even before he arrived.

"Wherefore do you, a founder of our Order, deny a papal request?"

Others nearby surrounded him, fearing that he would strike me.

"Let him go," I told them. "He has a right to his anger."

He pushed the others off, then bared his teeth at me.

"Do you fear to answer me?"

"Do you know why we lost Jerusalem? Do you?!"

The brethren gathered closer about me.

"It was not because the Muslims were more capable fighters. It was not because their leaders were wiser or more experienced in the art of war. It was because for every Christian who was willing to die for God and his fellow Christians, there were ten who could see only the gold, precious gems, and lands ripe for conquest! The Muslims were united in common cause. They saw the future. And the day that they forget their unity, that is the day that they will lose Jerusalem."

"If you love those heathens so much, why do you not go and live with them?"

I struck him. He flew across the room, smashing tables and chairs.

"Behold Goliath!" I shouted, mocking him.

Everyone laughed, though some helped the man to his feet. He wiped the blood from his mouth.

"Each man must search his own conscience," I advised them. "I may not agree with everything that the Cathars believe, but I do not agree with most people and what they believe either. Each man must make his own choice."

I left.

Several months thereafter, I was again at the Templar House in Paris, tutoring certain brethren in the use of Hebrew letters as numbers, when in came an unexpected visitor. Clad no longer in the garments of our Order, but in monk's robes, was Brother Benedictus. He had been searching for me. Really? Before his induction into the order of brethren that his clothing revealed, he had wanted to relate to me a story concerning his reasons for having left us to join a less bellicose group. I was rapt with attention:

"I killed many of them. I would have killed them all, that their souls might be saved from the fires of Perdition. For so it was, until we came upon a farmer and his family. Breaking down the door was our usual means of entry. I was the first inside. And I was the first to see him. At his feet lay the bodies of his wife and children, all without their heads. I beheld a bloody scythe in his hand. Tears were streaming down his cheeks.

> 'Did you think that I would let them die at your hands? I am the husband and father. This is what a man does. He protects his family from all harm. You think yourselves holy. What God would bless a blade? I curse you all. You who cannot see will see now. I have shown you the way of truth. I have answered your violence with eternal peace. You will not rob me of my family. They are mine. They will always be mine.'

"With a powerful thrust, he cut off his own head and fell before us."

He removed his scabbard and handed it off to me. I took it from him.

"I understand," I told him, looking into his eyes.

"I knew that you, above all others, would."

I followed him outside. He mounted his horse, then turned to me one last time.

"He was most correct. Truly am I cursed! Each time that I close my eyes, even to blink, I see them there in that farmhouse, and I know that never again will peace find a home within my soul."

He turned his horse into the western wind and rode away. Never again would I see him in all the remaining years of his penance.

More than ten years following the … *disagreement* between the Holy Father and myself, I journeyed to Toulouse, on the chance of locating again the tavern of the three sisters. When I came upon the road, where it was supposed to have been, I found nothing except formerly burned timbers, blackened, filling the cellar with their ashes. All about me had been smouldering for quite some time. I knew that I could not stand idle and allow an entire people to be destroyed.

Not far from that city lay a citadel, *Mont Ségur*. It had been under siege for the better part of a year, when I found myself in one of its towers with four Cathars. I had come thither in hopes of rescuing them.

One man (exceedingly fat) suggested that we escape with a rope.

I looked at it and laughed.

"This will not bring a single man to safety, let alone four. No. We must use three ropes."

"No," another (exceedingly thin) said. "Leave us here. You must take the grail."

"The what?!" I asked, refusing to believe his utterance.

"The grail," he repeated. "It is here," he said, opening a cloth of purple velvet to reveal a bejewled golden chalice."

"Forget that," I advised them.

"Forget it?" another asked, incredulously. "Why do you think the church has declared a war against us?"

"For possession of that thing?" I asked.

"It is our most holy relic," another said.

"It cannot be holy,"I told them, "for it is not a cup from which our Lord drank."

"How do you know this?" the first one asked.

"Believe me. I know whereof I speak."

They stared at me, then at each other, then at me, then at each other.

"We have risked our lives," continued the first, "and many have died, all for nothing?"

"It is not even real!" the thin one exclaimed to the first. "I told you this was not it. But did you listen? You never listen!" Tears began to flow from his already-reddened eyes.

"We have no time for this foolishness," I advised them. "Put that thing down, and we shall leave."

"No," said the first. "It makes no difference. Do you not see, all of you? Its truth is greater than the thing, itself. We must take it to safety."

I elected not to argue. I tied several ropes together, and guided the four upon their descent. Thanks be to God that only one (who was exceedingly fat) was ungainly in his climb downwards. In point of fact, he very nearly fell, which action would have probably killed all of them. I brought them to safety, however, I was the one who took their cup to its final resting place in a small church not far from the estate of the St. Claires, where it resides behind stones until this very day.

Did any of it matter? Still they took the cross. Still they came. The Holy Father had commenced this call to war, yet never thought how he might end it, if the enemies-in-question continued to rebel, as these had been doing for decades. He left the solution for those around him (or who would come after him) to determine.

One French king, Louis IX, journeyed to *Outremer*, (after having led a force to slaughter most of the remaining Cathars), and achieved there a greater degree of fame than even his best efforts on behalf of the Holy Father had granted him. He never destroyed all of the heretics, as no ruler or soldier did either. Shortly after his demise, sainthood was his reward, for having sent so many Christian *infidels* to the fiery depths below.

There were others certainly, noble (or ignoble, depending upon one's frame of reference), all until the last crusader stronghold of Acre passed once more into Muslim hands in that unforgettable year of 1291.

That action prompted me to see personally to the establishment of the Parisian Templar House as the new foundation for the Order. (That was a decision that I would soon come to regret.) There, I took leave of everyone. I considered my task complete, and it was time for me to leave the world of men.

It was shortly before his demise that Pope Gregory and I were reconciled. He felt that it was proper and just both for himself and for me, that we should forgive each other. I held him as he gave up his last breath.

Then began the years of my wanderings. I went as far to the east as the lands of *Chin*, where the people *did* have slits for eyes, (as a young Anna had once told me they did), and into the frozen wastes of *Rus*, the peoples of which evinced a devotion to our crucified Lord greater than any that I had ever seen. And each time, somehow, miraculously, my brethren would find me. I cannot say how I found myself in Scotland one day, convinced that I should have it known formally, that I would leave the Order and perhaps disappear into some cave somewhere to live out forever in mine own offal and filth, whilst praising God and His holy works.

As I left the Templar House in Stirling, I was beset by a tempest. My cloak did nought to shield me from the blinding winds and waters. At a loud peel of thunder, my steed bolted, and I fell, head first, into the muddy road. I turned over. Upon my back now, I opened my mouth, praying to drown, as perhaps Prince Bohémond, himself, might have done at the last. I cannot say why. Perhaps I had grown so weary after two centuries, that it seemed like the perfect time for a permanent departure. Whatever labours the Lord had seen fit for me to accomplish were now complete. If not, then nothing mattered anymore. The release of Death would be a blessing, for which I was well prepared.

Then it was that the storm ceased. So brightly did the sky grow, that I became blinded by the sun at its zenith. Like Samson, I felt myself eyeless in Gaza, at the mercy of others.

From afar came a whisper, as of a woman's voice, speaking my name. Upon the soft breezes it floated closer to me. I found that I could not speak, though my mind reached out to touch her. Was it Mary? Was it my precious Anna? She repeated my name, whispering it into mine ear. I felt the embrace of her lips upon me. The kiss was like no other imaginable. My entire body shook. I felt her breasts rub against my chest, as if fondling me. I grew ever harder. Into her moist hair she took me inside of her. I could not say how long we thrust into each other. I thought it days. Still her lips were upon me. Then I released. And the act took all my strength and will.

I lay there, feeling nothing, feeling the comfort of no one, for she was no longer with me. Then it was that my body shook again. This time each wound that I had ever received, (no matter how minor or insignificant), opened, pouring my blood into the muddy road. I felt myself floating, floating upon a red sea beneath me. Strange that I should think only upon a statue that I had once seen in a tiny church in *Outremer*. It was of Jesus upon the cross. So emaciated was he, that his bones revealed themselves through the thin flesh of his chest, whilst his distended belly hung over the cloth covering his nakedness. And upon that crucifix, he screamed in agony, that the entire world might hear his pain. Then I recalled the burial linen tightening itself around my face and form. Was it the suffering of man that ties one to his brethren? Though the Son of God, was He made flesh in order to experience birth, maturation, and death only? Is this what it meant to be Christian, to experience if not the wounds of Christ, then his agony of spirit, doubt, and finally acceptance. Doubtless was I that these three form the essence of the Christian mystery. One must die unto and into the Christ. In that way only are we reborn to Him.

Now it was that I had to render unto the Lord mine own life, freely, willingly, less any and all hesitation.

"Take me!" I cried aloud now, having found my voice once more. "Take me, for You know where I am. I am here, where You have found me. Whither shall I go, if not for You, with empty places inside, torn from my beginning, fitted with Your hands, this cycle of tears and forgetting, stopped only with Your laughter? You love like a nubile woman, itching for touch, like a careless boy, lost in gaming. In all places, in all things, I am ever … Yours."

"In righteous cause only," spoke her voice again, from so far away now.

So many times had we unleashed the Fenris-wolf to gnaw upon a lunar landscape and so o'erwhelm the world. Had man finally sent the creature on its way, never to be seen again? Thus I wondered as I lay there, tasting of mine own death.

And in that moment, in the high sun at midday, I realized that my life had returned to me, and I had been born into this world once more.

At that time came another voice, not the soft whisper of a woman, but the deep growl of a man.

"Fare ye well, my lord?"

It was somehow familiar to me, though I could not place it exactly. Momentarily I thought it might have been Brother Michael's particular tone, though overwrought with a Scottish *brogue*.

I felt massive hands lift me up. I was unable to see his face, for the sun was still very much afire in mine eyes, though I might have sworn the shape to be more lumbering bear than helpful man.

"How do you call yourself, kind stranger?" I asked of him.

"Dunstane of Inverness, if it be any business of yours."

A warrior, and without much patience for the rituals of greeting. Apparently I had need of such a gruff companion, and God did provide him for me.

"I have need of your services. I am blind."

"O, forgive me. I did not see."

"Neither did I," I added with a smile. "It is but a temporary affliction. When my sight is restored, you are welcome to stay with me, or leave if you desire. I am Guy de Lagery."

"Why, this is a day full of God's good fortune! I have sought you out for many a month now. Word has it that you wished the services of the finest swordsman in the land. I proudly submit myself to you as not only the greatest bearer of the blade, but the finest of men to be found anywhere."

"A proud Scot is a rare thing," I said with *eirony*.

"It is?"

"Now tell me; do I still bear any wounds?"

"Wounds? Have you been set upon? I'll shred their flesh, if I knew where they be. But no one else is about, my lord. And ye look as if they had not disturbed a single hair upon your head."

"No matter. I am healing. You are most welcome to join me, Dunstane, the Scot."

"*Dunstane, the Scot,*" he repeated. "Methinks I like the way that sounds."

"Somehow I knew that you would, my friend."

"And whither shall we go, my lord?"

"Whither God will lead us."

"God will lead us? You might be a damnèd sight holier than you look!"

Holy? Me? Now really, who ever heard a statement as foolish as that one?

Here endeth the Second Book.

LIBER TERCIUS

Et Spiritus Sanctus

CHAPTER THE FORTY-THIRD,

in which the lure of Paris calls me home to the regent's court royal, and O, what intrigues are to be found there!

As historians are so fond of listing royal personages and curt descriptions of them, in the ensuing years since his death, they have seen fit to render King Phillip IV de la France as *the Handsome One, le Bel.* However, if one were to look at portraits of him, even with a cursory glance, one might see sharp features betraying perhaps haughty arrogance—something in the eyes, I believe; or it may be the slight disdain that leaks from those selfsame eyes in droplets, as he looks down upon us all. There is no smile in any portrait. And each end of his mouth dips downward slightly to the side. The same may be said for the corners of each eye.

There is no warmth in this face.

By themselves these works of art may have had little more than slight historical interest or significance. What makes them so utterly fascinating is that they are so utterly false.

Phillip, somehow, miraculously, was able to accomplish something that almost all other regents have been able to control only minimally. Often a court painter has created an *eikon* of power and privilege that has lacked a particular blemish or scar. Often said subject might be shown in battle with his enemies, always as the stronger, the far more heroic participant. Though the same held true for Phillip's portrayals, his face was nothing like the curious studies of him. As I have herein written, he was called, *le Bel,* and I swear unto you, dear reader, that the name must have originated in either a mother's or a father's vain attempts to flatter a child as compensation for his inadequacies, or as a touch of bitter comedy from the Lord above, for Phillip was, doubtless, the ugliest man whom I had ever seen.

Wherefore was the reason, (divine or otherwise), in the man possessing mottled skin, upon which sat numerous warts? (Of these protrusions, the only one that I found to be truly disturbing was the large mound in the center of his brow, for I had ofttimes taken it to be the beginning of an eye. I wondered what things he saw with that curious *oculus*, things, which the rest of humanity never would or dared?) I could tell you of the magnificent crop of hair flowing like thick locks from his pate, as his portraits may attest, though, in truth, *hairs* might be a description more apt; thus an insult to nature they truly were. Very thin, and frequently mussed, they appeared as if no comb had ever passed gently through them, or as if he had arisen (at this very moment) from a night's fitful slumber. But I believe that his nose garnered all attention from elsewhere upon his person. It was not, strictly speaking, a *nose* in the way that you or I have come to understand the term. It was—what is the word that I am seeking? Amorphous! Yes. It lay there upon his face like a dollop of mud or *gesso*, waiting for a sculptor's hand to fashion it into something remotely pleasing to the eye. This, unfortunately, was not to be. Though if his appearance ever bothered him, he kept those thoughts to himself; nor did anyone ever mention it. (At least they never did so in or near his company.) He did, in fact, commission all royal portraits of himself to look very much like those of his father—(with slight variation)—a paragon of male perfection indeed! I assume that it was the vainglorious hope to attach his name to a kinder place in history than the one that he, in his heart, always believed would become his own, should anyone recall his actual comeliness (or lack thereof).

As I remember him now, he was little more than a child when first we met. And with the passage of time, he never seemed to age. Perhaps that was because his features appeared perpetually old. In short, his deformities were so harsh, that they became a source of virtually constant pain. In lieu of crying out from the agony, however, (an act, that I must confess, no one ever saw him do), he sought solace in drink, often, I might add. You may wonder, dear reader, why this French king was a seemingly endless source of fascination for me. I assure you, it is nothing more than my quest to uncover the essential truth of an individual, who was to accomplish what so few others had ever dreamed—the destruction of the Templars.

In the early years of the fourteenth century, I recently returned to Paris from Scotland, where I had made acquaintance of a fine swordsman and healthy drinker. Dunstane's hair was mostly gray, and as full as it was long; so, too, was his beard. His eyebrows were dark and thick. And whenever he wore a smile, his eyes would squint, nearly closing, whilst his entire face would transform into a veritable circle of laughter. His paunch was large and solid—the product of many years of gluttony. Despite his girth, he moved swiftly, and handled a sword better than any man whom I had ever known, or would ever know. And he was my friend.

The king had finished his speech and left the balcony. After having heard their leader's pronouncements, the crowd dispersed with a collective groan, as Dunstane turned to me.

"In truth, my lord, he is the foulest creature on God's green earth. Often I've heard the English say that monsters walk on French soil. I never believed it, 'til today."

After having made his innermost thoughts known to me, (as was his custom), he kept looking back at the empty balcony, as if a remnant of the grotesque visage had somehow still lingered behind to haunt him.

"Why we had to leave Scotland and come to this wretched country of yours is a great mystery. Mayhap when you think that I am worthy for the honour, you'll confess your reasons to me. 'Til then, can your business with the Holy Father wait 'til we've contented ourselves with a game of dice and a fine brew? You do have decent ale in this godforsaken city, do you not?"

The monarch was the reason why I had come back. Often he borrowed money from the Templars, and somehow always found an excuse not to repay them.

"Hmm, the privileges of regency, I suppose," was Dunstane's assessment of the entire situation.

"No doubt that is what the king believes."

"And you propose to change his beliefs? You are a man of deep and abiding faith in the impossible. This I have always said, have I not? I spotted a tavern not far from this square. A man should never have to argue the finer points of politics with the Holy Father on an empty stomach. I'm parched, I am. What say ye, my lord? Shall we?"

"We shall."

We did not leave the brewmaster's company until my purse was empty, as was my custom whenever I was in a tavern with Dunstane. The next day I left the Scot to sleep off his cups, and made my way to the Holy Father, the agèd Clement, in whose fellowship I had always found a welcome smile.

I did not locate him in the finished portions of *Nôtre Dame*, (contrary to my expectations), rather in the Abbey, *Sainte Genevieve*, a more modest house of God, set comfortably atop a hillock overlooking the city. I thought perhaps he had gone there to seek inspiration for the history that he had hoped to compose on the first Frankish king, Clovis, whose body was interred therein.

I passed through the vestibule, thence to the chapel. There, surrounded by a sea of multi-hued glass panels, the Holy Father was pointing out one artisan's handiwork to a select group of novices clustered about him. I caught the last portion of his statement:

"And there is the truth of truths, my brothers. When Adam bit of the apple, with which Eve tempted him, it was not long before our one-time parents suffered the expulsion from the Garden. So you see, a simple act may have far-reaching consequences. One must be ever-vigilant."

"And man went forth to toil in the fields," I added quite loudly, walking towards the group, "whilst woman cried out in the agony of birth. Such is our lot in life, for we are, all of us, exiles from Eden. Tell me, your holiness, what would have happened if Eve had refused at first to bite of that apple? Would we still be walking around shamelessly nude in Paradise?"

When he saw me, he smiled broadly.

"That is a question for our Lord, only, to answer. My brothers," he announced, stretching forth his arms, "welcome into our presence Sir Guy de Lagery, who has brought much honour to the Christian faith from one end of this world to the other."

They gathered round, but not for long. The Holy Father bade them leave, so that he and I might converse privately. His butler hovered about, before being asked, once more, to busy himself elsewhere.

An exceedingly large man, Pope Clement's face was heavily lined, its flesh sagging, jowly, as if he had consumed far too much of roasted meat and no less of drink throughout his many years of life. We embraced.

"As always, your arguments test an old man's patience. Were you this much trouble to your sainted uncle?"

"More so, I fear."

"O, of that I am most assured. It is good to see you again. You have been absent from our presence for far too long."

I informed him that the labyrinth of politics could ensnare even one who has little taste for the game, including myself, unfortunately. He took that to mean that the other members of the Order were not immune to its enticements.

"Scottish Templars have stood with Robert the Bruce," I concluded. "English royalty was most displeased."

"I am wondrous glad to hear of it! Those English are no better than beasts. Forever filthy, they are. And that language of theirs is monstrously harsh upon the ear. It is never as mellifluous as our blessèd tongue."

"Unfortunately, the English Templars have become the arm of an English king, who is as contentious as he is bold. The Scot, William Wallace, deserved better treatment at their hands. He might have even defeated the regent, had they not stepped in," I added with much bitterness.

"Was the man ever a threat to the church?"

"The Scots are a good, God-fearing people, a hearty race. You would trust your life to them."

His cheeks became flushed. He was angered that Jacques de Molai, the Master of the Templars, had not exercised greater control over his English chapter. (I had previously warned the Holy Father that the danger of their being used for royal whims was ever a real possibility.)

"Once more your words have proven true," he told me.

There had never been any affection between the head of the Order and myself, nor a shred of respect, for that matter, (at least not so on my part), and moreover, I usually let the man know the depth of my feelings, or considerable lack of them. I had often believed that the Templars had rewarded Jacques for his many years of dedicated service in *Outremer*, and his election to that position came at a most fortuitous time for him—when there was no clear choice remaining to assume the reins of leadership. If I am guilty of any sin or wrongdoing in my dealings with him, it was perhaps in my lack of tact. Whenever I think of what his future would hold, however, I curse myself. Did he not deserve to be given a fair portion of decent behaviour, even from someone who had no use for him?

"It would appear that Jacques has also proven himself to be as ineffectual a leader as you cautioned him that he might be," the Holy Father added.

In the vast social structure that forms our lives, there are positions, which call for the seasoned warrior to step forward, whereas others cry out for the impetuousness that accompanies only youth. Being the Templar leader meant being a combination of both.

"Your letters were most troubling. The old man has ever been a functionary, an administrator," I reiterated. "He has never been up to the task."

"I could ask him to resign. I would, except that I have always liked him, and always thought him honourable."

"If misguided."

He agreed. He knew that he had no choice except to call upon Jacques to rein in his knights. After all, they were the arm of the church, not of kings, and they would do well to remember their mandate.

"And speaking of royalty, have you seen our royal Phillip yet?"

In truth, I had not seen the regent since the day of his marriage. And when I looked upon his features now, I found it difficult to accept that his grandfather, the warrior Louis, who had been canonized not a decade previously, and who was of noble appearance, had ever brought forth such misshapen progeny.

"He is as curious about you as you must doubtless be of him," the pontiff continued.

"Only from a safe distance."

He laughed.

"No, he is no Medusa, despite all appearances to the contrary. In point of fact, his afflictions are many. In a less civilized age his parents would have placed the newborn outside the city's gates, there to be eaten by a pack of wolves. I have of late wondered if such cruelty would not have been more merciful."

"The populace might agree with you, especially since he seems determined to bleed them with further taxation."

"No! Not another one."

Indeed, this in a time when the system of barter was still all too common, especially in the outlying districts.

"If we had a Wallace," I suggested, "we might not have a *daemon* sitting upon the throne."

I had spoken as I did, because I wanted to see how the Holy Father would respond, whether he would take up the cause of the common folk, or simply repeat all that the king had told him that he should. During the times when we had met, (between my voyages back and forth to Scotland and other ports of call), I noticed that the church father did not appear particularly comfortable with my every mention of the regent. At such moments I thought that his skin had grown suddenly tighter, and was about to push his very organs out of his mouth. At this moment I had to know why.

In truth, I was not prepared to witness such a dramatic change. The figure standing before me now was no longer the pope, a man of courage and respect, not even the former archbishop, but a much simpler tradesman from a much simpler time—Bertrand de Grot. His eyes, overwhelmed by fear, flitted about to all the dark corners around us. Perhaps he was thinking that he might succumb to a poison similar to the one that had taken his immediate predecessor. (Of course, that was a rumour never to be proven either true or false, though more than a few believed it to be so.) Nevertheless, his eyes frightened me at a time in my life when nought could anymore.

"Never speak in that manner to a single soul," he whispered, "not even in jest. It is regicide!"

Was it no longer safe to speak one's mind freely in God's house, though His house be on French soil? What had happened to our magnificent land? In so rich a place as this I saw misery everywhere.

"This is not the young France I once knew," I told him.

Some things had indeed changed. The ruler had appointed a lawyer to the highest position at court, and did nothing without his counsel. This William de Nogaret had been the recipient of a new title created especially for him—*Advocate of the Realm*. And what I could not believe of him was that the man, himself, was an excommunicate.

"In service to a Christian king?" I asked. "How is this possible?"

"Yes. I have no doubt that the entire host of Heaven must be rattling their swords. However, the king trusts him, as he trusts no other. And in France today, the king's will, whether divinely ordained or not, must be obeyed."

De Nogaret was a family name not unknown to me, though I could not recall where I had first heard mention of it.

His holiness had called this king *a methodical regent, one who did nothing arbitrarily*. If Phillip had raised up this lawyer, then the man must have been very important to him, and possibly to the future of our people. Certainly, I concluded, that might not be a good thing.

"What else do we know of him?" I asked.

"Only of his expertise in jurisprudence. Little else, I fear."

I understood. I turned and began to walk away. I would inform his holiness of what I might discover.

"Exercise caution," he warned me. "Besides royalty, he may have many powerful friends at court."

I thought it a curious thing to say, considering the resources at our disposal, though I spoke not a word of it.

I left to pursue my research.

CHAPTER THE FORTY-FOURTH,

in which I create a coterie of observants, one of whom then proceeds to relate an exchange most curious.

I had never forgotten Archbishop Adhémar's advice that none in Konstantinople could be trusted. I must confess that the import of his statement has weighed heavily upon me, lo these many years. Consequently, I have rarely trusted a soul since. And whilst I had no particular cause to distrust our regent, neither did I have a single reason to put my faith into either his words or his works. So I set about the creation of a group of messengers, who would watch, (in secret), listen, (in secret), then report to me (in secret) of what had transpired at the court-royal. This labour was by no means difficult to achieve. There had been times in the past, when I would select a servant girl and regale her with tales of holy wars and brave knights. Often I tossed in the appearance of a dragon or two simply as a form of poetic embellishment. That would typically be all that was required of me. (On the other hand, if the girl were pretty, I would offer her far more of a romantic nature.) But as talented as these youthful maidens might prove themselves to be, (in numerous ways, mind you!), I found that the elderly were much more detailed in their telling of every single aspect of courtly life. Perhaps that was because they had to be quite proficient in their tasks, lest they incur royal impatience and wrath; or it might have been the many years of listening at key-holes that had made their keen acquisition of knowledge far more complete. And all that they required of me was that I listen to their words, or share their prayers. (Many of them thought that I was holy, and was, therefore, the perfect companion for these tasks. I hope that God will forgive me for not having made any attempt to dissuade them from that opinion, though I knew far better of it.)

My two chief accomplices in this duty would turn out to be women possessed of remarkable perceptive abilities. (The vision of the younger and the hearing of the elder proved priceless.) The younger, Theresa, had years of less than twenty. With skin like the finest Cararan marble, she was fit perhaps for a sculptor who might choose to fashion her as a youthful Madonna. Modest whilst in the performance of her duties, she became a randy wench with a maw of language most foul when in company amongst the others of her station. She it was who referred to the elderly Marie (my other helper) as *Madamoiselle Soixante, Miss Sixty*, referring both to the woman's age and to her lack of a husband. (Often I endeavoured to prevail upon the younger not to insult the elder, most especially in my presence. She was more agreeable about that than not.)

I preferred to keep my quarters far from the court and close to a small church. Its location provided me with a certain degree of privacy that was useful, especially when visited by either one of the ladies. Within less than a week of our arrival in Paris, Dunstane and I welcomed Marie in the late evening hours. After a prayer that we completed in due haste, (Dunstane was a good man, though not much for prayer), we sat about, sipping from a fine red that my comrade had secured for our pleasure. (O, how I had missed the aroma and taste of French wines!) Marie was not averse to the partaking thereof, I might add. She pulled down the hood of her cloak, revealing the long, thin head of gray hair that clung to her neck and the sides of her face like a second skin.

"I am most grateful to you for your kindness, my lord," she spoke, prior to her little sips. She warmed her hands now by the fire and related what she had heard this very night.

The king had been complaining to his advocate. But during what appeared to be an harangue concerning the nearly empty coffers in the treasury, the advocate mentioned my name. Apparently I was to be used in some scheme of financial acquisition.

"In what manner?" I asked.

She did not know, though she was able to relate the following conversation to me:

"How do you know that he will play along with this plan?" de Nogaret questioned his liege and master.

"It is his nature to seek reconciliation at all costs. Failing that, he will do what he is told. First and foremost, he is a creature of politics, as are we all. For him the church is secondary."

"But master, how can you be so certain?"

"How can you be so doubtful? Where is your faith in the essential indignity of man? After all, if men were pure of heart, we would have no need of lawyers now, would we?"

Their conversation ended, they erupted into mutual laughter.

Marie was not happy with the implications of what she had heard.

"This William is a man with many ideas in his head," she spoke, giving voice to her curious fears. "Sometimes he tells the king that he is working on something, and must excuse himself to complete his task. No one dares to speak to his highness in that way. Why do you think he allows this lawyer to dismiss him like that?"

Old yet wise she was, this Marie. If Phillip were to bend the rituals of courtesy for the man, then their relationship was so deep, that it was unlike any other. I wondered if it were simply the value of his advice, or the sharing of similar goals that was responsible. In fact, their connection might have been an amorous one, much as I cared little to ruminate upon what physical activities *that* might entail.

"As I recall, the queen has been dead these past three years, has she not?" I asked.

Marie nodded. She went on about the children, how much they missed their mother's attentions, for their father spent so little time with them.

I saw no sin in this. If he were guilty of anything, so was every other regent and nobleman. Of all those whom I had known, Hughes de Payens was the only one whose duties in *Outremer* and subsequent separation from his sons forever weighed heavily upon his heart.

"And the advocate, what is his marital status?

As much as she knew it to be true, she believed that the man was happy with his wife and daughter. Since she had not much else to relate, she thanked me once more. In turn, I thanked her for her aid.

The hour was quite late. I could not allow her to return to the palace with the numerous cutpurses and highwaymen abroad. (Under cover of darkness, and with stealth, they had created an even more unsavoury reputation for themselves than was their wont.) Dunstane, ever the gallant escort, bade me stay; he would return her safely. But before she departed, she told us that she would first have to go to an apothecary, there to purchase a poison. (Rats had been scurrying and gnawing about in her chamber, their noise depriving her of much needed rest.)

"Nonsense," I told her. "I have something far more effective than any purchase might provide you."

I removed a tiny vial from a small cabinet and handed it to her. She turned it over in the light of the fire, apparently admiring the aquamarine tint of the liquid encased therein.

"It glows, my lord! Whatever can it be?"

"A most powerful poison distilled from the venomous blood of Eqyptian asps, mixed together with sundry ingredients which are known to a select few only in all the world."

"Oooh! It must be priceless. I cannot accept such a gift," she refused, holding it forth.

"Take it, dear lady. I can think of no better use for it than to rid you of disturbing vermin. Place a piece of cheese on the floor. Remember to spill no more than two droplets upon the item. The creature will die shortly after swallowing its first bite. No more than two, mind you."

"Begging your pardon, my lord, but if my hand should waver and I spill a third?"

"The creature will die as before, but its body will begin to putrefy almost immediately. I fear the stench will linger for some time, despite all attempts to cleanse your quarters or fill its air with perfumery."

She assured me that she would remember, turning the vial over in her hands, still continuing to admire the appearance of the tiny object.

When they left, I looked into the fire, remembering how, upon the death of his Queen Jeanne, the king had applied for membership in the Templars, only to be rejected. Since all documentation was kept sealed, he never discovered why. I can tell you, dear reader, here and now, that it was I who had brought pressure to bear upon Master Jacques to reject the application. I had always believed that a monarch would use the Order for his own purposes, citing the importance of the fraternity and the faithfulness of good fellowship as two of the main reasons why his requests should be fulfilled. Jacques reluctantly agreed to abide by my decision, and consequently, it remained a sore point between us for some years. I believe that I never once thought of how that rejection might weigh upon a royal head, nor did I care. I was never more certain of any decision that I had ever made.

I had often received invitations for any number of royal functions. Most of these I had ignored. Of late I decided to avail myself of the opportunity to study his most royal French personage a bit more closely.

Within a day or two, Dunstane and I were at court, where the former marveled at the squares of black and white marble tiles, which formed the floor.

"It makes no sense to me," he offered. "Why is one colour not good enough? Is the man never satisfied?"

I bade him keep still, as the monarch approached. Nearing us, he raised a topic that I thought most unusual for discussion, *i.e.*, the consequences of my immortality:

"It must be a terrible thing to watch everyone whom you have ever known grow old and die," he spoke slowly, deliberately, I thought.

"Bearing witness is a terrible responsibility, my liege, perhaps the greatest."

"So you believe that you are still doing God's work after all this time."

"And I shall continue to do so, until the end of time."

"Such dedication to your own future is admirable. Consider this your home, Sir Guy. You are always welcome in our royal palace."

And with that, he and his entire retinue left to mingle with the other nobles and the occasional juggler or jester (or both). Dunstane studied him upon his leaving of us.

"Methinks I'm not likin' this man at all."

I watched him leave as well.

"What makes you say that?" I asked.

"Even his compliments are laced with venom."

I laughed.

"O, it may be nothing more than a bit of envy. Many men have been unhappy about the fact that I shall walk this earth long after they have turned to dust. Or, friend Dunstane," I said, turning to him, "it may be that he detests me."

"I never thought of it quite like that. But doesn't it stand to reason, that a man like you will remember a man like me? And in me own small fashion shall I have a bit of immortality, too, if only in your good graces, my lord."

I had never thought of it quite like that either.

"If the truth be known," I told him, "I believe that legends about you will spread far and wide without my help."

"Ah, you are most kind!" He lifted his goblet. "And if you will be a bit kinder, you will aid me to find something stronger than this piss that your people call wine."

"As Pliny wrote, there is truth in wine. And the truth in this wine is that servants have watered it down," I added, peering into my goblet. "And he has the audacity to call himself a Frenchman? Incredible!"

CHAPTER THE FORTY-FIFTH,

in which I meet with Master Jacques, after which Friend Dunstane berates me.

I had been putting off an inevitable meeting with Master Jacques since my return. The Holy Father pressed me to see him, lest the man suffer the ignominy of an imagined slight. (As one of the original founding nine, it was only fitting that I make an appearance.) The truth was, I had little desire for the pretense of mild affection, that I would be forced to display whenever in his presence. (The same held true for my appearances at court, except there the falseness was necessary to uncover the king's and his advocate's plans for me.) Reluctantly, I agreed.

The Order of the Temple was housed in a building second in size only to the palace. But it was, in fact, located in the far side of the city, away from the court. Besides the apparent difference that its circular form evinced, it contained numerous corridors, which led back to the main grand staircase and hall. (And in one respect this central hall was dissimilar to so many others in so many Templar Houses around the world; at either side of the first step of the staircase, there were no decorative columns. I heard that Master Jacques had insisted upon that omission when in conversation with the carpenters during the time of construction. He never gave a satisfactory explanation for this decision, though the Holy Father always believed it to be Jacques' impatience with symbols and the trappings of his station. The Holy Father was not pleased. However, the walls of this Templar House were indeed covered with floors of cypress and walls of fragrant cedar, as were those of the original Temple two centuries prior.)

Dunstane and I rode to the enormous stables, (located behind the structure), where attendants took our horses dutifully and fed them. I chose to use the rear door for entry, since a ceremonial greeting at the front was not my preference. (Nor did I care what efforts at greeting us the Master might have made.) Dunstane and I passed through the scullery, by various corridors, near sleeping quarters, until we arrived at the great hall, the height of which rose to perhaps as many as ten men standing upon each other's shoulders. There we found the Master seated upon what appeared to be some type of large chair, intricately decorated, and resembling a small throne. He was surrounded by his knights, all neatly assembled. These were wearing immaculately clean white tunics.

What I remember chiefly of Jacques is that he possessed the most perfectly manicured white beard that I have ever seen. Nary a strand of hair was too long or misplaced in some curled mode. It was as if his butler had taken hours to make certain that the old man maintain his appearance in a most dignified and forthright manner. And I must confess that the image was greater than the man, who had raised a sword against an enemy only in practice bouts.

I believe that my sudden appearance flustered him, as he jumped from his seat.

"I had hoped—we had hoped—all of us had hoped to surprise you, my lord."

I gave them my thanks and told them that, since there was always much work for us to do, we all had precious little time for these rituals, regardless of how pleased I might feel. They bowed. Some left. Some lingered a moment to stare, perhaps out of curiosity, for these must have been novices, who had never seen my face. The gaze of others was one of positive rapture. Of these I would have thought their look to be one of reverence, if I dared believe it possible. Of course, I might have been wrong.

The Master welcomed me. He said that all the Templar services were at my disposal, as well as the entire facility, itself, which he hoped I would consider a second home whilst in Paris.

"And who might you be, good sir?" he addressed Dunstane.

"Dunstane, the Scot," he spoke proudly, thrusting his huge paunch forward, and standing there, his hands poised at his hips, as if he were striking a pose for some Roman sculptor.

"He is my *seneschal* when the occasion arises," I explained, "and my friend always."

"And his protector, too, don't forget," he added. "I would die for him, if necessary."

Jacques then informed me that whilst free to do as I pleased, including an examination of the voluminous financial records of the order, my friend, who was not a Templar, could not be allowed any future access to the building. I assure you, this was not a wise statement to make. It was all I could do to keep from tossing the old bag of bones across the room and thereby crush the life from him. Then it occurred to me:

"Your butler is no Templar."

"True. All too true, though he has been in my service for a full ten years now."

"And Dunstane has been with me for five. Does your additional five years have more value than mine? Or is ten the magical number that you have created as the *formula* for entry by a non-Templar into these hallowed halls?"

It mattered little that I had not plunged my blade into his entrails; his face looked as if I had.

"I beg your pardon. It was not my intention to offend you. My concern is only with the security of our Order."

"As is mine. And if I look upon someone with absolute trust, does it not follow that others should as well, especially those whom I have looked after for two hundred years?"

His pain was so severe, that he barely had the strength to nod his assent.

Upon one of the upper levels Dunstane and I entered a large meeting room, a very large room. I surveyed the enormous table located therein, the many chairs positioned around it, and several *bureaus* against the walls. (Of these I recognized the Venetian designer's hand immediately.) The chairs were inlaid with gold dust sprinkled across their high wooden backs like a handful of stars strewn about.

"God save us from all foolish men," was my comment as I ran my fingers across the spine of one such seat.

Dunstane had folded his arms. O, I could see that he was not a happy man.

"I should probably be satisfied with how much you value our friendship," he began, for what I thought might become a lengthy critique, "though you have left an old man to wallow in his despair, a broken husk. And his only sin was that he had wanted to honour you."

I did not have the heart to tell him that I would have sought any excuse for an argument with Jacques, and my friend had provided me with a convenient one. Despite that, I *did* value Dunstane's friendship quite highly, so much so, that he may have been the only man whom I trusted during those turbulent years.

I reminded him that he knew me well enough to remember that I never chose my enemies capriciously. This kind man, whom he perceived as a victim, was in charge of the most powerful fighting force in the entire world. And Jacques barely had knowledge of how to wield a weapon. His purpose had been (until recent times) to keep the order's documentation. He knew a great deal about numbers and nothing about tactics.

"Ah, you've not been the same man since we set foot in this city. We should go home."

"This is my home."

"No, it's not. War is where you capture the comforts you cannot find here. I've never seen you so happy as when you were giving forth a battle-cry and cutting a man in two."

"This is war, Dunstane, albeit of a different sort."

"Have you returned to play a game of devilish politics with these schemers? Not a one of 'em has a drop of honour. If you ask me, neither one of us belongs here. You must have grown old when I took my eyes off ye. You fight now with words, instead of your sword, like all old fighters do. This Jacques is someone you would have never given two thoughts about before now. But if you think him incapable, tell the Holy Father. Don't punish him for it. Don't strip him of his dignity. You're a better man than that."

Was I? Was I really?

CHAPTER THE FORTY-SIXTH,

in which I witness the skill of a female warrior, then argue at court about royal finances, or the markèd lack thereof.

When Dunstane brought me to view a tournament, in a large field outside the city, he knew that I might take pleasure in watching one of its combatants defeat all the rest. What intrigued me far more than the knight's skill honed sharply in what must have been many campaigns, or the decidedly dark complexion, was the obviously feminine form. It was the second time that I had ever seen a breast-plate with two large mounds hammered out of it, so that a pair of breasts might sit comfortably therein during combat. Unlike Eleanor, however, this woman was no false Amazon. She tossed one rider off his mount, then another, with remarkable ease and efficiency.

"The more I live, the more I am amazed at this wondrous world and its infinite variety. What do you know of her?" I asked.

He chuckled.

"What makes you think that I know anything about her?"

He would not have attempted to impress me with her prowess, had he been ignorant of her history. And he knew that I knew it.

"The king has found himself someone far better than his usual crop of misbegotten failures, I wager," he went on. "This one comes from a place near Egypt. I forget its name."

I had not time to wonder of her origins, as her opponent fell off his horse, thanks to a well-placed thrust from her lance against his chest armour. She pulled off her helmet, and threw it down, exposing her hair. It was knotted firmly against her scalp, and sat in rows there like marshaled forces of tiny black pebbles neatly arranged. She circled the knight, who was rolling back and forth, unable to pull himself up due to his heavy metallic weight. She offered him no hand as aid. Finally, squires ran out to untie the straps, which bound his metal encasement to him. She laughed riotously, her sweat in droplets running down her face, catching the brilliant light at its zenith. She was as fierce as a lioness enraged. And the violence within her beauty was unlike any other woman's. In truth, she was in all things (I would come to learn) wholly unique.

"What do you know of her?" I asked again.

"With all due respect, my lord, you're no King Solomon, and even less is she the Queen of Sheba. Now, don't be thinkin' what you're thinkin'. She's a virgin, she is."

I could not believe it, for I could not recall the last time that I had ever met one, especially in Paris. How could he be certain? He said that she would either fight or drink with a man, though never give herself to one. He also said that she was both rare and dangerous. I nodded.

"No," he insisted, shaking his head, "not in the way you might like, and not in what she does, or who she is, but in what she might mean to future generations."

Now I knew Dunstane all too well, and philosophy had never been his strongest subject of study (if, indeed, study were something that he ever did). Besides, she was a knight, albeit female, no more than that. Did he expect me to take him seriously upon that point, whatever it might mean?

"Do you expect me to take you seriously upon whatever point you might be making?"

"She tells the women of the world that the day will come when they no longer need to stay in their homes and raise their children. They might decide not to take men to their beds altogether, but find comfort with other women!"

I had made acquaintance of several such women, though I thought better of mentioning that piece of my personal history at this crucial juncture in time.

"A woman like that," he continued, "will destroy the world."

"Or at least make it far more interesting."

He made a face gnarled with disgust. I ignored it as I watched her every move. She came over to the other knight and bowed, as did he. Then she walked off, her gait as assured and as strong as the sinews in her arms and legs—a most interesting sight to behold. Still, I knew that she would earn only the grudging respect of her comrades. Despite any of her possible accomplishments, she would never be more than a stranger amongst them. Why had the king placed her here in his service? Was he using her to mock these soldiers, who were ferociously proud? It was not every day that a man could claim to have been bested by a woman. I thought she amused her precious sovereign. I thought she deserved more than that. Pity.

"We were discussing a settlement of accounts, not an extension of the loan."

I had finished an explanation of terms, prior to Master Jacques' entry into one of the palace rooms. Despite its grandiose size, its high ceiling, and its many ornately framed portraits, it contained only a small table and four chairs. The king, his advocate, and I sat upon three; we had been awaiting Jacques to assume the fourth. (The advocate, if I have neglected to mention it already, was a slender man, of years no more than thirty, with piercing eyes, and short of stature. I distrusted him immediately.) Master Jacques sat upon the empty seat. He was ill at ease, staring first at his king, secondly at the advocate, and finally at me.

"His highness is fully prepared to make good all debts," was the advocate's response.

"Commendable," I said. "Now tell me how this is possible when rumour has it that royal finances are practically non-existent."

"You cannot believe everything that you hear," he countered.

"I have been hearing this for several years now. Is every story related by each individual wholly without merit?"

"Wholly," the monarch interjected, taking the initiative to clarify his position. "Now explain to me, if you will, why we must discuss these issues with a man, who is no more than an honourary member of the Templars, and not with the Master, himself? By the way, we meant no offense, Sir Guy."

Most certainly he did not!

"None taken."

"Sir Guy has spoken with the full support of our entire membership," Master Jacques averred. (The king frowned.) "However," he continued, "I might have preferred a more salient discussion, between him and myself, as to the nature of our appearance here, prior to this actual meeting."

Well done, Master Jacques! It seemed that he was finally learning the subtle art of insult for political expedience; whilst he showed to everyone his unflinching support of my humble self, nevertheless, he distanced himself from the import of my very words. Still, how intelligent could it have been to avoid insult to any of the parties involved? Was such an action ever possible?

The king smiled whilst addressing Jacques:

"Am I correct in assuming that you have no foreknowledge of his appearance here?"

"I had this knowledge. I was uncertain regarding the topic."

"This is most outrageous!" de Nogaret chimed in. "With whom are we to negotiate?"

"This subject is not open for discussion," I told him. "And I am here at the behest of the Holy Father, himself, if that means anything to you."

"Then you are most welcome," the advocate uttered immediately with a smile and a bow.

The look that Jacques gave to me was all the evidence I required to know that his holiness had never informed him of my presence here. And the only reason that he came was probably due to a royal summons, the nature of which was completely unknown to him, and which occurred only after I had made my own request of the king to appear. At what game was Pope Clement playing?

The king looked bored.

"Master Jacques and I have always had an understanding," he explained. "He knows that all debts will be paid … eventually."

Jacques nodded. I had no choice but to hold him up as a victim:

"Any decision made by a Templar Master is subject to scrutiny by the pope, as it may affect all our knights throughout the world."

That was all de Nogaret needed to hear:

"Are you saying that his holiness no longer has faith in the decisions which Master Jacques has struck with French royalty?"

A typical lawyer. What other abuse might he heap upon my language, I wondered?

"These decisions—" I began.

"Pardon me, my lord," the lawyer interrupted. "Those *agreements*, you mean."

"I am assured that you will correct me when I am in error, advocate, but if I recall my elementary jurisprudence, an agreement involves a mutual *understanding* of the parties involved regarding a particular issue."

"Indeed!"

It did not take much to impress him, did it?

"And how can a supposèd agreement be enforced, if one of the central parties has never been consulted?"

"Pardon?" the advocate asked. "Master Jacques—"

"Master Jacques could never approve such extravagant expenditure to any regent without the written approval of the Holy Father. What have you not understood, advocate?"

The absolute silence in the room endured for so long a time, that we were deafened by it. It was Jacques who spoke to end the stalemate:

"The Holy Father and I have a certain understanding where it concerns our country of origin and its regent. It is well within our mandate, as soldiers of Christ, to offer aid to those rulers who require and request it."

"Only during a crusade," I completed his thought, whether it pleased him or not. "And if the advocate doubts me, he would do well to remember that I wrote said rule with Hughes de Payens at the Templars' founding a very long time ago."

More silence. This time it was the king who ended it.

"It was not our intention to trample upon the Master's kindness, nor take advantage of the Templars' generosity. We are at a point in history where the systems of finance, which have previously existed, are no longer efficient. New methods must be devised, if we are to erect the future upon a solid foundation. Surely everyone here has wit enough to see this," he maintained, looking from one of us to the other. "We are currently in the process of creating those new systems for the continued existence of all decent Christian civilization. If we must step backwards occasionally for every step forward that is taken, then so be it. All of us must suffer a little in order to secure what tomorrow may bring."

A fine bit of speechifying. And what was his point exactly?

"I beg your pardon, your highness," I asked, "but how do you intend to resolve this situation here and now?"

"O, that is painfully simple," de Nogaret elected to respond. "We require another loan of an additional fifty thousand to balance everything."

My jaw must have dropped to the floor, for I could utter no further words.

"With that," he added, "we should be able to generate enough income to repay all monies and thereby cancel all debts. As you and the others of your noble Order often learned, it is necessary to spend in order to acquire, is it not?"

Before I spoke, Jacques interrupted.

"The Holy Father and I shall discuss it. I see no reason why it would pose a problem, especially since it means that the accounts can be cleared that much sooner."

The king and his advocate excused themselves immediately. Guards led us outside to the stables, where Jacques and I received our horses. We had not spoken a single word until that moment, when we were completely alone together.

"I meant no offense, Sir Guy."

I mounted my horse, then looked down at him.

"Of late you have made that statement more than once."

"I beg you to understand; it was my decision, and I must make it right."

"How many times shall I say this? It was never your decision to make. By doing so, you have set yourself above the papacy, as well as above the Order that you lead. And now you compound those crimes with a worse one. First, you approve a quarter of a million, when you did not have the authority to do so. Perhaps you knew that his holiness would have, at the very least, hesitated to sign such a lavish request, and you could not deny your prince his fondest wish. Mark well my words; you will never see that money again. I have always believed that along with old age comes a certain gravity of spirit, as well as a touch of wisdom. Congratulations, Master of the Templars; you have dispelled those assumptions. You and I have never been friends, but we were never enemies until today. You will discover that I can be a formidable foe; so, too, will this regent, whose approval you strive to covet."

CHAPTER THE FORTY-SEVENTH,

in which my observants relate events most strange, after which time I find myself in the presence of the advocate royal, who is both mysterious and most full of his own self-importance.

Where had all the money gone? Of the rulers whom I had known, not one was either wise or prudent about his fiscal responsibilities, though none would have ever stripped a royal treasury bare. Or was all this little more than the poor legacy of the regent's sainted grandfather, who would have spent all coin (including that of his descendants) to finance his *crusade* against the Cathars in his homeland? And the consequences? You see, though a human being is a fairly resilient creature, perhaps able to bear more agony than one would ever believe possible, even he has his limitations. How many more taxes, heaped upon each other, would the populace accept, before it began to deny its ruler his full purse? Yes, the fourteenth century was a spandrel, an exceedingly large hinge upon which doors opened and closed; still, was anyone truly prepared for what was to pass through those selfsame doors?

I always sent Dunstane away whenever Theresa arrived. (His presence would have been most awkward, considering that she would only relate what she had seen after fornication. And I must admit that I, too, appreciated a large degree of privacy, that only an otherwise empty domicile could grant.) As we lay together, she told me of an early morning session between the king and the pope. I thought it odd; why had the king not come to the other's residence as a sign of respect for the man's station? Instead, an ecclesiastical prince sat in a chair whilst a temporal one stood over him, shouting.

"What did he say to the Holy Father?"

"I couldn't come close enough to hear everything. I did hear him curse though. It was loud, very loud. It was the foulest thing that I ever heard."

She calling someone else's language worse than her own? Unthinkable! In any case, she continued:

"What type of man talks to a pope like that? Our prince must be very brave and daring. He must have a massive *scrotum*, like an ox has. Have you ever seen an ox's *scrotum*?"

I could not say that I had observed such large *pudenda* very often.

"They hang almost to the ground like the hairy balls of a jester's cap. I find it all disgusting. And I find our king disgusting. He never looks at a woman, no matter how much she flirts with him, not even the noblewomen at court. And he widowed not two years past!"

"Three, I believe," I corrected her.

"Whatever. Did you know that his personal guards are very respectful to women? I have never known guards not to try to have their way with female servants. I've been told that these look like Greek statues."

She was most correct. Upon first seeing the king's personal guards, I thought myself transported back through time to ancient Athens. I had no idea there were so many hirsute, young men in all of France, and all of them enlisted in service to his royal highness, apparently.

"Have you ever seen Greek statues?" she asked. "I haven't. Anyway, they always have private meetings with the king, especially in the evening hours."

Private?

"First he takes one inside, then, after a time, the man leaves, and another takes his place. This goes on sometimes all night."

All night?

"The king must be so exhausted after he speaks with them; that is probably why he sleeps for most of the next day."

"And who administers court functions during that missing day?"

"Why, the advocate, of course! Everybody knows that. Why don't you? You're supposed to be all high and mighty and very smart."

"What I lack in wisdom, I make up for in sexual prowess."

"True," she agreed, before she ran her tongue across her top lip, "all too true."

We embraced. She thrust her breasts (as white as swan's down) against my chest, as she sought out my tongue.

Afterwards, she paraded in front of me in a delightfully shameless manner, making certain that I would have an unobstructed view of each curve, most especially as she bent over. Of modest stature, she was quite slender, possessed of very small breasts but with long nipples, which grew hard immediately upon the merest touch or lick. (Only her legs were somewhat thick, though not so large as to be unattractive.) Her form was a source of constant pleasure for me, and in its own way perfect, save for a slight blemish, tiny, dark, and round, upon the side of her right breast. In all other things, in all other ways, she was most excellently wrought. I must confess, however, that each time when I looked into her face, I saw not a shred of innocence there. And I had to admit to myself that there were times when I found that tiny ember of truth a bit disturbing to watch.

She smoothed out her garments to look as fresh and as clean as she had upon entry. And for a moment, her face appeared free of a post-coital satisfaction that most people wear when the deed is done. A stranger might have thought her almost virginal …, almost.

She took the tiny sack that I had left for her at a small table, shook it to hear the jingling inside, and thanked me. I offered to return her to the palace. She declined. She thought the stroll would do her good. What she really meant was that one of her other lovers lived nearby, and she probably hoped to make a bit of further payment before the night was completely spent. (Far be it from me to begrudge anyone a bit of coin!) I thanked her for her efforts, and she wished me well with a long kiss, a massage of my *scrotum*, then a broad smile. But at the door she hesitated momentarily to turn around, to look at me once more. I thought that she had something further to say. She did not. She smiled only. And it was not as before; it was soft. I had not thought her capable of much tenderness (particularly as she was given to much of heat in her loins). Then she departed as quickly as she had come. O, the infinite varieties and wonders of Parisian romance! It was good to be home.

Whilst grateful for her observations, she could supply only one piece of the puzzle. The good Marie filled in a portion of what was lacking. Unfortunately, she could not recall the entire exchange, though she had heard something of its ending. I was surprised to discover that the thread of it had somehow led back to the possibility of a new holy war:

> "*Outremer* is a quagmire," the king said. "No matter which way one turns, he will be swallowed up. The Romans learned this lesson when they discovered the Hebrews to be a stiffnecked race. Today we must contend not only with them, but also with other swarthy races, whose customs are even stranger than their appearance, as well as fellow Christians, who know of or care little for the West. Consequently, western princes must respond in kind by ignoring them for the troublesome creatures they have all become."
>
> "In those lands our Lord was born."

"And what did God say to our forefathers? *Go forth and multiply.* Is this not what we have done? We have journeyed far from our ancestral home and set down roots elsewhere. This is our home now. We must look forward. That is the knowledge with which History impels us to face the future."

"What is the point of sailing headlong, rudderless, if one forgets where he has been?"

"Spoken like an old man enmeshed in memories."

"Without a commitment to tradition, there is no church."

"Sacrificing monies, soldiers, and supplies in order to support Pope Urban's dream of a Christian world has proven extravagant at best, pathetically stupid at worst."

"I shall not have you insult the holy work of the only man who united all Christian forces against their common Saracen enemy!"

"Saracen? Turk? Infidel? Unbeliever? How many more names can we use to debase an entire people? They have proven themselves far greater warriors, or barbarians, than two centuries of Christian blood have attempted to negate. If they want those lands so desperately, I say good riddance! It is time for western princes to concentrate upon the problems in their respective realms. The church will take its tradition of awe-inspiring miracles and bow to the pragmatic concerns of politics, or drown in the déluge of historical inevitability. Ecclesiastical princes will hold their fiefdoms only because landed princes allow them that privilege. That is the future for all mankind. I ... am the future."

Summoned to the palace, (or rather, I should say, *requested to appear*), de Nogaret welcomed me into his large study. Books and documents were everywhere, strewn about as if a passing wind had tossed all things with a careless hand. One could barely step upon a patch of carpet without crushing or tearing crumpled papers. And I was struck by the fanciful design of the floor covering, for I would have assessed it be of Muslim manufacture, possibly Persian. Strange that he should possess it. I would not have believed him to care for aught save items of a Christian manufacture. And when I saw him, I found myself riddled with a peculiar sensation. I can only describe it as a general nausea, similar perhaps to what Prince Bohémond must have experienced when he gazed upon a Byzantine courier one fateful night in his tent outside of the Nikaian walls.

"You are most welcome, Sir Guy."

He offered me a chair. We stared at each other across his desk. I waited for him to speak, but no words were forthcoming, only smiles.

"Is there something that you wished of me, advocate?"

He thought that it might be mutually beneficial for us to learn a bit more about each other, especially since we both had frequent business at court.

"Tell me," he asked, "does an immortal ever ponder the nature of mortality?"

I thought the query unusual as an introduction of amity. I cared nothing for this little man and his little excursions into his conceptions of truth, so I chose to respond, the quicker to be on my way.

"Every single day," I told him.

Was that merely as a curiosity on my part, he wondered? After all, the conception of dying must have been meaningless for me, whilst everyone around me doubtless feared it.

"No righteous man has anything to fear when he leaves behind this existence."

"O, but you see, how would you know this? You have never been to the other side, have you?"

"Faith answers all questions. Those who have ears to hear, let them hear."

"Obviously you remember your lessons well. Do you not find it rare that so many of the clergy concentrate in their sermons, not on heavenly rewards, but upon hellish torments? Why is that, do you think?"

"I suppose you have thought of it often, and are about to tell me."

"I like you; I really do. You are a man who can appreciate the essence of a given situation. I have made a study of this. Actually, I have spent most of my life in examination of the church and its actions. I have discovered that death is the one subject upon which the church's servants preach *ad infinitum*: eat of His body; drink of His blood; engorge yourself upon His suppurating wounds. As is quite evident to anyone, entire generations have been raised to be little more than bloodthirsty creatures. Is it any wonder, then, that in this glorious age, one in which man lives longer than before, one in which man may possess more conveniences than have ever been conceived, we pursue each other's possessions and resources with a lust for war whilst continually blessed by Holy Mother Church for our actions? Man is vile, corrupt. For millennia an aging Christianity has suckled him at its shriveled teat. But mark my words, the world is changing. Economics, finance—these will replace the church's profound influence upon man, as trading routes grow, as means of transport become more efficient, as the enormous world shrinks a bit more with each passing day. The church, too, will pass, albeit covered by the dust of *Outremer*."

What purpose did he have in trying to bait me? Did he not realize that I would kill him?

"Thus the world will become a *consortium* of trading interests," I summarized, "as the church becomes a memory."

"A concise statement!"

Bold words to speak to the church's own guardian. But he certainly meant no offense.

"Really? What did you mean exactly?"

"I speak only the truth. It is the nature of my profession."

And what a noble profession it was.

"And since I speak only the truth, you should accept most readily that not even you will be able to stem the tide of historical inevitability. What will you do one hundred years from now, when all this has come to pass? What will you do a thousand years from now, when the very reason for your existence has been eliminated?"

"I try not to think that far ahead. Being an immortal means that I should endeavour to appreciate every single day that the Lord has given unto me—a lesson that would not be wasted on the remainder of His mortal children."

I could see that he was pondering what I had said. A moment or two passed before he commenced a further query:

"Do you never grow bored?"

"Boredom is for the nobility, who cultivate idleness. My time is always occupied with something of consequence."

"Which is it for you? The acquisition of wealth? A new woman in your bed each night?"

"Are they the only two motivations for people's actions? In your conception of the universe, is there no selfless act?"

"To be human is to be selfish. Crawling about on one's hands and knees, if necessary, and clawing his way past his brothers and sisters is the only means for the child to make the largest piece of bread his own."

"You have my sympathies, William de Nogaret," I said, standing up and walking away.

"Why is that?"

"I think that you crawl around at every opportunity … still."

CHAPTER THE FORTY-EIGHTH,

in which Dunstane and I are invited to a joust, that yields an unexpected offer.

After having welcomed a visiting German dignitary to court, the king asked me whether Dunstane and I would care to participate in jousts as a display of French might to a potentially warring counterpart in the distant future. How could I refuse such a heartfelt request?

My comrade was the first to face his opponent. Completely uncomfortable in his armour, he was trussed up like a boar upon a silver chalice. In point of fact, whilst his squires clothed him, the much younger knight had mocked and laughed at Dunstane, perhaps wondering why a grizzled warrior would even attempt the contest. I envied the man his ignorance, for I, myself, had once fought the Scot when he became powerfully besotted in a tavern, and have barely survived in a single piece to tell you, dear reader, of it. I looked forward now to the resultant outcome with even more relish than I believe our royal host evinced.

The many standards were unfurled, as heralds blew upon their long trumpets. I walked over to wish my comrade a swift victory.

"When will this damnèd ceremony end?" he asked, his words struggling to escape from behind his visor. "It's hot as the Devil's loins in here, and equally dark, to my way o' thinkin'."

"Have patience," I spoke, trying to console him in his discomfiture. "And allow him to make at least one stroke before you butcher the arrogant whelp."

He looked about.

"Why? Is his lady present? She might prefer a man with experience, especially if he's the victor. What say you, my lord? Will she come to my bed this very night?"

I smiled, leaving his company.

Whilst the Holy Father appeared and assumed the empty seat next to the king, I elected to stay at ground, the better to watch my friend's prowess first-hand. Separated by a long wooden fence, no taller than a man's knee, both men sat straight atop their mounts at opposite ends of the field. They bowed their heads slightly to the regent, then each to the other. Together they charged.

The animals had barely arisen to speed, with nary a snort, when lances deflected the opposing blows. Dunstane slowed and turned long enough to see the young man twist his head around to watch him, as the latter's own horse continued to race away. Perhaps realizing that he would lose himself in the neighboring forest, the knight tugged at the reins, bringing the creature to a swift stop. It very nearly toppled the rider. I doubt that he expected to be jiggling back and forth for quite some time, before he lost his *momentum* and came to a final halt.

The contenders resumed their positions. I knew that Dunstane's lack of patience would bring an end to this amusement quite readily, so I had a squire fetch me a tankard of ale. I watched the young knight who appeared to crouch down slightly, as if to lighten all his musculature, much like a cat ready to pounce. But his armour kept him so rigid, that he appeared momentarily to have sunken down inside of it, and moreover, to have lost his very neck. Dunstane waited for the attack to begin. He was unmoving up there on his mount, a stalwart defender of the faith, or of honour, or of whatever lofty ideal one might conceive. The young man sped forward.

Dunstane began to move his body slightly to the right, as his opponent came towards him at his left. I believe that I had never seen someone thrust his entire metallic weight so much to one side of his steed without falling off therefrom. Indeed, lo and behold, his gamble avoided the lance, as he thrust at his opponent's chest, knocking him to the ground and sending up a cloud of dirt and small stones, which fell back down, pelting the young defeated victim with scratching noises. His squires ran out to raise him up. Once upon his feet again, the opponent bowed and gave word to his squires to inform Dunstane that the man had yielded.

My friend threw off his helmet. Laughing, I handed him the tankard.

"The child thought to defeat a Scot," I observed. "What *could* he have been thinking?"

"He's the right king of fools, he is. Yield, indeed! Ah," he said upon looking into the brewed contents, "drinking is a filthy habit, and one without which I cannot live."

He drank almost half of the ale in a single gulp. We both laughed. And as we did so, my friend looked over to the high wooden platform where the king and his entourage, together with the pope, had fixed their cheerful gaze down upon us.

"The king has not turned his eyes from us since we took the field," he remarked, then drank again.

"So I have noticed."

"'Tis a good thing that we watch him as closely."

"What choice do we have? He surrounds himself with equivicators and prevaricators, as well as a lawyer."

"Lawyers," he snarled through clenched teeth, "—truly the Devil's own spawn!"

The king tossed down a crown of laurels. It landed at the stallion's feet. I picked it up and handed it off.

"I would've preferred a bit of coin, but no matter," Dunstane said, placing the reward upon his sweating crown. "I'll make the best of it."

As for my contender, I had not expected that a woman would be pitted against me. Did the king believe that I would be more merciful and grant to her the swift stroke? If so, it was a ridiculous assumption. I had never been kind in battle, though this one were a game, and my antagonist female. Besides, I thought that she would appreciate the full thrust of my blade, less any hesitation.

I wore only enough armour to cover my chest. Upon seeing this, she did the same. Mine was not a brave action. (Death and I had a casual, yet amicable, relationship.) For her it was wholly different. Perhaps it was something that I witnessed in her dark eyes, as they grew even more full of shadow, though the light about us had taken on that unceasing amber common to the late afternoon. She assumed her position, straight, and mark this, dear reader, quietly powerful. Feline strength had found its home there, in each carefully delineated muscle, in the blood coursing through her fingers, whilst they clutched the lance. She held it so tightly in fact, that I thought I espied several red droplets falling from her palm. We began the gallop at the same moment.

Though there was little of wind, we created our own. I could feel it tear at my face. I knew that she felt the same. With firmness of purpose and full of might, we lunged at each other during the first pass, and we both struck! But our lances could not survive the contact. We circled round to stare into each other's faces, the broken remnants still in our hands.

I called to the squires for renewed weaponry. She did the same. We made a second attempt. Its result was no different; both items splintered off. It seemed to me that on this day royal lances were not so potent as they were wont to be. Neither one of us fell; the high back-supports of our saddles kept us rooted to our steeds. I rode up to her.

"I am prepared to continue for as long as you wish," I told her, "but your king, I fear, may grow bored if he is not witness to at least one death today."

"Is he not your king, my lord?"

"I serve only one Master, who is not of this earth."

I could see that my allusion had confused her. No matter. I rode back to my original position, as did she. This third, final attempt succeeded in knocking ourselves off our respective mounts. No sooner was she upon her back, when she jumped up, sword in hand. I walked over to where she stood.

"As you can see," I began, "I am unharmed. If you so desire it, you may attempt my execution."

She laughed, then sheathed her sword and removed her breastplate. The king declared the match a draw. We both bowed to him. She was about to leave the field when I stopped her.

"Wait. Tell me your name."

"You first. Whom did I have the privilege of meeting in battle?"

I told her. She smiled.

"It is no surprise that I could not defeat you. Everyone knows that Guy de Lagery is the lion of the Christians, who is older than time."

"Not quite that old, I assure you."

"You have had much experience at arms. No one has ever fought me as you have. Well done, Sir Guy. I am Makeda of Nubia."

Nubia? So that explained her militaristic acumen.

"Well done, Makeda of Nubia, though I must confess that some would consider your actions unseemly for a maiden."

"Who is the great unwashed multitude to judge me?"

"So, you care little for the judgment of your peers."

"My peers do not judge, for they fight at my side. My sword has brought me all the respect that I have ever required."

She turned to leave. I stopped her again.

"What do you wish of me, old man?" she asked, staring at my hand that was holding onto her arm.

"Only to know you better."

"I am neither noblewoman nor prostitute. How could you possibly be interested in someone like me?"

Apparently my reputation had preceded my presence here.

"I would not choose to love you," she continued.

Love? Had I mentioned love? I think most assurèdly not!

"I ask you again, what do you want with me?"

"O, love is a terrible disease, is it not?" I asked, releasing her arm, and utilizing her mention of the word as a starting-point for our verbal exchange. "I have yet to meet anyone who does not suffer from its symptoms. And you know what those are—the uncommon lingering gazes, the dryness of the throat, that odd little ache in the belly that ceases its rumbling only when the belovèd is near."

"I am immune."

Most strange! That bit of speechifying had always yielded the desired result for me before with the fair sex. I could see that she would require a different form of conquest. A welcome surprise, for I had always appreciated a good challenge.

"Except to the bitterness that you bear," I told her.

She turned to leave.

"I wonder what man it was responsible for the nourishing of it?" I continued.

She stopped and was about to turn to me again. Instead, she left with no more words.

The king descended to the field. He hoped to catch me before I departed as well.

"I have a proposition for you, Sir Guy de Lagery."

"O?" I asked, watching Makeda mount her horse and ride off. "And what is its nature, sire?"

He suddenly noticed that my attention were elsewhere.

"I see that she has garnered your admiration."

I turned towards him. "What? No, I—"

"I would not waste my time in a fruitless pursuit. Nubian women are faithful to their own kind only."

"Is she the only Nubian in your kingdom?"

"Indeed! *Ergo* her wish to maintain her virginity. She prides herself upon it, like all women," he said, trying to mask his disgust. "It is my firm belief that if a woman holds onto her hymen with as much fervent desire as that one appears to possess, perhaps the best thing for any man to do is to leave her be; for the man who takes it from her will suffer her endless devotion and relinquish all peace."

"Is she not devoted to your service?"

"She is dutiful. There is a difference."

Now that we had settled that piece of business, we had much to discuss. Apparently the southerners had grown restless again. (It occurred every decade or so, he averred.) And the king had need of a man like me when it came to dealing with them.

"I could be persuaded to offer you an appointment as leader of all forces against them. Would your service to a French king please you?"

Why did he want me to leave Paris? Did he fear the friendship between the Holy Father and myself? Or did he fear the influence that such a relationship might have upon whatever plans, which he and his advocate were hatching?

"And here I thought that you preferred to have my company at court, your highness."

Granted that my presence there was a source of constant awe and fascination, he thought it best that a man betake himself to the place where his services might be utilized to their fullest.

"And for whom would you have me slaughter them, my liege? For Holy Mother Church? No. As much as they detest our faith, for what we have already done to theirs, they should know the true identity of the one who has ordered their destruction. They would all be killed in *your* name. But if the truth be told, I must decline your generous offer. I would rather stay here at court. I find it a source of constant amusement."

Attendants brought up our horses, as Dunstane looked over the grounds.

"If this land belongs to the Templars, why do they allow the king to use it for his pleasure?" he asked.

"Politics."

"There's a great deal of that going on in this country. And here I thought Scotland had a bad time of it. I was surprised to see the Holy Father here. Does he never go to Rome?"

"I remember a time when popes considered tournaments a sinful waste of life and time. This pope hardly ever goes to Rome anymore, and he has courtly business on a fairly regular basis, it would appear."

"I hear that this king is making a new home for the papacy in a place called, *Avignon*. Then again, that might be a story only."

"This king wants mastery over everyone and everything he surveys, including everyone and everything he does not."

"What's boilin' away in that head of yours now?"

"I was thinking that the nature of people reveals itself in the fullness of time, because God created our world in such a way, that the truth of any situation can never stay hidden from human eyes forever."

"Now I don't rightly know if that's true, but if it is, I might say that God had placed a fairly sizeable wager on the future, since that's one game He has no intention of losing."

"Amen, my friend. Amen."

CHAPTER THE FORTY-NINTH,

in which Master Jacques is summoned to the court upon a pretext most curious.

Barely had several days passed after the tournament, when Jacques was summoned to appear at the palace. He thought the meeting with his king would be private, but when he arrived, he saw that the advocate was also present. They discussed a number of issues, primarily to do with matters of currency, loans, and the like. After the initial topics, the advocate made mention of one that had never before been raised in their civilized discourse; there were rumours. Neither the monarch nor his advocate advanced details of their nature; neither did they attempt to substantiate any of it. They alluded to a generalized form of unsavoury behavior without disclosing its details. Jacques was confused. He had no idea of how to defend either himself or his Order against accusations, which had never been uttered. The king advised him to look after his charges with a watchful eye, lest any one of them fail to live up to his oaths. Jacques left, more confused than ever about the capricious manner of the men who had tried to warn him of something wholly indistinct.

Ever since those years, I have often wondered when it was that the Templars began to trip and fall inexorably towards their own doom. As I think of it now, it must have been that very day, when the Master of the Order sat there, comfortably assured that he was in the company of friends, whose objectives and ideals were no different from his own. With conviction I can say absolutely that he had no idea how large that little seed of doubt about Templar behaviour would grow.

When I met with the Holy Father this time, it was beneath the grand window of *Nôtre Dame* at that critical time of day when the sun beams through its multihued glass panels to fall in rainbows at an observer's feet. (I had never failed to marvel at the artisans' handiwork, how they had transformed the image of a

Wheel of Fortune into an enormous portrayal in glass of a single rose.) His head was not raised, the better to view the inception of the gleam, but rather lowered at the play of light upon the stones below himself.

"You appear as if you have not slept much of late, your holiness. Do you wish to tell me why?"

He looked up at me. Embarrassment crossed his face now.

"You have lived far longer than is any man's right, and accomplished far more than most would have dreamed possible. Your life's legacy is assured."

What would my uncle have said about that, I wondered?

He had failed, he affirmed. He thought that he could persuade the king to offer his support for a new holy war. Alas, he could not. When it would be time for God to call him to His kingdom, he hoped to leave behind a legacy that would have honoured the papal line all the way back to St. Peter, himself. That may have been nothing more than his pride, and the Lord above saw to it that he would be sufficiently humbled for having placed his own desires above His Master's holy purposes. Nor did Jacques have any more success than he, himself, had. The monarch claimed that it cost a great deal to keep troops along the borders to protect against the English invaders. Skirmishes were a constant threat.

"If France and England are at war," I maintained, "then I have not heard a single declaration of it."

"This is no war; this is simple aggression."

He was wrong. There was nothing simple about aggression.

"Be that as it may, I beseech you, dear friend," he pleaded, "no disputations today. I have neither the head nor the stomach for them."

And with that, he dragged himself up from the pew, and, accompanied by his retainers, departed the cathedral.

Though he may not have wanted to hear the truth, it was self-evident. Only a war could justify the royal expenditures which had become commonplace. And since there was no war, the king and his minions had to nourish the possibility of one. After all, how else could one explain all the monies spent on galas and festivals and a court stocked with nobility, the number of which grew every single day? And did they not *all* depend upon royal generosity? One might have thought himself in the presence of Stephen de Blois at *his* court, though that runt of a man had been married to a very strong anchor, one that was determined to keep the precious ship of state afloat. Who was present here, who would dare to attempt the same with this Phillip?

That evening I related the above incident to Dunstane over a meal.

"You bother your head overly much with far too many thoughts of this king," he managed to comment between the chunks of meat in his already full mouth. "I've been thinkin' a goodly while on it, my lord, and if it's not too presumptuous of me, I wanted to share my thoughts with ye. I know what to do that will put you in a happy humour; I'll give you a gift."

And of what nature was his gift to be?

"Regarding this king, I'll kill him for ye."

I laughed. Not too presumptuous?

"You have to admit, this world would be a much better place without him. And it might not be a good thing for a man like you, with your fancy position in the church and all, to kill him. It's not like we're in a tavern and some bastard son of a whore passes a comment about me mother, or some other knavery. Besides, I don't like the way that he looks at you. Sometimes he's lookin' down his nose at ye, as if you were no better than the dirt at his feet. And other times I might swear that he was lookin' at ye the way that a man looks after a woman, as she walks away from him. Now that's a strange thing, is it not? No matter. It'll be me pleasure and privilege to do it for ye."

I welcomed the offer, though I did not wish for him to add more deaths upon his soul than those, which he already owned, and certainly not on my account. As it stood, he would have more than enough to explain to Saint Peter when he met him at the gates of Heaven.

"You're worried after the condition of my soul? That may be the kindest compliment that anyone has ever given me. Your concern touches me, my lord, right to the core of me heart," he said, slapping his chest.

I thought (momentarily) that his eyes began to water, though I could have been wrong about that. Nevertheless, he made me think about what the world might be, if things were different.

"I wonder what this world would be without kings?"

"Ah, you're talkin' foolishness now! There will always be a royal ass to fart in the face of his subjects."

Would there? The Romans, I believe, said that their emperor ruled in the name of the senate and the Roman people. Of course, there were occasions when he became too powerful to listen to anyone or anything, save his innermost thoughts of conquest. At those times he often managed to convince the senators, through use of threats, to approve his each and every decision. What if the senate had taken power from the regent?

"Not without the force of the army behind it."

"What would the people desire, I wonder?"

"A full stomach and a hard shaft are the only two things a man ever wishes to call his own."

"I believe that you underestimate the populace."

"Methinks I'm seein' the truth, that you, with all your grand age and wisdom, cannot recognize."

"We shall see."

"No. *You* will see. Thanks be to God that I won't be here for that battle; for if you think any prince will give up a shred of his might to please a commoner, then you know very little of the human heart."

"You may be right. I am not nearly so wise as I think I am."

As much as I tried to remove his attention from the previous subject of regicide, it would not be swayed. And even if I appreciated his offer, I had to admit that the Holy Father would frown upon such an act.

"O now, you'll never convince me that you take your orders from that old man."

"Have some respect!"

"Yes, yes, I know that he's a prince of the church with all the honours due thereof, or whatever, but you're a warrior, like me. We live by the sword. We don't have time for this politicking, this scheming. That's why the Devil created lawyers, so that good and just men like ourselves would drown in the fens and bogs of their incessantly confusing words."

I could not kill a man unnecessarily.

"Even a sinner like meself knows that it's a sin to kill, is it not? And you have killed very many men, have you not?"

Indeed I had!

"So what would be one more? Your soul's already damned. We're all damned! You don't see me weeping about it now, do you? If I'm going to spend eternity in one of Hell's chambers of torture, then I might as well do what I want and enjoy meself now, before the fiend takes me below. I'll kill this dark prince that brings misery to your motherland, then we'll go a-wenching. What say ye?" he asked, nodding vigorously.

"I believe, my friend, that all the philosophers and moralists who ever were could not posit a single argument against you upon that point. You are truly one of the most remarkable minds of this age." I raised my tankard. "Here's to you, Dunstane of Scotland."

We drank.

"Are we agreed then?" he asked.

"Perhaps later."

"O, you never let me have any fun anymore! Ever since we've set foot on this unholy land, you've gone all dour, like an old fishwife who's too tired to tell her gossips a single secret."

"Sometimes I do feel very old. Two hundred years are not four and twenty."

"That's not what the king's serving-girl had to say."

"What? Did she tell you herself? And to think that I relied upon her discretion."

"Discretion? From someone like her? You'd have far more success finding the grail."

"My friend, you will never know how correct you may be."

CHAPTER THE FIFTIETH,

in which Dunstane barely escapes loss of his long life.

"Bastard! Knave! Lecher! Base villain! Son of a whore! Scum! Scoundrel, who comes from an unfaithful lineage!"

So ended Theresa's tirade against her king. And what prompted such vituperation? The thrice-damnèd lawyer had hatched a plan, one that received his master's unusual approval, *i.e.*, veritable guffaws. It was so unlike the belovèd regent, that it frightened her. After I heard all that she knew of it, I reached for my sword.

"Death to all kings!" I shouted.

She stared at me, my arms outstretched, my legs spread wide, my blade raised high, and she laughed.

What in Heaven's name did she find so amusing? It seems that I had met her at the door whilst completely nude, in anticipation of our usual joining of several body parts, when she burst in.

"You might want to cover that other sword of yours, my lord," she suggested, pointing between my legs. "There is a definite chill in the air this evening."

She laughed again. O, women! What would a man's life be without their laughter at his expense? Nevertheless, I laughed as well.

Dunstane had taken up the habit of leaving my domicile long before my young informant crossed its doorsteps of an evening. He often proceeded to lose himself in a tavern's contents, until, his purse empty, he would be forced to drag himself back to a comfortable bed, almost always his own. (I had advised him not to take his horse along for these excursions, since a besotted rider and a swift steed might prove a dangerous combination for both.) Whenever he did not return, I found little cause for alarm. I knew that the capable fighter had many more years ahead of himself, though I wondered about that fateful day in the distant future, when his arm would hesitate, or his blow be deflected.

On that particular night he made merry with the tavern-wenches, stealing kisses, groping at half-covered breasts, and laughing as he stuck out his very long and very wide tongue at them. His vision was much clouded by ale, so perhaps he was amiss in having noticed five men seated together in one corner, quietly drinking, ignoring the women who cavorted around them. Whilst the Scot continued his carousal, the eyes of the five were upon him for the entire evening. And, as Fortune or Fate would have it, he had little success in finding a companion in whose bed he might pass the night. Perhaps he slurred his speech too much, or his brain was too addled, or (more likely) his current financial status (or lack of it) prompted him to trade the comforts of the ale-soaked tavern's air for the crisp rain that was beginning to fall outside.

He lumbered about for a short distance and stopped, as droplets began to fall down his hair and creep into his eyes. He held out his hand. He looked up, presumably to discover the watery source. Then he laughed loudly.

"Hear me, O Lord!" he called to the Heavens above. "May your children grow drunk, filled with the light of your Truth, that they may never again stagger through the weakness of their sobriety."

He roared with laughter once more, this time the rain filling his open mouth and nearly drowning him in the process. He grabbed at his throat, spat out the water, then frowned upwards, raising a fist thereto as well.

Completely soaked now, he did not wrap his cloak about himself more tightly, the better to keep himself dry, for he was quite warm and still perspiring. As he continued upon his journey home, perhaps he failed again to notice the five from the tavern, who were walking now behind him; or so they must have thought.

Their daggers drawn, they were about to set upon him, when he turned. Grand, old fighter that he was, Dunstane stood there, his sword raised aloft, his face as taut and as angry as it must have been in the first battle of his more youthful days. I emerged from the shadows near him, my sword also drawn.

"Five against one?" I asked. "I dislike the odds."

"It's two now," was one's response.

"I was hoping so very much you would say that."

They lunged at us forthwith. (I have never really understood that. In every battle that I have ever fought, my adversary ever parried with an initial thrust, exposing fully his chest, stomach, and limbs. Only once, as I recall, did I meet a Byzantine, who protected his exposed flank with a long dagger.) These men were no exceptions. They had vile tempers. And whilst they were quite proficient in mimicry of certain animal growls, their swordsmanship left much to be desired. It might have been the case that they had grown used to combat with drunkards, who were too weak to contend with anyone or anything, including their own abstinence.

As Dunstane pierced one man's chest, plunging his blade all the way to and through the man's back, I disemboweled another. (So rank were the contents of my victim's stomach, that I struggled to hold back the entire quantity of nourishment that I had eaten previously.) The others had no choice but to accept their ignominious defeat with some minor effort, leaving the mud beneath our feet soaked further with multitudinous shades of red.

Our evening's revels completed, we both looked up. The rain soaked our heads and blinded us. Imagine my surprise when I turned to see Dunstane, not smiling, mind you, but glowering. He hurried to me, brandishing his blade. I evaded his blow before it entered beneath my ribs in the very place where the old wound had brought me low in Konstantinople.

"Have you taken to following me now, for you don't think the old man capable of defending himself?" he roared.

"Why, you ungrateful, drunken swine!" I shouted back, pushing him off. "I should have let them run you through like a stuck pig at the feast."

"There's no use talkin' to you like this, all convinced that the whole world's wrong, save you."

I proceeded to relate the story that Theresa had told me, most especially of how the advocate had claimed that to defeat a man, one must first deprive him of his friends. He smiled.

"Ah, so it wasn't me you were trying to save then. It was yourself, 'cause you cannot live without me friendship."

I thought his assessment a curious twist; nevertheless, I agreed, albeit reluctantly. He rushed over and hugged me, picking me up, squeezing the breath from me, and filling the air with his laughter.

"Put me down, you old fool," I managed to choke out.

He sheathed his blade whilst looking at mine.

"Our cold metal has tasted hot blood this night. If there be a better way to live, I know nothing of it. Still, I'll never understand why you take such a liking to that big sword. Is it not too heavy a thing to wield swiftly?"

"It has been with me for a very long time. And I prefer to watch closely as Death takes over my enemy's visage."

"You're a strange one, my lord, but I like it!" A realization crept into his face as he looked around. "Where's the fourth and the fifth?"

"What? Who?"

"The fourth and fifth fingers of the king's hand? Where are they? They must've run away, the stinking cowards. Your ruler is scraping up the bottom of the barrel for some interesting friends these days."

"He's not *my* king."

"No? The man who is not your king wouldn't be trying to kill us now, would he? Be that as it may, we should betake ourselves from this pour. It's no fun when your outside's as wet as your innards. Let's to home and a warm fire."

If the advocate were not the recipient of my abject hatred before, most assuredly he possessed it now. And after all these years, I can still taste the bile that welled up into my mouth as I choked upon it that very night.

CHAPTER THE FIFTY-FIRST,

in which a quiet meal with the Templars leads to a confessional most disturbing.

Though he agreed with me that fundamental changes would have to be instituted in any future transfers of money between the Templars and the court, the Holy Father was most unhappy that Master Jacques and I were not on speaking-terms. I had to admit to myself, that even if I admired the papal desire to function in this given situation as a conciliator, I was reluctant to alter the current circumstances; or so that was the case until the Holy Father mentioned a possibility that had never occurred to me: with the forces of the church united against his wishes, the king might be disinclined to abuse his position where the Templars were concerned. A fine chess move, I had to admit, and most politic of him.

We all met at the Templars' House for an evening meal, of sorts. I say this for conversation, whilst not necessarily the motivating force behind all such occasions, is, notwithstanding, a welcome concomitant. This, however, proved not to be true.

Clustered around a very long table were the Master and several of the Templars, along with the Holy Father and his retinue, followed by Dunstane and myself. As we dined through our courses, we stared at each other, exchanged side-long glances, and kept our mouths closed, except to fill them with food or drink. Several papal comments, which were intended perchance to engage any number of us in even the slightest discourse, were ineffectual; nor did the wine produce any calming effect upon us, which result I found quite unusual. Instead of giving free rein to our innermost thoughts, as was its custom, the liquid cast a somber reflection upon our faces, as though we awaited something dire to occur. The chamber was more silent than a tomb.

Our repast finished, we gathered our strength to rise from our seats, but our combined efforts proved futile. Our stomachs laden now with much of food and no less of drink made our eyes as heavy as our limbs. My observation was especially accurate where Jacques was concerned. He had imbibed such an enormous quantity of the vintner's product, that he appeared to doze off more than once. His butler, who had been poking his head into our proceedings during the course of the entire evening, finally left his seat in the scullery and offered the Master his arm. The knights rushed over to offer assistance to the young servant. The old man would have none of it. He wanted only his butler and *myself* to help him to his chamber. (The others were averse to grant me such honour, nor did I seek it overly much.) Despite the unsavory image of an intoxicated Master, I did my best to restrain my distaste. I lifted him up on one side, as his butler did so to the other. We practically carried the heavy burden all the way to his bed, which was no mean feat, I can assure you. We sat him down.

"Never have I sought anyone's approval," Jacques mumbled. "You know that about me, do you not?"

Though he had spoken quietly, his statement was completely lucid, which fact surprised me. I chose not to argue, for often I had seen how drink could transform an otherwise calm individual into a raving beast. I did not want to be responsible for having harmed him in any way, should his demeanor degenerate, and I have to defend myself. I agreed.

"I have tried to do what was required of me," he continued, "tried to be worthy of this position."

As he spoke, his butler removed his clothing. I did not think that I had ever witnessed a servant who tended to a master with so much gentility and concern as I did that night.

"I have always wanted everyone to be happy."

A fool's errand, if ever there were one. I said nothing of this.

"You are happy, are you not, my lord?" he asked of me.

Most happy, I assured him.

"Sometimes it is so difficult to do what is necessary. O, I have never thought of all the times when you must have felt that way. I am so sorry."

I told him that there was no need to apologize, and that he should rest now. (Despite the fact that I had lost all patience with him, for his insufferable weepiness, I restrained my impatience quite well, I believed.)

He laid himself down and closed his eyes. His butler pulled the covers up to his neck, then kissed the top of his head. And at that moment it all became so clear. I had never known, until then, that the man's ministrations meant far more than those of any loyal servant. It was not the kiss; rather it was the way that he kissed, the meaning of which was unmistakable.

I chose not to ruminate upon this revelation for overly long. I returned to the company, believing that I had heard only the ramblings of an inebriated, old fool, ignorant that they comprised, for all intents and purposes, a confession. Shortly thereafter, I discovered that Jacques had granted another loan to the king—a smaller amount than those of the past, yet still in the tens of thousands.

In the ensuing days I proceeded to put into action an idea that I had formulated, once I had received certain crucial information. The advocate spent each day and night at the palace, save for several per month, when his master granted him the courtesy of returning to his manorial estate and his family sheltered therein. I was uncertain as to the time of his arrival, though I knew the appointed day of departure. Consequently, I had to follow him. I brought Dunstane along, as he would be most directly affected by my plan, save for de Nogaret, of course.

We rode at a comfortable distance—close enough to keep the carriage and its surrounding guards in clear sight, yet far enough away to remain undetected. Only once did the knights hear a sound that might have given away our location. (Dunstane's horse had stepped upon a fallen branch, cracking it further.) The petite *caravanserai* stopped. One of the men rode further into the forest to ascertain the presence of unwanted guests.

"Good," Dunstane whispered, watching the man pass us by. "They should all fear these highwaymen."

"Not good. We must be more careful. The next time that we attempt this, we cannot alert them. The element of surprise is everything."

"You mean, this is practice?" he asked, frowning.

I nodded.

"As you say," he acknowledged with a quiet anger.

Finding no one, the knight returned to his former position, and everyone continued on, including us.

Located in the hills, which encircled the city, the manor's architecture was plain. Though quite large, it resembled nothing more than a rectangle, of the sort that the English lords had often been so fond of erecting upon a tract of level rural soil. We watched from an outcropping of trees, as his family and servants welcomed the lawyer home. (And he had very many servants for so small a family!) But what held my fascination (even more than his wife's beauty, which prompted Dunstane to remark to me later that she was too good for *that ugly, lit-*

tle man, and was, in fact, somewhat taller than he) was the child that the mother carried. The girl was obviously crippled. It seemed that Dunstane was also looking at her.

"I've heard it said that her mind is feeble," he offered.

"*Feeble*, you say?"

He nodded. We watched the family for a time. We did not move. We even watched them return inside.

"'Tis a shame that the poor girl has a wee timorous beastie for a father, but there it is. It might not be a Christian thing to take him away from a child like that. Mayhap she needs him. Mayhap she always will."

"He is not going anywhere anytime soon. We should be patient."

"Have faith, my lord, faith in yourself, in your friends, and in your God. For when all is said and done, faith is the only thing that really matters."

"Then again, we could always kill him tomorrow."

"Or the day after."

CHAPTER THE FIFTY-SECOND,

in which I receive more than one surprise guest, then pay a visit of my own to a lonely soldier.

I received word that troops would be sent to quell the rebellious nature of the southerners. Once more I was asked to serve. This time the messenger was not the king, himself, but to my great surprise, a papal envoy.

When the Holy Father came to my humble quarters, Dunstane greeted him.

"No need to stand on ceremony, good sir," was the papal response. "See to it that my companions are fed, whilst your master and I are in discussion."

I thought that the Scot chafed under the weight of that word, *master*, however, he said nothing to the Holy Father about it, for which I was most grateful.

I rose from my seat by the fire to welcome him, commenting that I believed this to be the first time that he had ever visited my unassuming dwelling.

As soon as he entered, he looked about.

"You could reside anywhere in this city or anywhere in Christendom for that matter, yet you chose a modest home." What he found most surprising was the absence of any relics or remembrances, which were part of my personal history. "If I had not known better, I might have thought myself in a tent upon a Spartan battlefield."

I tried to make him understand that I carried my memories within me; they were enough to remind me of where I had been and what I had done when there.

"Nevertheless, you might want to write your personal history someday. There is every possibility that it would serve as a code of conduct for the knights of the Order."

"Is that a subtle command, your holiness?"

"Merely a suggestion."

"In that case, I shall ignore it; Guy de Lagery is no *paradigm* against which the lives of others should be measured."

"We could all do much worse."

He sat down in my most large and most comfortable chair. I placed a goblet, nearly full, in his hand. He looked down and swirled its contents. Then he sniffed them. Then he smiled. Then he drank. We conversed for some time regarding the nature of wine, its grapes, and how certain of these, sometimes in different sections of the same orchard, could yield vastly different aromas and flavours. But an analysis of current forms of viniculture was not the reason for his sudden arrival.

"The regent has asked me to perform a service, of sorts, for him," he explained. "He believes that he will not be able to convince you to lead his troops to quell a rebellion in the south."

"He is most assuredly correct."

"He also believes, furthermore, that I should be able to persuade you to do otherwise."

"He is most assuredly incorrect. What, exactly, have you promised him?"

"Only that I would discuss it with you."

So, he had decided to create a little war, after all, had he? The Nubian would be most pleased.

"Nubian?"

"The female warrior currently in his service."

The Holy Father made no attempt to conceal his displeasure at the very mention of her origin.

"I have seen you speak with this, this … woman. Why would you have anything to do with that sort of creature? She is a pagan, and her skin is as dark as dirt. Her presence in this Christian land is, itself, a sin."

"Then tell the regent that you want her sent into exile."

"He would not permit her presence here, if it were not for her military skills."

"O, I see. She does have some value, does she not? Besides, she fascinates me."

"Fascinates you? Yes, as a witch would her next cursèd victim. Tread lightly upon this ground, sir knight, for it is most unholy."

He went on about the duty of a French citizen to his king and country. I countered with the argument that I was bound in service to the Master of all masters, and no attempt at persuasion, not even from a prince of the church, could alter that commitment. I would not raise my sword against another Christian, unless it were to defend myself, or those for whom I cared. By the time that he had finished his third drink, he was in complete accord.

"How much simpler would our lives be," he asked with a certain degree of frustration, "if Eve had never bitten of that apple?"

A curious statement! How he had come to raise it as a point was beyond me. Despite his insistence, however, this was one subject about which the church and I had ever been at odds, I told him. Not content to remain an ignorant child, the mother of our race had striven to be more than what she was. The lesson was not that women brought evil into the world, but that knowledge, especially profound knowledge, never arrives without a great price—the end of blissful stupidity.

"You say that for you are overly fond of female ... companionship."

"And more than once have I been profoundly ignorant where they are concerned, only to grow much wiser about them later on."

"It has been said that the first step towards the achievement of wisdom is the recognition of one's own ignorance."

And it seemed that I had recognized that aspect of myself far more times than I cared to recall.

Before he left, he asked me once again if I would change my mind; I assured him that I would not.

After having seen him out, I bade Dunstane good night, and returned to the comforting fires of the hearth, there to finish my liquid refreshment. Upon entry into the chamber, I stood unmoving at the portal. Anna was at the fire, clad in that wonderful red silken garment that had once pleased me so very much. Her years appeared to be no more than five and twenty, or perhaps thirty. She was smiling.

"Greetings, belovèd," she welcomed me with more than a little tenderness.

"I must have imbibed far more than ever I thought."

"I am as real as you ... for a short time anyway."

I entered, walking towards her slowly. As I neared her, I put forth my hand to brush her cheek, then did so. Dear God, she was no illusory creature! Quickly she turned her head towards me and kissed me full upon the mouth. If those were not Anna's lips, then had I lost all memory of her.

"But how?" I asked.

"When we leave, we take our love with us. Yours has brought me back."

I stepped away from her, sensing all that she might actually be.

"Begone, fiend, *succubus*, or whichever of Satan's brood you are!"

She shook her head, frowning.

"Must you be so overly dramatic in your speech, my love? I know that it may be a personal failing of all the holy warriors who ever fought in Jerusalem, but I expected better of you. Why should my presence here pose a problem? You returned from the land of the Dead, did you not? Did you think that no one else would ever do so? There was this one Hebrew a long time ago—"

"Enough! Why are you here?"

"I was hoping that we might pass the time together."

She pushed aside a portion of the silk to reveal her nude breasts. (And they were lovely to behold!) I turned away, feigning disgust.

"Cover yourself, woman. You have no shame; you never did," I said, turning back once again to steal a furtive glance.

"O," she asked, covering herself again, "you wish for me to feel shame when I am naked before the man I have loved? Never have you acted in so disgraceful a manner!"

"Disgraceful? I? Regard yourself in this manner, before you regard me."

"I *am* looking at myself through your eyes, and I do not care for what I see. Never have I felt so unwanted."

She cupped her face in her hands and began to sob. I wished to comfort her, stepping towards her even, then thought better of it.

"I beseech you, no more tears. Please, my love."

She removed her hands from her face and looked up at me.

"Am I your only love?"

"O, this is absurd! Wherefore should I explain the great love of my life to a *phantasm*?"

"Your great love?" she asked with much excitement. "Am I still?" she asked shyly now.

"Will you explain your being here before cock crows at dawn?"

Smiling, she licked her lips, then began to push aside the fabric across her chest.

"Not that. Please."

She removed her hands therefrom.

"There is someone else. I know it. Who is this harridan?" she hissed. "I shall strangle the creature until her face turns red with struggle for life-giving breath, then laugh as it grows pale with lifelessness."

Verily, I had no doubt of it!

"Is it that servant girl, Theresa?"

I stared. Her query was completely unexpected.

"You know of her?"

"There is nothing about you that I do not know. That is both the blessing and the curse of all lovers, most especially the dead ones. O, wherefore do you indulge yourself with that prostitute? You could do so much better. Her thighs are horribly fat! Is it this Nubian?"

"If you know of her, then you must also know that I have not lain with her."

"Can you only love a woman who has given to you her body?"

"I cannot answer that question. I have loved only once. And you are supposed to know that."

"I wanted only for you to say it."

She folded her hands before herself, and looked down. Momentarily, she raised her head and smiled upon me.

"This Nubian is the reason for my return. I had thought it best to leave you with unspoiled memories of me. I love you too much to watch you suffer."

"How will this suffering come about?"

"You must listen to me, though your doubts will strive to stop-up your ears. Leave off these women. They will break your heart in ways which never I could, no matter how much I may have wanted to do so."

"How?"

"Have faith in my words. Even beyond death shall I love you."

She reached her hand towards me. Dunstane burst in.

"My lord, was there a commotion in here?" he spoke loudly, more of a shout really.

I turned to him.

"What? No. It was—"

I turned back to the hearth, only to see no one standing before it.

"My lord?"

"It was … the foolishness of an old man, no more."

"Methinks the drink sits not well with your mind tonight. Mayhap it would be best to leave off a bit more for the morrow."

"Maybe so."

The very next day I sought out Makeda at the palace, only to discover that she was at the field of tourneys, practicing her military art. There, atop my horse, I watched as she ran towards the effigy of a knight. She plunged her lance through it again and again, the pieces of straw filling the air about her once more like a billowing cloud.

"After you have ripped out its entrails," I called to her, "whom will you kill then?"

She stopped and turned. The fury was still upon her face. It endured but momentarily, before a smile appeared. She walked over to me.

"Have you returned for another match?"

I assured her that my humour was not a contentious one. I tossed a water-sack to her. She drank of it. I was certain that having been ordered to stay behind in

Paris, instead of being sent away with the other forces, had, at first, dismayed then angered her. I thought that she might have needed to speak of it with a confidant. (Part of me might have also realized that a conversation concerning her present status would endeavour to bring the two of us closer. Of course, I never admitted such a thing to myself at the time, especially after the previous night's warning.)

After having made our unusual greetings with each other, I asked a question that had been gnawing at me since the first time that I saw her fight upon this field: what had made her seek service in the army of a French and Christian king?

"I wanted to see all that the world had to offer."

I thought that it might have been the demands of her faith. If I remembered it correctly, Islam frowned upon a woman fighting in war, as a man would do.

"My Nubian heritage does not. Islamic rulers respect that aspect of our traditions."

And yet she had not been content to remain in her corner of the world, where there were many Islamic rulers who would have benefited from her skill.

"I grew up in the Muslim world. I saw its variety. I wanted to see what wonders there were elsewhere."

I did not believe that she had spoken complete truth, though I chose not to pursue that topic further.

"You are content with your place here, are you not?" I asked.

"I would rather be in my homeland, where my people once worshipped at the Temple of *Amun*, beneath the sacred mountain, *Gebel Barkal.*"

And as she spoke those words, there appeared a glint in her eye, as if the recollection of her time in the place of her childhood were more real than any life that had come thereafter. (And how many have I known, who ofttimes felt the same?)

She had done what she sought out to do, yet she was still unhappy. Perhaps it was true what people said: no one was ever satisfied with whatever he, or in her case, *she*, might possess.

"Are you satisfied?" I asked.

"Never."

"Exactly."

There was one thing that she should remember, I advised; she was in a Christian land. The cherished memories of her ancestors and their deeds might have appeared blasphemous to the local population.

She looked at me oddly.

"That is not true where you are concerned," was her judgment. "There is no hatred for me in your eyes. Tell me, why do you believe that the king has ordered me to stay behind, when he knows that I am the finest of his fighters?"

"I cannot speak for his actions."

"You bear no hatred for him, but neither do you love him, as any loyal subject should his ruler."

"I am subject solely to divine law. Rulers are nothing more than the forces with which I must contend as part of the human legacy—the history that has made me."

"I believe that you know why he wishes me to stay behind, even if you will not speak of it."

Whilst true that I possessed certain gifts, the ability to see into another's mind was not one of them. That revelation did not please her. She turned to depart.

"Why do you always leave when we are in conversation?" I asked.

"You cannot help me. You are of no use to me."

That statement cut me more than I might have realized possible.

"Is my help all that you seek?"

"I believe that I shall tell you something," she responded, upon returning. "I must warn you, if you speak of it to anyone, I shall climb the ramparts of *Nôtre Dame* and call you *liar* for all of Paris to hear."

An extravagant gesture!

"I assure you, I have kept secrets for more years than you have been alive."

She revealed to me (and it *was* a revelation, mind you), that she had been married in her homeland. The marriage did not endure. (She would not elaborate.)

"Now you understand why it is that I would never give myself completely to anyone who did not love me. I am unlike all the women you chase."

All?

"Moreover, for me," she continued, "taking care of a home and crops whilst my husband tends to his battles is a life that I no longer seek."

Had she sought it at one time?

"You have journeyed far to make that point," I commented. "And it was evident to me when first I beheld you, sword in hand."

She came closer and appeared to be studying me.

"When you look at me," she asked, "do you see the strange, the exotic, a curiosity perhaps? Or am I no more than a collection of holes for you to fill?"

I stared into the anger that was beginning to blaze in her eyes.

"I have caused you neither pain nor harm; therefore, it is wrong for you to hold me accountable for the sins of other men, most especially your husband's."

She reached up to slap me; I held her wrist as it neared my face. She pulled back now.

"Forgive me, Sir Guy. That was a gesture of weakness. You deserved better of me. So did I."

She said no more. She turned and left.

Shortly thereafter, I discovered why she had been kept in Paris. Was there ever any doubt that my suspicions would prove true?

De Nogaret wondered why his master kept the Nubian here, when she could have served him much better elsewhere.

"The swordsman of the church has an eye for her. He chose to stay. Like it or not, I cannot order him to leave. As she is here, something may develop between the two. It could become a potential source of manipulation at some future time."

"She has taken no man to bed in your service, thanks be to God. What sort of man would find a filthy creature like her appealing anyway? She is no cleaner than the horses she rides."

"Perhaps she prefers the lengthy members of such beasts. Any man would be a mere infant by comparison."

The king smiled broadly, much taken with his apparent witticism.

The advocate clutched his stomach.

"I beg you, my liege; please cease. The mere thought of it makes me want to retch."

"I have given them the opportunity to find each other," the king said with a smile. "If he wishes to play in a muddy hole, like a curious boy, who am I to refuse this child of the church?"

Their conversation ended in raucous laughter once again.

CHAPTER THE FIFTY-THIRD,

in which I reveal the advocate's genesis to the Holy Father.

The pope was most displeased to discover that I had been standing near the altar, staring at a representation of our Lord, and no one had informed him of my presence.

"I shall have their heads for this insult to you! Have you been waiting long?"

"Have you ever wondered what He might say," I asked, ignoring his query, "if He were standing here, watching all the Christian generations which have followed Him down that arduous road of faith? Would He be proud or disgusted, do you think?"

He looked now into the face of Jesus.

"A bit of both actually. Have you come to pray with us, Sir Guy?"

I turned to face him.

"I have come here to disclose certain truths, though before I do, you must tell me: did you know that the de Nogaret family were Cathars?"

The Holy Father remained incredulous. How could this be? Why would the king place a man like that in such a position of power?

"The king only looks like a beast," was my observation. "His mind is as sharp as a dagger."

From my many travels amongst Cathars, I had learned of (and subsequently recalled) the story of the de Nogaret family. I went on about how the advocate's progenitor had been the sole survivor of his family's destruction, when the knights of Pope Gregory rode into the cities of the south to crush those *unbelievers* under hoof and foot. The little boy's parents had hidden him beneath a pile of tubers in their root cellar. They bade him remain quietly there, until they returned. But they never did. After a time that seemed to drag itself forever, (and which may have been many days or a few moments), the boy climbed up and out. His village was in ruins, burned to cinders. The smoke choked him. He began to cry, when a neighbor rested his hand upon the boy's shoulder. It was an old man

417

come to rescue him, one who had escaped the sword, for he was, perhaps, too frail a thing to be of any consequence or harm. And he reared that boy upon the bitter bread of retribution.

"That poison has been festering in the blood of the de Nogarets for the past six decades. Is it any wonder that the man hides his unscrupulous manner behind codicils of law?" I asked finally.

"That creature will never be satisfied until he has brought Holy Mother Church to its knees. O, what shall we do?"

"I am not yet finished with my tale."

"No?" he wondered, devoid of all hope.

This de Nogaret was the son of a priest and nun, both of whom had renounced their vows for the sanctity of marriage, after he was born. My uncle would have been so pleased to learn of their decent Christian behaviour.

"This is terrible, my friend. You have spoiled what would have otherwise been an uneventful, unremarkable day."

"Truth has a tendency to do that."

He paced in circles about me for a time, his hands folded, their knuckles braced against his lips.

"Phillip is a Christian king," he spoke at last. "He will keep his man's baser impulses under control. Yes," he said, continuously nodding. "This will all be settled with little or no quarrels."

I could not believe what I had heard.

"Phillip and de Nogaret share certain unorthodox ideas about the future," I countered. "They are either visionaries or madmen. In either case, the church will have very little to do with their governance. What will you do with the burden of this knowledge, your holiness?"

"*I?*" he asked, taken aback. "What can I possibly do? I am one man only."

"You are leader of all the world's Christians. It is within your power, nay, it is your very duty to tie a rope around the master's neck and lead him around like the faithful dog that he should be."

"This is ... I mean to say, it is your duty, nay, *your* purpose, to control kings. I ... I have nothing to do with this sort of thing."

I had at times witnessed how fear can transform a strong man's legs into water. I did not believe, however, that I had ever seen it occur within a prince of the church; for that matter, nor had I ever seen this pope's face so ashen.

"Either you will allow me to remove this king's head, or you, yourself, will have to bear the responsibility for the demands which this truth makes upon us."

"He will not die by your hand."

I waited a few moments.

"I shall not ask this of you again."

"Not by your hand," he repeated.

"So be it. Regarding whatever actions he and his little fiend choose to take, their consequences will be upon *your* head. May God have mercy upon us all!"

CHAPTER THE FIFTY-FOURTH,

in which Theresa reaps the consequences of her affection.

One night Theresa stood at the closed door and was poised to depart momentarily, when she regarded me in a manner most curious.

"What?" I asked of her, then laughed. "Were you not satisfied?"

"Why do men always fear that they were not up to the task?"

"I was not thinking of my pleasure, but yours. Why else would you be staring at me so?"

"Forgive me."

Forgive her? When had she ever asked me for forgiveness?

"I was not at all displeased," she continued. "I did not wish to leave you with a false impression of our time together."

Now I was taken aback, for her speech and conduct had become the stuff of courtly romance. What, in Heaven's name, had prompted this sudden *meta-morphosis*?

"I have realized something about myself," she revealed.

Ah, that was its cause! I was most relieved; I thought that a devil or angel might have taken possession of her soul, and I was not comfortable with either possibility. In addition, I was not prepared for how long she would take to gather her thoughts into a coherent form for enunciation. At last, she achieved her task.

"I have wondered about the sort of woman you find desirable."

Why ask me such a question now? Had I ever made her feel that I wished to be with someone else when we were together?

She shook her head, but looked downward and away from me slightly, as if she were ashamed. (Ashamed?) At this point I began to fear for the effects to which her revelation might have subjected her.

"My dear Theresa, what has happened? Will you not tell me?"

"The women at court are beautiful."

"And well they should be! Their ladies-in-waiting expend a great deal of time and effort in making them look that way."

"You could have them all, if you so desired it."

"I desire no dainty damsel. In truth, I believe that I never have; though there was an occasion a century or so ago when I—O, that matters little today. What do those women have to do with you? Has any one of them made you the victim of her casual cruelty?"

"A courtly maiden is the only type of woman you could ever love. Is that not true?"

"I loved a princess once. I had different dreams then. I thought that the two of us could find some happiness together. Strange how that time seems like only several days ago."

The colour faded from her face, and left only its pale remnants.

"If you love her that much, you should probably try to be with her again. I shall miss you when you leave."

"I am not going anywhere. She has been long since buried in the cold earth. Why have you brought me down this road?"

She struggled to respond. I placed my hands against her cheeks, and pulled her face close to mine. We kissed.

"There is nothing that you cannot tell me," I assured her.

"No other man has ever been able to make me feel what you make me feel."

I was heartily flattered, considering her presumably vast experience.

"And this is a bad thing?"

She smiled, though it was not in her usually effusive manner.

"More than once have I thought that I would give up all other men … for you."

I stared into her face and realized that Plato had been most correct; often the eyes formed a lookingglass into the very soul, itself. And at that moment I knew that she had unburdened her heart, certainly for the first time, to me at any rate.

"Why, Theresa, I do believe that you love me!"

"Never would I say that to a man and give him that much control over my life. And I refuse to start now! But you are the only man who has ever tempted me to change all that."

"Sweet lady," I told her, stroking her cheek, "I would never demand that you alter the essence of who you are. The very nature of our relationship is one of mutual respect and liberty." I smiled. "I am, after all, like no other man."

There was a moment quite brief, albeit quite visible, when I thought that I had struck her, so quickly did she turn from me. Had I but known that she sought a different response, I would have given it up without hesitation. (At least I believed then that I would have.)

With equal rapidity, she turned back with a smile.

"Good for you!" she exclaimed. "I would not expect to be so mistreated in the way that you do all your other ladies."

She was about to leave. I decided to make a confession that I hoped would comfort her in some small manner.

"Ever since my return to Paris, you have been the only woman in my bed."

She smiled wryly, believing, I supposed, that I had lied. She kissed me, and that kiss was not full of heat, as was its wont. It was tender, yea, soft even. It was as if another woman's lips had touched mine.

"You are a terrible liar, Sir Guy of Lagery. I would not have you any other way."

I thought I espied a tear upon her leaving, or it may have been nothing more than a play of the candlelight.

In recent days I had elected to follow the pope's advice, as I began to write down the summation of my adult experiences, even if the only eyes to see their development would be mine. (I was still convinced that the work would provide meager aid to any Templars in their desire to understand either the holy wars or my life.) At such a moment, dissatisfied with a particular bit of phraseology, and rubbing a pumice stone across the letters to erase them, I failed to notice Dunstane's presence. In point of fact, he was standing over me, steadfast and silent, though he spoke no words to disturb my concentration. I believe that he never stepped into a room so quietly as he did that evening.

"I barely heard your entry," I told him.

Still he did not speak. I had lost all patience with him, and was determined to let him know this when I looked up. His face was horribly pale.

"Have you seen a spirit?" I asked.

"Very like, my lord."

I had never witnessed so much pain wrought into his face, as it was that night.

"What has happened, Dunstane?"

"'Tis a shame what they have done to that poor lass. Too terrible for any words, it is."

"Girl? Which girl?"

He refused to answer. Then it was that I realized the full import of his statement. No, he did not have to give voice to a single word of it.

He led me behind the rear of the house, into the stable. Upon a mound of hay he had rested a woman's lifeless body. (He had found her lying facedown in a muddy pool, not far from my home. His curiosity bested him, as he turned over the form to see the face. When he recognized it, he brought the woman here.)

I knelt upon the pile and brushed aside the hair from her closed eyes. I could not help thinking that some might have said this a proper finish for a girl full of sin. Of course, her only sin was that she had become a part of my life, and she paid for that participation with her own. I looked at the muddied blood surrounding the gaping hole in her neck. O, my poor Theresa, I was so sorry for what had been done to her. And I never suspected, until the very moment that I saw her lying there, that I had been watched as carefully as I had watched others.

I stood up now.

"Someone killed her," I said. "That was his sin. I never loved her. That was mine."

"Where shall we find him, my lord?"

"In the taverns no doubt."

"Do you think he went thither to drown his sorrows afterwards?"

"Nay, my friend, he went there to celebrate his victory over a defenseless woman. And what a brave man he must believe himself to be! We shall find him this night, spreading his newly acquired wealth, for this action has a lawyer's stench hovering about it."

"And shall we send him to the Lord of the Pit?" he asked anxiously, revealing a broad smile and every tooth in his mouth.

"Very like, my friend," I responded with equal glee.

It was not the first tavern, nor the fifth inn that yielded the knowledge necessary to complete our task. Eventually, we came upon him—a poor man made newly prosperous. Somehow, miraculously, he had managed to develop a sudden coterie of friends, and they surrounded him as if he were a lost brother, come home at last to partake of their good fellowship (and ale-drenched breath). Upon seeing him, Dunstane and I exchanged a nod; we recognized him as one of the missing pair who had attacked us then fled the night of that déluge.

We pushed through the crowd, making our way towards him. As I placed my hands upon his shoulders, one of his comrades, a contentious fellow, had the audacity to spit at me. I raised my blade and touched his hand with it, albeit barely. He howled in pain. All noise in the tavern ceased.

"He comes to baptize with fire and sword," Dunstane offered as explanation to the patrons, all of whom ran out rather quickly, I would have to admit.

Upon seeing our faces, the man's own laughter sank into despair.

"What do you want with me?" he managed to ask.

"The spirit of a young woman calls out from beyond the grave. She accuses you of sending her to that cold place."

He jumped up and began to run. Dunstane tripped him, then bent down and rubbed his face into the dirty floor.

"Shall I step on him and crush him like the bug he is, my lord?" he asked, looking up at me.

"Bring him outside. His presence has soiled this establishment enough."

I threw several coins upon a table, which action brought forth a smile upon the tavern owner's formerly distraught appearance.

Dunstane dragged the man up from the floor and into the middle of the road. Surprisingly, there was no one about. It was as if the entire city had been given over to *phantoms*.

Upon his knees now, the man pleaded.

"What do you want?" he asked me. "I am a Christian. You're supposed to protect Christians."

"Not the evil ones."

"O. Really?"

I nodded.

"What will you do with me?"

"Are you that stupid?" Dunstane shouted. "He will send you all the way to Hell, knave."

"Hearken unto me, killer of women," I announced loudly. "The suffering there is without end. Your only salvation is confession."

He thought upon it momentarily.

"For all my misdeeds?"

"Who has paid for your services?"

"For which thing, my lord?"

"For the young woman's death!" I howled, beyond all patience.

"It was my friend, Master Squink."

"Squink?!" both Dunstane and I asked of each other simultaneously.

He revealed to us that one Master Squink had both paid him for her murder and had put together the group of five who had attacked us previously. (Squink it was who escaped that night as well.)

"And who was his benefactor?" I asked.

"A very important person at court. That is all I know. I swear it upon my wretched life."

"And a most wretched life it is!" Dunstane agreed.

"Will you grant me mercy, my lords? I shall leave Paris never to return. This I swear."

"He's done a godawful lot of swearing this night, he has," Dunstane said.

"What shall I do, Dunstane? Shall I show him kindness?"

"No!" we answered simultaneously.

"Show no mercy!" Dunstane demanded.

"Not even a little bit?" the man asked.

"Not a drop of it," Dunstane responded.

"O, you never let me have any fun anymore," I said, walking over to the man. "Defend yourself," I addressed him now.

"This is an execution?" he said, rising.

"It certainly is."

I allowed him his several lunges, parrying the thrust each time. Finally, having grown bored with his ineptitude, I sliced his head off his neck as if it were a lanced boil. (Despite the pleasure with which I had accomplished the task, it did not give me as much delight as I thought the cracking of his spine would have. Nevertheless, I have learned to adjust to life's disappointments, even if they are of my own making.)

"This homicide has sought a certain remuneration. I have paid him well, have I not, Friend Dunstane?"

"Very well, my lord. Methinks you've paid the city's rats with equal generosity. They'll be likely to pay you with thanks for their feast in the morn, I'll wager."

Later that night, at the de Nogaret household, a servant interrupted the master's meal (and that of his entire family as well) to inform him that two knights were outside, wishing to speak with him. He had no idea who they might be; nevertheless, he comforted his lady and asked her not to delay their eating, as he would doubtless take some time to see about this business.

Truly he had no idea what vision would greet him at his doorstep. Dunstane and I sat calmly atop our mounts, as the little man looked up at us.

"This is quite a surprise!" he exclaimed. "I had no idea that you knew where my home ... was."

The hesitation in his speech may have been due to his recognition, that the red liquid pouring from the small sack that I held, was coalescing into a thick pool of blood upon the soil below.

"We know that and a great deal more," Dunstane said.

The advocate appeared to be confused. I thought it best to make certain that he knew exactly how to take my friend's meaning.

"I cannot believe that you have paid very much for his services," I began. "Unfortunately, such men are everywhere in these troubled times."

I tossed the sack at his feet.

"I have brought the Gorgon's head. It is my gift to you. Open it and look inside."

He was hesitant to do as I had asked, though he acquiesced ultimately. The scream froze in his throat.

"Now that you recognize his face," I continued, "you may recall his large frame. I have left that in the road for other vermin to feast upon. I deemed his head to be a fit and proper illustration for the de Nogaret family to see how the husband and father facilitates royal business in this city. I shall share a single lesson that I have learned in my very long life: the coward knows no peace, for there is always someone or something else that he may fear. I cannot conceive of such horrible existence. I would rather be dead. Your master will be most cross with you. He is someone or something to be feared, is he not? I have often heard that you were a capable councilor. O, forgive me, I mean, *are* a capable councilor. Pity, that."

We turned our steeds to depart, but stopped, as he called out to me:

"You forget, Sir Guy; *vengeance is mine,* says the Lord."

I turned back to face him.

"And you forget, advocate; I am the Lord's vengeance."

CHAPTER THE FIFTY-FIFTH,

in which Marie changes her vocation.

There are moments when all conviction, planning, or holy blessings cannot prepare one for each unexpected turn of events. Perhaps that explains how I arose one day with a full absence of joy; not that I faced each dawn with a song, mind you, but I immediately found myself wrathful, as though I had not slept during very many nights. And that was not a good omen.

With the lateness of the evening and still no appearance by Marie, I sent Dunstane to the palace to discover her whereabouts. Upon his return, he informed me that she had been removed to a convent outside of the city. There she would be attended by the Sisters of His Most Precious Blood, who were determined to make comfortable her final days.

My friend related the above information quietly. His face downcast, it was painfully obvious that he was not prepared for the telling of it. (He had, in fact, developed a respectable fondness for her, and had even taken to referring to her as, *the old girl*.) More than saddened, I was angry at the unremitting Frailty, that always made of age Its veritable nest of comfort.

Dunstane was eager to gather together our horses, and he was most unhappy when I informed him that he would not be coming along. He refused to understand why he was compelled to stay behind; his duty was to remain at my side. Yes, I had no doubt of it, however, the Holy Father would have to function as a witness to Marie's decline. This he could not understand either, though he knew it pointless to argue with me.

He left the room to prepare my horse. I removed a small vial from a cabinet. (It glowed like the previous liquid that I had presented to Marie, except this colour was blue.) I was uncertain (even when I did suspect) that it might be of some use. Of course, if it were, then—Still, I preferred not to think upon the true meaning of that possibility.

428   The Lions of God

The Holy Father was most displeased to be pulled from his bed in the middle of the night, though *I* were the cause. If it had been anyone else … (I shuddered to think what punishment he might have demanded, had it been.) I told him that the two of us would ride alone to the convent. The cardinals were most unhappy with that prospect. At the very least they pleaded with him to take a coach led by their brothers, or call upon my Templar brethren as escorts. But when the pope looked into my eyes, he knew that there was no other way. He said that he would be protected by my guardianship, and there was no better sword to defend him in all of Christendom. (Nevertheless, he was most unhappy about riding on horseback, as it had been some years since last he found it necessary to perform that task). We left.

Riding there, he gave voice freely to his feelings about what was transpiring this night:

"All this effort for a sick, old woman! I hope that she values your friendship as much as I."

The Sisters received us with kindness, despite their reluctance to allow two men into their *sanctum*, even if one were the prince of the church, himself. They did, however, warn me to keep a bit of distance between the poor woman and myself, as her body was emitting a strange (yet potent) odor. That piece of information was the first hint of my initial suspicion proving itself true.

When we approached her, the Holy Father's hand flew up to cover both his nose and mouth. She did not stir. There was no doubt that she stood at Death's door. Her gray pallor was the final form of evidence that I required.

I bent down upon one knee, reached over, and brushed the hair from her brow as a gesture of comforting. (I did not believe that she was aware of my presence.) I opened her mouth slightly. My companion thought me mad. He had no idea that I would pour a portion of the aforementioned liquid down her throat. Then I stood up.

Not long after, the smell about her began to dissipate. It was at that time she opened her eyes. Upon seeing the two of us, she smiled. She reached up and held my hand tightly. She had no idea where she was, or how she had come to be here. Her last remembrance was of a certain dizziness that occurred after having partaken of some wine in the scullery. (I had no doubt that it had been left for her to find, though I told her none of this.) Once informed of her location, she confessed that she was most glad to be in such a quiet, peaceful place. And she thanked me for tending to her.

I knew that she had grown unhappy in service to the king, especially in recent years. I asked for and was granted a meeting with the prioress. (His holiness offered to be present, though he accepted my desire to speak alone with her.) I wished for Marie to be admitted into the order. The prioress was reluctant; their resources were few; the dear woman would have to be looked after on a reasonably consistent basis; and their resources were meager. Had she mentioned that fact already? Yes, I understood.

I placed a bag of coins upon her bureau. This was not for Marie, I insisted; it was for the greater glory of the convent and their devotion to our Lord, and both our actions would make the Holy Father quite happy, I assured her. She smiled broadly, revealing a mouth of very yellowed and few teeth.

Before we left, the Holy Father was generous enough to pray with me at Marie's bedside. She was genuinely touched by his concern for her. And I was grateful for his kind blessing upon her.

As I made my final good-byes, I noticed that the paleness in her eyes had not faded with the cure. (Apparently the substance that she had previously imbibed had already completed its infernal work. There was no manner in which I might rectify this bit of *lawful* business.)

Riding off, I informed his holiness of what I had suspected and ultimately discovered to be true. This knowledge did naught but augment his uneasiness concerning the current state of affairs.

"Sometimes I forget that, along with your advanced age, you may have acquired far more esoteric practices than are a man's typical habits. Such knowledge may be useful, as it was today, however, this entire matter is an unwholesome business. I shall be glad to leave here."

"What I have learned is of no use to her anymore. Death has called her to his kingdom. She will journey thither within the year."

"Why did you wish me to see this?"

"There is only one man who could be responsible—the king's advocate."

"How can you be certain? The bottle was left to stand there by the cupboard. Anyone might have drunk from it. And anyone might have forgotten to return it to its former place of storage. There is no proof that his hand has ever poured a single drop of any elixir into it."

I concurred. The one lesson that the practice of poisons had taught me was that it was very difficult to prove their usage.

"That explains why cowards prefer them to swords," was his general understanding.

"Emblematic of the advocate's nature as well," I added.

"Tell me how the death of this woman will be of any benefit to him. She is agèd, sickly, and most evident to all, quite powerless."

"Ever since my return to Paris, she has been my ears in the royal court."

He was silent for a time. I pushed him for a response.

"What do you wish me to say?" he asked. "Is it possible? Indeed. Is it more than likely? Doubtless. Is there proof? Absolutely not!"

"You have witnessed her illness and the means of its partial cure."

"And in what tribunal have we revealed this cure?"

"Your word is law! Everyone will believe it."

"Shall I call for a man's head when I have not seen him commit a crime? Everyone will believe only that I have seen a holy man perform a deed of miracle for a kind, old woman."

Now it was my turn for silence, as I stared at him. He turned from me. I was not quiet for very long.

"It had never occurred to me that a French pope might be reluctant to condemn the actions of a French king's most trusted councilor, especially since said councilor does nothing without his royal master's knowledge of it. Is that why you asked me to return here, to Paris?"

"What do you mean?"

"Perhaps the Holy Father sees it all, and fears worse. If I uncover the truth of things, even a French king may have to compel his man to assume the burden of the blame and suffer an execution. Such action might prompt royal ire to strike against the man responsible for this revelation. And if said man were, say, a pope, committed to truth and protected by an immortal knight, he might be willing to risk his safety, all for the sake of a justice that is fast disappearing in his homeland. And all of this will come to pass in the pope's own good time, will it not?"

"If only I were as committed to the path of truth as you say!" he confessed with a sneer. "You have grown well-versed in politics, Sir Guy."

"I know nothing of politics. I know well the human heart, in all its grandeur, in all its grossness."

"You have done well by this woman, and I have every conviction that you will do well by me. After all, yours is the hand of reprisal, put upon this earth to render all enemies of God and His church useless. Everyone knows this, including me, the king, and his thrice-damnèd lawyer," he said, then spat.

"Hughes de Payens once called me, *a lion of God*. This king and his advocate believe that I have grown soft and lazy in my dotage. They will soon learn how loud is this lion's roar."

CHAPTER THE FIFTY-SIXTH,

in which the Parisians inform the king, in no uncertain terms, that they would prefer other fiscal policies.

During our return, a great noise was carried upon the wind. I was reminded of the first time that I heard the Turks riding in the distance, shouting when they came upon us, screaming as their swords met ours. Only, this occasion was not a battle in *Outremer*, it was a war of the common people against their king.

His holiness and I watched from a hilltop, as the great tumult encircled and burned Paris below.

"It would appear that the peasants have decided that they will no longer pay their taxes," I observed.

The Holy Father glowered at me.

"Do you believe this a comedy?"

"It is essentially tragic, though it is not without its comic elements, like most things in life, I suppose."

"Do you have any idea how many people will die because of this?"

"Very many."

"I cannot believe you to be so callous."

"Me? I am not the one responsible for this rebellion. The king has finally sown what he has so long reaped."

"Right or wrong, he is this country's leader. If the people rise up against him, they will be punished severely, and rightly so! They will shatter the very foundation of this land. For them there can be no mercy."

He looked down upon the smothered populace, his jowels flapping to and fro.

"And no justice either?" I asked.

Together we waited for the wrath in their bellies to burn itself out. And after three days, there were a great many clouds of smoke rising above the city, but there was not very much noise. The Holy Father was reluctant to leave our encampment. I reminded him that no harm would come to him, as long as I were at his side. That assurance would have been sufficient for him before, however, with this most unexpected turn of events, it was as if his entire world had shattered to bits. He was uncertain of everything now.

Thankfully, the houses of God were still sacrosanct; they had been left untouched. Having deposited his holiness at *Nôtre Dame*, in the safe hands of the cardinals, I returned to see if my home had suffered any damage, or if it might have been burned to ash. Having passed the remnants of many such structures, I was relieved to see that no harm had come to it. (Dunstane had probably sat high atop his horse, in front of the *aedifice,* his blade raised aloft, should anyone dare to come near; Dunstane, ever the brave soldier.)

He greeted me with a hug that I believed I had seen certain bears perform, in traveling shows, for their masters. After having put me back down so that I might regain my breath, he related that he had not left the domicile during the riot; he wanted to be present when I should return. Besides, he was uncertain whether he should join the war or not. Despite his initial inclination to attack the king, (a Scottish habit, he confided to me), he had no idea how his actions might reflect upon my position, what with my connection to the church and the pope and all. I thanked him for his discretion.

"Have you seen the royal troops?" I asked.

"A fine pack of killers they are," he spoke solemnly. "The people never had a chance."

And Makeda? The Nubian? Had he seen her at all? No, he had not. And it suddenly occurred to me that I might never see her again either, this fearless warrior-maiden with the annoying habit of perceiving the truth in a man's eyes.

Now that the churches and my property were safe, there remained but one other structure to see—the Templars' House.

When we reached it, we discovered that it, too, had remained quite intact. (A surprise, considering that Phillip would have prevailed upon Jacques to use his Templars, alongside royal troops, to break the rebellion. Following that, the people would have doubtless become enraged and stormed the building. But neither situation ever occurred, as I was to learn.)

We found Phillip upstairs in the very same room where Dunstane had formerly voiced his impatience with me. The king looked even more unkempt than was his wont. (I found out later that he had left the particular chair upon which he sat only to take his meals or to relieve himself.) He had been there for three very long days. He stared at me now with the wild eyes of a feral cat.

"Where have you been, brave fighter," he asked, "when your kingdom needed you?"

"I have been away on church business with the Holy Father."

"Always this business with the church. You should have been here for your king!" he roared, rising from his seat.

"God is my king. I have always been here for Him."

He sat back down, his body bent over upon itself, as if his very entrails and spine had been ripped therefrom.

"The war is over, your majesty," Master Jacques offered, hoping, I supposed, to function in his newfound rôle as peacemaker. "You may return safely now to the palace."

"Have I crushed them all?" Phillip asked.

"So it would seem," was my response.

"Now am I happy," he concluded with a smile.

His attendants lifted him up from the chair.

"Enjoy your life, your majesty," I said. "It is a gift."

"Is that what you call it?" he asked, walking over to me. "Perhaps that is how it is for you, the recipient of a miracle. But what of me? When you look at me, do you see God's mercy, His kindness, His benefaction? I ... am ... an *abomination*! I have been betrayed by the Creator of us all, Who saw fit to fashion my form from the misshapen fragments of humanity; betrayed by my sire and his belovèd, who could not bear to look upon me, though I sprang from their loins; betrayed by everyone and everything." He stepped closer and whispered in my ear. "Where is my gift?"

He walked away, his attendants leading him downstairs, as I held back Jacques, the better to discover why the king had sought refuge here.

"It was the only place in which he felt secure," was the response.

He had, in fact, ordered Jacques to keep all of the Parisian Templars here and not participate in any battles outside, so that he might have the best protection possible. (At that moment he trusted no one, save God's holy warriors, it seemed.)

"I am grateful to God that you are unharmed," Jacques continued.

"I cannot be harmed. But you know that already. Go soon to an apothecary, and ask his recommendations for what substance might benefit you. This forgetfulness of your extreme age is most disheartening."

Upon our return to the residence, Dunstane and I found Makeda on horse-back, near the stables. Her face was haggard, as though she had spent several days in long battles. Blood from a small cut had dried upon her cheek. The blood across her scabbard was dried as well, and I suspected it not to be her own.

Dunstane took charge of the horses, as she and I went inside.

I offered her a drink.

"I never drink," she told me. "Today will be an exception."

She emptied the chalice instantly.

"How many of them have you killed?" I asked.

"How do you know?"

"Firstly, you are not the only one who can look at a person's face and see what troubles lurk therein. Secondly, the defense of the realm is your purpose."

"For some time now I have lived as a knight. In the past days I have become a killer."

"Taking life is *exactly* what you do! Did you think that your position would never demand the worst of you? This king is no saint. He will use anyone as it suits him. As for his people, when families are starving, everyone feels that he may have nothing left to lose, so protestations become a civil war. It has happened several times before, and it will surely happen again. You should probably learn how to harden yourself against the pain that you feel, or you should leave off service to this crown."

She walked over to me, stared at me.

"Maybe one is not meant to live for very long, because the more years he has, the colder grows his soul."

"I am not a cold, undead thing that was once a man. When I look at you, my blood begins to boil."

"You should see a physician," was her retort, with an added smile.

"Will you not let me kiss you, or is that a sign of too much weakness?"

"We are not weak creatures, you and I. We take what we will, when we will."

She thrust her chest at me. The meaning of that action was unmistakable. With my sword I cut open her tunic at its center. I threw my blade upon the car-pet, and cradled a breast in one hand. Simultaneously we reached towards each other's face, and our lips met with such force, that I thought each tooth in my mouth had shattered. We tore at each other's garments, as the blood from her face, hands, and torso rubbed against and smeared mine. We fell to the floor.

Shortly thereafter, Dunstane came in, watching from the doorway, as two bodies lay nude, entwined upon the carpets.

"Her, too?" I heard him say aloud. "Now the women are throwing themselves at him. Would that I were as fortunate as he!"

He left quietly, after having watched us a bit further.

CHAPTER THE FIFTY-SEVENTH,

in which the king is most aggrieved over the memory of his belovèd Jeanne.

Into a small chapel of the palace stepped Dunstane and I. Guards led us there and had the good sense to leave us be, that we might pay our respects in solitude. This small room, with its very high ceiling and circular shape, was where the stone effigy of Queen Jeanne lay. After the men left, the silence was broken only by the fierce storm outside. Against the tall, variegated glass, that stretched from floor to roof, and formed, in essence, the entire perimeter of the chamber, it drove its hard rain like so many fists. It was a wonder that no pane cracked at all.

"He's angry with his children tonight," Dunstane commented, looking through one of the windows.

I could not disagree with him.

I walked over to the stone *gisant.* Studying her face now, I had to admit that the sculptor had indeed captured her in a semblance of quiet dignity. She had been possessed of an ethereal beauty, of the sort that one might find upon the visage of a female saint in portraiture. It was a thing most rare, and for that reason, perhaps, she was loved by the common-folk and all who had the good fortune to have known her. I had met her only once, upon her day of matrimony, yet it was enough for her gentle manner to have found a lasting place within my heart.

She lingered there in slumber, her form forever young. I reached out to touch it, when her widowed husband entered.

"We thought it most unusual when the guards apprised us of your presence," he began.

I informed him that I had chosen to avail myself of the invitation that he had made me some time previously, *i.e.,* that I should look upon his castle as my home.

"I have come to ask forgiveness, your highness."

He stared at me in quite skeptical a fashion, or so I thought.

"I could not bring myself to return to France when I heard of her passing. I have never been comfortable with the act of mourning. I suppose it is a weakness of mine. I should have come to see her much sooner in any case," I continued, returning my gaze to her features.

"What has prompted this sudden departure from your usual habits, if we may be so bold as to inquire?"

"I have recently lost someone who was dear to me."

"Ah! Did she pass in the comfort of a night's sleep, as did our Jeanne?"

"Not quite. She gave up the ghost when a sword passed through her throat."

"A most vile creature must have been guilty of this crime. Tell us, Sir Guy, did you kill him swiftly or slowly?"

I had not expected such a query. The advocate must have already informed him of my actions.

"I never said that I found the man responsible."

"Now it is our turn to ask for your forgiveness. We assumed that you would not be able to rest until you had deprived him of his continued existence."

"In point of fact, you are correct, your highness. I took his life, though not so slowly as I should have."

"It is a good thing to slake one's thirst for another's blood. It would not do at all to have knights riding around our kingdom, seeking to impart their own particular type of justice. What would the common-folk think, to say nothing of our most faithful nobles?"

"The man was quite easy to find, despite the assistance that he had received from others."

"Assistance? Was a group of men responsible for her death then?"

"She died at the hands of one man alone, though others had paid him handsomely for the deed."

"She must have been a very important lady."

"She was insignificant to all, except to me."

"Part of a man's measure is the number of powerful enemies he can claim. In a curious way, we suppose that you should feel flattered."

My hand tightened around the hilt of my sword. The only thing that stopped me from its use was a papal prohibition against the permanent removal of that broad grin from this regent's face.

"As unique as she may have been," he continued, "I warrant that she was not so wondrous as my Jeanne."

I was taken aback, surprised that he had left off his usage of the royal *we*. O, it must have been a rare moment of vulnerability.

"She was a beautiful queen, your majesty," Dunstane offered. "You are very fortunate to have known the kindness of such a lady."

I believe that he was moved, but momentarily, by Dunstane's honest appraisal of both himself and the object of his adoration, for the appearance on his face now was one of absolute peace.

"Was there ever a woman like this in all the world?" he asked, bending to his knees, and running his hand slowly across her face. "Helen of Troy would have been plain by comparison. My most beautiful Jeanne, she was, a woman without malice. Can you conceive of such a thing? In all the royal courts, in all the world, there was none with heart so pure. More than wife to me, she was my most faithful helpmate. And no matter what I told her, she bore it all with equanimity of spirit. And I told her everything."

Apparently he had had great need of a mother-confessor. I wonder if she were satisfied with the rôle into which he had thrust this kind, unsuspecting lady?

He stood up now.

"She fulfilled her matrimonial obligations with all deliberate kindness. She gave to me three sons and two daughters. And she treasured her children as few queens have."

"A remarkable woman, your majesty," I observed, "and most rare."

"This lady whom you have lost, was she as dear to you?"

Most dear, I assured him.

"Then our mutual pain is one more thing that we have in common."

"O? And what else do we share, your majesty?"

"Why, our French blood, of course! We are both faithful to the demands, which it imposes upon us. Of me it asks to make harsh decisions when the occasion demands it."

"And of me?"

"We have not yet made that determination. However, we believe that all will be revealed within the fullness of time."

"I look forward to that revelation."

"As do we."

In an old district, where once stood many houses of prostitution, and where now could be found innumerable small churches, one might stumble upon an ornate structure, the home of the Philamos family. Former Greek traders (of Persian carpets) with the Byzantines, they had settled into a comfortable life of occasional indulgence in this, their newly adopted city. Their sole surviving descendant, the current Master Philamos, was a jovial sort, much given to the partaking of fine wines and sundry other amusements. He was rotund as well, and wore sheer garments far too large for his circular shape. As a result, the cloth hung from him and billowed about as he walked. Moreover, he was the first of a new class of men, an intermediary, who brought different people together for different reasons, for a modest fee, of course. As regards his domicile, it was used for the gathering of noblemen, most of whom were married and with families. He would allow them the use of his rooms for perhaps an afternoon, and sometimes for a full day and night. And whatsoever any two men (or the occasional third) did in those rooms was a subject never open for discussion. All temporary occupants of the household always claimed that its proprietor was a man of the highest discretion. He was an individual much loved, and much sought after, *i.e.*, by a particular segment of the population.

And lo, the queerest of occurrences came to pass during that same wet evening that the king and I exchanged our observations about the depth of each other's pain. Royal soldiers stood at the front door. They broke it down, tracking mud across the carpets. Then they smashed through each door of every room, seeking a certain pair of individuals. Their activities, having been sanctioned by the crown, ceased only when they came upon the two men in question, *in flagrante delicto*, as the advocate would later refer to the manner of their corporeal positioning. There were several others in the building at that time, but they were all permitted to go free. Only two men were dragged out of the house, along with the current Master Philamos, who was forced to go along, despite his constant protestations of innocence in all things. When word of Master Jacques' arrest (and that of his barber) came, it was a wonder to all. I, alone, was not in the least surprised.

CHAPTER THE FIFTY-EIGHTH,

in which everyone is put through his respective paces.

Upon the field the Templars were put through their military practices under the watchful eye of the finest swordsman in France, Dunstane of Scotland. (The Holy Father had summarized what little he had learned of Jacques' arrest, and asked me to look after the knights as a temporary measure. Their attention being focused upon their physical acumen was necessary as well. Rumour was one lady that he had no desire to see set up her house and flourish in this land. I was afraid that his wish had already arrived too late to make any difference at all.)

In the afternoon I rode up to Dunstane. Together we watched the members of the Order as they attempted to fight each other.

"How goes it?" I asked.

"My lord, had I as many years left to me as you, I cannot say that they would change much the pitiable sight that I have seen here today."

Thus, the fruit of Jacques' labours.

"I cannot believe that the king had thought it safe to be under their protection," he continued. "Thanks be to God that no one stormed the keeps."

"Work them hard. And when they break, work them harder. They must be made ready. Only God knows where it will all lead."

I had very nearly left, when one of the brothers came to me. Gilbert de St. Claire was a lad of years no more than five and ten. His hair was pale and his thin beard red, very like those of his ancestor, the noble Hughes. Inquisitive as always, he was concerned about the Master, whom he had come to look upon as a paternal substitute, I surmised.

"Is it true?" began his inquiry.

Though I knew what he was asking, I told him to be more specific. (The sooner that this issue was laid to rest, the better would it be for all concerned.)

"Did the Master do everything that has been said of him?"

Rumour—she could spread throughout a city faster than a plague; a pox upon the wench!

"You are needed upon the field. Wherefore do you concern yourself with anything else?"

"Concern?" he asked, bewildered. "We are all brothers. *The agony of one is the agony of all.* That was the first lesson that you taught to the Order."

"*Never allow the sins of one's forebears to become one's own.* That was my second lesson. What Jacques may or may not have done has nothing to do with how you will perform today. Your concern now is for yourself and for your brethren. Do not bring shame upon anyone."

"Forgive me my impertinence, lord; I do not wish him to die."

Try as I might, I could not keep at bay this twinge of embarrassment. He had not brought shame upon me, but rather, nourished my own—a quality of character that had obviously not disappeared from the de Payens bloodline in the intervening centuries.

"If guilty," I swore, "then no one may be able to save him, except God. If innocent, I shall not allow him to suffer."

That evening, as we lay together, Makeda rolled over and began to caress then kiss my chest. (For one whose life was hard, she was possessed of the softest lips, which have ever touched mine own. I hope that the spirit of Anna, wherever it may be, forgives me for having written those last lines.) I was thoroughly enjoying her tender passions, when she stopped. I opened my eyes to see that the appearance of her face was sedate, grave. O, I knew it meant that a confession was forthcoming.

She struggled to speak.

"I must tell you something."

And she trembled. From time to time had I felt a woman tremble near me, (ever in bed, it seemed), prior to her unburdening her heart to make some sort of confession. Rarely was it as serious a remembrance of past actions as they might have assumed it to be. This time, however, was painfully different.

Yes, I had heard that statement several times before, even though I did not believe it time enough for her feelings to have developed so deeply for me. Then again, it would not be the first time that I had underestimated a woman's affections.

"I can bear no children."

O, I had not expected that piece of truth. Then began the balance of her earlier tale, in which a farmer's wife, having grown tired of being beaten daily for the lack of fruit from her barren womb, took a knife, (that she, herself, had carved from a stag's horn), and cut her husband's throat as he slept. It was not idle curiosity that had sent her in journeys across the world; it was Islamic and Nubian law, which demanded her execution. The woman whom she had been she buried that night. And somewhere, during the time of her flight, she took that same knife and carved a lion's head into her arm, as emblematic of the spirit that had always set her soul aflame.

"You must hate me," she said at last.

I caressed the scarred shape of the feral cat. How could I hate her? Though there was blood upon her hands, I could not deny the innocence in her eyes.

"Why?" I asked. "You have been most honest—a rare quality in anyone, whether female or male."

"Is such a thing not a sin in your world?"

It certainly was! But I found it difficult to sympathize with a farmer who beat his wife more often than he did his cow.

"You are unlike all other men."

"And I was wondering when you would notice that."

With the night's passage, I also made my confession: we were perfectly matched, for I, too, was as barren as she. Upon hearing this, she wept. I thought the agony of having relived her experiences during the retelling of them were responsible. I have since come to realize that it was probably due to her recognition that she was not alone in her torment. And perhaps she even felt a bit of sympathy for a man, who would see the dawn rise for untold centuries, but who could never see it shine upon his own infant's face.

During the following day, after the training exercises, I noticed that Dunstane appeared to be staring at me. Odd, I thought.

"There's something different about you," he began. "I can't quite say what it is."

I never thought I would discover something new here in Paris. Then again, I always had.

"And what might that be?"

"For the first time in many years I am happy, for I have learned that love may come in all colours."

"O, Heaven forfend! You'll not be tellin' me now that you've tossed away your heart to that dusky maiden, are ye?"

"Does her complexion disturb you?"

"'Tis not the shade of her skin I'm thinkin' 'bout. She's a woman. And a woman's a woman for a' that. I take them or leave them as they come and go. This one is bound in service to the evil king of this godforsaken land. Her allegiance will never be to you. Try as you might, you'll never have her heart completely."

"Have faith, my friend. The human heart does not betray another so easily."

He made a face whilst staring at me.

"How can one have lived so long and learned so little?" he asked. "In fact, with all the women you must have known, do you not grow tired of the chase?"

How could I? Was not each one different from the next?

"Whilst their faces and forms may be different, they all claw at ye in the same way: *when shall we marry?*" he asked, in imitation of a high-pitched, shrewish lady, "*is this spring time enough for planning?* Once you've had them, your freedom's no more your own."

"And have you never thought to seek a maiden's fair hand in marriage?"

"And lock meself away behind the portcullis of a marriage-tomb, never to drink with former comrades-in-arms or throw the dice in a tavern's back-rooms? I think not, my lord. I think very much not!"

"I think it a sin that you have not had any sons to whom you would pass on your … *values*, shall we say?"

"Now I never said that I had no brats of me own. At least, there are none that I know of anyway."

I laughed.

"You never mention it, though I've always wondered, now that you have, have you never sired a brood, my lord, not a one?"

I shook my head. I suppose that I must have worn an unusual expression, for he noticed something that prompted an additional question:

"Have I said something now to offend you, my lord? Forgive me my very large mouth, if indeed I may have done so."

"Each gift comes with its own distinct price, my friend. A wise physician once told me that not having any children might have been the price that I have had to pay for mine. When I realized that he was probably correct, I began to learn how to live with the absence of something that all men take for granted. These Templars are my concern now."

"O, now, you can't tell me you'd barter back your immortality for the chance to be a father?"

"That choice is no longer mine to make."

As I watched them struggle more against their own inadequacies than against each other's attacks, I felt Dunstane's eyes upon me still. It would be some time before he would return his attention to the field and continue his loud roarings.

CHAPTER THE FIFTY-NINTH,

in which I visit Master Jacques at his new place of residence.

We French have excelled at a number of endeavours in our long history, namely, the creation of new instruments of torture. One such device was not a machine, *per se*, but a type of location for imprisonment. Dug deeply into the earth, so deeply in fact, that one would needs place a long ladder down into it as its sole means of entry or egress. This hole, fashioned like a *hookah*, (or like one or two women and men whom I have known), was thin at its top, with a massively rounded bottom. We had come to call it by a gentle name, so sweet in fact, that one might have thought it a diminutive form for a babe's plaything. Simply a hole, it was where enemies of the realm were tossed and forgotten over time. And it was in one such *oubliette* that I found Master Jacques.

Having climbed down to the bottom, I looked back up to determine if the guards had betaken themselves from the line of sight. Once assured of this, I removed my cloak, and untied a number of items which I had bound to myself: a loaf of bread, a sack of wine, one of water, and a portion of dried meat, the better to nourish the old man. He concealed them post-haste. He thanked me now for my generosity, but more so for having come here in the first place. (The fact that his holiness had asked me to do so was a topic that I chose to omit from our conversation.)

"I wanted to apologize to you," he began.

O, I had absolutely no patience for him to assume, once again, the burdens of another's sins by making them his own.

He barely smiled before he went on to relate that he was already old when selected for this position. I had urged him then to be certain that he could handle all that would be required. He thought me arrogant and prideful. The truth of it was, he never cared for the ways in which others fawned over me, as if I were Jesus' own representative made into immortal flesh. A man, like myself, given over to much of sensual excess, could make only a mockery of God's love, he was most assured.

He speaking of excess about *me?*

If I had known that he wanted to insult me today, I would have probably stayed at home.

"As I said," he continued, "I disbelieved most of what you told me. I should have realized then that your concern was never for yourself. Somehow you knew what was to come. The only one whom I believe capable of seeing into the future is our Lord, yet you *felt* that my acceptance of this position would not turn out well for anyone. I should have recognized a true leader when I saw him."

He looked up to make certain that watchful eyes were not upon him, as he drank from the water-sack.

"Tell me, Sir Guy, do you believe that I am evil?"

"What I believe will have no bearing upon your case."

"The opinions of all the rest are meaningless to me. I care only what you think."

What a strange turn of events! A man who bore me no affection had become my staunchest ally. Had I but known this sooner, I might have treated him with a bit more kindness. (At least, I believed that I would have done so.)

"I have seen so many things," I said, "strange things, fantastic things, terrible things. More than once have I heard of an individual who would take another of the same sex to bed. If it be the will of God that such people exist, then perhaps I am in no position to judge their mating habits. I leave them to their Creator."

"Regardless of what the Holy Book teaches us?"

"I am a guardian, not a priest. If fornication of all sorts is a crime, then I, before all others, am incapable of redemption."

He laughed.

"Even now your generosity of spirit refuses to condemn me, though I am most assuredly guilty of the charge. Poor Francis was arrested with me," he said, referring to his butler. "I wonder if he lives still?"

Only later would I discover that the aforementioned butler was now housed in a small yet adequate estate on the outskirts of the city, where he would live out the rest of his days in relative peace, until some hitherto-unknown disease (or poison) rotted his flesh and took him screaming into the night. I never did learn if he were the one who had informed the advocate where the Templar Master might be that day. On the other hand, it could have been Master Philamos who was responsible, but that jovial Greek soon disappeared from the eyes of all men, so no one was ever able to question him if that were true.

I feared that Jacques would admit to the act, for I knew enough about him to recognize his unfailing honesty. His future was now inevitable, and the only way to alter it was to escape from this prison. The consequence of that action might result in another revolution, one that will have been fomented by my involvement therein. His holiness would never agree to it, as its ultimate finish might be the death of the king by my own hand. Still, Jacques was head of the Order—one that I had sworn to protect with my life.

"If you wish to leave here," I offered, "and all of France, I shall place my sword in your defense. You have only to ask me for it."

"Again I am grateful to you; however, I have no wish to put the entire city through any more turmoil than it has so recently known. I have no choice but to submit to the judgment of a French court."

"This advocate loves no one, save his own family. To him all men are no more than dirt beneath his feet. He will hold you up to ridicule, insult you, then condemn you."

"Only the king may do that."

"The advocate is the hand of the king. It squeezes when the king commands it."

"If it is God's will, then I shall live to see numerous tomorrows. If not, then I must make ready to ask St. Peter for forgiveness of my many sins. Of you I must ask one more kindness."

I nodded.

"You, alone, have the wisdom and the power to succeed where all others have failed them, myself most of all. I beseech you, though I have no right to ask, watch over my Templars. Protect them, if you are able. Their legacy must not end with me."

"I cannot say if you will find redemption in God's eyes, but you have found respect in mine."

I held his hand, as he began to weep.

I was called to a meeting with the Holy Father (without the benefit of Dunstane's presence) in a small chamber at the rear of *Nôtre Dame*. When I saw him, I could not believe how pale his face had become. Moreover, it seemed to me that he had not eaten in several days. He bade me sit, as he paced about. (This he had never before done.)

"A key issue concerning the future of the Order must be considered. Someone should lead the Templars, and very soon now."

I disagreed.

"You must prevail upon this king to have Jacques released."

He stood perfectly still.

"With all due respect both to your achievements and to your good name, Sir Guy, have you lost your mind? Jacques' arrest is not the tale of a poor man who has stolen a bit of bread. His sin is most grievous. If judged guilty, no one and nothing will be able to save him, most especially the church."

"Let us not pretend, your holiness, that the Law is anything but a mistress who will perform her master's bidding. This monarch has surrounded himself with people who take great pride in their work. Have you ever seen his jailers in the performance of their duties? They will strap a man shirtless, down upon a table, his spine facing the roof of his cell. They will heat iron pincers, and dig them into his back, until they have grasped a significant amount of flesh. Then they will begin to peel off sheets, and the blood will flow like water. Master Jacques' years are more than sixty. If interrogated, he will say whatever this belovèd regent wishes him to. I beg you, do not allow this to happen."

"The only one who can help him now is God."

"Then you will do nothing for him?"

"He has already admitted his guilt to me!"

"To me as well. You can still grant him sanctuary."

"After having committed *that* sin? Surely you jest."

"Who cares what he has done?"

"Who cares?! *I* care. Every Christian is supposed to care. That includes you. Your responsibility is to uphold church doctrine, not challenge it."

"Are you going to presume to tell me how I should act?"

I do not believe that he had anticipated such a response. He sighed.

"My apologies. I have been somewhat short-tempered these past days. Grand fool that he is, Jacques believes that he will find some sort of justice at the royal court. His naïveté knows no bounds."

The Holy Father could not have been more wrong. Jacques expected only a swift judgment. "He has no wish to sully the name of the Order with his own misdeeds," I explained.

"Did he say that to you?"

"Not in so many words. It was implied."

"I could care less for his implications or inferences. He is what was. The Order must continue."

I concurred.

"Perhaps you should confer the duty upon Gilbert de Saint Claire," I suggested. "As a descendant of the de Payens family, he is perfectly suited for that position."

"Come now! He has barely left behind his childhood."

"I was less than a decade older when I felt the hand of God upon my face."

"You were a man nonetheless. Gilbert has a sharp intellect—a necessary quality in any capable leader. I must confess, however, I am less than pleased with his fondness for jurisprudence. It would break my heart, were he to leave Templar service to become one more advocate in a kingdom that is rife with them. He may yet mature into the holy knight whom we all hope him to be. Until that moment, someone else is destined to assume the reins of leadership."

I nodded, and was about to suggest another name when I noticed a papal smile that was positively beatific.

"Holy Father, are you well?"

"I am finer than I have ever been, for I am filled with an inspiration wholly divine!"

He said nothing. He continued to smile. At that moment, I, too, was struck by a realization, though there was nothing heavenly about it.

"Impossible!" I offered at last.

"Why? You were one of the original founders. Who better to serve the needs of God, His church, and His knights?"

I would hear no more of it. Still, he persisted.

"Do you not see the truth, my friend? Other Masters have helped the Order spread throughout the world. That much is a matter of history. Some, however, were not so pure of heart. You have stood your ground, where others have faltered. You have always been here for them. This is the reason why you were born. Everything that you have ever experienced has been leading you here and now to this moment. How can you deny what God has allowed a simple, old man like me to see as absolute?"

His fists were clenched. His very face had grown enflamed. Every particle of his being spoke with passionate conviction. Would that I had felt the same!

"This is madness."

"Yet from this madness will emerge more sanity than this nation has seen in many a year. You must accept. More than your duty, it is the history that has made you."

"I have never desired the Master's title."

"It should have been offered long ago. Today you and I shall rectify that error, Sir Guy de Lagery, Master of the Knights of the Temple of Jerusalem! Amen."

CHAPTER THE SIXTIETH,

in which the Holy Father and the king share a pleasant conversation that turns rather quickly.

Once more the Holy Father came to my residence, fell into a chair, and emptied an entire bottle of its contents before telling me of what had transpired between himself and his king.

"Sit, Sir Guy," he commanded me, "long will this night be."

Having been summoned, the pope arrived at the royal palace to find the king in a large room, smiling, seated behind a very large table, upon which sat a large bottle of wine and a goblet. A single empty chair was placed on the opposite side of the table.

"Your message said that the matter was urgent," his holiness began, as he looked at the royal portraits of Phillip's ancestors hanging on the long walls around him.

"Do sit down. I hate having to speak to someone whilst he stands over me, as if I were *his* vassal."

The Holy Father endeavoured to make himself comfortable, despite his new-found wish not to be present at court.

"A drink?" the king offered.

The pope looked at the open bottle and the half-filled goblet and decided that he would.

"I would not deny myself a small cup, if offered."

"Nonsense. You will have a chalice full, as befits your position in my glorious kingdom. You there," he called to a servant girl who was standing at one corner of the room, "what is your name again?"

"Françoise, your majesty," she spoke softly and with a bow.

"How quaint!" the king said to the pope. "The populace has run out of names, so today's sons and daughters must spend their lives being called after the countries in which they reside. I wonder what names the English and Germans are using in these times?"

"One might say that people everywhere have unusual ideas."

He agreed, as the smile left his face, perhaps remembering recent events.

"You there, girl. Bring a chalice for Pope Clement, or he will excommunicate you here and now!"

The girl raced out of the room to search for a cup. Her king laughed most heartily. Her pope wore no expression at all.

"Why have I been summoned, your majesty?"

The king ran his index finger around the circular lip of his cup. Having watched his own action, he turned his eyes now to his guest, as he began something of a response:

"She is lovely, is she not?"

"Who?"

"That quiet, unassuming girl. Her form is slender, almost boyish."

"I had not noticed."

"I have never believed that the forms, which God, in His wisdom, gave to us, were inherently sinful."

"That is blasphemous, your highness."

"It is tradition. Since that is its nature, it may not necessarily be correct, or do any justice to the truth of the situation."

"Do you believe, because you are of the blood royal, that you can select which of our Lord's commandments you may choose to obey?"

"Created in His image, are we not beautiful creatures?"

The pope turned away.

"Perhaps not all of us are so fortunate," the king completed his thought, a touch of bitterness in his voice.

"Again I shall ask, what do you wish of me, your majesty?"

"This business with the Templar-Master gives us pause." He perused a document that lay upon his bureau. "Have you ever studied this emblem of theirs? Two men sit astride a single horse. Are these noble knights clad in any garments at all, or are they simply naked, cavorting about?"

His holiness said nothing, as Phillip continued:

"It has been said that one of the horsemen is Hughes de Payens. Now tell me, Holy Father, do you believe that Sir Hughes is the one sitting behind, giving, or the one sitting before, receiving?"

The pope's face reddened.

"Is there no end to your disgraceful tongue?"

"I would not say, *disgraceful*, though I have been told that it is quite long and capable of giving much pleasure."

The regent smiled, as his guest arose, presumably to depart, then thought better of it and sat back down.

"Prison is not an easy thing for anyone to bear," the pope averred, "not simply for the incarcerated, but especially for those who may have called the man *friend*. And Master Jacques was ever a friend to me. Now, what of Templar business does his highness wish to discuss?" he asked a third time.

"Yes, I suppose so, but there is a matter of greater significance here. The crown has need of a loan, so that it may rebuild the damage done to this city by an unruly mob. Without its Master, who will supply the letters of credit, or the gold?"

Before he had an opportunity to respond, the pope received the awaited chalice. The girl was all out of breath, as she had obviously run about swiftly during her search. He thanked her for it. Since there was nothing further, the king dismissed her, then filled the chalice. The pope looked into it, and then decided not to drink of the contents.

"You wish an additional loan?" he asked.

"Have you seen the way that we are forced to live now? Each residence resembles a peasant's own hovel. Are we no better than those filthy, vulgar creatures? We hold our throne by the very righteousness that God has granted to our bloodline, though to look around this city, one would never know it."

"God did not place you upon the throne of France. Your father did that."

"You make it sound as though I were undeserving of my most honourable position."

"Never would I dream of offending you in that manner, your majesty. My concern is solely for the spirit of man, his eternal reward or punishment, not his current temporal circumstance."

"Is that why you requested the return of Sir Guy to our kingdom? Or is he the sword that you rattle before me, that I may never forget the might of Holy Mother Church?"

Now it was Pope Clement's turn to smile.

"I am a simple man. Such deviousness would not be proper in a pope."

The king refused to believe him.

"And why not?" he asked. "The popes? You speak of them as if they were God's messengers. They have been as wicked a group of men as any who have ever drawn breath. They preached a love of poverty, whilst living in luxury. They demanded chastity, whilst fornicating in secret, some having fathered illegitimate heirs. They have wanted us to obey the word of our Lord, whilst they slandered those who would not bend to their will. Like all men in power, they have used their position to enhance their lives at the expense of others."

Certainly the Holy Father could not agree. Whilst some might have indulged the worst aspects of their natures, others had proven themselves to be true *fishers of men.*

"*Fishers of men?*" the king asked with a visible repulsion upon his face. "What in Hell's name does that mean? *Fishers of men!* You mouth church doctrine with the same lack of understanding from which all zealots suffer. Go hunt them, go find them," he commanded, pointing hither and yon. "Good Christians all, there is not a single decent man to be found in any nation."

"Does that include you, sire?"

"Most especially me."

It was probably at that very juncture in time, when the pope believed that the regent had spoken with utter veracity, as he had never before done.

"Have you called me here to insult my position," he asked of the king, "or simply to bait me?"

The king assured him that they were friends, were they not? And as friends, he was certain that the pope would sign off on the proper documentation necessary to expedite the loan. Unfortunately for the king, the pope had to admit that he would be unable to do so.

"I fear not. You will have to ask the current head of the Order to accede to your wishes."

"The current head of the Order can do nothing, for he rots in his cell."

"O, pardon. It has all happened rather quickly, so I may have forgotten to inform you. I have asked Sir Guy to take over the position of Master, and he has agreed to it."

Phillip's mouth fell open, and his eyes widened so, that they appeared to bulge out, blindingly white, from his very head.

"What have you done?" he was able to ask finally.

"What was necessary. The Templars need a leader, a man with profound experience in international relations and—."

"And he is a drunkard!" Phillip shouted, rising from his chair. "Never forget that he rarely sleeps alone. And he has the wealth of Croesus to waste as he sees fit."

"I have never seen him drunk. And as for his sleeping arrangements, he has agreed to act with a bit more discretion than is his custom, especially in front of the other men. Moreover, if anyone is found in his bed, it will be, most assuredly, a woman. Regarding his fiscal conditions, I have come to realize, in my old age, that having wealth is not always so sinful a thing as my predecessors have claimed it to be."

Phillip fell back into his chair. For some time he said nothing, until his eyebrows shot up to either side of his head, and he clutched the edge of the table, and he thrust his entire face forward, towards the Holy Father.

"An immortal knight who wields a magic sword that none, save he, may touch, is the stuff of legend," he averred. "And this is no ordinary man."

"Indeed!"

"You think him holy. What if he is not? What if he has made a pact with the Devil?"

"This talk is foolish."

"Is it? He has walked the world for more than two centuries. In that time he has killed more men than, by his own admission, even he can count. How has he made our lives better? What has he done for the church?"

"I refuse to listen to your ravings."

"This is neither madness nor jealousy. This is truth. The First Holy War liberated Jerusalem. But every subsequent battle ended in a Christian defeat. That is the way of all things diabolical. Give to the unsuspecting victim exactly what he wishes, then remove it from him a piece at a time, until he has nothing of himself left. All of his efforts have not caused the people to worship him; they *fear* him. He haunts the dreams of grown men and children alike. He should be cast out from all mannerly society. In this kingdom we bow down before statues of the Christ who died for our sins; we do not bow before an unwholesome thing made flesh!"

The Holy Father jumped to his feet and stared down at the king.

"He is the lion of God, made immortal to protect the church until the end of time! You will *not* perpetuate this slander against the holiest man in Christendom."

The king had jumped back in his seat, clutching at his chest. It may have been the first time that the pope had ever spoken to him in such a fashion. In any case, Phillip sat bolt upright now.

"Holiest, is he?"

"For many years now you have indulged the worst aspects of your nature, whilst condemning the same in other men around you."

"Take care how you speak to a king. Rumour has it that the former pope was poisoned, shortly after a disagreement with us. That was most unfortunate."

"Understand this, King of France, for you there can be no redemption. Your soul is forfeit."

The king stared at the pope; the smile never left the regent's face.

"If that is so, then there is no limit to what I may do next."

The pope spilled the contents of his chalice on the carpet, then threw the cup against a wall.

"The Devil take you!" he shouted, then fled the room and the castle as quickly as his own feet and his horse's hooves could carry him.

CHAPTER THE SIXTY-FIRST,

in which one confession leads to several others, which leads to several others, which … know no ends.

Besides the usual numbers of *hangers-on*, or practitioners of petty knavery, I was to discover later that the advocate had his own group of dedicated watchers and/ or listeners. These men reported to him on all manner of events, which had already transpired. (As you can well surmise, dear reader, they were not terribly efficient in the collection of information as regards future events; thus, the first taste of a civil war that the regent, above all others in his kingdom, did not expect.) Nevertheless, this *Royal Order*, as they had taken to calling themselves, with a certain degree of pride in their profession, (be it warranted or not), were very good at uncovering the sole voice that had provided the spark for the popular flame of rebellion. And when he learned that the man's name was *Squink*, the advocate was not a happy, little lawyer.

Into the bowels of the earth below the castle, Master Squink was led in chains. As he was beaten, burned, scarred, he was also informed, (in no uncertain terms), that his sometime-master, the illustrious William de Nogaret, was far from pleased with this sudden twist of events. After all, the man had been paid handsomely for a number of tasks, and not a one of them had ever been traced back to the royal court. Yet somehow, in a series of unusual coincidences, (or if part of a much larger divine or *daemonic* plan, I cannot say), Master Squink had given voice, in a tavern one recent evening, to the general dissatisfaction and hunger of the city, *en masse*. And the patrons cheered him, and lit torches, and spilled out onto the road, where they gathered others for their march. And as their Anger rode across the wind and set fire to the houses of the nobility, they followed the lead of Master Squink, who called for the palace to be burned to ash.

Of course, without any prior planning, the spontaneous outburst was quickly snuffed out. And Master Squink was nowhere to be found, when royal troops retaliated with their own slaughter.

Now the advocate was in a bit of a quandary. He could have this former servant ripped apart into quarters, or pounded relentlessly, until death was assured. But the satisfaction would be a temporary measure, and would, in essence, nullify the man's previous usefulness. Somehow he had to rectify this situation. Then it was that he felt a moment of inspiration (whether divine or *daemonic* I cannot say). He would put into practice an idea that he had previously considered only momentarily. He would turn a man's confession (under much duress certainly) into a revelation about the Templars. And in the process, he would also end the scarcity of funds in the royal treasury. The idea was brilliant, for though false in nature, it contained a particle of truth. A lie like that would be very difficult to disprove. He was much satisfied and much taken with his own brilliance that fateful day!

So, before he ordered an execution, he compelled Squink to admit to a particular statement, to which the advocate had the jailers agree as valid testimony. When all the necessary preparations were complete, de Nogaret ordered the death of his former servant. But something unusual prevented that. Squink began to quote (rather swiftly) from the Fifty-First Psalm, albeit in a confusing order of somewhat more confusing phraseology:

"Have mercy on me, O Lord, for my iniquity has not washed my spiteful tongue out, nor cleansed my bowels of my sinful nature, and I desire no truth in my broken bones and curse my tongue that cannot sing songs of deliverance, for I have slaughtered bulls on your altar for much bloodthirstiness. Amen."

The jailers traded glances with the advocate, who was reasonably well-versed in the correct terms of that particular psalm (as he had heard it in various forms during many a confession). And so well did he know it, that he could have easily had the execution continue. Nevertheless, he decided against it. The servant might prove himself useful once more, the occasion permitting. And unscrupulous men were not so easy to find, despite society's current assessment of itself.

Though Jacques had already confessed to what he believed was his very sinful behaviour, he was now called upon to admit to one or two ancillary matters, which pertained to his conduct with other members of the Order. Upon hearing what he was asked to pronounce, however, he refused. And so began the torture of poor Jacques, with the advocate in attendance.

During the first day he was not able to say much to the advocate, (who had taken it upon himself to conduct personally this interrogation), for the old man often fainted, was awakened with water splashed upon his face, then fainted again. It was during the second day that the advocate had the jailers ply their efforts with a touch more leniency. And this time, Jacques was able to speak, though he often asked why he was being made to suffer when he had already confessed to his crime.

"In a place such as this," the advocate replied, "each word becomes truth."

"Including the lies?"

"Most especially those. Now, let us begin. Who else has been a party to these heinous actions?" he demanded to know.

"I am the only heretic in the entire Order; the sins are all mine."

"Perhaps you did not understand my intentions. If there is any possibility for confusion, please allow me to clarify. The evil that one man may do is virtually meaningless to the nation as a whole. The wrongdoing of an entire group, that masquerades as the holiest of holy men, now *that* merits further discussion. Have I explained myself sufficiently? The only manner in which you will leave this place, whilst still alive, is by revealing all the others who are part of your conspiracy."

"There are no others. I swear. Where is the justice in this land? I want justice!"

"Really? The only justice that you can receive in this kingdom is whatever its divinely ordained leader chooses to mete out to you. That is exactly what you are experiencing at this very moment. It is all perfectly legal, and therefore, perfectly just."

Later that day Jacques told him that he would not lose this battle.

"Look around you, old man," the advocate said. "You have already lost."

Upon the third day Jacques informed his captor that God would not let him suffer endlessly, though his sins were great. The lawyer reached for the crucifix that dangled from a chain about his prisoner's neck.

"Do you believe that this little strip of metal will save you?"

Jacques made no response.

"For whom do you maintain your silence? If for your fellow sinners, fear not; they will all confess, as you will very soon. If for God, then you waste your efforts. Do you think that God takes notice of something like you? Crippled in body and mind, you are beneath our contempt. You are no better than the vermin, which crawl around here at your feet. Who are you? What are you?"

"God's child," poor Jacques spoke between dried, cracked lips.

The advocate laughed most heartily, as he tore the item from Jacques' neck. And by the day's end, he had everything that he had endeavoured to create.

It was a commonly held belief of the time, that during ceremonies in the black arts, the Devil would be conjured. Once present, he would evince his supposèd superiority over God and man by sticking out his buttocks for all and sundry to kiss. It is my fervent belief that the advocate recalled this tale when he was creating his charge.

The crowd assembled below, the advocate stepped onto the balcony, unfurled his scroll, and began to read aloud therefrom:

"*Wherefore on this, the fourteenth day of July, in the year of our Lord, one thousand three hundred and seven, Phillip, by grace of God, Regent of France, King of Navarre, Normandie, Poitou, Anjou, and Toulouse, amongst others, brings charge against the Poor Knights of the Order of the Temple of Jerusalem, also known as the Knights Templar, also known as the Templars; said charge being moral corruption in the highest, resultant from idolatry in the initial cause, and from copulation between men in the secondary cause.*"

The crowd gasped.

"*That said Templars did hereby and willfully and with all malice of forethought kiss an idol fashioned in the shape of the Devil's own head, one Baphomet, as the diabolical thing is so termed; that said Templars did also hereby and willfully and with all malice of forethought kiss the head of their Master's penis when inducted into the Order, and did subsequently lie with him and give unto him their buttocks for his misuse and pleasure.*"

The crowd gasped again. One member of the court, who was standing nearby, and who had apparently never learned the value of silence, spoke:

"Consorting with the Devil?" he asked. "So *that* was how they became so wealthy. And all this time I thought that one needed do no more than be born into the landed gentry."

Those standing around him, who were not nodding in agreement, were laughing.

"*As these most corruptible actions have been brought to light, they now obviate the necessity of a trial,*" the advocate concluded. "*The king will convene a trial seven days from today. That is all.*"

He rolled up the scroll and smiled.

CHAPTER THE SIXTY-SECOND,

in which the most prized possession of the Templars is revealed.

It was very late of an evening, long after prayers were finished, when I led the members of the Order to a portion of their residence near the scullery. I threw aside the carpet, revealing a long door that had been cut into the wooden floor. There was much noise about how none had ever seen it, for the Master had refused to allow the carpet ever to be removed from that spot. I pulled up the metal ring that was its handle, and the door opened to one side. A staircase had been cut into the rock below, and I made my way down with a torch, urging the others to follow in like manner. A labyrinth of long passageways brought us finally to the end of one hall, where stood an enormous boulder. I pressed firmly at a point near its top, its base, its left side, then its right. A very loud gnashing sound appeared to come from inside the stone. Several moments later, dirt and dust filled the corridor as the rock turned. Pivoted as an open door in the middle of a large frame, it would allow a single person to pass through at either side. I walked in. The others followed.

The circular room was enormous. All of us were able to stand inside of it with ample space between. The only items present were a small table, and a golden bust that sat upon it. Dunstane walked over to examine the face more closely.

"She's a lovely creature, she is, my lord. Who is she?"

"The Holy Mother, of course."

"Begging your pardon, my lady," he addressed the statue, backing away quickly and bowing all the while. "I meant no offense."

"Never would I dare to hope," Gilbert exclaimed. "I thought it a story only, part of Templar legends."

"As your new Master, I have brought you here to witness our greatest possession, our most holy relic. From this day onward, you will be known as the *Lions of God*, for you have protected her from all harm. Behold, the power of our Lord. Dunstane, give me the battle-axe."

I had asked him to bring one along, knowing that I would have need of it now.

"No, Master!" Gilbert cried out, attempting to stay my hand, and suspecting, full well, what I would do next.

Dunstane picked him up and placed him off to the side.

"He is your Master," he reminded Gilbert. "Have faith that he will do what is right for all."

I took the handle and raised it, but stopped in the air. I hesitated briefly, endeavouring not to recall the moment when first I saw it in a Byzantine garden. I brought the point down with all deliberate force, and the bust shattered in two. A cloth fell out of it. I returned the axe to Dunstane, and held up the contents now for all to see.

"Behold, my brothers, the burial shroud of our Lord, Jesus!"

To a man, everyone in the room clasped his hands and fell to his knees. (All except Dunstane. He was a good Christian, though not one for obeisance.)

"Rise, my brothers," I told them.

As they did so, a chorus of observations filled the room: "*Behold the face of Jesus! There are the wounds in his hands! Look at his feet! There are holes in his feet!*"

And so they went on for a time, heedless of Gilbert, who decided to come closer for a better view. The young man was ofttimes much given to the commencement of his actions, long before he ever gave a moment's consideration to their consequences. And that night was no different. He pushed aside others to see the face upon the cloth more clearly, when one poor knight fell, thus knocking over Gilbert with him. The torch from Gilbert's hand flew up. All of us, to a man, reached for it, and consequently, not one of us was able to retrieve it. It came down upon the cloth with all its naked fury. As the fibers sizzled and burned, I tore off my tunic, held the shroud against me, and threw myself down upon the soil.

"Bring water!" I shouted. "Hurry!"

I lay there, the weight of my body against the linen, the proximity of my chest strangling the flame.

A short time thereafter, Dunstane and several knights returned and threw buckets full of water upon me, soaking the cloth as well. I stood up now and saw Gilbert nearby, his hand covering his mouth, his eyes wide and full of fright.

I handed off the cloth to Dunstane. The others about me marveled at how the burns upon my chest began to heal over with new flesh.

"I've never seen the like," Dunstane whispered, aghast. "Are ye in much pain, my lord?"

"More than you will ever know, God willing," I spoke through clenched teeth.

It was not exactly how I had intended the night to pass. Yet despite the near-tragedy, it was crucial that Templar business be conducted and completed.

I stared at Gilbert.

"Take your hand from your mouth, child," Dunstane told him, "and show to your leader his proper respect."

"Forgive me, my lord," Gilbert seemed to say barely shy of a plea, his eyes full of water.

Each man glared at him with a tangible hatred in his eyes.

"It was a mistake," I said loudly, addressing the members, "a very stupid mistake," I added now, looking at Gilbert, "but a mistake nonetheless. And if you wish to rectify your behaviour, Brother Gilbert, you will do exactly as I say."

I told him that at dawn he would leave with Dunstane and four other goodly knights of my friend's selection. Together, this brotherhood would journey to the highlands of Scotland, there to be welcomed at the ancestral manse of the Saint-Claires, his family's home. In a stone vault deep below ground, they would wall up the shroud, never again to be beheld by the eyes of men.

The entire brotherhood bellowed at me. How could I deny Christianity its most holy relic? And the face, did not all men deserve to see the very form of our Lord at the moment of his death?

(I had not the heart to admit to them that the image of the person contained within the cloth was a sinner's. I thought it best that they believe as they would. I had learned that sometimes faith needs a miracle of sorts to nourish it. And who was I to deny anyone a belief that he needed most?)

"When will you learn, my brethren," I asked, "that our legacy is not the display of Christian wonders for all eyes to see, but their protection, that all the generations to follow us will still be blessed by their continued mercy and His divine love?"

"But Master," one Templar asked, "how will people know this to be true, if they do not see the holy relic?"

"Have you ever stared into the eyes of God?"

He shook his head.

"Yet you believe. That is what it means to have faith. And we are the guardians of the faith."

No one else spoke after that.

Back upstairs, I turned to Dunstane. His disappointed look could mean only one thing: he did not wish to leave Paris.

"You must return with Gilbert to Scotland. He will be safe with you."

"Begging your pardon, my lord, but this I cannot do. I have sworn myself to your side, and there I'll stay, until I die, or until you've had your full of me."

"The others may need your help."

"I cannot help but feel that you will need it more in the days to come."

I thought about the implications of his statement and smiled. I placed my hand now upon his shoulder.

"You will leave my side, Dunstane, though not today, I suppose."

"Prophecy, my lord?"

I did not answer.

And not having insisted that Dunstane go with the others was a grievous error, for during the journey, two of the Order overcame their companions, seized the shroud, and fled. Apparently, they were determined that the object be worshipped publicly, not hidden away forever. And in time it would surface again somewhere in Italy. And within the year Gilbert, wracked with much guilt over his actions and those of the other members, left the Order permanently. Consumed with justice, or the lack thereof, he became a lawyer, one who brought much honour and dignity to the profession, if such a thing were possible.

But for now, and before he left with the others, Gilbert returned to his chamber, and removed, from a small chest, a very strong and thick leather lash. He pulled down his vestments, revealing a series of long, thin scars across his back. He knelt, raised the scourge, and began to beat himself with it.

"*Mea culpa*," began his sometime-apologies to his Lord, and the leather slapped him.

"*Mea culpa*," he continued with a second cut that was now open slightly and bleeding.

"*Mea maxima culpa*," he finished, as his clothing ran red.

CHAPTER THE SIXTY-THIRD,

in which the acquisition of information is purchased at a price most dear.

In the morning I bade Dunstane make the horses ready. (Some information had come into my possession, and I thought it best to act upon it sooner rather than later. The servant-girl, Françoise, had become my new and dear friend.)

"Whither are we going, my lord?"

"To the Jews. The king has plans for them."

"What business does he have with the Jews?"

"He has a great deal of business to do with their moneylenders."

Dunstane said nothing as he thought upon it a moment or two, only to realize the full import of my statement.

"O my lord, he must owe them a king's ransom!"

"Very like."

At their temple an attendant opened the wide oaken doors for us. We walked down towards the altar, where the rabbi stood, reading from his *torah*. He turned around. The man was quite elderly, small, and with a very long beard. We must have been an unwelcome sight, for there was much of trepidation in his eyes.

"What is it that you wish, my lords?"

I introduced us both. I was certain that he studied my appearance. He recalled reading, in an obscure treatise written by Moses ben Maimun, the name of a Christian knight who had once come to visit with him.

"Was that your forefather?" he asked.

"In the time when I knew him, he promised that he would never write about me. I see now that his every word was not complete truth."

The old man very nearly fell over, as his face turned pale. Dunstane grabbed him and brought him to a nearby pew. Momentarily, all was well again.

"If a man, untouched by time," he began, "walks into God's house, then it can mean only one of two things: either he has come to announce the creation of Paradise upon the earth, or he has come to tell of its imminent destruction. I can see upon your face that not much of happiness is to be found there."

I told him of what I had learned, how in three days the advocate would declare all debts owed to Jewish moneylenders null and void, and his people would be forced out of Paris and all of France, or stay behind and be butchered. I believed it was better to leave now.

"So soon?" he asked. "It seems that we have come to this place only a short time ago."

I offered aid in the only ways I could. Several of my Templars would protect them during their passage out of Paris and its environs; I would also see to it that their valuables were turned into necessary currency. He took my hand, smiled, and thanked me.

"You may be angry now," he told me, "but if it is any comfort to you, our blessèd Moses included your name in a very short list of the men whom he had come to admire. I beg you, do not hold that against him. I ask you, moreover, not to hold it against us as well, for you must understand that you have been a friend to the Jewish people. There are those amongst us who mention your name in our prayers, though Maimun asked of us never to do such a thing, no doubt out of respect for you and your wishes. Yet, if God wills it, there will always be a few of us alive who will continue to do so until the end of time."

Now it was my turn to smile.

Despite my presence at the Templar House, I kept my own residence as a place where I might conduct private business with Dunstane, the subject of which I had hoped to keep from the Templars until necessary.

"In Scotland ye have all the lands up to the *Firth* of *Forth*," he counseled me. "There the men will find safety in the company of good Scotsmen, when they leave here."

"I wish I had your faith. These days I find it difficult to believe that any nation is safe from the evil in the hearts of men."

Our discussion concluded, we both heard someone banging vigorously at the front gate. Dunstane went to see who it was. I heard loud arguments from the interior vestibule, when the door to my living chamber flew open. Makeda ran up to me, holding a sword to my throat.

"In what Christian Hell were you spawned?" she shouted.

Dunstane followed behind, bent over. At the doorway he clutched his crotch.

"I'll kill her, if it pleases you, my lord. It would please me to no end."

"Take one step towards me, Scotsman, and I shall separate your master's head from his neck, before you can take a second one."

Dunstane was about to lunge forward at any rate.

"This is a lovers' quarrel," I told him, "nothing more."

"Methinks otherwise, my lord."

"Leave us, Dunstane. No one will die today."

He did as I had requested, albeit reluctantly. I turned to the swordswoman standing near my throat.

"Dearest lady, if you had wished for our time together to be at an end, you had only to tell me of it. I already have sufficient drama in my life." I pushed aside her blade.

"I trusted you. And you lied to me, as all men lie."

"I have never lied to a woman I love."

She stared at me, oddly, I thought, as her head appeared to nod towards one side. But her eyes were full of sadness. Perhaps she believed what I had said, for it was the absolute truth. (I hoped that she did so, in any case.) Then she let fall her sword, and fell, herself, into a chair.

"You have no idea how long it has been since I opened my heart to another," she sobbed. "I believed you when you said that you could never sire offspring."

I knelt at her knees, and looked up into her dark eyes.

"As I believed you."

I reached to caress her hand. She slapped it away and rose to pace about.

"Would you care for a drink?" I offered, also rising.

"Do you French ever do anything except drink?"

"Sometimes we make war; sometimes we make love."

"O, why did I ever leave Nubia?"

I had to know why she would make such a ridiculous claim about my virility.

"I am with child," she admitted finally.

The full chalice that I was holding now fell to the carpet, spilling its contents everywhere.

How could this be? She had killed her husband who beat her with what he believed to be as justifiable cause, an empty womb. And I? I had never fathered—. No. Perhaps it was her husband who had been barren all along. Perhaps she did not cherish the mask of her virginity as much as she had claimed. I could feel the heat upon my face, burning my cheeks.

"What other man has taken you to his bed?" I shouted.

She crouched down like a cat, and lunged forward now, sword in hand. I did not raise my own, but allowed her to pierce my face, chest, and arms. And each time the wound closed as quickly as the metal left the hole that it had made. She stopped.

"You are not of this world!" she exclaimed, staring.

I barely touched her sword-hand with my blade, when the searing pain caused her to drop her own. She cried out.

"Still you have not answered my question," I reminded her, returning my sword to its scabbard.

"You are the Devil of legend these Christians all mention with great fear," she said, struggling to speak and clutching her hand. "What monster has stolen my heart and corrupted my body with his poisoned seed?"

I tried to calm her, lest she spend the entire day filling the room with a flurry of metaphors. It turned out that she had sought a physician (thankfully not the royal one), when her monthly *menses* did not arrive as it had always promptly done. After a very painful examination, he confirmed her suspicions: she was more than one month with child.

He might have made a mistake, I insisted. Experience had taught me that the hints of earliest pregnancy often signify the absence of any child within the womb. She refused to believe that. She could feel it growing now inside her.

I chose not to disagree. She was far too distraught to accept any other rational explanations for how the physician might have erred in his *diagnosis*.

"How can I be certain that the child you carry is mine?" I asked, still determined to uncover the truth.

She eyed me with a palpable disgust.

"I have opened my heart and my body for two men only. My husband was the first."

I stared into her eyes. And I believed her immediately. (The practice of dissembling was never part of her nature. She had always considered that a common tradition among Christians, and beneath her dignity to do.)

"I ask your forgiveness for having doubted you," I said finally.

"I have not come here for that. I came to kill you. But you cannot die."

"I cannot die, except at God's own hand."

"Then we are finished."

She walked to the door.

"Wait. This is a miracle-child! Both pale and dark, both Christian and Muslim, it may unite the world in ways of which we dare not dream."

"This child will be neither dark nor pale, neither Muslim nor Christian. It will be detested by all peoples and belong to none. It is not a blessing. It is a curse. And curse you for having given it to me!"

Barely had I time to ponder the possibilities of fatherhood, when his holiness called me to his chamber. He rolled up a scroll and handed it over. He had finished reading the advocate's subsequent charges against the Order. Subsequent?

"By all means, read it. It contains diction that is too florid for the worst of the ancient Romans. Despite that, its Latin vocabulary might amuse you."

I gave it a cursory examination, then handed it back. I was not in the least impressed. It had seemed that there was no end to the *litany* of Templar misdeeds and sundry crimes against nature.

"I fear the results of this attack may continue for many years ahead," he went on.

Had he asked to see me out of fear for what might happen to the brethren?

"That and several other issues."

He stood up and removed from a cabinet a bottle of wine and two glasses. He filled both and gave me one of them. We wished each other good health, and drank.

"This is a very difficult time for Christians everywhere," he remarked. "I received word today from the Master of the Hospital, that he has been compelled to move the entire order to the island of Rhodes for their continued safety. The Byzantines were most unhappy about *that*."

"It may not be the last time that the Hospitallers will have to do this."

"Yes, I agree. Everything is changing, and not necessarily for the better. The Muslim world is spreading apace, and I can do nothing but complain of it."

He drank again. There was much in the list of charges that disturbed him. Mention had been made, more than once, of a figurine, or magical *head* of sorts. He knew that Templar practices had never been kept secret from me. He was determined to discover the essential truth behind the fictions.

"What is this object of reverence?"

I informed him that no Templar ever worshipped an idol.

"That is not an answer to my query."

"I cannot say what it is."

"Cannot? Or will not?"

"Long ago I made a promise to one of the finest men whom I have ever known. If I reveal what it is, the spirit of Hughes de Payens will haunt me until the end of my days. I believe that passage of time will endure far into the future, so, if it pleases you, Holy Father, I decline to discuss it."

He was unhappy with my decision, yet he chose to leave the topic, for the time being. (He would not ask me to break my vow of silence, unless it were of my own choice.)

"When you are ready, you will tell me. For now, we have other matters."

He rubbed his beard, as was his habit when lost in thought.

"I have never been a particularly intelligent man," he confessed. "O, I have prospered where far more capable men have not, to be sure. However, I have been able to keep my wits about me under the most pressing of circumstances. I consider that ability a gift from the Lord on high. And I tell you this, Sir Guy de Lagery, in order to make you realize, that if a foolish, old sot like myself can recognize that Parisian Templars are fast disappearing, then so can other men. Drink up. I have more bottles handy."

We drank in silence for a time, until the bottle was empty. He uncorked another and poured again.

"You will have to stop sending them away," he admitted finally.

I had wondered how long it would be until he arrived at the essence of this discussion.

"I shall not allow any one of them to be sacrificed, especially by a king of their homeland," I informed him in no uncertain terms.

"Damn you, man! With all your profound age and experience, you still refuse to accept the obvious demands of politics. Jacques has already given evidence to these heinous crimes."

"So would any man under the mere threat of torture."

"Jacques is not any man. And that makes all the difference. Some will have to stay behind. Some may have to die."

"If any of them die, so, too, will the Order."

"Long after I have returned to dust in the ground, the Templars will still be here. You will see to that. I have every confidence in your abilities. Why do you think I asked you to be their leader? I, too, am not without a certain awareness of which direction the winds of the future will wend."

Once more I pressed him:

"All these struggles can be easily surmounted, if you will but permit me—"

"Enough! I shall not have the burden of his blood upon your shoulders."

He lifted the bottle and regarded it.

"I was mistaken about their number. I wish I had several more of these, for I have no doubt that today will be a very long day."

He placed it back down and looked at me now.

"You are most holy. There is nothing that I can say to hinder you from leading what we both know is no celibate life. Despite your choice, I *can* stop you from piling sin upon sin as regards the deaths of others. You see, the older that I become, the more I realize that wanton killing is the foulest type of action that any man may take, and I believe, the one for which there can be no salvation. As long as I am pope, I shall forbid you from taking the life of a king."

I walked over to him, stared at him.

"What do you want of me, old friend?" he asked.

"What I have ever wanted from someone in a position of power—the truth."

"Is that all? Better you had asked for a burning bush to speak on a forgotten mountaintop. That is a far more common occurrence to find."

"The time has come, your holiness. I would know everything that you have ever done in concert with this regent, and I would know it now. This day I shall be *your* father-confessor."

"Who are you to speak to me in this fashion?" he roared. "I am the head of Holy Mother Church!"

"And I am its sword."

"Damn you again. You always know exactly what to say." He looked at the empty bottle. "Finally I have the courage to speak without duplicity. This is a rare day indeed!"

Late into the evening he spoke. There were times when his anger was passionate, and he stormed about the chamber like a manic swordsman, flaying this way and that. And there were times when he sat quietly and wept.

"I would ask for your forgiveness," he said at last, his eyes red like two hot coals.

"It is not my place to give."

"I ask for His forgiveness every day. I wonder if He hears my voice?"

"He hears."

"How do you know?" he asked, pleading to confirm his suspicions. "How can you be certain?"

"I have heard His voice, and since that day, I have never been the same as once I was."

"O! Perhaps it would be best if I pray without asking for a response of any kind."

"That might be wise."

Before I left, I knew that there could be no more appropriate occasion to solicit a promise from him than at that moment. (It was perhaps a dishonourable thing to do to a man when bent by his own vulnerability, but my responsibility was to a higher purpose.)

"Yes, some things are going terribly wrong. For that reason, you must keep an oath that you will now make unto me."

"If I am able."

I told him that he would have to issue an edict, that all properties belonging to the Order be donated to the Hospitallers, should the Templars ever be disbanded. He refused to believe what I had asked of him. For me there was no doubt that it would be the conclusion to which all of the advocate's machinations had proceeded.

"I swear it, though it will no doubt displease the lawyer greatly. For that reason, alone, it may well be worth the effort," he concluded with a fit of laughter.

Not very much time passed before three elderly members of the Order came to me with the same judgment that I had mentioned. For them it was nothing more than the proper way to finish a life of service. I argued against their decision; we would endure; it was necessary not to lose faith. But I had to admit to myself, that a piece of me could not disagree with them. Consequently, two Geoffreys, one *de Gonneville*, and the other *de Charney*, along with another of the many Hughs, whom I had come and would come to know, this one *de Pairaud*, would join Jacques in whatever fate awaited him. And like our Lord, Himself, had done thirteen centuries prior, these men would take upon themselves the sins of others, the better to cleanse the human spirit after they had departed this life.

May God bless and keep them forever in the warmth of His eyes. Amen.

CHAPTER THE SIXTY-FOURTH,

in which I try, again, to reason with a most unreasonable woman.

Once more I found Makeda on the Templars' field, except this time she was on horseback, staring at a hacked version of a straw effigy. I rode up to her, hoping that we might speak. Upon hearing me, she turned.

"I want you to stop sending letters," she spoke calmly, coldly.

I had recently paid several royal servants to bring my correspondence to the soldiers' quarters, hoping that she might be moved by their content. If she were, she was not evincing any feeling now, except minor irritation.

"Since all the men cannot read, they create stories about what you have written. They say that you wish me to join the Templars. That possibility has created an uproar. No one ever expected a woman to find a home amongst that sainted brotherhood of *eunuchs*."

I bit my lip before I spoke:

"They are not eunuchs."

"I suppose not, especially since their former leader finds the fragrance of a man's sweat so appealing. My people have no name for such creatures; we simply kill them. What does the educated and pure white nobility of this land do with men like that? What do you think your king will do?"

Once more I denied that he was my king.

"Yes, you keep saying that, yet he does what he wishes and answers to no one. Some have said that you are most happy, for now you are the leader of the most powerful army in the world. Tell me, Master of the Templars, will you gather your troops from all across the world and march them to France, here to Paris, to usurp the throne of your most detestable king?"

"If I had truly wanted to be leader of the world, I would have taken that position long before now."

She did not believe that Phillip would recognize the purity of my motives. In fact, she was certain that he thought all men to be very like himself.

"He may fear you," she cautioned me, "and a frightened king is capable of anything."

Whilst grateful for the conversation that she had denied me in recent days, and moreover, quite impressed with her grasp of the current state of affairs, nevertheless, I also knew that she would not wish to speak of her obvious condition that had become a barrier between us. I had no choice, therefore, except to raise that issue.

"How did your comrades know that it was I who had written?" I asked.

"Your choice of servants is poor. They all worship you and speak of what an honour it was to serve you."

O, that was not a good thing! I had hoped that she could maintain a certain degree of anonymity, but that was probably a foolish idea; her large stomach would soon reveal all that she might have hoped to conceal. What was worse, I did not wish for Phillip to have this knowledge either, at least not until she and I were married.

"And you said nothing to dispel their assumptions?" I asked.

"Why should I? Why should I care what anyone else thinks? Besides, I have never found your language easy to read. So, stop your letters!"

I informed her that I had had little choice; she would not see me.

"That should tell you everything."

"We have to make arrangements for the future."

She withdrew her sword, and appeared to be studying how she might toss it at the effigy.

"Now put down that sword! You might hurt yourself and our child as well."

Her nostrils flared.

"Who are you to tell me what I may do?"

"I am the father."

"Do you have a womb? Show it to me, man of miracles. Then I shall rip this thing out of mine and shove it up yours!"

I have never placed my hands upon a woman to beat her, as I have heard some other men do. (There are so many other far more pleasing things, which a man may accomplish with his hands, when a woman is present.) But her anger ignited my own. It took every bit of my strength to control the fire that was now burning behind my eyes. Before I spoke again, I swallowed the gall that had crept into the back of my throat.

"Then you have decided. And did you think never to consult me?"

"Consult you? As if you were a royal councilor or a physician? You are nothing more than a knight. You kill other men with the blessing of your pope, as you march beneath banners with the wooden symbol of your Lord's death stitched into them. The soldiers of this king have no such delusions about themselves. They would rather risk a youthful death fighting in one of his campaigns, than die old and bent over a plough. That is why they take up the sword in defense of this land. Only a holy warrior like you can waste centuries dreaming of his honourable duty to a bleeding victim that he calls his *God*."

"If the king has no honour, then why should his armies?"

My question mattered little. She ignored it, as she continued to wave her sword in front of herself. I watched her, thinking that offtimes have men believed themselves to be masters over the women in their lives. But more so than not have I seen the myriad ways in which these *masters* can be easily manipulated by a *come-hither* stare, or a most innocent and most beguiling smile. In short, most women will do what they will; such actions are not man's provenance alone. And between us, on this day, was a very real course of action that stood high and mighty, like a great stone monolith. Right or wrong, I had to make her understand.

"Mark me, Makeda of Nubia; mark me well."

She stopped, though did not turn to face me.

"I have waited two hundred years for a child of my blood to be born. Should any harm befall the gift that God has given to both of us, then no one and nothing will be able to stop my thirst for others' blood."

She let fly the blade, and it entered and passed through the straw figure at a point below the heart.

Whilst Makeda and I unburdened ourselves, each to the other, the advocate felt it important to speak from *his* heart upon the current demands of kingship (or so my newfound friend, the winsome Françoise, informed me):

> "I think it is apparent, my liege, that a ruler maintains his power not simply through the force of his will, but also with the support of his people."
>
> "The people?!" the king asked with repugnance. "They are *my* subjects. Am I to become theirs?"
>
> "This has nothing to do with the indulgence of their whims at the expense of your dignity. The exercise of power is all about artifice. The appearance ... is everything."
>
> Lost in thought, the king walked away. After several moments, he turned to his trusted advisor.
>
> "What, exactly, am I supposed to be doing, that necessitates the appearance of righteousness?"

"I would never presume to tell my prince *what* to do, but merely *how* to do it. The Templars must not be destroyed in one swift stroke."

"No? We have gone through a great deal of effort to expedite this matter. Why cease now?"

"It will require very careful planning, if the crown is to receive a papal blessing. All of us are products of our age. Clement wields great power. And regents sometimes have need of those who wield great power, if they are to maintain their own with minimal threat. Once you have that in hand, you will hear a great hue and cry raised across your lands. The people will praise you as they call for the blood of their enemies. You will rule their hearts, even as you send them to their deaths in wars, or tax their families beyond endurance."

"I have always admired your pragmatism, through the forms, which it sometimes assumes surprises even myself."

CHAPTER THE SIXTY-FIFTH,

in which the regent and I share one final conversation.

Having assumed that the Holy Father would probably not attempt to remedy the current situation, I, myself, called upon the king. To my surprise, I discovered that I was no longer welcome at court. To the surprise of the royal guards, I left them wounded (not fatally, mind you) as they tried to bar my path inside. I found his highness seated upon the throne, giving audience to several of his councilors, including de Nogaret. (The advocate was most unhappy to see me there, if the fear upon his face were any indication of it.)

"Must you be so irritating," the king asked, "*all* the time?"

I informed him that I had come to ask him to desist from his attacks upon the Order.

"The charges must be documented in a court of law," the advocate interjected.

"Never address me again," I told him, "if you value your life."

He stepped back several paces. The king was less than pleased with what he had witnessed.

"If you cannot exhibit civilized behaviour," he said, "perhaps you should be chained up with the other hounds."

"Will you do nothing to stop this?"

"Stop it? Why would we want to do that? We must see this through to its inevitable judgment. That is the way of all civilized nations, where grievous crimes have been committed."

"The Order was born of French blood spilled upon the soil of the Holy Land. Your own grandfather was its most ardent supporter. He fought at their side. He looked upon them as his brethren. Will you not trust the judgment of a saint?"

"Our cherished grandfather, may he rest his soul, would not have bothered with the formality of a trial, had he lived to see this dark day. Regarding our obligations, never presume to tell a king what they may or may not be. You should bother yourself with business elsewhere, holy knight. In fact, with your tales of brave warriors, fair maidens, fire-breathing dragons, and miracles abounding, you should probably go where people appreciate such fables. I hear the English so love them, that they have created a veritable *industry* in book production. You should go there, crusader. They will laud you.... We have outgrown you."

I could bear no more. I raised my sword and shouted for all in the chamber to hear and never forget.

"I, who fought alongside Richard the Lionhearted against the armies of Saladin, shall not stand idle!"

He stood up quickly now, absent of all difficulty or pain, as I had never before seen him do, and he smiled most viciously.

"You think to best me? Which dark gods were present at your nativity? I can enumerate all those who there at mine."

"Some wars can never be won, regardless of how powerful a king believes himself to be. It is a lesson that my long life has taught to me."

"Why, if you were any other man—"

"If I were any other man, I would be dead, would I not? Look upon me and remember that I am immortal, ageless, and indestructible. Who and what are you?"

The entire chamber was as silent as the grave. Suddenly, the king laughed.

"Who am I? King of France. Try to remember that on the way out of my palace."

I returned to my chamber, hoping to seek solace in an old, comfortable chair. I cherished what I prayed would be a time of solitude, whilst Dunstane busied himself at the Templars' House, making preparations for the rest to leave.

Upon entry, I found items strewn about or thrown over and cracked to bits. And there was a telltale passage of red droplets along the floor, leading towards my bed. I followed, only to find, upon my bedclothes, a larger red pool, as if someone had lain down there to die slowly, softly.

It was then, I believe, that my heart stopped, for my entire body grew absolutely cold. In this stain of liquid and bodily tissues were the fragments of what might have been.

At first I ran my finger in a small circular pattern at its very center. Then the pattern grew larger, as my hand reddened. Then I did the same with my other hand. Then I clutched at the fabric and held it to my face.

I sensed the presence of someone else in the room. I turned to see Anna standing there, as she had stood formerly before the hearth. She was holding one hand over her mouth, as the tears fell from her eyes to the floor below.

"Look here," I said to her. "Look at what is unspeakable."

I turned back to the bloodstained clothes, and felt my belovèd's hand upon my hand. I turned to her once more. She was no longer there.

I roared. I jumped up, and with my sword, I shredded each of the fabrics, until the room was filled with their pieces floating down.

I fell to the floor, screaming. And the cry that dragged itself from me that day, taking all of my strength with it, was the voice of the damned. I know that now. I understand what it means to be deprived of all hope. What did it matter that I would always have a tomorrow to make things right? The Anger, born of Agony, had fled from me. I was left Its mere shell.

My uncle believed that I would never die. He had no idea how a man may die slowly, bit by bit. The Darkness, that had come into my life at the very moment when I recognized Its truth, left behind Its mark upon my soul. For I swear before God and you, dear reader, that it has never healed, lo, these many years since.

CHAPTER THE SIXTY-SIXTH,

in which a legal proceeding is put before all to witness and cheer.

Long have we held that there is a type of blind faith nourished by all forms of daily routine, in that the sun will rise, and crops will yield their bounty. Then arrives the unexpected moment, when the pastures burn, and the sun's yellow gleam grows scarlet. At such a betrayal of expectancy the world is forever altered.

A royal decree brought the first of the Templar trials into one of the grand lecture halls of the university. I cannot say why. Perhaps a French regent thought it proper for the educated amongst us to see (first-hand) the workings of French jurisprudence. Perhaps he required a completely open *forum* to illustrate to the world that he had nothing to hide from other nations. Or perhaps it was all the advocate's idea.

Surrounded by students and educators, who were doubtless fascinated with the possibility of which *theses* would be argued either for or against each other, the advocate stood up proudly. He laid out all the previous charges, as the three Templars and their leader, Jacques, were brought in, fully chained.

Covered in the typical brown habit of a monk, and with the hood pulled down to cover most of my face, (as I did not wish to call attention to myself), I watched from the portal at one of the corridors leading into the hall. I had never seen the poor Master so gaunt as I did that day, his eyes sunk deep and low into his head. And he kept clenching and unclenching his fists throughout the entire time that he stood there next to the others.

As each charge was read, the noble three said nothing. Only Jacques responded to them. There was no sentiment in his voice, no feeling whatsoever. As if he were making a statement of fact, he declared calmly and clearly, that everything previously mentioned was absolutely true and was nothing but the truth.

The three looked at him, as if he had lost his wits, though added nothing, either to confirm or to deny.

I do not believe that anyone of the educated population was particularly satisfied, for there was no *dialogue*. The advocate had turned the proceedings into a lengthy *monologue* concerning the betrayal of the Templars: betrayal of our Lord's commandments; betrayal of the regent's trust in their once proud and merciful actions; betrayal of the people of France and all other good, Christian nations, who had always admired their *reputed* decency; betrayal of all things natural. And what did the four letters at the end of each Templar document represent? Long did he labour to discover the truth of it, however, discover it he did. *D.S.M.M.* could mean one thing only: *Diaboli Sancti Mundus Meus—My World (Belongs) To The Holy Devil.*

The entire assemblage gasped.

The once proud brotherhood had become a hotbed of heresy, he continued. The Templars were more bestial than beasts, and any surviving Templars anywhere should be brought into custody forthwith, to answer for their most bestial behaviours.

He then held up a scroll, whose wax seal revealed the imprint of the Holy Father's ring. (And as I looked about, I suddenly realized that his holiness was not present, nor could a single prelate of any stripe be found herein.) And the royal lawyer proceeded to quote from the document, to the effect that, according to Aquinas, in his *Summa Contra Gentiles*, as quoted by his holiness:

"*The good of the nation is greater than the good of a single man or group of men.*"

And since there was not much good left of which to speak in the current Templar group, the pope had no choice but to support the current royal regime and condemn one and all. The audience, to a man, laughed.

Only I did not. (I never believed that the Holy Father was determined to secure his political position at the expense of the knights who were devoted to him. To this very day, still I find it difficult to accept, though I am, grateful, that he kept his pledge to me, and gave all of the Templars' former property and possessions to the Hospitallers, whose dedicated service made them most deserving. And not only did that action rile the advocate; his king was also most displeased with the decision. Unfortunately, or fortunately, as the case may be, neither man lingered in thought for very long upon it. More of this shortly.)

His attack now complete, the advocate awaited an appreciation from his spectators. Everyone arose from his seat. Most cheered, albeit halfheartedly.

I returned to my residence, where I informed Dunstane that, like it or not, he would have to leave very soon with the rest of the Templars, whom we had placed for safety in the homes of several trustworthy Parisians. This was the time for my holy work to begin, and he would be very much a part of it. He laughed.

"I always said you were a holy man. Right proud am I to be of service to you, my lord. Worry not. I'll be lookin' after them. But what of you? Who'll be lookin' after you?"

"My work here is not yet finished. I shall join you when I am able."

"Why do I think you're lyin' through your teeth?"

"They will need my guidance, and they will have it shortly. For now, we have lost all necessary time. There will be other trials. And any noble or peasant who is dissatisfied with his life and is jealous of what the Templars have achieved, will bring his testimony to the advocate's *carnevale*. And the list of crimes against humanity will continue."

"If you're so determined to have me go, I will. But I refuse to like it!"

"I would not have it any other way."

I had word that Makeda would soon be leaving Paris as well, never to return. I had not yet gathered my thoughts to speak with her, if at all. I knew only that I had to see her one final time.

I found her once more on the field of tourneys, standing next to her horse. With much of sadness in her face, she looked across the empty fields.

"How did you know that I would be here?"

I told her that it was an obvious choice for one who knew her.

"I did not think that you would ever see me again," she said.

"Yet we are here."

"I wanted to remember this place. It was where we met. Have you come to say good-bye, my brave knight, or to kill me?"

"I have never killed a woman, though there may have been one or two who deserved such a kindness from me."

She told me that she had chosen to leave in the service of the *Elektor von Sachsenhausen*—the German leader who had previously watched tournaments here with the French regent.

"He was much impressed with my abilities. He believes that they will serve me well, when I lead a contingent of his troops in the Holy Land."

And to what end?

"He seeks the burial shroud of your god. He has discovered an ancient text that tells him that it can be found in a sacred mountain somewhere in Tripoli. A man named *Joseph* left it there."

I thought, momentarily, that I should try to convince her of the foolishness of this German errand, but she would not have listened in any case.

"Is that where it is?" I asked, smiling. "Verily, I had no idea."

"He believes that if he claims it as his own, it will grant him power over all peoples."

"Over you?"

"I am to lead his armies. I shall journey across the world—"

"In order to subdue other races?"

She turned her face from me. I wondered if her eyes were filling with water; not that it would have changed anything between us. I was not yet prepared to offer her tenderness of any sort. She turned back to me now, her eyes as feral as once they were.

"As the years pass, I would rather that you never think of me except with hatred. It will be so much easier for both of us, if that is true."

She mounted her horse.

"You have known many women," she said, grabbing the reins, "but you have never known me as well as you believed."

"That much is certain."

"There was a time when I prayed both day and night for a child. I want you to know that if I had given birth to our child now, no one and nothing would have ever been able to make me leave it. But the mother, that I had hoped to become, is someone who died many years ago beneath the sacred mountain in a land far away. There is no more room left for softness in my heart. I am what my Destiny has made of me."

Not until I heard those words did I begin to let go of the hatred festering inside of me. Still, it would not go quietly.

"Your Destiny, or your choice?" I asked.

She did not respond. Despite her arrogance, and her crime against both of us, I wished her well.

"God go with you."

"Your God?" she asked, mocking me with her laughter. "I shall soon see his burial garments."

She stopped laughing, and for a brief moment, I thought I saw what might have passed for some gentility in her eyes.

"I shall also remember your kindness to one who was most undeserving of it," she concluded.

Watching her ride away, I wondered if she would have stayed behind, had she known that she and her troops would all be dead within six months, victims of the Caliph's forces? Would the truth have made any difference at all?

Dunstane, who had been observing us from a thicket of trees, now rode down to me. We both watched her, until she was no longer in the line of sight.

"Sometimes the best way to love a woman," he began, dispelling the silence, "is to let her go."

"Tell me, Dunstane; was it her choice, alone, to still the heart of our child?"

"I don't rightly know, my lord, but I do know that it was her belly. And a thick belly sometimes interferes with how well one may wield a sword. I can attest to that struggle," he said, patting his paunch, "personally."

I sighed.

"She could have been a mother."

"But she is a warrior. Do you not believe in forgiveness?"

"It is something that mortals should do, since their lives are circumscribed by time. I am not subject to such temporal concerns, and therefore, cannot forgive. For me the memory of a single hateful act will not endure for a month or for several years, but for an eternity. How can one forgive what one will never be able to forget?"

"Then you should probably go after her and kill her, if that is the only way to make peace with your pain."

"Does a man's love count for nothing in today's world?"

"Probably not. More's the pity."

On the morrow I rode with him and the rest of the Templars to the outskirts of the city, where we dismounted and bade each other *farewell.*"

I took Dunstane's hand and told him that I was sorry for our experience here to have finished so miserably.

"Ah," he asked, "how could one have lived so long and learned so little? The story is never about the destination, but always about the journey. 'Tis a hard thing to say good-bye, for it is has been my very great honour to serve with you, my lord."

"No, old friend. Between us, I am the man much more honoured."

We embraced, then I pushed him away.

"O, you sentimental, old fool," I shouted. "Begone with ye!"

"Why, you're nought save a foul-mouthed sinner! Does no one in this godforsaken country keep a civil tongue in his head? You're all a bunch of heathens, is my way o' thinkin'."

And with that growl Dunstane mounted his horse.

"God be with you, Dunstane of Scotland!"

He smiled.

"And with you, Sir Guy of Lagery. I ride off now to see once more rainbows over the highland hills and castles atop the lofty crags of Stirling, whilst dragons swim in the deep of the *loch* below. In the Scottish land I'll make my home, for God, Himself, is there, the bravest Scot of all. And when I look up into the night sky, I'll know that the stars are lightin' their way for your safe return to the brethren and your friend. And I warrant you'll remember this old Scottish warrior with fondness in your heart."

"All the days of my life."

"Damn right you will!" he bellowed, laughing most heartily, as he rode off, at a full gallop, into the wind.

CHAPTER THE SIXTY-SEVENTH,

in which commence the executions, and the dramatis personae sing out the final act.

The Romans called it *Lutetia*, a nomenclature that possessed perhaps a ring of poetry about it. Lord knows, it is far grander a thing than *Island within the City*, which is what *Ile de la Cité* is at the heart of Paris. Soon after Julius Caesar conquered it, the native population, the *Parisii* gave to history and the future city that would develop around it their name. As the centuries grew into a *millennium*, a tradition emerged there as well. I cannot say how it began, if in an emperor's determination to frighten a lawless populace into submission, or as the result of an argument between two drunken peasants, or as the continuation of a quaint Roman custom, but public executions were held upon that soil, the better to be watched by native Parisians. And it was there, upon this small island, on a bright noon filled with the last of the late winter's chill, that Master Jacques and the few remaining Parisian Templars met their end.

The March winds were particularly intense and unforgiving that day. They swept through and around the platforms and scaffolds with an unearthly howling. Despite the bitter chill, the crowds poured across the bridges and walkways to seek out a comfortable place for viewing the forthcoming ceremony. The contingent of archbishops, bishops, abbots, and prelates of all sorts was led onto the platform that had been designated for ecclesiastical use only. The nobles were brought onto a smaller platform adjacent to the *holy* one. The peasants either sat upon the dirt or stood about, babes seated upon the shoulders of their most curious parents.

The entire royal court was ushered onto the highest planking, that had been constructed for today's purpose. The regent never wore a smile so great, nor laughed so gregariously as he did that day. And all those who clustered about him did exactly the same.

Again clad in holy robes, the cowl pulled down to cover my face completely, I grasped at the arm of the Holy Father before he climbed the staircase to his seat. He eyed me curiously, (or he may have witnessed a glint of the sun upon the hilt of my sword, that was beneath the other sleeve) and informed his entire company that he had sufficient time to hear the words of one of his brethren.

We stepped away from the crowds, which were beginning to assemble.

"You should not be here," he told me in whispers. "Most believe that you have already quit this city for parts unknown, and that is a very good thing."

I thought it best to confess to him now what the true nature of the infamous *head* turned out to be. I assumed that Brother Hughes would forgive me, as the object no longer existed. So I discussed in detail what it was and what it contained. The Holy Father appeared to faint. I held him up, until the crisp air brought him around once more to a clarity of vision.

"How can you know this?" he asked.

"It was my gift to Hughes de Payens at the founding of the Templars, not two hundred years ago."

"Is it still here in Paris?"

"Worry not. It is somewhere safe. I would not allow this king and his legal servant to soil it with their blood-soaked hands. And this is the final time that you will have bound mine own. I wish you well, Holy Father. Enjoy the celebration. After today, you will not see me in this life again."

The advocate walked over to the four accused personages, unfurled his scroll, and read his charges, as a matter of formality, really, since the Master had already confessed to their absolute truth. Consequently, said advocate expected the four to acknowledge that fact once more, if only for the recordskeeping of the chroniclers. He declared them all guilty as charged, after a cogent analysis of the facts, then looked at them with his broad smile, and said that if they wished to make a final statement, it might be the proper thing to do, should they seek redemption of their souls.

Both Geoffreys and Hugh declared their innocence before God and all that was holy. Master Jacques, however, wished to say a few more words. And in the process, he stood straight and tall, as if a youthful dignity had now been restored unto him. And lo and behold, there came a miracle that day. No one knew why or how, though I was convinced that God had given a sinner strength, when he needed it most:

"We are now and have ever been God's chosen warriors. He, alone, is our Master. We shall stand in the brilliant light of His judgment with nothing to fear, for we have kept hidden nothing from His eyes. We are proud of our French blood and its heritage of brave kings and faithful knights. What does it mean to be French? It means that one must fight for the liberty of all men. That is the French truth. But you have forgotten that truth this day. And for that reason, I shall speak the truth that I have been too afraid to announce. The charges against the Order are completely false!"

The advocate dropped his scroll. The entire assemblage yelled, murmured, and pointed at the four Templars. One of the bishops (who resembled remarkably Baldwin's physician, Fausto) turned to the pope to say that Jacques had blasphemed and should be put to death immediately, the better to take the Order's ill-gotten gains and disperse them to bishoprics everywhere. The Holy Father smiled wryly and shook his head. I wonder if he found something to admire in poor, old Jacques at that moment? It was then that the bishop noticed my appearance and smiled slightly to me. A chill sped along my spine.

"These falsehoods were fabricated by William de Nogaret with the full support of the king. Scribes!" Jacques called to two young men who were seated in a corner, writing away. "Make certain that you do not delete my words. I want all the generations which follow me to know what I have done."

With difficulty the king stood up and called out for a restoration of order. The crowd became silent. He sat once more.

"I have fornicated with a man," he continued. "If that be a sin, then there are many here this day who should be standing with me."

Once more the crowd raised its voice, though what emerged as audible sound was a chorus of *ohs* and *oohs*. (Several noblemen laughed slightly and eyed each other suspiciously.) The king's face revealed that he was more than offended; he was sickened by the tragic farce that this hearing had become.

"What I have done are the actions of one man. No other Templar is guilty of my crime. The Lord above knows this to be true. So does our royal advocate. So does our royal highness!"

De Nogaret picked up his scroll and studied his royal master's face.

"Make your conclusion now, master Jacques," the advocate demanded. "We are ready to begin the consequences of our judgment."

Jacques smiled, albeit briefly.

"Hear me now, King Phillip, Pope Clement, and Royal Councilor, William de Nogaret, you have betrayed the Lord, His people, and His knights. Woe unto the enemies of Liberty, for they are without salvation. For that reason, you will all follow us within the month. May God have mercy upon your souls. Amen."

I suppose there was no doubt as to what the king would say in response. Jacques and the others were quite prepared.

The king arose again, but this time he needed the arms of those nearest him, for he had little strength left in his legs.

"Burn their every last vestige out of my kingdom. Do it. Now!" he declared.

Royal executioners obliged. The piles of wood at the base of their stakes were set aflame.

Amongst those present, many nobles and peasants wept piteously, whilst others derided the screaming victims as the villainous scum they were. Then it was that the strangest of things occurred: the winds, which had so ferociously whipped everyone about, died to the barest whisper. (The significance of that event was not lost upon even the simplest of minds, as the jibes and caterwauling ceased.) And as my innocent brethren gave up their breaths, a light poured forth from them, more brilliant than any that I had ever witnessed. Perhaps it was the light of their souls upon the long journey home. Perhaps it was no miracle at all, only a chance meeting of flame and drafts, which consumed everything in its wake. Who could say? Who could be certain?

And heard I did a chorus, as of angels weeping piteously. I could not bear the horrid sound, as they bemoaned their wailing. But to the dirge were all others deaf. Only I am alone here to tell you of it.

I had forgotten how long it takes for someone to die whilst being burned alive. I was grateful for that former ignorance, though it was fast disappearing.

Despite the crowd, the pope believed that one particular set of eyes was staring at him with such intensity, that he could find no peace. He rubbed his eyes and turned round to see me.

"In His judgment He is righteous," I told him, then turned to leave. As I did so, he clutched at his throat and began to choke. The discomforture lasted but a moment. Then all was well, or so it appeared to be.

Within little more than a week after the burning of the heretics, Pope Clement V, who had never been ill a single day in his life, fell suddenly from his chair to his table, thence to his floor, and gave up the ghost. Thirty-three days after the burning, I surprised Phillip inside his castle. Instead of calling for his guards, he shared a drink with me from his vast stock. (I supposed that he wished to make amends of some sort.) As we sat together, I would have very nearly sworn that he had been determined to have me partake from one particular chalice, as opposed to the other, so as a former practitioner of poisons, I switched our cups. (Not that it would have mattered really; I have drunk of poisons before, and am still here to tell you of it. I do not believe, however, that he knew this to be so.) Imagine my consternation when he, who had never been well a single day in his life, choked soon after the first few sips and fell, cracking his head open upon the stone floor. It was truly a miracle, for he did not die. He lingered in his bed for several weeks, screaming often throughout the day and into the night, as suppurating wounds appeared all over his flesh, the fetid stench of which floated in the air throughout his chamber like *miasma* above a bog. Neither doctor, nor apothecary, (nor theologian, for that matter), was ever able to comfort him in his distemper during those final days. Despite the stench, this presumably loyal monk (for so I appeared in my earthen robes) kept vigil at his bedside, where I watched him sink deeper and deeper. Before he closed his eyes, the final words, which he heard, were mine:

"I do hope that you can understand me, your highness. I would hate to believe that I were wasting my precious time here. I have been giving a great deal of thought to a subject that may be very dear to your heart, namely, what it means to be a Frenchman. I have concluded that Jacques was most correct when he said that it is invariably bound up with the prospect of liberty. Perhaps it is true that fighting for the liberty of all is what it means to be French. You probably cannot grasp the essential truth of that concept, spoiled son of the wealthy that you are, but your descendants will. I want you to know that I have had a dream of late, a dream of the future. And in it are very many people, huntsmen, herdsmen, farmers, peasants all. Interesting to note is that these gentle tenders of the land are in riotous tumult! The common folk are smashing and burning the homes of the nobility throughout France. And I am watching this violence take place from a lovely grove, wherein I sit comfortably atop my horse, laughing loudly. Such is my gift to you and all the generations to follow your line; for you should remember your psalms as you journey to await your last judgment, Phillip, that they who sow in tears shall reap in joy. Amen."

His eyes had stared wildly, to the point of nearly tearing the flesh around the sockets, when the lids fell back to their usual half-somnolent glaze. Then the choke filled him and left with its final gasp, his chest sinking down, his head tilted now to the left.

I am uncertain if he had the presence of mind to grasp all that I had uttered as my meager attempt to comfort the poor wretch. (It was the Christian thing to do, was it not?)

Before the king's lifeless body was interred, his attendants entered his chamber only to discover that somehow, miraculously, the former regent had been cut neatly into twenty-three pieces. Some have said that those fragments represented the twenty-three Masters of the Order of the Temple of Jerusalem, and that they had crawled out of the earth to avenge themselves and their line against him. There were, in fact, soil, loam, and pieces of a burial shroud, which could be clearly seen upon his bedclothes and floor. (From time to time people have asked of me how such a thing might have happened. I have always responded that I had no idea. But in an age when people everywhere believed that there were no more miracles to be had, everyone was compelled to admit that there are always miracles of one kind or another. Those who have eyes to see, let them see. Christ commanded it, did he not?) Though guards had been posted outside his door all throughout the night and into the following dawn, not one had seen a living soul or heard a solitary sound. The night had passed as quietly as a placid wind across the headstones of the dearly departed.

Not so the morning gossip. Everywhere, from the royal court to the marketplace were bruited about cries of fear, cheers for justice. The king's end became the matter of legend. God would remember the poor in their prayers. Despite all the iniquity of their lives, God would not let His children fall.

And so it came to pass that there was a resurgence of faith. The cathedrals were filled to bursting. A new age was dawning, one in which God would raise man from his humble station and welcome him as a truly noble child, despite the lowliness of his birth, and one worthy enough to receive His many legacies.

Perhaps these ideas or similar ones filled the head of the eldest princes as they, too, ascended to the throne, only to die shortly thereafter. (Unlike their father, they had never been sick a single day in their lives.) Perhaps none of these ideas ever occurred to them at all. The only ones who know are keeping their counsel in the undisturbed earth.

Some have said (most notably the English, the Germans, and even one Italian poet named Dante Alighieri) that the sins of the father were visited upon the children. Not being a priest, I am loathe to hazard such summary judgments.

The English, the Germans, and many other peoples never believed that the Templars were guilty of any misdeeds. Either this belief, or the ties of blood between a French king and a French pope, never sat well with non-French royalty, but whatever the cause, the English struck first. They entered into a war with

France that lasted more than thirty years. There have never been accurate counts of how many died during that time. I prefer to leave this bloody labour in the hands of future historians, who may possess far greater patience (and strength of will) than I to accomplish such a task.

As for the advocate, he ordered his servants to pack his belongings, as he was determined to leave France indefinitely. No one really knew why he was in such a hurry to depart, especially under cover of darkness. It may have been nothing more than the overly long amount of time he took to dispose of certain courtly records, which contained his signature, or the judicious editing of same that he performed, so as to reflect the current royal position upon all matters, which, certainly, matched his own. (His family he had already sent away to the Iberian Peninsula for their safety.) Before he fled, he decided to sign several official documents, one of which claimed that five thousand Templars had already been imprisoned and were awaiting execution. There were others, certainly, of a similar nature, in that they mentioned further crimes by the Templars against the state.

His holy labours completed, he revealed, one last time, that he was still a creature of habitual comforts. He appeared to have partaken of a wine that, unbeknownst to him, contained a potent draught, *Nepenthe*, that sent him immediately into a deep sleep shortly after the first sips. In his dream-like slumber he was somehow conveyed to a small church in the Loire Valley. The sky had thickened to a single palette of white, as the first snowflakes of December fell over what had been formerly the rolling hills and greenery of the region's bucolic landscape. Once there, he was brought into that structure. It was very old even then, and it possessed a very tiny and very sturdy vault below ground, composed of large stones and mortar. Somehow, miraculously, William de Nogaret awoke inside this vault. Forgive me. I should say, rather, that he awoke inside a closed coffin, (that had been placed inside the aforementioned vault), his hands and feet bound securely, a cloth stuffed into his mouth. For several days and nights thereafter, muffled sounds could be heard rising up through the floorboards and dirt into the church proper. Some even said that the church was haunted. But after a time, the sounds ceased to contend with the chorus of parishioners' voices raised in prayersong, and all was well with the world again. No one ever found that coffin, walled up in the vault below that tiny church. Pity, that.

Regarding Dunstane, my old friend, he found himself back in Scotland one fine day, (in a tavern, no less!), when another customer made a most grievous insult against him (either real or imagined, I cannot say, though I believe it may have had something to do with someone's mother). Both men unsheathed their swords and threw themselves into the heat of battle. (Though Dunstane was much older, I have been told that the patrons wagered *for* him, after they saw how he handled himself.) They matched each other cut for cut, until Dunstane failed to parry a single thrust. He stood there now, looking at the new hole in his stomach, then at the other man, then back at the hole again.

"Now look what you've gone and done, you heathen," he said. "You've killed me. Damn you. But thanks be to God for me good arm!"

He flung the sword at his foe, who, perhaps from surprise, stood quite still, thus providing a perfect target. The man took the blade in and through his neck, then fell over quite dead.

"Ooh, me stomach," Dunstane choked, reaching for the tankard of ale that he had left a-table. "I think I'll have another."

He sipped, then fell over dead, a broad smile upon his face.

And for that Squink fellow, I chanced upon him entering that very same tavern from which he and four other cohorts had followed Dunstane on that very wet night long before. Much later that day, when he left, (alone this time), I followed *him*. Good fighter though he was, he was not my match. And since I made certain that he not escape this time, I proceeded to perform a bit of *surgery* upon him. I took out his tongue, took off his right hand (his sword-hand), and his left foot. (I had no idea why I selected the left one really. For me it represented some type of balance between left and right or right and left, I supposed.) Afterwards, I rushed him to a physician, who applied numerous fires to the separated sections of his form in order to *cauterize* the wounds. It was an evening of much muffled screaming and more than a few of the patient's tears. I paid the medical practitioner handsomely for his efforts, and I tossed the newly remade Master Squink out upon his buttocks. The man spent the rest of his days and nights as a beggar in the streets of that lovely city. And it was there, upon one bright morning, that his hunger caused his stomach to growl, and the pain of it was so severe, that he bent over and fell, face-down into a pile of horse manure, where he choked and gave up the ghost. The rats of Paris must have been grateful to me once more for having provided them with so tasty a morsel.

Finally, Jacques' experience with financial matters yielded several intriguing suggestions, one of which included a recommendation that the Order base itself in the mountains of the Swiss, whose gentle people knew how to keep both their business transactions and their counsels quite private. And some of his ideas had merit, for somehow, miraculously, no one ever found the majority of the actual monies and/or precious metals and jewels, (as well as the various documents and mallets used for the letters of credit), which were in possession of the Templars—an interesting fact that pleased none of the then current rulers.

There was much that came later: the immolation of Jeanne d'Arc; peasant uprisings across the known world; the great city-states and their even greater conquering fleets; the countless slaughter attributed to the Black Death; and even more crusades. These things and so much more have I witnessed and endured, yet I find that I no longer feel the need to narrate my continuing genesis. I began writing this tale in the year of our Lord, 1453, the year in which Jerusalem and Konstantinople have fallen to the Ottoman Turks. The once proud Byzantine emperors ruled according to an ancient motto that was inscribed in stone at the founding of their empire: *basileos basileon basileuon basileusin—kings of kings who rule over kings.* The great kingdoms are in other hands now, for the time being. And I am in Paris once again, traveling *incognito*, seeing to the business of old friends and potentially new enemies. As I walk the streets here, I remember an incident that occurred when Dunstane walked in upon me, as I perused a letter from an old friend, the painter Giotto di Firenze.

The man had only recently completed a series of frescoes in a chapel for the Scrovegni family of Padua. The works consisted of narrative events in the life of Christ, with various members of the patron's family standing near Him. I supposed that the entire brood needed to legitimize itself in some fashion by relating its current head, Enrico, to our Lord. (Apparently, the church had refused to allow Enrico's father to be given a Christian burial, as the elder had spent much of his life in the accursèd practice of usury. Upon its completion, the family and the church were once more reconciled, as the patriarch was given a proper Christian burial.) No matter. I was sorry that I had not witnessed the admixtures of his practiced hand. (No one ever caught the profound truth in that interplay of light and shadow as well as he did, in my opinion, to be sure.) Despite my revery, I heard clearly my companion's very negative judgment concerning all things creative, new, and noteworthy:

"I care nought for those childish scribblings! Give me a tavern's song of a bawdy wench and the fire in her loins, or the tale of heroes and the tears of an honourable death. I wish I were a bard, my lord, for if I were, I would sing of bold adventures and strange creatures from the end of the world. There you would ride upon a snow-white steed, clad in the finest of silver, across the heather in the fierce winds of March, sallying forth to slay a dragon or two. And all the people of all the towns would put aside their many toils simply to see the most blessèd knight of Christendom pass them by."

"You should have been a poet, friend Dunstane."

"Mayhap when I'm too old to raise me sword anymore, I'll sit by the fire and write tales of wonder, if I could but learn how to write first."

This artist had been a friend of the Templars. He had honoured us with secret images, the meaning of which had often eluded most spectators, except for us, certainly. This chapel was no different. Upon the wide walls of an archway, below several sacred representations, he had painted a birdcage upon either side. Nine birds were within each cage. The nine were the original nine founders of the Order.

"If it be God's will," I said, "his creation will endure long after the reason for it can be barely recalled."

"'Tis an extravagant gesture, methinks."

"This Enrico probably feels that his sire will spend far less time in *Purgatorio* now. Is that not worth any price?"

"I think not, my lord. This entire situation stinks of manipulation and not a little of greediness. And if the Lord above takes Himself a good whiff thereof, I shudder to think of what may happen to the poor fools involved therein."

"Only Giotto's work will remain. Art is the only thing that ever endures."

"Except for you."

"There you are wrong, old friend. I do not exist. There is not now, nor has there ever been a man named Sir Guy of Lagery. Remember my words."

"Always," he responded. "Always."

And so began my slow but eventual disappearance from the hearts and minds of men. Knowing that I shall be the one who lingers in shadow, watching the mortal parade, is a great comfort to me, far more than Dunstane could have ever dreamed possible. What is the expression that Brother Michael was always so fond of? O, yes, "the more things change …"

D.S.M.M.

Here endeth the third book.

EPILOGUE

He closed the book. Just then he became aware that someone was watching him. He turned around. A young man dressed in a suit was standing at the doorway entrance, holding a sword. Inexplicably, Mr. Paine felt the need to blurt out a question:

"Mr. Aghapos? I didn't hear you come in."

"Yes, I get that a lot. Good afternoon, Hugh. It is *Hugh*, isn't it?"

With a puzzled look, Mr. Paine stared at the other man.

"Did anyone ever tell you that it's not polite to stare?"

"Sorry. I thought you'd be much older."

"I get that a lot, too. Well, what did you think?" he asked, pointing to the folio.

"You don't seriously expect me to believe this, do you? There's not an ounce of truth to it. I mean, all that business about the shroud is … well … Really!"

"An *ounce* of truth? Weights and measures? Is that how you gauge the validity of a person's life? I guess Brother Hughes was right; faith is so transitory a thing, that it often fades away if there are no relics about. I'm sorry that you find the tale so incredible. I have no choice except to believe in it. You see, it's my autobiography."

Mr. Aghapos needed only a moment to notice Mr. Paine's skeptical look before tossing the sword onto the table.

"Go ahead. Touch it …, if you dare."

Mr. Paine seemed to be debating his next move. Several moments later he held his hand over the item in question.

Quite shocked, he looked over at Mr. Aghapos.

"I can feel its heat!"

"Are you sufficiently convinced?"

"I see a curiosity; there are no miracles here."

"Oh, ye of little faith!"

Mr. Aghapos placed his arm on the table, then reached for the sword and cut off his hand at the wrist. Hugh screamed as he watched how blood vessels, tissues, musculature, and bone stretched towards each other's half to reconnect. Mr.

Aghapos lifted his wrist and studied the scarring upon it, that was now fast disappearing.

"I must be getting old. Wounds don't heal as quickly as they used to. But they still hurt like hell! I keep forgetting that."

Mr. Paine jumped back, away from the table, knocking over his chair.

"Relax," Mr. Aghapos urged him. "I won't bite, maybe growl a little is all."

"This is insane! I'm an atheist, or I was until today. Are you going to kill me?"

"Atheist are you? May God have pity on you. Now why would I have you read my book, if I had every intention of killing you?"

"I don't know. Maybe it's in retaliation for having mentioned your name in mine, isn't it? That was the whole point. You were determined to maintain your anonymity."

"And that's the *only* lesson that you got from it? I see I didn't do my job very well. My uncle would have been most displeased."

"The truth is, I would've never known your name," he began to speak at an alarmingly quick rate, "if chroniclers of the period hadn't written about how Dunstane mentioned it all the time. He was obviously fond of his former employer and friend. Don't blame me. Blame *him*! I'm—I'm completely innocent in this."

While Mr. Aghapos laughed, Hugh stepped back, moving ever closer to the door.

"God bless that old soldier. He could never keep his mouth shut, once he had a bit of ale in him. As for your mention of my name, I have to admit, I wasn't happy about seeing it. You will, of course, write another book that repudiates your previous findings, as they relate to me. The rest can be left unaltered. You're not planning to leave, are you?"

"Not at all!" Hugh shouted, standing absolutely still.

"Good. We're not finished yet. I want you to perpetuate the legacy that your ancestor began."

"Ancestor?"

The family of Hughes de Payens had split off into two branches: the Paines who lived in America and in Scotland, while the St. Claires became the Sinclairs, who resided in Scotland to this day. Mr. Aghapos believed that Hugh's family originally departed the old sod for America several hundred years ago.

"And here, in this land, the French-Christian blood of your ancestors mixed with many others, including a great-grandfather who was Jewish. Then came the introduction of Afro-American blood with your mother, and here you are today.

I fancy myself something of an amateur historian, you see. Have I omitted any pertinent facts?"

"I think I need to sit down," Hugh said, picking up his chair.

Mr. Aghapos found it most interesting that Hugh's ancestors should pick America as their new home. Perhaps it was because so many of them were lawyers, and, after all, America was a nation created by lawyers for lawyers. Hugh made a face when he heard that last statement.

Mr. Aghapos stopped speaking to look up and around.

"I can't help but feel that somewhere the restless spirit of William of Nogaret is laughing at me," he commented.

"I really wish you'd refrain from insulting the profession of both my parents."

"You chose not to follow in their footsteps. There may yet be hope for your bloodline."

Hugh made another face. His impatience had gotten the better of him, as he questioned why he was *really* here.

"You are here because I am here. And we are here because today America is the center of the world. At this center our journey is to begin."

"Journey?"

"I have known the players on all sides for the past thousand years. And when I wasn't fighting one, or attempting to make peace with the other, I was watching. I have seen incompetent rulers at the helm of state, who sacrifice a young generation for their own unspeakable agendas. I have lived to see multi-national corporations transform into war profiteers, because their chairmen are determined to maximize profits, even on the spilled blood of other people's children. The Holy Land is a curious place. Despite the current heavy traffic or occasional luxury hotel, the people are the same now as when the first Crusaders passed through the Damascus Gate. Long ago our tools were swords, then letters of credit and checkbooks. Today it's all about secured internet lines and the latest suicide-bombers. You see, the war never stops; only its machinery changes with each new generation. It is time for you to take your rightful place with us. We have always needed competent historians and translators, especially in as dangerous a time as this one appears to be. You will be inducted into the Order, where you will continue your work."

"What order?"

"The Templars, of course!" He laughed. "You didn't think that I would allow them *all* to be executed, do you? I shall tell you what I told them upon their departure from Paris: *we must be stronger than what we were in order to become better than what we have ever hoped to be. Never again shall we stand idle, while the rulers of nations try to burn away the last vestiges of who we might have been.* That sounds pretty good, don't you think? My old friend, your ancestor, Hughes de Payens, would have approved of it wholeheartedly. I can tell you, it impressed my brethren to no end. Besides, today the Templars are needed more than ever."

"Wait a second. If my father's a Templar, why don't I know about it?"

It seemed that the elder Mr. Paine had been uncomfortable with the position, when the choice to join was offered to him thirty years before.

"Thirty?"

"Actually, living is the toughest thing that anybody can do, and no one gets it right all the time. I believe that his refusal to join us was a grievous error on his part. He was never very clear about the reasons why. I assumed that it had something to do with his distaste for our calling, and ours for his profession, I suppose."

"Maybe he just didn't want to be part of some super powerful, secret organization. Did you ever think of that?"

"We're not a bunch of hired assassins, not usually anyway. We have tried to maintain the peace for seven centuries, though we used our efforts *behind the scenes*, as one might say."

"You mean, you've killed a hell of a lot of people, haven't you?"

Mr. Aghapos stared at him.

"Do you really want to hear the tale of every person who had the misfortune to give me a hard time?"

"Not particularly. No."

Hugh was silent for a few minutes before he spoke again. All this … this stuff was causing his head to spin. There were a thousand questions for which he had no answers.

"Well get a grip, man," Mr. Aghapos advised him. "We don't have all day. My schedule's pretty full, I'll have you know."

"You're worried about a full schedule, because you haven't done enough in the past thousand years? You must be kidding me, right? Wait. In order for your knights to have survived, you were probably involved in all sorts of international financial transactions. *Knights*, I suppose, is a good-enough term?"

"That will do. But we were Templars then and are Templars now. Try to get your terminology correct. That's the first lesson of an historian, isn't it? At any rate, Jacques could often be a much better accountant than he was a Templar-Master, when he put his mind to it, that is. I think he would be proud of what we have achieved."

"My God, you people must be everywhere!"

"A rather obvious conclusion. I am grateful that you have finally gotten the gist of it. Nevertheless, I have the distinct feeling that you and I are not always going to have an easy relationship."

"That much is certain, if I decide to go with you, that is."

"You must! The spirit of Hughes de Payens would not have it any other way. The Order was once the sword of the church. Today it is the guardian of civilization. We stand between the tyrant and his prisoner. Through foundations, we feed and house the poor. We restore the art wrecked by war. Now, it is time for us to leave. Don't sit there, gawking about. Come with me. The dragon has once again raised its scaly head. Shall we sally forth and slay him?" he asked loudly, raising the sword aloft and cutting a wide swath through the air with it.

"Now I think I'm going to need a drink."

Within the month, in the town of Siena, Italy, Mr. Aghapos led Mr. Paine into the church known as, *Il Duomo*. Passing the numerous columns composed of alternating layers of white and black marble, they crossed the stone floor and stared up into the royal blue of the vaulted ceiling alit with golden stars. In the vast open gallery a frieze of the busts of all the popes who ever were looked down upon them. The men stopped in front of one.

"Is that him?" Mr. Paine asked.

"Indeed."

"He doesn't exactly look like he's too thrilled to be here."

"I suppose he isn't. It's unfortunate that the object of my annual pilgrimage should look down upon the parade of humanity with such utter disdain."

"Why would you want to remember him like that?"

"I keep hoping that the artisan who carved him in that manner did so because he believed my uncle to be responsible for all the blood shed during all the crusades. I sincerely hope that it is not because of where his soul spends eternity."

"You don't seriously believe in an afterlife, do you?"

Mr. Aghapos scowled.

"Sorry."

"Farewell, dearest uncle," Mr. Aghapos said, looking up once more. "We shall see each other again within the year. Until then I hope that your soul finds some peace." He turned to Mr. Paine. "I have seen enough. Remember his face; it is a warning."

"About what?"

"That if all your actions proceed with conviction, then you might momentarily attain your goal. But once in a very great while, you may want something that lasts longer than a fleeting moment," he added, looking up a final time, "otherwise, what you reap may return to haunt you until the end of time." He turned to walk away. "Come. We must to Rome, where you will meet the current pontiff. You will have much work to do in the ensuing months at the Vatican Library."

"Wait," Mr. Paine called out. "I must know. Did you ever memorize the names of the fifty thousand angels and speak directly with God?"

Mr. Aghapos stopped.

"And did He answer you?"

Mr. Aghapos turned around

"Are you a believer now, Brother Hugh?"

"I don't know. It just seems like the most appropriate question to ask in a place like this."

"In a house of God, you mean? Well, I hope that you will forgive me for adopting the old Talmudist practice of the Hebrews, who often answered one question with another. What makes you think God is a *He*?" he asked, smiling, before he burst into laughter and continued on.

Mr. Paine rushed to keep up with the other man's swift gait, but turned back momentarily to stare once more at the carved replica above. The sun was just beginning to filter in through the gallery windows, and it shone upon Pope Urban's visage. In a sea of whitish-gray stone, his was the sole face that glittered a brilliant red.

Fin.